THE
GAY PLACE

THE GAY PLACE

BEING THREE RELATED NOVELS

The Flea Circus

Room Enough to Caper

Country Pleasures

BILLY LEE BRAMMER

*With a new introduction
by Don Graham*

UNIVERSITY OF TEXAS PRESS

AUSTIN

Copyright © 1961 by B. L. Brammer
Copyright © renewed 1989 by Sidney, Shelby, and Willie Brammer

Introduction copyright © 1995 by the University of Texas Press

Printed in the United States of America

First University of Texas Press edition, 1995

Reprinted by special arrangement with Houghton Mifflin Company

∞ The paper used in this publication meets the minimum requirements of American
National Standard for Information Sciences—Permanence of Paper for Printed Library
Materials, ANSI Z39.48-1984.

Library of Congress Cataloging-in-Publication Data

Brammer, Billy Lee.
The gay place : being three related novels / Billy Lee Brammer. —
1st University of Texas Press ed.
p.   cm.
Includes bibliographical references.
Contents: The flea circus—Room enough to caper—Country pleasures.
ISBN 0-292-70831-9 (paper)
1. Texas—Politics and government—Fiction.   2. Political fiction, American.
3. Governors—Texas—Fiction.   I. Title.
PS3552.R282G3   1995
813.54—dc20   94-24649

Is there then any terrestrial paradise where, amidst the whispering of the olive leaves, people can be with whom they like and have what they like and take their ease in shadows and coolness?

— FORD MADOX FORD

In the fall of sixteen
   In the cool of the afternoon
I saw Helena
   Under a white moon —
I heard Helena
   In a haunted doze
Say: "I know a gay place
   Nobody knows."

— F. SCOTT FITZGERALD

these three
are for these three
     sidney
     shelby
     willie

Introduction

FOR OVER three decades now, Billy Lee Brammer's *The Gay Place* has carried the aura of a legend. The legend is partly true. Brammer was a supremely talented writer who wrote one very good novel but was never able to write another. Frustration and anxiety dogged his subsequent efforts, and his life ended prematurely at age forty-eight from a drug overdose. According to this version of the legend, he belongs in the company of such promising one-book authors as Thomas Heggen (*Mister Roberts*) and Ross Lockridge (*Raintree County*), novelists whose early triumphs were never duplicated and whose lives came to ruin from, among other causes, the pressures attendant upon their initial successes. Neither Heggen nor Lockridge ever wrote that crucial second book, and both eventually committed suicide.[1]

Like Heggen and Lockridge, Brammer certainly felt a sense of anxiety occasioned by the lofty praise of his first novel. It garnered glowing remarks from the kind of names that matter. Gore Vidal, for example, proclaimed it "an American classic," and David Halberstam ranked it alongside *All the King's Men* and predicted it would be read "a hundred years from now."[2] Such praise registered strongly upon the young author. When Larry L. King read to Brammer Halberstam's rave review from the *New York Times Book Review* in 1961, Brammer responded, "Oh, Jesus, now they'll be waiting to pin my ears back if I can't do it again."[3] But *The Gay Place* was not a commercial success. It went into a second printing—and then onto the remaindered table.

Brammer's decline and death have more to do with the stark and indisputable fact of prolonged drug addiction than with the anxiety of achievement. His second wife, Dorothy Browne, has said: "Tragic? Yeah. But only at the very end. And it certainly didn't

have anything to do with Lyndon Johnson. It had to do with addiction."[4] Many of Brammer's friends insist that his life was essen-
tially a happy one. Film director Robert Benton, a longtime friend
of Brammer and Nadine Eckhardt, his first wife, says, "I don't
think Billy went through the sense of torment that Fitzgerald went
through. I never knew him when he was not some kind of extraordinary optimist, or wasn't filled with a kind of hope or generosity
toward everyone around him."[5] Jan Reid, journalist and novelist,
reports that Brammer never exhibited any signs of "that tortured
writer sense about him."[6] Ronnie Dugger, Edwin (Bud) Shrake,
Larry L. King, Willie Morris, Gary Cartwright—writers and friends
of Brammer's—all remember him with great respect and affection.
Recalling Brammer's habit of staying up all night writing, Shrake
has observed: "If it was 5 a.m. and you wanted company, you could
count on Bill."[7] There is also a sense of loss, of wasted gifts. King
has written of the frustration he felt upon hearing of Brammer's
death: "And I felt, too, a quick surge of irrational anger. But even
as I recognized it as such, a part of me began yelling at my old
friend's ghost: *Goddammit, Billie Lee, why'd you get yourself so screwed
up you only left to the world a fraction of your talent?*"[8]

For Brammer was a card-carrying intellectual and a writer's writer.
His conversations were an important part of his influence. Willie
Morris recalls that "the long talks we had at his house or under the
trees at Scholz's were, along with talks with Ronnie [Dugger], the
first real conversations I ever had with anyone about the power and
beauty of the written word."[9] Journalist Kaye Northcott has suggested that Brammer "was just as important to the Austin underground as Ginsberg was to the beats. They were both mentors,
teaching the impatient how to cope with an imperfect world."[10] A
"middle-of-the-road anarchist" in Gary Cartwright's phrase, Brammer "was always ahead of the game. Instead of writing, he was cuing
the rest of us on what to expect."[11]

Born in 1929 in Dallas, Brammer enjoyed a conventional middle-
class upbringing. He played sports at Sunset High, and sometime
in early adolescence discovered a lifelong passion for books. He

attended college at North Texas State College, which, though no Harvard or Yale, was stimulating enough if you read and yearned for contact with ideas. There Brammer wrote columns for the campus newspaper, adopting a sophisticated, more-superior-than-thou tone regarding such local campus fixtures as fraternity and sorority life, and there he met Nadine Cannon, whom he married in 1950. Following graduation in 1952, he held newspaper jobs in Corpus Christi and then in Austin, where, in 1955, he became associate editor of the sprightly new anomaly in the Texas of that era, a liberal weekly called the *Texas Observer*. Life in Austin in the mid-fifties, by all reports, was pleasant to the point of rapture. The small capital city of some 80,000 citizens had a legislature full of colorful solons and lobbyists, and it had a university growing in prestige. In such a stimulating atmosphere Brammer began to work on a novel called "The Heavy Honeyed Air," set in Austin. It never came together, though. It consisted of isolated pieces and somehow just didn't work.[12]

In 1955, too, the catalytic event in Brammer's life and work occurred: he joined the staff of Senator Lyndon B. Johnson and moved to Washington. The senator hired Nadine as well; hiring couples was a generous Johnsonian habit not without its benefits to the senator—his aides worked very long hours, and this way it was all in the family. Johnson's vitality energized Brammer, stimulated his imagination, led him to work assiduously on The Novel. Larry L. King remembers those days of intense creativity: "When we were young Capitol Hill flunkies together, Billie Lee wrote *The Gay Place* on candy bars and hot Jell-O water swigged from a milk bottle; he claimed the strange combination gave him 'energy rushes.' He obviously found stronger fuels later on, though I am convinced that in those distant days (1958–61) Billie Lee was no dopehead."[13]

In 1957 Brammer got a publisher's advance on the basis of "Country Pleasures," a short novel about a governor named Arthur Fenstemaker who visits a movie set in far West Texas, has a fling with a female aide, and dies in bed. The contract was intended to provide the means whereby Brammer would complete a longer novel about the governor. The result, in 1961, was *The Gay Place*. The title, of course, sounds faintly archaic now, the word "gay" having undergone a permanent sea change within just a few short years of the book's publication. The author's name on the title page is of interest, too. It read "William Brammer," an East Coast emendation of his Christian name, Billy Lee. A letter to Brammer from a Houghton Mifflin editor, Dorothy de Santillane, explained the company's position in detail:

> *No one, I repeat no one, up here thinks "Billy Lee" is possible. With all respect to your parents who gave it to you with such evident love (it is a very "loving" name) it has not the strength and authority for a novel which commands respect at the top of its voice.*
>
> *We are going to call it "by B. L. Brammer" and if we are asked we shall answer "Bill L. Brammer." This is official.*[14]

THE TEXAS LITERATI have made much of this change. William Broyles, the founding editor of *Texas Monthly*, for example, has remarked that he was "still Billy Lee, no matter if editors in Boston mistakenly believed that people named Billy Lee didn't write great books."[15] Yet in his signed articles for the *Texas Observer* he used the name Bill Brammer. The preference for "Billy Lee" seems at times something like inverse snobbery to claim him as even more of a down-home hipster with a good ol' boy name.

The title page bears a curious subtitle: "Being Three Related Novels *The Flea Circus, Room Enough to Caper, Country Pleasures*." The three novels involve the repetition of characters, settings, and themes. It is interesting that the publisher chose not to call it a trilogy, perhaps because trilogies typically appear in separate volumes (Dos Passos's *U.S.A.*, for example). Shrake has pointed out that if Brammer had published the novels separately, say two years apart, he "would have been a lot better known."[16] That way, he might more easily have had a career. Instead, everything was contained in one volume, making it difficult—indeed, as it turned out, impossible—for him to produce the next volume. There is something to this argument. Brammer's "second act," as Paul Cullum has called it, echoing Fitzgerald's famous remark about there being no second acts in American lives, never happened.[17]

After *The Gay Place* Brammer worked for *Time* magazine in 1960. He quit in 1961 to write full time and never held a permanent job again. In 1961 he and Nadine divorced, and in 1963 he married Dorothy Browne. Things looked very promising that year. Columbia Pictures announced plans to make a major film of the novel. Paul Newman would play Roy Sherwood and Jackie Gleason, Arthur Fenstemaker.[18] Eventually the project was abandoned, partly, it is thought, because of the ascension of Johnson to the presidency. That November of 1963 in Dallas, hours after the assassination, Brammer received offers to write magazine articles on the new president. A bit later he got an even better offer, a contract to do the first biography of Johnson. What writer, after all, knew LBJ better than Brammer? But it was not to be. The new president forbade access to Brammer, partly, everyone believes, because the first lady had read the book and was not amused. Johnson himself told Brammer that he had read a few pages and found it too dirty to continue, but there is no evidence that Johnson ever read a novel; he was too busy living one. In any event, the project was dead in the water.

All through the sixties and seventies, friends and admirers expected, hoped, prayed that Brammer would write another novel. And he worked on one for a long time. That, too, became part of his legend. The book was called "Fustian Days," but it never got beyond a mass of pages, revised endlessly, that was never shaped into a coherent whole. Larry McMurtry has claimed that the early sections of "Fustian Days" were the best thing Brammer had written but that the rest failed to sustain such promise.[19] Larry L. King reports that he read "perhaps 150 or 200 manuscript pages" of "Fustian Days" in 1964 and that they "bordered on the brilliant." [20]

The "Fustian Days" manuscripts survive today in the Southwestern Writers Collection at Southwest Texas State University. There are seven folders of material ranging from a few pages to several hundred.[21] Some sections are fairly clean, others are extensively revised; the sections overlap and repeat each other. But from what remains one can see something of Brammer's unfulfilled intentions. "Fustian Days" consists of three books: "Sonic Goddam Boom," "Secret Muzack" (alternately titled "Eatin' Little Babies"), and "And It Don't Hurt the Meat Much." They deal with the lives of Roy Sherwood and Neil Christiansen, the protagonists of the first and second books of *The Gay Place*, now living in Washington, D.C., and somewhat lost and directionless without the spirit of Arthur Fenstemaker to breathe life and purpose into them. A couple of passages are enough to suggest the self-conscious artistry that almost paralyzes the fragments. Brammer writes in one section:

> *We ought now to be getting round to the* story *part of this story: the real and human document part . . . complex, absorbing . . . leavened with symbol and the subtlest* ennui *. . . Before we are overrun with the dancing girls I thoughtfully contracted for earlier in the evening in behalf of those among us whose tastes might run to excess.* [22]

A page later in this prolonged meditation on style, he writes: "Wild prose, hah? I learned how, writing speeches for southern politicians, whose rhythms are unmatched in all of modern literature."[23]

There were other, far lesser fragments of unrealized efforts. "El End Zone," dated April 27, 1965, is a wild, obscene, gonzo-style interview of an author named Maelstrum (obviously Brammer himself) who at one point lists all the substances fit to smoke, inhale, or eat, beginning with pot and running through Seconal, cocaine, ether, "Elmer's goddam glue," and on and on. There is a one-page fragment titled "The Angst Book" or "Avez-vous Dexamyl?" There are aperçus scrawled on unmarked pages, of which this one is typical: "Absinthe Makes the Hard Grow Fonder."

No one was more aware of his problems as a writer than Brammer himself. He wrote King in 1968: "This is not another of them pleas begging assistance, so you should immediately relax the scrotum; lend some ease to your careworn sac. Which is not to deny the *need* for help, God wot: wise counsel or some new miracle drug or just maybe a plain unprettified boot in the arse: any old damn gesture is welcome currently." A few sentences later, he summed it all up: "Writing is just so murderously hard for me in recent years— unaccountably so—though my skull feels livelier than ever."[24] The anguished-artist thesis may be the correct explanation; on the other hand, perhaps not. At least one friend, Gary Cartwright, has argued that Brammer in some sense "chose" not to write the next novel, that he preferred "living" to writing and that "everyone who knew the man profited."[25] Perhaps Brammer himself made the best, most trenchant assessment of what happened, writing in 1976:

Bestowed from birth with a lucy-in-the-sky twinkle and irreverence for every thing, [I] bounced around the sub-culture after leaving LBJ, writing unfinished masterpieces by the score, ingesting hogsheads of drugs and acquiring a local image as the best approximation of guru and human wonder around. [26]

The wide-open counterculture enticements of the exploding sixties were irresistible to a bohemian, jazz-loving, methedrine-dependent intellectual of the fifties. The sixties promised everything, and Brammer went hog-wild in the decade of revolution. He got on Ken Kesey's bus and schlepped down to Mexico; he journeyed to San Francisco and Europe; he pursued drugs and women and had a long binge of it—in fact on into the next decade. And then, February 11, 1978, the clock ran down. His daughter Sidney, one of his three children to whom the novel is dedicated, remembers the day when she was called away from her classes on the University of Texas campus to claim the body of her father. He had died of an overdose in a ratty apartment where he was living at the time. His last job was as assistant hors d'oeuvre chef at the Driskill Hotel. It would cost about $3,000 for the funeral, and so far as Sidney knew, her father was penniless. She didn't know where the cash would come from to pay the undertaker. But Brammer had provided in a manner that any novelist would appreciate. He had tucked away $3,000—just enough to cover the funeral costs—in the toe of one of his boots.[27]

The Gay Place is the most famous roman à clef in Texas writing. That may not be saying very much, but in Texas it matters. Or it used to. Willie Morris, author of a brilliant Texas book himself, *North toward Home*, has amusingly recounted his experience upon seeing himself in the pages of his friend's novel:

> He had this protagonist, Willie England, and I had just returned from England. And he was the editor of a small weekly literary/political journal, in the unidentified capital of the largest state in the Southwest— and I had just taken over the Observer. And I said, "Billy Lee, at least Thomas Wolfe changed the names and addresses."[28]

With the passage of time, however, the identities of the actual people grow dim. The most famous roman à clef in American writing is *The Sun Also Rises*, yet today only specialists know the names of the actual people out of whom Hemingway fashioned Lady Brett Ashley, Robert Cohn, and all the rest. In this case, one towering presence comes alive off the page in a novel replete with the people in Brammer's life: Arthur "Goddam" Fenstemaker, perhaps the best portrait yet of the *personality* of Lyndon B. Johnson, the larger-than-life figure who intrigued, beguiled, and dominated Brammer's imagination until finally Brammer understood the man in a way that biographers such as Robert Caro seem not to have.

Although it has been widely assumed that LBJ was the sole impetus behind the creation of Fenstemaker, the character may be more of an amalgam than previously recognized. Two real-life political figures have been suggested: Earl Long, Louisiana's colorful governor whose sexual hijinks with stripper Blaze Starr were widely reported in the mid-1950s,[29] and Beauford Jester, governor of Texas from 1946 until 1949.[30] The only Texas governor to die in office, Jester succumbed on a train on July 11, 1949, in circumstances closely resembling those surrounding the death of Fenstemaker in *The Gay Place*. Other characters based upon real-life prototypes include Sweet Mama Fenstemaker, a weak satirical picture of Lady Bird; Hoot Gibson Fenstemaker, a right-on depiction of LBJ's brother-in-the-shadows, Sam Houston Johnson; Jay McGown, Brammer himself; Ouida, Nadine; and so on, right on down to the children. Several liberal politicians of the era have been nominated as the basis for Roy Sherwood, but one leading candidate, Bob Eckhardt, former liberal congressman from Houston, disavows such identifications: "There's not much of me in there, and I knew Brammer pretty well."[31] Malcolm McGregor, former member of the House from El Paso, is another figure thought by many to be represented in the novel.[32] There can be no doubt, however, about the authenticity of the meeting place in the novel where liberals, lobbyists, and university professors gather to talk and drink. The beer garden dubbed the Dearly Beloved Beer and Garden Party in the novel is a meticulous rendering of the site and ambience of Scholz Garten, the famous old German watering hole on San Jacinto Street in easy walking distance of the capitol and the university.

As to the novel's dependence upon facticity of time and place, Nadine Eckhardt has commented, "Every time I read *The Gay Place* I can't believe how much he got in there. He used *everything*."[33] Nadine plans to write her own memoirs of that period. About the fifties there is this to be said: There is a secret, as yet unwritten, history of the remarkable women of that era, bright and talented women, who came to maturity before the women's movement and who often gave up even the idea of a career for the sake of husbands who lived, as the saying goes, in a man's world.

The Gay Place is also a what-if novel that asks the question, What if LBJ had been the governor of Texas? In retrospect, the governorship looks like small potatoes to a man whose ambition was always national. Johnson never aspired to be governor. During the Eisenhower era, the governor of Texas was Allan Shivers, a *Democrat* who supported Dwight D. Eisenhower, not Adlai Stevenson, in both 1952 and 1956. For this and other sins imputed to him, he was the bête noire of Texas liberals in the fifties. The liberal hero, Ralph Yarborough, was never able to be elected governor, so Brammer made it up: he elected LBJ in the province of his mind and set him at work upon the lives and imaginations of a handful of penny-ante state politicians. The result is a portrait of Johnson that is profoundly true in two respects. Brammer, better than anybody, captures the style and humor of LBJ as well as the authenticity of his commitment to social and economic justice.

The first words uttered by Arthur Fenstemaker evoke the LBJ persona. The governor, like Johnson an inveterate telephonist, rings up Roy Sherwood and identifies himself as Arthur "Goddam" Fenstemaker. Immediately the governor invites Roy to come to the mansion and "break watermelon" with him. It's LBJ to the *n*th. Fenstemaker's name, incidentally, has provoked some interesting commentary. Lon Tinkle, a well-known Southwestern book reviewer of the day, thought the name meant "fence-mender,"[34] which is plausible, but Al Reinert, a journalist and friend of Brammer's, convincingly argues that the word derives from the German "window-maker," meaning illusionist or visionary.[35] Throughout the three novels Fenstemaker speaks in the unmistakable rhythms and tones of a word-drunk Southern politician, a consummate rhetorician who is half-Isaiah and half skirt-chasing egomaniac. From many wonderful examples of Fenstemaker as master politician, this one stands out. The governor is explaining his theory of politics:

> *"You want to overturn the existin' institution, that's fine. But you got to be sure you know how to build a better one. The thing to do is work* through *the institution—figure a way to do that—to make a change and build a city and save the goddam world from collapse. You got to*

work through that institution, Roy . . ." Then he leaned back and flashed his shark's smile, saying, "An' I'm that institution currently . . ."

This is Fenstemaker/LBJ, the arm-twisting, snake-charming, "cornpone Buddha," the ultimate wheeler-dealer. But there is another side of Johnson that Brammer also captures better than just about anybody. This is Johnson the liberal, the genuine post–New Dealer who wants to improve people's lives and economic conditions. In the novel, Fenstemaker expresses real concern over such issues as integration and education. In the opening chapter he asks his Negro butler if things are getting any better for his people. And he means it. He energizes Roy Sherwood into passing an education bill. It's a part-way measure, and the pure liberal ideologues denounce him for it, but, like LBJ, Fenstemaker is a half-a-loaf politician.

The sincerity of Johnson's interest in improving the lot of down-and-out Texans is something that Brammer is very convincing about. A little-known radio speech that Congressman Johnson gave in 1938 sheds some light on the accuracy of Brammer's portrait. "Tarnish on the Violet Crown," it was called, an interesting title since Austin had been dubbed "the City of the Violet Crown" since the 1890s, owing to the twilight coloration of the hills surrounding the city beside the Colorado River. O. Henry is credited with coining the phrase. Anyway, here is Johnson in 1938:

> *Last Christmas, when all over the world people were celebrating the birth of the Christ child, I took a walk here in Austin—a short walk, just a few blocks from Congress Avenue, and there I found people living in such squalor that Christmas Day was to them just one more day of filth and misery. Forty families on one lot, using one water faucet. Living in barren one-room huts, they were deprived of the glory of sunshine in the daytime, and were so poor they could not even at night use the electricity that is to be generated by our great river. Here the men and women did not play at Santa Claus. Here the children were so much in need of the*

very essentials of life that they scarcely missed the added pleasures of our Christian celebration.

I found one family that might be called typical. Living within one dreary room, where no single window let in the beneficent sunlight, and where not even the smallest vagrant breeze brought them relief in the hot summer—here they slept, here they cooked and ate, here they washed themselves in a leaky tin tub after carrying the water for 100 yards. Here they brought up their children ill-nourished and amid sordid surroundings. And on this Christmas morning there was no Santa Claus for the 10 children, all under 10 years old, who scrambled around the feet of a wretched mother bent over her washtub, while in this same room her husband, and the father of the brood, lay ill with an infectious disease. [36]

A staff writer for the congressman probably wrote this piece (Brammer, after all, years later, answered personal family correspondence for Johnson when he worked on his staff), but no matter: it came out under Johnson's name; it expressed his sentiments. The 1938 radio address contained the essential premises of the Great Society, Johnson's sixties updating of Rooseveltian liberal policies. Brammer saw and understood this side of Johnson in the fifties when many other liberals did not. Ronnie Dugger, for example, held a quite different view of Johnson. Writing of Brammer's novel in 1966, Dugger remarks,

From reading an early version of some of the book I knew I would resent Bill's politics in the novel—both his contempt for the Texas liberals, so many of whom I knew to be people I would go to the wall with, and his adulation, a kind of disillusioned hero worship, of his Lyndon Johnson figure, Governor Fenstemaker, with whom I would not. [37]

As a novelist, not an ideologue, Brammer sought to capture the whole complex personality of Johnson. A 1957 memo from Brammer to Senator Johnson suggests the measure of his admiration: "Your strength, as always, again emerges from a joint mutual admiration society: Classic liberals and classic conservatives who can recognize a man for his abilities and honesty rather than whether he fits the mold of their own partisan views."[38] In any case, he got more of Johnson into his novel than many biographers have been able to.[39]

The roots of Brammer's conception of Texas and how it might be corraled in fiction can be glimpsed in the pages of the *Texas Observer*, the liberal weekly founded by Ronnie Dugger in 1955 and for which Brammer wrote a number of pieces in those exciting mid-years of the decade. Typical *Observer* articles dealt with social and political themes of the day: "Negroes Still Take a Back Seat," "Shivers Backs Ban on Integration," "Our Separate But Unequal Schools—Negro Facilities Lag in Some Serious Ways," "Negro Boy Murdered in East Texas," "A Teacher Views Our Schools' Shortcomings—Sees Wasted Time, Effort, Money, Talent, Intelligence," "The Slums of Texas," and "Forgotten Texas—Our Aged Citizens Are in Poverty and Filth." Segregation, Education, and Poverty were central to the liberal agenda, and each finds its way into the texture of *The Gay Place*, which is sometimes wrongly described as a novel about the ultra-rich or "Super-Americans," the title of John Bainbridge's 1961 book about Texas.

The *Observer* was as interested in the powerful as in those without power and frequently ran knowing articles on the inner workings of the political process. In May 1955, for example, Ronnie Dugger produced a long article titled "Austin Lobbyists at Work—They Inform, Squire, Cajole, and Bribe." At one point he quotes a state senator who sounds as though he stepped out of the pages of *The Gay Place*: "Where's a goddamn lobbyist? I want somebody to pick up the check for my hotel bill, you can't find one around here."[40] In another anecdote Dugger tells of four members of the House who spent an evening dining and drinking at a private club and cheerfully allowed a lobbyist to pick up the tab—a grand total of $20. The earnest young liberals of the *Observer* staff seem to have been fascinated with the simple, eternal fact that people in power enjoy using other people's money and that lobbyists are by nature engaged in precisely this most predictable of transactions.

Brammer himself wrote a series of articles devoted to explaining/exposing another invisible influence-peddling connection, the activities of behind-the-scenes political operatives. "The Political Hucksters—'Hit 'Em Where They Live' " (May 9, 1955) dealt with power brokers such as "Phil Fox, the king of the political hucksters of Texas." This article also records an incident in Dallas in which Barefoot Sanders, a liberal member of the Texas House, was accosted by an opponent denouncing him as a Communist and Sanders engaged the man in a fistfight. This incident seems to underlie the sequence in "Room Enough to Caper" when Neil Christiansen physically removes his red-baiting opponent from a political banquet. Brammer also reported on the visits of the most powerful man in the U.S. Senate to his home state. "The Senator at His Precincts" (May 9, 1956) described Lyndon B. Johnson's convincing grass-roots persona at a precinct meeting in Johnson City; "Lyndon Comes Home" (August 24, 1955) described Johnson's loss of weight and fragile appearance following a heart attack; and "Pow-Wow on the Pedernales" (October 5, 1955) offered an insider's view of a political strategy meeting held at the Johnson ranch.

The *Observer* had broader cultural interests as well. Issues in those years were as apt to carry a review of an international work like Simone de Beauvoir's novel *The Mandarins* as of something more locally resonant like Stanley Walker's *Home to Texas*. There were finely honed naturalistic slice-of-life stories about life among working-class Texans, such as Winston Bode's "South San Antonio" (November 21, 1956) and "The Shearers" (November 28, 1956). And there were many pieces that dealt with literary issues pertaining to the Southwest.

In a biting review of a novel about Texas by an "outsider," Robert Wilder's *The Wine of Youth*, Dugger deplored the errors, the reliance upon gross, exaggerated stereotypes, and the general absurdity of passages such as the following, which describes a supposedly typical Texas social event:

Someone would say let's have a barbecue. The next thing they would be on their way to a ranch a hundred or so miles distant, halting to send telegrams to friends in New York, California, Dallas, Houston, Fort Worth, Beaumont, telling them to hurry on over and eat a piece of meat. Since everyone in Texas knows everyone else, the barbecue might last for weeks.[41]

Dugger denounced such treatment as "inept and inaccurate nonsense." Here was a phony, outsized Texas that had nothing to do with the diverse and complex state that he and Brammer were exploring in their journalism.

Brammer, perhaps inspired by the fact that Warner Bros. was filming *Giant* at Marfa, reviewed Edna Ferber's 1952 best-seller, the most famous outsider Texas novel of the era. In "On Rereading 'Giant'" (July 4, 1955) he declared the novel "richly-conceived and rottenly written" and went on to complain of Ferber's distortions: "Instead of portraying Texas as proud, primitive, super-patriots obsessed with sheer bigness and magnitude, which many of us are, she made us out as oil-rich robber barons and feudal lords, buffoons and mountebanks, which, it is hoped, few of us are." Brammer ended his reflections by taking up the question of what the modern Texas novel should be. He cited the recent observations of Harrison Smith, a *Saturday Review* editor, who suggested at a conference in Corpus Christi that Texas fiction had typically dealt with either a mixed population or the very wealthy and called for a writer to deal with "middleclassers who have come from other places." Brammer agreed and concluded: "These are the people who make up the state of mind that is Texas. Miss Ferber failed to sense this. Perhaps the next novelist will."[42]

The next novelist, it seems, was waiting in the wings. His name was William, Billy Lee, Bill Brammer. We know little about the genesis of that first novel, "Country Pleasures." But again the pages of the *Observer* offer clues. Around the same time that he reread Ferber, he visited the set of *Giant* in Marfa and wrote an account of his observations. Most of what he reported in "A Circus Breaks Down on the

Prairie" (July 4, 1955) appears in the opening pages of "Country Pleasures." The article begins with a description of the eye-catching false-front Victorian house constructed by the film company:

> *Some miles out from town, south on Highway 67, there looms large on the horizon a macabre structure which should remain for years a curiosity for West Texas cattle and cowpokes. Sticking starkly out of the prairies is a three-storied Victorian mansion, all gingerbread and lightning rods, rococo and utterly inelegant.*[43]

In the novel the Governor's party first glimpses the house in a passage that owes much to the original journalistic description: "Everyone strained to catch sight of the prefabricated Victorian mansion towering above the floor of the ranchland. The mansion loomed on the horizon like a great landlocked whale, gingerbread bas-relief against the backdrop of bleached dune and mountain and gunmetal sky." Other details in the *Observer* article are woven into the scene in the novel. Brammer reports that the local grass was sprayed with green dye to make it greener, and in the novel the viewpoint character, Jay McGown, the Governor's aide, cries: "They even dyed the grass green near the mansion. . . . It wouldn't respond to the water they piped in, so they dyed it green." Another detail that fascinated Brammer the reporter was trucks full of tumbleweed imported from California. In the novel these details are set forth by the Governor's colorful brother, Hoot Gibson Fenstemaker. His explanation of how the tumbleweed will be made to perform is a good example of Brammer's perfect-pitch dialogue: "It don't tumble. . . . Even when there's a good wind. It just don't tumble. So they brought out some big blowers—big 'lectric fans—to make the tumbleweed tumble when they shoot the moom pitcher." Curiously, Brammer's central image for describing the spectacle of the movie company that gave the article its title is shifted to another subject in the novel. In the article Brammer writes: "It's as if a vast, traveling circus has broken down in the midst of this desolation and set up shop for some kind of performance." In the novel the circus description applies to the college attended by Jay McGown and his ex-wife, the blonde bombshell Vicki McGown: " . . . you could have mistaken it for a great, shapeless circus that had somehow broken down on the edge of the city."

Clearly the trip to Marfa and the visit to the set of *Giant* stimulated Brammer's creative imagination, as he set to work on "Country Pleasures." There is another tantalizing possibility about the sources of his plot idea of placing the governor in the midst of a Hollywood crowd. There was an immediate precedent for this in real life. That same year, 1955, Governor Allan Shivers appeared in a Paramount production titled *Lucy Gallant*. Toward the end of the film Governor Shivers introduces the title character, played by Jane Wyman, to an audience assembled to see a Neiman Marcus–like style show. Brammer would likely have known about this film, and in any case he certainly could have read Dan Strawn's tongue-in-cheek review, "A Gallant in 'Gallant,' " which appeared in the *Observer* in November 1955. There is one odd echo of the Shivers business in the novel. The character who directs the film, based on George Stevens, who also appears in the circus article under his real name, in the novel is named Edmund Shavers.

Brammer's novel remains interesting on both the regional and the national level. In the Southwest it occupies an important space in the emergence of contemporary fiction set in the region. Published the same year as Larry McMurtry's *Horseman, Pass By* and one year after John Graves's *Goodbye to a River*, it did not, however, reap local rewards. Both Graves and McMurtry received cash prizes from the Texas Institute of Letters. Brammer, in fact, lost out to his friend, McMurtry. The three books and their takes on Texas are most instructive. Graves's book is a nonfiction narrative in the elegant folksy mode favored by J. Frank Dobie. Old-time Texans loved the book, and still do. Part elegy, part wry comedy, and part high pontification, *Goodbye to a River* is the culmination of the Dobie-Webb-Bedichek evocation of a pastoral past in decline.

McMurtry's novel is also elegiac. Its portrait of the old cattle-man Homer Bannon, whose values derive from the land and are founded on the old West Texas Protestant virtues of work, thrift and possession of cattle and land, has a deliberate end-of-an-era tone. In McMurtry's rancherly allegory, Hud, the hard-driving, hard-drinking, hard-everything stepson, is supposed to stand for an unprincipled modern generation that has replaced love for the land with lust for money, women, and oil. Between them, observing, appraising, judging, is the adolescent narrator, Lonnie Bannon, the sensitive youth, the proto-English major. *Horseman, Pass By* contains some brilliant writing and is the first believable account of a Texas male adolescent in Texas writing. (Katherine Anne Porter's Miranda stories, written in the mid-thirties, are the first great portrait of coming of age in Texas, a fact ignored, however, by both Dobie and McMurtry, between them the two chief progenitors of the patriarchal legend of Texas.)

Dobie admired Graves's book but had deep reservations about those of McMurtry and Brammer. Though he found McMurtry's portrait of the old cowman "good in places," he judged McMurtry overall as lacking in "ripeness."[44] (McMurtry was twenty-four at the time.) Of Brammer's book, however, Dobie had nothing good to say. He inscribed his overall assessment in the flyleaf of his copy:

> *Not a character in the thick novel who is not cheap. Some talk about what a great man Governor Fenstemaker is, but he never appears more than an astute fixer, babbling now & then a good phrase. We are in the middle of politics for 175,000 words and nobody actually every* [sic] *does anything but drink and drink & drink to boredom & screw, & screw & screw to death—the great governor's climax. I expected satire, inside views & a little wisdom at least. Bill Brammer has been with Senator Lyndon Johnson for some time.*[45]

Thus the official voice of Texas literary judgment. Dobie said much the same thing about Edwin Shrake's *But Not for Love* (1964), an urban novel inspired by Brammer. "Over drinking of everything but water. Pages & pages of talk that reveal nothing but more drinking, more smoking [sic?], mere facility on part of the author, no character development, no integration with plot."[46] In such reactions it is not easy to tell whether the basis of Dobie's dislike is primarily aesthetic—thus the complaints about length and lack of conciseness—or moral—the degenerate (or is it merely modern?) conduct of the characters.

The Graves and McMurtry books inhabit Nostalgia Ville: a river, a ranch. But not *The Gay Place*. Brammer's vision of Texas is urban, and in this conception lies one of the important insights the novel has to offer. Typically it is Fenstemaker who makes the point. He is fulminating against a right-wing red-baiting McCarthyite: " . . . what he doesn't know is that most of us came into town one Saturday a few years ago and stayed . . . We're urban, by God. All of a sudden the people in the metropolitan areas outnumber the rednecks . . . They come into town—they buy little houses and color television and Volkswagen cars." This is new Texas, ca. 1958, and Brammer's novel accurately predicts the continuing urbanization of the state so that by now, in the mid-nineties, the demographics are around 82 percent living in cities and suburbs—urban, by God.

Brammer's novel is also topographically all-encompassing. Its famous opening pages reveal a helicopter-like survey of the variousness and immensity of the Texas landscape. Texas as a transitional region of Gulf coastal lands, Deep South–like pine forests, rocky Hill Country, and Western prairie and grazing lands are all caught in the zoom lens of the pictorial imagination. But mostly, Texas is urban in the post–WWII era, and Brammer was the first powerful novelist to make this claim. (There had been earlier Texas urban novels, for example, Philip Atlee's *The Inheritors* [1940], and George Williams's *The Blind Bull* [1952], but none had anywhere near the impact of *The Gay Place* upon aspiring young writers.)

Early in Chapter 1 Brammer detaches his novel from the agrarian tradition. Roy Sherwood wakes up in his car with a hangover. (Most of the characters in the novel have hangovers most of the time.) Groggy but in good spirits, he first hears, then sees, a family of Mexican American migrant workers. This family's relation to the land is itself modern in a literary sense, as they are no landholding farm family with roots in the nostalgic legend of agrarian Texas. And they quickly disappear in this novel, which moves on to its real subject—urban people and political power, not land.

At the national level, beyond Texas, *The Gay Place* is a searching and reflective document of America in the fifties. Brammer touches upon many of the dominant themes of the era, including the conflicts in ending segregation, the role of money and influence in government, and the Cold War atmosphere of lingering McCarthyism. Brammer's fifties are recognizably those of stereotype and legend: an era of comfortable if not bloated affluence, a sense of American power at the apex of its arc, a nation at peace. It is also an era of political quiescence, of liberal paralysis, of what Brammer called, in an *Observer* piece in 1961, "the apathetic conditions that obtained overall." Looking back at the impact of the *Observer* under the leadership of Ronnie Dugger, Brammer characterized the era in extremely negative terms:

> *Dugger and the Observer survive, and the revolution is on the record for all to see, obvious to anyone who remembers how it was in Texas during that hysterical, No-Think half decade of the early Fifties—our own mid-century Inquisition—when nearly everyone lay torpid and uncomplaining in the clutch of the Peckerwood and the Ignoranti.*[47]

"Our Hookworm Belt complacencies," he called the era in another piquant phrase from that article.

At the same time Brammer captures hints of cultural change ahead. Hipsters and politicians talk of Zen and Buddhism and existentialism and jazz. There is a sense of imminent cultural revolution waiting just 'round the corner. Brammer knew what his old friend David Halberstam has recently shown in his book *The Fifties*, that the Eisenhower era was a lot more complex and interesting than retro television sitcoms would suggest. In "Room Enough to Caper," he also proved prophetic. This story of a young man with good looks, intellectual savoir faire, and excellent political instincts—in short, a great campaigner in the coming telegenic age—is ahead of its time. Not until the Robert Redford film *The Candidate* would there be as searching a study of the politician as hollow man, a man capable of winning elections but without any sustaining vision, without any reason or motive to serve beyond ego satisfaction.

Narratively, too, Brammer's book reached far beyond Texas for its models. Brammer was extremely well read. It is hard to imagine another Texas novelist of the period leading off a book with a beautifully apt quotation from Ford Madox Ford's *The Good Soldier*. Though the novel is often compared with Robert Penn Warren's *All the King's Men*, its narrative procedure derives not from Warren's first-person, tough-guy vernacular but from classical American social realism, the rhythms of F. Scott Fitzgerald, whom Brammer deeply admired, Fitzgerald in turn deriving in part from Edith Wharton and Henry James, novelists who sought to express the manners and morals of the day. In "Room Enough to Caper" and "Country Pleasures" Brammer also incorporates Joycean interior monologue (probably filtered through William Styron's *Lie Down in Darkness*), something else that sets him apart from regional writing of the period. There are stream-of-consciousness sequences in both of these books. There is also a rich allusiveness, from Dave Brubeck to George Orwell to the Bible. Much of Fenstemaker's memorable talk derives from the cadences of Isaiah. Brammer is on record about this influence, remarking in 1961, "The only researching I did for the novels was a re-reading of the Old Testament (in its old-style prose) and I've never enjoyed anything more."[48]

The most important literary source is T. S. Eliot. The interior monologue section of "Room Enough to Caper," for example, elides the young senator's voice with Eliot's vacillating, indecisive Prufrock and the novel's full-throttled man of action, Arthur Fenstemaker:

> *Am no presiding officer.*
> *Wasn't meant to be.*
> *I'm the goddam* Prince*! An easy tool.*

Other specific Eliotic echoes from "The Love Song of J. Alfred
Prufrock" include "I grow old" in one of Neil's self-reflective moments and "all those scattered buttends" in Sarah Lehman's stream-
of-consciousness reverie in Chapter 15 of "Country Pleasures,"
which recalls Prufrock's "all the butt-ends of my days and ways."
Unmistakable also, and very funny, is the actor Greg Calhoun's pas-
tiche of Eliot's "I will show you fear in a handful of dust" in "Country Pleasures" (which title in turn derives from one of Eliot's favorite
poets, John Donne.) In the actor's hands the famous line from *The
Waste Land* becomes, "I will show you death in a handful of bust."

More importantly than these verbal echoes, the method of *The
Waste Land* informs *The Gay Place*. Like many post–*Waste Land* novelists, Brammer adopted the mythic method (which Eliot in turn
seems to have taken over from Joyce's *Ulysses*.) Put simply, the author underpins the narrative with a mythic substructure, playing off
the present against the past. "Room Enough to Caper" makes the
most abundant use of the method, as protagonist Neil *Christian*sen
returns home at age thirty-three, at Easter time, to face a crisis of
personal belief. Should he run for the Senate or not? Does he believe in anything or not? At one point he ponders Christ's passion:
"They just didn't make passion like that any more. He tried to remember the last time he'd seen real passion, but nothing came to
him. It was all a cheap imitation, a fraudulent compound of polemic, spleen, and seasons of rut." Filled with indecisiveness, he
thinks at one point: "If I could read that script I just might walk
on the goddam water." Here one of Jesus' miracles is layered with
Fenstemaker's signature blasphemy. Later Neil thinks of himself as
a "dime store Jesus." The whole Christian subtext is summed up in
Neil's brother's meditation on God in our time, quoting from an
unidentified source: "Some lines came to him . . . 'For anyone alone
and without God and without a master, the weight of days is dread-

ful. Hence, one must choose a master, God being out of style . . .' "
If *The Gay Place* has a god, it is Fenstemaker, but he proves a completely secular deity, one unable even to save himself from perdition and destruction, no matter how much Isaiah he quotes.

Like the best of novels, *The Gay Place* captures its own era and speaks to our own in rhythms that we remember.

> *Don Graham*
> *J. Frank Dobie Regents Professor*
> *The University of Texas*

Notes

* I wish to thank the University Research Institute of the University of Texas for a grant that supported my work on this essay. My thanks also to Nadine Eckhardt for granting permission to quote from the Brammer Collection of the Southwestern Writers Collection at Southwest Texas State University; to Dick Holland, director of the Southwestern Writers Collection, for help provided by him and his fine staff, and to Winston Bode for some excellent oral history research.

1. For an interesting account of these two authors' lives, see John Leggett, *Ross and Tom: Two American Tragedies* (New York, 1974). Reviewer Garrett Epps has cited resemblances between Brammer and Malcolm Lowry, in "Deep in the Heart of Texas," *Washington Post Book World*, February 4, 1979; clipping file, Southwestern Writers Collection, Southwest Texas State University, hereafter SWWC.

2. Quoted on jacket of *The Gay Place* (New York: Random House Vintage, 1983).

3. Larry L. King, *None But a Blockhead: On Being a Writer* (New York: Penguin Books, 1987), p. 252.

4. Paul Cullum, "Billy Lee Brammer and the Second Act," *Austin Chronicle*, March 16, 1993, p. 22.

5. Ibid.

6. Ibid.

7. Joe Frolik, "Author Dies Money Poor, Friend Rich," *Austin American-Statesman*, February 14, 1978, clipping file, Center for American History, University of Texas.

8. King, p. 252.

9. Willie Morris, "Billy Lee Brammer, 1929–78," *Texas Observer*, March 3, 1978, clipping file, Center for American History.

10. Kaye Northcott, "Billy Lee Brammer, 1929–78," *Texas Observer*, March 3, 1978, clipping file, Center for American History.

11. Gary Cartwright, "Billy Lee Brammer, 1929–78," *Texas Observer*, March 3, 1978, clipping file, Center for American History.

12. Al Reinert, Introduction to *The Gay Place* (Austin: Texas Monthly Press, 1978), p. xiii.

13. King, p. 252.

14. Dorothy de Santillane to Bill Brammer, June 3, 1960. SWWC.

15. William Broyles, Foreword to *The Gay Place* (Austin: Texas Monthly Press, 1978), p. i.

16. Quoted in Frolik.

17. Cullum, p. 20.

18. "Filming of Texas Movie to Be Started at Austin," *Houston Chronicle*, February 10, 1963. Clipping file, Center for American History. Brammer's daughters Shelby and Sidney coauthored a screenplay adaptation of their father's novel, "Come and Join the Dance," in 1988. A copy is contained in the Brammer Collection, SWWC.

19. Quoted in Reinert, p. xxv.

20. King, p. 252.

21. There is also another manuscript of "Fustian Days," consisting of 275 pages, in private hands. Cullum, p. 22.

22. Untitled ms., p. 16, folder 9, SWWC.

23. Ibid., p. 17.

24. Bill Brammer to Larry L. King, August 23, 1986. Quoted in King, pp. 253–254.

25. Cartwright, "Billy Lee Brammer, 1929–78."

26. Brammer papers, SWWC.

27. Sidney Brammer, interview with Don Graham, April 7, 1986, Austin, Texas.

28. Dave McNeeley, "The Courting of Willie Morris," *Austin American-Statesman*, November 15, 1983, p. 9. Ronnie Dugger has also been identified as a prototype for Willie England. About this Dugger has written, "I knew

my friend Bill had a character in there named Willie England that the Guessers of Who said was either Willie Morris or me or each and both of us" ("Observations," *Texas Observer*, November 11, 1966, p. 11).

29. Nadine Eckhardt emphasizes the dominant influence of LBJ but also says that Brammer was very interested in stories about Earl Long that surfaced during those years. Interview with Don Graham, September 12, 1994. Jay Milner, a journalist and friend of Brammer's, reports that Brammer claimed to have "based the Fenstemaker character as much on Louisiana Gov. Earl Long as LBJ, but it is generally assumed that LBJ was his primary model." "Austin Writer Never Followed Up on Success of 'Gay Place,'" *Houston Chronicle*, March 6, 1968, sec. 8, p. 8.

30. Journalist Anita Walker Howard, who worked with Brammer on the *Austin Statesman*, says that Brammer repeatedly told her that Fenstemaker was based on Beauford Jester, citing particularly the parallel deaths. Interview with Don Graham, September 12, 1994.

31. Jan Reid, "Last of a Breed," *Texas Monthly*, May 1994, p. 52.

32. Winston Bode discusses this possibility in his newsletter, *Austin Ear* (September 30, 1993), p. 2.

33. Cullum, p. 20.

34. Lon Tinkle, "New Novel by Texan Lampoons Politicos," *Dallas Morning News*, March 5, 1961, clipping file, Center for American History.

35. Reinert, p. xiv.

36. Lyndon B. Johnson, "Tarnish on the Violet Crown," radio address, December 25, 1938, Center for American History.

37. Ronnie Dugger, "Observations," *Texas Observer*, November 11, 1966, p. 11.

38. Bill Brammer, Memorandum to Senator Johnson, May 11, 1956, p. 4, Lyndon B. Johnson Library, University of Texas.

39. In a survey of books about LBJ, Larry L. King has claimed that Brammer's novel is "the best book about Lyndon B. Johnson." "Lyndon Johnson in Literature," *New Republic*, August 3, 1968, p. 30.

40. Ronnie Dugger, "Austin Lobbyists at Work—They Inform, Squire, Cajole, and Bribe," *Texas Observer*, May 23, 1955, p. 2.

41. Ronnie Dugger, "Wilder's South Texas—Novel Teaches Little about Ourselves," *Texas Observer*, July 13, 1955, p. 6.

42. B.B., "On Rereading 'Giant'—'Enormous,' But 'Incredible,'" *Texas Observer*, July 4, 1955, p. 7. The debate about what Texas literature should strive to be was continued that summer in an article by John Igo. "South-

western Novels—Our Writing Lacks Something—But What Is It?" *Texas Observer*, August 3, 1955, p. 6. Igo concluded that "a southwestern story to our way of thinking must use the two cultures here (side by side or merged) as a background for those things which could happen only where these two cultures [Anglo and Hispanic] meet."

43. Bill Brammer, "A Circus Breaks Down on the Prairie," *Texas Observer*, July 4, 1955, p. 4.

44. Quoted in Don Graham, "J. Frank Dobie: A Reappraisal," *Southwestern Historical Quarterly* 92, no. 1 (July 1988): 7.

45. Ibid., p. 6.

46. Ibid., p. 7.

47. B.B., "A Personal Reminiscence," *Texas Observer*, August 25, 1961, p. 6.

48. Untitled article, *Dallas Times*, March 19, 1961, clipping file, Center for American History.

The Flea Circus

"What matters it how far we go?"
    his scaly friend replied,
"There is another shore, you know,
    upon the other side.
The farther off from England,
    the nearer is to France;
Then turn not pale, beloved snail,
    but come and join the dance."

— The Lobster Quadrille

"I don't want the old blues to die because if
they do I'll be dead, too, because that's the
only kind I can play and sing and I love the
old style."

—Big Bill Broonzy

One

THE COUNTRY is most barbarously large and final. It is too much country — boondock country — alternately drab and dazzling, spectral and remote. It is so wrongfully muddled and various that it is difficult to conceive of it as all of a piece. Though it begins simply enough, as a part of the other.

It begins, very like the other, in an ancient backwash of old dead seas and lambent estuaries, around which rise cypress and cedar and pine thickets hung with spiked vines and the cheerless festoons of Spanish moss. Farther on, the earth firms: stagnant pools are stirred by the rumble of living river, and the mild ferment of bottomland dissolves as the country begins to reveal itself in the vast hallucination of salt dome and cotton row, tree farm and rice field and irrigated pasture and the flawed dream of the cities. And away and beyond, even farther, the land continues to rise, as on a counterbalance with the water tables, and then the first faint range of the West comes into view: a great serpentine escarpment, changing colors with the hours, with the seasons, hummocky and soft-shaped at one end, rude and wind-blasted at the other, blue and green, green and gray and dune-colored, a staggered faultline extending hundreds of miles north and south.

This range is not so high as it is sudden and aberrant, a disorder in the even westerly roll of the land. One could not call it mountain, but it is a considerable hill, or set of hills, and here again the country is transformed. The land rises steeply beyond the first escarpment and everything is changed: texture, configuration, blistered façade, all of it warped and ruptured and bruise-colored. The few rivers run deep, like old wounds, boiling round the fractures and revealing folds of slate and shell and glittering blue limestone, spilling back and across and out of the hills toward the lower country.

The city lies against and below two short spiny ribs of hill. One of the little rivers runs round and about, and from the hills it is possible to view the city overall and draw therefrom an impression of sweet curving streets and graceful sweeping lawns and the unequivocally happy sound of children always at play. Closer on, the feeling is only partly confirmed, though it should seem enough to have even a part. It is a pleasant city, clean and quiet, with wide rambling walks and elaborate public gardens and elegant old homes faintly ruined in the shadow of arching poplars. Occasionally through the trees, and always from a point of higher ground, one can see the college tower and the Capitol building. On brilliant mornings the white sandstone of the tower and the Capitol's granite dome are joined for an instant, all pink and cream, catching the first light.

On a midsummer morning not very long ago the sun advanced on the city and lit the topmost spines of hill, painting the olive drab slopes in crazy new colors, like the drawing of a spangled veil. Then the light came closer, touching the tall buildings and the fresh-washed streets. The nearly full-blown heat came with it, quick and palpitant. It was close to being desert heat: sudden, emphatic, dissolving chill and outdistancing rain . . .

It was neither first light nor early heat that caused the two politicians to come struggling up from sleep at that hour, but an old truck carrying migratory cotton pickers.

The younger of the two politicians was named Roy Sherwood, and he lay twisted sideways in the front seat of an automobile that was parked out front of an all-night supermarket. Arthur Fenstemaker, the other one, the older one, floundered in his bed-covers a few blocks distant in the Governor's mansion.

The old truck banged along the streets, past dazzling store fronts and the Juicy Pig Stand and the marble façades of small banks in which deposits were insured to ten thousand dollars. The dozen children in the back of the truck had been first to come awake. They pulled aside the canvas flaps and peered out at the city, talking excitedly, whooping and hee-hawing as the old truck rolled north, straining, toward the Capitol grounds and the Governor's mansion, where Arthur Fenstemaker slept, and the supermarket where Roy Sherwood's car was parked.

The truck came to a sudden stop and began, with a terrible moaning of gears and transmission, to back into a parking space next to Roy Sherwood's car.

Roy heard the commotion and blinked his sore eyes in the early light. He struggled to untangle his long legs from between the steering wheel and seat cushion, and he was able, finally, to sit up and examine the truck. He unrolled a window and leaned his head out, taking deep breaths, blinking his eyes. The children in the truck watched him gravely for a moment and then began to giggle. Their laughter subsided abruptly when Roy called out to them: *"Buena dia . . ."*

There was silence and then a small voice answered back: *". . . dia . . ."*

Roy smiled and opened the car door. He stood on the cool pavement for a moment, weaving slightly, trying to hold his balance. He was dizzy with fatigue and an hour's poor sleep and possibly a hangover. "One hell of an awful *dia*," he muttered under his breath. The children were laughing again, and fairly soon he began to feel better. The driver of the truck climbed down and came round to Roy's side to stare at him. The fellow had a murderous look — a bandit's look. He was wearing a

wrinkled double-breasted suit coat over what appeared to be a
polo shirt and uncommonly dirty and outsized denim slacks. He
stared at Roy with his bandit's eyes until Roy lifted his hand in a
vague salute. Then the Mexican smiled, showing hilarious buck
teeth, lifted his arm in the same indecisive gesture and almost
immediately turned and walked toward the supermarket, flapping his feet in gray tennis shoes.

The children attempted to engage Roy in conversation. Roy
came closer to the back of the truck, trying to understand some of
it, cocking his head and listening carefully and interrupting now
and then: "*Qué?* . . . *Cómo?* . . . *Despacio,* for chrissake, *despacio* . . ." The children giggled hysterically; two or three
adults in the front cab stared at him, looking uneasy, and finally
Roy gave it up and waved goodbye and wandered into the supermarket.

The inside of the store was aglow with yellow light. Everything was gorgeous and brightly packaged. Only the people —
the cashier and the Mexican gathering breakfast staples and Roy
himself — seemed out of phase with the predominating illusion.
Roy looked all around, examining the market with as much wonder and concentration as might have been demonstrated in viewing Indian cave mosaics or a thousand years old cathedral. He
stared all around and then he uncapped a bottle of milk and tore
open a bag of cinnamon buns. He wandered over the market
eating and drinking, pausing occasionally to stare enraptured at
a prime cut of beef or a phonograph album or a frozen pizza or
a stack of small redwood picnic tables. There seemed no limit to
what the market might conceivably have in stock. Roy decided
the pussy willow cuttings were his favorite; they were a little
fantastic: out of season, out of habitat . . . He wondered if the
pussy willow had been shipped fresh-frozen from the East, like
oysters or cheese blintzes. He moved on; he had something else in
mind.

He located this other without difficulty — a tall pasteboard box
containing twenty-four ice cream cones, maple flavored. The box
of cones was part of it; the plastic scoop stapled to the outside of

the box solved the next most immediate problem. He carried the cones and the scoop to the cashier and then went back to pick up two half-gallon cartons of ice cream.

Outside again, at the back end of the truck, the children and two or three of the older Mexicans crowded round to watch. Roy left off serving after a while, letting one of the older girls take his place. There were a few accented whoops of *Ize-Cream . . . Aze Creeem,* but the children were unusually quiet for the most part, sweetly, deliriously happy waiting in line to be served. Presently, he returned to his car and sat in the driver's seat to watch. One hell of a crazy *dia,* he reminded himself. Not to mention the *dia* before and the night or the goddam *noche* in between.

He turned now and looked in the back seat. It was all there . . . All of it . . . All his art objects purchased during his twelve hours travel on the day before: the button-on shoes, the iron stewpot, the corset model, the portrait of President Coolidge, the Orange Crush dispenser with its rusted spigot, part of an old upright piano. Everything except . . . But he remembered now. The television set, one of the earliest models, big as a draft animal, with a seven-inch picture tube . . . He'd left it in knee-high johnson grass fifty miles outside town. He grunted to himself, thinking of the television set: it was a terrible loss; he'd been blinded by the wine on the day before and thoughtlessly left the television behind. He grunted again and re-examined his treasure in the back seat.

The Mexican children were finished with their ice cream, and he could hear their singsong voices rising in volume. The elder, the old bandit in gray tennis shoes, came out of the supermarket carrying his grocery sack. He moved past Roy, nodding, showing his wonderful teeth.

"You need a stewpot?" Roy said suddenly.

The Mexican was jerked back as if suspended by a coil spring. His face twitched, but he managed to smile and mumble an incomprehensible something in Spanish.

"Stew pot," Roy repeated. "Fine piece of workmanship . . .

You need one? For free . . . *por nada . . . Tiene usted una stew pot-to?"*

The old Mexican gasped in alarm, altogether mystified. Roy climbed out of the car and opened the back door, pointing to the soot-covered vessel. It was very much like the ones in which neighborhood washerwomen had boiled clothes during his childhood. He loved the stewpot. But now he knew he must *make the gesture.* It was part of being a public figure. He addressed the Mexican: "Here . . . You want it? Desire you the stew pot?"

Roy struggled with the pot; it was big as a washtub. The old man accepted it on faith, smiling as if vastly pleased. He bowed politely and turned toward the truck, carrying the stewpot with great dignity. The children in back greeted him with strident questions. Roy sat in the front seat of the car and watched, wondering if he ought to make a speech. They'd never understand a word, but he could make pleasant sounds. It was no matter. His Mexicans back home never understood anything, either. You just paid their poll taxes and showed them where to mark ballots when election time came round. He'd made a speech the night before. One of his best. Parked alongside a narrow river, he and the girl had lain on a picnic blanket and finished the last of the wine and the chicken. Then he had climbed a huge magnolia tree and plucked a great white bloom from the top, before descending to one of the lower limbs to make the presentation speech. He'd never been in better form. Though there had been some difficulty about addressing the girl. Using her name seemed to take all the fire out of the occasion. "Ladies . . ." he had said in the beginning, but it wasn't quite right. Nor "Fellow ladies . . ." He'd made a number of attempts: "Dear Lady" and "Most High and Mighty Ouida, Bride of My Youth, My Rock, My Fortress, My Deliverance, Horn of My Salvation and My High Tower . . ." But that had been too excessive for what, basically, was meant to be a ceremony of some dignity and restraint. He'd finally called her "My Dear Miss Lady Love . . ."

He thought he might step outside the car and possibly stand on the Orange Crush dispenser, addressing the Mexican children briefly, but after a moment the truck started up with a great thrashing sound and began backing out of the driveway. Roy sat for a moment, rubbing his eyes, and then he got his own car started and proceeded slowly down the main street of the city behind the truck carrying the cotton pickers. After a block or so, he grew impatient with the business of waving at the children, and nodding, and blinking his lights, and waving again; and finally he raced the car's engine and passed them by. A noisy, high-pitched cry came from the children; their flapping arms caught his vision briefly through the side windows. He grinned oafishly, studying his face in the mirror. "I have a way with crowds," he said aloud to himself. "I have gifts of rare personal magnetism . . ." He listened to the dying cheers from in back, and he thought he detected a clanging in the midst of it, a series of bell tones, deep and dull and flattish, metal on metal. My old iron stewpot, he thought . . .

Arthur Fenstemaker heard the cheers and the children's laughter and the groan of the truck's motor blended with the blows struck on the stewpot. He lay in his bed on the second floor of the Governor's mansion and listened thoughtfully. He was reminded for a moment of an old International he'd driven in the oil fields years before. The Mexicans were blocks away now, and he opened his eyes, still wondering over the sound from the street below. He reached for cigarettes and matches. After a moment he lay back in the bed, gasping for breath. He left the cigarette burning in a tray and pulled himself closer to Sweet Mama Fenstemaker. His right arm was pressed under his own huge weight, but he did not want to turn away just yet. Sweet Mama smelled goddam good; she nearly always perfumed herself at bedtime.

The Governor lay like that for several minutes, listening for sounds in the house or from the street, pressing his big nose against his wife's skin, until the kitchen help began to arrive downstairs. Then he rolled off the bed and went to the bathroom. He brushed his teeth and smoked another cigarette; he swallowed pills and massaged his scalp and began to stalk about the second floor of the mansion. He looked in on his brother: Hoot Gibson Fenstemaker lay sleeping quietly, knotted in bedclothes. The Governor turned back to his dressing room and stared at himself in a full-length mirror, sucking in his stomach, shifting from side to side. He slipped on gartered hose and shoes and a robe, and again stood listening, leaning over a stairwell and cocking his head. Soon he could hear the limousine being eased into position on the concrete drive. Fenstemaker strode down to the end of the hall and opened a casement window. A highway patrolman circled the car, examining tires, polishing chrome. The Governor put his head through the window and yelled: "Hidy!"

The patrolman looked up, squinting against the sun, trying to smile.

"Hah'r yew, Mist' Fenstemaker," he said.

"Nice mornin'," the Governor said, looking around.

"Hassah!" the patrolman said.

The patrolman stood on the concrete apron, gazing up at the Governor. He kicked a tire with the heel of his shoe; he patted a fender of the car. He stared at the Governor, and finally added, ". . . Sure nice one . . ."

Fenstemaker turned his head, looking over the city from the second-story window. The mansion was constructed along Georgian lines and was situated on a small rise that placed it nearly level with the Capitol dome and some of the office buildings downtown. Mist blurred the hilltops to the west, and occasionally, a mile or more away, lake water flashed in the sun. The smell of flowers, blooming in profusion in the backyard garden, was fused with the harsh bouquet of compost heaps and kitchen coffee. Fenstemaker pinched his big nose and took deep breaths. The patrolman continued to gawk at him.

"I'm not goin' anywhere right off," Fenstemaker said.

He pulled his head back inside and rang for his coffee. He

sat at a desk in his study and shuffled through papers. The butler arrived with a small coffeepot, dry toast, juice, and a half-dozen newspapers.

"You had your breakfast?" Fenstemaker said. "You had your coffee?"

"Yessir," the butler said.

Fenstemaker sipped his coffee and shuffled papers.

"I hope it was better than this," he said. "Siddown and have some more."

The butler poured himself a cup and stood blowing on it, waiting.

"Siddown for Christ sake," Fenstemaker said.

"Yes sir."

"Goddam."

"Sir?"

"I'm just goddammin'."

"Yes sir."

"Let's get a new brand of coffee," Fenstemaker said. He made a face.

"I'll tell the cook."

"Nothin' tastes like it used to," Fenstemaker said. "Not even vegetables."

"Sweet potatoes especially," the butler said.

"Not even goddam sweet potatoes," Fenstemaker said.

The two of them sipped coffee. The Governor turned through the newspapers, talking but not looking up. "You think it's gettin' better?"

"What's that?"

"Bein' a colored man. You think it's any better?"

The butler looked at him desperately. "I got a good job," he said.

The Governor did not seem to pay attention. He went on talking and turning pages. "Maybe little better, I guess . . . Discussions goin' on. . . . Least *that's* not like it used to be. Hell! I remember old Pitchfork Ben Tillman — the things he said . . ." Fenstemaker broke off momentarily, peering at the newsprint, then went on: "Of course bein' better still don't make it very good. I was thinkin' yesterday, signin' my mail, how I'd feel if I wrote a public official about, you know, my rights? I was lookin' over what I'd been sayin'. 'Well now this sure is a problem, involvin' grave emotional questions, and we can't tolerate havin' second-class citizens in this free country and I'm sure gonna do what I can . . . Try to make reasonable progress toward a solution . . . Sure keep your views in mind . . .' Why *God damn!* Some cornpone Buddha say that to *me*, I'd set a bomb off under him."

The butler grinned. "I think most colored people vote for you," he said. "Even when you don't say things exact . . ." He began gathering cups and saucers.

"I'm a damned good politician," Fenstemaker said. "I know how good I am and I ain't doin' much, so what about the others not so good? Goddam and hell!"

"You want another pot?" the butler said.

"Yes," the Governor said. "Switch to that ersatz stuff — I think it's probably better than this . . . And some fruit. They got any watermelon down there?"

"I'll see," the butler said. "They don't, we get you some."

The Governor's brother, Hoot Gibson Fenstemaker, appeared at the door. He rubbed his eyes and smiled, looking deranged. "You get me some coffee, Jimmy?" he said. The butler nodded, carrying the tray. Hoot Gibson stepped inside.

"Mornin' Arthur."

"You enjoy that party last night?" the Governor said.

"Sure did. I like parties here."

"I think you danced with every lady."

"I think I did," Hoot Gibson said. "I liked that orchestra, too. It was like Wayne King."

"I remember at college you had some Wayne King records," the Governor said, looking up from the papers. "And Henry Busse. What in hell ever happened to Henry Busse?"

"He dead?" Hoot Gibson said. He thought a moment. *"Hot Lips!* I booked old Henry Busse once for the gymnasium. A dance. Made two hundred dollars promoting old Henry Busse . . ." Hoot Gibson's eyes went cloudy, thinking about Henry Busse. He sipped from his brother's coffee cup.

Fenstemaker looked up patiently. "Don't make that noise," he said. Hoot Gibson gripped the cup with both hands and stared at the coffee. The Governor read the papers. Hoot Gibson picked up one of the sheets and glanced over the headlines. "I think I got a hangover," he said.

The Governor cleared his throat but did not comment.

"I might go back to bed awhile," Hoot Gibson said.

"Take some aspirin and sleep another hour," the Governor said.

Hoot Gibson stood and stretched and scratched himself. He loosened the drawstring on his pajamas and retied it. "I think I'll do that," he said. ". . . You got anything for me today?"

The Governor looked up and said: "You remember that fellow talkin' to me and Jay last night? Up here — out on the screen porch?"

"That new lobbyist?"

"That's the one."

"I know him. He's workin' the Capitol nearly every day now."

"Well suppose you keep an eye on him," the Governor said. "Follow him around. Or get someone to do it for you. Find out where he goes, who he's seein'. Do that today and tonight. Maybe tomorrow. Don't for God's sake let him know he's bein' watched. Give me a report — and don't come around *tellin'* me about it. Write it up."

Hoot Gibson looked vastly pleased. He vanished down the hall, humming to himself.

The Governor signed some papers. He looked at the clock — it was nearly seven; nearly nine in the East. He reached for the phone and got the long distance operator, making notes of persons he could call in the Eastern time zone. He talked with an economist in New York. They discussed investments; Fenstemaker asked questions about the stock market; he complained that none of the big investors seemed interested in municipal bonds. "I got some mayors in trouble," he said. "They need help. You got any ideas?" He listened to the economist's ideas. They complained to each other about the goddam Republican high interest rates.

Fenstemaker rang off and placed more calls; he talked with his two Senators, a union official in Philadelphia, a college professor in Boston. The professor was a nephew whom he'd put through college a half-dozen years before. "Listen," the Governor said, "those are wonderful speeches you been sendin' down — especially if I was runnin' in Oyster Bay or Newport. But I'm not, happily. Try to remember I'm way the hell down here in coonass country . . . You forget your beginnin's? You need a little trip home? Might do you good . . . I need some ideas . . . You got good ideas . . . But I want 'em in speeches that sound like Arthur Fenstemaker and not some New goddam England squire . . ."

He completed the calls and turned back to the papers on his desk. An assistant had left him a note attached to a hand-written letter: *"This may interest you, though I advise against reading it when you're trying to shake off a low mood. It is very sad."*

He read the letter attached:

Sirs:
We the people of the 9th grade Civics class at Hopkinsville feel that you the people of the Government should try to conquer the world here before you try to conquer outer space. We feel that there may be some kind of gas on the moon that is under the surface and if a rocket hit it, it may open the surface of the moon and these gases may escape and get into our own environment and kill us. So we feel that you should leave well-enough alone. We feel that if the Good Lord had wanted us to conquer outer space he would have put here on earth instruments instead of people. We would like to know what you think about this issue.
                                                    Sincerely,
                                                    THE 9TH GRADE CLASS

Fenstemaker rubbed the back of his neck and pulled on his nose and sat staring at the names of the 9th Grade Class at Hopkinsville. He put the letter down and reached for the phone.

"Jay . . ."

Jay McGown's voice came to him feebly; then it got stronger. There was music being played on the radio in Jay's room. The music ended and an announcer talked about a cure for piles.

"Sir?" Jay was saying. ". . . Sir?"

"What in hell's goin' on there?"

"Sir?"

"You think we got a chance on that school bill?"

"School bill? Sure we got a chance," Jay said.

"I got your note and that letter," the Governor said.

"Ah."

"Let's take a run with that bill this week," Fenstemaker said.

"You think this week's really the best time?" Jay said. "Old Hoffman's still in the hospital. We'd need him. He wrote the damn thing. At least his name's on it."

"Who's that? Who wrote it, then?"

"A lobbyist for the schoolteachers. A lawyer from the education agency."

"Who else?"

"Me."

"Well let's take a run with it," Fenstemaker said.

"Who'll we get to floor-manage?"

"Who's on the committee?" the Governor said.

"You know that committee better than I do," Jay said.

"Name some," Fenstemaker said. "I forget."

"Who you want me to name?"

"Name some."

Jay named some of the members.

"They don't sound so good to me," the Governor said.

"They aren't," Jay said. "We'd probably end up with half a bill. Old Hoffman's not much, but he won't lose us any votes. He knows how to manage a bill."

"How 'bout Roy Sherwood?" Fenstemaker said.

"Roy's a good friend of mine," Jay said.

"So?"

"But he's not exactly one of our boys."

"Maybe he just never got invited in," the Governor said.

"He's pretty damned independent," Jay said. "And lazy. That's a bad combination."

Chimes from the college signaled the half hour. The highway patrolman polished the limousine on the side drive. The butler came into the room with an enormous slice of watermelon. Fenstemaker broke off a piece with his hand and began to eat. There was a silence on the phone while the Governor ate watermelon. Then he said: "He help write that bill? He do anything at all?"

There was another silence before Jay began to answer: "That's right. He helped a lot. Fact is, he was the only one on that lousy committee who gave a damn. With Hoffman gone."

"Well old Hoff got it reported out for us before he went to the hospital," Fenstemaker said.

"How'd you know about Roy?"

"It just sort of came to me in the night," the Governor said.

"Well I thought you might disapprove. My getting him to help us. He's a friend of mine, like I said, and we needed some help from someone on the committee. Desperately."

"All right," the Governor said. "That's just fine. I'm delighted. You think he could carry it?"

"I don't know. I really don't. He's never worked a bill in three terms here. I'm not even sure he'd accept the job."

"Well I'll just ask him and see."

"You think he could hold the votes we've got? He might scare some off."

"See about that, too," the Governor said. He paused, and then added: "He ain't worn himself out on Earle Fielding's wife, has he?"

There was a pause before Jay answered: "That piece of information just come to you in the night, too?"

"Everything does," the Governor said, his voice warm with

pleasure. "Borne on the wind. Like a cherub. It do fly . . . Listen . . . We'll just see how old Roy reacts. Okay? Take a little run. Pull out all the stops and try to get this thing through. Maybe tomorrow. We can't afford to wait much longer. They'll be building up opposition soon's it appears Hoffman's well. We put off any time, we lose votes and we lose hard cash in that bill . . . You want some cash for Hopkinsville, don't you? We'll just have to get that goddam thing through in a hurry. Can't afford to have any great debates . . ."

Jay was silent on the other end of the line while Fenstemaker talked. Then the Governor rang off without formality. He dialed another number on the phone and waited during the six or seven rings. He pressed the disconnect and dialed again. After another interval, Roy Sherwood answered.

"What're you doin'?" Fenstemaker boomed.

"Sleeping," Roy Sherwood said. "Real good, too."

"Hell of a note," Fenstemaker said. "World's cavin' in all round us; rocket ships blastin' off to the moon; poisonous gas in our environment . . . Sinful goddam nation . . . laden with iniquity, offspring of evildoers. My princes are rebels and companions of thieves . . ."

"*What?*"

". . . A horror and a hissing . . ."

"Who the hell is this?"

"Isaiah," Fenstemaker said. "The Prophet Isaiah."

"I'm going to hang up in just about three seconds," Roy said, "but first I'd really like to know who the hell this is?"

"Arthur Goddam Fenstemaker. Hah yew?"

"I think it really is," Roy said after a moment. "Governor? That you?"

"Come over the Mansion and see," Fenstemaker said. "You like watermelon? I got some damn good watermelon. You come over here and we'll break watermelon together."

Roy's response was plaintive but respectful: "It's awful early in the morning for breakfast."

"Nearly eight."

"I know," Roy said. "That gives me nearly three hours sleep."

"Well, you're a young man. I needed five."

Roy was silent.

"You come over and talk to me about this bill?" Fenstemaker said.

"What bill's that?"

"That school thing you did for Jay. Damn good job."

"Thanks. I appreciate it. But what do you want to talk about?"

"About when you're gonna get off your ass and pass it for me."

"*Pass* it. Hell, I'm just the ghost writer. Passin' it is your —"

"I mean take charge in that madhouse."

"Hah?"

"I mean floor-manage for me."

"You sure you got the right man, Governor? I never in my life —"

"I got you, all right," the Governor said. "Roy Emerson Sherwood. Non-practicin' lawyer. Family's got cattle, little cotton. Never struck no oil, though. Elected sixty-third Legislature. Re-elected without opposition to sixty-fourth, sixty-fifth. Never did goddam thing here till you wrote that bill the other day . . ."

"You got the right man, I guess," Roy said.

"You help me with that bill on the floor?"

"When you plan to bring it up?"

"Tomorrow."

"*Tomorrow!* Godalmighty —"

"Day after, maybe. Come on over here."

"Governor, I couldn't learn the *number* that bill, condition I'm in right now. Let me sleep a little. Just a little. Let me think about it."

"*Sinful* goddam nation . . . Laden with iniquity . . . **My** princes are —"

"Al! right," Roy said wearily.

"How you like your goddam eggs?" the Governor said.

Two

THE TWO young men sat out under the trees in straw-bottomed chairs, barking their shins against the wooden tables. They sat waiting, looking glum. Record music came from a speaker overhead, somewhere in the trees. The music was turned loud so it could be heard above the noise from a next-door bowling alley. There were periods of relative quiet when the bowling slacked off and the records changed, during which they could hear half-hearted cheers from a lighted intramural field a block away, near the college, but the record music predominated. The sounds from the bowling alley ruined only the ballads.

Roy Sherwood looked around and groaned.

"You don't like music?" Willie said. "And a gay party atmosphere?"

"I like music fine," Roy said. "I just don't like these gap-toothed teddy boys raping some old favorite with a chorus of ex-truckdrivers behind them going 'ooh-ah, oom-ah, ooh-ah.' " He looked around the beer garden impatiently. "Can't they turn it down?"

"That would be a violence to the whole idea of the Dearly Beloved," Willie said.

"Exactly," Roy said.

Willie said: "It's not so bad. What was it Rinemiller was saying the other day?"

"Rinemiller's a sewer," Roy said.

"He said it was *genuine*. Simple and alive and —"

"A sod and a sewer," Roy said conclusively. He looked around for the waitress.

They sat talking. There were twenty or thirty others, mostly young people, out under the trees, sitting at the unwashed tables, and through the windows of the building the boiled faces of some of the old-time customers were visible. It was still very early in the evening: the lights had just now come on, and the Dearly Beloved Beer and Garden Party was only partly filled.

A waitress finally appeared. She was a pretty girl, wearing a white uniform with a faded checkered apron. She smiled and said: "Ike and Mike — my favorite customers."

"Stop calling us that," Roy said. "Think of something else." He did not look at the waitress, but gave his attention instead to a group of undergraduates and their dates just now arriving.

"You don't like Ike and Mike?" the girl said.

"It's just that neither of us wants to be Ike," Willie said.

The girl nodded. "You want menus?"

"Some of the light," Willie said.

"How about a pitcher?" the waitress said.

The two young men hesitated, looking at each other, numbed momentarily by the weight of decision. The bowling eased off some next door. A singer's voice came to them through the trees:

> *Tew . . .*
> *Spen' . . .*
> *One . . .*
> *Naaaht . . .*
> *Wishyew . . .*

"Let's get a pitcher," Willie said.

"We wait for Huggins, he'll buy pitchers for everyone," Roy said. The waitress swayed slightly to the music, looking away, her eyes foggy.

"You strapped again?" Willie said.

"No. Trying to avoid it, though. I'm budgeting myself. Watch the pennies, the dollars take care of themselves."

The waitress leaned down and rested her elbows on the table. She looked at the young men closely. "It's only *seventy-five cents*," she said.

"It mounts up," Roy said. "And I'm out of work."

"You make thirty dollars a day, for God's sake," the waitress said. "I read it in the paper."

"Only when we're in session," Roy said. "And that money's got to last me the year round. Otherwise, I'd have to practice the law. Or live off lobbyists. You tryin' to corrupt me?"

"Two glasses of the light," Willie said. "And when you see Huggins come in, ask if he wants to order some pitchers."

The waitress nodded.

"I'll get your lousy fifteen-cent beers," the girl said.

She turned, walked across the garden and up the stone steps into the building.

The beer garden was shielded on three sides by the low yellow frame structure, a U-shaped Gothicism, scalloped and jigsawed and wonderfully grotesque. The bar, the kitchen and dining spaces were at the front; the one side and the back were clubrooms for the Germans who came to town once or twice a week to bowl and play cards. The Germans had bought half the block years before and built the bar and clubrooms. During the hard times of the 1930's they had begun leasing out the front part as a public bar, an arrangement that had proved so profitable that it was continued through the war years and was now apparently destined for the ever-after.

Just prior to the war there had been rumors of German-American Bund meetings in the back rooms. People in town talked about seeing goosestepping farmers through the windows, their arms raised in fascist salute. But nothing was ever proved; no one ever came forward to substantiate the claims, and after Pearl Harbor it was nearly forgotten. There was even a little plaque got up to honor certain of the clientele gone off to war; there were waitresses who boasted of being Gold Star Sweethearts. Business — and the beer — had always been good, before, during, after the war, and even in recent years when some of Roy's and Willie's friends had petitioned for a change in names: when they wanted to call it the *Weltschmertz.*

The waitress brought the two glasses of beer. She came toward them, both hands occupied, weaving between the bare tables and the crowds of people. The place was gradually filling. "Thirty cents," the girl said.

Roy insisted on paying. He pushed out a half dollar. The waitress hesitated with the change. "You want some pennies?" she said. "Let's see — ten per cent of thirty is . . ." Roy waved her off.

"I'm going to be short the end of the month," he said. "I got to get in good with my friends."

"You don't have any friends left," Willie said. "They're all furious."

"As it should be," Roy said. "They're all sewers."

"They disapprove."

"Stuffiest bunch of bohemians ever existed," Roy said.

Willie shrugged. "It's just they don't think you ought to be hoo-hawin' around with a fellow legislator's wife," he said. "Even a fellow *ex*-legislator's wife."

"Or even a fellow *ex*-legislator's *ex*-wife," Roy said.

"She's not Mrs. Ex yet," Willie said.

"I got censured today," Roy said. "My district caucus."

"Oh, Jesus . . . What does that mean?"

"Don't know," Roy said. "They've never had occasion before. No precedents." He laughed horribly. "They even went into executive session . . . I started to make a point of order about whether this sort of thing was germane. I suppose it was. Since they called the meeting on account of me."

They went on drinking. They had two more glasses apiece. The beer was close to freezing cold, with slivers of ice floating on top; if you took too much right off, it made shooting pains in the back of the eyes. They had two more glasses.

"You see?" Willie said. "We should've ordered a pitcher."

"I thought Huggins'd be here by now."

"Not on Tuesday nights," Willie said. "He remembers about the bowling on Tuesday nights and comes late to avoid the noise."

"Awful place," Roy said.

"He probably paid an early call at the whorehouse," Willie said.

"I wish I had his money."

"You got his money," Willie said. "I wish I had anybody's money. I wish I had yours."

"It's a myth about my money," Roy said. "It's all tied up in a trust fund until I'm seventy-five years old."

They were silent for a time, watching the college students come and go. The noise from the bowling alley subsided, and the German farmers appeared, filing out, carrying their equipment in little bags. It was much better with the bowling ended, though the record machine continued to play at full volume.

"They think we're deaf?" Roy said, looking up at the trees, scowling, as if the liveoaks were personally responsible. "I'm going inside and raise hell . . ." But he did not move from the straw-bottomed chair.

After a moment, Willie said: "That's why you're being so insufferable tonight."

"What's that?" Roy said.

"Because you know everyone's disappointed with you."

"The hell with everyone," Roy said. "They're all a bunch of sewers."

"I'm on your side," Willie said. "I like her. Even —"

"Even what?"

"Even," Willie said. "Even-even. She's got, as the phrase used to go, a repu*tation*. Most eligible married woman in town."

"You're a sewer," Roy said. "You're middle class."

Willie was silent for a moment. Then he added: "Censured, hah? You think they'll keep it quiet?"

"It'll get around," Roy said. "I just hate for it to get back to my family. They're liable to have me impeached." Again he laughed. "Have a recall election and send one of my cousins up here, instead."

"Who else knows about this? So far."

"Only the people I've told," Roy said.

"*Told?* Who the hell you told, for God's sake?"

"You. You and one other."

"Who's the other? Your mistress?"

"She's not my mistress," Roy said immediately. ". . . No . . . Not her."

"Who?"

"Arthur Goddam Fenstemaker."

"Godalmighty. How come him?"

"Well I think he knew about it, anyhow. The way he talked. Sonofabitch knows everything goes on. We had breakfast this morning."

Willie looked stunned. "You? You and the Governor?"

"At the Mansion, even," Roy said. "Eight o'clock. I've had three hours sleep the last thirty-six."

"How come?" Willie said. "How come you're suddenly on the inside? Or did you just break in on the Governor at breakfast?"

"Last-minute invitation," Roy said. He told about the phone call that morning. He didn't embellish; he was entirely matter-of-fact; Willie could count on his friend being absolutely candid. Roy Sherwood didn't ordinarily talk about himself, though when it was unavoidable he did so with objectivity, standing off and re-garding his own conduct with an amused and occasionally be-wildered curiosity.

Willie smiled and signaled to the waitress for more beer. "Your life is suddenly very complicated," he said.

"Try to resist writing me up as a sellout artist just yet," Roy said.

"Trust me," Willie said. He attempted a look of cynicism; tried and failed. He couldn't play the role. He was a tall, well-constructed young man (though not a really very young one any more) whose innocent face, blue eyes and straw-colored hair had brought about the speculation among friends that he secretly posed for soft drink advertisements depicting unimaginably wholesome teenagers grinning at one another next to drugstore soda fountains. He struggled, with singular unsuccess, against this portrayal. He was thirty years old and rather liked to think of himself as a thoroughgoing degenerate, and if he failed in exhibiting himself as such, it was probably the result of his conveying precisely the reverse image years before at college. In those days he had not only presented the façade of unreconstructed wholesomeness, he had lived the role with conviction: as a member of the glee club, football player, honor student, debater, summer camp counselor, and author of some of the most earnest and tiresomely obvious editorial essays ever to be published in the college newspaper. The years since graduation had, to use his own phrase, muddled his vision and corrupted his ideals — and he was unqualifiedly pleased with the transformation. He might have looked like the same person from all outward appearances, but inwardly, he insisted, he had changed. He was currently editing what he preferred to call his "little left wing weekly newspaper," and he was happiest when anyone belabored him with the charge that he was a mere political propagandist.

If Willie, then, first impressed with his innocent good looks and tired-eyed naïveté, his companion at the bare wooden table in the beer garden was a study in villainy, a road-show Rasputin, dark and bent-nosed with what certain of his women friends occasionally described as a "sensual" face. The characterization invariably depressed and annoyed Roy. He did not consider his face sensual by any standard, and he did not much like women, either, though he thought about them most all the time. He simply felt they were up to no good. He had been married once, for a few months in 1945 while serving in the Navy. He had met the girl at a USO dance and married her soon afterwards, on the mistaken assumption that he had got her pregnant on the first date. Now he could scarcely remember the way she looked. Not that there had been a great many women in between — it was just that after the naval service and his divorce while still on sea duty, after four years as an undergraduate and then law school, an attempt at private practice and then entering politics, the whole business of his youth and early marriage seemed as vague and fanciful in the memory as some unusually strenuous but otherwise undistinguished weekend assignation.

As politician, Roy Sherwood had little to worry about so long as he behaved himself. He called himself a "conservative States' rights Democrat" — it was a little game he played with people back home — and his seat in the Legislature had practically been conferred on him, like a title. His grandfather, father, and older brother had served the same district before him — an uncle had even put in twelve years as a Congressman in Washington. If anyone ever got rid of Roy, it would be his family, not his constituents. And Roy tried to tell himself he didn't especially give a damn, anyhow.

The waitress came with a pitcher of dark beer. Huggins was following close behind.

"Hah yew men tonight?" Huggins said.

"Hello, Pancho," Willie said.

"Hello, Frank," Roy said. He turned to the waitress. "Get Pancho a glass for his own beer, will you honey?"

Huggins dragged over a chair and poured beer. He was about average height, spindly in the limbs but lumpish through the middle: a spectacle, really, for anyone who had not got used to him. There came a time when he seemed unreal even to his friends, a little too much to believe. People came to accept his appearance, his seedy, gaping face, unmanageable hair, disproportionate weight (food-thin, whiskey-fat), but there were moments, inevitably, when the idea of Huggins, alien and uneasy in ski sweater and baggy corduroys, strained all credibility, when he seemed the most nearly perfect Undesirable anyone could imagine. During the past year he had tried to do something about himself by calling on the Brooks Brothers traveling representative, but the mail-order wardrobe made no appreciable change, succeeding, instead, in merely parodying the whole natural-shoulder mystique.

There was family money behind him, but no more than was used to support many of his colleagues in the Legislature. Yet his friends ordinarily made some pretense of assuming responsibility during adjournment: managing family businesses, experimenting with breeds of cattle, speculating on oil properties, holding down ceremonial positions of one kind or another. Some friends felt the least he could do was *open* a law office if not take any action so drastic as to constitute actual *practice* of the law, but Huggins couldn't qualify. He had, at last count, tried and failed seven times to pass the bar exam.

He was a winner, all the same. He was unbeatable in his home district, having been elected and re-elected to successive terms of office since his freshman year in college just after the war. The year before he had registered his greatest triumph, defeating a blind lady justice of the peace while "campaigning" in Europe and Mexico.

Huggins sat at the table, grinning at Roy and Willie, looking terrible. He paid for the beer, still grinning, looked up and said: "I cashed a check out on the highway."

"You're in for trouble if an opponent ever gets hold of your canceled checks," Willie said.

"Maybe I'll start making them out to cash," Huggins said.

"Make one out to me," Roy said.

"They got a new girl out there," Huggins said. "She said she was from Mount Holyoke. Where's that?"

"South Hadley, Mass.," Roy said.

"Couldn't be," Huggins said. "She had an awful twang. But she was something to look at. That's the beauty of whorehouse syndicates — always bringing in new faces."

"You're gonna get caught in a raid," Willie said.

"Don't write me up if they do," Huggins said. He turned to Roy. "You need some money?"

"Sure."

"What's the matter? Family cut you off?"

"I never was on," Roy said.

"They're down on Roy," Willie said. "They want him to come home and help his brother try a case."

"I heard you were mean as hell in a courtroom," Huggins said.

"I'm mean everywhere," Roy said.

"I remember your brother my first term here," Huggins said. "He was an awful conservative."

There seemed nothing that could be done about Roy's brother, so they concentrated on a new pitcher of beer. Soon a crowd of people — a great, tortured gang of them — appeared at the entrance and headed directly toward the table. Some were in evening dress, some in khakis and tennis shorts and tropical worsteds. There were eight or ten in the party, and after a drawn-out interval of handshaking and high-pitched laughter, tables being pushed together and trips to the ladies' room and inquiries about beer and jukebox preferences, they were settled.

A girl named Ellen Streeter sat between Willie and Roy. She was splendid looking, with marvelous legs, and Willie watched her closely, examining her sweetly freckled and slightly over-baked chest and shoulders, feeling unaccountably sad. He had been secretly in love with the girl for several years, but had never got anywhere with her. No one ever seemed to — and he had only recently given up from exhaustion. Willie sat watching Ellen Streeter, who watched Roy, who was giving his attention to Alfred Rinemiller, at the other end of the table, whom he regarded as a monumental sewer.

"How've you been?" Willie said to the girl.

"Fine. I went to a party last night with a bunch of hoods. My date has the football card concession in town. They smoked marijuana."

Someone wanted to know how Ellen Streeter could afford to be seen with such a crowd. A woman across the table said it was because she was a virgin. "Ellen's notorious," the woman said. "Everybody knows about her. Virgins can do things like that."

Ellen looked resigned. "What can I say? I don't advertise — I don't put it in the want ads."

Roy lost interest in Alfred Rinemiller for a moment and turned to stare. "You don't advertise what?" he said.

"That she's honest," one of the women said. "Is that the right word?"

"How do girls get that way?" Roy said.

"It's just that you start out thinking you ought to save yourself," Ellen said. "Now *there's* a lovely expression. For someone special. You start saving and the longer you wait the more special it seems the fellow ought to be. So after a while there's really no one anywhere who is as special as all that. Except maybe that Shah at Harvard."

Roy smiled. "It's a problem, all right," he said. He turned round to listen to what was being said at the other end. Rinemiller was talking, so he tried hard to hear it all. Harry Belafonte sang to them from the treetops about how it was loading banana boats.

"I told him off," Rinemiller was saying. "I gave him hell."

"Who?"

"Old Fenstemaker."

"What about Fenstemaker?" Roy called out.

"He gave me one of his hard-sells," Rinemiller said.

"How?"

"He called me in and said, 'Looky heah, Alfred, wooden yew much rathuh git haff uh loaf than none at all? Then whyn't yew git buhind me on this heah legislation . . .' "

It was a pretty bad imitation of the Governor, but there was some laughter around Rinemiller. Roy squinted and started to say something but then changed his mind and got to his feet. Somebody had a bottle of gin and was ordering ice and setups. Some of the others were examining menus. Roy walked behind Willie, leaned down and spoke into his ear.

"I'm going."

"Comin' back?"

"Maybe."

"What?" Ellen Streeter said.

Another woman leaned over. "What're they whispering about?" she said. Crazy Kermit suddenly appeared. They all had a great affection for Kermit because he was genius gone to seed — gone slightly askew, in fact — and it was very sad. He had a Ph.D. and insisted on regarding all his friends as doctors of philosophy.

"Hey, Doctors," Kermit said, moving round the table, shaking hands. "Hah yew Good Doctors?"

There was a young man with him from the college whom he introduced as Jobie. The boy named Jobie moved behind Roy and smiled at everyone. He spoke to Roy.

"We've got to hold on to our principles. We've got to shape issues and advance the fundamental concepts of economic and social enlightenment."

"*Whaat?*" Roy turned and stared.

"We need more liberal intellectuals like you in politics," Jobie said.

"I'm a conservative States' rights Democrat," Roy said. "Excuse me." He turned and walked away.

"Where's he going?" Ellen said to Willie. They watched him heading up the stone steps and through the bar. "Where?" someone else said. "He coming back?"

Some of the others looked up. One of the women said: "Earle Fielding's going to be furious when he gets back to town."

"He's already back," Rinemiller said. "I talked with him tonight."

"It's shameful," one of the women said. "The least they could do is wait until Earle . . ." Her voice trailed off. She seemed to have forgot what exactly it was the least of which Roy and Earle Fielding's wife could do.

"I don't know what he sees in her, anyhow," Ellen said.

"It's a growing disgrace," Willie said, looking at his beer.

One of the girls at the other end of the table changed subjects and began talking about making ceramic jewelry in a ten-dollar kiln. "It's an art, honey," she was saying, "it really is. Like chicken sexing . . ."

Three

Roy knew George Giffen was paying his evening calls because the lights in the front room were dimmed and only the flickering of the television shone through the window blinds. He did not bother to knock but eased open the door, looked around, and walked inside. George Giffen sat on the carpeted floor, his back against the sofa, staring at the television. He looked up quickly, said, "Hey, hello, Roy," and returned his gaze to the action on the screen. Roy nodded, walked past Giffen and began to pour himself a glass of whiskey. He sang quietly under his breath:

> *Buckle on your overshoes . . .*
> *Whenna wind blows free . . .*
> *Take . . .*
> *Good . . .*
> *Care mahsef . . .*
> *Ah belong to me . . .*

Giffen stirred but did not look up again. Roy wandered into one of the bedrooms. The girl, Earle Fielding's wife, sat on the edge of a youth bed, reading a story to a boy of about five or six. The boy lay there bored, scratching himself.

"You hadn't ought to read him that Milne stuff," Roy said. "It's mainly for grownups nostalgic about their lost youth."

The girl's name was Ouida. She turned round and stared. The child screamed: "Hey, Roy! — let's play the game."

"No," Roy said.

"Let's *play*," the child insisted.

"Not on your life," Roy said. "I've lost interest in that game."

"What's the game?" Ouida said.

"Charades," Roy said. "He gets down on the floor and crawls

around making an awful noise. I'm supposed to guess what he is. He's always a roothog. Always. No imagination."

"I know that game," Ouida said.

"I know it, too!" the boy said, kicking at the covers bunched up at the end of his bed. "Let's play it *now*."

"You ought to go to bed, Merton," Roy said.

"What?"

"Sandman's comin'," Roy said.

"Name's not Merton."

"Well don't hold me responsible . . . I just thought — well, I've never really been very good at —"

"It's Earle Cummins Fielding," the boy hooted. "The *Third*."

"Yes . . . Well . . . It comes back to me now."

The boy pulled the covers over his head. "Leave me alone, please," he said. "I'm trying to get some sleep." He jerked the covers back again and howled. His mother bent down and kissed him and then redraped a sheet over his head.

"How long Giffen been here tonight?" Roy said.

"Not long," Ouida said. "He'll be leaving soon. This is one of the poor television evenings. We've already had our boy-girl talk."

"Be *quiet*," the child called out from inside the covers.

They switched off lights and moved toward the front of the apartment. Roy paused, refilling his drink and making one for Ouida. Giffen was coming out of his semi-hypnotic state. He had got to his feet, and though he still glanced nervously from time to time at the television screen, he was able to communicate with Roy and Ouida. A television announcer was talking about a "real smoke" and drawing on the end of a cigarette as if it were an after-dinner delicacy. Giffen glanced at Roy and said:

"Where'd you go today? I saw your secretary doin' your votin' for you."

"Once a week I withdraw," Roy said. "I disengage. Tension and all. I went out on my boat."

Giffen had no opportunity to reply because the commercial was ended and the closing scenes were coming on. He sat down immediately. Roy and Ouida went into the kitchen and began to pick at bits of food left over from the child's plate. Ouida washed dishes. She was thin and pale, yet handsome and full-mouthed with sunburned hair pulled up and pinned in back. She held plates under the water and dabbed at them with a paper napkin.

"How're you feeling?" Roy said.

"Fine."

"You sure?"

"Yes."

"You look good — better all the time."

"Thank you."

Roy looked inside the refrigerator and removed a piece of chicken. A section of skin had been peeled back and there were small teeth marks where some of the white meat had been torn away. Roy pulled the skin over the eroded section and took a bite. He stared at Ouida. She was wearing tight-fitting denim slacks, a plain blouse, loafers and thick white socks. He got his attention focused on a part of her leg, tanned and polished-looking, between the thick sock and the tapered cuff of the slacks. She sat at the breakfast table with legs crossed, and Roy could not keep his eyes off the bare part of her leg revealed between sock and cuff.

"I gave blood today," he said. "Told 'em to credit your account."

"You shouldn't have done that," Ouida said. "I've got the money even if the insurance doesn't cover it."

"It's all right," Roy said. "It's only my life's blood." He made a hopeless gesture. The girl came over and kissed him. He brought his arms up around her and pulled her in closer. "I think," he said, "that we ought to call another committee meeting. Pass a new unanimous-consent agreement."

"Why's that?" she said.

"I'm no longer satisfied limiting the fun and games to just kissin'," he said.

"How come?"

"I don't know. Weak in the head, maybe. Losing all that blood today."

"Make up your mind," she said. "It was your idea to begin with."

"That was when *you* were weak and defenseless," he said. He kissed her again.

He had known her for several years, since his first term in the legislature, but they had been seeing each other for less than eight weeks. Ouida and her husband, Earle Fielding, were either separated or estranged or divorcing or just having trouble — it wasn't quite clear to their friends, even after Earle had gone off three months before to organize Democratic Clubs in the Middle West. Ouida was still in town and showing up at most of the parties, and at one of these on the lake one evening Roy and Ouida had got a little tight and disappeared in one of the boats. Afterwards, even though he had not seen her for ten days, people talked about them. They had not seen each other until the evening she called to ask for help. She wanted, she said, someone to take her to the hospital. He told her she didn't sound at all sick, and at first he couldn't understand, her voice rising and fading, laced with drunken laughter. All he heard clearly was the last of it. "I think," she said gaily, "I'm bleeding to death."

He had come right over and found her passed out on the living room floor. He roused a neighbor to look after the boy and drove her to the hospital. On the way she began to come out of it. "I'm sorry," she said. "I'm pie-eyed, and I'm really very sorry I got you into this. I thought you'd be a rock to lean on. There wasn't anyone else. I think I'm having a miscarriage."

At the emergency room entrance they'd both been a mess, blood-smeared and haggard, Ouida in her nightgown and Roy in patched khakis. He held her in his arms, Ouida alternately laughing and crying, and rang the bell. She was still giggling and crossing herself when the nurse came to let them in. "Trick or treat," Ouida announced. She'd damn near died that night.

He had given blood and sent flowers and rented a television and arranged for special nurses, and he had been seeing her constantly since her release from the hospital. Recently, they had "caucused" and passed the unanimous-consent agreement.

Now he sat staring at the patch of bare skin on her leg, between thick sock and cuff, a few inches above her ankle.

"I missed you all day," she said. "You think that's a bad sign?"

"I don't know anything about signs," he said. "Talk to your analyst. Talk to your son. Have a serious discussion."

"I don't know any psychiatrists," Ouida said, "and I don't think little Earle would understand."

"Understand what?"

"That I've got to stay on good behavior, and I began missing you today."

"Well," Roy said, "it probably doesn't make any difference."

"What do you mean?"

"People are already talking," Roy said. "I'm the only company you've had since Earle left. Except for George Giffen, Melancholy Lover. You ever miss George?"

Ouida rolled her eyes. "I never have occasion to miss George," she said. "He's always here, wanting to watch television or talk about girls and why it is he's afraid of them. Tonight he was disturbed about Huggins."

"Why Huggins?"

"George thinks something's got to be done about Huggins, because Huggins is interested only in fallen women. He says Huggins doesn't have adult relationships."

"Like George does?"

"Like George does."

"Huggins likes the brothel circuit because it gives him a sense of security," Roy said. "He told me that once. He says he feels easier with women he's paid for."

"Well George doesn't approve. He says he likes *our* relationship — his and mine. He says it's adult and I make him feel clean."

Roy smiled and chewed on a piece of chicken and stared at Ouida's leg. Ouida said: "Are people *really* talking about us?"

Roy nodded and mumbled: ". . . bunch of sewers."

"But *why?*"

"I guess they think we're havin' an adult relationship."

"What are you looking at?" Ouida said.

Roy pointed at her leg and started to explain, wondering how he could possibly get the idea across, but then Giffen appeared. He stood in the kitchen doorway and said: "Where've you been, Roy?"

"Drinkin' beer," Roy said.

"Really? What was doin' at the Friendly?" Giffen could never get the name straight. He was a first-term member of the House, and since coming to town he had persisted in identifying the Dearly Beloved Beer and Garden Party as the Friendly Tavern. Or most of the time just the Friendly — possibly as a result of the others calling it "the Dearly."

"You mean the Garden?" Roy said.

"Yes," Giffen said. "What was doin' at the Friendly Garden?"

"The usual."

"Huggins there?"

"Yes."

"Who else?"

Roy named some of the others. Giffen's eyes bulged for no apparent reason. He began to fidget, jingling the change in his pockets and clacking his heels together. There were fascinating events taking place all over town. With the evening's television out of the way, Giffen seemed restless to look in on whatever was "doing." He leaned over suddenly and kissed Ouida on the cheek. The movement gave her a start. None of the girls had really got used to Giffen coming upon them and reaching out; it was a relatively new experience for George himself, in fact. He had recently come to realize that he could touch women in pub-lic — that it was both permissible in the company of good friends and that he was capable of doing such a thing. It had been like a revelation, opening limitless possibilities. In private he was terrified of women, but in a social situation it was becoming increasingly difficult to keep him off. Ouida referred to him as "my very tactile person."

"Earle looks bad," Giffen said matter-of-factly.

"Who?" Ouida said.

"Earle . . . He doesn't look so good."

"You mean little Earle? What's wrong with —"

"No, no . . . Big Earle . . . He looks terrible."

"You've seen him?" Ouida said. "Where've you seen him?"

"This mornin'," Giffen said. "Downtown. He was drinkin' before noon. I'm worried about him."

"I am, too," Ouida said. "Especially when he comes to town and doesn't call or even come by to visit his son. He say anything?"

"You didn't know he was here?"

"Of course not. He say anything at all?"

"I only saw him a minute," Giffen said. "I told him I'd been lookin' in on you and little Earle — just to head off any malicious stories that might be goin' round. About you and me, I mean."

"That was probably very wise," Ouida said.

"I think I'll take a run-by the Friendly," Giffen said.

Ouida and Roy were silent, looking at one another.

"You seen my new car, Roy?" Giffen said.

"Yes."

"You said Huggins was at the Friendly?"

"Yes."

"Had he been out to that place again?"

"What place?"

"That cat house."

"He didn't say."

"I've been worried about him," Giffen said. "He goes out there all the time. It's getting so it's a crutch for him."

Again they were silent. Giffen took a deep breath; his brow furrowed; his eyes bulged. The phone rang, and Giffen said:

"That's probably Earle now. He's probably been tied up all day."

Ouida answered, listened for a moment, turned and said: "It's for Roy. I think there's a madman on the other end."

"Really?" Roy seemed delighted with the prospect. "What'd he say?"

"He said something about you're being down in the short-rows — what in hell does *that* mean? — and for me to send you home to sleep as soon as you're finished talking. To whoever it is."

Roy went over to take the phone. Giffen kissed Ouida again and laughed.

"Hello," Roy said.

"Who is it?" Giffen called out from behind him.

The voice came to Roy, rasping and hilarious: "Goddamit, Roy, you got to cut out all this hoo-hawin' and get serious. You ought be home studyin' that legislation. You ought have it set by God to memory. You goin' be home early tonight?"

"Are we down in the shortrows?" Roy said.

"Goddam right," Fenstemaker said.

"What does that mean?"

"Cotton pickin' expression. You ever picked cotton? Bet your daddy ginned a lot of it, exploitin' them masses. How many tenants you got on your family land?"

"I don't know," Roy said. "I never looked real good. I was probably too busy joining the N Double A C P."

"You better not have," Fenstemaker said. "Not recently, any-how. I got to keep you clean till this bill's passed. You study it this afternoon?"

"Yes, sir," Roy said.

Giffen called out again: "Who the hell is it, Roy?"

"You got it down real good?"

"Yes, sir."

Giffen looked at Ouida. "Who's Roy sir-in' like that?" he said. Ouida shook her head.

"You gonna be ready tomorrow?" Fenstemaker said.

"No," Roy said. "Not about to be. I could memorize everything, and I'd still need to talk to you about how to handle the
damn thing. I don't know how to work a bill. Never did it in my
life."

"You know, goddamit," Fenstemaker said. "But that's a good
answer. You'll never know as much as I know, unless I teach you,
and I'm gonna teach you tomorrow. Day after all right?"

"For what?"

"The *bill*, dammit and hell. You think you be in condition to
work that bill then?"

"Maybe."

"Okay. Now go home and get some rest. You ain't learnin'
nothin' over there with old Earle's wife. Least I hope not. You
know he's in town?"

"I just found out," Roy said.

"Well . . . You gonna get the hell out of there?"

"I wasn't plannin' on it," Roy said.

"You nutboy liberals . . ." Fenstemaker began.

"I'm a conservative States' rights Democrat," Roy said.

"Well that's worse," Fenstemaker said. "Don't go round talkin'
like that or you'll be a total loss to me. 'Stead of just a calculated
risk."

"Your risk," Roy said. "Not mine. I didn't initiate this crazy
business."

"You goin' along, though, cause you're okay," Fenstemaker
said. "Go home and go to bed. You hard-peckered boys need
more rest than I do. Goodnight."

The connection was broken immediately, and Roy stood there
with the receiver in his hand, staring at the wall.

"Who was it?" Giffen said.

Roy turned round and poured himself a fresh drink. "Just a
political enemy," he said, "giving me a bad time."

"Really?" Giffen said, genuinely excited now. "How come you
sir-in' him like that?"

"I don't know why," Roy said. "I guess he had me rattled."

"Well . . ." Giffen began. He did not know quite what to say. He was reluctant to question anyone about political enemies — he'd never had a political enemy in his life. Everybody loved George Giffen in his home district. "Well . . ." He kissed Ouida again and said: "I guess I better move on to the Friendly before they close it on me . . . You seen my new car? I got a new Alfa. Come out and take a look."

Roy said he'd seen the new Alfa, and Ouida said she'd seen it several times. Giffen nodded and waited a moment for Roy to go on talking about his telephone conversation. When it was apparent that there would be no discussion, he waved goodbye and headed out the front door. In a minute they could hear the car sputtering in the drive. Ouida said: "What was all that about?"

"Arthur Fenstemaker," Roy said. "I'm suddenly one of Fenstemaker's prince consorts or something. He's got me handling a bill for him."

"How'd he know you were here?"

Roy shrugged. "How's he know anything? He knows, all right, though. He even told me Earle was in town and suggested the better part of valor."

"Apparently everybody knows Earle's in town but me," Ouida said.

"I didn't know."

"You want to leave?"

"Not especially," Roy said. "What I'd really like to do is sit down here and look at that place on your leg." He showed her where. "It's about the most desirable section of a woman I've ever seen," he said.

"Well," she said. She sat down and examined her leg and said: "Looks like we're making real progress. You think you might kiss me some more?"

"I might kiss that place on your leg. Or lay my head up against it — that might be even better."

"I thought you were all set to change the rules? What about that meeting you were going to call? That other vote?"

"Renewed convictions," Roy said. "I'm feeling stronger — got whiskey in my veins now to make up for all that blood I lost."

"I thought you were making pretty good sense there for a while," Ouida said. "Remember what you pointed out? If we're going to be talked about anyhow, we might as well . . ."

"I don't want to get me in trouble," Roy said, smiling.

"*I'm* the one who's going to be in trouble," Ouida said. "I could mess up the divorce — if there's going to be a divorce — and lose custody of the boy and bitch up everything, and *I'm* not complaining . . ."

He leaned forward, splashing whiskey on his wrist, and kissed the place on her leg.

"Kiss me here," she said, showing him where. He kissed her throat. She moved her arms around him and touched the back of his neck. "I like you here," she said. "It's nice to find a neck that's not shaved . . . In Florence last year, when Earle was running around with that lady parachutist, I'd go out walking in the afternoons just to look at the backs of men's necks. They all had such nice shaggy necks."

"We're both sick," Roy said. "You like hairy necks. I like that place on your leg."

"Listen," she said. "You made the point — I didn't. If we've already made spectacles of ourselves, why not — if we're going to suffer the consequences — take advantage of it?"

"I want to have a semi-adult relationship," Roy said. He kissed her again, for a longer period of time. "You make me feel clean all over," he said.

She backed off from him, smiling, slightly flushed. "You've got your *propensities* all in a conflict," she said. "And they used to run in such clean straight lines . . . Where are my art objects, by the way?"

"Storage," Roy said. "All in storage . . . Except for the iron stewpot. Which I've donated to charity."

"Let's go have a beer," Ouida said. "Let's go by the Dearly Beloved and give those people something really to talk about."

"What if Earle's there?"

"What if he is?"

"All right," Roy said.

"Will you tell them you're my lover?"

"If you want . . . I'll post it on the bulletin board, alongside the bowling scores."

"I'll go next door and get the baby sitter," Ouida said.

He sat listening to record music. He thought about going out to the car and returning with several of the art objects. They might interest the boy; Earle the Third might have some fun with the corset model or the Orange Crush container. As for the Coolidge portrait, Roy had resolved to be entirely selfish about it: he couldn't possibly give up the portrait of President Coolidge. Though he'd nearly been forced to part with it the night before when he was stopped by the policeman. He remembered the policeman distinctly; the fellow had stopped him on the night before just after he'd dropped Ouida at home. He hadn't been driving recklessly; rather not recklessly enough to avoid suspicion. He remembered driving down the main street of the city at two in the morning, holding the last of the wine in his lap, driving very slowly and perhaps weaving a little, bending his head to get a better look at the lighted Capitol dome and the awful store fronts. Then the nice policeman had come upon him from behind, honking and flashing his red light. He had come round to Roy's door, sniffing his breath and demanding that he walk the chalked line. Roy would have liked to go back now and find that chalked line, pry up a section of the street and take it home to hang above his fireplace for all his friends to come see: he'd walked the goddam chalked line as if he'd been training for it for years. Then the policeman had noted the backseat full of the art objects. "What's all this?" he said. "Looks like you've been looting a store . . ." He was prepared to take Roy into the station house then, until Roy produced his legislator's credentials with the cards signed by the Governor and the Speaker of the House and the Chief of Police and the captain of the Rangers.

The officer had become all fatherly and protective at that point, looking after his favorite young politician, and Roy had been permitted to drive on, inconvenienced only by the relinquishing of his half bottle of wine . . .

They'd traveled all over on the day before, all day and all over three counties, hundreds of miles through the hills and the low country, and never being, so far as could be determined by the semi-precious county maps (provided all high state officials) more than thirty or forty miles away from the Capitol dome. They had traveled over the backroads that led through the hills and down and out and past Indian forts and historic creeks, ancient iron bridges and endless small towns. Ouida had been charmed by the towns; she repeated the names aloud all afternoon: *Pflugerville* and *Utley* and *Bastrop* and *Rosanky* and *Spicewood* and *Drippin' Springs* . . . After the first hour on the road and the first bottle of wine, they fell into a rhythm for the day, with rather special rituals to be observed and referred to only in fixed, vaguely esoteric terminology. What had begun as a plan for nothing more ambitious than a picnic in the country was soon transformed into a sort of progressive dinner on a grand scale . . . chicken leg in Rosanky . . . slug of wine in Bastrop . . . deviled eggs in Drippin' . . . with backyard dancing and speeches out under the elm trees, organized games and favors for the guests. Roy, it soon developed, had a *propensity to consume,* which he indulged at every opportunity, usually on an *art object.* Ouida decided everything was either *quaint* or *charming;* she sent a number of postcards to friends in the city (the highest buildings of which were frequently visible from the hills), mentioning a charming iron bridge or a quaint corn silo and noting how, despite the uncommonly warm days, they'd slept under blankets every evening. And there was the business about the legends . . . *"Legend* has it," one of them would say, glancing at the guidebook until resorting to invention, "Legend has it that the charming stone privy we just passed was once inhabited by immigrant German noblemen who, forsaking the pomp and ceremony of European drawing rooms, came to the New World during the last century seeking economic freedom and Cherokee poontang . . ."

They bought art objects all over three counties. Roy would see one of the phony antique shops up ahead and would immediately hit the brakes, saying, "I've got a sudden propensity to consume." "That's a good thing," Ouida had said to him once. "I've got a terrible propensity to use the ladies' room . . ." They had bought the stewpot during the first of their antique store stops. The others were irresistible after that: Ouida had wanted the corset model; farther down the road he had picked up the Coolidge portrait, and there followed in easy succession more than a half-dozen purchases through the day. The ghost town had been the climactic event. The ghost store, rather. What little remained of the town was now converted into a group of decaying, pitched-roof farm outbuildings. But the store itself yielded up a treasure: high button shoes, patent medicines, hard black farmers' hats, faded sunbonnets, the pasteboard containers collapsed and mildewed and strewn with rat droppings. The store had been closed down — never to reopen — during the first year of the Depression, its stock intact and still on display. There were WARNING signs all about, with painted KEEP OUT admonitions and underscored notations in finer print that trespassers *had* and *would be* prosecuted. Roy assured Ouida there was nothing to worry about. If called to account for their actions, they would identify themselves as members of a special legislative committee appointed to investigate small business failures.

Now he sat in the front room of the apartment, listening to record music, trying to recall the speech he'd made to her from the magnolia tree on the evening before. Scarcely a particle of it came to him now . . . He couldn't seem to get past those opening lines: *"Most High and Mighty Ouida . . . My High Tower . . . My Dear Miss Lady Love . . ."* When memory failed him, he continued mumbling to himself, an extemporaneous speech made under the breath: "I am come to you today, My Friend, a

chaste . . . a *chastened* man . . . *censured* is the word for it
round here, and I want my one lady friend out there to know —
I'm sure she'll be *gratified* to know — and I'm *proud* to state, My
Friend — that (where was I?) my . . . (oh yes) only regret is that
I have but one married lover and lady friend mistress to give up
for my country . . ."

"Where ya'll going?"

The little boy had wandered into the room, rubbing his eyes,
interrupting Roy's speech. Roy tried to mark the place mentally where he had left off in the discourse with himself. He
turned to the boy and said, "Hello, Earle Cummins Fielding.
The Third."

"Will you come see me tomorrow?"

"Yes."

"Will we go out on your boat?"

"No."

The boy got down on his hands and knees and crawled round
the room, snorting. He looked up suddenly and said: "What am
I, Roy? Hey, what am I?"

"Armadillo?"

"*No!*"

"Platypus?"

"No . . . What's a platypus?"

"I think," Roy said, "I'm almost certain . . . it's a species of
roothog."

"Hey! That's it!" He got to his feet and said: "When we going
out on your boat?"

"Soon," Roy said. "It's bound to be soon."

There was a sound of footsteps on the front porch, and the boy
moved toward his bedroom, vastly pleased with himself. "Have
nice time," he said, looking back and grinning before he vanished
down the hall.

Four

THERE WERE several tables pushed together now to accommodate all their friends. The beer garden was filling rapidly, and dancing had begun on a small concrete slab. Someone had taken Willie's chair next to Ellen Streeter; he had circled the tables several times, examining people, before settling at the far end, across from a young man named Harris McElhannon. Willie liked Harris all right, but it was Harris's date that drew him to this end of the table.

"Hello, Willie," Harris said, barely looking up, his attention fastened instead on what the politicians were saying at the other end of the table. Willie sat down and stared at the girl, who seemed to have her mind on better things than politicians. After a minute or so, Harris turned back to his date and said: "Cathryn, this is Willie . . . Willie — Cathryn Lemens. Cathryn teaches at the college."

Willie and the girl exchanged glances and Harris turned back to the politicians. She was nothing really extraordinary, Willie decided, but she was a new one. That was something. They were such an incestuous bunch, any unfamiliar face was a welcome addition. Giffen, Huggins, and Rinemiller had already come round to greet Harris, exchange a few words, and look over the girl. Now Willie commenced his own inspection. The girl smiled at him absently. Fats Domino sang to them about getting married and going to Paris.

Harris got abruptly to his feet and stared around menacingly, grinding his teeth, flexing muscles in his arms. They were all used to Harris by now — he had once told a legislator's wife with whom he was carrying on that Alan Ladd in the motion picture *Shane* had changed his life. He wore specially tailored shirts with three-quarter length sleeves and tight western trousers with piping along the pockets that suggested a small child's cowboy outfit. He was a salesman of used cars.

"Excuse me," Harris said, setting his jaw and moving off in short strides toward the men's room. He was actually a very attractive young man. He was out of law school by a year or two, and when he was not involved in someone's political campaign, he worked in used car lots, selling on commission. It did not much matter where Harris found employment. His family had a good deal of money and could be depended on for generous contributions to anyone's campaign for whom Harris might have a special affection at the moment.

The girl looked at the dancers on the slab for a time and then lost interest. She turned to Willie and said: "What did he say your name was?"

"Wilton England."

"Wilton . . . ?"

"Wilton *Jubal* England, matter of fact."

"I thought he called you Willie."

"Guess he did."

"Willie England?"

"Yes."

"*Oh!*"

"Hmm?"

"You're the one with the newspaper," the girl said.

"That's right," Willie said. "You read it?"

"Sometimes."

"You shouldn't bother."

"Why not?"

"It's a bore," Willie said. "It's like a prayer meeting."

"I don't think it's so bad," the girl said.

"I'm worn out from editing those awful ambivalent essays the faculty members send me. About the human situation and all. Even worse is having to read my *own* copy. Proofs. And corrected proofs. And corrections of corrected proofs. We've got lousy printers, but they're sincere liberals."

The girl smiled and said: "Feel better now?"

"No," Willie said. "You like teaching?"

"It's all right. "I'm on a fellowship — working on my master's."

"I'll bet you're brilliant," Willie said. "I can tell about these things."

"I was Phi Beta Kappa," the girl said. "Would you believe it?"

"Sure."

"But an absolute cultural vacuum. I really don't *know* anything. All I do is memorize . . . You want something from memory?" She did not wait for Willie's reply but started right in:

> *Come let us mock at the great*
> *That had such burdens on the mind*
> *And toiled so hard and late*
> *To leave some monument behind,*
> *Nor thought of the levelling wind.*
>
> *Come let us mock at the wise;*
> *With all those calendars whereon*
> *They fixed old aching eyes,*
> *They never saw how seasons run,*
> *And now but gape at the sun.*
>
> *Come let us mock at the good . . .*

"And so on . . . See? That's Yeats."

She had spoken the lines without expression, running them past, uninspired, one behind the other like passing freight cars. She smiled brightly. Willie murmured approval. Harris returned to the table with George Giffen trailing him. Giffen sat next to them, his face twitching.

"Hey, you hear about Rinemiller, Willie?" he said.

Willie said, no, he hadn't heard.

"Rinemiller's runnin' for the Speakership. Takin' pledges already. I just pledged him my vote."

"That's real good," Willie said.

"You know what I *think* about all the time?" the girl said.

"What?" Willie said.

"Rinemiller make one hell of a good House Speaker," Giffen said. "Don't you think so?"

"Yes," Harris said.

"Sports cars," Cathryn said to Willie. "I sit around grading themes in my office and my mind's not on comma blunders or run-on sentences at all. I have little fantasies about riding around town in a red roadster with my hair flying, looking chic and adorable . . ."

"Like in the magazine pictures," Willie said.

"Yes," the girl said.

"You say you got a roadster?" Giffen said.

"No," Cathryn said. "I say I *want* one."

"I got a new Alfa," Giffen said. "You want a ride in it?"

"Harris is my date, George," Cathryn said. "But I suddenly find you irresistible."

"Go ahead," Harris said, gripping himself. "I'm willing to make any reasonable sacrifice to get Giffen away from this end of the table."

"Come on . . . Come on . . ." Giffen was saying. He stood behind the girl and held her chair. She finally got to her feet. Giffen put his arm around her and kissed her neck. "Hey!" he said to her. "We're good friends, hah?"

"Can I drive it?" she said to Giffen. She looked around uncertainly at her date. Harris continued to concentrate on conversations at the other end of the table.

"I'll check you out on it," Giffen said. "It's Italian. You can't beat foreigners for workmanship. It goes like a bomb . . ."

Cathryn and Giffen moved off toward the parking lot. After a few moments, Harris rose and moved down to the other end of the table. Willie sat alone, thinking about money.

There was an argument underway at the opposite end. Rinemiller, Huggins, and some of the others had ambushed a state senator who had been drinking with friends on the inside. It was like a gang war — someone from the enemy camp had wandered onto alien ground, and they were giving him a terrible time. Willie could hear most of it from where he was sitting. The older man was flushed in the face. He held on to his glass of beer and looked off into the trees. "You want a Soviet America?" he kept saying.

Ellen Streeter came round from the other end. "Hello, Harris doll," she said. She looked at Willie. "You left me," she said.

"It's not true — quit demagoguing," Willie said. "You just got taken over by a mob of admirers. One of them took my chair."

Ellen Streeter smiled and touched his hand. He wondered if he ought to start dating her again. It was like high school, when boys and girls had crushes on each other from one semester to the next. Except that now the subject of his secret desire had developed faint wrinkles round her nice neck.

"Who's your girl?" she said to Harris.

"Teacher at the college."

"She has nice legs," Ellen said. "You don't see good horsy legs like that any more."

"Don't be unkind," Willie said. "You don't need to."

"I've got to," Ellen said. "Here that girl is already out of college and teaching — and I thought she was just some defenseless little freshman about to be seduced by Harris."

"I will . . . I will!" Harris assured them.

"Harris is a real snake," Ellen said. "You know that, Willie? He took me out one night and I was nearly deflowered. It all happens before you know it. He's a snake — honest to God he is."

"I'm passionate," Harris said.

The two of them got up to dance, and Willie sat alone again. George Giffen and the new girl, Cathryn, returned to the garden, appearing almost simultaneously with Roy and Ouida. There was terrible confusion for a moment while introductions were made. Giffen leaned over and kissed Ouida. He explained how he had just taken Cathryn for a ride.

"Tell them how it goes, honey," he said.

"Like a bomb," Cathryn said. She thought a moment and added: "I forget how it corners."

Harris and Ellen Streeter returned from the dancing slab, and there was another great shifting about while an effort was made to introduce everyone and find additional table space. When they were settled, Ellen Streeter sat across from Ouida and began to talk:

"I saw Earle today. I thought he looked a lot better."

"Everybody saw Earle today but me," Ouida said.

"You haven't seen him yet?" Ellen said. "Heavens! You'd think a man would want to see his family the minute he got into town."

Conversations sagged a little all around them; people left off in mid-sentence, struggling in the gathering silence to find words — any words — with which to crutch the moments. Even the inanimate world seemed to connive at focusing attention on the one clearly understood conversation at the table: one record expired on the jukebox and another was not immediately put to vibrating the evening air. Ellen Streeter went on: "I suppose you're meeting him here, then? He told me at lunch he was coming out."

Willie searched his empty head for some subject with which to engage Ellen Streeter in conversation. Roy turned in his chair and considered retreat to the men's room. The new girl, Cathryn Lemens, not yet among the *cognoscenti,* was almost immediately aware, all the same, of unease at the table. She tried to think of something to say, but she could only join the others, mute and disabled, her mind gone blank even as concerned sports car capabilities. She looked at Harris, who was beginning to smile fiercely in anticipation. Harris had no favorites — it was just that he liked to go with winners, and Ellen Streeter at the moment seemed far and away ahead of the others. Alfred Rinemiller's was the last voice going at full volume, and now even the intensity of his remarks began to flag. He ended one of his favorite political stories and attempted to begin another, but no one was listening.

"He's coming here, is he?" Ouida said.

Ellen Streeter laughed with wonderful assurance. "Oh yes," she said. "Did he tell you about his plan?" She looked at the others. "Earle wants to have a tennis tournament while he's in town. Out at the ranch over the weekend. He was calling it the Egghead Mixed Doubles Invitational Tennis Tournament and Civil Rights Conference. He didn't tell you any of this?"

"Not that I recall," Ouida said.

"Well you'll hear all about it tonight. He's all excited." She paused for a moment, considering, and then went on: "He'll be pleased Roy brought you out — he's been so busy all day."

It seemed at first that Ouida was addressing someone else at the table. "I remember," she said, "a really weird experience we had in Europe. Earle had fallen in love with this lady parachutist, and we were separated for about a month and we were talking about a divorce. So he called me for lunch one day and brought the girl. She was English and jolly and all and something of a bum. She talked constantly at lunch, patting Earle's hand and giving me the business. *'Dearie,'* she would say. *'Dearie,* I know this is terribly difficult for you, and I've been worried whether you're having any fun. I mean are you really *doing* anything — alone as you are in a strange country.' I tried to remember how all those brave women look in the television soap operas, and finally I said, 'Oh, yes, *Dearie,* there's lots to do. There's the swimming and the tea dances and the parachute jumps and the Red Cross work, and of course there's still Earle. Earle and I screw every Wednesday at noon . . .' "

There was a gasping for air all round the table, and then things started up again. A record came on and a singer whooped about the romantic problems of sixteen-year-olds. Cathryn Lemens began to giggle; Willie sat back in his chair, positioned in a half-sprawl, head lolling, staring at the treetops and smiling; Harris McElhannon laughed and beat the table with the palm of his hand and showed his good white teeth. Rinemiller began another story and George Giffen smiled wanly. Giffen had not quite understood the point of Ouida's remarks, but he cared deeply for Ouida and knew enough to smile. Roy stared at Ouida for a long moment, grinning, vastly pleased. Willie still could not think of anything to say, but he succeeded in getting Ellen Streeter away from the table by asking her to dance with him. A waitress arrived and they all ordered steaks.

Ouida smiled back at Roy. "Let's all dance," she said. "Let's do a mambo or the dirty boogie."

Five

THEY MOVED round in the small space of the concrete dancing slab, holding each other lightly. Willie danced with Ellen Streeter; Roy with Ouida. Harris came along and asked Ellen if she would go out back and neck with him, and Ellen said she supposed she might, and Willie went to the tables and returned with the new girl named Cathryn. The music was harsh, thumping in their ears. Occasionally, they could hear Rinemiller's laughter from across the garden. George Giffen skulked about the edges of the dancing space, telling himself this was the way life really was. They did some crazy steps and changed partners and then changed back again. They were all a little tight, stiff-tongued and slack-jawed; aggressiveness sagging into an uncharacteristic sentimentality. They changed partners again, perspiring a little in the warm evening air. Willie danced with Ouida; she seemed uncompromisingly happy.

"You and Roy . . ." Willie began.

"What?" Her warm breath was in his face, smelling faintly of spearmint gum and expensive cosmetics. The interruption muddled his thoughts, and for a moment he forgot what it was he had started to say. Then he remembered.

". . . are my favorite people. All-time favorites."

Ouida smiled and kissed him on the mouth. "Me too," she said. "I am my all-time favorite. Then Roy, then you."

"Am pleased," Willie said. "Happy and content by that ranking."

"Why is he so low-geared?" Ouida said. She had her eyes on Roy, but Willie had to ask to make sure.

"Who?"

"Roy —" she said, "how come he's so low-geared?"

"We're just good friends," Willie said. "I never inquired about his gears."

"I mean he could practice law or help in his family's business or run for an office that would keep him busy the year round," Ouida said. "Is he a good politician?"

"I think he's pretty good," Willie said. "It's not a compulsion with him like with some of the really good ones. He practices law occasionally. He gets on the phone once a week and tells his brother how, at least, and he takes a case sometimes on holidays. He tried one last Easter. Or maybe it was Palm Sunday — I forget."

He stopped talking and concentrated on the dancing. Ouida had her arm up over his shoulder and her hand touching the back of his neck: an intimacy which rendered him nearly inoperative. Harris and Ellen Streeter returned and began to dance: in the small space of the slab they constituted lethal objects. Harris barreled past Willie and Ouida, singing to himself: "Chantilly lace and uh prutty face an' uh pony tail an' uh *everthang* . . ." Willie and Ouida steered away from Harris and changed partners with Roy and the new girl named Cathryn.

Willie danced with Cathryn, taking her hand and placing it at the back of his neck. "Do that," he said. He held on to her and they moved round the slab; he negotiated variations on the box step he'd learned in junior high.

"You're a terrible dancer," Cathryn said.

"I've got a natural rhythm," Willie said. He kissed her lightly on the mouth and then wondered if he were infected with George Giffen's illness.

"Harris is still ignoring me," Cathryn said. She watched Harris and Ellen Streeter dancing but did not seem really to mind.

"He senses how I feel about you," Willie said. "He's leaving us alone."

"Is he successful with women?"

"Success comes to Harris with depressing regularity."

They danced in silence for a time. The absence of talk made Willie nervous. He said: "Ask me some stupid questions."

"All right," the girl said. "What do you want out of *life?*"

Willie thought a moment. "Nothing," he finally said. "I got everything."

"*Every*thing?"

"Almost. Except for a few accessories. Like reasonable clothing and clean shirts every day. And a couple of mutton chops waiting for me in the evenings. Grilled without condiments — you like that? And pie with a piece of Stilton, and pulled bread and a pint of Club Médoc. A good fire in the grate. A comfortable woman to keep me warm in bed and to brush my bowler and fold my umbrella in the mornings."

The girl looked ill. She had drunk several glasses of beer and then switched to someone else's gin and tonic. She stared at Willie desperately.

"And a London tailor," Willie said. "And a charge account at the Colony."

"I don't feel well," the girl said. "Can we sit down?"

They returned to the table. Roy and Ouida had already given up the dancing, and now they sat at the table looking bored with everyone. Willie wished they would leave before Earle Fielding arrived — if he did arrive — though he was unable to explain why he should feel this way: Roy could take care of himself; all of them could. Willie decided he was growing impatient with the rich and near-rich and deadbeat and dependent — all of them — his hipster pols.

Steaks were served, crackling in iron plates, and conversations flagged as people got serious over dinner. Alfred Rinemiller approached from the other end and sat across from Roy and Ouida. Roy nodded, picking at his food. "Hello, Alfred," Ouida said. He was a large, handsome man with an oversized, vaguely leonine head. He pushed hair back from his eyes and gave Ouida his rogue's look. He had necked with her for a quarter of an hour once, two years before, on a hotel bed during a political convention with friends wandering in and out and her husband Earle sick on the floor of the bathroom. Rinemiller was certain that Ouida still remembered this with pleasure.

Giffen sat close by, looking strained, spreading himself too thin. It was difficult trying to keep track of the conversations all around him, but Giffen was there, giving his best, shifting ceaselessly from one group to another. He looked at Ouida and clapped Rinemiller's shoulder.

"You-all hear about Alfred runnin' for the Speakership?"

Ouida nodded. She started to answer, but Giffen's attention was already shifted to conversations elsewhere, and they were left to deal alone with the beached and flopping wet fish of Rinemiller's ambition. "Nice to know about," she managed to say.

Rinemiller shrugged and said something about ventures and gains. He turned to Roy and said: "Appreciate your support, Good Buddy."

"You'll probably get it," Roy said without enthusiasm.

"How about right now, though?" Rinemiller said. "I need as many pledges as possible to get this thing off the ground. How about it, Roy?"

Willie interrupted, and Roy gave his pledge in silence — to do something extraordinarily nice for Willie one of these days.

"I heard you had an audience," Willie said.

"What's that?" Rinemiller said.

"I heard you and Fenstemaker had a little visit."

"That's right," Rinemiller said. "How'd you hear about it. You hear too much. Don't understand how you birds . . ."

"Best tradition of a free and independent and fearless press," Willie said. "I walked into his reception room and looked at his engagement book . . . I tell you, it took guts."

Giffen's face came near again. He redraped an arm round Rinemiller's shoulder. "How 'bout that, hah?" he said. "Ole Alfred's gonna be our next Speaker . . . 'Bout time the Liberals in the Lower Body had a man on whom they can depend . . . on . . ." Giffen's remarks were ignored by the others now. His voice faded as he lost track of his own thoughts.

"What passed between you two old pros?" Willie was saying to Rinemiller.

"We just visited," Rinemiller said.

Giffen looked at Roy and whispered: "Who're they talkin' about? Who's Alfred been visitin'?"

When Roy did not respond, Ouida explained to Giffen.

"Was there a laying on of hands?" Willie said.

"No comment to the press," Rinemiller said.

Willie thought a moment. He could not push Rinemiller too far. Rinemiller was one of the original board members of the corporation organized for establishment of the weekly newspaper; was, indeed, the one member most responsible for securing the editorship for Willie England.

"Not even to your own press?" Willie said. "You ought to take advantage of your sympathetic correspondents before our little non-profit organization folds."

"Anything comes of it, you'll be the first to know," Rinemiller said. "I believe in that business about rewarding friends and giving those who aren't as bad a time as possible."

Roy wondered what Rinemiller and Fenstemaker had really talked about and whether the Governor had spent the day rousing young people in support of his programs. If there was a threat implicit in Rinemiller's remarks, it did not disturb Roy: he was more immediately concerned with the possibility of having to work with Rinemiller on the Governor's public school legislation. He remembered Rinemiller's imitation of the Governor earlier in the evening and now he hoped it hadn't been just a performance for the others.

The new girl named Cathryn pulled on Willie's arm. "Mencken," she said, "talked about gay fellows who tossed dead cats into sanctuaries . . . See? I memorize . . . What're they talking about?"

Willie started to answer, but Kermit's strident voice came from directly behind them: "Trouble is, there's no more sanctuaries. They been overrun by all them moneychangers."

Crazy Kermit still had his young friend named Jobie in tow. They stood behind Willie and Cathryn, the two of them in identical black shag sweaters and soiled back-buckle khakis. They swayed slightly, together.

"Here he is, Jobie," Kermit said. "You met him while ago, but you didn't really know who he was. Willie — Jobie's got something for you. Give it to my Good Doctor Willie, Jobie."

The young man named Jobie began removing sheets of yellow typescript from a manila folder.

"What is it?" Willie said. He stuffed bits of meat and potato into his mouth, hoping the spectacle of his eating might hold the visitors to as brief a transaction as possible. He knew all about the boys from the college with their yellow typescripts.

"It's called *No Way Out — The Dilemma of the Modern Radical*," Jobie said.

Willie continued to eat. Harris, sitting nearby, looked up startled.

"No Way Out," the young man repeated. "Our culture is ossifying. We are become a nation of conformists — automatons if you will — with backyard barbecue pits and corporate security . . ."

"Wish I had some corporate security," Willie said.

". . . smug and complacent, terrified, in reality, by the awful reality of . . ."

Someone else interrupted to order fresh ice and setups. Jobie went on.

". . . of . . . today's window dressing world. There's *no way out*," he emphasized. "There's only hope for the young — the radical young — those few not yet corrupted and housebroken by the pressures of conformity in modern society. They have got — these young — to make an affirmation in the dead and empty air."

Harris looked up, drowsy with food and beer. "Make a what?" he said amazed. He held a large piece of beefsteak in front of him on the end of a fork.

"An *affirmation*, man," Kermit said. "Dig those people, yes!"

"Goddam right," Harris said moodily. "We're all dyin' of the fallout." He regarded his piece of beefsteak for a moment and then poked it into his mouth.

"That's fine," Willie said. "That's real good." He reached out for the typescript. "I'll take a look at it at the office tomorrow."

The young man held on to the papers. "I'd prefer," he said, "to bring it by myself and be present when you read it. There are some allusions, references, that might need to be explained."

"Fine," Willie said. "Bring it by." Jobie started to speak, but Willie anticipated the next question. "Bring it by tomorrow after lunch. I've got an hour then," he said.

Kermit and Jobie wandered off to another table. It was nearly closing time now, and the waitresses were moving about, picking up empties, urging customers to finish their beer before curfew. Huggins came down to the end of the table with a gaunt, moist-eyed girl alongside him. The girl carried a guitar.

"Where'll we go?" he said. It was always a terrible decision to face at the midnight closing.

"We could all go home," Roy said. "There's a new place."

"Whose home?" Huggins said, grinning.

They discussed people's homes — other people's homes, mostly. No one volunteered shelter for the party.

"How about Harris's apartment?" Huggins said.

"How about yours," Harris said.

"It's a mess there," Huggins said. "And my phonograph's broke."

"I'm tired of Thelonious Monk, anyhow," Willie said. "I think he's basically a reactionary."

Some of the others joined them from the other end to discuss housing prospects. The girl with Huggins hung the guitar round her neck and struck a few chords. The jukebox was turned off inside and customers moved out of the garden. The girl began to sing as the others discussed places to go. The girl sang in a flat, unhappy voice about slaves following the Big Dipper north to freedom. Waitresses gathered up glasses and pitchers and bottles and stood just inside the building, next to the bar, looking out at the young people grouped round the main table and the girl playing guitar.

"Let me take Cathryn home," Willie said to Harris.

"If you want," Harris said.

"Let me take her," Giffen said. "In the Alfa."

"Don't I have any voice in this?" Cathryn said.

"I'll take her," Harris concluded. "I brought her — I'll take her. I got a sense of responsibility in these delicate matters."

Earle Fielding came walking across the grounds from the parking lot. Ellen Streeter was the first to see him — she ran out to greet him, taking his arm. The others hooted a greeting from a distance and then fell silent as Earle approached.

"Where you been all day?" someone yelled.

Earle, coming closer, said: "Hotel room. Making plans for our little party over the weekend — all of you heard about it? The Egghead Invitational Mixed Doubles Tennis Tournament and Civil Rights Conference . . ." He broke off suddenly, noticing Ouida for the first time.

"Hello, Earle," Ouida said. Roy, sitting next to her, shifted in his chair and struggled against the temptation to rise and move off a few feet. He noted with relief that Giffen was on the other side of Ouida and had his arm draped round the back of her chair. Earle Fielding came directly over to his wife.

"Hope you don't mind, baby," he said. "We're planning this thing at the ranch — you think your parents would object?" It was as if he had been away from the city a few hours instead of several months. It was not until Ouida mentioned the advisability of bringing their son out to the ranch for the weekend that Fielding showed any emotion over his own return home.

"Yeah . . . *Yeah* . . . You've got to bring the boy out," he said. "I haven't seen him in . . . Jesus . . . We've got to spend some time together, maybe go huntin'. I bought him the goddamdest deer rifle you ever saw . . ."

"He's too little," Ouida said. "He couldn't lift a gun."

"Yeah . . . That's right," Fielding said. Someone got his attention and he turned to talk to the others about the party. The folk singer started on the same song again.

Earle Fielding stood with the others and talked about politics. He was a tall, big-shouldered man, slightly jug-eared but with a handsome college boy's face. Once, people had talked about how he would be Governor in fifteen or twenty years, but that was when his marriage was sound and he was still unscarred in politics. A year ago he had resigned his seat in the legislature and was drunk for several months, leaving his wife now and then, moving into nearby bachelor apartments whenever there was trouble between them. Everyone agreed that he had "got hold" of himself recently. He was not tight in the middle of the day as often as before, and he had begun to travel a great deal, ostensibly on family business but nearly always checking in with local politicians over the country and making occasional speeches for one enlightened candidate or another. He had made many friends and secured these liaisons with large cash contributions. It was generally assumed that Earle would seek office again, something on a statewide level, or possibly land an appointive position in the party. He had been educated in the East, as had his mother and sisters, but his position was not undermined by the defection: the Fieldings were as sound historically as they were in business; their wealth could be traced back to the frontier.

Earle's father and uncles had been responsible during the 1930's for forcing through the legislature a series of anti-labor bills, and no one was more aware of the brutal social forces at work behind the legislation than Earle. Several years before, in college, he had sat through a series of lectures dealing at length on the labor laws of his home state and the manner by which they had been enacted, afraid to speak out in discussion period for fear he might be revealed as a member of the same robber-baron gang of Fieldings that had perpetrated such crimes against the people.

Now it was Earle's hope that he would have a personal hand in overturning these statutes. He liked, in addition, to make frequent attacks on the depletion allowance for oil, from which a sizable amount of his own wealth was derived. Earle's conservative critics had not yet got around to denouncing him as a traitor to his class — they merely regarded him as a damn fool.

"Where'll we *go?*" Huggins insisted.

"Giffen's?"

"He's got no whiskey. Only sherry."

"How about my hotel room?" Earle Fielding said. "They gave me a whole suite of rooms."

Someone laughed. "Earle owns the goddam hotel."

"Only half interest," Earle said. "How about it? I got a case of whiskey there. We can talk about the tennis tournament and our civil rights conference and electin' Alfred to the Speakership and the next revolution. How about it?"

Most of them looked pleased. They were on their feet almost immediately, ready to move on, laughing and talking around the unpainted tables, the garish lights from the bar and restaurant reflected on their innocent pink faces. They began to walk slowly toward the parking area. Ouida held Roy's arm, but reached out to get Earle's attention.

"Should I tell Earle Cummins you're home?" she said.

Her husband considered this for a moment.

"You coming with us to the hotel?" he said.

"I've a baby sitter to relieve," Ouida said. She held on to Roy's arm in the darkness of the parking lot.

"Well, hell — I wish you would," Earle said. "I'll call later . . ."

"When? I hope not in the middle of the night. Or what's left of it."

"In the morning. I'll call in the morning. Tell little Earle I'll be by to see him in the morning if I can't get home tonight . . . You got a ride?"

Ouida said she would get a ride with George Giffen or Roy. Earle clapped Roy's shoulder and said: "How you doin', Roy? You castin' some good votes?"

Roy said he was only interested in bad votes.

Giffen had been walking behind them, and now he came up even. "Hey," he said, "I hear you say you needed a ride home?"

Ouida gripped Roy's arm and tried to ignore the question. Earle turned back to them. "I'll tell you what," he said. "Roy — why don't you go with George in that hot rod and I'll take Ouida home in your car. Meet you both at the hotel — here's the key. I'll take Ouida. That way I can talk to her a few minutes."

Roy backed off but then changed his mind. He told Earle he thought he would probably go on home but would be happy to lend him the car for the night. Earle said that wouldn't be necessary; he'd get Alfred Rinemiller to drive them. Earle wandered off looking for Rinemiller. Giffen stood around for a moment. While he stared at the others, Ouida kissed Roy and urged him in a whisper to come by later. Before Roy could answer, Fielding and Rinemiller returned and led Ouida to one of the automobiles. He would have to call her later and run the risk of Earle's still being there, possibly even answering the phone.

There were some noisy exchanges: giggling conversations between the others, grouped round their cars: half-muffled laughter and catch-phrase goodbyes blended with the grinding of gears and the sputtering of radios being tuned in on the single after-midnight station. Giffen said goodbye to Roy and went off in a loping stride toward the others, trying to catch up. Willie, Ellen Streeter, the new girl, Huggins — all had vanished from sight. Cars moved past; occasionally someone would dangle an arm out a window and whoop at him. Roy climbed into his own car and sat for a moment, lighting a cigarette, fooling with the radio, fidgeting, wondering how much longer he could go without sleep. Or release. His stomach rumbled; his eyes burned and his mouth felt numb and shrunken from the drinks. He wondered just how much Earle Fielding knew — and if information was necessarily limited this first day back, how long it would be before he did know something? He wished Ouida would explain, but she wasn't talking — couldn't or wouldn't; it was never quite clear which. Roy knew only slightly more about the Fielding marriage than the others. Perhaps Ouida in her confusion knew even less.

He got the car started and drove slowly through the darkened streets. Heading west, toward the lakefront, he passed Ouida's apartment and noted Rinemiller's car parked in the drive. He moved toward his own place. On the radio, an announcer hawked a product: genuine cultured South Sea Island pearls . . .

Six

ARTHUR FENSTEMAKER chewed on a cold cigar and dribbled whiskey down the front of his silver dinner jacket. He paced about the second-story front gallery of the mansion, humming to himself, a little off key. He snapped his fingers, grunting, humming, sniffing the midnight air. He reached down inside his trousers and adjusted his undershorts. His assistant, Jay McGown, sat nearby, looking out over the city. Across from Jay, a large gray-haired man sat with hands folded, watching the Governor.

The butler brought them drinks. There was dance music coming from a group of Latin musicians belowstairs, and out front the guests in evening clothes wandered back and forth across the grounds and lounged on the whitewashed steps.

"I got to settle this in a hurry," Fenstemaker said, biting on the cigar. The gray-haired man offered a light, but Fenstemaker waved it away. "They don't let me smoke," he said, "but they didn't say nothin' about chewin'. I invent new vices ever' day." He spit into a potted palm and went on: "Just got few minutes . . . Let's get this business over with."

He took hold of his drink and put it to his mouth, swallowing hard. Then he handed it to the butler. "You get me a better one, Jimmy? Like you'd make for yourself?"

"Miz Fenstemaker said half jigger."

"I know all about that," the Governor said. "But goddam! All it's doin' is makin' me drink twice as much and I end up goin' to the bathroom all night long."

"Miz Fenstemaker . . ."

"She ain't here, Jimmy. Now's our opportunity."

"How 'bout three-quarter jigger?" the butler suggested.

"All right."

The colored man moved off with his empty glasses.

"Looky heah!" Fenstemaker said, and the gray-haired guest jumped perceptibly. The Governor stopped, thinking for a moment. He turned to Jay McGown. "You see that, Jay? That three-quarter jigger stuff? That boy's already learned somethin' about effective accommodation and compromise!" He laughed loudly and told the gray-haired man all about the butler being elected captain of his precinct over in niggertown. The guest, now totally mystified, jumped once again when Fenstemaker repeated the exhortation: "Looky heah, now . . ."

"Yes sir?"

"You want to take this business to the District Attorney?"

"I don't know, Governor. I just don't know. That's why I've come to you. I thought —"

"I'll get the D.A. on the phone right now — he's a personal

friend of mine. I'll get him over here right now to listen to this
damn thing, you give the word."

"Governor . . . I . . ."

"You wanna set little trap, instead? You had some good practice, it seems. You got some money, marked bills? Might even
try it on the District Attorney. Just for practice."

Fenstemaker had his face down next to the gray-haired man's,
their noses nearly touching. The visitor was pressed against the
leather chair. "Governor," he said, "I keep telling you I just . . .
don't . . . know. This never happened to me before. That's why
I come to you for advice."

Fenstemaker straightened up and talked over the fellow's head.
"Knew enough to tape-record that conversation. That's knowin'
somethin'. That's knowin' more'n I know . . . You even made
him count out that goddam money right out loud so it would get
on the tape. Why hell, man! *You know.* Don't give me that
stuff. That old dog don't hunt no more — that cow's been bred
and milked and damn near slaughtered."

The visitor, looking holy, determined to keep the conversation
on a high plain, shook his head from side to side and laid his hands
open. "Governor . . . I . . ."

"How many others you bribed?"

"Governor . . . !"

"You give me some names? Just like to know myself out of
curiosity. I deal with these people every day, understand."

"Governor . . . I never in my life . . ."

"You must've dangled somethin' a-front of him first conversation you had to make him go for the bait that way." Fenstemaker
examined the end of his cigar, as if it were a foreign object only
recently extracted from his throat. He went on: "What in hell you
say to him to make things develop the way they did?"

"I talked to him about the legislation. That's *all.* We went
out and had a drink. We got friendly. You know? Hell — maybe
I bragged on him some. We got us a couple dates for the night.
You know? *Friendly.* Then he starts talkin' about runnin' in

a statewide campaign and how he needed money for a race like that and how he could sure use a contribution from us. That was the first indication, Governor."

"So actually all you did is make a little contribution to his campaign . . . That's about all it boils down to."

The guest sat up straight in the leather chair and crossed his legs, looking resolute. "I think you'd agree that, under the circumstances, it amounted to considerably more than that, Governor."

Fenstemaker was silent for a moment. Then he said: "I think I just might dump this right back in your lap . . . Really none of my business."

"Sir? You wouldn't just . . ."

"Jay — go get me that reel of tape off that machine," Fenstemaker said.

The visitor was on his feet, following Fenstemaker and Jay McGown across the old pine floor. "Governor, I just come to you for advice. I don't want a lot of bad publicity. I don't want any scandal. I don't want to hurt anybody. I just want a fair shake before that committee. And I don't like a shakedown racket of any sort . . ."

Mrs. Fenstemaker appeared at one of the jalousied doors. The Governor looked up, smiling. "Sweet Mama . . . ?"

"They'll all be leaving soon downstairs, Arthur, and I thought . . ."

"Be right down," the Governor said. Mrs. Fenstemaker nodded and moved off toward the stairs.

"I can understand you're busy," the visitor said, still following Jay and the Governor. Jay picked up a reel of tape and handed it to Fenstemaker, who looked it over, balanced it in his palm, and held it out toward the visitor.

"Governor, you're the only qualified man to judge."

"Take it to the goddam District Attorney," Fenstemaker said.

"I just didn't want to cause any trouble. I thought it might all be handled without . . . I didn't want to damage that boy's career . . ."

"Damage!" the Governor hooted. "It's plenty damaged already, mister. That boy's ruined — one way or another — even if it never comes out in the open. I'll see to that personally."

"I think you ought to be the judge how it's handled," the guest concluded.

"Tell you what . . ."

"Yes, sir?"

"I'll let you know."

"Sir?"

"I'll let you know, for Jesus sake. I'll call you when I decide something."

The gray-haired man smiled. "I'm deeply relieved that you . . ." His voice trailed off as Fenstemaker turned and left the room.

Downstairs, a half-hour later, Fenstemaker poked at Jay's shoulder with his big hand, sipping a Scotch drink he'd managed to lift off one of the dinner guests. "Coonass is what it is, Jay," the Governor said. "Real cedar chopper stuff. God damn it's depressing." He paused and gulped his drink. "You ever sell me, Jay, I hope to Jesus it's for something big, something really important to you."

"That fellow's scared," Jay said. "I don't know which of them is worse."

"Coonass," the Governor repeated, shaking his head. "It's like learnin' everybody screws . . ."

At Earle Fielding's hotel suite, at nearly the same hour, the young people sat in overstuffed chairs or flopped on the deep-pile carpet, holding on to each other, talking politics, discussing the weekend's possibilities.

"You see the trophies?" Ellen Streeter asked someone. "Where are the trophies, Alfred?"

"Earle put them away somewhere," Rinemiller said.

"Let's see the trophies."

"Wait for Earle," Rinemiller said.

"He'll never get back," someone said. "Probably already jumped in bed with Ouida." There was laughter round the room, and the fellow added: "Or maybe he's set up a patrol outside his place to catch old Roy Sherwood sneakin' in."

Rinemiller got to his feet and went into Earle's bedroom. In a moment, he returned with the tennis trophies, a half dozen of them, already engraved for the winners of championship and consolation brackets.

"They're lovely and old-fashioned," Ellen Streeter said, taking them from Rinemiller. "Little gold figures. Like Alice Marble and Don Budge." She looked up at Rinemiller and some of the others and asked what they were doing. Rinemiller, Giffen, Huggins, and several girls were bent over a cardboard tournament chart, filling in names. "Seedings and pairings," Alfred Rinemiller said.

"Seedings and pairings," Ellen sang to herself. "Cockles and mussels . . ."

Harris and the girl named Cathryn sat across the room. Harris had his sleeves rolled up above the elbows, and Cathryn stared at his brown muscled arms.

"You're gorgeous," Harris said to her, making the muscles jump.

"You're gorgeouser," Cathryn said. She looked at his arms. Harris stared down her dressfront. "Where'd Willie go?" Cathryn said.

"You want Willie?" Harris said. His voice was high and careless. "I'll go get Willie, you want him. I'll *take* you to Willie, for God's sake . . ."

Cathryn looked up in amazement. "Who's Willie?" she said. "I don't know any Willie."

Ellen Streeter came over and sat with them. Harris shifted his attention to Ellen, wondering if he ought to attempt, one last time, to seduce her.

"Where's Willie gone?" Cathryn said to Ellen Streeter.

"Yeah — where in the world is he?" Harris said irritably. "We've been worried nearly to death about where Willie's gone."

Ellen shrugged. Harris asked her who she was dating for the tennis tournament. She made a face, rolling her eyes, as if about to describe a female operation from which she was not quite fully recovered. "George Giffen," she said.

"Tell you what," Harris said. "You help me find Willie, and I'll take you home tonight and even to the by-God tennis tournament. Okay?"

Ellen Streeter smiled, looking at Cathryn. Cathryn made a gesture of innocence. She said: "I only asked where Willie might have —"

George Giffen came upon her from behind and placed both hands on her bare shoulders. "Hah, honey," he said. "You gonna be at that tennis thang?" He massaged Cathryn's shoulders, making her wince.

"I haven't a date," Cathryn said.

"You really ought to come," Ellen Streeter said. "It's the most glittering social and cultural event of the season. Last year, we —"

"Don't worry," Harris said. "I'll get you a date. I got a fellow in mind. He's not here now, but . . ."

"Last year," Ellen continued, "we had what was called a Seated Drunk With Frictional Dancing."

"I got this young fellow in mind," Harris said. He took hold of the pasteboard chart on which the pairings had been outlined. He wrote in Cathryn's name next to Willie's. Then he thought a moment and put in Ellen Streeter next to his own. Giffen looked over his shoulder. "Hey," he said, "Ellen's *my* date for the tournament."

"You don't understand these things," Harris said to him. "This is a *mixed* doubles tournament. That's the whole point."

"It's like free love, doll," Ellen said, smiling at everyone.

Night insects buzzed round Willie England's head. They came piling in through the open windows of his second-story loft, seeking him out, feasting on his bare arms, cracking against walls and lightbulbs, banging window blinds and struggling in the turbulence of an ancient overhead fan. The fan stirred the air and flapped papers on Willie's desk. He sat there typing, waving a hand in front of his face whenever the insects came near. He picked steadily at the typewriter keys, rising only to refill his glass of water or change a record on the phongraph. He had selected the music with great care — Benny Goodman, Rex Stewart, Stravinsky, Prokofiev, Jelly Roll Morton — but he heard none of it, really. He was nearly finished with the issue of his newspaper, and his concentration was intense and absolute as the end came into sight.

He was several days ahead of schedule, and the printers would be enchanted. It was the earliest he had closed out the paper in months, and everyone indirectly connected with his one-man operation could now count on a monumental weekend drunk. Especially the printers. He thought of them, tight in a roadhouse or cultivating gardens or making love to their wives, or whatever it was printers did in their spare time. Whatever anyone did. The printers were his connective, the last narrowing umbilical that tied him to grim reality. What the hell *did* people do in their spare time these days? He hadn't looked lately, not in years it seemed: not since he had been plucked from the one dull world and set down in the other, infinitely more gorgeous sphere of politics and rebellion. They'd set him down in this other place — Rinemiller out front, inspired with the idea of a free and independent truth-telling newspaper reporting on the melancholy activities of corrupt officialdom, Rinemiller out front, with Earle Fielding and others like him not far behind, paying the bills. They'd thrust Willie into this glittering world, and the experience had been exhilarating. All he had to do was print the truth, like Rinemiller said, and he'd shaken the universe a little. As much of it as he could see, in any event; the trouble was that he was seeing less and less of it now. He wondered what in hell people were *doing,* all those people who didn't drink beer at the Dearly Beloved, the ones not included in weekend tennis tournaments.

He sat thinking about all the world's dull people. He swatted insects and examined page dummies and decided it was not such a bad issue he had put together. Nothing that would send anyone to the penitentiary, like last year, but good minor league reporting all the same. What disturbed him now was that he was still going through the old motions, laboring like the elephant of the year before and producing, instead, one tiresome mouse after another. Perhaps all they needed was a new cast of characters or one last big-time villain? They were running short of evil, and it was becoming more and more difficult to find any significant amounts of muck to rake. He thought about the good old bad days. There had been a time at college when he had dared invoke such multiple disasters as to bring about oddly beneficial results: stirred a controversy and got his picture in *Time* Magazine and been given a year of study abroad.

But all that had passed, passed dead away. He'd lost his first newspaper job for printing a wirephoto of Sugar Ray Robinson in dancing clothes, surrounded by a dozen white (white as could be!) chorus girls. He'd got another job soon enough, but he'd never regained his vision, his cheerful libertarian's optimism; not, at least, until Alfred and Earle and the younger politicians came round to buy it back for him.

He shoved his chair away from the desk, conscious for the first time in more than an hour of a cigarette in his mouth and music coming from the phonograph. He rose and washed his face in the open lavatory. He was drying himself when he heard the commotion outside, in the parking lot next to the old office building. He looked through one of the open windows but could see nothing. A car horn honked and someone yelled: "Willie! Hey Willie!" Harris's voice was high-pitched, impatient. Willie squinted in the darkness and could see the outline of Harris's automobile. He shouted hello.

"I've brought you a love gift," Harris yelled back. There was the sound of a doorslam, and then the car pulled away. Someone remained on the gravel below. "Who is it?" Willie called out, and Cathryn Lemens answered: "How do I get up there?"

He directed her to the fire escape and waited in the window to help her up the final steps. She dropped down from the window ledge, looked round the deserted loft, and brushed thin strands of hair out of her face. "You've got me for a tennis partner if you like," she said.

Earle Fielding bent down over the small boy and listened to the whispered protests. Earle tried hard, but understood none of it; the child wheezed and groaned and rolled over in his sleep, turning his back on the father, and whatever it was he might have been attempting to communicate was lost altogether on Earle. Earle straightened up and looked about the room, picking out familiar objects of the child's world, illuminated in the half-light coming from the hall. He shuddered a little, nostalgia gripping him for an instant; he struggled with an emotion compounded from desire, from an overwhelming sense of loss, of failure. He wondered when it was that everything had started going haywire for him, and whether, given another chance and all the intelligence and common sense in the world, he could make anything from the shambles. He walked down the hall to Ouida's bedroom, thinking about this.

"He looks good," Earle said. "The boy looks real good."

"He's neurotic," Ouida said, brushing her dark hair at a dressing table. "He's sweet and bright enough, but he needs a man around. He misses you."

"Perhaps he needs a brother or sister," Earle said. "Let's have another baby." He smiled, not knowing what he meant by his own remark, unable to judge how Ouida might take it. She did not seem to take it any perceivable way. She looked up at him sharply, questioningly, and continued brushing her hair.

"I don't think so," she finally said.

"How're you feeling?" Earle said. "You all right now?"

"Yes," Ouida said. She stopped brushing and looked at her face in the mirror. She applied dabs of cream on her forehead and on either cheek.

"Sorry I wasn't here," Earle said. "You pregnant when I left?"

"If I wasn't," Ouida said, "I didn't waste any time getting into trouble."

Earle flushed and paced round behind Ouida, watching her rubbing the cream on her face. "I mean I'm sorry I wasn't here," he said. "If I'd known, I would never have left town."

"I was all right," she said. She began pinning her hair on top of her head. "I had some friends looking after me."

"Who?"

She looked at him and smiled.

"My legions of lovers, Earle," she said. "They were lined up at the hospital entrance, donating blood."

Earle sat on the corner of the bed, smoking his cigarette. "It's no goddam joke," he said. "I talked to the doctor long distance, you know that?"

Ouida shook her head.

"He said you could've died. He told me that on the phone."

"I don't think it was all that serious," Ouida said. "I felt fine."

"I would've come home then, but he said you were being released. I would've called you, but I didn't know what exactly I could say."

"Your friends waiting for you at the hotel?" Ouida said.

"I love you," Earle said. "I think I really do love you — despite everything."

"What does *that* mean?"

"What?"

"Despite *every*thing . . ."

"I mean our troubles. Why we can't seem to keep the faith in any sense of the word."

"I kept it," Ouida said. "I think I've kept it a long time."

"You have to expect that in men," Earle said. "Men are going to go off on a bat of one kind or another. It's inevitable . . . You have to expect it."

"You have to expect it with women, then," Ouida said.

"You're a grown woman — you ought to act like one. You've got a child. You ought to have a couple of 'em."

Ouida did not answer. She began to undress. Earle watched as she pulled stockings off her dark legs and slipped out of her skirt. He continued watching dolefully until she stepped behind the closet door. In a moment she was back in view, wearing a gown. "I'm going to bed," she told him again.

"Who're you seeing currently?" Earle said.

Ouida giggled and rolled over in the bed, her face away from him. "George," she said. "George Giffen. I see George nearly every night."

"Who is it?" Earle said. "Who the hell is it? I know there's someone special. I know you pretty well by now. I can read you like a goddam book, you're so transparent."

Ouida rolled back over and looked at him, her eyelashes wet, face trembling.

"Well who's it been with you the last three months? Or the last year? Or half the time we were in Europe? Or the month in Cuernavaca? You started this libertine business, Earle. You started it — exulted in it. I didn't. I never did."

"All right," Earle said. "I take full responsibility. I started it. I suppose it's up to me to end it then. So let's end it."

"The way you've been wandering off and coming back again — I'd think you'd abandoned any right, any capacity even, for starting or ending anything."

Earle was silent for a time. Finally he said: "Should I stay here tonight? You think it would be good for the boy for me to be here when he wakes up."

"For a change. Sure. He might not recognize you . . . Stay anywhere you want . . . Goodnight." She rolled over again, pulling the covers up over her head.

Earle sat on the edge of the bed several minutes, finishing his cigarette. He kicked off one shoe and debated with himself. He might, he thought, go sleep with the boy. Or make a bed on the front room couch. He thought about sleeping next to Ouida, wondering if everything could be miraculously resolved by morning. He thought about the others at the hotel suite and realized, with relief, that he was wide awake and nervous and in no condition for sleep. He slipped the shoe back on and walked through the apartment, rattling Alfred Rinemiller's car keys in his pocket.

They were still talking politics in the hotel suite. Rinemiller, Huggins and Giffen sat together, attempting to work out the problems. Earle Fielding's guests had gone through four of the whiskey fifths; Earle was still nowhere in sight, and they were all a little crazy drunk.

"What we really need," Rinemiller was saying, "is some new faces at the state level. A young people's ticket for Governor and Lieutenant Governor and on down the line. We do all right in the House — not too badly in the Senate — but we haven't elected a single man at the state level . . . Same old hacks moving up every year."

"Young man's ticket," Giffen put in.

"Might even run a nigger," Huggins said. "Let's run a young buck nigger.

"You ought to run for Governor, Alfred," Giffen said.

"Not me — I had Earle Fielding in mind," Rinemiller said.

"You ought to run," Giffen repeated. Huggins was silent, thinking about running a colored man for Governor.

"Earle's the natural for the race," Rinemiller said. "He can afford to spend a hundred thousand, put on real campaign."

"You run with him, then," Giffen said. "You and Earle make perfect young man's ticket. Governor 'n Lieutenant . . ."

"I wanna get a nigger in there somewhere," Huggins said.

Harris brushed past, dancing with Ellen Streeter. Harris asked Ellen how about it. How about what? she wanted to know.

"*You* know," Harris said. "I could really lose my head a little over you, El, but you never give a man a chance."

"What chance?" Ellen Streeter said. "You've got your chance."

"I mean there's got to be more . . . *Got* to be . . . I'm that kind of person. For a relationship to mean anything at all to me, it's got to be adult . . . mature."

Ellen looked at him puzzled. "Adult . . . ?" she said.

"I can't be serious about a woman otherwise. I got to make love. It's a dirty habit I picked up long time ago."

"It *scares* me," Ellen said. "It really does. Always has."

"You're *thirty years old*, El."

"Who says I'm thirty?"

"You do. Two years ago when you told me you were twenty-eight. When I was tryin' to lay you couple years ago."

"I'm not thirty yet," Ellen Streeter said.

"Twenty-nine, then," Harris said, holding her close and speaking into her good-smelling blond hair. "How 'bout it? You can't go through life this way. You're missing out!"

"You make it sound so pretty, it's a real temptation," Ellen said.

Huggins wandered by, two girls on either arm. "We're gonna run a Negro man next Governor's race," he was saying.

Rinemiller continued to sit with Giffen. He puffed his cheeks and rubbed his eyes. "I could do it, George," he said, breathing heavily. "I know I could. Earle and I could put on a great campaign."

"I know you could," Giffen said, attempting to nod his head but succeeding in a mere lateral movement of the eyeballs.

"I got friends all over," Rinemiller said. "All over. All kinds. Not just liberals — fatcats, conservatives, too. Businessmen. Captains industry. Could put together real tough little co'lition. Unbeatable. I know this business, by God . . . I know politics if I know nothing else. And people like me, you know that? Like me right off. Make friends ev'where I go. Can't esplain it — just a quality I have."

"That's *true*," Giffen said. "There's that quality . . ."

Earle Fielding arrived, flanked by two bellboys carrying fresh ice and soda. Earle's appearance seemed to give the party renewed vitality; people attempted to get hold of themselves, straightening mouths, tightening jaws, laughing a little. Earle moved across the room and handed over the car keys to Rinemiller.

"We got it all figured, Earle," Giffen said. "We gonna run you and Alfred for Governor and Lieutenant Governor next year."

"And a black man for Attorney General," Huggins said.

Earle smiled. Someone handed him a drink. He hoisted it as in a toast. "Throw the goddam rascals out!" he said.

"Yeah!"

"Yah!"

Rinemiller excused himself and went into the bathroom. He stood over the toilet bowl and blotted at the perspiration that had flashed across his forehead. He thought about money, standing there weaving over the toilet bowl, wishing he had only half — a quarter even — of Earle's. He decided, standing there, realizing that he was somehow, incredibly, not going to be sick, the future almost automatically suffused with limitless opportunity, that he really should work on Earle Fielding about their running together. If not next year, some year soon. Earle was a good and valuable friend and one hell of a fine politician. No one better. Too bad about Earle and Ouida, he thought.

He turned and lurched out and lay down for a few minutes in one of the vacant bedrooms, holding his head. Presently, he turned over and reached for the telephone. He dialed the number, and on the third or fourth ring Ouida's voice came on.

The child, he thought. Oh Jesus I hope I didn't wake that boy. Little Ole Earlie.

"Ouida," he began, "I hope to Jesus . . ."

"What . . . ?"

"Ouida?"

"Yes."

"How are you, honey?"

"Fine . . . Who . . ."

"You think I could come over see you? I need to talk."

"Who . . . Alfred? Is that you, Alfred?"

"This Alfred, honey. You think I might cover over an' visit?"

"The two of you? You and Earle? You want to spend the night here?"

"Yes . . . I mean no. You and mean . . . *Me* . . . Is what I
me. Sit talk few minutes. You'n me. Always felt . . . Had a
special feeling . . . That time we kissed . . . Remember? That
time? Had feelin' 'bout . . . Didn't wake the boy, did I?"

"Alfred . . . I'm already in bed. I'm sorry. Really. Perhaps
we can talk this weekend at the ranch. Would you like that?
You'll come out, won't you?"

"Yeah, yeah," Rinemiller said. "Ranch." He repeated it again
— *"ranch"* — as if it were an insight into something. It was not
until he rang off that he remembered everyone was coming to the
ranch for the weekend. It wasn't a country house rendezvous with
Ouida after all.

Still . . . he was able to tell himself there was some promise
in what she'd said. She hadn't hung up on him, hadn't said *No,
Alfred, hell no and go way and quit buggin' me.* She was nice
enough on the phone. He tried to remember what it was like
when he had kissed her in the hotel room two years before, his
hands touching her dressfront and Ouida gasping every time he
pulled her hips against his. He lay back in the empty bed now,
wondering about the Fieldings. There was record music coming
from the front rooms. Fats Domino sang it to him . . .

> *Ah'm gonna be uh wheel someday*
> *Ah'm gonna be some bah-dy*
> *Ah'm gonna be uh real gone cat*
> *'N then Ah woan wahn yew . . .*

Willie's phonograph droned on in the second story loft. Willie
sipped wine from a peanut-butter glass and watched the girl, who
sat cross-legged, like a small boy, on one of the work tables. She
was slim and small-boned, neck and arms like flower stems; yet
oddly voluptuous, full-breasted and going heavy in the hips, like a
dancer who had never quite taken her work seriously. Her
clothes were a puzzle too; she exuded a kind of chic provincialism,
and he considered the conflicting images: Cathryn visiting smart

little dress shops, looking for something a bit different; Cathryn bending down on her knees in a glum college dormitory, tracing off a fifty-cent dress pattern. He couldn't determine which it was with her, and now that he'd asked, he was afraid he might have said the wrong thing.

"I had no business," he said, hesitating, searching for the right words.

"Why not?" she said. "I *wish* I were a debutante. The truth is, my father's a traffic cop. He has to renew a note every year at the bank to send me spending money."

"Still," Willie said. "I had no business making smart cracks."

He had taken a good look at her and suggested that she was either very rich or very poor — that she was definitely not middle class.

"I was thinking tonight how long it's been since I carried on a normal conversation with anyone," Willie said. "Without talking in the secret code. You know what I mean? I can't remember the last time I carried on a really *dull* conversation — I mean commonplace stuff. The weather, neighbors, family. *Realism.* Paddy Chayefsky. You know?"

She nodded her head. Her sweet laughter filled the big room.

"Anyhow," he said, "I'm glad you're not a rich girl."

"*I'm* not glad about it," Cathryn said. "Why should it please you?"

"It's easier," Willie said. "It's easier on my tender jazz-age psyche. I get a terrible case of the nostalgia in the evenings. I have this thing about girls I like. I've got to know all about them — everything. I'll want to see your yearbook pictures and old love letters and photographs when you were coming to puberty and who it was first kissed you. And whether you were in the senior play. All that stuff. I always want to live it over again with the girl and feel poignant because I wasn't there. Wasn't there to see how pretty you were when you were thirteen, for example."

"I was terrible at thirteen," Cathryn said.

"It'll be easier with you," Willie said. "Not as much fun; I mean not as poignant — no real pathos — but I won't be agonized about it. With rich girls it's different. Their young girlhood is about as remote to my experience as playing stickball on the streets of New York. My father was a salesman for the National Biscuit Company. Growing up was bloody dull. So I sit around wishing I had been sent off to dancing school when I was twelve; sorry because my family never vacationed in the same resort town year after year — you know? The way it is in resort towns when you see the same good families reappearing every season? I hitched East on vacation few years ago, and it had a terrible depressing effect on me. Just looking at all those damn prep schools stuck away in the hills. I visited Cambridge and lay alongside the river and looked at those crazy spires at Harvard. I was melancholy for a week. Damn near ruined me . . ." He looked at the girl and grinned. "See? I make one hell of a revolutionary."

Cathryn slipped off her sandals and pulled her bare feet up on the worktable. "Fascinating," she said. "I never had this problem."

"It's this new social mobility," Willie said. "Damned lousy democratic way of life. And it's worse down here where there aren't many really old and good families left. What we've got is new money; status hasn't solidified. You like that? You can move up — or at least drift in and out. It's bad enough having to come to terms with the money itself . . . Very conspicuous consumption . . . You become acquisitive; you want things. But even then it's not enough. You end up wanting the impossible things — like a new childhood."

"All I want," the girl said, "is a red M.G."

"No unhappy thoughts about your misspent youth?"

"In my youth I wanted a red M.G."

"You'll get it," Willie said. "You're bound to."

"*I*'ll end up a schoolteacher driving a five-year-old business coupe!"

"Maybe it's because of my age," Willie said.

"What is?"

"All this wishing I'd gone to summer camp and attended Choate School and Harvard and married a girl from one of those junior colleges you never heard of. Maybe it's because I'm getting old. Because I'm thirty.

"You don't look thirty."

"Only as young as you feel," Willie said. "I feel thirty. And shallow and superficial and defeated. Compromised. No more revolutions. I missed all that, too. I need an enthusiasm. I feel about ready to sell out. Except nobody would buy me off . . ."

"Good heavens!"

"I don't ordinarily groan this way," Willie said.

"Reading that paper of yours I thought you were irrevocably committed to the class war," the girl said.

"I want a red M.G.," Willie said.

Roy Sherwood lay across the bed, propped on his elbows, smoking a cigarette. Through the open window, from a great distance, he could hear the college towers clanging the half-hour. Only he hadn't any notion what hour. One or two or three in the morning — it was all fuzzy in his head — and it was not that he wished so much for sleep now as simple, primitive release. Escape of any sort. Willie was right, he decided. My life, my wonderful, uneventful, irresponsible well-ordered life, is suddenly become complicated. He looked out through the window, marveling over the moonlight that seemed more spectacular than a noonday sun. I only want, he said to himself, to be left alone. Damn their souls — all of them — Ouida, Earle, Ellen, old Fenstemaker, Willie, even. Were they all out there, lurking in the shadows, ready to sandbag him with ambitions? He sniffed the gardenia bush through the window and rolled over on his back. He wondered if Earle Fielding really was outside, waiting for his next move, looking for the lights to dim.

Ouida came down the hall and sat on the bed. She smoked his cigarette.

"I hope that wasn't Earle who called," Roy said.

"No," Ouida said. "It was Alfred. I can't imagine why, either. Have I ever given Alfred any reason to think . . . ?"

"Nobody gives Rinemiller any reason to think," Roy said.. "He does it all by himself. What'd he want at this hour?"

"To come out here. To see me. Just the two of us. He wanted to talk. Just the two of us . . . He kept saying that . . . I can't imagine . . ."

"Keep away from him," Roy said. "He's up to no good."

"Oh?" She lay alongside him and kissed his face. "What are you up to?"

"Good," Roy said. "Good works. I'm the world's greatest lawyer, politician and Zen archer, and I'm up to true and good and beautiful works."

They lay on the bed in the back room with only light showing from the kitchen and dining area. There was a faucet dripping somewhere, and occasionally the Fielding boy loosed a sad complaint in his sleep. They traded the cigarette back and forth and Roy fretted with the radio. In a few minutes, he thought, he either would or wouldn't make love to Ouida, and however it went, whatever success they might have, there was no release in sight. Life had become intolerably complicated in a few short weeks, and he wondered if this was what he had been unconsciously working toward all along. Avoiding any positive steps, one automatically narrowed alternatives. Resisting commitment of any kind, one was exposed to pitchmen of every sort. A pox on the irresolute! He'd get Willie to write it up, newsmagazine style: As it must to all men, the awful weight of responsibility came to State Rep. Roy Sherwood one day last week . . .

He wondered how long it would be before his father or uncle or older brother called, wanting to know what in hell all this talk was about his being censured. Who's this married woman youah carryin' on wif, boy? You can't behave, we send Cousin Sammie up theah take you place and brang you back fah to practice the law. Lahk you should be, anyhow.

At breakfast that morning Fenstemaker had thought it a great joke. Roy considered Fenstemaker a moment, deciding he was either a dirty old man or the world's second greatest lawyer, politician and Zen archer. The Governor had tugged on his big nose, sitting there at breakfast in the Mansion, and said, "You good boy, Roy, but that ain't good nuff. Up in Washington right now, in the Statler, they already made the beds and swept the rooms — and ev'body's out runnin' round makin' history. Lots of history been made on top of a woman, but you ain't gonna make it that way. Not just yet, anyhow . . ."

Ouida sat up and snuffed out the cigarette. "I'm going to undress," she said.

"Wish you wouldn't," he said.

"Why?"

"You'll make things awfully difficult."

"You're a dud, you know that?" she said. "I thought we were all set to change the rules."

"It's just . . . Well, Earle's in town. Rinemiller's calling you on the phone. Your boy down the hall here, he's whooping in his sleep. It's an unwholesome environment . . ."

She held on to his hand and he began to speak again: ". . . I'm basically a poet, fundamentally a poet . . . Shy, sensitive, communicating on several levels of consciousness. *Ambivalent* is what I am . . ."

"All right," Ouida said, smiling. "I'll wake the sitter. We'll go somewhere else. Where shall we go?"

"I'll think about it," he said. He lay there thinking.

"What about your house?"

"My cat's there," Roy said. "Name of Sam Luchow. A shy, sensitive basically ambivalent cat. I wouldn't want to give Sam Luchow the trauma. He's anxious enough as it is . . ."

Theories spun round in his head, schoolboyish and implausibly proper, vaguely Freudian. What he wanted, actually, was *not* to have Ouida. Would he have preferred to wander on out the front door and spend the next year rooting in his own bedcovers, pawing the ground, moaning about his unrequited love? It could not be entirely that. He did not want to get himself hopelessly involved with a girl he cared far too much about. Carnality had been such a tyrannizing factor between them from the beginning that he felt some effort ought to be made to establish another set of values before embarking on the obvious.

But then she pulled open her dressfront and lay against him, and his last uneasy conviction flailed the air and died. Her skin smelled wonderfully good, and they had some lighthearted beginnings.

Later, he pulled himself from bed and, partly dressed, bent down to kiss her fluttering heart. But she would not let him leave, coming awake in his arms and beginning to cry, and it was dawn before he got out of the house. He paced off the distance to the car and was just stepping inside when Earle Fielding grabbed him, whirled him around, and clipped him lightly on the chin.

The motion was all so smooth and effortless, so lacking in violence, that Roy could only sit on the damp grass and smile, looking about the neighborhood, watching the weird morning light touch the tops of houses. From a railroad siding miles away a single switch engine thudded against a boxcar. The lawn's moisture was coming through the seat of his trousers. He touched his jaw and attempted to look serious.

Earle stood above him, embarrassed. On stage. His movements were oddly wooden as he circled warily. Finally he bent down and extended a hand.

"Aw hell, Roy," he said. "I'm sorry."

Roy looked up at him, still serious.

"You want a sonofabitch," he said, "I'll be your sonofabitch, Earle."

Fielding began backing off and waving his hand. "Naw," he was saying. "Jesus . . . forget it . . ."

Half a block down the damp street, the engine in Rinemiller's car exploded like a cannon in the stillness of the dawn. Roy sat back down on the grass and watched Earle and the auto vanish over a hill.

Seven

FENSTEMAKER roused him at eight with awful exhortations, a compound of biblical wisdom and Hill Country homily. Roy groaned
and looked out through the window at the quiet surface of the
lake, wondering about the hour. There were no fishermen in
sight, nor had the water-skiing contingent from the college arrived.

"Jesus . . . " Roy said. "What's the time?"

"How long, America, O how long," Fenstemaker was babbling.

Roy turned round the face of his clock, blinked in the harsh
morning light and groaned again. Fenstemaker badgered him
mercilessly. Roy protested: "I'm a sick man, Governor . . . I
had three hours sleep night before last; I gave blood yesterday; I
got in late again last night . . . this morning . . . I'm getting a
nervous tic . . ."

"You get over here in an hour?" Fenstemaker said. "I got
somethin' important . . . How soon you get over here?"

Roy said he would come as soon as he had strength enough to
shave and dress. "I'm sick, Governor," he said. "I got the
neurosis."

"You tie your shoelaces?" Fenstemaker said.

Roy said maybe he could.

"You're all right, then," Fenstemaker said. "Psychiatrist friend
mine says man's not really disabled emotionally till he gets up in
the mornin' and can't decide which shoe to pull on first . . ."

Roy gave assurances he would get to the Capitol sometime before noon.

"Bring your friend," the Governor said.

"Who's that?" Roy said. For a terrible moment he thought the
Governor was going to start in on the business with Ouida.

"That Willie," Fenstemaker said. "Bring that Willie person. I got somethin' for the both of you."

Then the Governor rang off with characteristic abruptness. Roy got slowly to his feet, washed, shaved, fed his cat, and ate a bowl of cereal. He tore off the cereal boxtop for the Fielding boy and listened unhappily for a moment to the sounds of fun and games commencing on the lake.

Willie's offices were in a semi-abandoned building several blocks from the college. It was a large frame structure put together during the war to house Navy V-12 personnel. There was good reason to doubt whether it could ever again survive another national emergency, but efforts were being made from time to time, very much in the manner that building construction progressed in Mexican towns, to restore it for use as office space. A new stone veneer rose halfway up the front; window screens were being repainted and striped linoleum laid along the first-floor hallway. Brightly colored asbestos paneling was used to partition off the ground-floor rooms. There was no way to reach the second floor from inside: only half a stairway hung from its fractured supports, leading up to nowhere. Willie's guests had to climb the fire escape outside.

Willie worked alone in the unimproved quarters upstairs. He had the whole upstairs — a space roughly the size of a basketball court — the dark floor littered with waste paper, cheap newsprint, candy wrappers, beer cans, soft drink bottles, and numerous pasteboard boxes on which the word FILES had been drawn in black crayon. There were also three enormous, new and shining metal garbage cans. Willie had a single desk, a typewriter and stand, a makeshift worktable put together with sawhorses and thick plywood, an ancient wicker chair, a broken-down sofa, a clothestree, a leather ottoman, a fading, partially collapsed beach umbrella, a phonograph, and remnants of what appeared to be an army shelter half. A smell, an inexpressible something compounded of commercial detergents, sawdust, new paint and rat droppings, clung to all the upstairs.

Willie had secured these offices through a rental agent friend, an ex-pipefitter who had not yet got over his uneasiness from deserting the labor movement. The agent had recommended the building to Willie's sponsors, advising that work on the newspaper could be conducted in the upstairs space free of charge until such time as the newspaper became a moneymaking proposition or restoration of the upper half of the building was resumed. The likelihood of either seemed infinitely remote at this time.

Roy climbed the fire escape and found Willie bent over his desk, talking with the young man from the college, Kermit's friend, named Jobie. Roy sniffed the incredible air of the loft and said hello.

Willie looked up, nodded, and went on talking to the boy. "You make some persuasive points . . ."

"I know the prose is rather splendid," Jobie said, "but the content — do you think it really says something to the common man?"

"Yes . . . Yes . . ." Willie said, nodding, looking up at Roy for help. "I think it says a great deal." Roy decided it was simply in Willie's nature to be gentle on all occasions.

"Is it true you have a large number of, uh, working class subscribers?"

Willie nodded. He looked at the window for a moment, as if searching for the right words. "Yes . . ." he said. "The unions conducted subscription campaigns in all the locals."

"You'll use it then?" Jobie said.

"I imagine so," Willie said. "It's a bit long — forty pages — but —"

"Plus the footnotes . . . ?"

"Yes . . . Well . . . We've got to be *realistic* about space. We're necessarily limited to . . ."

Roy sat down in the wicker chair and read an old issue of the newspaper. He knew Willie would carry Jobie's article in one form or another, possibly in installments of several weeks. Life for Willie had become a progressively desperate, never-ending struggle to get the pages of the little journal filled and sent to the printers. There was never any advertising that amounted to much: an occasional beer ad, an "institutional" endorsement from one of the unions, legal notices sent over from sympathetic lawyers. Those eight to twelve pages each week yawned at Willie like a voracious sea monster, a scavenger, swallowing up everything, meat and vegetables, gold and dross, whole or in part, whatever garbage and flotsam was washed close by. Roy sat in the wicker chair and turned through the pages, glancing over an article written by Kermit, the Mad Doctor, entitled *Radical Pacifism — A Way Out.*

Out of what, Roy was not able to determine on so brief an examination, but he did note that Willie had managed to stretch Kermit's "monograph" over three pages, breaking up the gray spaces with line drawings clipped out of a 1934 issue of the old *Scribner's Magazine.* He looked up, wanting to commend Willie as a newsman in the best tradition, but Jobie was still talking fiercely.

"You have an art critic?" the young man wanted to know.

Willie shook his head and said he had never exactly given any thought to the possibility of carrying art criticism. "But we're certainly not bound by precedent," Willie added. "You have anyone in mind?"

"You might want to look at some *small* things I've done," Jobie said. "Lately I've been very much interested in the idea of the *mot juste* in art — have you ever thought of that? The painter striving much as Flaubert to arrive at . . ."

"Yes . . ." Willie said, jerking his head up and down.

Roy got to his feet and said: "That's the wonderful thing about this newspaper . . ." Jobie looked at Roy, delighted. "It *is* a wonderful thing," Jobie agreed.

"Any work," Roy went on, Willie giving him a grateful look, "any work that is honest and genuine — anything of a special lyric or *human* quality, as primitive as it might seem to the academician, as bewildering as it might appear to the, uh, working class type, will nonetheless have great appeal to Willie as art . . . a *folk* art that is *indigenous* to the region . . ."

Jobie strode round the workbench, waving his arms. "That's it! That's exactly what I had in mind! There are some revolutionary things being done here . . . In the arts . . . This is a frontier . . . You won't find such vitality in . . . anywhere else. This is where new things are being done. I have a friend experimenting with ceramic murals, using the native soils to produce a tile painting that will reflect not only the *images* of the region but its very *fundament* as well . . ."

"I hope you'll excuse me for breaking in," Roy said. "Willie and I have an appointment downtown."

"I do some painting myself," Jobie said.

"We're supposed to be at the Capitol in fifteen minutes," Willie said. He looked at Roy. "That right?"

"Though I'm normally a writer," Jobie said. "I've had some shows."

"It'll take us ten minutes to get there," Roy said.

"Of course sculpture is really the most exciting, the most *plastic* of . . ."

"Play the recorder?" Willie said suddenly.

"Pardon?" Jobie got his eyes in focus and looked at them.

"Clock's out of order. You have the time?" Willie said.

"Nearly eleven."

"We've got to leave."

They climbed out of the window and walked down the fire escape, blinking in the sunlight, trying to keep their balance so as to avoid holding on to the metal railing which rubbed off, dusty and black oxidized, on the hands. They dropped the young man off near the college and headed the car toward the Capitol grounds.

Eight

THEY CLIMBED the great stone steps and headed down the main corridor of the Capitol building, taking a back elevator that let them off at a third-floor passageway near the Executive Offices. They sat waiting for a few minutes, watching the nice-legged secretaries moving back and forth. Occasionally, the Governor's voice could be heard through the thick walls, a little like Grand Opera from a great distance. Jay McGown passed through the reception room, looking gloomy and efficient. He stopped and talked with them.

"He ought to be ready for you," Jay said, looking back toward the Governor's conference room. His attitude was not so much one of anxiety; Jay had more the quality, characteristic of those constantly exposed to Arthur Fenstemaker, of having peered steadily at the scene of an accident, experienced a revelation, seen death and redemption, God and Lucifer staring back, and somehow, incredibly, survived.

Jay started off toward the pressrooms down the hall. Almost immediately the Governor came banging out of his office, one arm draped round the shoulder of a state senator. The senator grinned at everyone, eyes glazed, the Governor leading him as a blind man toward the door. Then Fenstemaker turned, a great happy smile on his face. "Come on in, you two," he said.

They got to their feet to follow him inside. Fenstemaker had already collapsed in his chair, stretching out, neck and spine resting against the leather cushions. They sat across from him and stared. Fenstemaker pinched his nose, moved a big hand over his face as if probing for minute flaws in a piece of pottery. He rubbed his eyes, sucked his teeth, punched holes in a sheet of bond paper with a gold toothpick. He stood and paced about the room and stared out the windows and scratched himself. "Well goddam and hell . . ." he said. It was like a high mass, a benediction.

"Let me do you a favor, Willie," he said.

"What kind of favor?"

"I don't know. Anything you ask. I just want to get you obligated," the Governor said, grinning and winking at Roy.

"Don't know of anything I want offhand," Willie said.

"Think of something."

"How 'bout some more of that Scotch whiskey then — the smoky twenty-five-year-old stuff you served me last month."

Fenstemaker smiled, showing his shark's teeth. "Hell and damn," he said. "That's no favor." He swung round in the big chair and opened a side panel of the desk. There was the sound of ice clacking in metal tumblers, and he pushed drinks across to them. "Look at this," the Governor said, setting a seltzer bottle on the desk top. "Damndest things . . . Used to see 'em in the movies when I was growin' up. When I could afford a movin' picture show." He held the bottle in one hand and pressed the lever, sending a spray of water across the room. For a moment there was a fine mist suspended in the air between Roy and Willie and the sunlit windows. A lovely rainbow appeared.

"You're a mean sonofabitch," the Governor said, staring at the seltzer bottle. Roy wondered if he was talking about the bottle or his guests, until he repeated himself. "You're a mean sonofabitch, Willie," he said, still smiling.

"I'm lazy and no-account," Willie said. "But not mean, especially."

"You ever think about old Phillips?" He referred to a minor state official now serving a term in the penitentiary who was convicted on several counts of theft and conspiracy from evidence developed in Willie's news columns.

"I think of him," Willie said. "I keep thinking how I wish he'd come back and do it all over again. I'm running out of people to expose."

The Governor spun round in his swivel chair, grinning. "Well you keep tryin', Willie," he said. "You keep tryin'. What's your circulation now?"

"About the same as it was. About ten thousand. But only about six of it paid. We give away a hell of a lot of copies."

"That's not much," the Governor said. "Ten thousand's not much."

"No."

"How much money you losin'?"

"Lots."

"I imagine so," the Governor said.

"I try not to think about it," Willie said. He looked unhappy for a moment, thinking about it.

"Where's the money come from?"

"I'm not supposed to say."

"You got to say now," Fenstemaker said. "I give you that Scotch whiskey."

"Various sources," Willie said, raising his glass as in a toast. "I don't know who-all. Rinemiller helped raise the original amount. Got it from people like Earle Fielding . . . Some others . . . Hell! You probably know who they all are."

The Governor laughed and leaned toward them. "But it's not your circulation, Willie — it's the *quality* of your goddam readership."

"Suppose they can all read," Willie said.

"Now goddam I mean it," Fenstemaker said. "Anybody who really cares about politics subscribes to your little paper, even if they don't necessarily subscribe to your point of view. People who shape thinkin' — policy makers, lobbyists, lawyers, judges, small-time politicians."

"There's been no one else printing a lot of this stuff," Willie said. "I suppose something's better than nothin'."

Fenstemaker looked delighted. "Exactly!" he said. "Whole basis my philosophy!"

"What's that?"

"Somethin's better than nothin'."

"Half a loaf?"

"Slice of goddam bread, even," Fenstemaker said. He changed moods suddenly. "Now about these hospitals . . ."

"*What* . . . ?" Roy and Willie leaned forward, trying to follow the course of Fenstemaker's conversation.

"Hospitals," the Governor said. "You care about the hospitals?"

"Sure."

"They're a God-awful mess."

"Worse than that," Willie said.

"I got this little bill . . ."

"I know," Willie said.

"I got the votes," Fenstemaker said. "At least I *think* I got them. It's not much of a bill — not half enough of an appropriation — but it'll close up some of the worst places and build some new ones and bring in a few head doctors. And this little bill can *pass* is the main thing. I'll put it through next week if I don't get everyone all stirred up and worried about taxes and socialism and creepin' statesmanship. You gonna help me, Willie?"

"How can I help?"

Fenstemaker slapped his desk and showed his teeth. "Oppose the goddam bill!" His face beamed. "But just a little bit, understand?" he said. "Don't get real ugly about it."

"I don't understand," Willie said.

"Those fellows in the Senate — they think this is all I want, they'll give it to me. But if somebody's runnin' round whoopin' about how good this is, settin' precedents and havin' a foot in the door and braggin' on how much more we'll get next year, then all my support'll get skittish and vanish overnight."

"I see."

"Only don't oppose it too much, either. You raise hell and *your* bunch won't go along. They'll introduce their own bill askin' for the goddam aurora borealis. I need their votes, too. Just oppose it a little bit — oppose it on *principle!*"

The Governor paused a moment and considered the problem. "I want," he said, beginning to laugh quietly, his sad eyes blinking, "I want unanimous consent and dead silence!" He roared his laughter at them.

Willie stirred and looked at Roy. Then he looked at Fenstemaker and said: "That all you wanted? We taking up too much of your time?"

"Oh, *no!*" Fenstemaker said. "Hell no. I got you two here for somethin' else altogether. Just a minute." He leaned across his desk and punched a button. A girl's voice came on the speaker.

"Yes, sir?"

"Hah yew, honey?"

"Just fine . . ."

"Jay in there?"

"Yes, sir."

"Tell him to get that machine of his and bring it in. Tell him I'm ready for a little transcribed soap opera."

He leaned back in the chair, resting on his spine, looking as if he were in great pain. "How you get to be one of those goddam elder statesmen?" he said.

Nine

IT WAS such an improbable story it had to be true. If it were simply some hoked up yarn designed to discredit an enemy, old Fenstemaker's inventiveness would have served him better; there would have been some style, some magic, a sense of possibilities.

Fenstemaker didn't insult a man's intelligence — you could nearly always count on that — and this story here was so coarse and bumptious there *had* to be something to it. Otherwise, the Governor would have devised a folktale with source material for his own amusement. Fenstemaker would have invented a better story.

Willie sat listening, trying to set bits and pieces to memory, wondering if he should take notes. The Governor was sprawled in his big chair, looking out the window, beyond the granite ledge where two bizarrely plumed pigeons clucked and strutted, flapping their wings for balance in the careless wind. Roy sat like a bronze figure, cigarette ash spilled down the front of his dark jacket, and Jay McGown stood next to the machine with his hands on the switches. They played the recording all the way through, listening in silence, and then once again, stopping and backing up the tape and commenting on the undecipherable sections before proceeding.

"Once again, Jay," the Governor said, and Jay McGown spun the reels like a scientist at the controls. There was scarcely any doubt — the voice, one of the voices, was Alfred Rinemiller's; the other identified by Fenstemaker as a lobbyist for a group of loan companies. They sat and listened all the way through one more time . . .

— Who'd you say?

— Huggins. He's chairman of the committee and a good friend.

— And you think you could change his mind . . . ?

— I think so. I could work on him. I've done him favors and he knows it.

— Well listen . . . We got to be damn sure. There's a lot ridin' on this. We got to be absolutely certain about it — that's why I'm down here. Our future's at stake — there's a whole pot of money we could lose with just a change of a few percentage points on the usury limitation . . .

— Then you understand it's going to cost you money to save money.

— We know that. We've done business down here before. It's just we want to be dead sure. We can't afford to go throwin' it around. We can't afford it. We've been burned before.

— I'm just telling you you've got my word. Ask anybody. You can depend on it. I can keep the bill in committee, but — hell — you understand — you got considerations.

— How many?

— There's a lot of sentiment this year for some kind of legislation in the field.

— How many considerations?

— I don't know. There's Huggins . . .

— He's a rich boy. What the hell's he need —

— Rich family. He only gets a limited amount from them, and he spends most all of it. And he likes women . . .

— We've all got our weaknesses . . .

— That's his. Women. And he's known only the inexpensive ones. I can get a couple who . . .

— Hell! You do, hah? Whyn't you get 'em up here, then. We'll have a little party.

— You pay?

— Only kidding. Listen — how much now? You got yours. I thought that would be enough. You realize how much you got there?

— Yes.

— How much? Count it.

— I believe you.

— Go ahead . . . count it . . .

— It's all here.

— How much.

— Seven-fifty. Just like you said.

— Now you goin' to deliver the goods just like you said?

— You've got my vote. I have a good deal of influence on the committee. Enough to stop the thing from being reported out.

But it's going to take some work. I expect more for that work. And it'll cost *me* some hard cash to bring it off.

— How much, goddamit?

— Five thousand.

— You're crazy.

— Take it or leave it.

— You're out of your mind.

— You want your money back? Here . . .

— No, dammit, I want your *vote*. But you bring up this subject yourself of what you can do for us in workin' on the others. And then you say five thousand for Chrissake. I could buy up control of the Senate for that much.

— Fat chance . . . All right then. What's your offer?

— Half.

— Half? Half of what?

— Half of five . . . That's twenty-five hundred. And I tell you, mister, we've never thrown money around like that in the history of this organization.

— It's not enough.

— The hell it isn't!

— All right.

— And we want to be damn sure.

— You can count on it.

— I mean *damn* sure. You're gettin' only a thousand of it now.

— *What?*

— And the balance when we're certain the bill's dead for this session.

— Well now how can I be sure I'll get the rest of it?

— You can count on it, my friend.

— There's no assurance.

— What assurance you give us? And besides — I haven't got that kind of money. Not that much. I'll have to go tap our directors, and that'll be a touchy business. "They'll think *I'm* gettin' to *them*. Puttin' the money in my own pocket.

— All right. But they'd better come across. Otherwise, they're liable to find this legislation looking right at 'em again next session. And I'm the boy who can make sure it passes. Think that one over . . .

— Well now it seems you have a very good point there.

— Yes.

— So we're all protected.

— That's right.

— How 'bout a drink?

— Fine.

— Bourbon?

— Anything else?

— No. Just bourbon. Like I said, we're a small outfit. *Five thousand!* Why godalmighty, man, that's half my salary for a year.

— Bourbon's fine.

— Seven-Up?

— No . . . Soda.

— We don't have any . . .

— Jesus . . .

— There's a cold-water tap in the bathroom . . .

The tape came to the end of the reel and continued to spin noiselessly in the big padded room. "That's enough, Jay," the Governor said. Jay McGown packed the recorder and left the room. For a few moments they were silent. The Governor stared at his spotted pigeons on the window ledge.

Willie said: "Why'd this fellow bring it to you?"

"I don't know. He's a kind of screwball — doesn't really have much idea what's going on down here. He said he didn't know what to do with the evidence, as he called it, so he brought it to me."

"Just like that?"

"Yes. And I wish to God he hadn't."

"Sounds like something for the grand jury," Roy said. "What the hell's wrong with people? Rinemiller gone out of his mind?"

"Well now this fellow's put it on my back. Listening to what he said in that conversation, he wouldn't look so good in the courts himself. Even if he was just stringin' Rinemiller along . . ."

"He did a pretty convincing job of it," Willie said.

"Yes. So he brings this tape in — just this morning — and puts it all on me. I almost suspect *he's* trying to make a deal. Seemed to think Rinemiller was one of my boys and maybe if I'd just take care of that bill for him personally he wouldn't be out any money and would be willing to forget everything."

"He say all this?" Willie said.

"No. Just a feeling I had. He's supposed to come back to discuss it after I've had time to think it over."

"He mention calling in the law?" Roy said.

"No. He just kept saying it was a very serious matter. Very serious."

"He has a gift for understatement," Willie said.

"Well," the Governor said. "What do you think?"

"For God's sakes don't get me in on it. You know Rinemiller's an officer in the corporation of the newspaper?"

"I knew he was connected," the Governor said. "Otherwise, I wouldn't have let you know about it."

"How do you know I still won't print it?" Willie said.

"I'd be pleased if you would, as a matter of fact. Make the decision for me."

"I just might," Willie said. "It would probably ruin me, but I might if I could get that lobbyist to talk. Who's to say definitely beyond doubt it's Rinemiller?"

"It would bitch up a great many things," Fenstemaker said. "It would put you out of business, and probably take away all those great gains you people made this year in the elections. You know Rinemiller campaigned strictly on the issue of being a liberal? He kept calling himself that. Capital *L*."

"Why'd you want me in here?" Roy said.

"Well, you're a friend of Rinemiller's . . ."

"Rinemiller's a sewer."

"All right, then. I called you because you're about the only one of the bunch I'd put any faith in. You've got good sense. You're always honest with me. I respect you. I want your advice."

"On what?"

"I dunno. How to deal with this thing, I suppose. Tell me what you think? I don't know whether to lay it all out in the open or call Rinemiller in and let him squirm a little or let that fellow have it back and see what he's planning. If he's got a plan."

"What's that?"

"He mentioned the possibility of paying off Rinemiller in marked bills and having some state police there to grab him when he takes it."

"That would be interesting."

"I really don't think he wants any of that, though."

"You think he's bluffing?"

"He might be. Just to see what *I'll* offer *him*. Goddam. He would have me opposin' that legislation for the next four years. And I happen to believe it's needed. Had it in my campaign platform."

"Why you letting him pull you in?" Roy said.

Fenstemaker poured a glass of water, used it to wash down a pill. He got to his feet and paced around the room, pausing in front of a mirror to look at himself. He smiled, baring teeth and pink gums, tapping the enamel with his blunt finger. He turned round and said: "We haven't heard Rinemiller's side of it, you know. That recording might be faked."

"I hope so," Willie said.

"And whether anybody believes it or not, I care about those people downstairs. I care about your bunch, Roy. We got the same objectives — we just disagree on methods. Something like this here, it'll set us all back, disgrace the whole bunch of us, and blow the session all to hell. I got a program to worry about."

"Well," Willie said, "most of our people got elected on the corruption issue, and I suppose it would be only fair to go right back out again for the same reasons . . ."

They were silent for a time. Finally, the Governor suggested they think about it for a few days. They all agreed to think about it. Arthur Fenstemaker's collapsed features came together; he smiled and put an arm around each of the two young men.

In the reception room they stood and talked about seeing each other again in several days. Jay McGown was bending over one of the secretary's desks, making corrections in a television script. The Governor suddenly reached across, took several of the sheets of paper, and began to read aloud. Then he looked up at the ceiling for a moment.

"This is too prissy, Jay," he said. "Can't you brag on me some without it soundin' like I'm diggin' my toe in the ground?"

"It's a problem," Jay said, "bragging on you when you're making the speech yourself . . ."

The Governor looked resigned to another defeat. "Well forget it then — take that stuff out about receiving honorary degrees. I never even got the B.A., anyhow . . ." He turned to Roy and Willie and said: "Everybody's tryin' to blur my public image."

Then he stalked back inside the office.

Ten

THEY LEFT the reception room and walked down the marble stairway, moving past portraits of dead governors and senators, Confederate battle scenes and endless bronze figures in pioneer dress. There had been an early adjournment in the House. Committee meetings were underway in the back rooms, though a good crowd remained on the floor of the main chamber. Members and their secretaries milled about with lobbyists and newsmen and pageboys. Roy and Willie walked down the middle aisle and stopped to talk with Huggins.

"Hah yew people?" Huggins said. He leaned back in a leather swivel chair, feet propped on the desk. He munched on a banana.

"What's going on?" Willie said. "We miss anything?"

"You just missed," Huggins said, swallowing hard, "you just missed witnessing the nearly unanimous passage of a resolution expressing the will of this body in regard to bastardy."

"And how does this body stand?" Roy said.

"Firmly against it," Huggins said. "Almost unanimous. Except for me and about five others. We're for all those unwed mothers. They're mainly ladies of color, understand. Somebody here's tryin' to figure a way to keep 'em from havin' one baby after another. Gonna reduce the compensation on the welfare. Got to cut costs somewhere, I guess."

George Giffen came over. "I heard," Giffen said, "I heard you and Willie been in to see the Governor."

"How'd you hear that?" Roy said.

"Giffen's got a pipeline," Huggins said. "I got a theory Giffen just lurks outside the reception room all day long, makin' notes on who goes in and out."

"Fill me in, George," Willie said. "I need a part-time man to keep me posted on what goes on round here."

Giffen grinned, pleased with himself. He mentioned the tennis tournament. They sat talking about the tennis tournament for a few minutes. Then they all got up and left and talked about tennis some more over cold beers at the Dearly Beloved. Roy didn't stay long. He had two beers and then waved goodbye. On the way out he hesitated near the pay phone, wondering if he should call Ouida. His eyes were beginning to burn; he was growing dizzy from the beers and from lack of sleep. He was afraid, moreover, that any moment Earle Fielding and Rinemiller might come through the doors — and he was already embarrassed for both of them. Just thinking about it. He realized suddenly, unhappily, that he could not make the phone call. He couldn't explain why; he only knew it was impossible and he was too worn out to begin the laborious assembly of self-justifications. He left the Dearly Beloved and drove directly home.

The phone rang several times during the afternoon, badgering him in sleep. When he could not bear it any longer, he rolled out of bed, putting the words together, hoping he could think of enough words to give to Ouida. But it wasn't Ouida calling. His brother was on the long-distance wire. *Oh Jesus*, he thought. *Here it comes* . . . But again it wasn't what he expected. His older brother wanted some advice on a case, or, more specifically, wanted Roy to handle an appeals case before the high court at the Capitol.

"You got all the books there," Roy said to him. "You know all about the law — I don't."

"I'll send you a good brief," the brother said. "We'll send you everything. Just want you before that court. You're better than any of us here at that sort of thing."

Roy said all right; he'd do it, thinking he had better begin courting favor with someone at home and remembering at the same time that he really was a pretty good lawyer. He remembered once, a year out of law school, when an uncle died and his father fell sick and the brother was off in the Pacific on Naval Reserve duty, he had been suddenly confronted with nine criminal cases all by himself. It had just about killed him, but he'd won them every one.

His brother was about to ring off, satisfied, when Roy asked him how long he'd been trying to call.

"Just now," his brother said. "Just now called. First time."

He felt better about Ouida. It was such a murderously petty business, but now he was out front again. At least he'd made his gesture by answering one call. He flopped back on the bed, and within the next half-hour the phone jangled twice more. Then it was silent for a time. He lay on his bed in the lake cabin and tried to bring back sleep. One more hour's release would work wondrous cures; he was certain about it. He lay thinking of sleep, and the more he thought the more it receded from him; the less there seemed of all possibilities. It could be a key, a diminished return, money in the bank. But there was only torpor. He lay in the bed, limp and wide awake, fully conscious yet inoperative, perspiring in his underwear. Sleep resisted him as the sunlight held the day. He leaned on one elbow and looked outside toward the blue-spined hills, the lilac-colored slopes. The sun was down but not yet forgotten; there was light enough still for all the young-muscled people on water skis. A half-dozen boats stirred the surface of the lake, churning circles in the region nearest the cabin, and for a moment, in the retreating light, he was partly tempted to call Ouida and suggest a ride upriver. That was one way to get her out of the apartment, out of his cabin, away from the Dearly Beloved and Fenstemaker and his family and all the others. They'd got wonderfully tight together one afternoon on the lake, drinking wine and lowering the puny ship's flag to half-mast and raising insane toasts for Arbor Day. That was it. He remembered now. They'd celebrated Arbor Day, nearly drunk, drinking wine in the boat one afternoon.

He rolled over, stretching, trying to relax. The cat came to the bed and stalked across his body, taking up a position in the window sill. Roy slid off the bed and went to the door, holding it open. "Sam . . . Sam Luchow," he called. "You want out, Sam?" The cat regarded him patiently and did not move. Roy returned to the bed and shut his eyes. In a moment he opened them again and stared around the room. He had occupied the cabin nearly three months, but there was scarcely a change in it since he had unpacked the first day. A pair of suitcases lay open in a corner, containing a laundry bundle of shirts and underwear he'd never botherd to unwrap. There were rumpled suits hanging zigzag fashion in the cedar closet, and a plastic bag of winter clothes was draped across the back of the single easy chair. The floor in and around the closet was littered with great wads of jumbled bedsheets, pillowcases, sweatshirts and bathing robes and decaying hotel towels. On one bare wall he had pinned an outsized campaign button that spelled out *A D L A I*, red on black, and on the wall opposite was the ancient oval photograph of *Our President Calvin Coolidge,* who peered out glumly, bound in celluloid collar.

Roy examined his room, deciding it could only be identified as the tourist home lodgings of some lunatic recluse who had suddenly taken to travel. He wondered what Ouida would think of his cabin. He supposed something should have to be done. But where to start and where leave off? Once underway, should he keep on setting things in order, all his life, his work, his junk-pile romance, preparing his laundry bag of splendid emotions for some final adjustment, an ultimate dislocation, acknowledging once and for all the ceaseless demands of public ambition and private loves? It seemed a crime to seek power from either source unless he was prepared to assume the responsibilities. And looking round his ill-furnished fraud of a life, he could not convince himself that he was prepared for any such thing. There was Fenstemaker, by contrast, who dared to seek it for whatever wealth of largeness it might bring him. "I tell you boy," he'd said that week at breakfast, "there ain't nothin' else but power an' change an' improvement. The rest — an' I think I misquote some English socialist on this — is all a mere middle-class business . . ." The Governor had leaned across the table, bigger than life, stabbing at egg yolk, and put the idea to him: "Ain't no use fomentin'. Learned that long ago. Ain't no use 'cept in the last extremity. You want to overturn the existin' institution, that's fine. But you got to be sure you know how to build a better one. The thing to do is work *through* the institution — figure a way to do that — to make a change and build a city and save the goddam world from collapse. You got to work through that institution, Roy . . ." Then he leaned back and flashed his shark's smile, saying, "An' I'm that institution currently . . ."

He rolled over in his middle-class bed and closed his eyes again. The cat stalked back across the covers and curled at his feet.

Darkness settled round them, and out on the lake the motorboats
vanished one by one . . .

The landscapes changed, colors blending and fading and separating again, outlines quivering and growing less distinct in a
fusion of grays and greens and washed-out mauves. Rinemiller
raised his glass of whiskey to the twilight and the burnt-orange
root beer sign across the street. "Divorce is a terrible thing," he
said.

Earle Fielding was silent for a moment. "Let's have a parachute jump," he finally said.

Rinemiller looked through the highball glass. "But sometimes
it's for the best," he said.

"I feel like makin' a jump," Fielding said. "It makes a man
feel like a man."

The others chatted back and forth across the dining table.
There were a half-dozen of them in the Mexican café. They sat
in a little bunch at one of the tables, talking, watching the sun go
down. They called the proprietor Mack the Knife, though not to
his face. He was a huge Irish-Mexican, black-mustached, gold-
toothed and sinister.

"All the people down here do is get dronk and chase each
other," Mack the Knife said.

"You're not being fair," Willie said. "It's this way all over —
it's a sick world, Mack."

"Not in Detroit," said Mack the Knife, who had been in Detroit.

"In Detroit, yes," Willie said. "You just weren't aware of it.
Too busy on the assembly lines making all your money."

"I am a self-make man," said Mack the Knife.

"I know you are self-make," Willie said. "Here — have some
of your good self-make Mexican chianti . . ." He held the bottle
out; Cathryn, sitting beside him, offered her empty glass. The
others talked incessantly and at the tops of their voices. Mack
the Knife always came over to their table, making time with the

women, preferably large blondes like Ellen Streeter and, as a matter of good form, unattached.

Mack the Knife grinned. "You craze *cabrones*," he said. "That's no goldam self-make. A brought it all the way from Monterrey and the State of Nuevo León in my pickup truck." He looked around, proud of the establishment. "Everything in here I did," he said.

"I know you did," Willie said. "That's how it is possible for you to build yourself an authentic State of Nuevo León Mexican restaurant . . . Have some chianti."

"How 'bout some good Club Ninety-Nine brandy," Mack the Knife said. "Why doan you buy a bottle? Every bit as quality as a Five Star . . ."

"The chianti," Willie said, "is quite quality enough."

Mack the Knife took an empty seat next to Cathryn. "You want some of the Ninety-Nine?" he said to her. She shook her head and smiled.

Willie said: "All she wants is a red M.G."

"I'll buy you one," Mack the Knife said. "Buy you one for cash tomorrow." He had been born along the border, on the Mexican side, and come across as a teenager — he could not remember at what exact age — following the cotton and wheat harvests into the Middle West. In Michigan he had found work on the automobile assembly lines, saved his money, and returned to build his own restaurant. Now he was very rich, owning, in addition to the restaurant, a loan company, a catering service, a tamale factory and an apartment house.

"You mean it?" Cathryn said.

"Goldam right I mean it. I doan kid around."

Mack the Knife got to his feet and told Cathryn to think it over. He waved goodbye and moved across the room, directing abuse in Spanish at the waiters and busboys. Earle Fielding talked about how he would like to jump out of an airplane. Harris and Ellen Streeter discussed the problem of Ellen's frigidity. George Giffen was attempting to get his secretary tight. Huggins talked with Rinemiller about the race for the speakership and how many pledges Alfred had received from the House membership up to that time. Willie tried not to think about Rinemiller, who sat directly across from him. He wondered if Arthur Fenstemaker could somehow resolve or explain away the matter of the bribe — its offer and acceptance — before Willie himself might be forced to make a decision. He put his hand on Cathryn's knee.

"Don't," she said.

"Why not?"

"Because it feels terrible good," she said.

He left his hand there and tried not to think about Alfred.

Arthur Fenstemaker arrived in his hotel suite, three floors above the banquet room where he had given a banquet address. He lay down on the sofa, holding his head, massaging his eyes, groaning quietly to himself. His brother, Hoot Gibson Fenstemaker, crawled about on the floor near the sofa, looking for a lost shirt stud. "It was mah dyemond one," he kept saying.

"That's no goddam diamond," the Governor said.

"Mah dyemond one," Hoot Gibson repeated.

Jay McGown sat nearby, telephone receiver in hand, holding for a long distance call. He looked at the Governor. "I think you did all right downstairs," he said. The Governor did not reply.

"Yew made good speech, Arthur," Hoot Gibson said.

"I don't think they heard a word of it," the Governor said. "All of 'em sittin' there half drunk, thinkin' how important they were, greatest group since the goddam House of Lords . . ."

"They heard you, all right," Jay said. "You nearly scared 'em to death with that talk about taxes and spending. It wasn't exactly what they were expecting from their own candidate."

"I'll deal them the blow of an enemy," Fenstemaker said, "the punishment of a merciless foe . . ."

"Mah goddam dyemond one . . ."

"Because their guilt is great and their sins are flagrant . . ." He looked down at his brother and said: "You look in your trouser cuff?"

Hoot Gibson examined his trouser cuffs. The Governor twisted round on the sofa, reached down and retrieved the shirt stud next to the leg of a coffee stand. Hoot Gibson got to his feet and went into the kitchen to make drinks. Jay brought the telephone over. "Here's your call," he said.

Fenstemaker took the receiver and said, "Hello-Charley-how-in-hell-are-you-anyhow?" He listened for a moment. "I'll be damned," he said, and then repeated himself, ". . . I'll be damned." He looked at Jay, holding a hand over the receiver, and said: "Charley's very special client's asked him to rig a jury for him." He laughed and talked into the phone:

"Well now listen now, didn't I warn you about this bird? He's not just rich — he's mean and stupid. You should never have got involved . . . I don't care how much he offered. You're the best trial lawyer round here and there's no need for you to —" Again he broke off, listened, and spoke to Jay McGown: "Charley thought the bastard was innocent!" He listened for a few seconds more and then went on.

"Charley, they'll drink your blood if you let 'em. That insurance company of his just didn't happen to collapse — it wasn't the goddam law of gravity . . . He milked the business dry and stuffed the profits somewhere — I don't know where, maybe up his ass — no tellin' where — but he got away with it for four years and now he's hired a smart lawyer like you thinkin' he can buy his way out . . . All right? Now listen. You tell him you've gone and bought off two or three of 'em and you got two or three more on the jury who're waverin', can't make up their minds. Then you take his money an' give it to the orphan's home or the Salvation Army shoe fund or somethin'. Just do that and then go ahead and try the case best you can. Your conscience'll be clear . . . You got your ethics intact . . . All right . . ? All right . . ."

He hung up the receiver and lay back on the couch, holding his head. "Jesus," he said. "All my ruined cities . . ."

Hoot Gibson returned with the drinks. The Governor put the glass to his mouth and swallowed hard. "I think I'll talk to Roy Sherwood," he said. "See if you can get Roy for me, Jay."

Jay took the phone again. He looked at the Governor and said: "You going to tell him about this afternoon?"

"I dunno."

"How's he doing? You think he'll be all right?"

"No way tellin'," Fenstemaker said. "No way at all . . . Just goin' on a hunch. Can't ever tell about these far-out boys. You dump a responsibility on them, and sometimes all they'll produce is a very wet bowel movement . . . Git 'im on the phone."

Jay dialed the number.

Eleven

THE QUESTION came to him forcibly that morning, a little before noon, as he stood outside the Governor's Office in the Capitol building. He had with him an enormous black notebook, its thick pages neatly indexed with pink tabs, and a freshly inked speech, eight pages triple spaced, strange words dazzling him in oversized type — a "reading copy" Jay McGown said. Jay stood next to him, fumbling with manila folders and copies of the committee report, law books and news releases. Roy stared at Jay and at the bundle of printed matter and the gleaming marble corridors down which Arthur Fenstemaker had just now slouched. He wondered about those times in the past when he had asked himself the question, when some abstract force seemed to have separated him from awareness of what had gone before, leaving him bereft of reason, all justification, to grapple with the bald moment. *What,* he would ask himself, *What am I doing here?*

It was as if the question had been poised on his lips for years, always asked and forever unanswered. It had come to him once in Alaska, as he stalked a bear, cold and blinded with tears, on a hunting trip with his father; and, again, one evening in 1945 at a squawling party given in the U.S.O. in Norfolk, Virginia, as he perspired in his dark sailor suit and danced with his bride of three days. And even before that he had asked himself the question: fumbling in the cramped darkness of a Model-T Ford, barking his shins against the pine dashboard, in his first fantastic attempt at seduction.

The question had been coming to him for so long it had become a sort of ritual, a trick of the imagination, in which he was thrust back in time and then forward again, coming upon the moment as a stranger and viewing whatever experience was at hand with the limited awareness of one who might just now have stumbled on the scene. How come I'm *here* of all places? he would ask himself.

He turned to Jay McGown and repeated the question.

"Makin' goddam history," Jay said. "You heard the Governor . . ." He stared at the speech copies and added: "You see any errors in this stuff?"

Roy shook his head. "How should I know?" he said. "I'm just the author of the bill." He stared at the print. "You write the speech?" he said.

Jay nodded. Roy said: "I never in my life had a speech written for me."

"Then this here's a moment of unparalleled magnificence," Jay said. "You got yourself a ghost — you've arrived as a major public figure."

They walked down the marble hall and into the chamber of the House of Representatives. Jay began distributing copies of the bill and the committee report and Roy's remarks, yet unuttered. The chamber was steamy and half filled. It was a time just before convening when lobbyists and secretaries and newsmen and people with any sort of authority were permitted on the floor to pursue the legislators. Roy went to his desk and began his last-minute studies, checking notes, thumbing reference books, making penciled changes in the speech. He stared around, glancing at the back of the chamber, watching the clock. Arthur Fenstemaker came upon him from behind. He pulled over a chair and sat down. He asked Roy how he was. Roy said he was wondering what he was doing there.

"I never thought, when I was growing up, about getting into politics," Roy went on. "And when I did, finally, right after college, I never thought I'd take it seriously. Just a means to an end. I forget what end."

"I remember," Fenstemaker said, "selling Real-Silk Socks — that's a trade name — durin' the summers at college. The limit of my ambition then was to sell enough of those goddam Real-Silk Socks to be manager of district sales and sleep with my secretary. The district manager had a secretary . . . You ready to take a little run?"

"Yes."

"It's all set up," Fenstemaker said. "I had to talk to the Speaker. About puttin' the bill up on the Calendar, ahead of some minor stuff."

"I thought he was against the bill," Roy said.

Fenstemaker showed his marvelous teeth. "He's an honorable and reasonable man, Roy," the Governor said. "All I had to do was threaten to ruin him." He got abruptly to his feet and headed up the aisle without looking back, pausing occasionally to whisper in a member's ear. Roy resumed his studies. A pageboy brought a telephone extension to his desk and plugged it in. Roy picked up the receiver.

"Where've you *been?*" Ouida said to him. "I called all yesterday afternoon and half the night, and —"

"I fell asleep — passed out actually," Roy said. His voice sounded timorous. He thought suddenly about how nice it would be on the lake that afternoon; the emotion was unsettling. He was quickly, peculiarly charged with desire — right there in the middle of the day, on the floor of the House of Representatives — and the hell, he thought, with Earle Fielding and Fenstemaker and —

"I called five or six times," Ouida said. "Where were you?"

"In bed . . . Unconscious . . . I didn't wake up until . . . it was too late to call."

"I'm going out to the ranch a day ahead of time," Ouida said.

"Ahead of what?"

"That insane tennis tournament. I've got to get out there early to clean up the place. Arrange for a cook, have the courts rolled . . ."

"Courts?"

"*Tennis* courts. They're playing tennis, remember? That's the kind of tournament it is."

"I'm still asleep," Roy said.

"What I called about — what I was calling about last night — was to ask you to come with me. We'll be miles and miles from everything. I've already got a baby sitter to stay in town with the boy. We can be alone out there — we'll have the whole evening and night and next morning together. The others won't be arriving until the afternoon."

"I don't know," Roy said.

She wanted to know what was the matter and he tried to explain, and then she still wanted to know.

"What's all this got to do with Fenstemaker?" she said. "I'm not in love with Fenstemaker. You in love with Fenstemaker? You obligated in any special way? I don't understand any —"

He tried again to explain. "I happen to *want* to do this," he said.

"All right. Forget it. Go back to sleep."

"Look," he said, "I'll try to get loose later this afternoon. I can't promise but I'll try to —"

"Forget all about it," Ouida said. She hung up.

He put the receiver down and sat there still holding onto it, wondering if he should call her back and attempt once again to explain the curious, the very trying circumstances. Look, he would say to her, I don't know why I'm here about to make a speech. I never in my life thought I'd be. Or that I'd get a phone call from a lovely married lady with girl-sized bosoms and hair the color of maple syrup and just about the most desirable shin-bones I ever in my life saw. Calling to argue that I ought to be out in the country to watch her walking barefoot, wearing cotton underpants, all around a ranch house that's having its . . . its *tennis* courts rolled. I don't know why, lady. I'm not now and never have been a well man . . .

The boy returned and disconnected the phone extension. Willie England came down the aisle and sat next to him. "How's it feel to be a member of the Governor's team at last?" Willie said.

"I'm on nobody's team," Roy said with finality. "Wouldn't drink a cup of coffee with some of the buggers and fourteen-carat sons of bitches that swoon and genuflect around the Governor. I just happen to —"

"Okay . . . *Okay,*" Willie said. "I think it's fine."

They sat in silence for a moment, looking round the great hall. Red and white lights flashed on a large board behind the Speaker's rostrum. A slim young man moved along toward the front, stepped up on the raised platform and banged a gavel.

"This House is coming to order," Willie said. "Suppose I'd better clear out." He hesitated and then added: "You know anything new about Rinemiller?"

"A little," Roy said. "Fenstemaker called me last night. He call you?"

"No," Willie said. "Guess he thought he'd given me enough miseries . . . I *still* don't know what to do about it. Am I supposed to expose my own employer? Chairman of my own board? You think Fenstemaker might do something himself? What'd he call you about?"

"The fellow with the recording machine. Looks like he's back doing more business. According to Fenstemaker, anyhow."

"Oh, Jesus," Willie said. "Who is it this time? I hope to God it's not another friend of the family."

"Another House member," Roy said. "He wouldn't tell me who. Just said the fellow had taken another member up to his hotel suite and spent part of the afternoon. Fenstemaker must have spies everywhere. Nobody's safe. He thinks the guy's given up on trying to work through the Governor's Office and is back buying votes again."

"I'm not going to think about it," Willie said. "I got to go look for a new job."

Willie retreated up the aisle. Roy studied his legislation until Huggins appeared beside him. "What's all this I hear about you and Fenstemaker?" he said.

"It's true," Roy said. "Come round tomorrow and share my mess of pottage."

"How'd all this happen?" Huggins said.

"I haven't the foggiest idea," Roy said. "Maybe he just knows real class when he sees it . . . You give me some help?"

"Help? What kind of help?"

Roy wrote down the names of some members with whom Huggins might have influence. "Help me pass a bill, for chrissake," he said. "You don't want to be an obstructionist all your life."

"Sure . . . I'll help," Huggins said, looking mystified. He turned and moved up the aisle, picking out members to visit. A succession of speakers, from the rostrum and then from the floor microphones, inveighed against one thing and another. Their voices droned on; House members wandered in and out, drinking coffee from paper cups, reading newspapers, waving to friends in the gallery. Fairly soon the Speaker gaveled for order and called up a series of minor bills that were briefly described and passed without objection. Willie walked past alongside a committee chairman, talking and taking notes. Roy bent over his notes, try-ing to remember all of Fenstemaker's instructions. Voices raged around him. Rinemiller and Earle Fielding came down the aisle and stood next to his desk.

"Hey, Roy," Rinemiller said. *"Hey,* Roy . . ."

He looked up at Earle and Alfred. The two of them stood

there, pursuing him, like old debts. "Just trying to get this stuff set right in my mind," he said. "Before I have to get up there and make a fool of myself."

"Wanted to let you know I got a little amendment," Rinemiller said.

"That's fine," Roy said. Rinemiller smiled. Earle Fielding stared at him tragically for a moment and then turned away, focusing his attention on the speaker's rostrum.

Rinemiller said: "My amendment calls for three hundred thousand more than is in the bill."

"You have my good wishes," Roy said. Earle Fielding did not look at him again.

"You mean that?" Rinemiller said.

"Mean what?"

"You'll accept the amendment?"

"Hell, no."

"Why not?" Rinemiller said. "Godalmighty, Roy, you think the money in that bill's adequate?"

"Half a million dollars wouldn't make it adequate," Roy said.

"All right, then. So we're agreed. Let's stand up and make a real fight on this thing . . . For an adequate bill . . . Let's see who'll be counted for the folks. Fenstemaker goes too far with these accommodations of his. I'd rather lose than —"

"I'd rather win," Roy said. "In this instance, anyhow. This bill would pass. I don't think it could make it if we start tampering with those appropriations figures."

Rinemiller backed off a step or two, looking resigned. "You sound like Fenstemaker," he said. "Already got you spouting the clubby line."

"Go ahead and introduce your amendment from the floor," Roy said. "It might get accepted. I know some people who'd vote for it just to weaken chances of the bill itself on final passage."

Rinemiller and Fielding wandered off. Roy stared at them. He wondered if he should go talk to Earle. If not now, then later. And if he couldn't think of what exactly to say, he'd get Jay McGown to prepare a few words and see they were distributed to the press-radio-television gallery.

"That was all very interesting," Willie said.

"You hear it?" Roy said.

Willie nodded. His attention faltered for a moment as one of the secretaries moved past, smelling good.

"What'd you think?" Roy said.

Willie raised his hands in innocence. "I don't know," he said. "I'm going to stop making judgments. After hearing that tape yesterday, I don't know anything for real sure. But Alfred made a point about Fenstemaker. Sometimes he goes too far. Sometimes you've got to stand up and holler."

"Yes," Roy said. He rubbed his eyes and thought briefly of Ouida. There seemed no use in arguing anything. Willie moved off again and Roy attempted to concentrate on his notes. He thought, instead, of Ouida, building a hurried fantasy of how it might be with Ouida at the ranch, or better still at the lake cabin, with the sounds of fishermen beaching their boats and the sour-water smell mixed with pine and the yeasty ferment of silage, coming awake like that, early in the morning in Ouida's perfumed arms. Ouida had been partly right. Another evening wouldn't be the same as the one that was most immediate. None of the evenings was. He was nothing like his person of two or three nights before, nor even of that morning.

Jay McGown walked past, hesitated, and came back to whisper into his ear.

Red and green lights splashed across the voting boards and a faint riffling sound was heard as the automatic computers went to work on the tally. Roy leaned over and pressed his switch. A young man strode past, watching the board, holding one finger above his head; another member followed a few steps behind, signaling with two fingers. The young men glared at each other and separated. The midday sun gleamed chalk-white through the windows, and two flags flapped dismally in the torpid heat outside. Roy wondered how the carp were biting.

"You're all set, then?" Jay said to him.

Roy nodded. "You got any new converts?" he asked.

"Few foot-draggers giving us trouble," Jay said. "Some of the fascists." They both smiled at the word; it seemed almost archaic. Jay said: "They're shaken — a few of them — about you managing the bill. They think something's wrong."

"There probably is," Roy said. "Wish I knew what it was."

Jay moved on. Roy repeated to himself: I wish I knew. What it was. What in hell did Fenstemaker expect of him? He could nearly hear it now . . . Behold, my friend, I have gone and set the land before yew. Go in there yourself now and possess it, as I have already sware it unto yew and your children and their seed after them . . . He began to tremble slightly, the way it had been at one time with girls, or the time with his father, leveling gunsights on the Kodiak bear. It must've been the size of an upright Model-T, the bear, and he'd had one of the old Fords once, trembling even then, the first time he had propped himself mile-high at the steering wheel. The bear was bloodied and poorly killed, and the T-Model nearly impossible to stretch out with a girl in.

He heard the Speaker's voice droning from the rostrum, and then he was on his feet and plodding along in crazy slow movements, feeling monstrous and obtrusive, even in the stadium-sized chamber, toward the front microphone. He stared round the big room, took a deep breath, blinked in the stark light. He laid out his notes and the reference books and the speech Jay had written for him, gaped foggily once again at all his thieves and princes and rapscallions, and began, finally, to talk about the bill. He talked for a quarter of an hour, shifting from his notes to the prepared text and back again to the notes. Then he stood there revealed, waiting for the others to start in. He answered most of the questions right off, and when he couldn't pull it out of his head, he turned through the thick pages of the reference books to find answers before questions were half out of mouths. A succession of amendments were proposed, defeated, proposed again in different form and beaten again. He accepted some minor

changes, after pausing to reflect and in one instance straining to
see Jay McGown nodding approval at the back of the hall. Alfred
Rinemiller got to the back microphone and talked for ten minutes on his liberalizing amendment. Roy did not comment, but
moved immediately for a vote; and Rinemiller was beaten badly.
Roy motioned Huggins to the front microphone to relieve him
while he went to haggle with someone at the back about obscure
points of law in administering funds. When he was finished
there, he turned to see Huggins in furious, full-wind debate with
an old man, a member of twenty years standing, who had risen
to decry the whole concept of such legislation. The old man
hooted at the top of his voice, shaking his gnarled fist, charging
that an unholy alliance had been formed between Fenstemaker
and "minorities." Fenstemaker and people such as Huggins, the
old man claimed, were leading them all down the road to government control and socialism. Huggins stood there at the front
microphone for a moment, amazed. "I ain't even talked to the
Governor about this bill," he said finally. "I just thought it
looked all right to me."

"You think it's all right, that's enough to convince me it's all
wrong," the old man said, waving his hands and looking about
him for agreement from the others. Roy came down the center
aisle and stood next to Huggins.

"Don't argue with the old bastard," he said. "Ignore him."

"What?" Huggins said. "We can't do that, can we? He's mis-
stated the whole thing — he's even *invented* stuff about it. Godalmighty, you can't let it go unanswered."

"He's just an artless old man," Roy said. "Let it go . . . Forget it. It ought to be obvious to everyone. He's got a reputation
for it. But you get into an argument with him — hell that's
what he *wants* — he'll have you defending every point in the bill
for the next two hours. He can go all day on something like this.
I've seen him. So've you. Ignore him. Otherwise, all our support might take a walk to the washroom. Don't answer him.
Just nod and sit down."

"You're the straw boss," Huggins said. He walked off and sat at his desk, looking unhappy.

The debate resumed. Roy stood silent at the front microphone and let the opposition talk. Finally, with critics repeating themselves, their forensic gone dreary and uninspired, there were complaints from all around them for a vote. Roy made the motion then, and the Speaker banged the gavel and Fenstemaker's bill was up for passage. Roy walked back to his desk and the lights began blinking on the big boards. He pushed the switch at his desk and heard one of his opponents say with satisfaction, "It looks like a red board." Someone else said: "Mebby not. It's too close to tell." Roy looked at the boards and then across the chamber. Arthur Fenstemaker had appeared at the back, and Roy saw him there, slumped against a marble column, hands in pockets, staring up at the board. Then the Governor's eyes focused on him and Roy got to his feet. He moved toward Fenstemaker; he could hear the noise of the electric computers and then the click and a sudden shout from all around. Fenstemaker's face beamed. Roy turned to look. The red and green lights had vanished and the totals had been flashed. Fenstemaker had his arm and was roaring in his ear: "Ten votes! How 'bout that, my friend. You got home with money in the bank! Ten goddam votes!"

He clapped Roy on the back and pulled him toward the marble column. Huggins was on his feet down toward the rostrum, requesting confirmation. There were some late votes being cast, but not enough to change the outcome. "You did good job, Roy," the Governor said.

"I just followed instructions."

"You did real good job . . . Pretty goddam remarkable demonstration for just a few days' homework. Hah? How you like those skids bein' greased?"

"I like it fine," Roy said. They walked outside together. Jay McGown joined them, and then Willie. Fenstemaker suggested they all go to his office and have a drink.

They walked down the halls together and through the reception room and into the Governor's office. Fenstemaker got out the whiskey and Jay made drinks. Hoot Gibson came in and stood around grinning for a time until Jay gave him a glass of whiskey; then he told Willie a long, incoherent story about bringing Henry Busse and his orchestra to the college for a dance fifteen or twenty years before. Willie said he thought he remembered Henry Busse. Roy sat in one of the big chairs and closed his eyes, thinking distractedly of Alfred Rinemiller and what would happen to him. Nothing, possibly. It all seemed to depend on so many people. Fenstemaker was flushed and grinning. He waved his glass as in a toast.

"Then, my friends, then we did beat them as small as the dust of the earth . . ."

Roy got up and excused himself for a moment. He found a phone in one of the back offices and dialed the number. The baby sitter answered, announced that Ouida had gone off to the ranch for the weekend and asked if there would be a message. Roy said no — no message he could think of.

"You wawn talk to *Mister* Fielding? He's right here."

Before he could answer, Earle Fielding's voice came on.

"Roy? That you Roy . . . ?"

He broke the connection and wandered out the door, down a stairway and into the afternoon heat. On the way home he stopped at a liquor store and bought a bottle of whiskey. He would either drink from it straight on his way to the ranch or mix a few sours with which to brace the late afternoon on the front porch of the cabin. It seemed like another awful decision to make.

Twelve

IT WAS ONLY a half-hour's drive out into the country. He knew the way nearly by instinct. Four or five years before, toward the end of what they now called the *crypto-fascist* era in politics, when the young people were just beginning to stir about, there had been parties at the ranch almost every week, all during one session of the Legislature. They were only a small group of them, the first organized liberal activity since the years of the plague. They'd driven out to Earle's place once or twice a week to talk and plan and play and get drunk. He knew the route by heart; he'd driven it all that year, in one direction or another, and half the time he'd been drunk. He was drunk now, like old times. He had brought along a pint of whiskey for the express purpose of retaining the glow of well-being achieved earlier in the evening.

He swung the car easily through the front gate and headed up the hillside toward the big house. Lights shone through the bastard Gothic windows. She would be waiting up for him. His heart pounded exquisitely, painfully, as he sat hunched over the steering wheel, staring at the house. He took a deep breath and wiped his face and had one last swallow from the pint bottle. Then he got out and banged confidently on the front door.

"My God!" Ouida said, standing away for a moment and regarding him.

"You see?" he said, smiling. "I did come . . ."

"Yes," Ouida said. "Well . . . Come on in. Where are the others? Anyone else coming out early?"

"They were talking about it," Rinemiller said. "Don't know if they ever reached a decision. I had to get out of there — we were having dinner at Mack the Knife's — I had to get out or

Earle would've had me flying him up so he could make a jump for your rooftop . . ."

He walked inside, set his small bag down on the gaudy tile of the entranceway, and looked around, examining the imitation hand-hewn beams that supported the walls, the bare timbers stretching across the ceiling; staring up at the balcony that led off to the bedrooms on either side. There was a *bidet* in one of the baths; he remembered that much — and wagon wheels for chandeliers: all in the worst possible taste of first-generation wealth. It was a perfect barn of a place for weekend parties.

"Looks just the same," Rinemiller said with satisfaction. He could not quite meet her eyes just yet. He stared round the room, commenting on one object and another.

"Is Earle back on one of his parachute obsessions?" she said. "I thought — hoped — all that had maybe passed."

"He was on it tonight," Rinemiller said. "And neither of us was in any condition to fly." Finally he managed to let his eyes come to rest on her. She looked splendid: dark cotton tennis shorts, blue oxford cloth shirt with sleeves rolled up to the elbows, white sneakers — it all seemed to strike just the right note of reverse elegance, high-grade licentiousness.

He moved over next to her. Ouida touched his arm and then let it go and then backed off and came close again. It was as if each was testing the other's reactions. Ouida stood in the center of the room, next to Alfred, looking round in an effort to find something — anything — to comment on. The place seemed notably absent of stage props and conversation pieces.

"We'll have a drink," she said.

"I have a case of whiskey in the car."

"No . . . There's plenty here."

They walked into the kitchen. Ouida found the bottles; Alfred struggled with the ice trays.

"Early in the morning," Ouida said, "the man comes to fix the automatic icemaker. It always freezes up when there's no one here . . ."

"The house looks fine," Alfred said. His voice banged around inside the kitchen, sounding idiotic. He tried to get control of himself and think of something to say.

"Did you have much to do?"

"The help was here till an hour ago," she said.

"They're just down at the bottom of the hill?"

"Yes," she said. "Just down the hill."

They sipped their warm drinks and looked at each other.

"Since you're the first," she said, "you can have the pick of the rooms . . . On the boy's side of the house, of course."

"I thought being first would entitle —" Rinemiller broke off midway, changing his mind; he searched his head desperately for something else with which to complete the statement.

Ouida did not seem to notice. "Get your bag and I'll show you around upstairs," she said.

". . . Entitle me to more priority than that."

What the hell? he thought. If she didn't want to play this particular game, he should think of something else. Their conversation had always bordered on the ribald, anyhow. After a couple of drinks they'd both be able to ease off and accept one another.

They climbed the stairs, paused for a moment next to the balcony rail, looking down the well at the great center room. "Who was it swung out on the chandelier that night?" he said.

Ouida thought a moment, trying to remember. She shook her head. "I recall the face — a friend of somebody's. See up there . . . ? The bolts are still pulled halfway out. It's a wonder he didn't kill himself."

"Earle had to pull him back to the rail with the net from the swimming pool."

Ouida laughed. "We should've left him hanging there. Had him stuffed and bronzed. You know? Like baby shoes. *There'd* be a conversation piece."

They moved in and out of several bedrooms. "This one's fine," Alfred said.

"No towels," Ouida said, looking about the room. "Go ahead and unpack. I'll get some."

She left the room and walked down the hall, circling round the balcony and reaching her own room at the other end of the hall. She looked at herself in a full-length mirror and then sat at her dresser and applied fresh lipstick. This, she told herself, was doing a *lot* of good. She looked at herself, make-up half applied. Am I going to discourage Alfred by making myself pretty? No, she thought. But at least she *felt* better. *Damn you Roy.* She said it again. *Damn you!* This could all have been avoided if he'd only . . . And now there was the problem of keeping Alfred off her spoor for the rest of the night. And probably the morning. Perhaps the whole hideous weekend. I'll swing, she said to herself, out on that chandelier. And hang there all night long. She finished applying her make-up, humming a few bars of an old song, found some towels and walked back toward the other end of the house.

Downstairs again, they mixed fresh drinks. This time Alfred poured the whiskey and made it doubles. Ouida stirred ice with her finger, put the glass to her lips, swallowed and made a face. But she did not protest. I'll need it, she decided. Get little tight, think something.

They sat on one of the big sofas and listened to phonograph music, and it was not so bad — not really. It was rather pleasant for a fact. The thought made her feel better. They sat smoking cigarettes, their heads lolling from side to side, talking about some of the weekend parties of years past. Ouida began to talk perhaps too volubly about her early marriage. "God! he was something," she said. "You don't know. I was a sophomore and completely dazzled. He'd just graduated and he'd been every-thing — just *everything* — summa cum all that stuff, president of his club, a boxing champion. He'd even won the short story prize — he'd written this story, first time in his life, don't think he's written anything since, and won the college prize. He was a second lieutenant and on his way to Korea and we had met at this party during the holidays in New York. We had a week. My God! I felt like Susan Hayward and Edna St. Vincent Millay. There he was in that uniform, gorgeous, going off to write me sonnets and be killed. I got it in my head he *had* to leave me pregnant. I wanted to leave him something and he would leave me something. Fantastic. And you know Earle — he insisted we get married. *One week.* It was a lovely week, though . . ."

Rinemiller leaned sideways and kissed the corner of her mouth. Ouida held his hand and looked off toward the empty fireplace. "We were both just too spoiled and self-indulgent and nutty and incapable of forgiveness. Absolution." She lay back in his arms, feeling a sense of great happy release. She had never in her life succeeded in looking at herself so objectively. It was wonderfully therapeutic — she thought idly of going to an analyst. She smiled, thinking next time she saw her priest they would have a cocktail together. Then, as suddenly as it had come, the feeling was gone, passed in the night, and she was plunged into melancholy; impatience and restlessness nagged at her, imperiled what little there was left in life of pleasure and tranquillity. It was all so damn tragic, she thought, and she began to cry . . .

Rinemiller had been battling lassitude and wishing he had not drunk so much. He pitched sideways for a moment and then struggled upward, holding on to Ouida, one hand on her breast, hoping he was not going to be sick. Her wet cheeks were against his for the first time, and he pulled back to look.

"Hey . . ." he said. He had been with women who cried, but he had never regarded Ouida as one of that sort.

"What is it?" he said.

Ouida sat up straight on the sofa, brushing at her cheeks with thin fingers. "Nothing," she said. "Really. Excuse me a minute . . ." She walked very calmly up the stairs and down the hall to her bedroom. There, she blotted at her face with tissue and touched up her eyes with dark make-up. She stared at herself in the mirror for a time; her cheeks were scarlet, but the high color was growing faint. She walked across the room and sat on the bed and picked up the telephone. He deserved it, she thought to herself; it would serve him what for, or something, in kind, the selfish, low-geared . . . Just like Earle with his parachutes and lyric poems and aimless politicking all over the country. Even Alfred, sprawled out on the sofa downstairs, groaning about his future and how it was for him as a small boy, wanting to play Governor and do his lousy good works, all of them so sexy and panting and hirsute and trying desperately to palm off their manhood. Or find it. She'd tell Roy something all right — she'd give him hell. How'd he like to know she was spending the night alone in the big country house with none other than —

"Hello?" Ellen Streeter said.

"Hello," Ouida said. "Hello? Operator . . . I think I might —"

"Hello," Ellen said.

"Who is this?"

"This is Ellen. Who's this?"

"Ellen who?"

"Jus' ole Ellen. Who'n the worl' could this be? Sounds like a divorcée of note . . ."

"Is Roy there?" Ouida said. "I'm calling Roy."

"He's here, but he's occupied at the moment. Gone to the bathroom."

"Well how long —"

"Oh not long at all. I shouldn't imagine. Fifteen, twenny minutes. You like to hold?"

There was a silence. Each of them debated whether to hang up on the other. Ouida said: "What are you doing there?"

"*Me? Doing here?*" Ellen giggled.

Ouida was silent.

"Well I'll tell you, *dearie,*" Ellen said. "You see there's the swimming and the Junior League and the Cotillion in the fall and water skiing in the afternoons, and then of course there's Roy. You remember that nice fellow, dearie? Roy? Roy and I screw just about every Wednesday noon . . ."

Thirteen

". . . LILYAN TASHMAN," Roy sang softly, staring at his strange face in the bathroom mirror, "was not kissed by an ashman . . ."

He relathered and pulled the razor across patches of dark skin. He rinsed his face and the blade. And the whiskers — they lay along the sides of the lavatory, trapped in soap film. *I will free myself,* he said, drawing more hot water, washing the whiskers down. *All worldly attachments . . . impulses . . . personal and egotistical . . .*

Saying this, he dropped, one by one, razor, blades, powder, cologne, deodorant, mouthwash, vitamins, styptic pencil, lighter fluid, tincture merthiolate, glycerin suppositories, comb, military brushes — the works — into a wastebasket.

All of it, he thought. *I shall keep my soul fixed on the Eternal Soul: performing my worldly duties without fear, hesitation, self-seeking or remorse. Divest. Disengage. Krishna, I am come. To stand on head and practice the Yoga. I shall find spiritual elevation. Shall brush teeth in an honest solution of salt and soda . . .*

He shut off the hot water and emerged from the bathroom . . . bare-chested . . . disengaged . . . looked at Ellen Streeter for a moment, and walked into the small kitchen. He explored the empty cabinets, faintly strewn with dust. "Don't I have any salt?" he said out loud. "Any bicarbonate?" He stood over the sink and looked through a small window at the dark water of the lake.

Ellen followed him into the kitchen. "You don't have anything in here," she said. "I was going to fry some eggs. No eggs. Not even a frypan."

"All I want is salt and bicarbonate of soda," Roy said, staring gloomily at the lake. "Pretty damn thoughtless of you to come visiting without a little something — little salt, little soda . . . Just a small gesture — but the kind that's appreciated."

"What do you want it for?" Ellen said.

"What? What indeed." He turned and faced her, spread his lips and rubbed a finger across the enameled surfaces. "My teeth," he said. "To brush teeth."

"Use your toothpaste. I saw toothpaste in there."

"Toothpaste," Roy said, "is a worldly, egotistical attachment. The symbol of my fall into this state of helplessness. Salt and bicarbonate will release me from all that — clarify my understanding and make my true course clear . . ."

Ellen smiled and moved back to the front of the cabin. Roy thought a moment, went into the bathroom and retrieved his toothpaste from the wastebasket. He began to brush. He stared at himself in the mirror, touching his face, and then disinterred the shaving lotion. When he was finished, he joined Ellen on the rock porch that overlooked the lake. They sat in canvas chairs and smoked cigarettes steadily, commenting on the record music coming from a club on the far side of the lake. The music blended with the sound of water slapping against rocks and insects droning round their heads.

"What's open this late?" Roy said. "Think of someplace and I'll take you."

"I'm not hungry," Ellen said, "and there is still some beer in the refrigerator. If nothing else. Ever thought of brushing your teeth with beer?"

"Yes," Roy said.

"And I'm not dressed to go out. Know what I've got on under this robe?"

"Lovely golden legs," Roy said. "Worldly attachments . . ."

"Damp bathing suit. It's going to give me sinus."

"We could go swimming," he said, swatting at insects.

"Only in the nude. Otherwise, the damp suit will give me sinus . . . Or does Ouida have exclusive rights on you in *that* department?"

"The bathing suit," Roy said, "is a great allegory of man's spiritual crisis. We keep wanting to crawl back to the sea, to get right with the Lord, achieve eternal union with God. But the bathing suits get in the way. Vain, self-seeking, worldly attachments."

"I know where most men want to crawl . . ."

"Worldly impulses . . ."

"You've been making a spectacle of yourself — you know that?"

"Ventures and gains," Roy said. "One has to run certain risks, defy the social order, to . . ." The cat came pacing across the concrete and sprang into his lap. ". . . if one expects to find the ultimate reality of Sam Luchow. Hah yew, Sam?" The cat looked up at him and then began to gnaw on his hand.

"She's bankrupt — you realize that?" Ellen said. "I'm a bitch and all, but I *have* held on to a few values. Ouida's worthless."

He was silent, thinking.

"Is she better than I am? At . . . lovemaking? Is that it?"

He wished now he could have said he really wouldn't know about Ouida's capabilities. "Not noticeably," he said.

"I've never asked you this before . . ."

"No you haven't."

". . . but why is it you stopped coming round to see me? I've been dropped by others, with even less ceremony, but never by anyone who proposed marriage on one day and stood me up for a date on the next. I wonder about that sudden cooling."

"You said no."

"I was young and stupid," she said.

"So was I."

"You said you loved me. Change your mind in twenty-four hours?"

"No . . ."

"Then why —"

"Praise the world but never the inexpressible . . . I quote somebody . . . You can never impress the Angel with your splendid emotions. Show him some simple thing that has weathered until . . . I forget the rest. Snaf-snaf-snaf-snaf. Hem-hem. Hum-hum. Speak to him things. He'll stand amazed . . . And so forth. How the hell can I express what's goin' on inside my head? I loved you — sure — maybe I still do . . ."

"Then why? I'd have gone on sleeping with you."

"That's unimportant . . ."

"It wasn't to me," she said. "You realize you were the first and there haven't been any others since? You believe that?"

"Your reputation's intact."

"Oh balls."

"Speak to me of things . . ."

"Roy . . ."

"Worldly attachments . . ."

"We made love twenty-eight straight days."

"Count 'em — twenty eight."

"Roy, for God's sake . . ."

"And on the twenty-ninth day I rested. And proposed marriage. And you said no. So I packed and moved out here. To forget."

"Roy, be serious for a minute and —"

"I *am* serious," he said. "You know why I moved? Because people got in the way. Because there was a foul-voiced woman across the alley who kept saying goddam and goddam and throwing things at her husband and beating her kids. Because there was a fellow appeared at the garbage pile downstairs one day with a boxer dog, looking for rats. Killed thirty-seven rats so far, he told me. Hell of a dog. Crazy for rats. Stick around, he said — the boxer dog sniffing through the Kotex boxes — he'll find a rat; stay and observe. There was this rich broad lived upstairs, stopped me in the hall one day and told me all about her trip to Mexico. The people, she said, were so wonderful and simple; they had a *verve* and a *zest for life* and a *joy de vee* that she was so completely simpatico *about*. It jus' cast a *spell!* Because an old Negro woman stopped me on the street one day and asked for a quarter for busfare so she could get to the hospital to visit her daughter. Who was having her womb scraped. Her *womb* scraped! Because there were Mexican kids starving across town and all Fielding and Rinemiller and the others were talking about was how to force Fenstemaker to come out against the loyalty oath for chrissake. Because . . . How the hell do I know?

Because I was a menopause baby and the only boy in the dorm at military school who hadn't had a circumcision, and we'd made love twenty-eight straight days and you wouldn't marry me and there was the Mothers' March on Polio the next night and a debutante party the night after. How can I tell you why?"

Ellen got to her feet, dropped her hairbrush into the pocket of her robe and pulled the collar round her neck. "Well . . ." she said, looking at him for a moment and then bending down to kiss his forehead. "Lots of luck."

"I'm sorry," he said.

"Ask me over again sometime," she said.

"Door's always open."

"I'll try to remember to bring salt and bicarbonate."

He got to his feet and moved next to her. They kissed for several minutes. "Go home," he finally said. "I'm having an affair with a married woman and I shouldn't get involved with a virgin at the same time."

"Ask me for a date," she said. "For the weekend."

"I'm already committed."

"Then follow me around out there when you're not playing tennis. Pursue me. Like I'm wanted."

"You're wanted," he said.

"Badly . . ."

"You're wanted badly."

"Not enough," she said.

"I'm bored," he said, "with abstract gods and loves that are little more than social habit."

"What does that mean?"

"I don't know. These insights just seem to come to me."

He walked her to the car and said goodnight. When she had driven away, he strolled for a short distance along the lakefront. He stood watching the water and then pulled off his shoes and socks and clothes, setting them in a neat pile a few feet from the water's edge. They'll find them here, he thought. Should he run back to the cabin for his billfold? To stuff into the trouser pockets as some means of identification? He decided against it, and stepped off into the water. It was cool and exhilarating, but the mud bottom felt awful against his feet. He moved farther out; the depth did not seem to reach beyond his hips, so he lay flat in the water and began to swim, with smooth effortless strokes, and when he looked back he could see the distance covered — considerable — yes, a *substantial* distance — a good fifty yards. The lights in the cabin gleamed feebly; there was a thin path of reflection leading directly to him. He let his legs sink and then his head went under and then he broke the surface again. Plenty deep, he thought. Enough to drown an elephant in. He floated on his back, gaining strength somehow, and when he realized he was not going to sink he began to swim again, round in circles at first and then following the trail of light, finally pulling himself onto the slippery rocks. He walked naked and shivering up the stone steps into the cabin.

He sat on the edge of the bed, bunched in bedcovers, staring round the room. He looked at the cat.

"Who'd have fed you, Sam?" he said aloud. The cat's ears twitched forward and then fell back. "Who'd have fed you, hah? Seems to me a man's got to have *some* sense of responsibility . . ."

Fourteen

THE STRIDENT song of two grackles waked him late the next morning. He lay listening to the birds, attempting to isolate the sylvan smells that filled his head. The grackles were camped outside on a ledge, annoying the cat with their shrill calls, feathers glistening in the sun like sheets of carbon. The cat crouched in the window, peering through the screen, growling to himself. Roy lay on his side watching all this, feeling better with the sweet smell coming off the hills. The phone's ringing finally got him out of bed.

"What I called about," Ellen Streeter said, "was to inquire how you're getting to the ranch."

"Driving," Roy said. "The last trip on water skis was just too hard on all the family."

"Your car?"

"Yes."

"Alone?"

"I think."

"Would you take me?"

"All right," he said. "In about an hour . . . I thought you had a date."

"I did. But Harris called this morning and broke it. He was furious because I said I was going straight home last evening and went to your house instead."

"In about an hour," Roy repeated. "I've got to bathe. And iron my Indian madras underwear. Feed the cat. Kneel toward Mecca. All kinds of things."

Ellen said that would be fine and rang off. Roy smoked a cigarette and ate a bowl of cereal. He pulled on a pair of khaki shorts and walked outside to retrieve the clothes he had dropped along the lakefront on the night before . . .

Sometime during that night Ouida had untangled herself from Rinemiller's dead embrace and wandered half asleep, the smoke and whiskey smell of him still clinging to her skin, down the hall to her own bed. Thinking of this next morning, the gesture was dimly consoling. I have *some* standards, she said to herself. She had come awake in her own bedroom, and who could say, for that matter, what really had happened during the night? They'd both been drunk — helplessly, monumentally drunk — struggling up the stairs together, fumbling in the dark with buttons, buckles, underwear snaps. He had stretched out alongside, kissing her arms, and when she rolled over, languidly returning the kiss, Rinemiller was limp and gulping air, already fast asleep.

At some remote hour, she liked to think, she had clutched her clothes to her breast and fled down the hall. But she knew there had been something in between, sometime before and after, with the phonograph music still thumping on the ground floor. Alfred had regained consciousness and taken hold of her in the night, resuming the familiar progression of events, mounting in awareness, until such point when they were both seized by wild, bed-groaning flights of anarchy, at once spirited and aimless, in quest of something long since passed from sight and mind. She could not recall where it had taken them or how it was ended; there was more the memory of exertion than exaltation.

She had come awake early, in her own room, and immediately set about putting the house in order while Rinemiller shuddered with his bad dreams in the upstairs bed. Window draperies stirred with the rustle of dead leaves on the lawn. Servants moved about noiselessly; the gardener rolled the courts and pruned hedgerows bordering the massive rock fences. Ouida sat in the kitchen, talking with the cook and listening to popular songs on the cheap radio.

George Giffen arrived at noon, stalking into the big house, smiling and confident, breathing Dentyne in her face, taking her in his bear's clasp like a sugar daddy come to call. Then he bolted up the stairs to shake Rinemiller awake. She could hear their movements from the kitchen, tracing their progress from bedroom to bath and back to bedroom. They would be coming down the stairs soon, and she wished suddenly for all the guests to arrive, the whole pack of them descending at once to bring some privacy to the manse. She was relieved to have Giffen around to help her face Rinemiller. She'd need an army, though, to deal with Roy. If he came at all. She wondered if he would. Had he been aware of the phone call? Had that slut told him? Perhaps he had been in the same room all the time, listening to Ellen

Streeter rattling on. She would need the crowd, in any event, to cushion the shock of renewal . . .

I have a horror, she thought, of salvaging operations.

She remembered Earle going off to war, brandishing his lieutenant's bars, just after they were married, and the horror of his coming back. The feeling advancing not so much from fear he might have changed, but rather just the reverse — that he hadn't changed at all. Returned, instead, just as he had been in the beginning, packaged and shipped home in one of those germ-free, sterilized plastic bags. Good as old! Exactly as remembered in her high school hopes. It was the trouble with all of them. Didn't anyone ever change? She ought to try to make that clear sometime . . . Don't you see, lover? The magic's all gone. We had something once, but you never changed . . . Impale them with your love and they were the same as dead, gone fixed and rigid and beady-eyed: my wax museum of propped-up paramours. So few of them grew large in her eyes with the passing of time. If Roy should come, she hoped he would have changed in some small way, put on weight, added a quarter inch in height, succeeding in an overnight alteration. With even the slightest change, they might become old lovers all over again.

She sat alone at the kitchen table, wishing the others would arrive, all of them new and exotic and miraculously strange-visaged. When she grew tired of waiting, she prepared a tray of gin drinks for herself, George, and Alfred. They would feel so much more secure with cold drinks in their hands. She had the refreshments ready by the time the two men came down the stairs.

Giffen had changed — my heavens, she could see that. All of a sudden changed. And so had Alfred, though it could not be called progress of any sort. He seemed to have gone off in the other direction, retreating, pale and timorous, into a fog of indecision. Here she'd been uneasy about meeting his glance, and there was scarcely anything to meet. His face was vague, eyes all glassy; his rogue's smile little more than a joke. She asked him how he felt.

Rinemiller touched his gleaming forehead; there was goose-

flesh risen on his arms. "I've got an awful hangover," he said. He
looked at Giffen, and added: "Ouida and I got tight last night. I
think I must have drunk a quart of whiskey. It didn't occur to me
until this morning that I never had anything to eat . . ."

George Giffen grinned at everything and talked endlessly, appearing to gain strength as Rinemiller lost ground. She could not
imagine what had got into George. A success of one kind or another. Perhaps he was in love. My God. She could not begin to
conceive such a possibility, but if this was what had happened to
him she knew there would be only the single, sudden change and
little else. What siren painter had got him fixed and immobilized
for his first and only sitting?

They sat talking, drinking gin. Only Giffen demonstrated enthusiasm for the moment. Ouida and Rinemiller exchanged
some preliminary banter, avoiding meaningful glances at one another. At the first sound of cars on the drive they all three rose as
with immense relief and moved out to the porch to greet the visitors.

By the middle of the afternoon nearly everybody had arrived.
The front grounds resembled an abandoned movie set, as if players and technicians had retired to a distant commissary, leaving
their papier mâché stage props flapping in the wind. There were
guests about, but most of them had either gone inside to drink
or headed off round the back to play tennis. Luggage was piled
on the front lawn; the grass was strewn with clothes and books
and sporting gear. Someone had got halfway through the job of
setting up equipment for badminton and croquet, and then given
it up suddenly when no one expressed interest in playing.

Roy staggered slightly with the light bags. He moved along the
concrete walk, past the carnival litter. Harris glared angrily at
Ellen from the front steps. He stood and watched them approach,
popping his knuckles. Roy deposited the bags on the porch
and sat down to rest. Ellen sat next to him and opened a small
thermos.

"Like a cocktail?"

Roy shook his head, leaning back on his elbows, breathing hard. Ellen held the plastic cup toward Harris, who turned round immediately and walked inside. After a moment, Willie appeared and helped carry some of the parcels upstairs. Giffen cruised up and down the long circular front drive in the Alfa, ferrying people to and from the tennis courts. Ellen went riding with George, and Roy followed the others into the house.

He found Ouida in the kitchen, overseeing the preparations for a picnic dinner. She looked up and said hello; she picked nervously over a turkey carcass.

"Need any help?" he said.

"No." She peeled off a strip of white meat and nibbled at it, not looking at him.

"Looks like my mother's kitchen when her bridge club meets," he said.

There was no answer. He went to the refrigerator and found a bottle of beer. Then he stood next to her and said: "Are you still annoyed because I didn't come out yesterday?"

"No. I knew you were busy."

There was another silence. She wrapped sandwiches in wax paper and said: "What did you do last night?"

"I went home to bed. Not much sleep the night before. Remember?"

"Were you advised about my phone call?"

"What call?"

"Last night," she said. "I think you were occupied. Shaving, picking your nails, something like that . . ."

"No," he said. "I wasn't advised."

"Strange . . . And she did *promise* to give you the message."

"What message was that?" he said.

"Slipped my mind," she said lightly. She turned away and carried a plate of sandwiches into the dining room. When she did not return, he looked through the door. Ouida was talking with her husband and Rinemiller. Earle Fielding was wearing white overalls. A parachute harness was laid out on the dining table.

Roy walked through the kitchen and out the back door, heading toward the tennis courts.

Cathryn Lemens sat in the deep grass next to the courts, watching the others. Harris and one of the girls had begun a doubles match with another couple. There was a great amount of inexpert smashing by the men; the girls lobbed the ball back and forth. Harris served with a twist and charged the net repeatedly. His male opponent took a savage swing; the ball whanged off the wood of the racquet and looped over Harris's head. Harris and his partner stood with their backs to the net, watching the ball bounce. Harris turned to her and explained patiently:

"When I rush, you fall back to the baseline."

"Where's that?" his partner said, admiring his dark arms.

The game resumed. Roy came over and sat next to Cathryn. She looked at him and said hello. She was a very special sort of girl, he decided, although it was impossible to determine whether she was worth a damn. It was difficult with all their women. Except with Ellen Streeter. With Ellen you could be fairly certain — she always flashed those warning signals: *You're going to bed with a thief, my friend, and there's every likelihood of your pockets being picked over in the night.* There weren't many women so candid and unpretentious, so frankly corrupt, so willing to acknowledge personal ruin, as Ellen Streeter. He found this quality somehow exhilarating. Once he had believed that disorder and unrestraint were the hope of the world; then he had come round to thinking exactly the reverse — that carelessness in their private lives symbolized a general dereliction, a decline of the public ethic. But all such assumptions foundered on the hard-rock facts of Ellen's misconduct. She wasn't licentious; she'd come to him with her chastity relatively intact. It was something else with Ellen — it was her heart and head that were sullied. He wished he could understand half as much of Ouida. Confused, depressed, in love with her, he was nonetheless bewildered by the patchwork terrain of her emotions. He knew nothing, really, about the girl; he could only reason that whatever tortured aberrations came to the surface were the nearly direct result of her failed marriage. It would require more than well-intended advice from her cocktail party priests to save her from ruin. He wished he had not slept with her just yet.

He watched Willie's girl. She sat gripping her dark knees, following the desultory progress on the tennis courts. Don't dump on old Willie, he said to himself. Then he repeated it aloud. The girl turned to him, smiling.

"What did you say?"

"I said I hope you won't give Willie a bad time . . ."

She pulled off her white sneakers and moved her bare feet over the grass. The day was altogether splendid; the sky was vivid blue; a southerly wind stirred the tops of trees and tumbled thin white clouds across the horizon. Down the hill, below the courts, a Mexican laborer bent over a sawhorse, cutting wood for winter. The sound of birds came to them from a cluster of deteriorating elms. The tennis foursome left off playing to search for lost balls. Cathryn said: "I don't give men a bad time. More often it's just the other way around."

"Willie won't be like that," he said.

"Some men seem compelled to dump on themselves if they can't find a woman to do it for them."

"Not Willie."

She thought a moment, and said: "He's too serious — and not serious enough. I mean he's not so deadly intent on the immediate objective, as, say, Harris over there. But then it's obvious how he feels. It's all over his face. It's very difficult for him to make serious let's-go-to-bed talk. He's jaded already, and for no apparent reason."

"He used to date Ellen Streeter," Roy said. "You know her? She gave him the business night and day. It's a kind of magic quality she has."

They were silent, watching the others resume the game. He asked her where Willie was.

"He went off with that Giffen person," Cathryn said.

"In the car?"

She looked behind her, toward the house. "I don't think so," she said. ". . . There they are . . ." He could see Willie and George Giffen moving across the higher ground. Willie waved; Giffen flashed his demented smile. They came directly across toward the courts. Roy lay on his back, watching the thin clouds soar past, listening to the sounds of the game in progress. They were all such amateurs, he thought. Risen out of innocence, out of grace, passing into awareness and a kind of hollow sophistication with hardly a corrupting experience — a genuinely horrific crime — come in between. And there were parallels. You could trace the wornout course of their piddling derelictions right alongside their politics. It wasn't enough; not enough to break through into awareness and good intentions; not enough, moreover, to stand away and point to how the public and private business ought to be carried on, clucking your distaste and disapproval. It was insufficient — in fact, it was ruinous. He wondered about the Governor. Had he somehow managed to transcend into some blessed state, passed them all, perilously close to the abyss until reaching a point of holy ground from which he could view the whole speckled landscape, viewing it without a tyrannizing emotion? At least he remained operative — old Fenstemaker — he knew what absolutely had to be done; he could engage himself and then withdraw without losing that commanding vision. Even when the vision itself was not as prettified as it might once have been. The truly able, it appeared, had only so much time to squander on disillusion and self-analysis. Then those destructive vanities were turned round and put to the business of doing what had got to be done. The truly gifted, as opposed to the merely clever, were too busy running things to be bothered. He thought briefly of his cat Sam Luchow, battling himself against a mirror.

The two faces, Giffen's and Willie's, appeared upside down across the blue sky. Roy rolled over and said hello.

"Ready for tennis?" Cathryn said to Willie. "I want to live like the idle rich. It's what I came for."

"The tennis," Roy said, "gives you only a glimmer of the whole sweet picture. I suppose you haven't heard about the pigeon shoots?"

"The what . . . ?"

"Pigeon shoots," Willie amplified, "subtitled The Decline of Western Civilization . . . They come from all around for the pigeon shoots."

"They fly in from all over," Roy said, "to shoot pigeons."

"*Pigeons?*

"Menace to society," Roy said, nodding sagely, rubbing his chin.

"Hundreds of pigeons," Willie said. "Imported. Along with a full-blooded gypsy from Castile, Spain, or someplace, all dressed up in silk knickers and cummerbund, green-turbaned, like a Shriner's convention — everything, all the trappings, except possibly a scimitar on his hip. He throws the pigeons."

"I don't believe any of this," Cathryn said.

"It's the God's truth," Willie said.

Giffen stood around, grinning.

"I couldn't invent all this, could I?" Roy said. "Listen — this fellow, the gypsy, he *throws* the pigeons. Throws hell out of 'em, like a shot from a gun. Makes a living doing it, throwing pigeons . . . Underhand . . . This way . . ." He paused to demonstrate, and then went on: "He throws pigeons faster than those trap-shooting gadgets, and these birds are live — not clay — they zoom off like goddam rockets . . ."

"I don't understand . . ."

"Rich man with a gun — my daddy used to come to these things — rich man stands in a circle with his shotgun, pretty near the pigeon tosser. When the pigeons are launched and flapping, he blasts away . . ."

"*Awful . . .*"

"It's a *sporting* proposition," Willie said.

"The ones that are missed," Roy said, "the ones that aren't blown to pieces — they're free to fly back to town and take up residence. Crap on the Capitol steps. The good life."

"Read your Gibbon," Willie said. "There must have been a Roman Empire equivalent to all this."

"I refuse to believe it," Cathryn said. "I just want to be rich and healthy — not depraved. Let's all play tennis."

"Whenever you're ready," Willie said.

"In five minutes, then," Cathryn said, getting to her feet. "I'm going to the ladies' room to freshen up. Put something on my head." She started across the lawn toward the house, brushing grass off her backend. Willie turned and watched her part of the way; then he looked at Roy.

"George just told me a fascinating story," he said.

Giffen looked pained. "Come on, Willie, I don't want this to get around. I wasn't supposed to talk about it."

"You told me — now tell Roy."

"I wasn't supposed —"

"For God's sake, tell him. Or I will." He turned to Roy. "George had lunch and dinner with an eminent lobbyist yesterday. They spent all afternoon together."

"Who's this?" Roy said.

Giffen mentioned the name. Roy sat back and listened. Giffen told the story, breaking off the narrative now and then to moisten his lips, making periodic exclamations . . . "Ain't that somethin'?" . . . "I couldn't believe it . . . Such a crazy damn thang to ask a fella to do . . ."

"How much was his offer?" Roy said.

"Five hundred."

"And you gave him a definite, categorical no thanks?"

"A *what?*"

"You told him no . . . Positively."

"I threatened to bash his goddam face in," Giffen said, "if that's positive enough."

"That's positive, all right," Roy said.

"Five hundred dollars," Giffen said in wonder. "For that little old vote of mine . . ."

"So what else you tell him?"

"Nothin'. Just that — and go to hell. Then I went ridin'. I must've ridden around half the night thinkin' about it. Drove out here first thing this mornin'. I could hardly sit still. I had to tell *some*body . . ."

"So you told Willie," Roy said.

"No — I told Alfred. This mornin'."

"Oh, Jesus . . ."

"What's wrong?"

"You'd have done better telling your priest."

"My priest?"

"What did Alfred tell you?" Willie said. "Tell him what Alfred told you."

"He said not to talk about it with anyone. He said it might get me in trouble."

"Well he's mistaken," Roy said.

"That's what *I* thought," Giffen said. "Can't see how it would get *me* in trouble when it was *him* that got out of line."

"Exactly," Willie said.

"Let's think about this," Roy said.

They sat thinking. In a few minutes Cathryn returned. She sat next to them and tied a scarf round her head. "I believe you now about those pigeon shoots," she said.

"Why?"

"There's a crazy man in the house — what's his name, Fielding? — says he's going to jump out of an airplane . . ."

Fifteen

THERE WAS to be a jump. Ellen Streeter came down from the
house, carrying a tray of iced drinks — something cool for pressing against their foreheads, she said — to repeat the story of Earle
Fielding's jump. Someone was playing "Imagination" on the
piano inside the house, playing it from memory with a great flourish of missed or off-key notes. Presently, someone else began shaking bean-filled gourds; the tempo increased as still another joined
in with bongo drums. They could hear all this from where they
were sitting, next to the courts; even the players left off with their
game for a moment to listen. They all imagined there would be
dancing in the main room of the big house. Roy wondered if
Ouida was in there helping make the music. He could see her
with the castanets she had bought in Majorca, prepared to join
the dance, clomping her hard heels against the terrazzo floors.

It was fantastic, Roy decided: somewhere there were people
who refused to be corrupted. He looked at Giffen sitting next to
him: beet-nosed, pock-marked face, a ruin of mentality who still,
all the same, simply could not be bought off. Or was it that Giffen
had no emotional attachment to money? Could he have been
tempted by something else? A girl, higher office, a more expensive sporting car? No. He thought not. Somewhere in George's
church-haunted past the basic right and wrong of things had been
drummed into his consciousness. In his narrow world there were
moral delineations one did not question. Those preachments
stayed with you through the years. Except for the proud individuals who had cut themselves loose from all that, enlightened, got
religion of quite another sort. Then you could no longer rely on
instinct alone to keep out of trouble. It was the first shifting
about of intellectual furniture that set them free; the trouble was

once they had begun using more of the head, abandoning the computer-machine data that had been fed to them like pablum during childhood, they had to *keep* thinking. And there was no determining where *that* would lead them.

There was old Fenstemaker. Could he be — had he been — corrupted? He hadn't time; too busy tending to things. He could corrupt, all right — Roy had heard, had felt that call girl's song — but he himself, old Fenstemaker, was incorruptible. Fenstemaker hadn't a selling price; he sold things . . . people . . . but never himself. There was a point in Fenstemaker's code beyond which existed neither profit nor pleasure. He'd developed his own set of values; there seemed no one like him, anywhere, for weighing ends against means.

Ellen Streeter lay in the grass and hummed to herself. The music from inside stopped abruptly and a half-dozen persons came charging out the door in a run. Roy watched them pile into the cars: Rinemiller, Earle Fielding, Huggins, some others. Ouida stood on the porch, waving goodbye.

"There they go," Willie said.

Ellen got to her knees and waved. "Earle's says he's going to hit that pasture over there," she said. "Shall we walk over?"

"It'll be a while yet," Giffen said. He looked after the retreating automobile, almost wistfully. "Rinemiller's flying the plane . . . I wonder if he could teach me . . ."

The tennis players gave up their game to come sit on the grass overlooking the small pasture where they could witness Earle's descent. They chatted for a quarter of an hour, until the small plane came in sight, circling overhead.

"I don't like this wind," someone was saying. "See out there — it's beginning to kick up."

Roy had turned to look at Ouida on the porch when he heard a scream of pleasure from one of the women and someone else shouting, ". . . There he goes . . . There he *goes* . . ."

They were all on their feet, stumbling along, eyes fastened on the speck that was Earle Fielding, white-overalled against the blue sky. The speck grew larger; Fielding rolled over slowly and they could see he was nearly spread-eagled, holding the air on his outstretched arms and then turning again, as if searching for some agreeable position in an enormous feather bed.

"It's not going to *open* . . ." a girl cried out.

"Sure it is," Harris said. "He's just waiting, giving us a little show. That's the whole point of —"

And then the chute billowed out, swelling to full bloom, brightly colored nylon flashing in the sun's glare. Earle jerked crazily through one vast pendulum swing, arms reaching up for the lines, sailing with the wind. He did not appear to be coming down anywhere near the pasture.

Roy looked back once again to see Ouida on the front steps, open-mouthed and undecided, and then he was running ahead of the others in yellowing, knee-high pasture grass, brushing past enormous sunflower stalks and occasional clumps of dwarfed mesquite. He paused once to get his bearings; Earle soared overhead, a thousand feet in the sky. Giffen drove past in the roadster, stopped and backed up. Roy climbed in, and they started off across country, bouncing over old wagon ruts. "Where is he . . . ? Which way . . . ?" Giffen was shouting. Roy watched the sky and gave directions. They reached the top of a small rise at the instant Earle came plunging down in a boulder-strewn space near the river, jerked puppetlike on the end of the lines. He bounced once and a second time; the chute began to collapse, caught the wind, then became entangled in a mesquite bush. Roy and George Giffen got out of the car and ran downhill toward the river. Earle lay twisted on his back, mud-smeared and grotesque, arms pulled above his head as if taken from behind by an invisible assailant. They bent over him.

"God damn . . ." Giffen said, horrified.

Earle's eyes fluttered and a whisp of a groan escaped from his lips. He struggled to sit up.

"Are you hurt?" Roy said. He poked around on Earle's back, feeling idiotic.

"All over," Earle said, turning his head from side to side.

The others arrived and circled round. Earle brightened noticeably. "How'd it look?" he said to them. "I thought I might try a figure eight, but I put off too goddam long."

"The wind . . ."

"You missed that pasture . . ."

"By about half a mile . . ."

"I don't think I could've hit it if I'd dropped straight down," Fielding said. "Once we got up I couldn't even *see* the pasture. I was all turned around."

They helped him up the hill and let him stretch out in the back seat of one of the cars. They started back toward the ranch.

The Mexican laborer, down in a hollow sawing wood, looked up as the procession of cars passed by. He smiled, and on a crazy impulse waved his floppy hat. Although no one looked at him from the car windows, he shared a little of their excitement. He had stopped sawing wood to watch the parachute jump; it was the first time he had ever seen such a thing.

Sixteen

OUIDA waited on the front lawn. "Is he all right?" she yelled to them. She moved closer to see. Earle sat grinning in the back seat. Then he got out of the car, put his arm round his estranged wife and planted a long kiss on her mouth. She pulled away after a moment, astonished. He had been drinking inside before the jump without any noticeable change coming over him. Now he beamed his new confidence, as if crazy drunk. He sat down and rested under one of the oak trees.

Ouida stood and watched after him until Rinemiller arrived. Alfred came over and talked with Earle for some time, discussing the jump and the peculiar characteristics of the light plane he had piloted. Ouida suggested that Earle go upstairs and bathe, but he continued to sit out under the trees, wearing the mud-smeared overalls like a battle dress.

Willie and Cathryn went to play tennis. One of the men wandered around the grounds, waving the cardboard on which the tournament brackets had been drawn up, stressing the urgency of completing first-round matches before dark. Otherwise, he warned, the next day's quarter finals would be a mess and there'd be little time for serious drinking.

Roy told George Giffen to wait for him while he went to make a phone call. George walked over to the courts and watched Cathryn's bosom bounce up and down.

Roy completed his call and wandered down a dark hall toward the front of the house. He met Ouida emerging from the lavatory. She carried a damp towel.

"I thought I'd at least wash that muck off Earle's face," she said.

He stared at the towel; he gaped at Ouida; she moved closer and touched his own perspiring forehead with the towel. He was conscious of the profusion of dartweeds and cocklebur that had got lodged inside his trousers during the run across the field. He shifted slightly, scratching his leg. She gave him a great open-mouthed kiss, held on for a minute and then stepped away.

"I'm sorry," she said, holding the towel up against his face. She was close to him again; their hips nearly touching; her eyes all soft and wise with understanding; she kissed him again and held the wet cloth to his face. She kept kissing and drawing back a few inches, looking at him and resuming the kiss, her face coming at him, turned to one side and then another. It was like a movie love scene by Hitchcock: all that soft talk going on, mouth to mouth . . .

"I'm sorry," she repeated. "I hadn't any business . . ."

"I didn't know you'd called . . . That goddam Ellen never . . ."

"Oh, Roy, I was just so jealous, and everything seemed hopeless, I . . ." Her hair was gardenia-scented and her fresh mouth tasted of expensive whiskey.

"Things all mixed up . . ." he said.

"I know . . . Isn't it —"

"I should have come on out here last night."

"God, I wish you had! If you'd only . . . So ridiculous . . . I was furious 'cause you didn't and you were mad at me for being so demanding and we each took it out on the other . . ."

"I should have driven out."

"I've really no right to pry into your personal life. I shouldn't care who you're going to bed with. It's just that girl I can't stand. Anyone else . . ."

"To bed? No, I . . ."

"Anyone else I don't think would set me off like it did. God, I'm sorry, dearest . . . We're really so much alike, let's declare a truce. Would you promise me you won't have anything more to do with her?"

"Sure, I — There's never . . . not last night at least . . . been anything betwee — Not since, Jesus really there —"

"Oh, promise will you, Roy? It's terrible, what these things do. I hadn't intended, but last night, after that call, I couldn't help it . . . If you'd heard what she said on the phone. I let Alfred make love to me, pretending at first it was you and then beginning to like it and knowing it was him and liking it because it was the worst thing I could think of . . ."

"Rinemiller? My God, you —"

"He came out last night. That's why I called. Hoping to get you to come help. He was practically in a state of caterwaul, and pretty soon, after that phone call, I was the same way. Oh Roy, I . . ."

"Rinemiller? He was *here* . . . last night?"

"Yes . . . It was awful . . ."

She kissed him again. They were very close in the hallway; piano music had resumed in the main part of the house, and through the windows they could hear the fellow with the tournament card calling off the names of first-round contestants. Her mouth searched his face; the back of her blouse had grown damp against his hand, and the hallway steamed a little.

"I'll be here again in just a minute," she said. "Will you wait? Right here? I'll take this to Earle and be right back. There's a small bedroom down the other end of this hall. No one knows about it. I'll take you down there and we'll lock ourselves in. The hell with all these others . . . We'll never have to come out . . ."

He stood there gasping for an answer. She kissed him once more and then headed toward the front of the house. He stood in the dark for a short time, his face and neck gone sticky with perspiration. He went into the washroom and drew another towel across the flesh under his collar. Then he walked toward the rear of the house to make his phone call. On the grounds in the back, near the courts, he found Giffen.

"Let's go for a ride in your Alfa," he said.

Giffen was delighted. He got quickly to his feet and looked around for the car, sighting it at the side of the house.

"I want somebody else to hear your story," Roy said.

"Listen — I don't want to get in any trouble . . ."

"This way," Roy said, "you can be sure of keeping out of trouble."

"How's that?"

"Don't you want to go visit the Governor?"

"*Sure* . . . I always wanted . . . but . . ."

"He wants to hear this story," Roy said. "Old Arthur — him and me, we're great friends. He's got a place out here, just up the river, and he wants to talk to *you*, George."

Giffen was not yet convinced. He thought about Cathryn's bosom and the crazy afternoon he'd spent with the lobbyist and bending down to kiss the Archbishop's hand the week before —

all this, the sinful emotions and the righteous ones, nagged at his sense of order. He decided, finally, to go with Roy to see the Governor in the hope that Fenstemaker might in some way relieve him of responsibility. Roy had said earlier he should have told the priest. But what was the point of telling a priest you'd just done the right thing?

They climbed into the roadster and sped toward the main highway.

Seventeen

HE HAD CALLED Fenstemaker's country place, but he had not thought to talk personally with the Governor. Now he wondered if it had been a mistake. Barging in like this might only cause confusion, and further agitate George Giffen. And perhaps Rinemiller had been right — right for the wrong reasons, thinking only of himself, but a source of sound advice nonetheless. Why should he have presumed? It was really none of his business. Let George carry his burden round with him until he had told enough people so that the story was absorbed by the local folklore, became a part of the public domain. Let Fenstemaker find out on his own good time. He wondered how all this should concern Roy Sherwood.

The little roadster ground up the hills; Giffen kept his eyes on the road, looking unhappy. Roy wished he had thought to talk the matter over with Willie.

The Governor's country mansion, a hideous Gothic-cum-Federalist affair, stuck out on the terraced hillside. Giffen stared in wonder; to his innocent gaze the gaucherie signified only wealth, vast power, a way of life unrevealed. For Roy it was merely an eyesore. The grotesque, the absurd, the bizarre — he'd grown up on it, new-rich vulgarity leavening his environment so completely that the conception itself had become a tired cliché, no more tormenting to his senses than the crude wink of an old streetwalker.

His vision of real wealth, affluence — the abundant Life — was conditioned on a level of experience entirely remote from his own. It had nothing to do with pigeon shoots, parachute jumps, twenty-five-year-old whiskey or replicas of rambling summer houses seen at Newport. Even the private railroad car — his grandfather's — still parked alongside the cattle ramp on a spur near home — had no part in shaping his own touchstones of opulence. He thought about this as Giffen steered the roadster through the front gate of the Governor's property. He thought back, attempting to lend a single identifying symbol to the idea, and finally he hit on it . . . laughed aloud . . . wondering what primrosed image of bearskin rugs and cerise Cadillacs clouded Rinemiller's mind . . . For Roy it had been simply a radio program in his youth, a harmless interval of exotica falling between the Metropolitan Opera and the special overseas broadcasts from the Royal Hawaiian Hotel in Honolulu. Tortured Saturday afternoons, he remembered, in Fort Stockton. Just off the El Paso highway and the bald slopes of the mountains. You'll know you're there by the sound of the spluttering radio . . . He had dreamed of creamy-complexioned women in short skirts and fur hats, stepping out of prewar Packard convertibles, enormously chic in the shade of monogrammed roadhouse canopies . . . He moved his lips, repeating the words aloud:

". . . From Frank Daly's Meadowbrook, just off the Pompton Turnpike (was it Merritt Parkway?) near Little Old New York we bring you the music of Charlie Barnett and his . . ."

Giffen stared at him in astonishment.

"What'd you say, Roy?"

They were parked in an open space near the main entrance to

the house. There was music coming from inside and from loud-speakers nesting in the trees, the sounds blending to produce a notably unpleasant effect of mismated stereophonics.

"Let's go see old Arthur," Roy said.

They left the roadster and headed up the front steps. Roy peered through the blinds: two secretaries labored over electric typewriters, strangely empurpled in the fluorescent glare. He turned and walked round the side of the house, Giffen at his heels. They did not see Fenstemaker right off — not until they were nearly directly upon him. He lay floating on a brightly colored air mattress at the far end of the pool, the breeze stirring lambent blue eddies against his large arms. He lay face down, big nose nearly touching the water. He wore khaki swim shorts; a check-ered golf cap was pulled down almost to where the ears joined the skull. There was even, Roy noted, a buckle on the back of the cap.

They stepped up on the blue marble surface and walked round to the other side, coming to a stop a few feet away from where the Governor lay. He still did not seem aware of their presence.

"Afternoon," Roy said.

Fenstemaker opened one eye and squinted in the sun. "God-dam," he said. He reached down at his side, fumbled with a pair of dark glasses, and set them on his nose. He paddled over to the bank and slid his big body across from mattress to marble. Then he looked up at them again, sitting with his feet dangling in the water.

"You should've let me know you were comin' out," he said. "Planned a barbecue or somethin' . . ."

"You know George Giffen?"

"*Sure* . . . Sure I know George . . ." Fenstemaker extended a great freckled hand. Giffen grabbed it and said something incom-prehensible.

"Get ya'll a drink?"

They shook their heads. Roy lit a cigarette and looked over the grounds. Giffen maintained the semi-crouch position he had as-sumed when bending down to shake hands with the Governor.

Roy dragged a canvas chair to the bank of the pool and sat down. Then, with as little prefatory comment as possible, he made George repeat his story. As George droned on, Fenstemaker lowered himself in and out of the water, gasping happily as if being immersed in steam. He did not seem really interested in the story, although he did appear vaguely pleased about something when Giffen was finished.

"Would you repeat all this in court?" he said suddenly.

Giffen stammered for a moment. ". . . If you think it's the right thing to do," he said.

"Got no choice," the Governor said. "I'm gonna call the District Attorney in just a few minutes. Could you stay here and talk to him if he comes out tonight? Stay and have dinner with me?"

An ecstatic grin spread across Giffen's face. "Yessir," he said. ". . . Sure I will if you think it's the right —"

"I'm about ready to see that son of a bitch is put away. With George's testimony, I think it'll be a cinch . . . You told him hell no — that right? You're the key to this whole business, George, you got to realize that . . ."

"That right?" George said. He gazed at Fenstemaker with unquestioned devotion.

"Sure as hell is . . . People damn fortunate to have a man like you in the Legislature. Gonna look tremendous to the folks back in your district, too. Gonna work out perfect all the way. It's a goddam bird's nest on the ground . . ."

They talked some more. Roy insisted that he had to get back, and agreed to drive the roadster. Fenstemaker said he would bring Giffen into town next morning in the limousine. George would spend the night and they could have a good long talk. "You mind having to miss your party over there at the Fielding place?" he said. George shook his head . . .

"Whatever you say, Governor . . ."

"That so?" Fenstemaker said, vastly pleased. "Well then why don't you walk right up that litle rock path there and tap on those glass doors and tell one of my girls to bring us something to drink . . . Scotch all right? Roy? . . . Tell 'em Scotch and one of those fizz bottles and a pitcher of water . . . And tell 'em to put some different music on that phonograph . . ."

George stood in front of them, moving his head up and down; he turned and walked quickly toward the house. The Governor pulled off his dark glasses and began talking rapidly to Roy:

"How'd you get him out here? Have any trouble?"

"No . . . Willie got the story first. I just —"

"I was worried. Goddam I was worried. I been out here all afternoon wonderin' what in hell I ought to do. Ain't that somethin'? An honest man. I'd have thought Rinemiller would succeed in sellin' him the wrong load of cotton. You must've got to him before —"

"You *knew* about all this. How —"

"I got my sources," the Governor said.

"But how'd you know he talked with Rinemiller?"

" 'Cause Rinemiller called that fella early this afternoon. From the Fielding place . . ."

"How'd you —"

"Well now I don't *tap* lines, and I don't tape-record conversations — but I'll sure as hell listen in on one. Hell! I've had a suite in that hotel for years. Half the help there owe their jobs to me. Including the switchboard operator."

Fenstemaker lay in a hammock and pulled the golf cap down over his eyes; he curled his lips slightly and sucked on a tooth.

"What'd he tell him?" Roy said. "What was the phone call about? You say Alfred called in to town?"

"He called to throw a scare into that lobbyist. Told him Giffen was goin' around tellin' people he'd been offered a bribe. But that he'd managed to shut him up . . . And now he was ready to shake him down for George's share — and more. He chewed the fella good and proper, apparently. Scared hell out of him. I don't think the lobbyist was just playin' along, either. Didn't sound like it."

"But why," said Roy, ". . . . why would he come to you with that tape one day and then turn right around and try to buy off somebody else on the next?"

"Coonass," the Governor said. "Coonass operator's all he is.

First he tries to sweat me into doin' somethin' for him — tries to
bargain with me for Jesus sake. Gets the idea I'm just a coonass
tradin' politician. That I'd make a little deal just to keep the boat
from bein' rocked. He never once thought I'd try to haul Rinemiller in before a grand jury. He thought I'd rather have that tape
to hold over Rinemiller's head. He figured me for a cheap pol —
that son of a bitch just doesn't *know* cheap pols — figurin' *I'd* want
Rinemiller runnin' around loose and ready to do what I told him
to do more than Rinemiller stuck off in prison for a few years . . .
Ah, goddam. All the time he was goin' right on tryin' to bribe
himself some more votes . . . Ain't he in for a kick-in-the-pants
surprise now!"

Giffen was coming back down the path carrying a tray of bot-
tled drinks and glasses.

"What about Rinemiller?" Roy said quickly. "What are you going to do about Rinemiller?"

"I'm not sure," the Governor said, rolling off the hammock to
greet George.

"Hey, you needn't of done that," he said. "One of the girls
could do the servin'."

Giffen set the tray down, smiling, silent. The Governor poured
drinks for them. Roy sat back in the canvas chair; he watched the
hills change color; he picked burrs and dartweed off his socks and
from inside his trouser legs. There were no more heroes, he
thought. There were only the fallen clergymen like Rinemiller,
honest and simple people like Giffen, and the pretenders like himself. And the Fenstemakers, of course, who couldn't care less.
Heroic attitudes didn't amount to much for the Fenstemakers.
They were fakirs, medicine men, illusionists — making miracles
with mirrors and sleight of hand and finding, suddenly, that their
dross was somehow incredibly turned to gold. What an act! Who
the hell needed a hero?

He finished off the drink and got to his feet. The Governor
talked with Giffen, rattling on implausibly, without relevance, in-
dulging himself: the witch doctor in repose.

"It's damn good Scotch whiskey," Fenstemaker was saying. "The best there is . . ."

"I'd like to try some in a snifter at room temperature," Giffen said.

That was giving the old man what for . . . Now where in heaven had George ever heard an expression like *that*? His liquor salesman possibly. Room temperature? The whole goddam planet was cooling off to room temperature. Fenstemaker's cosmic sleight of hand. No more heroes; not even any real sinners; sin was simply dullness and bad faith; heroism an empty gesture.

"It's really the fusel oil in whiskey that gives you a hangover," Giffen went on learnedly. "The alcohol insufficiently distilled . . ."

"It's that goddam fusel oil all right," the Governor said. "It must've been what ruined so many cedar choppers out here in these hills. Years ago. Jesus I remember that busthead stuff they distilled . . . Insufficiently as you say . . . It nearly crippled you . . . Poor boy's gout was what it was . . ."

Eighteen

It was nearly dark when he started back. The color was gone off the hills, blurred hummocky outlines dividing the gray sky from the blacked-out lower slopes and the featureless plain. Then the sky itself was shrouded in gloom as boiling stormclouds gathered in the distance, piling up in bunches, sailing over the valleys and small plateaus. He steered the roadster along the narrow road, picking up speed, the first drops of rain exploding against his forehead. A breath of cold enveloped him like a sudden chill; lightning flashed behind, reflections bouncing off the small windshield and exaggerating the slag-heap shape of hills on either side. The air expanded and there was a clap of thunder that made him jump. The collapsed convertible top flapped like a windsock in his ear.

Beyond the next rise the big ranch house lit up the sky, windows gleaming. He raced the car ahead of the downpour. His face and shoulders were drenched, the rest of him scarcely damp at all. There were more cars in front; he had to search for a parking space. The property suddenly resembled a huge, fashionable roadhouse — a gambling hall — all it needed was a checkered canopy extending out from the entrance, searchlights, a parking attendant, a uniformed doorman.

Lights shone through every window. Or nearly every window. There was the place down the hall Ouida had mentioned: the empty bedroom no one seemed aware of. He wondered if it was still available. And was Ouida? Perhaps he should have left a note, sent up a signal flare from Fenstemaker's blue-dappled pool. But there was really no point in feeling obligated. It was she, after all, who owed him a thing or two. Was he going to be stuffy about that business with Rinemiller? Yes he was — he was going to insist on it, in fact. He thought about what kind of love those two had contrived to make. Their dark bare writhing shadows fouled his vision. And what, he thought, of Rinemiller in the light of day? *I'm not sure,* Fenstemaker had said. If Fenstemaker wasn't sure, who in hell was? What could be constant, aside from the earth's inexorable cooling (down to room temperature), if not Arthur Fenstemaker? Sure he was sure. It was unthinkable . . .

Music rumbled from inside the house: neither phonograph records nor tinkling off-key piano, but the *live* sounds of stringed instruments and accordion. Someone had even thought to hire a hillbilly band. He ran along the drive and up the front steps as the raindrops beat down on his head. The door was wide open. Hell of a lot more people than in the afternoon. The musicians were off in a corner; he could see only the top of the bass fiddle; there were dancing couples in between and clusters of people strewn along the walls, clogging doorways, lining the balcony overhead. No one really noticed his entrance, or even cared; he wondered if his absence had left any kind of gap at all.

Possibly Willie, just possibly his friend Willie had missed him. And Ouida — she would remember his broken engagement. Or had that idea been abandoned even as her season of heat began to turn with the planet's relentless cooling to room temperature?

Someone touched him on the back and pushed a drink into his hand. He was there — suddenly, officially — recognition come at last. He was identified, set apart, brought miraculously to life. He put the drink to his mouth, swilling fusel oil, and looked about. Across the room he could see Willie and Cathryn; they sat together on a couch talking with some others. He looked closer and saw that they were with Harris and his tennis partner and Ellen Streeter. They all sat there, defining one another. He looked round for Ouida. She was nowhere in sight, and this seemed to inflate her value to him. He searched for Rinemiller's face, and found it, with relief, suspended in the doorway to the kitchen. Alfred stood there talking with Earle and Frank Huggins, plotting grand strategy for some mythical campaign for the governorship. Just everyone was there — and scads of others. Kermit and his red beard floated past; he had his arm round a stunning, high-hipped colored girl. Kermit sang a little song:

> *Got a date with a Negress*
> *And I'm filled with elation . . .*
> *I'm a liberal who's vig'rous*
> *Fav'rin misceg - ahnation . . .*

Someone pawed at Roy's back. He turned to face Jay Mc-Gown; one of the Governor's pretty secretaries held on to Jay's arm.

"Ah."

"Ah."

They made noises of recognition; everybody was coming to life. Jay introduced the girl. Roy said: "I've been out to see your boss."

"I heard," Jay said. "He called here little while ago. To talk to Willie. Said he wanted to give Willie first crack at the story because he rescued Giffen."

"That's good. Giffen was nearly ecstatic. I'm glad Willie got to him early. Otherwise . . . The Governor say anything to you about Rinemiller?"

"No," Jay said. "And I didn't press him about it. I thought you'd know something."

"I don't know anything," Roy said. "I'm beginning to wonder if I ever did."

"I gave up long time ago," Jay said.

Roy reached across for another drink as a tray passed by his head. He watched the high-hipped Negro girl move through the crowd alongside Kermit. His father once had told him of seeing a lynching in his youth, around the turn of the century, the scarred, black naked body dangling from a flagpole outside a downtown office building. His father had taken one look and run all the way home to hide under the house. Roy remembered a time when he was nine years old, playing games with a colored boy who followed his mother to work occasionally, the mother working as a domestic in a big home the next street over. *Make him call you Mr. Roy*, some neighbor had advised. And he had — the idea struck him as altogether perfect. The boy had called him *Mist' Roy* all one day. Except on the next he'd only said it when Roy was close by; when there was a distance between them he'd stand off and call him just plain unprefixed Roy. Then a chase would ensue, and when he'd been overtaken, the boy would collapse, giggling, out of breath, repeating *Mist' Roy, Mist' Roy, Mist' Roy* . . . Smart-alec nigger, the neighbor had observed . . .

Jay went on: "You did real well yesterday. You ought to be out front more often. These people need some leadership. You and Huggins ought to get them organized . . ."

"I couldn't organize a crap game," Roy said.

"The hell you couldn't. Get up front and let 'em just look at you if nothing else."

"I don't even campaign back home," Roy said. "The elections are foregone conclusions. It's in the family. All they do is send the Mexicans into town with their poll tax receipts and tell them where to mark the ballot."

"Here comes Rinemiller," Jay said.

Alfred approached them, weaving slightly. He extended his hand toward Jay. "How's the Governor's wiper?" he said, smiling to assure them it was a joke.

"Bought and paid for," Jay said.

Rinemiller turned to Roy and said: "George Giffen around here? You went riding with him this afternoon, didn't you? You seen him since then?"

Roy couldn't resist it. Rinemiller would find out soon enough, anyhow.

"George is over at the Governor's," he said.

Rinemiller's jaw went slack for an instant. Then he hauled it back up, like a drawbridge. "Fenstemaker's ranch?" he said, controlling his voice. "What's he doing there?"

"I can't say. I just know he's there."

"How come? What's he got that's so important to Fenstemaker?"

Roy shook his head. Alfred looked around. Jay and the secretary shrugged.

"He coming back soon? I need to talk with him."

"I don't know," Roy said. "There was some mention of his spending the night."

"You were there? What's it all about?"

"I really don't know," Roy said. "All I did was show him the way . . ."

". . . Fantastic . . ." Rinemiller said, shaking his head. He turned without formality and strode off across the room.

"Got to go," Jay said.

"You leaving now?"

"Governor wanted us out there with him. Big party. Dinner on the ground with the District Attorney . . . See you later."

Jay and his girl moved on through the crowd toward the front of the house. Willie came over.

"You know anything I don't know?" he said.

They exchanged information on Fenstemaker and George Giffen.

"He's even said he'll try to get the prosecutors to sit on all this a few days until I can get a press run started," Willie said. "I might have to put out a two-page edition to keep from being skunked by the dailies on my own story. But old Fenstemaker is being very cooperative."

"What about Rinemiller?" Roy said. "What's going to be done about him?"

"He wouldn't go into it," Willie said. "But he did say something strange."

"What was that?"

"He asked me what ought to be done. He said he realized my little publication might be ruined. Rinemiller being on the board of directors and all. He asked *me.* As if it were *my* decision . . ."

"Well . . ."

"Well."

They looked at each other in confusion. Willie caught sight of Rinemiller moving across the room. "Son of a bitch," he said. "It's not just that it would mess up my operation — but it could defeat some good people at the next election. Force some of them out and keep some others from getting in . . . Son of a bitch . . . Why couldn't he have said hell no, the way Giffen did?"

They were silent for a moment. Roy said: "He had more imagination than Giffen. And not as much discipline. He had a larger conception of himself — he wants to go farther, faster, than the rest of us . . . If you accept the premise that a politician's first obligation is to get elected, or re-elected — and I'm inclined to; perhaps because I've never really had to work at getting anything

— if you accept this, then you could probably see Alfred justifying what he's done. Every step of the way. He believes in himself. He thinks he can do some good. But he knows it's impossible — it's entirely hopeless — if he loses. He took a good look at himself and decided he had everything but money. He's as able as Earle Fielding, but Earle's got plenty of money and sources for even more. So Alfred sets out to solve his most immediate problem . . ."

"You're too damned easy on him," Willie said.

"Sure I am. But I was just trying to see it from his point of view. The everyman politician with a cause. Most politicians accommodate themselves this way. One damn self-administered absolution after another — ends and means. But there's a limit to how far you can go. The good ones know this. They realize — certainly Alfred must have been at least *aware* of it — that you can only go so far. If you carry your justifications any farther, it's a risk and it's wrong. I mean if you're Rinemiller, you know it's a risk. If you're Giffen, you just know it's wrong. If you're Fenstemaker . . . well. The good ones know there are limits. The really great ones don't even have to think about it — it's instinctive. There's really no decision involved, because there's none required, nothing to decide . . ."

"Now you're being too hard on Fenstemaker," Willie said. "I can't believe any of his problems are easy to solve. You can't just write it off to instinct . . ." He smiled and added: "If you accept the premise, of course, that he's one of the great ones."

"Mahatma Gandhi and Rasputin," Roy said. "The Prince of Darkness and the goddam Mystic Angel. If I ever back off from Fenstemaker, it won't be because I lost faith. Just the reverse. Because I might put so much faith in him I'd stop believing in myself. Can't have that. Matter of self-preservation."

"Well," Willie concluded, looking back at Rinemiller, "there's something to be said for politicians. I can't think of what it is right offhand, but . . ."

They gave it up at that point. The hillbilly band had begun to make a music to which it was nearly possible to dance, and people moved into the middle of the room, taking hold of one another in a stuporous clutch. Roy and Willie walked out of the way and stood next to the wall. Cathryn found them there. She appeared suddenly out of the crowd and took Willie's arm.

"I'm hungry," Cathryn said, putting her head against Willie's shoulder. "I'm drunk and I'm hungry." She closed her eyes.

"We'll go to the kitchen," Willie said. "Some Southern fried chicken for my Southern fried lady love."

They moved off through the crowd. In the kitchen they helped Cathryn onto a high stool and brought the food to her. She chewed on a wing and said:

"I may be fried; I suppose I'm Southern, but this chicken is neither. It's barbecued."

"They have a Mexican who does it," Willie said. "He knows how to barbecue a Southern fried chicken."

"This barbecued chicken," Cathryn said, "is fraught with ambiguity."

"Yes," Roy said. "I have the feeling that if you could somehow break through that deceptive crust of skin you would find peace. Perhaps even God . . ."

"I dreamed I found God . . . at the Mixed Doubles Tennis," Cathryn said.

"I knew I loved her the instant I set eyes on it," Willie said.

"What?"

"The chicken . . . That symbolist chicken."

"I feel better," Cathryn said, wiping her mouth with a napkin. She held Willie's hand. "Let's take a walk along the river."

"Shall we bring a six pack?"

"A two pack will do," Cathryn said. "I feel better, but not sober. And some cigarettes. I'm out of cigarettes."

Willie looked at Roy. "Two pack," he said. "I suppose that pretty well excludes you . . ."

"I suppose," Roy said. He raised his hand. "Bless you, children. I hope I've helped show you the Way."

Willie and Cathryn left through the side door without looking back. Roy sat on the stool and took a bite of chicken. Presently Willie reappeared at the kitchen door. He looked through the screen and then stepped inside. "It's wet out there," he said. "You suppose there's a blanket available?"

Roy put his piece of chicken down and thought. "We can take a look around," he said. They walked toward the stairs; Roy hesitated and then said he'd heard someone mention a bedroom on the ground floor. They went back in the direction of the hall.

They found it at the very end of the hall, after looking into doors along the way that revealed nothing more than storage space for linens, china, silver, and a few bath and beach towels. The last door swung open and Roy reached round the corner and switched on the light. Ouida rolled over on the bed, propped herself on one elbow, shielding her eyes.

"Pardon," Roy said. "Thousand pardons."

It was really a very old bed. A chenille spread was bunched at the foot; intricately carved posts, painted yellow, rose from each corner; Ouida's clothes were hung on one of the posts. She sat up on the bed in her cotton underwear, rubbing her eyes. She made no attempt to cover herself, so they stood there looking.

"What *time* is it?" she said.

"Little after nine," Roy said.

She could not seem to hold her eyes open in the light. Finally, she slipped off the side of the bed and walked past them into a small bathroom and began washing her face. While she bent over the lavatory bowl, Willie said: "We were looking for a blanket. Should I take one off the bed here?"

Ouida returned to the bed and sat on the edge of it for a moment, blinking. "How long have you been here?" she said to Roy.

"Couple hours."

"Where in the world did you *go?*" She was not cross, especially; it was more as if she were disappointed and a little impatient in dealing with a small child.

"I had to take George Giffen over to Fenstemaker's ranch."

She sighed and made a gesture of resignation: Roy's answer did not explain anything, but it was too hopelessly confused to go into any further. She looked away from them, thinking.

"Blanket . . ." she said aloud.

She got to her feet again and went to the closet and pulled down a heavy Mexican serape. Willie took it from her.

"I suppose," she said, "you wanted this for the out-of-doors?"

Willie said yes. He thanked her and headed down the hall. Roy remained where he was, liking the looks of her good legs and her hips and her small behind and the soft roll of her abdomen encased in cotton underwear. Her wisp of a brassière was like something from a subteen shop. She returned to the bed and sat with her legs hanging off the side. She got a cigarette lighted.

"I was sick after you left," she said. "God, I was sick."

"Are you feeling better?"

"I think."

She propped herself against the back of the bed and sat smoking, holding an ashtray in her lap.

"Shut the door and come sit with me awhile," she said.

He sat at the opposite end so he could see her better. It occurred to him that he had spent nearly all one night in bed with her but had only the vaguest impression of how she looked. She was like a little girl just going into woman.

He was breathless for a moment, thinking back, struck by the little girl image. Once, on the promise of three gasoline ration stamps, he had driven across town to a neighborhood of broken-down-flatbed trucks and decaying church buildings, where a small girl of twelve or thirteen sat waiting on an ancient front porch swing. The yards were smeared with chicken dung, and she had come toward him, holding the gas stamps out for him to see as if to demonstrate the absolute, manifest goodness of her promise. He was home from military school and had met her the night before in a cheap movie house. Next to the water fountain. Munching on popcorn. The two of them bored with the movie. They had sat together on one of the back rows, kissing interminably. She promised gasoline stamps if only he would come take her someplace the next evening, and there he was with the family's prewar Buick parked out front on the ruined street. "Someplace" was a wooded gravel pit she knew about, and after kissing and holding on to her small breasts during the final quarter hour of twilight, he suggested they move into the back seat. She slipped over the top, and before he could get a station fixed on the radio and extract two cigarettes from the pack above the visor, she had pulled off nearly all her clothes. She sat in a corner, small and lovely in her cotton knit underwear and thin brassière, waiting for him, explaining, once he had joined her in back, that her older sister had instructed her in how it was done. She sat watching him, smiling faintly, waiting for something. Instead, they sat together in back, holding on to each other, until it was time to go. Outside her house he tried to return the gasoline stamps, but she wouldn't accept them. Her father had come out on the porch, drunk and abusive, and there had not been time even to promise he would call.

He never seemed able to call, nor did he see her again, and now he sat at the end of the four-poster bed, watching Ouida in her rich girl's cheap underwear, wishing he had. The memory of the child in the back seat of the old Buick filled him with regret. Where was she now? Whoring in New Orleans or disguising her innocence as an aging car hop along the border — he would have called her now under any circumstance. He could not remember her name. The street where she lived no longer even existed; a four-lane highway had long since supplanted those diseased neighborhoods. But the small girl, in his memory, seemed to embrace all of virtue in a world of barbarisms.

Ouida was talking. He had not been paying attention.

"I was so sick . . ."

She was still going on about that. He turned round on the bed and stretched out beside her. She continued to sit up with her shoulders resting against the back of the bed. She put her hand out and touched his face. He felt he should say something; he'd been silent for several minutes.

"You look like a little girl," he said. He could not see her; his head was turned the other way and one arm was flung across her bare legs.

"Let's get out of here," Ouida said. "Let's go someplace where everyone looks different."

Nineteen

CATHRYN had waited in the front room while Willie looked for the blanket. She stood next to the side door, watching the progression of events at the party, trying, but not in the least succeeding, to share in the general rapture. The cowboy musicians were clearly drunk now, and they were playing overtime in exchange for whiskey and an opportunity to dance, every so often, with the women. The noise in the house had risen to such a pitch that it was nearly impossible to determine its individual components. It was just noise: bad music and loud talk, interspersed with whoops of maddened laughter, held together by the continuous thumping of bass chords. She watched Harris and Ellen Streeter grappling with one another behind a potted palm. Ellen was pale and stoic looking. Harris had kissed her and now had backed off, glaring at her. Ellen said something — it was impossible to hear any of it — and then Harris pulled her roughly against the wall. She shook loose and stepped away, as if gauging the distance, and then swung her small fist, cracking Harris smartly across the bridge of the nose and a corner of one eye.

Harris blinked in astonishment; he reached up and touched the nose and eye. Ellen watched him for a moment, then turned and walked off into the crowd. Harris's face had gone red all over, and a single large teardrop advanced from the corner of the sore eye, spilling down his puffed cheek.

Willie appeared with the serape. "You ready?" he said to Cathryn.

"Just a minute," Cathryn said. She told Willie about the blow Ellen Streeter had struck Harris behind the potted palm. They stood there for a few moments, watching Harris, who looked their way for an instant but did not seem really to notice anyone. He had a pocket handkerchief out and was blotting at both eyes. His face was still very red. Finally, he walked off in the direction of the bathroom.

Willie and Cathryn turned to leave, but Rinemiller reached them as they moved toward the side door.

"You there this afternoon when Earle made the jump?" he said.

Willie said yes, and Rinemiller said, "I mean were you there when he hit the ground? Did you see him when he hit?"

"No," Willie said. "Giffen and Roy got there first. I'm not certain whether they actually saw him land — but they were there first. What's matter?"

"It's Earle," Rinemiller said. "He pitched over in the kitchen a few minutes ago. Still passed out. Maybe it's the booze, but I got to thinking maybe he cracked his head harder than he wanted to admit to himself this afternoon . . ."

"Well let's go have a look," Willie said.

"He's out *cold*," Rinemiller was saying as they pushed through the crowd. "His goddam eyes are all up in his head. His skin's clammy and he looks awful . . ." He paused for a moment, thinking, and then added: "But no more awful than most drunks, I suppose."

The party was still going good; people moved past and in front of them, looking reckless and extravagant and gloriously muddled. One of the women had been persuaded to sing, and she was going at it vigorously, in an occasionally off-key light opera voice, describing how it was when the Deep Purple fell.

In the kitchen, Earle Fielding was sprawled on the linoleum, his long legs half under the table. A sofa cushion had been slipped under his head, and there was a crowd gathered, pushing in close to see. Willie bent down to get a better look; he peeled back one eyelid but was uncertain about what exactly he was looking for; he attempted to take a pulse count; he kept losing it. Finally, he straightened up and said to Cathryn: "Wait here a minute. I'm going to go find Roy."

He headed out of the kitchen and down the back hallway toward the little bedroom where he'd last seen Roy and Ouida. The bedroom door was closed, but light shone at the bottom, against the polished tile. He put his head against the door panel to listen. He rapped lightly and then once again, with more authority. He turned the knob and stepped inside. They'd left only their impressions on the unmade bed; other than the bed, there was little else. Willie wandered into the small bathroom, switched on the light, examined the tile floor, shook the dry shower curtain. He stared at himself in the mirror above the lavatory. His face seemed as bleached and pallid as Earle Fielding's. He splashed cold water across tender eyelids. Then he switched off lights and left the room and moved back up the hall. Cathryn was at the other end, next to the door to the front bath. She took his arm and said: "Everyone's gone crazy — really."

Willie glanced at Cathryn and then, through the bathroom door, at Ellen Streeter. Ellen sat on the edge of a low tub, pressing a washcloth against the side of her face. Willie and Cathryn stepped inside, and Cathryn said: "Feel any better?"

Ellen smiled faintly and nodded her head. She got to her feet and stood in front of a mirror, holding the cloth away from her cheek to examine the bruise. She sat down again on the edge of the tub. Willie asked what happened; Cathryn stared at Ellen and said: "Harris socked her back. Right outside the door here. I saw it all . . . The son of a bitch."

"Men is men," Ellen said, looking up and smiling again.

"Jesus . . ." Willie said.

"You'd have to collapse on the floor and scream and swallow

your tongue to get any attention around here," Cathryn said. "Think I was the only one who noticed."

"Where's Harris?" Willie said.

"Wandered off somewhere," Cathryn said.

"Sure you're all right?" Willie said.

"Yes," Ellen said. She got back to her feet and looked in the mirror. "Harris and I have now exchanged black eyes . . . We ought to buy us some boy-girl look-alike sweaters."

Willie left Cathryn with Ellen Streeter and returned to the kitchen. Earle still lay sprawled, half under the small table. Rinemiller and Huggins were maneuvering over him, as if about to lower grappling hooks.

"I couldn't find Roy," Willie said to them. He stared at Earle, and added: "We ought to get him into town."

Rinemiller nodded and got hold of Earle Fielding's two feet. Willie and Huggins struggled to get a firm grip under each arm. The three of them began a slow, shuffling move toward the kitchen door. Cathryn appeared and Willie told her to go out front and bring the car around. Cathryn made a languid gesture, as if resigned to the inevitability of witnessing one delirious incident after another.

A few people stopped and stared and smiled as they carried Earle to the car. One young man, locked in an excess of pleasure with his date in the backseat of a car, let loose of the girl and looked out the window as they moved past carrying Earle.

"Hey-hey!" he called to them. "You all gonna be back now? Anybody drops out the tournament, screws up the pairin's for everyone else . . ."

They got Earle stretched out in the back of Rinemiller's car. Huggins sat alongside the unconscious figure, and Alfred moved up front to drive. Willie and Cathryn followed in another car. The rain had started up again, and they drove along the soft roads toward the main highway, alternately accelerating and slowing with the downpours as the stormclouds sailed overhead.

Twenty

THEY HAD DRIVEN in silence most of the way into town and along the gleaming streets; fled across soggy lawns, rainsheets flashing against the stone walls of the cabin. They walked through Roy's three rooms, turning on lights, silent and self-conscious, touching hands. Roy got some music started on the phonograph; Ouida sat on the side of the bed, combing the dampness from her hair. Rain drummed on the expanse of lake water. They sat listening to the weather, talking a little, waiting for her hair to dry. They kissed until the whacking of their pulsebeats made it nearly unendurable, and then they switched off lights and lay in darkness, listening to the lake sounds; presently they were communicating in gasps and half-sentences and muffled laughter, and Roy could very nearly convince himself that they had something, the two of them there, something amounting to more than mere mathematics and consecutive, counted-on-the-calendar fornications; a prize that outshone thrust and parry, challenged parts, and the mingled secretions of comparison shoppers.

And then, the two of them passing into sleep in simultaneous exhaustion, he could not be sure. For an instant he could hear the singsong chants of children, the sounds outdistancing ancient discords; ephemeral fragrances came to him in sleep: pine and cinnamon and fish-water, and he remembered an old friend from college telling him of making love to his wife of ten years in the backyard mint bed, next to the water hydrant, thrashing in sweet leaves, in the dark of night, laughing and talking and whispering Solomon's Song: *Thou art fair, my beloved, yea, pleasant, and our bed is green.* And he could not be certain. Memory, reason, poetry, failed him in sleep. He was unable to recall even the wife of his youth, his sweet dumb blonde mirage of a wife, swilling Nugrape

Soda in the Norfolk U.S.O. — where was she now? And where was Ellen Streeter, his lover of a leap-year month? Or the child who'd been so accommodating in the backseat of the prewar Buick? Or even Ouida, sitting cross-legged on the bed, romping about in her cotton underpants, small breasts swelling and going flat with the shift of her weight? There was only the idea of them — he'd nearly forgotten all the details in the short space of their absence. Now they were no more than an idealized montage, symbols of desire put together from all his women. He hoped they were somehow, each of them, with him in the bed, beneath the covers. He was certain he could feel one or all of them up against him as he passed into the deepest hour of sleep.

In the morning there were flecks of lipstick round his mouth. He blinked at himself in the bathroom mirror, wondering how long it would be before Ouida came awake and how soon he would need to construct a face, an attitude, with which to ease a wife at dawn. He went out on the rock porch and stood in the gray light to wait for the milkman. When he got back inside, Ouida was awake and ravenously hungry, boiling eggs and munching vanilla wafers. She was barefoot, with a pair of his bleached khakis tied round her waist, good hips filling the seat, trouser legs rolled to the first flare of calf muscle. They sat across from each other at breakfast, and Roy struggled with the right noises, the alien faces, until the phone's ringing rattled the dime store silver service.

"I hope they haven't tracked us here already," Ouida said. She sat pinning her hair and watched Roy hesitating, his hand on the hooked receiver. He picked it up, finally, and said hello.

"You give up on the party?" Willie said to him.

Roy said yes he had; he'd withdrawn from public life; he'd divested himself of all worldly attachments.

"Yes . . . well listen," Willie said. "I've got to get in touch with Ouida. I can't find her anywhere."

"What you need her for?" Roy said.

"You know where she is?"

"She's around," Roy said. "I've got a pretty good idea."

"Yes . . . Well . . . Listen . . ." Willie said. "Earle's in the hospital — nothing really serious — I mean he's not going to die or anything — but I thought Ouida ought to know."

"What the hell happened?"

"He's got a concussion, it turns out. That parachute jump. Got clonked on the head after his helmet was knocked off. Something like that."

"I'll tell Ouida," Roy said. He got the information about which hospital and what room and how many special nurses. And the doctor — he'd forgotten to ask about the doctor: after telling Ouida, he had to call Willie back and ask about the doctor. Ouida cleared the breakfast table and began dressing, and Willie gave him the doctor's name and more reassurances.

"He was unconscious most of the night," Willie said, "but he began coming out of it about an hour ago. He's not quite sure what's going on, but he'll be all right." Willie's voice was smoke-strained and full of exhaustion. "Rinemiller and I took turns sitting up with him."

"Alfred? He was with you?"

"Yes."

"How's he acting?"

"He grumbled about Giffen a few times — wondering where George was — but otherwise he —"

"You say anything to him?"

"No . . . What in hell would I say? Weird feeling just being there with him. Now I'm going home to bed and think about whether I ought to expose him. Know where I can get a good job?"

Roy said no, but that Willie might think about running for a seat in the Legislature. They hung up. Roy put on a clean shirt and tie and then walked outside with Ouida for the drive to the hospital.

The big country house was silent. Cars were parked all along the drive, creaking in the morning heat. Inside the house a Mexican maid moved through the main room, emptying ashtrays, collecting bottles and sandwich crusts and half-filled glasses of whiskey. Huggins lay asleep in his underwear; he lay on one of the sofas, wrapped in the serape Willie had left behind the night before. He had got back from the hospital at two or three in the morning, waved a liquored goodbye to the cowboy musicians, and collapsed on the couch. He made horrible sounds early that morning, but the maid did not seem to notice. She went into the kitchen, switched on the dishwasher, and then walked out back and down the hill to look in on her husband and children. Huggins stirred on the couch, murmuring to himself, as the dishwasher shuddered on the kitchen floor. Huggins opened his eyes and stared at the ceiling. He struggled to an upright position, sitting on the edge of the couch, and fumbled with cigarettes. Then, he got to his feet and wandered into the kitchen, stared at the dishwasher and rinsed his whiskered face at the water tap. He chewed on a turkey wing and took a swallow of vermouth from an open bottle. He rubbed his damp face again and squinted in the morning light.

"*Anybody here?*" he yelled suddenly. He walked back into the main room. "Anybody in this *house?*" He lay back down on the sofa and fell asleep.

He did not stir again until George Giffen arrived. George came bounding up the steps after the Governor's limousine had dropped him on the front drive. Giffen did not immediately notice Huggins on the couch; he wandered round the big room, examining rubble, staring at the paneled walls, listening for anyone moving about upstairs. Then he came near the sofa, stopped, and poked at Huggins.

"Hey, Pancho. Let's play some tennis, hah?" he said. "Come on — I just got back . . . I missed out on everything yesterday."

Huggins did not move; breath barely fluttered across his parted lips. Giffen sat down and removed one shoe and began meticulously to scratch his foot. Presently he could hear people shuffling around on the second floor, and soon the plumbing began to groan as showers were put to use.

Twenty miles upriver from the Fielding ranch an old army command car banged along one of the backroads, lurching across culverts and coming to a stop next to a small low-water bridge. Arthur Fenstemaker got out of the car and sniffed the air. He was dressed in fresh khakis, a starched dress shirt with frazzled collar, and lace-up boots. He had the checkered golf cap pulled down tight so that it covered the tips of his big ears.

Fenstemaker stared at the water pushing over the small dam, hands on hips, his head working up and down as if in solemn agreement that, yes, it certainly was water, lots of water. He watched for a few moments and then returned to the cab of the open command car. Jay McGown sat in front alongside him. There was a thermos cooler at Jay's feet, and between his legs the guns were stacked: a three-inch magnum, a jungle carbine, a pump action.

"Open me a beer, Jay," the Governor said. "Goddam I like a cold beer in the mornings."

Jay opened cans of beer for the two of them. Fenstemaker started the engine and the old car jumped ahead, moved over a hill and then slowed again. Birds flapped overhead. Fenstemaker pointed. "Ain' that lovely?" he said softly. He took hold of the pump action, poked it out over the windshield, and fired two shots quick and successive. The dove fell nearly straight down. Fenstemaker laid the gun across Jay's lap, stepped outside and went to get the bird, crippling along like an old man whose joints were stiff and sensitive. Then he was back inside the car, holding on to the bird, and they moved off again, in the direction of the ranch house.

They left the car in front and walked inside. Jay stored the guns while Fenstemaker cleaned his hands. One of the secretaries came down the stairs.

"Any calls?" the Governor said.

The girl nodded and named several people. "And Willie England . . . just now . . . just as you drove up. He's holding for you on the downstairs phone."

"Tell him I'm still out inspectin' my lands," the Governor said, smiling. "Tell him you don't know when I'll be comin' in."

The girl went off into another room, and Fenstemaker began sifting through a stack of correspondence. Jay McGown said: "How come you're avoiding Willie? After all you told him this week?"

The Governor unlaced his boots. The golf cap was now pulled down to where it nearly covered his thick eyebrows, giving him the partly sinister, faintly comic look of a worried horse player. Then his face brightened and he said: "I been sucklin' my babes . . . Time the chicks got out the henhouse and foraged for themselves . . ."

He pulled off his trousers, hoisted plaid bathing trunks, and walked outside toward the pool.

Twenty-One

EARLE had a private room with a television. And a view, a really lovely view, as Ouida pointed out, standing next to the picture window, the expanse of glass and the cheerfully colored plastic blinds that revealed the stretch of turf and oak and redbud falling away from the building in uneven terraces. The room was large and brightly lit and now rather resembled a florist's showroom. The sweet pungent smell of flowers filled the room; they were all about; they'd been brought in all during the afternoon: luxuriant and wildly colored. Everyone at the ranch had left off tennis for a while to contribute to Earle Fielding's flower fund. Roy thought there must have been a hundred dollars' worth of flowers in the room. Even Arthur Fenstemaker had found out about Earle and had sent an enormous mixed spray: iris and glads and some kind of lily that should have been past its season.

Soundless figures jerked back and forth on the television screen. A dark ha'red singer moved her lips and gestured insanely. She had enormous breasts that seemed to rise up and nearly out of her gown with every deep breath, defying physical laws, like a half-finished bridge. Roy sat staring dully at the silent screen.

"I don't know why the hell they all had to send flowers," Earle said, thrashing in the white sheets. "They could've sent whiskey or books or cigarettes. I feel like a goddam fairy under-taker in this room."

"I think the flowers are lovely," Ouida said. "And so is your room — look out there. Aren't the grounds pretty in the rain?"

"I wonder if it washed out the tennis tournament," Earle said.

"Alfred thought not," Ouida said. "He was on the phone, talk-ing to them out there. He says they're still playing."

They sat looking out the big window at the rain and the ter-raced grounds. It was a very modern hospital. There were picture windows in nearly every room, with the colored blinds. The hallways were wide and soundproof, and the white-jacketed peo-ple padded up and down outside the door all the afternoon, grin-ning at each other. Such a happy place. Perfumed air. There was scarcely a hint of ether or antiseptics, even in the hallways. Ouida tilted the blinds slightly; she lit a cigarette and handed it across to Earle.

"I'll take some of the flowers home with me," she said. "Cheer up the apartment."

"Take me home," Earle said. "I'll cheer it up."

"You're sick."

"I'm fine. I feel fine."

"I saw you a few minutes ago. You nearly fell off the john stool. You're weak — you're a convalescent."

"I want to go home," Earle said.

"Which home?" Ouida said. "*My* house? The hotel? You can't even remember which hotel. I ought to go check you out and get your clothes. Waste of money you're not being there."

"I've got half a case of whiskey there," Earle said. "Don't forget the whiskey."

"Which hotel?" Roy said.

Earle looked at them, agonized. He tried to remember.

"See? You're a sick man," Ouida said.

"It'll come back," Earle said impatiently. "I'll remember. If I just don't try so hard — let it sneak up on me. Some things I remember. Some things I don't. I remembered about the whiskey, didn't I?"

They were silent for a few minutes. Ouida looked through a paperback book. Roy turned up the sound on the television. The two men sat watching a variety show. Roy wondered how much Earle Fielding remembered; how much was lost to him and how much was coming back. Some things and some things. Would he know (or did he now know?) about his being with Ouida these past months? Would it all come to him in a flash of rage and perception? Or only part of it, like the whiskey? Remembering only that there was a phantom lover pursuing his legal wedded. How soon would he remember it was Roy? When would he recall swinging on him outside Ouida's window in the Cuckold's dawn? While wornout toms and pariah dogs sniffed back-alley garbage.

He got to his feet and went down the hall, returning in a few minutes with the afternoon papers. He dumped them in Earle's lap and said: "You got a little headline. All about the parachute jump and your accident. Next year you can campaign for office on the free publicity."

"Let's see," Earle said, spreading out the front pages. Ouida put down her book and came over to read the stories.

"And you're registered at the Carlton," Roy said. "I just called the hotels and asked for Earle Fielding. It wasn't too difficult."

"But I wasn't in, was I?" Earle said, grinning. "They know where I was?"

"You ought to thank Roy," Ouida said.

"I would've remembered," Earle said abruptly.

Roy wondered if it was coming back to Earle Fielding already. Or perhaps, memory failing, he was plodding along on instinct and sorting out the sons of bitches, unable to remember precisely *why* but only that they *were*.

He watched the clock. In a few minutes the visiting hours would be ended for the afternoon and he would be able to leave gracefully, all the time protesting against the hospital rules. He wished Ouida could leave with him. Though he had no special plans for the evening, he wanted very much to take her along. It was difficult to separate his feelings, to tell himself exactly why he wanted Ouida. He hoped it wasn't entirely the throb of old desire; he hoped that wasn't all of it. What the hell? Maybe spend the evening watching television. He half wished he could go home and put young Earle to bed. Just a quiet evening in another man's home. He was ready, he told himself, to embrace it all, wherever and whatever it was: wife, children, victory gardens, neighbors, evening television. Was it some protective shroud of conformity he sought? It seemed only a matter of exchanging one for another.

But Ouida did not go with him. Earle asked her to stay, and Roy left alone, saying goodbye and promising to call early in the evening to inquire if any errands needed to be run. Like taking Earle's own wife home to bed, Roy thought. He left the hospital and drove directly to the cabin, to feed the cat and try to understand what it was he wanted, what could be asked for and what, at the minimum, could be attained.

The rain let up at midafternoon. The sun's heat came through the cloud cover, steaming the streets, quivering upward through the damp air. The city was quiet; people stayed inside, sitting under fans, sipping iced drinks, barely stirring. A single diesel train prowled the rail yards, stacking freight cars one behind the other. The beer garden was vacant, damp leaves plastered against the tops of the rough tables, loudspeakers dangling from the trees, vibrating with songs that went ooh-ah oom-ah ooh-ah. Roy lay in a lounge chair on his stone porch, gasping for the cool air that came off the lake. Arthur Fenstemaker moved slowly. down the front steps of the Capitol building, reaching for a pocket handkerchief and rubbing it across his forehead and along the back of his neck.

"Goddam," the Governor said under his breath. "Hell and god-dam."

He waited out front while Jay McGown brought the limousine round to meet him. He was perspiring through his silk shirt, and the air-conditioning in the car did not seem to solve anything.

"Drive around some," he said to Jay.

Weekend afternoons he liked to call on people, roaming the city and the countryside until something or someone caught his imagination, though on this particular afternoon there did not seem an indulgence left in the world for him. The limousine moved off through the quiet streets. They rode for half an hour, circling past the Capitol grounds, slowing for children and a few gawking pedestrians, heading up into the hills, parallel to the river, back into the city again and close by the college, coming near the ball park and the beer garden and the hospital and slum neighborhoods and a Mexican cemetery that was speckled with picked flowers and brightly colored pieces of glass and stone. Presently, they headed toward Roy Sherwood's cabin.

Roy got uneasily to his feet when the limousine pulled in the drive. Jay McGown stayed behind in the car while the Governor climbed the rock steps, staggering in the heat. Roy got him a bottle of cold beer; Fenstemaker gripped the vessel in both hands and turned it to his mouth. He wiped his face and said: "The douche-bag's bust, Roy."

Roy nodded and waited for Fenstemaker to get past his introductory parables.

"Rinemiller — smart bastard — he's been placin' some side bets. Coverin' his flanks . . ." He looked up suddenly. "You hear about Willie?"

Roy said no; he hadn't heard. What was it about Willie?

"He's gone and wrote himself a story. About Rinemiller and the lobbyist and old George Giffen. He stopped his weekend press run this mornin' and put the new story in."

Roy said he supposed that was good. Willie had been worried about what to do. Now he seemed to have decided on the right thing.

"Nothin' good about it at all," Fenstemaker said. "Willie made the mistake of leavin' a copy of the story at Rinemiller's apartment — wanted to do right by Alfred, somethin' like that, give him plenty warning — and that was all the son of a bitch needed."

"What do you mean?"

"Like I said — side bets. It give him time to cover his flanks. He was runnin' all over the Capitol this afternoon, callin' press conferences and claimin' he's been libeled by his own newspaper."

"Before Willie's story is even out?"

"That's right. He says the business with the lobbyist actually boiled down to his tryin' to trap that no-account in the act of offerin' a bribe. That he was gonna turn him in. That he took the money as evidence."

"Well how does he prove all this?" Roy said. "People just supposed to take his word for it? You've still got that recording. It all sounds pretty desperate to me."

Fenstemaker shook his big head. He squinted in the sunlight and stared fascinated at a water skier circling round a sailboat. Occasionally the sounds of music and laughter came to them from across the lake.

"No . . . Hell no . . . He's quicker'n that. He says he told Earle Fielding about his plan three days ago. Before Willie ever wrote his story."

"That *still* sounds flimsy," Roy said. "Earle fell on his head yesterday — out of an airplane — he's been in the hospital since last night and he's got a memory problem covering all the last three-four days. He couldn't even remember his hotel."

"I know," the Governor said. "But he remembers Rinemiller tellin' him about this. He backs him up . . . I talked to him."

"Oh, Jesus . . . He does?"

"Worse than that, even," Fenstemaker said. "So does his wife."

"*Whose* wife?" Roy said.

"Earle's wife . . . Mrs. Fielding . . ." Fenstemaker paused and smiled vaguely. "Believe you are personally acquainted with that lady."

"Ouida says it's true?"

Fenstemaker nodded. They were silent for a moment. The harsh outline of the hills grew faint in the afternoon's iridescence.

"Well . . ." Roy said, "Willie can always salvage something. It's not too late to pull that story and let the paper go as it was originally."

"But he's not gonna do it," Fenstemaker said. "He's keepin' it in."

"You sure?"

"I'm always sure," the Governor said, smiling. "I got a more reliable intelligence staff than the goddam C. I. and A."

"Why's he doing it?" Roy said.

"He says he knows Rinemiller's guilty. I called and told him I know it, too, and that we can stick him one way or another later on. But he don't want to wait . . . He can't wait . . . Rinemiller's havin' him removed. Tomorrow. Already called a meetin' of Willie's board of directors."

"They're taking him off the newspaper?"

"That's the way it looks."

"Godalmighty, he's the best thing ever happened to those people. Look at what he's done! Last couple years. They can't just flush him like that."

"I'd go plead his case to them personally if I wasn't certain that would make it worse," Fenstemaker said. "That's part of the problem. Rinemiller says Willie's sold out to me — that I fed him all this distorted information. And those people got no real love for me, I can tell you."

"Nor me, I imagine," Roy said. "Not if Alfred's been talking to them."

Fenstemaker stood next to the porch rail, looking out over the lake, scratching the seat of his pants. "I got Willie mixed up in this thing," he said, "and I can probably take care of him afterwards. But I don't think he'd be happy with any job I could offer him. And besides — I *like* that goddam little paper. And it wouldn't be quite the same without Willie runnin' it. Reminds me of old Linc Steffens when I was growin' up . . . Though old Steffens fell in with the Reds. Suppose it's in the cards for all of us to get carted off to the mourner's bench once or twice in a lifetime . . ." He straightened up suddenly and wiped his face. "I got to go," he said.

"What're you gonna do?" Roy said.

"I don't know what-all," Fenstemaker said. "I just don't know. You call me, you get an idea . . . I got to go . . . I think we'll arrest that lobbyist tonight or tomorrow — if he hasn't already left town."

Roy stood on the porch and watched Fenstemaker descend to the limousine parked below. He waved at Jay McGown and then went inside to the telephone and dialed Willie's number.

A girl's voice came on. At first he thought he should hang up and redial, but then he realized who it was.

"Cathryn?"

"Yes."

"What are you doing?"

"Is this Roy?"

"Yes."

"I'm cooking," Cathryn Lemens said. "Tamale pie. It's all I know how to cook."

"Willie got a special craving for tamale pie?"

"I doubt it. But it's all I know. A gesture."

"You his new housekeeper?"

"Nothing so ambitious as that," Cathryn said. "Maybe an overnight guest. Apprentice mistress."

"I shouldn't think there's any danger of your wearing out your welcome," Roy said.

"Maybe it's a sort of training program," she went on. "I really haven't decided quite *what* I am just yet . . ."

"Whatever you decide, I approve."

"You ought to," Cathryn said. "You got me into this . . . You gave me that lecture."

"What?"

"You hoped I wouldn't treat him badly. Remember? Well now I'm just trying to show the tenderest possible solicitude. I kiss him. I brag on him. I make the tamale pie. The works . . ."

"You needn't have taken me so seriously," Roy said.

"Well maybe I'm here with my good works at a good time," the girl said. "He seems to have a problem."

"That's what I heard," Roy said. "That's what I'm calling about. He there?"

"Try him at the office," Cathryn said. "I think he's still working. Do something. Make a miracle. Solve his problem and then send him home."

"I'll call him there," Roy said. They rang off, and Roy tried the newspaper office. Another strange voice came on, careless and a bit incredible.

"He's not presently available," the voice said.

"Who's this?"

"This is Jobie . . ."

"Who?"

"Jobie Burns . . . I'm the art editor . . . May I help you please?"

"This is Roy Sherwood. Where's Willie?"

"Ah, Mr. Sherwood. You will remember me from the other day here at the office and the evening before at the Dearly Beloved. I would like sometime to discuss with you the problems a liberal public official encounters in trying to apply his idealism against practical political considerations. Coming to grips with the more unsavory aspects of democratic —"

"Where did you say he was?"

"Pardon?"

"Willie for chrissake. Where the hell is he?"

"To the printers," Jobie said. "He has driven to the printers. To examine page proofs, as we call them. We have a rather special edition out this evening. It could become quite a point of controversy among our friends. I have my own doubts about the advisability of carrying this particular story, as a matter of fact, but I, of course, am not the editor. I have been sitting here, however, wondering whether it will be possible for me to continue my formal association with the newspaper. I do not want my views to be compromised by what may . . . by what shouldn't be . . . As the art critic, I mean, I am not concerned with politics *per se,* though I sometimes contribute essays of a philosophical nature that will quite naturally touch on the *Zeitgeist,* the underlying political and intellectual questions of all our —"

Roy hung up.

Twenty-Two

THE RAIN resumed, thunderheads piling up in the distance and moving on the city in the same progression as the evening before. Roy lay in his bed, fixed against the mattress, wondering if he should rise up and go make his miracle. He'd have to learn how first; he'd need to call Fenstemaker and find out. He wondered if his old magician had got his pills and portents hopelessly muddled.

He could hear the rain coming, rattling the cedar breaks on the far side of the lake and then the big drops on the water, like frogs. The cotton curtain shifted and began to flap softly against his face; cooler air filled the room suddenly, the smell of damp cedar, and Roy waited until the first drops split against the window screen, covering him with fine spray, before rolling out of bed.

He stood in the dark in his underwear for a moment, listening to the rain. Then he switched on the light and saw the cat's wet fur against the door screen. The cat looked at him uncomplaining. The porch glistened in the red and white neon of a beer sign a hundred yards beyond. Raindrops whanged against porch furniture and water began to rush along the gutters, boiling round the stopped-up drains. Roy let the cat in and began to dress.

When he had his trousers pulled on, he sat on the side of the bed and wondered where he should go, whom he should see first, how he should spend what remained of his weekend. The real question was whether he wanted to spend it with Ouida. And if not with Ouida, what was there left of the weekend? And the days and weeks to follow? There was Fenstemaker, of course. He could possibly learn something from old Arthur. There seemed so much to learn — from all his abandoned studies. He would need to get wrapped up in something: juvenile crime, public housing, pensions for the aged? Or the *grave*, the really *weighty* issues of our time. Like the excise tax on telephones. If he refused once again to go home and practice the law, he would have to find something . . . anything . . . to seize his interest. Two years before he had simply gone traveling over the state, looking up old friends. Not friends, actually — and not really seeing them. Just names, terribly familiar names from the card index of childhood. He just looked up names, all day long, all over the state. He'd go into a public library and exhaust an afternoon examining city directories. The directories gave him nearly everything he needed to know about the names. Were they married? Had the married ones made babies? And the occupations: pole climbers, plumbers, oil men, brokers, shoe salesmen — productive citizens every man-jack one of them. It had been an exhilarating experience, running down the names; discovering, as if it were revelation, whether they were renters or homeowners. Occasionally he would venture out into some roseate suburb, looking for a face, driving past a numbered house to catch a glimpse of a face grown old, possibly a little compromised, clipping hedges, washing new cars, playing catch with children.

Those names, those occasional faces, were wonderfully reassuring. Life rolled on. There seemed always to be enough names and faces to fill in the gaps where some of the others had left off and deserted. This was reality, the genuine article — it was like stepping down off the stage and moving past the footlights to find an audience of flesh and blood people after all. Silent . . . vaguely preoccupied . . . ground under, some of them, by the weight of days — but people live and pumping all the same.

The public life? It was a joke. There seemed no life less public than the politician's. What they had was a fantasy world, populated with kings and priests and brigands and court jesters and camp followers. There was no getting round or out of it. The thing to do was accept, embrace, believe. Who could be certain whether Miss Alice abandoned reality when she went off down the rabbit hole? Like the wire fence round mental institutions. On which side were the zanies?

Rain pounded the cabin. Smells of pine and fish and cedar filled the room, registering in his unconscious, evoking a nameless, faceless nostalgia, another dusty unpaid account, old sounds and smells setting off the emotion inside him. He could not recall a particle of the event, if it was so much as that; there was only the sensation. He thought of the small girl, peeled down to her cheap lingerie in the backseat of the old Buick. What directories would reveal the fate of his gum-cracking thirteen-year-old lover? A crisscross listing for the year 1943, he thought insanely. Once he had got the neighborhood, the street, the family's name established, there would be other sources available to an important public official. Once he had got the name. He could make it his life's work, a massive research project, and then he would go to wherever she was and pluck her from her brothel world.

He thought, suddenly, of Ouida, and wondered if he were being fair. Here he was filled with regret for all his lost loves, his child-whore in the backseat of the Buick, and here was Ouida now, at this moment, ruined and waiting. Half a life from now would the groaning in his head complain of Ouida?

He thought about this as he continued to dress, and then he made a run through the rain for the car.

She sat close to him on the couch, reaching out periodically to touch his hands. Once she leaned over, took one of the hands and kissed it. The streets had been full of reflected headlight patterns; there were flooded gutters in the low places, and the car and the glare and the pounding rain constricted the spirit. It was fantastic how, in so short a time, in the space of a crosstown drive, one's temperament could be changed. He wondered what it was he'd planned to do for her. He'd nearly forgotten all of it; though not really forgotten. Not the what of it but why? Now he could not begin all over to reconstruct the justification. Not when the edifice of thought itself was flabby and insubstantial. He tried to get his mind to working. New conviction eluded his blunt grasp, like orange seed. He sat next to her in the front room, watching her hoist the dress to unsnap her hose.

She fluffed out her hair and patted his hand and reached up to touch the dampness of his head and shoulders. She crossed one dark leg and then the other, pulling off the hose. He kissed her once, very slightly, and then she got to her feet.

"It's early," she said. "We can drink some whiskey before dinner."

She walked behind him toward the kitchen. He could hear

the tray of ice popping under the hot water tap. He sat there unable to move. He stared across the room at a pile of enormous plastic toys; fire trucks, rocket ships, an army of Martians, armored tanks and foreign cars. He looked at a fashion magazine; a tall, bored, open-mouthed model stared back at him, her chin slightly uptilted, a fur wrap slung round her neck; her black-rimmed eyes were awful and the pink tip of her tongue seemed capable of spearing insects. The tall woman stared at him from a darkly lit barroom of polished oak and brass. Did the woman love? Was she loved in return? He marveled over the possibility. Ouida returned with the drinks.

"It really is early," he said, as if confirming a miracle. "You want to go by the garden for a beer?"

"No."

"Want to go out for dinner?"

She shook her head, smiling.

"We can watch Saturday night television," he said.

She sat sideways on the couch, facing him, waiting for his whiskey mouth. When he kissed her again, she shuddered a little and seemed to cave in.

"You want to rough it on the cotton pile . . . ?"

He had to hold on to her to prevent her from falling. Her face was against his and he could barely hear her voice.

"Maybe," he said. He held on to her and reached for his glass. "Maybe it might be better. If we sort of back off from the bedroom. You know? Go off in the other direction — make camp on the couch, or the floor, like you suggest. Or maybe outside in some consecrated mint bed — I wish it weren't raining, though the rain of course might lend an agreeably violent stimulation to the business — or the front lawn or the backseat of the car. Or standing up even, like kissing goodnight. I tried that once at college, front of a boardinghouse — it's a real sweat. And then when we're far enough from the bedroom, maybe we can make another run for it, having learned a thing or two . . ."

"What . . . ?" She was still in his arms, and he wondered if she understood any of it as he slogged along, trying to explain . . .

"I mean a bed's for lovers, isn't it? While some of those others are just places for letting off steam. The bed ought to be something special — like reaching the summit. You know? And we just jumped right in. I keep thinking we should've waited. Until we were sure another place wouldn't have been more suitable. You know? Like a telephone booth . . . It's a theory I have, anyhow . . . Just formulated . . . Just now . . . Did Alfred really tell you about the bribe?"

"What?" she said again, faintly, her face against his, staring past his shoulder.

"Did Rinemiller really tell you he was offered a bribe? From the lobbyist. The one he's supposed to be getting the goods on."

"Why do you ask that?" she said. "How did you know about all that?" She no longer clung to him but rested her shoulder against the back of the sofa, one bare arm draped over the top. She began to smoke a cigarette; her tongue flicked out and she touched it with a fingernail, plucking off a particle of tobacco. She seemed, for the first time, a little bored.

"I've known about it all week," he said. "I heard a recording."

"So there really is one, then," she said. "Alfred thought it was a bluff."

"No . . . It was the real thing. When did he tell you about it?"

"Do you think I would have to testify?" she said. "Earle said I wouldn't if they didn't indict Alfred. And they probably won't. Will they? Now that it's obvious he wasn't doing anything really wrong. Isn't that right?"

"When did he tell Earle about it?"

"Oh, Earle doesn't remember anything. He just wants to. I told him when it happened and he wanted to think he could remember so he just remembered . . . Wish fulfillment."

"You had to tell Earle?"

"Yes."

"What the hell is all this, Ouida? Rinemiller's supposed to have two firm witnesses ready to testify. If that son of a bitch —"

"Do you think he really did do what they said?" Ouida broke in.

"I *thought* he was guilty . . . I was certain of it until today when I heard that he had witnesses to testify otherwise. You and Earle."

"Why are you so disturbed about it?" she said. "You act as if you had some stake in it."

"Goddamit Ouida . . ." He had been up, moving about the room, and now he returned to the couch and took her face in his hands. The rain pounded the house; a television throbbed against the wall of the next apartment. He held on to her face; her thin arms came up, encircling his neck, and her eyes, flecked with green and revealing the barest mirrored image of the overhead lights, began to fill with tears. "When did he tell you about all this?" he said.

"Today," she said. "At noon."

"For the first time?"

She nodded her head, not looking at him. Her voice came from deep inside her swelling throat. "I couldn't see how it was all so important, and —"

"Willie's losing his job . . . You're about to perjure yourself . . . And there's a goddam burglar running round loose . . ."

". . . and *Earle* wanted to believe it — Alfred's his friend," she said. "And then Alfred . . . I mean if I hadn't helped, he would've messed everything up."

"What do you mean?"

"He told me he was desperate — that he hadn't any choice."

"Choice between what?"

"Between . . . He said if I didn't help, he'd have to force me to help. He was going to Earle and tell him all about you and me — and then even about *him* and me, the other night at the ranch, about how I was nothing but a slut and Earle ought to leave me and get custody of the boy. And I think he would have, Roy. He was crazy. He could have messed up everything . . . So . . . I . . . just decided to help."

They were silent for perhaps a minute. As time expanded, each of them seemed to have shrunk perceptibly, away from the moment and each other. "Godalmighty," Roy finally said.

Ouida began to get hold of herself. She stood up and started on another cigarette. Then she fastened her red eyes on him and said: "Don't you get into this. Keep out of it. Please. You could only make things worse. Alfred might say anything, the state he's in. Keep out of it. Don't rock the boat. You could mess it all up, too . . ." She put out her cigarette and swallowed the last of her drink and turned to him again. "I'm going to bed."

After she had vanished into the back rooms, he continued to sit on the sofa, wondering how everything had come unstuck. He stared at the little filmy pile of her hosiery at his feet, and, finally, he was able to move, to stand and find his jacket and direct himself toward the door.

Twenty-Three

THE NOISE at the front of the cabin triggered a dream: bits and pieces caroused through his head during the moments he wrestled with sleep. Someone was pounding on the door, and he came awake sore-eyed and feverish. The cat stirred at his feet, stretched and began to complain. The room was filled with morning light, and the noise up front persisted. Roy rolled out of bed and searched for his trousers. He thought about the dream, concentrating on it, hoping the stray pieces would not vanish in the morning air, unnamed and irretrievable. He moved toward the

front of the cabin. The pounding continued until he began to
shift the bolt.

Rinemiller stood under the slight shelter of the eaves, lashed by
the rain. He did not speak but stalked past Roy and then turned,
waiting, in the middle of the room, water spilling off his slicker,
his forehead glistening.

Roy closed the door and hoisted his trousers. His mind seemed
blank: gone slack in another moment of truth. Rinemiller was
there, finally, come to call, and Roy was suddenly furious with
everyone, all the politicians, for going off and shooting birds, battling tennis balls, playing with parachutes. It wasn't right they
should be gone or still in bed when Alfred came round. Roy wondered why it should be his responsibility.

"You're Willie's soulmate," Rinemiller said. "You got to stop
him."

"Stop him from what?" Roy said.

"I give you credit for not being totally ignorant of what's been
going on," Rinemiller said. "Don't act so goddam innocent . . .
That paper — that's what. That story he's written. You've got to
stop him from publishing it today."

"Isn't it already out?" Roy said. "He was at the printer's when
I called him yesterday evening."

"It's not out yet . . . It's printed but not yet out . . . I've got
to stop him before he starts distribution."

"He's your employee — not mine," Roy said. "I can't stop him
from doing anything he's set on."

"You could reason with him," Rinemiller said. "You might try
to talk some sense into that crazy bastard. Maybe he'd listen to
you. I've tried everything else. I'm havin' him fired this afternoon . . . Called a meeting of the board. But by then it could
be too late. He's got to be stopped this morning. I'd get a goddam restraining order if it weren't a weekend."

Rinemiller's greased face seemed about to crack; he dripped
water, hands stuck in the pockets of his coat; he did not move off
the damp spot in the center of the room.

Roy said: "You're not going to stop him — and I couldn't if I wanted to. He's going to get that story out. He'd do it even if he had to run it off on a mimeograph."

"He's a damn fool, then," Rinemiller said. "He's really pulling a rock. Why the hell — just why? I'll never figure out."

"He thinks you're guilty," Roy said. "And I know damn well you are."

"You're a whore — you're both whores. You and Willie both," Rinemiller said. "Fenstemaker's bought you off and I'm not really much surprised. You've been ready for the sellout. You've never been with us. You've never had the guts to stand up and —"

"Oh shut up and go away," Roy said.

"Never in your life — not once . . ."

"Go away," Roy repeated. "It's early in the morning and I've got to spend the day trying to figure how to prevent you from hauling everybody else down the abyss with you . . . Go on home, Alfred . . . Go badger some more of your witnesses. You stink. You're a god damn sewer."

"I just wish I could prove you had something to do with this story," Rinemiller said. "I'd sue. If Willie had any money, I'd sue him."

"Wish I *had* had something to do with it," Roy said. He sat down on the bed and smoked a cigarette. Through the window he could see the rain beating on the lake surface, but beyond the hills there was a faint break in the overcast, a wisp of improbably blue sky. Some crazy college students sped past, moving upriver in a large outboard, towing a water skier. Rinemiller continued to stand in the middle of the room, fixed on the damp spot. He stared round the room, looking impatient and slightly wall-eyed.

"You got any coffee?" he said.

He was insane, Roy thought. In just a minute he'll give me his fraternity grip and call me a whore again. He said: "What the hell were you going to do with all that money, Alfred?"

"What the hell you think?" Rinemiller said. "Buy myself a new blazer jacket and join the Book-of-the-Month. Go to hell." He walked into the small kitchen, found a clean tumbler, and drew a glass of water from the tap.

"Have you heard yourself on tape?" Roy said. "You didn't do too badly. Though you really ought to work on your diction. You tend to slur —"

"I haven't had that privilege," Rinemiller said, setting the glass down. "I wasn't invited to the premier in Fenstemaker's office . . . I'm going to get that son of a bitch, too. One way or another. Never thought of asking me. Never give a man a chance at all. Face his accusers. Never thought of getting my side of it. Just invited people in to hear his lousy tape recordings . . . I'll bet he's had some second thoughts since yesterday."

"Imagine he has," Roy said. "Probably wishes he'd left Willie and me out of this and handled it all himself. I don't think he'd ever have let you get off so easy."

They both jumped a little when the phone rang. Roy walked over and picked up the receiver.

"Roy, dearest . . ." Ouida's voice was weak and full of exhaustion.

"How are you?" The question sounded ridiculous in his head, but he could think of nothing else to say to her.

"Do you love me?" she said. "Do you care anything at all about me?"

"I imagine so," he said. "There's certainly that possibility."

"I thought I was going to die the night you took me to the hospital. And I really didn't care. Not till you came by. We didn't know each other very well then. I needed you, though — someone — to lean on."

"You sure did," Roy said. "Otherwise you'd have sat there all night, watching the television and bleeding to death."

Rinemiller glanced up, frowning, from the kitchen. He had a small coffeepot from the cupboard and was trying to measure with a teaspoon. He drew water and then put the pot on an open burner. He began to rinse a cup and saucer.

"Do you love me, Roy?" Ouida repeated.

"Yes," Roy said.

"Say it."

"It's . . . hard. It's damned difficult. I'm trying to learn how."

"When did you know?" Ouida said. "How long . . . do you think you've loved me?"

"Off and on," Roy said, "for three or four hours."

Rinemiller came into the room, rubbing the cup with a dish-towel. "Don't you ever wash your goddam dishes?" he said.

"Who was that?" Ouida said.

"It was just Ellen Streeter," Roy said. "Ellen spent the night here with me."

"Who was it?" Ouida said. "Who's there with you? It sounded like Alfred."

"A legislator of note," Roy said. "A famous recording artist."

Rinemiller made a wicked gesture with his hand. Roy made it back.

"Is it Alfred? Is he there?" Ouida said.

"Yes," Roy said. "You have hit the nail on the hammer."

"Let me talk to him," Ouida said. "That's what I called you about. I've been trying to get Alfred on the phone since seven o'clock this morning. I need to talk to him . . ."

Roy held the receiver out for Rinemiller and said it turned out the call was for him. Rinemiller got to his feet and reached for the instrument. Roy pulled it back at the last instant and said into the mouthpiece, "I love you, this is goodbye."

Then he gave the phone to Rinemiller and walked over next to the screen door and stood there looking out, scratching his bare chest, attempting to listen to what was said and understand what was happening to him that morning, while all the time the bits and pieces of the dream kept coming back from his interrupted sleep. He had been stopped by police while out driving late at night and taken to the station because he had no identification on him and was wearing only pajama bottoms. The police were coarse and impatient with him. He did not seem able to explain why he was what he was. They wouldn't believe it when he emphasized he was a solid, respectable, responsible citizen. With important connections, moreover. Who just happened to be riding through the city in pajama bottoms. They pushed him around, but the abuse wasn't so annoying as the fact they just didn't understand. Then Arthur Fenstemaker appeared, coming through the station house shaking hands, moving from one officer to another, gripping everyone. And he had thought, here, at last, was someone who could help. But the Governor had only looked over at him, winked an eye, and strode on out of sight. Toward the end of the dream the police were getting more abusive and it appeared he would never be given an opportunity to make that one phone call. And he was uncertain, for that matter, just who he might have called . . .

Someday . . . he thought . . . Someday I will be alone and in trouble and inadequate for the moment. The more I will rage, the more I will be pushed around by the law. Arthur Fenstemaker will be out campaigning for re-election, flapping his huge arms, gold teeth gleaming in the Kleig lights, quoting from Isaiah, and the authorities in some perverse sequence of events will be singularly unimpressed by the power catchwords I will have thrown out to them.

He sat on the edge of the bed, watching the coffee boil. Alfred Rinemiller had hung the phone up and was now sitting across from him, beginning to cry. It was horrible to see the big, handsome, bushy-haired man cry that way. Alfred's face was swollen and inflamed, and he sat across from Roy blowing his nose, repeating over and over again, "God damn her soul . . . God *damn* her soul . . ."

After a few minutes, he seemed to have got control of himself. He straightened and even managed to show a little of his old arrogance. "Earle will stick with me," he said. "I'll fix that bitch with Earle, and he'll back me up. He'll remember what I told him Thursday night. He'll testify to what I told him Thursday night . . ."

Roy sat watching in wonder. It was fantastic. He really believed what he was saying; he'd convinced himself.

"You didn't tell Earle anything Thursday night."

"Who says? Who the hell says?" Rinemiller seemed prepared to debate the point endlessly.

"You weren't even with Earle Thursday night," Roy said.

"Who says?"

"You were with Ouida Thursday night. You were shacked up with Ouida Thursday night."

"Who says?" Rinemiller repeated, his voice high and shrill and breaking slightly. He began, once again, to cry. His expression gave way and was twisted then into an awful distortion. After another minute he got up to leave.

"Hold on," Roy said. "Wait up. Sit down and I'll tell you what you ought to do. I'll give you my counsel — no fee involved. I don't hardly ever give it away, either. Not often even for money."

Rinemiller sat back down.

"Incline your ear to wisdom," Roy said. "I quote the Governor of our state, who reads the Good Book . . . Bend your heart to understanding . . ."

Twenty-Four

RINEMILLER lived in a huge, shapeless apartment building, a fawn-colored structure with a façade of dwarfed porticos, in a neighborhood of abandoned manses and old-time grandeur very near the Capitol. The building ran the length of a block and then doubled back, serpentine fashion, ranging over alleyways and between parking lots in an arrangement of small courtyards, interior gardens. Enormous windows looked down on the gardens, which were spotted with occasionally sunless and frequently overfed shrubs. There were rows of azalea and jasmine and bloomed-out mimosa, with a cluster of bulb plants set in the middle, struggling against the changing season. Roy walked between the shrubs and flowers, staring at the ground-floor entrances, trying to distinguish one from another, until he found Alfred's rooms.

He had visited here once before, late one election night, the apartment full of people drinking and whooping and falling silent on the quarter hour to listen to returns coming in on the radio. Now — empty and unclaimed, with its gruesome blend of modern and ranchstyle — it could have been mistaken for a furniture showroom. Except for the few books and magazines strewn about and the stacks of freshly laundered shirts and underwear on the bed. Roy stood in the bedroom and stared at the pictures on the wall. He'd seen hundreds like them, mostly in hotels and apartments: Paris street scenes, Impressionist imitations, fuzzy pastels. There were some books on the night table; he thumbed through them without interest — the Ickes *Diaries,* the *Addresses and State Papers* of James Stephen Hogg, a volume on the German General Staff, two political biographies, a paperback on anthropology. The bedspread was pulled tight and squared on the ends, military fashion. Draperies hung motionless in the heat of the room; a scarlet water bird, three feet tall, gawked at him from the shower curtain, spotted with mildew.

But where was Alfred? Was this all there was of him — just a few irrelevant scraps, not even the print of his big head on the machine-tooled pillowslip? It was depressing that a man should leave so little behind. There ought to have been more. Alfred owed it to himself to leave more than this. Or were they all meant to wander pointlessly in a vacuumed world of fresh-pressed linen, handy blade dispensers, and Gideon Bibles? There wasn't even a ring in the tub.

He began gathering up things, the books and laundry, sheets and towels and washcloths and old magazines, stuffing them into one of the pillowcases. When he had picked up all the loose ends, he sat for a time on the front-room sofa and wondered why he had ever let himself get involved. Am no gentleman's gentleman, he thought, no stormtrooper floorwalker come to set things right. It wasn't all that important — the others could take care of themselves. Willie could have; and Ouida, she would have managed somehow. Old Fenstemaker made his compromises, surely, an endless succession of them. Was there a point on his scales where mere convenience left off and necessity queered the balance? He wished one of Caesar's divines were available to show him where.

He stood and walked outside and wandered through the courtyard gardens. The inside of the car was like a chicken roost at midday. He began to perspire almost immediately, and he pushed along at a faster rate of speed, the blast of hot air searing eyelids and nostrils. He bought a bottle of beer at a drive-in grocery and then drove slowly toward the hospital.

He could hear their laughter in the perfumed corridor. The sounds, high and puckish, echoed off the vinyl floor. Nurses and dark-skinned attendants soft-shoed back and forth, pacing off their disapproval. Roy ignored the looks they gave him and headed toward the point of disturbance.

They were all there, most of them, and Earle was happy and loquacious. His friends had finally come and thought enough about him to bring a drink. Ellen Streeter, Huggins, Harris McElhannon, a half-dozen of the others, crowded round the hospital bed, clutching their paper cups of gin like front-row tickets. Earle sat amid the disordered bedsheets and examined a new bottle of brandy. They all looked up and gave a little cheer when Roy came in the room.

They'd driven into town to begin another party. The one at the ranch was a shambles; they'd never even got around to playing the finals of the tournament. Too many bugged out: first Earle, transported to the hospital; Roy and Alfred and Ouida and Willie and Cathryn. And Giffen. No one knew what happened to

George Giffen — he'd come and gone and come back again and now he was vanished still again, clean out of sight. This morning they'd simply given up on all pretense and formality and got stoned before noon and presented the winners' trophies to the Mexican kids down the hill. And now they were back in town searching for a party, a beginning. Was there anyone willing to offer up a house or apartment as a point for starting?

There was none.

Roy considered Rinemiller's place, but then thought better of it. Couldn't desecrate holy ground. And besides, Alfred might be there; lying in state on the striped bedspread.

The floor supervisor came into the room to say they must be quiet or leave. So they decided to leave, promising to come back with more to drink if Earle needed any. All he had to do was give the word. Send up a signal. They'd call in on the hour. Roy stood near the picture window and examined the room. They'd decorated it for Earle. There were fewer flowers, but now there were mobiles suspended from the light fixture on the ceiling; there were books and magazines and a Picasso print and half a roll of pink toilet paper strung like bunting round the end of his bed. There was a new martini pitcher, stacks of greeting cards, a bedpan with Earle's name stroked in gold along the side, a feather fan, an embroidered cushion. Someone had even brought a pair of hamsters, they explained, but they hadn't been successful in smuggling them into the hospital.

Ellen Streeter came over to say goodbye to Roy. Her cheek was still discolored, but she'd done an amazing job with her make-up. She looked very pretty, suntanned and somehow rested. She asked if he would join them later, and Roy said it was just barely possible.

"We'll be at all the obvious places," she said. "At one time or another . . . We'll leave a little trail for you to follow."

"Maybe we'll cross paths," he said.

"I know all about that," she said. "Like ships in the night. Quit squandering your lousy radiance and focus on someone who needs it."

"Needs what?"

"Help."

He did not reply but only looked closely at her mauve-painted eyes. She repeated: "I need help. From the no-good man that ruined me. You could come by my house later. I've got a new record — Jelly Roll Morton. He introduces some of his own work. 'Creepy Feeling.' And some others. *This tune,* he says, *was wrote 'bout nineteen-two.* The album's all hermetically sealed. Like a virgin girl. Can you come listen?"

Before he could answer, Harris and Frank Huggins moved past and took her by either arm, guiding her toward the door. He got one last look at her spoiled face before they disappeared down the corridor. For a moment he thought of going after her, but he knew it wasn't just a question of giving help — it was no doctor-patient relationship; rather one of fever victims struggling to breathe a healing into each other's mouths. He hadn't the strength; he doubted, moreover, if he had any help to give to anyone. But he had to see. Did his splendid emotion amount to anything more than good intentions? He turned to face Earle, who was preoccupied for the moment with all his gifts. The tinseled mobile spun above their heads, moving in the blast of an air duct. Earle opened his bottle of brandy and poured a little into two sterilized glasses.

"Let's have some of this stuff, Roy," he said. "Sure glad you came by."

"Where's Ouida?" Roy said.

"Home with little Earle. Baby-sittin' problem on Sundays."

"I got everything from your hotel room," Roy said. "I checked you out and paid the bill."

"Damn good. That's great," Earle said. He raised his glass to Roy and took a swallow. "You seen Alfred today? I thought he'd sure come around, but he hasn't yet."

"I saw him this morning," Roy said. "We had coffee together. He didn't tell me his plans, though."

"You hear about that crazy story? That one about Alfred. He told me about it yesterday. Hell of a goddam note."

Roy nodded and said: "That's what we talked about this morning. Alfred was in a sweat about Willie's story."

"Hell of a goddam note," Earle repeated. "What's Willie tryin' to do? Everybody knows Alfred couldn't be bribed."

"You seen Willie's story?" Roy said.

"No."

"You heard about the tape recording?"

"No. What recording is that?"

"The one the lobbyist made when he offered the bribe to Alfred. When Alfred accepted. It goes into a lot of detail . . ."

Earle was silent, watching the mobile twirl.

"You didn't know about the recording?" Roy said.

"Alfred might have mentioned it," Earle said. "He was pretty excited when we talked."

"When did he first mention this to you? Yesterday?"

"Yesterday," Earle nodded, "and earlier in the week. Right after the lobbyist made the offer."

"When was that?"

Earle waved his hand with assurance. "I don't remember exactly. I still got a little fuzziness about last week."

"Thursday night?"

"That's it — Thursday night."

"Couldn't have been Thursday night," Roy said. "I know where Alfred was Thursday night, and he wasn't with you."

"What the hell!" Earle said. "Some other night, then. He told me. I know that much."

"You sure Saturday wasn't the first time he told you? You'd have to do better than that on a witness stand."

A nurse came in with a little tray of pills. She looked at the decorations and smiled at Earle. Earle tossed off the brandy and then swallowed the pills with a glass of water. He made a face; his stomach rumbled.

"Thursday goddam night," he said. "Thursday night was when we talked." The nurse looked mystified. She turned and went out the door.

"Believe me," Roy said, "it wasn't Thursday night. Or any other night last week."

"It was one of those nights . . ."

"*Come on, Earle!* Don't take any oaths for Rinemiller unless you're damn sure."

"I'm sure, I'm sure . . ."

"Listen — if you'd heard that recording you'd understand. It was the real business, Earle. No kidding around about it. Alfred accepted fifteen hundred dollars from that guy. It was counted out right there, one-two-three, on the tape. And Alfred's still carrying it around with him, I suppose. You know what happened Thursday? Thursday's the day the same lobbyist offered Giffen a bribe. And old George turned it down . . ."

"Old George . . . ?"

"George turned it down. Didn't hesitate. Then he told Rinemiller about it — that was George's mistake — he asked Alfred what he ought to do about it. And Alfred didn't say anything to George about trapping a lobbyist. All he did was tell George to forget it, stay out of trouble, and then he called into town — from *your own ranch,* Earle, and tried to shake down the lobbyist for *more* money to keep Giffen quiet. He was playing every angle. And doing fine until Willie told him what he was going to print. So then he runs over here to remind you what he *says* he told you earlier in the week. To get an alibi established. From his best friend . . ."

"Best friend," Earle said dully. "Jesus, I can't let my best friend down . . ."

"He wasn't anybody's friend last week," Roy said. "He was just real hungry. Real ambitious."

The nurse returned with a tray of food. She set the tray down on Earle's lap and fled immediately. Earle looked down and lifted the cover on one of the hot plates. A puff of steam rose up in his face. He poked at the meat and the baked potato.

"I've got to go," Roy said.

"Where's Alfred?" Earle said, still staring at his food.

"Probably sitting around wondering what he ought to do. I scared hell out of him this morning, but all I really succeeded in doing was to leave him immobilized. He'd better get off his bum and start building a better defense than he's got."

He turned and started to leave. Earle called out to him: "Roy . . . Wait . . . second."

"Yes?" He came back to the bedside.

Earle chewed dismally on the roast beef. He put his fork down and said: "You wanna . . . tell me anything about . . . you and Ouida?"

Roy sat down. "Well," he said. "I guess your memory's not so bad after all. I'm sorry about the other night."

"I don't know anything about the other night. What happened the other night?"

Roy started to explain, but Earle was grinning and seemed nearly about to laugh. Roy said: "Well . . . I'm sorry about the other night. It really wasn't as bad as it might have seemed. Hope you believe that . . . What do you want to know about Ouida and me?"

"I've heard some talk," Earle said. "First hour I hit town last week I heard about you being censured. Alfred told me that. And then I'd heard some other things while I was out of town. And then there was the other night, of course . . ." He smiled again and went on: "What I mean is, it doesn't look so good for either of you. It's grim — it's depressing. It's no way to court a woman."

"Well I'll put a stop to it, then," Roy said. "I promise you it won't —"

"I didn't mean that," Earle said. "I didn't mean that at all . . . Unless you're lookin' for an excuse to shake loose?"

"Ouida's something special . . ."

"She's an exciting woman," Earle said. "She's got some qualities that . . ."

Roy sat nodding his head in agreement. He got to his feet suddenly and said: "I've got to go. I really do. I'll talk to you later . . ."

He was talking and moving sideways toward the door and he finally waved and turned out into the corridor. He rode the elevator down three floors and walked through the hospital, past waiting rooms and the receptionist's desk and the coffee bar. He headed out a side entrance and went to his car. He sat there a few minutes until he began to perspire again and then removed his coat. He switched on the radio, searching for a station, listening for a time, very attentively, to a commercial announcement. The voice, deep and tremulous, discussed body odor. Some music came on; Roy sang it aloud: *"Ah-wah, ooh-ah, oom-ah."* He paused and repeated to himself: "These are my *active* years — years when I *perspire,* like millions of tiny *fountains."*

He attempted to recite a little lesson he had learned. Thin puffs of wind rattled the trees and the hedgerows. The cool air was like a gift . . . A man, he said to himself, a man whose thoughts dwell only on sense objects soon learns attachments. From attachment is born love; from love springs wrath, and from wrath is confusion born. From confusion comes wandering of memory and wreck of understanding, and with wreck of understanding man was lost . . .

This dissatisfied him. He tried another: An Agent of Goodness who is free from attachments, speaks not of himself, his constancy or vigor, and is unmoved by success or failure . . . Relinquish . . . renounce . . . sweet sounds and sense objects, casting aside passion and hatred, turning everlastingly to passionlessness, away from force, pride, desire, wrath, possession . . .

Well, it wouldn't do. It just wouldn't. If that sort of thing really caught on, they'd all capsize. Who the hell qualified as an Agent of Goodness? Who was it passed the judgment? How'd anyone ever accomplish good while casting off attachments, passion? Gimme a sweet sound any old day — a sweet sound and a snifter of Zen. At room temperature.

He got the car started and steered it down the drive and out into the street. He felt unaccountably pleased with himself and a little sick in the stomach. Back among the living. And (what was the phrase?) the low farce of left-wing politics. He made a short speech to himself: "This is a holy war, my friends, against spies, murderers, pimps, burglars, Chinese bandits, foreign isms, alien-minded mongrels, utopian praters, saboteurs, subversives — a battle between God-fearing principles and pagan ideals . . . Is there an honest man here who'll — *I say, is there an honest man here?* Nobody here. Well, my friends, we'll just have to make do with what we've got, what we had last time I looked, which is pimps, thieves, spies, rapscallions and robber barons, fops, charlatans, mountebanks . . ."

He resisted a queasy sensation. The late afternoon was warm and the damp air clung to his face, soaking his shirt collar. He fashioned a new *koan* for himself. It would bring enlightenment, make his course clear. Nice cream *koan:*

We know, my friends, the sound of a meal going down. But what is the sound of a meal coming up?

He sped along the pastel streets.

Twenty-Five

Roy sat out under the rain-softened trees, smiling at his buff-bronze pitcher of beer, dark and light, trying to get cockeyed. He owed it to himself — he hadn't been *really* drunk in weeks. It was the least he could do. He sat there smiling, tapping his foot. Popular songs pounded his eardrums. The beer pitcher perspired on the bare table. He refilled his glass and signaled to the waitress. What was it that fellow had said? Man ain't got no fuckin' chance. Noble sentiment, but he was an uninspired thief to the very end, lifting his phrases from good-bad books. Man ain't got no . . .

"You want another?" the waitress said.

"Yes, Georgia love," Roy said.

Her sweet, gap-toothed face hovered a mile above him. He looked up and smiled, blinking his eyes in the moist air.

"Where's your friend?" she said.

"You mean Ike or Mike?"

"No . . . The one just here."

"Gone," Roy said. "Left this vale of tears."

The girl swooped low in front of him, resting soft-freckled arms on the table. "How come you're so nice to me tonight? It's not like you."

"I found peace, honey." He tried to keep his worshipful eyes in focus.

"Stop pullin' my leg," the girl said. She went to get his beer. He sat unthinking, dull in the head, until she returned. She refilled his glass and set the pitcher down. Roy fumbled with damp dollar bills.

"A man's cupidity, Georgia, is . . ."

"Man's *what* . . . ?"

"Avarice . . . inordinate desire . . . It's a good-bad thing . . . *thang*. Ambivalent. You got to have it — it's necessary — but it's subject to abuse. Get you into trouble. Like sex. You know like sex? You got to discipline yourself, focus all that radiance on noble objectives. Propagate the species . . . Build a city."

The girl looked back toward the bar, pulled out a chair and sat down.

"You're *drunk*, you know that?" she said. "I've never seen you drunk. That why you're so friendly tonight?" She looked at him in wonder.

"This theory I have, Georgia, is brand, spankin' new. Never been explicated before, not more than a million times. You may quote me. Go now and tell the others."

The girl leaned toward him, on the edge of her seat.

"Listen," she said. "It's early yet. Take it easy. You've got hours."

"Are you honest, Georgia?"

She leaned back in the chair, smiling.

"You mean like Ophelia?"

Roy was vastly pleased. He said: "You amaze me sometimes, love. No . . . I mean honest like good and bad, right from wrong. Are you *virtuous* that way?"

The girl kept looking in back of her, toward the bar. Finally, she stood and collected empty glasses. She stacked them. One on top of another. She tilted her head, thinking.

"I don't know," she said. "As much as anyone else, maybe."

"Well you work at it," he said. "You work at it. It's a damn precious commodity."

The girl smiled at him and said she would. "Take it easy," she said, pointing to a clock hung from the trees. She turned to go.

Roy sat alone, drinking his beer, moving his lips, *oom-ah ooh-am,* to the sounds of the music. The garden began to fill with people. Occasionally, someone would come over and speak to him, Roy nodding and smiling, struggling to his feet to pump hands. A familiar face floated toward him. He attempted to identify the young man, but failed. A hand was extended. Roy took it, clutched it.

"I wanted to apologize, Mr. Sherwood," the boy named Jobie said. "I hope you don't think I hung up on you yesterday. We must've been cut off. I tried to find your number so I could call back and explain, but it wasn't listed."

"That's all right, that's all right," Roy said. He flashed a winning smile. "It's nothing."

Jobie nodded his head eagerly, jerking it up and down. He began to talk rapidly about how he *knew* Roy would understand — he was obviously a cut above these other political types; he was a man with whom a lasting *rapprochement* could be estab-

lished. Roy shook the boy's hand, nodding back, saying *yes . . .
yes . . . yes.*

Ellen Streeter, Harris Huggins, and some of the others appeared. They came across the garden in convoy, fending off
torpedo stares by their sheer number. They noticed Roy, yelled
a greeting, flapping their arms. They encircled him, dragging
chairs round the table, banging their shins on the bare wood.
Ellen sat next to him and clutched his arm.

"You *came!*" she said. "I didn't think I'd ever see you again.
Not even for the Jelly Roll Morton."

"I came," Roy said, nodding his head, acknowledging the fact.
He belched softly, putting his hand to his mouth. Ellen smiled
her love at him, herself a part of the love object. The others
talked a stream of incoherence, words raging back and forth
across the table. Roy got to his feet and asked Ellen to dance.
They walked arm in arm to the concrete space and moved around
easily, close together, until they both began to perspire a little
in the heat. They stood apart, looking at one another, listening
for the sounds of the next song. A wisp of blond hair was stuck to
her forehead; her lips were slightly parted, and she seemed, in
that instant, all that anyone could desire. Roy noticed Willie
and Cathryn coming through the doors, taking a table some
distance away from the others. Amazing conduct. They had not
even looked around to see who was there. Roy took Ellen by the
hand and went to Willie's table.

"Hah yew?"

"Ah'm fahn. Hah yew?"

They sat across from them. Willie was grinning. He had his
arm looped round the back of Cathryn's chair. He picked at her
bare shoulders unconsciously.

"You write your story?" Roy said.

Willie nodded. He reached in his pocket and brought out a
folded copy of the newspaper. The stories about Rinemiller,
Giffen, the lobbyist and Fenstemaker were spread across the
front page. Roy looked them over carefully. Ellen glanced at the

paper, looked away and then stared back again. "Rinemiller?" she said. "Is this Alfred he's talking about? Taking a bribe?" She stared at the smudged printing. Roy said yes and looked up at Willie.

"Any repercussions?"

"There were supposed to be," Willie said. "But they never seemed to repercuss."

"Really? What happened?"

"I felt I ought to tell Alfred. I left him a copy yesterday, and he came around later, furious, threatening me with everything but the rack. He said he was calling a board of directors meeting and was having me discharged. He said he had an alibi, and it sounded like a good one. It had something to do with Earle Fielding — I'll tell you about *that* later. Anyhow, I couldn't get in touch with Earle so I went ahead and printed the paper. This evening the board met to consider Rinemiller's charges. No Rinemiller. He just never showed. We waited two hours. Nothing. I called Earle Fielding and talked to Ouida and she said that Rinemiller didn't have an alibi after all. So . . . we just sat around and waited another hour and then we left. Those board members were bewildered. They'd driven in from all over at Rinemiller's request, and he never showed."

Roy sat there grinning, trying to keep his balance in the chair. "That right . . . ?" he was saying. "That so . . . ?"

"Couple of them raised hell about writing the story even if Alfred *was* guilty. Said we had no business getting our own people into trouble — that they weren't paying good money to defeat themselves. One of the others suggested we at least wait and see if there's a grand jury indictment . . . ."

"And you prevailed," Roy said.

"Mostly," Willie said. "They decided to hold off, ride it out. Or try to. They don't like it, but I think I convinced them it was better the story came from us instead of someone else."

"Clean up our own house," Roy said.

The waitress came over, carrying Roy's half-finished pitcher of beer. "You want this?" she said. "You don't take it, those others at your table will." Roy said yes he would take it. The girl set the pitcher down and said hello to Willie.

Roy got up abruptly and said he was going to the men's room. Willie ordered dinner and followed Roy inside. "He's been here for hours," the waitress said to Cathryn.

"Alone all that time?" Cathryn said. "That's a bad sign."

"There was another fellow with him at first," the waitress said. "They came in together, but the other one left."

"Who was it?"

"One of that bunch," the waitress said. "One of the politicians."

Roy and Willie returned. Roy put dimes in the jukebox and danced with Ellen until Harris came across to the slab and cut in. Roy lurked round the edges of the crowd, watching the others. He put some more coins in the machine, concentrating, studying the music, making a conscious effort to pick the songs he liked least of all. Huggins came over and stood next to him. They gazed inside the record machine, watching the colors change, reds and greens and citrine yellows. Huggins told him all about Willie and Rinemiller and the lobbyist. Roy stood open-mouthed, gasping his amazement. "You mean you hadn't *heard?*" Huggins said. "It's all over *town* this evening." They discussed what these revelations would mean for their own futures.

Huggins leaned against the jukebox, talking, while Roy pushed coins inside. Suddenly, Huggins straightened up, his eyes widening, staring toward the front.

"Jesus!" he said. "Guess who's comin' in with Giffen."

Roy squinted through the colored glass, studying the record mechanism. He did not look up. "Fenstemaker," he said.

"Old Arthur Fenstemaker," Huggins said. "Jesus. He goin' to sit here and drink on a Sunday evening? He'll lose the drys next election."

Fenstemaker and Giffen came across the big room. Some of the men at the bar turned and gazed in astonishment. One of them yelled hello to the Governor. Fenstemaker stopped, swung round, and gripped the fellow's hand. He moved round the bar, a victim of his habit, shaking hands, clutching arms, bending his head sideways and a little forward, talking into ears, blowing into faces. He worked his way across the room, coming near the jukebox. When he saw Roy, he brightened visibly and walked directly over to them.

"Hello Roy . . . Mr. Huggins . . ."

They said hello to the Governor.

"I want to thank you, Frank, I want to . . ." The Governor spun his magic. Huggins showed his gold teeth, stretching his lips, his mouth an uncapped jar of amber jelly. "You and Roy here did a wonderful job last Thursday. Not just for me. For the people, for the folks . . ."

Huggins started to say something, but Fenstemaker had him by the arm and hand, manipulating the appendage like a pump handle, propelling him along the side of the wall toward George Giffen. "George," he said, stroking the two of them, "you and Frank here — I understand they call you Pancho, Mr. Huggins — George, you and Pancho get us a table out there under the trees. We'll be with you in just a minute."

Huggins and Giffen backed off, heads dipping, gesturing toward a bank of unoccupied tables. Fenstemaker waved at them and then turned to Roy. He smoked a borrowed cigarette and took a deep, happy breath.

"You've been a busy man," the Governor said.

"Not so busy," Roy said. He stuck another dime in the phonograph. The music clacked in their ears.

"The blind man smells a feelin'," Fenstemaker said. "Besides, I had my agents out lookin' at thangs."

"Samson was blind," Roy said.

Fenstemaker's voice rose an octave; his eyes began to go out of focus. "How come the heathen rage and the people imagine a vain King?" he said.

"How come?" Roy said. "Tell me how come."

"Vanity of vanities, all is vanity," Fenstemaker rumbled. "You tryin' to play Superman or somethin'? What the goddam hell you say to Rinemiller to make him run for cover like that?"

Roy sat down at an empty table near the record machine. His dry tongue felt enormous, swelling inside his mouth. Fenstemaker signaled to a waitress and sat down next to Roy, waiting for the beer.

"What the hell you do?" he repeated.

"Nothin'. Just talked."

"You scared him. You made him run, goddammit."

"I saw him catch that cab," Roy said in wonder.

"You *called* the goddam cab. Hoot Gibson *saw* you do it."

"You told me once," Roy said, "that all your princes were rebels . . . and companions of thieves . . . How *is* Hoot Gibson, anyway? I noticed him sitting at the table here this evening."

"Smarter than he looks," Fenstemaker said. "Lot smarter. At least he does what I tell him. And he don't go round tryin' to play God."

"All you ever told me was get off my ass. I may not have that just right, but —"

"Destruction upon destruction . . ." Fenstemaker mumbled under his breath. ". . . the whole land is spoiled . . . Everyone loves a bribe — yea — and runs after gifts. Goddam and hell, Roy. I was surprised you just didn't go out there with him and *put* him on the blasted plane. You make the reservation?"

Roy spread his palms, making a gesture of innocence, of helplessness. "It was one I had," he said, "an old one . . ."

"He leave everything behind?"

"I packed a little bag for him. I made him promise to write."

"God *dammit,* Roy . . ."

"It was his doctors," Roy said, "recommended a long trip. A sea voyage, preferably. But you know how it is booking passage this time of year."

"All right, now, okay. You made him run when I thought he

was gonna get off free. Practically an admission of guilt. Where's he gone? When's he comin' back? What'd you say to him?"

Roy was silent. Cymbals clashed, male choruses moaned, all the glamorous people in the beer garden clomped their feet. Roy shut his eyes and tried to concentrate on the music. Fenstemaker's presence in the garden seemed to give the place an illusion of permanence. Roy said: "He'll be back. He's not such a bad guy. Not much of a thief at heart, you know. I tried to tell him that. How he'd have to come back 'cause he's got no place else to go."

"I was workin' all afternoon on this," the Governor said. "I badgered that goddam lobbyist for three hours, tryin' to get him to talk about Giffen. All he'd say was he never heard of him. There was George right in front of him, and Hoot Gibson swearin' he'd seen the two of them together and Giffen *himself* more than happy to say the fellow had offered him a little proposition. And the lobbyist just looked at George as if he was a total stranger."

Roy opened his eyes. Cathryn walked past, heading toward the ladies' room. She smiled, and Roy smiled, and Fenstemaker never ceased to smile, showing his marvelous teeth like a sideshow saint, some leering Buddha, and across the old beer garden Huggins and Harris and Ellen and the others could be seen crowding round Willie and George Giffen, just now arrived, all of them smiling insanely.

"How you know he's comin' back?" Fenstemaker said.

"He'll just be back," Roy said.

Earlier in the evening (Was it an hour? Hours? He couldn't recall), there had been the last words with Alfred, the two of them haranguing one another on the long distance. Alfred had placed the call to him collect at the beer garden to advise that he had changed his mind, that he was coming home to begin the fight all over again.

— Where are you? (Roy had said) Didn't you catch that plane?

— Monterey. I got off. I don't know anybody in Mexico City. Why should I want to go to Mexico City?

— Your idea. Not mine.

— Man ain't got no fuckin' chance in Mexico City. What could I do there? I'm comin' home — I'm up for Speaker next year.

— You'll be up for more than that if you aren't careful.

— I can beat this thing. They've got no case. You sold me on this defeatist stuff when I was agitated. When I was disturbed. I know better now. I'm comin' back . . . I got witnesses . . . I'm supposed to be there for that meeting . . . to get my favorite newspaper editor sacked.

— Come on, then, and quit breakin' so much goddam wind about it. If you're so sure of yourself. But I'll tell you one thing. It's even worse now than when you left. *Both* your famous witnesses have copped out on you now. I had a little talk with Earle. And your lobbyist friend is already under arrest. And you're not going to sack Willie — even if I have to haul a tape recorder into that meeting and enlighten those blind-bastard stockholders. And take a deposition from Earle. And maybe bring Ouida with me if necessary and make her tell *all her* story . . .

— For chrissake tell me what I ought to *do*, Roy . . .

— I told you once . . . I told you all morning. Make a plea. Madness . . . Insanity — not far wrong there, you know. Temporary aberration . . . Extenuating circumstances. Admit everything. Your lobbyist friend continues to deny it all — you heard about Giffen's proposition, didn't you? So you're ahead of your co-conspirator. You can testify against the villain.

— I'd be ruined. You know that.

— Then stay there. Catch the clap in Mexico. I don't care. Come back and try to bribe yourself a jury with that cheap seven hundred you got off the lobbyist.

— I could've been Speaker next year . . . I was gonna run on a statewide ticket with Earle . . . I could've —

— Wait fifty years. Maybe your constituents will forget . . .

But it would take one of those monkey gland operations for you ever to become a real politician, or even an inspired thief . . .

Fenstemaker leaned across the table and poked Roy's arm. "I want to know how come," he said. "How'd you get all this done behind my back?"

"I didn't do anything," Roy said. "Just had a talk with Alfred. We had some beers here earlier. Then he decided he ought to get away for a while."

"You give him the airline ticket — you call him the cab? You get in trouble doin' that Roy . . . Aidin' and abettin' somethin' or other."

Roy shook his head. "He's not even indicted yet, and he won't stay long — he hasn't the guts to vanish off the face of the earth. I just needed to get him out of the city for a while. To give me some time. To work on his witnesses and get Willie out of this jam. He'll show up again. After he's had himself a woman in Mexico — if he can manage an erection, the condition he's in — after he's all whipped down, he'll be back."

Fenstemaker seemed to have been taken by a tremor, by a massive agitation. He trembled as if he were about to launch himself, propelled by his own rhetoric. He began to talk, endlessly, aimlessly, grinning and frowning, waving his empty beer glass. Cathryn had come back from the ladies' room, and now she paused for a moment directly behind the Governor, staring in fascination. Roy tried to get his attention, to signal him, flag him down, but Fenstemaker was aloft and soaring, somehow fabulous, quivering past God and Mother and States' rights and the Freedom-Loving Peoples, the Copts, the Spics, Starving South Asians, the Infantile Paralysis, Will Rogers, Cancer Cures, the Scout Law, Mental Health, Thrift, Virtue, Mischiefs of Whoredom, Kings and Pawns and Court Jesters and assorted Agents of Goodness . . .

Roy rose to his feet as Fenstemaker paused for breath. "Governor," he said, "I want you to meet a friend of mine — Willie's great and good friend, actually — Cathryn Lemens. Cathryn, this here's the good Governor Fenstemaker . . ."

The Governor pulled himself back and around, eyes distended, took Cathryn's hand and kissed it. "Hah yew, Miz Lady," he said. "Yew got yoursef tew good friends in Roy and Willie heah . . ." The accent seemed to be dulling his lucidity. He paused, took another step back, stared at Cathryn and winked at Roy. "Her face is most sweet," he finally said, "yea, altogether pleasant . . ."

He had them on either arm now and was moving toward the big tables. "They're both good boys," he was saying. "Except Mr. Sherwood's been goin' round obstructin' justice . . . Let's go over here and see Willie and Mr. Giffen and Mr. Pancho Huggins. I want to ask 'em all to lunch in my office this week. So we can get together. And talk about the goddam revolution . . ."

When they were seated, Roy asked Cathryn to dance. He put some more coins in the jukebox. Drums and horns and choir voices clanged about them in the great beer hall. They walked through the crowd and scuffed their feet back and forth on the concrete slab. A little breeze rustled the branches above their heads, and through the complex of limbs and damp leaves they could see the steep sky and fantastic starscapes.

"It's lovely out," Cathryn said.

"It is! It really is!" Roy said. There seemed no denying it. I'm going to be all right, he told himself. I thought I was going to lose myself for a while, but through the miracles of science and modern medicine —

"The Governor was very pleased with you about something," Cathryn said.

"He was. I think he was," Roy said.

— No reason why a person my age . . . watch what he eats . . . sensible hours . . . little duck pin bowling —

"Here comes Willie after us," Cathryn said.

Some of the others were following him. Fenstemaker was heading up the stairs, waving goodbye, leaving as he had come, shakin' hands, pressin' flesh, and Willie came toward them on the dancing slab.

"I was thinking," Willie said, "that we could all go to my apartment. I've got some brandy."

The others were ringed behind him, ready to move on. Everyone nodded in agreement. They walked up the steps and through the barroom and out front, waiting along the curb, watching cars roll past. The tops of tall buildings were visible against the evening sky. A claque of newsboys appeared, whooping about the attempted bribe of a legislator. Giffen bought a copy and looked at himself on the front page. They began climbing into cars; some of the young people were already moving past, waving their arms. Roy held a door for Ellen Streeter. She came next to him, fair and sweet-smelling in the glow of mercury vapor lamps, all hermetically sealed. He embraced her lightly, and in the one motion seemed to embrace the whole pack of them, the pretenders to all the unlikely thrones, unable to sort one from another, unable to determine if they were real or last week's illusions. He waved goodbye, and Ellen protested loudly, and he waved again, walking back behind the car, and stepped inside the barroom.

He went directly to the phone booth and fumbled with change. He dialed Ouida's number, but then pressed the disconnect before the first ring. His coin came back to him, bread on the waters, and he held on to it for a moment, thinking, wanting to do the right thing. Then he put it in the slot again and dialed. He had some difficulty, in the beginning, trying to get through to Earle in his hospital room, until he told the switchboard operator who he was — Arthur Fenstemaker — and how he had important business to discuss with Mr. Fielding. He was put through immediately then, and he thanked old Arthur under his breath before Earle came on.

"Earle?" he said. "I wake you, Earle?"

"Hell, yes," Earle Fielding said. "I was sittin' straight up in bed, fast asleep, readin' the early editions. That's an amazing story about Alfred and Giffen and that lobbyist. You seen it?"

Roy said yes, he'd seen it.

"I guess you were right all along," Earle said. "About Alfred, I mean. Still . . . it's a goddam shame."

Roy said it was; it was awful. Then he began: "What I called about was . . ." His voice was fading slightly, and Earle was saying, "What? What's that?"

"What I called about," Roy said, "was to ask permission to take your boy for a boat ride tomorrow. Or maybe a picnic in the country, by the river, under the Utley-Webberville High Bridge . . ."

Afterwards, there was no need to use another coin. He left the barroom and got into his car and drove directly across town to the apartment. The door was open and the lights were dim and George Giffen was sprawled on the floor, his head against a sofa cushion, watching television. He could hear Ouida singing to the little boy in the next room, and he paused for a moment, standing next to George, listening to the sounds. Giffen flapped a blind arm at him, still staring at the screen. Roy moved toward the hall and stuck his head round the corner of the partition. Ouida sat facing the door, singing; the boy was bundled under bed-sheets, giggling deliriously. Ouida did not see him right off, but when she did look up and begin to smile, Roy waved and ducked back and sat down next to Giffen on the floor and closed his eyes.

Room Enough to Caper

"*I've had eighteen straight whiskies . . .
I think that's the record . . . I love you
but I'm alone . . .*"

— DYLAN THOMAS

There's room enough to caper on this lengthy stage . . .

— *The Gallows Ball*

One

THERE WERE two other passengers aboard the old attack bomber
that carried the very junior Senator home for Easter. There was
the young man named Stanley, a long-time friend, and the very
pretty little schoolgirl whom they had met only that morning.
The Senator's name was Neil Christiansen, and he wanted desperately to sleep. But the two younger people wouldn't hear of it.
They wanted so many other things. They wanted first of all to
talk and have a United States Senator — even a very junior — for
an audience. The seatbelts were annoying and they would have
liked to unfasten them; they would have preferred another brand
of cigarettes and certainly something else, *anything* else to read
besides *Business Week* and *World Oil* and the dreary *Journal of
Commerce*. They wanted a fourth for cards too, but Neil had already made it clear to them that he wasn't to be regarded even as
a third.

The two young people fell mercifully silent for a moment,
thinking. There was the colored steward who sat up front,
strapped into one of the reclining seats, but the girl said she
didn't feel especially demo*cratic* on this particular morning.

There was another silence, and then she said: "We could get one
of the pilots to play cards. It's been done before. We don't really
need *both* pilots."

"We do today, honey," Stanley said. "They're both busy plotting the weather." He stared out the window, looking glum, and
added: "I think we're in a typhoon."

"You don't plot weather," the girl said. "You plot courses . . .
you *chart* weather . . . I think. They're just sitting up front
worrying about the weather."

The girl was eighteen years old and a freshman at Sweet Briar.
Such a pretty little girl, Neil thought. She'd changed from her
saddle oxfords to I. Miller pumps for the flight home from school
on the Easter weekend. Her father was a vice-president, and at
eleven o'clock that morning, with the weather raging outside
and the old attack bomber nearly caving in, she wanted a martini.

"Very dry," she called out, moving her head dreamily from side
to side.

The colored steward, strapped in the reclining seat, failed to
respond, but at such a distance and with the kitchen supplies
rattling round in the galley the girl could not be certain if he
had heard. She turned back to Stanley.

"Give him his walking papers," Stanley said.

"Can't do it," the girl said. "My father's only a vice-president.
We can complain, but we haven't yet got authority to discharge
the help."

The old bomber rocked along; the sky was the color of grubby
linen. The turbulence was periodic, almost rhythmic, and occasionally there would come a reverberating thud followed by the
clatter of pots and pans and canned goods spilling out of the galley. The first time it happened they thought the old plane was
breaking apart. It was an A-20 from the war, converted into a
passenger ship of conventional oil country opulence for use by the
company's junior grade executives. Earlier that week one of the
Washington representatives had mentioned to Neil that the company plane would soon be flying south, and the possibilities had
seemed endlessly appealing in the beginning. The idea of special

treatment and semi-privacy had been partly responsible for his decision. But there were some convincing and less snobbish arguments to be advanced. The private flight would be faster, for one thing: a more or less direct course from one capital city to the other. There would be none of the schedule conflicts, delayed departures, cancellations, tiresome layovers or missed connections that seemed always to plague him at crucial moments on commercial flights. He needed all the time he could get at home on this Easter weekend — and it was, Neil thought, grinning foolishly to himself, a goddam lot cheaper.

But he was paying for it now, he decided. One way or another — a year off his life or a pound off his own middling young flesh — he would pay. There seemed to be even less privacy with just the three of them and the steward on board. And there was the weather; the weather was at the heart of his problems at the moment. One of the larger commercial airliners could have at least got out of the turbulence by climbing to the higher altitudes. But he had been informed shortly after take-off that the pressurizing system on the old attack bomber had somehow, suddenly ceased to function, and now they had been forced to flap along for two hours through the middle of a spring storm that seemed to have embraced the whole eastern seaboard.

Neil lay back in his seat, gripping the armrests as the old bomber pitched violently. He tried to remember what it had been like twelve or fifteen years before (how long *had* it been?) when he'd flown the Mustang fighter. Goddam hot pilot . . . A riot . . . It must have been . . . Like driving Andrea's M.G. for the first time . . . And nothing like this weak-ribbed A-20, sideslipping worse than a rowboat on the downside of some monstrous swell. He looked round the posh interior of the plane, noting padded walls, deep pile carpets, creaking card table and uniformed steward, and was reminded of certain elegant, meticulously restored Georgetown row houses, their pasts incredibly recaptured with a faint whiff of antiquitous plumbing and half a century of historical rat droppings.

The plane seemed to give up the struggle for a time and ride with the wind. Stanley and the girl resumed their conversation.

"But what do you really *do?*" the girl wanted to know.

"I go to movies — lots of movies," Stanley said. "Then I go home and write long, involved, arty criticisms. I finally sold a review last week to some hipster magazine. Fourteen bucks!"

"I mean what do you do for the Senator?" the girl said, looking first at Neil and then at Stanley. "I thought you worked for the Senator."

"Only part-time," Stanley said. "Only on assignment. I float around a little. I'm a ghost errant."

"You write speeches for him?"

"I *compose* speeches, honey," Stanley said. "Mind the genteelisms — I try never to miss them."

The girl's expression was suddenly, improbably serious — and somehow comic. "Do your real, your compulsive interests," she said, "lie in art or politics?"

After a moment Stanley realized she really was serious, and he tried not to smile . . . not just yet. Like an interview with a college journalist, he thought. And now Neil had heard the question too; Neil was turned round in his seat, staring, smiling faintly, waiting to hear his reply. "They don't mix," Stanley finally said.

"What?"

"They don't mix — art and politics — like Scotch whiskey and Pepsi-Cola they don't mix . . . I mean how can you keep the *issues* in perspective? You imagine writing an epic poem and expecting to *Say Something Important,* like in Lippman's column? If I let an issue creep into one of the speeches I'm composing for Neil, it just sort of erupts and runs bloody all over the prose."

"He's right," Neil said, smiling at the girl. "The speeches he writes for me are rarely ever flawed by even the suggestion of issues . . ."

"Can you imagine," Stanley said, "can you imagine *real people* going around agonizing about fluoridation and dental caries or recognition of Red China or the goddam hydrogen bomb?"

The old plane lurched downward and sideways; blankets and pillows and small bags descended on the passengers from overhead racks. There was an extended sensation of free fall, and then they were pulled up brutally against their seats. They lay fast against the cushions until, as suddenly as it had come, the pressure eased. A flash of pure sunlight could be seen through the windows, and one of the pilots appeared up front, smiling, as if it had all been happening right on schedule.

"You survive that last bump?" he said cheerfully. "We're about out of it now. There's perfect weather from here on in . . ." He moved down the aisle and began clearing the litter. The steward rose and joined him, setting kitchen stocks back in cupboards. The pretty little girl finally got her martini. Neil and Stanley had whiskey. It was half past noon, and the steward had begun to prepare frozen TV dinners in the oven.

Stanley raised his glass in a toast. He wished them a happy Good Friday.

The hours of His deepest passion, Neil thought . . . They just didn't make passion like that any more. He tried to remember the last time he'd seen real passion, but nothing came to him. It was all a cheap imitation, a fraudulent compound of polemic, spleen, and seasons of rut. *Whare's all mah passion?* Earlier that morning, dressing for the flight home, he had stood staring at himself in the bathroom mirror . . . "I grow old . . ." he had said aloud, and Stanley's voice came to him from the next room: "You're the Very Junior Senator — that ought to help some." It wasn't really much help, though, and least of all on this Good Friday with the two younger passengers there beside him. He felt nearly feeble next to them, with none of the compensations of age. He was the Very Junior Senator and there were nice gray patches in his dark hair and some interesting lines appearing at the corners of his eyes and round his vaguely dissipated-looking mouth. But all that was irrelevant . . . frivolous . . . He welcomed the one thing but could not avoid the queasy notion that he was losing all of the other. A most difficult year: like a young girl approaching

her menses. Was there some precarious balance one struck between wisdom and resignation, passion and repose?

He sighed, settling in his seat as the steward placed the steaming precooked dinner in front of him. The thawed vegetables
were of incredible shades of green and orange; they simply
weren't convincing. He picked at the tray of food . . . Ersatz
stuff? . . . In the space of a few seconds he was visited by a great
weariness. He pushed the food away and settled in the chair,
lowering the backrest. He felt certain that he would be able to
fall to sleep. God! How monumentally bored he was with all
tired young men — and by the melancholy notion that he might
qualify as one of them. He closed his eyes.

"Do you really manage to make a living out of all those part-
time jobs?" the girl was saying to Stanley. "Fourteen dollars for
an article isn't going to take you very far."

"No . . . No . . ." Stanley said. "Neil's really the source of
most of my income. We were roommates at college. We're old
friends . . . This is a real boondoggle, honey . . ."

Two

AFTER two martinis and an owly-eyed sip at a third, the girl had
passed abruptly into semi-coma. Her disablement came without
warning; there was no intervening period of distress or giddiness
or quietude. One moment she'd been sitting there, chattering as
before, pausing only to poke food into her mouth or taste the gin,
and the next she had simply ceased to function. She still sat there

nearly upright, plump hands resting on the edge of the dinner tray, green-painted eyelids in a three-quarters droop, her mouth slightly parted. It was as if a beautifully turned out machine had developed a sudden, chronic imperfection. Like the pressurizing system on the attack bomber, Stanley thought. He moved his hand in front of the girl's face; he touched her cool forehead; he leaned close and spoke into her ear — "Hey, honey, how's it feel?" — but there was no response. He sat back for a moment and cleaned his plate of food. He leaned forward again and speared the remaining bits of roast beef and potato from the girl's plate. He smoked a cigarette. Then he signaled to the steward to retrieve the trays and he began the laborious business of lifting and pulling on the girl until she was stretched out the length of the reclining chair. He slipped off her new pumps and propped her feet on an overnight case. Then he took another seat across the aisle.

Story of my life, he thought. The goddam past is prologue, and I continue to comfort my drunks . . . Should have left them all to soil themselves!

He opened a small notebook and began to mark source material for a speech Neil was scheduled to deliver on the following day. He hadn't any idea of the subject matter; all he could manage at this point in the writing — in the *composing*, rather — was the assembly of half-thoughts and once-rejected phrases. But he left off the note-taking after a minute or so and again addressed himself on the problem of tending drunks — all his favorite people, fore and aft, front and back, down through the years. Perhaps he could go into the business! He'd had, God knows, enough practice. There ought to be a demand for an attractive young man of good health and pleasant disposition with a lifelong experience at . . . What? They hadn't been drunks exactly; not alcoholics in any event. His mother and father hadn't drunk themselves to death; his uncle at the farm was no lush, and neither for that matter were Neil and his younger brother John Tom Christiansen. It was just that he seemed always to be putting a

friend or relative away for the evening. People were always getting snockered in his presence, and he was invariably somehow
sober enough to help.

It suddenly came to him that all were dead except Neil. All
but Neil: Mother, Father, Uncle, and fat John Tom. Strange
. . . And thoughts of death had never much concerned him. No
matter. None of them had choked to death on a whiskey bottle,
and there were others still live and kicking who were periodically
liquored up in Stanley's presence to the point of helplessness . . .
He remembered Neil at college, back from the war with his
drawerful of medals and the enormous stack of books stolen from
Rec Room libraries. Neil had been tight nearly every evening
(and many of the days) during that first semester. And John
Tom half boozed during most of the next. Still . . . it had been
a marvelously rewarding year. There was a beach they'd driven
to on weekends: he remembered it was compared at the time
with Cannes and Nice and Marseilles — they were near the same
latitudes, weren't they? There was a corn products factory
nearby, constantly belching smoke and disgorging workmen.
There was a naval gunnery range a mile away, and clearly in
sight from the yacht harbor was a cluster of offshore oil rigs. Even
the season had been a little absurd, though it never seemed really
to matter. It was a year after the war when the first new cars had
two-by-fours for bumpers and the women wore shoulder pads and
rather resembled Joan Crawford. He was only seventeen at the
time and there was no way of ever remembering all those boozy
episodes during which he'd undressed Neil and John Tom and
directed them to bed. It was experience that counted in handling
drunks, not so much one's age . . . He remembered helping his
mother and father, first one to the bathroom and then the other,
on the evening after Roosevelt's funeral. How they'd mourned!
White horses and helmeted soldiers and blue-uniformed Navy
women, the slow procession down Constitution Avenue. God!
*I mourn'd and yet shall mourn . . . I give you my sprig of li-
lac . . .* They'd watched the procession earlier and then gone

back to the Willard, in a steamy little room, where his mother had read the Whitman to him until evening. Whitman's funeral song for Lincoln. All the family had been a little batty about politics. He could remember when he was ten falling asleep in Carole Lombard's lap, but the experience hadn't meant half so much to him as shaking hands with Jim Farley or Hopkins or Louis Howe or seeing Bilbo in his last days. Or Forrestal or Frank Knox or Wallace or Mister Cordell Hull. His parents had talked of them endlessly, the way some families gossiped about the neighbors. And how his father would have ragged him today! Writing speeches for southern politicians! Well it was the old man's fault; it had been his decision to send his son down south to the farm after the mother's death. And down south the son had remained. He really must have been insufferable when he descended on the farm that first year; a preposterously chic and worldly New York City prepschooler. At the farm they'd just called him tacky. The farm was his uncle's — how many times had he put *him* to bed, half out of his mind on Jack Daniel? — it had been his father's homeplace. And it was to the farm that he had been exiled soon after his mother died and his father realized the son wasn't going to be chic and worldly about the new lady friends visiting the apartment.

Who had helped the old man to bed, breathing hard, complaining of bad whiskey, after Stanley had gone off to the farm? He supposed they all somehow survived without him. And maybe the old man had never really needed help, not until toward the end. He'd been something of a public figure (an anachronism now, if he were alive: the sort glibly dismissed in nostalgic accounts of an era as just another left-wing journalist), but there was still a whiff of excitement and trench coat intrigue surrounding him when he'd sent his son to the farm. He had a syndicated column and a news commentary on the radio — he'd even grown a goddam beard. It was all in that grand manner that passed out of fashion toward the end of the war . . . Passing out of fashion was what probably killed the old man . . .

Dazzling sunlight shone through the windows of the plane, and Stanley rubbed his eyes, wishing now that *he* had succeeded in drinking himself to sleep during the flight south. He looked over at the girl across from him; the girl groaned softly as she slept: her pumps pulled off, her forehead gleaming, the hard line of her girdle visible against the skirt she'd bought to wear home Easter. He was reminded of a cousin on the farm, a lovely dark-haired girl with whom he had played endless kissing games during the first year. He remembered her distinctly . . . up to her beautiful arms in the backend of a troubled cow, praying over a new calf. *O God please God,* she kept saying, *make it live God please.* The sale of that bull calf had financed her first semester at college . . .

Three

THEY LEFT the brilliance of the day behind, coming down through the cover of clouds, the old plane rocking and shuddering in the turbulence of the lower altitudes until, very suddenly, the graveled roofs of new houses and the little wooden figures of people appeared a few hundred feet below. And then they had touched ground and were plunging along the narrow runway.

Neil had slept solidly until that moment. Now he came awake to find Stanley and the girl on their feet, gathering belongings, pulling hats and coats and bags from the overhead rack. Neil moved into the washroom and stood staring at himself in the mirror. He pulled his tie up against the collar and brushed his hair. He rinsed his mouth, using a greenish astringent from a small vial. "Christ!" he said aloud, and then to himself: Is there a politician here with bad breath? Bring him out . . . Let's have a look at him!

There was a fine mist falling; the warm air seemed suffused by it, stale, ubiquitous. They climbed down a small ladder to the pavement alongside the refueling apron and made a little clumsy run for the shelter of an attendant's shed, their light bags knocking against one another. Neil was hatless; he wore a wrinkled brown raincoat over his silk suit. Stanley held an umbrella between them and looked at the girl. The girl looked at Neil. The run had brought some color to his face and there were minute droplets of moisture collecting in his dark hair, barely visible in the poor light. He seemed all at once a remarkably good-looking man. His smile made the two young people feel altogether pleased with themselves.

"They should have our luggage in a minute," Neil said. "I suppose they'll send a limousine down here for us." He looked toward the airport terminal several hundred yards away. Once again he told himself he should have traveled by commercial airline. There would have been no inconveniences of this sort. And it would have looked a good deal better. He felt no obligation to anyone for the plane ride. It had simply been available to them, and he *was* making an address the next day to a group of independent oil men. That was how the plane happened to be made available. Still . . .

"There's a station wagon headed this way," Stanley said.

Neil nodded. "That's the one. Thanks to the pilots. They must have radioed ahead . . ."

A young man in blue work clothes loaded the bags and held the car doors for them. Neil noted with pleasure that the young man's work trousers had a belt in the back; his shirt was a rough Oxford cloth with button-down collar. "Lousy day," the young man said, steering the car toward the terminal. "But it's supposed to clear by Sunday . . ."

There was a crowd inside the terminal: an Easter weekend

collection of students and servicemen and plain-faces, subtly agitated. The two men shook hands with the pretty little girl, expressed the hope they would meet again, and waved goodbye. Stanley went to the desk to make return reservations. A brusque young man with gray teeth confronted Neil. He stared at Neil, and Neil stared back, wondering if he ought to speak.

"Senator? Senator Christiansen?"

Neil nodded and smiled. "That's right."

"When did you get in? We've been looking for you."

"Just now."

"Oh? We've been looking the last two hours . . . I didn't see a plane out front."

"Really? It was just now . . . Just a few minutes ago . . ."

The young man introduced himself. Other newsmen now began to appear. Neil recognized some of the faces; he knew one or two of the reporters by name. He wished Stanley would hurry. There was still a chance he could avoid these people. In another minute it would be too late. They were already clearing a space for him in a corner and bringing over a leather lounge chair. They crowded in close, some standing, some half squatting, all of them with their notebooks out.

"Let's get the pictures over with first," Neil said.

The photographers at the back gave a little cheer. They moved in closer and had him turning his head and mouthing fool answers to nonexistent questions for several minutes. Then they wanted to stay there and get some shots during the conference.

"We want you *ani*mated," one of them explained.

"All right. All right . . ."

"You have a general statement to make about the record of the Congress up to now?"

Neil gave them some vague reply. It was a good record, actually — it just wasn't going to win any substantial support in this part of the country.

"Whattaya think of your first nine months?"

"Ten months. Don't shortchange me. I've got the least seniority as it is." They all laughed at this.

"Well *ten* months then . . ."

"Well it's a tremendous experience of course. I've learned more at this job than any I've ever had. Especially since the first of the year. I got to Washington during the last six weeks of last year's session, you know. It was like taking over a case just before the jury goes out. All I could do was try to listen and learn and keep out of the way and vote for what I thought was right . . ."

"We've heard a lot about some of those votes . . ."

"So have I," Neil said. "Isn't it curious he's waited till now — that fellow — waited ten months to mention those votes? I was here all during the fall. I would've been happy to talk about them then. Isn't that when we're supposed to face the music?"

"Maybe he thought folks would be sick and tired of him by now if he'd started that early," one of the reporters said.

"Maybe they're suffering already," another said. "And it's only been a couple weeks."

Neil smiled at them. Perhaps he had two newsmen on his side! "That's a reasonable assumption," he said.

"Can we quote you on that?"

"You can quote yourself on it." Now he'd gone and lost his partisans. He tried to catch sight of Stanley, but there were too many reporters closed in around him. Planes were droning overhead . . . He was beginning to perspire through the silk suit.

"What about that 'people's choice' business?"

"He has a real gift of phrase — a sense of irony."

"And the Senator Nobody Knows . . . ?"

"Well . . . I don't like to think *nobody* knew who I was. I *have* run for — and won — elective offices before. Some people must know me . . . Obviously the Governor knew me."

They all laughed again.

"He says you're the white rabbit in the Governor's top hat. He pulls you out — presto — and puts you back again . . ."

"He says you're the errand boy . . . the hound dog on the old plantation . . ."

"He says all these things? Well . . . I'll tell you something. And this is the God's truth. I just didn't believe it when the wire came I'd been selected for this job. I knew the Governor — sure — I'd even campaigned a little for him. But I couldn't say we were intimates. This thing was a complete surprise — I was staggered. I just didn't believe it. Until you fellows started calling me on the phone and the photographers came around. There'd been no hint of it. I hadn't seen the Governor in three months — and I hadn't *talked* with him for any length of time in more than a year. I'd been on a fishing trip. I didn't even know Senator Morris had died until a week after it happened. I found out there was a vacancy existing on the same day I was appointed to fill it . . . Hey — what do you say we knock it off? I've got to run. I'll try to have something for you before the Easter recess is ended . . ."

"About your having won elections before . . . He says you got yourself elected through college — that the legislature paid your way through law school."

"Well . . . I'll say *he's* certainly found a home in the legislature. Did he ever do anything at all before he started running for office?"

The reporters smiled. "That's too far back for anyone to remember," one of them said. "You made up your mind?"

"About what?"

"About running for a full term?"

"No."

"You've got ten days to decide."

"I know. Maybe I'll have something before I go back. I'm just not sure."

"Are you getting much encouragement to run?"

"Oh yes. What you'd expect. I wouldn't call it a great groundswell of public sentiment or anything — but nobody's threatened to come up there and haul me back kicking and screaming, either. People don't seem outraged by the idea that I might consider trying to get *elected* to the job. And that's been a comfort . . ."

Again, the newsmen responded with laughter. He was good copy. He hadn't yet learned the clichés. Either that, or he just didn't give a damn.

"There's one thing that's impressed me more than some of this other business," Neil went on. "I really didn't know there were so many nice people. Does that make sense? Somebody's always coming around just trying to help — somebody up there or somebody down here. They've been awfully good to me. When I left the legislature I thought I was through with politics. I had to get out and make a living. Since then — and up to ten months ago — I'd forgotten how many nice people there were in the world . . .

Then he smiled up at them and added: ". . . Not that there still aren't a few sons of bitches around . . ."

Before the laughter subsided Neil could hear Stanley's high-pitched voice at the back of the crowd . . . "Don't quote him, you guys! For chrissake don't quote him on that."

"If we did he might be a cinch to win," one of the reporters said. The crowd grew thin, and Stanley came over, looking distressed.

"You think you're Will Rogers or something? You got to stop talking that way . . . Unless you're ready to practice law again. Or go on the stage."

"I'm about ready to give it up. I don't think it's exactly my milieu. Damn! I need a shower. My clothes are about to dissolve on me. I hate it, Stanley. I really hate it."

But it wasn't true — both of them knew it wasn't. Stanley had seen the way Neil responded to a crowd or a crisis, a group of newsmen or a gaggle of old women or a challenge of one kind or another. He had it — Neil really had it, whatever it was, in the make-up of some few men who seemed able to get high on their own adrenal fluids. It was what had made him a war hero — it must have been. It was certainly part of what Stanley sensed those ten years ago during the first months they were together, in the little one-windowed room at college with the "busy" wallpaper and the weekends at the beach and later when Neil began dating Andrea and decided he would have to get into politics if he had any hopes at all for marrying her and finishing law school.

The trouble was, his tones were mixed. Sometimes he just

didn't care; it seemed so absurd. I want to be Adlai Stevenson
with hair, Neil told himself as they moved through the crowded
terminal. All those nice people — they don't know me yet but
maybe they will next year. I want to be Adlai Stevenson with
hair. And win. Down here in the Hookworm Belt. And I don't
think it's possible . . .

"I got a cab," Stanley was saying. "The bags are already loaded.
And there's a message for you . . . This number."

Neil looked at the slip of paper for a moment, half hoping.
Then: "It's the Governor's. Anything else?"

"No."

They headed through the swinging doors. Neil was mumbling
under his breath.

"What's that?"

"Stevenson with hair . . ."

"What?"

"I want to be Adlai Stevenson with hair."

"Win or lose?"

"Win . . . Or either . . . Or both . . . There was just this
one message?"

Stanley nodded. Then he said: "Did you call Andrea? Is she
in town?"

Neil shook his head. "I don't know. She was up in the hills
last week with the kids. That was the last I heard. She just knows
I'm coming. I guess."

The mist continued to fall, though the light seemed to improve
even at the late hour in the afternoon. There was a mauve lu-
minescence halfway up in the sky where the sun ought to have
been. It was a Good Friday afternoon with people moving about
all over the city, more than the usual activity, all of them starting
out early for the holidays. There would be some parties underway in an hour or so . . . The cabdriver affected an Eastern accent. Had he picked it up from watching television? The way
cabdrivers are supposed to talk?

"Where to, Mac?"

"I'm not Mac," Neil said.

"What?"

"I'm Mr. Stevensonwithhair . . . You don't recognize me?" Stanley was gasping for his breath in the back seat.

"Whaaat?"

The driver seemed genuinely concerned. He looked at Neil closely and lapsed into the native accents.

"What was that yew said?"

"The hotel district."

"Yessir."

"The hotels. We'll get rid of this young man downtown and then I'll tell you where . . . Or whare . . . er . . . whirr. Then I'll introduce you to Miz Stevenson. Withaire!"

Four

Now THEY WERE in the better neighborhoods. They had moved through the commercial district and the Capitol grounds and dropped Stanley at his hotel, and now the cab rolled on past the endless old-frame dwelling places of forgotten first families to a higher level where, occasionally, if one looked back, a glimpse was caught between trees and rooftops and church spires of the torpid little river that half-mooned the town. From these highlands the original settlement seemed always to be changing faces, like a painted dowager, burgeoning in all directions in rockfront, ranchstyle subdivisions. These higher levels represented the city's middle period, and time had mercifully softened the landscapes, the strident designs. Luxuriant trees and shrubs pushed next to the big obtrusive homes — the replicas, gold and dross, of Tudor mansions, Spanish villas, Edwardian manor houses, edifices vaguely reminiscent of the Georgian, the Colonial, and the inevitable "California bungalow." Age now gave the neighborhoods a kind of absolution from their original sinful ways. Now they were not so much bizarre as merely eccentric and (charitably) somehow charming. At least Neil preferred to think this was so. He had even contrived to give an identity to his own home, a florid and truculent structure of ornate flutes and columns and interior arabesques. He called it Coonass Gothic.

It was early evening as the cab moved through this section of the city, and in the dim light Neil could barely distinguish one home from another. They all ran together in a purplish wash of pitched roofs, gables, towers, and massive porticoes. Between them lay flowering shrubs and great white-blooming magnolia trees. Neil sat staring through the back window. The cab slowed and turned into a narrow drive. The man who talked in strange accents looked back at him.

"Zis ah place?"

"It looks like it," Neil said. "It rather resembles it . . . I spent a little time here once . . ." He peered out through the gloom . . .

When the driver had gone, he stood for a moment in front of the big house . . . alone for the first time since . . . He could not remember the last time. He was conscious of an incredible quietude, in himself and around him. The dampness clung to trees and grass and graveled walks. There was only the slightest rustle in the tranquil air and he was utterly alone. The cabdriver had fled — Stanley was off in some pink hotel room doing his flexing exercises — all those airport people had met and caught their planes . . .

He moved across wet flagstone and let himself in the front door. The downstairs rooms were empty; from the second level came the sounds of children at their bath. He switched on lights and set his bag down in a hall before pausing in the main room, examining books and pictures and straightening small objects. He sorted through a stack of phonograph records; they were old ones mostly: Ellington, Ray Brown, Basie, Jimmy Rushing, Red Norvo, Mildred Bailey, Teddy Wilson. In a moment, the sound of the music filled the room, and he turned and headed up the stairs.

The two children, both girls, wet and glistening, confronted him midway. He smiled down at them; he thought they were his; he remembered them from last time. "Daddy! Daddy!" they screamed. He thought about committee reports he'd read on amounts of Strontium-90 in the bones of children to age four. The girls jumped up and down, screaming, one of them holding onto his hand and the other embracing a leg. An enormous Negro woman in white uniform loomed at the top of the stairs. He walked on up, the girls clinging to him. On the second landing he stooped down and kissed their wet faces. He sat on the edge of a bed and talked with them for several minutes, speaking in an adult, unpatronizing way as if he had forgotten how it was you were supposed to communicate with children and old people. They told him about their beagle dog, lost and later found; they showed him gaps in their sweet smiles where baby teeth had worked loose; they talked about measles and an epidemic of "monks" in the neighborhood. The older one stood facing him while the other brought out props to illustrate her sister's babbling commentary on books and pictures and puzzles and new ballet slippers. They asked if he had been following the Saturday morning television shows; they sang a little song in Spanish; they told about a large family that had moved into the house across the street — four children and a batch of parakeets; they gave him a detailed report on the girl next door who was twelve and who had recently begun to develop "breasks."

At last he sent them off to prepare for bed. The Negro woman moved in and took charge. She smiled at the children and then at him.

"Miz Chris'ensen went out 'bout five. Say she call if she was late."

"Thanks. Let me know when they're ready for bed."

He went back downstairs and stood in the big room for a few moments, listening to the music. It was Ellington — an old composition but a fairly new record. He remembered there was an old shellac version of it somewhere in storage, one he had bought before the war, his freshman year in college. He remembered pushing a secondhand lawnmower out into these neighborhoods twice a week that year. It was miles from the campus, but he had earned enough money at yard work to pay for nearly all his room and board. Sweet melancholy, he thought — and all of it now seemed so unimaginably remote.

In the kitchen he spooned out meat and vegetables from open pots. He poured some whiskey. There was a pitcher full of an aging martini mixture in the freezer, gone cloudy in a film of ice. He walked back toward the front of the house, humming to himself, sipping the whiskey. The piece of paper with the telephone number was still in his pocket — he would have to make the call . . .

"Capi-tawl . . ."

"Is the Governor in?"

"Who are you calling please?"

"Governor Fenstemaker . . ."

"Who is calling please?"

"This is Neil Christiansen."

"Mister . . . Christian? I'm afraid —"

"Christiansen. Neil Christiansen . . . I'm returning the Governor's call."

"Mister Christiansen returning a call . . . I'll check our rec —"

"Yes. That's right . . ." Then he thought: *What the hell? Throw your weight around.* "Listen," he said, "this is Senator Christiansen . . . In Washington . . . I'm calling long distance, so will you please —"

"Oh! *Sen*-ator . . . I'm *real* sorry . . . I'll ring the Mansion."

He stood and carried the phone from the hallway into the other room, holding the instrument in one hand, the drink in the other, executing a little dance step. He lowered the volume on the phonograph and lay back in an overstuffed chair. It seemed he had just got settled, holding the receiver to his head, when he noticed the glass was nearly empty. He sucked on an ice cube and wondered if there was time to pour another drink. "Operator . . ." He said, ". . . Operator."

"Just a moment, Senator," she said.

He lay back in the chair again and closed his eyes. He opened them almost immediately and stared at a painting partially hidden by a vaguely oriental lamp that was suspended from the ceiling. He had not seen the painting before. It was unmistakably his wife's work — there were a number of her oils hung throughout the house — but this one was new to him. He sat upright in the chair and stared across the room at the picture. It was himself and yet not quite himself, a portrait of him, younger and older, grinning like death with white-glazed eyes as in a poorly done piece of sculpture. Then he realized it wasn't himself . . . but his brother. He lay in the chair with his head against a rough-textured Mexican cushion, his eyes closed, for perhaps half a minute. He started up suddenly, unaccountably, as if his whole body had been seized by a furious bunching of the nerves, some enormous tic, a spasm of old horror, wonderful and ecstatic. He heaved a great sigh and from upstairs came the sweet singsong voices of the little girls.

"Senator . . . Senator . . . Senator . . ."

He brought the receiver up. "Yes."

"I have Governor Fenstemaker for you."

"David McNeil Christiansen," the Governor said. His voice was loud and always reassuring. "I think you ought to use that some — the full name — part of the time at least. *Neil* most of the time, but occasionally the whole goddam works. Names are important."

"How are you, sir?" Neil said. He was trembling slightly and he wondered about another drink. There was a decanter of sherry on a small table nearby; he reached across, got hold of it, and splashed half a glassful over the ice. It had a nutty, sour-mouth taste.

"Whattayou think of that, Neil? You agree with me?"

"You mean the name — in campaigning?"

"Exactly. Your last name's too long — like mine, Fenstemaker — too much name for political purposes. Tom Moore — that's a good political name for an unknown. You can remember a name like that. Fenstemaker . . . Christiansen . . . They're too much. But you can reverse the psychology. You can make the name even longer and they'll sure as hell remember *that.* The full name has a nice sound to it, and it registers visually, whereas —"

"Assuming, of course, you're in a campaign," Neil said.

"Assuming — yes. Am I assuming too much, son?"

"Well. It's just that I really haven't decided. Really. You'd know if I had."

"Get me a fresh one . . ."

"What, sir?"

"I was talking to the butler," the Governor said. "I've got this great old dark-complected butler who . . ."

Dark-com*plexioned,* Neil said to himself. And he really ought to have one in his own white-columned mansion. Someone standing by at all times to replenish those sweating highball glasses. He'd call him Gunga Din. And equip him with a syringe so the stuff could be fed directly into one of the main arteries. He touched a distended vein on his forehead and wondered if it led to the brain.

The Governor was talking between loud smacking gulps of whiskey.

"You're in town, aren't you?"

"Yes. Got in late this afternoon."

"That girl must have been confused . . . Neil?"

"Yes?"

"There's only a few more days, son. You got to make up your mind soon."

"I know, I know. Tonight . . . Tomorrow . . . Sunday. I'll be sure by then."

"Well how do you feel? As of now."

"I feel that perhaps I'll lose . . . That I'll be murdered. I don't much like that feeling."

"Nobody does," the Governor said happily. "But nothing ventured, nothing by God gained! And you can take that bastard. I *know* you can. Hell! I just didn't pick you in a lottery. Hell and damn! I looked all over for someone I thought could take that sonofabitch. He ran against me once, you know. And by God he was the favorite in the early polls. But I stuck him — I *harpooned* him. And I think you can. He panics in the stretch."

"But everybody *knows* him. And nobody knows me. After ten months as Senator I'm still just a cipher to most people. Who *knows* me?"

"I know you. A lot of 'em do — more than you think. You using your frank?"

"About four hundred times a day."

"Good . . . Good . . . You get those lists I sent you? Those mailing lists are worth a goddam fortune. It took me ten years to put those names together. Even *I* couldn't afford to buy them now."

"Yes sir, I got them."

"You got some speeches coming up?"

"A couple tomorrow. A few more next week if I decide to get into this. So I've got to decide by Sunday. Otherwise, I'm just wasting my time in public."

"You stick with it, son. You're doin' just fine. You got a good press. The reporters like you — I can tell. And I can goddam well take care of the publishers."

"You don't think he's hurting me? I think he's hurting me."

"With a few people, a few people. But listen — he's been beating you over the head with a talisman — a goddam good luck horseshoe. It's perfect! You couldn't ask for anything more. He's puttin' your name right up there. You're somebody! You'd be nothin' without him. By their enemies ye shall . . ."

"You think so? I feel like I'm already on the defensive."

"Listen — You just play it cool. Give them that boyish, air-conditioned smile of yours on the television once a week, for a while and don't pay attention to the *extremists*. That's what he is — an extremist. Goddam I'd like to get a liberal in there, some wild man at the opposite end, and let him give you hell too. I just might find one — I'll try. But listen — you remain aloof from all that whoopin' and hollerin'. You just give them the old smile and the image of the wholesome young man trying to do good job, and keep makin' those pretty speeches. Who's doin' those speeches for you?"

"A friend of mine named —"

"Listen . . . You just stay above it all. You just keep doin' your job up there. Fly home couple times next month, make some speeches, film some for the television, and then stay out of it. Ignore the campaign. Tell 'em you're not coming back until the last week. You can tear all over the state in four or five days and accomplish more that last week than you ever thought possible."

"Then I shouldn't debate him? Neither of us has even filed yet, and he's already challenging me to debate him."

"Oh hell no. You're *above* all that now. You're too busy workin' for the folks."

"All right."

"Never get into a pissin' contest with a polecat."

"Well . . . That's wonderful. You've put it beautifully — your characteristic eloquence."

"Damn right . . ."

The Negro woman was calling to him from upstairs. He tilted the decanter to his mouth and finished the sherry.

"I have to hang up," he said. "I'll talk with you tomorrow. I've got to say goodnight to my little girls."

"Fine. They're beautiful children. And Andrea! You ought to have them up there with you. You ought to get them on the television sometime."

"Well I don't know about that . . ."

"Well . . . I don't blame you. You'll be by tomorrow, then? Nine in the morning too early for you?"

"No . . . That's perfect. I've got to make this speech in the early afternoon at —"

"I'm talkin' to the same people tomorrow night. I'll give you a plug. Hell! I'd talk about you forty-five minutes if you'd make your announcement in the afternoon. That would be a perfect —"

"Maybe I'll know something by then. Right now . . . I'm just . . . not sure. I've really got to go . . ."

"Fine. That's fine . . . *Senator*. You like the sound of that? You think about what I've said . . ."

He set the phone down and increased the volume on the phonograph. He turned the records over. The maid called him a second time, and he headed up the stairs.

The girls were in their beds, giggling against the pillows. Their cheeks were flushed, and they were so lovely — there was so much of their mother's vitality and abundant good looks in them — that he had to sit there speechless between the beds for a moment, reaching out to touch their bare shoulders.

"Read us a story . . . A sto-*ree.*"

He read *Winnie the Pooh*. It seemed to have an oddly therapeutic effect on him. The girls were notably unmoved. They wanted to know if he would watch *Tom Terrific* in the morning. They remembered *Tom Terrific* as one of his favorites. He told them he would be able to watch *part* of it. And that, of course, was always the best part.

"*Which* part?"

"*That* part. It's my favorite part. My all-time favorite part."

"Which *part* is that, Daddy?"

"The part I always *watch*. Which part do you think I could *pos*sibly mean? I've never seen the other part."

"I like the other part best," the younger one said smugly.

"I like Daddy's part best," said the older.

"Go to sleep," he said to them. They kissed him fiercely.

The maid was finishing the dishes when he got back downstairs. She talked with him for a moment about her daughter who was in law school at the college. She wondered where in the world a colored girl would ever be able to practice law. He said he would give it some thought. Then he wondered if he could possibly risk putting the girl on his staff. He decided he couldn't — he would get her a job in the Government. Justice Department. Or Internal Revenue. She could hide out in one of the agencies and send huge sums of money home to help get the other brothers and sisters through college. But then he had to remind himself that he might not be in any position to help. It depended on whether he decided to stay on — and on whether he could win if he did.

The big old Negro woman, complaining of her corns, vanished into a bedroom off the kitchen. She had seven children in her own home across town. They always seemed able to take care of themselves.

He poured another whiskey and sat in the overstuffed chair in the front room. Once he got to his feet and studied the painting closely. The face was all bright colors; the rest of it somber grays and browns. He returned to the chair; then almost immediately he was up again and heading toward the kitchen; back in a moment with the whiskey bottle. He slumped in the chair, quiet for a period of time before he was conscious of a voice in the room. He did not immediately recognize it as his own.

> *No more these pure oases:*
> *These bubble-cups are burst.*
> *Neither fables nor faces*
> *Can appease my thirst.*

Fables nor faces? How 'bout *feces?* He edited the line mentally. And then:

> *Songster, my crazy drouth*
> *For thy daughter craves —*
> *Hydra without a mouth*
> *That saps and enslaves.*

He rather wished they were his own lines, but he should not be a perfect ass about it. Wasn't it enough that he could remember them? Whose were they then? His dead brother's? No. That late fellow only quoted them. We are all such quoters and *poseurs*. Whatever happened to the old-time manufacturers of such lines? The inventors, the innovators, the real genuine aboriginals? Out of the business, gone out of the business — it's the way things are in this welfare state, gentlemen. No incentive to write lines like *that* any more. Now we are all sewn from some miracle fabric spun out of test tubes. Better living through chemistry . . .

He dialed for information; then he dialed the number of Stanley's hotel. They put him through, but there was no answer there. Or anywhere. No answers. Only the low mournful signal of some distant distress. He put the receiver in the cradle, and almost immediately it rang back at him. He picked it up again, put it to his ear . . .

"Big Emma, honey, you've really got to stop using the phone so much, so long. I've been trying to get through every fifteen minutes and — Just a sec — I *know*. I'm coming, you louse, but I've got to make this phone call. Don't you understand some people in this great happy world have got respon — Hello. Emma? Big Emma? Listen —"

"Is it lice or louse?" Neil said.

"What . . . ? Who —"

"Who-what?" Neil said.

"I'm sorry I must have the wrong — Who is this talking please?"

"David McNeil Christiansen. It's the full name, you see. It sounds good and the visual image is really very nah —"

"Neil? Neil, talk nonsense to me, sweet . . . Go ahead."

"I . . . I . . . got in about seven. The girls are lovely. They really are. Perfectly delightful. Why is it you're such a good mother?"

"Are you being sarcastic?"

"No."

"Because I spend all the day with them. We invent games. We put on plays. We put dresses on the dog and wear lipstick and paint our toenails and —"

"Next week they learn the cha-cha. And the week after, feminine hygiene?"

"Oh Neil. You never let me know . . . Are you going to bed, going out, waiting up . . . What?"

"I'll probably stay around here."

"All right. I'll be home shortly." There was a note of impatience, of disappointment in her voice. "Do you want me to come home?"

"Yes." He did not know why. But he rather imagined he really did.

"All right. Goodbye . . ."

He began to lower the receiver, but then he heard a clicking and another voice on the line. It was getting to be like a party. Just *every*one was there. So many nice people on the phones. The voice was insistent, a little irritated.

"Yes . . . Yes . . . *Yes* . . . ?"

"What?" Neil said.

"Yes sir? Can I help you sir?" It was a prissy voice, he decided.

"Where am I," Neil said. "I haven't had the pleasure of —"

"This is the night clerk, sir."

"What?"

"This is . . . Oh, I'm sorry. You must be calling *in*. I thought you were the party in . . . I'm really very —"

"What am I calling?"

"The Skyliner, sir . . ."

He broke the connection and poured himself another drink. One of the girls cried out in her sleep from upstairs. "No!" she was insisting to some unknown accuser. He sat on the edge of the chair for a moment, listening, but she did not sound another protest. "No!" he said to himself, aloud in the empty room. Lee Wiley was singing about the old ace in the hole on the phonograph, and there was the scent of gardenia mixed with nextdoor roses on the heavy, honeyed evening air . . .

Five

HE WAS AWAKENED by the absence of sound. He stirred in the chair, his eyes still closed. Something was wrong, hideously wrong, the evening all out of joint. For a moment he was unable to isolate the disturbance in his head. Then it came to him that there was no sound in the room, not even the usual roaring in the ears. He opened his eyes and looked at Andrea. She was standing next to the phonograph; she had turned down the volume.

"Get some music on the f.m."

She punched buttons and spun the radio dial. He wondered if he ought to rise and kiss her — if he *could* kiss her — but before he was able to move she walked past him and seated herself in a sling chair.

She was breathtakingly pretty. How was it? How come the romantic image persisted? Why didn't the ankles swell, the calves collapse, the sweet mouth sag? Here was Andrea — altogether more desirable than at any time in his experience; never farther away from him, never more unattainable, than at this moment. She smiled.

"How long will you be here?"

She was wearing a loose-fitting cotton knit dress, bare-armed and open round the throat. The pumps were linen, some kind of Paisley print. There was a notable absence of jewelry and she still apparently disdained cosmetics except for the eyes and mouth. She was slim and nearly flat-chested and he sat there gaping at her.

"Well?"

"I . . . don't know yet. It all depends on what I decide."

"Decide? Decide what?"

"Whether to keep this job — or try to keep it."

"Oh. Well, if that's what you want . . ."

"That's the point. If I knew what I wanted, there wouldn't be —"

She got to her feet suddenly and stood looking through the open glass doors onto the terrace. "God! The weather has been wonderful. Little showers in the afternoon and then the evenings are just unbelievable. I thought I might drive to the beach with the girls next week . . . Unless you're still here."

"Perhaps we can all drive down together if I'm still here," he said. But then it occurred to him he ought to be making speeches, public appearances, at every opportunity, if . . . "The girls really are fine," he said.

"Aren't they. I've never enjoyed them so much as these last few months."

"Would you like a drink? I'll make you one."

She turned to him, not really looking; their eyes did not meet. "Yes," she said. "Some kind of gin — I've been drinking gin." She stared at the new painting.

"How about that stuff in the freezer?"

"No . . . Emma should have thrown that out a week ago. Just tonic. Tonic will be fine."

He got to his feet and went into the kitchen. She was sitting in the sling chair when he returned with the drink. She took a long swallow. "The bank called me this week," she said.

"What?"

"The bank. The vice-president at the bank. He called this week. Very discreet. He sounded like a god damned undertaker, he was so discreet. He knew it was just an oversight on our part

— these things happen to everyone at one time or another. Oh he was very discreet and understanding and circumspect . . ."

"What is all this?"

"We were strapped. The account was overdrawn."

"Oh Christ . . . How much?"

"I forget . . . Several hundred. I got some of my bonds out of the box and put them up to cover the overdraft. But we're still strapped." She sat there smiling at him. She kicked off her shoes, unfastened her hose and slid them off her dark legs. She pointed at him with her feet. "Isn't that something? Like the first year we were married."

He sat looking at her pretty arched insteps. He decided he was getting funny about insteps.

"Well, they're mailing my check here this weekend. Go down Monday and get your bonds back."

"If we're overdrawn that means we'll probably be short again before the end of next month," she said.

"I know . . . I'll take care of it." He had no idea how he would take care of it. Unless he arranged to borrow it from Arthur Fenstemaker. The Governor had money — endless amounts of money. He could always say he needed some pre-campaign funds. Pre-campaign funds and no campaign. He could sell his brother's bookshop. It was the bookshop, John Tom's bookshop, that was draining them. John Tom had always managed to make a little profit. But for more than a year now the bookshop had been a steadily losing proposition. A few dollars, a hundred dollars, and then a few hundred dollars a month. That was the famous missing few hundred dollars. How the hell did you sell an interest in a bookshop? What were they worth? All those books, those obscure volumes. Twenty thousand? Fifty thousand? More than that? Who's to judge? He would have to find an appraiser. Where did you find an appraiser, and better still, a buyer? Of rare books. He would have to ask someone at the college. Or he would apply for a small business loan, keep the bookshop for sentiment's sake. All that sentiment. He would pass a special bill in the Congress for sentimental owners of small, marginal bookshops.

"I could get some help from Dad," Andrea said. "He'd be more than —"

"No, no, I won't need it," Neil said. Not, for God's sake, old man Baker. He had managed to avoid doing anything so desperate as *that* up to now. He'd never been able to keep Mrs. Baker out of the picture — she insisted on the house in this neighborhood and arranged through friends to have Andrea hooked up with that Junior League crap and had even got them into the Country Club years ago. Years ago. But they had survived without the old man's money up to now. He had just about killed himself trying to avoid it. Up to now. He had run for the legislature while he was still in law school to prevent it. He had by God to excel if only to keep the old man off his back. He had turned down a good job with a good firm to go into private practice. For the same reasons. Private practice. Very private and not really much practice: just a few retainers for occasionally visiting old friends in the State House and explaining the really significant aspects of legislation. He probably knew less about the law now than during his senior year. Hell! He would pitch over in a faint if he had to try a case. Or brief some hotshot trial attorney who *was* going to court.

He tried to think of ways of making a living if he did not hold on to the Senate seat. Right back into very private practice: not so much practicing the law as practicing *on* the law. Or he could go into the rare books business. If he really set his mind to it and worked like the devil, why he could probably clear a cool three-four hundred a month from the bookshop. Enough to pay the rent and keep them in gin. They could just let the other obligations slide until the sheriff came after him with a net, or a shroud.

"Well I'll just let you handle it, then," Andrea said.

They were silent for a time. The radio stations in town went off the air; the big speakers began to sputter, and he stood and switched on the phonograph again. He asked Andrea about friends of theirs. Well how are *these* and *those* and *them?* She told him all the news that flowed on in endless alternations of attraction and reaction, gossip and event . . . He did not know what possessed him to ask the next question. It just came blurting out of him.

"Well how are the Christiansens — what about them?"

Andrea looked up at him coolly. Her gaze was level and imperturbable; she did not have to ask what he was talking about.

"I don't know," she said finally, "I just don't know . . ." She was silent for a moment, and then: ". . . Are you happy? I've been very happy, very content these last few months . . ."

"If not exactly continent," he said.

"What?"

He made no reply.

"I mean I've felt really serene for the first time in years," she continued. "It's a nice feeling, I can tell you. I do exactly what I want to do. Life is awfully well ordered. I don't sit around wishing I were in Taos or Aspen or Cuernavaca. If I wanted to go I would go. But I don't, you see. It's like the alcoholic with the booze hidden in the commode. I can rest easy 'cause I know it's there . . ." She laughed quietly to herself, as if looking inward. "I feel like a great happy bird."

"Well that sounds fine," he said. He seemed to have found something fascinating on the label of the whiskey bottle.

"Do you want a divorce?" she said.

He continued to stare at the bottle. "I . . . don't . . . think so," he said.

"I suppose it *would* rather bitch up your politics."

"Oh hell. It's not that — it's not that at all." But now that he thought about it, it was — it certainly was.

"Well . . . Like I said, I'm content. It's entirely up to you."

"But god *damn*," he said, "how long does this go on? Where does it end? Where does it lead to? It's like working without pay. Is it just going to be an interminable *blah?*"

"Is that how you feel?"

"Well. I think I love you — or as if I'm teetering on some brink, half in and half out of love for you."

"Really?" She appeared to think this faintly amusing. "I don't believe I feel anything. Anything at all. For you or anyone. I was just so tired, so God-awfully exhausted when you left . . . I've just been enjoying being alone . . . I feel saintly."

Now Neil was amused. He started to say something, but she continued to talk.

"I think it would probably be a lot better for you . . . politically, at any rate, if we just let things ride. For appearances. Perhaps someday I might want a divorce — I might want to remarry. Who's to say? I like things as they are. I'm happy."

"Appearances? I never knew you thought much about appearances."

"Well, there are the children to consider, and —"

"Where's the Skyliner? What is it — some motel?"

She ground out her cigarette as if she were about to leave the room. But she stayed in the chair and looked at him. "What did you do — have the operator trace the goddam call?"

"You wouldn't believe me if I told you."

"I wouldn't — you're right — I really wouldn't."

They were silent, looking at each other.

"Well what were you doing there?"

"You wouldn't believe me if I told you," she said. She smiled. It seemed to satisfy nothing. Then she said: "God! Here it is again. You'll never understand, but I was feeling so good until I knew you were in town. And now here it is again."

"You don't feel any of this is a husband's prerogative, then?"

"What do you think you are?" she said. "A priest in the confession box? If I went around wondering what you've been up to while —"

"You wouldn't believe me, etcetera," he said.

They fell silent for a time, like half-primed athletes, breathing lightly.

"Oh Jesus . . ."

"You're right. Oh Jesus. And I felt so good all day." She left her cigarette in the ashtray and got slowly to her feet. "I'm going to bed . . ."

"Where shall I sleep?" he said.

"With me if you like . . . I don't care . . . If you'd rather not you'll have to get some linens out for the other bedroom."

He stood and looked around. He pulled the glass doors shut and switched off the phonograph. After a moment, he got his bag from the hall and followed her up the stairs. He undressed and hung up his two suits. Andrea was in the bathroom. He moved on down the hall, looked in on the bare cubicle reserved for guests. A few feet beyond he could hear the children breathing softly in their sleep. He checked their covers and returned to the main bedroom. Andrea was slipping out of her clothes; she was silhouetted against the french doors — there was a false balcony leading off — and she was uncompromisingly lovely in the soft light.

"Damn!"

"What's wrong?"

"I . . . can't . . . get out of this thing."

"When did you start wearing girdles?" He moved up behind her and began unfastening hooks.

"It's the clothes this year . . . You have to."

When she was out of it, she continued to stand there, looking out through the doors and across the narrow balcony, her back still turned to him. He could see her bare shoulders begin to tremble, and when she finally moved to face him tears were running down her cheeks.

"Oh, Neil, what's happened . . . ? How did all this happen . . . ?"

She was up against him, crying softly. "I don't know . . . I don't know . . ." He had his face next to hers; her hair brushed lightly over his eyes. He stood there holding her and wondering if he would ever know anything . . . They pulled the covers

down to the foot of the bed and lay on the faintly perfumed
sheets . . .

"Ah Neil . . ."

"Oh love . . ."

"Oh God I love you, I really do . . ."

"Ah . . ."

"Ah that's . . . it's like . . . not being married . . ."

For a moment they both seemed stunned; it was as if she had
collapsed under him. Then she slipped sideways and was on her
feet, sobbing, grabbing at the covers at the end of the bed. She
vanished down the hall.

For a long time afterwards he could hear her sniffling in the
other room. He lay there in her bed, perspiring against the
soft, sweet-smelling sheets. There was a place along his neck
where she had dug her nails. When he could no longer hear her
in the next room, he pulled himself from the bed and began to
dress again.

Outside, the moon suggested some hideous, oversized medicine
ball. The wind moved through the rank foliage, and the houses
across the street and on either side resembled cheap stage props.
Andrea's roadster was parked out front. He did not much like to
drive the little car, but he did not want to bother with moving it
out of the drive. He climbed in, stretching his legs, and got it
started. The sound of the motor was awful; it screamed like a
wounded animal all the way down the street . . .

Six

STANLEY had been working continuously since his arrival at the hotel in the afternoon. He had sat there, cushioned by foam rubber pillows in a hard-backed chair, for nearly eight hours — except for an interval of twenty minutes when he had gone down on the street to buy the early editions. And some cellophane-wrapped cookies and crackers (peanut butter in between). And a banana . . . several candy bars . . . a bottle of whiskey . . . and chocolate cupcakes. Along with a carton of strawberry-flavored soft drinks he identified as "Country Red."

Now the banana, the crackers, the cupcakes and cookies were gone. Consumed. A single candy bar remained. Two of the big red drinks had been drained much earlier in the evening. Soon after midnight he split the seal on the whiskey and began taking sips from the bottle. He had been working nearly continuously since sundown and the black-topped desk was littered with pencil stubs, wadded typescripts, sheets of onionskin and cheap bond, candy wrappers, looseleaf notes, and a fine spray of cigarette ash. He now began to fit his portable typewriter into its traveling case. To his right, at the foot of the bed, were the neat stacks of paper, the completed speech drafts. He stood and moved into the bathroom, returning in a moment with a sterilized glass wrapped in wax paper. He removed the paper and poured himself a drink from the bottle.

There was Mexican music coming in on the radio. Occasionally an announcer exhorted everyone listening to send him a check or money order in the amount of one dollar ninety-eight cents. A genuine gold-plated Ten Commandments charm bracelet would be immediately dispatched by return mail.

Stanley lay on the bed, balancing the glass of whiskey on his thin chest. He kicked off his shoes and began massaging his eyes with the tips of his fingers. The fingers were stained with tobacco and his eyes burned worse than ever. He pulled himself up, set the drink on a night table, moved into the bathroom and washed his face. He looked at the radio, loosed an oath at the fellow selling charm bracelets, and began to undress. He stood in front of a full-length mirror staring at himself in his too-large underwear. He shook his head and sighed and began doing flexing exercises in front of the mirror.

He was tall and spindly with a caved-in chest, and he had been doing the exercises since his first year in college when he and Neil and John Tom had lived together in the unrelieved heat of a decaying quonset hut. Neil and John Tom had stolen the quonset hut off government land, from an abandoned Army camp; transported it fifty miles in a borrowed flatbed truck and set up housekeeping like a pair of redneck squatters in a kind of servicemen's hobo jungle in a woodsy trailer park a few blocks from the campus. They had charged Stanley twenty-five dollars a month for room and board, which gave him *carte blanche* on whatever decomposing wet-rot was made available in the icebox and alternate nights on the only mattress that was innerspring. He remembered the old icebox clearly — loudly and clearly: it was constantly dripping water into a shallow pan underneath. At least once an evening it was his responsibility to empty the pan. Each of them had his chores, John Tom would explain; everybody pitches in to help. Neil and John Tom called it the co-op.

He lodged constant protests against the inequity of it all — at twenty-five dollars a month, for Chrissake, they ought to have been hovering round him with silken comforts and viands and enormous feather fans. But he could never bring himself to desert. It would have been the same as leaving some wonderfully ribald stag party just before the dancing girls came in.

John Tom was the younger of the brothers; he was only two years older than Stanley and this helped span the gap between Stanley's generation and Neil's. The distance was enormous and not entirely a matter of age differentials. Neil was a war hero.

He had begun in Stanley's imagination to resemble a *Terry Lee* or a *Captain Easy* — some incredible soldier of fortune out of a comic-book world. He'd won not only the Air Medal and DFC as a fighter pilot, but a Silver Star and Purple Heart for infantry action. He had been shot down over Normandy, and instead of trying to get back to his base at Coventry, he had joined some footsoldiers and slogged into Paris carrying an M-1.

The M-1 was still around the quonset hut that year for all of them to see. Sometimes they used it for a door prop; occasionally as a window stick. Most of the time it was pushed under one of the narrow bunk beds, gathering dust, but for a full month, he remembered, Neil went around polishing the gunstock and wetting the sights, threatening to shoot the first Nazi who walked through the splintered door. He had been trying to work himself into some kind of disability over the war — hoping he could get a monthly compensation from the Veterans Administration as a "spiritual casualty" — but the effort was unsuccessful. Even when Stanley and John Tom testified in his behalf.

There wasn't much else in the quonset hut: some beat-up furniture, a handmade bookshelf for the volumes Neil had never returned to the USO and Rec Room libraries, a few pen and ink drawings by John Tom and one enormous mural, streaked by water and dappled with mold, painted in the shower stall. And there were Neil's old records — Chick Webb, Fletcher Henderson, Billie Holiday, a bunch of others — along with a windup victrola his parents had passed on to him when he entered the Air Corps. John Tom had an ancient LaSalle automobile. Neil occasionally rode around on an old Harley-Davidson motorcycle.

And there were the barbells, of course. John Tom's barbells. They were always around, going to rust. Sometimes John Tom would notice them on the floor and would pause reflectively for a moment, staring. Then he would spit on his hands and squat down as if he were about to hoist them in one clean, swift movement. . . . Then he would hesitate again, straighten up and turn away.

"Come on, Stanley," he would say. "Let's get out front and do

some calisthenics, some flexing exercises. Those iron things'll give
you the hernia."

Stanley had been standing in front of mirrors, doing the flexing
exercises, since that first year in college, but it never seemed to
bring about any noticeable difference in the way he looked, least
of all the miraculous transformations touted by John Tom. But
who could say what kind of wreck he might have become without
them? He stood there now in front of the hotel room mirror,
mashing his thin arms, perspiring slightly. He lay down on the
bed again and remained motionless for a few minutes. Then he
sat up, reached to the foot of the bed for the typescript, and examined his work.

There was the one main speech — fourteen awful pages of it
— along with an attached news release capsuling its contents so
the lazy dumb bastard reporters would know what to say. If you
didn't take them by the hand and show them what it was all
about, they would miss the point altogether. The other speech,
an alternate, was shorter and vastly more appealing. He had told
the robber barons in convention assembled just what sons of
bitches they were. In a nice, oblique way, of course. But he felt
sure they would grasp the point, the God's truth of it. He had
simply unloaded on them — explained how any notion of a tax
cut was imbecilic in the extreme; made the obvious point that
big government would just inevitably get bigger; appealed to
their better natures (like a chicken bone stuck sideways in the
windpipe would appeal!) to realize the absolute necessity for a
relaxing of trade barriers. And so on.

Looking over the typescript, Stanley realized this would be his
definitive work. "I've never seen me looking better," he said
aloud. "A credit to old Daddy-Pop." He would show the two
speeches to Neil and then they would form a little circle, joining
hands and chanting obscure market quotations, as bare-breasted
native women moved in close to set fire to a trash pile in the
center — old looseleaf notes, onionskin, the morning papers, banana peels, half-eaten candy bars, cellophane wrappers, grubby

hand towels, and the wadded typescript of the second speech, his definitive work.

Neil could use it if he decides not to run — and if he's lost all interest in making a living at his law practice. They would call it the Stevenson-with-Hair speech.

He smiled and lay back on the bed. Old Neil. Old Neil and old John Tom. He wished they were all back at that beach again, years ago. When the two brothers seemed to know. What was behind those gilt-edged rootbeer signs. All the answers to all the hard questions. You know? *I* didn't know, he said to himself, but Neil and John Tom must have known. He supposed they had forgot. Ah! Some lines came to him . . . "For anyone alone and without God and without a master, the weight of days is dreadful. Hence, one must choose a master, God being out of style . . ."

Well, he had set his heart on old Neil, his own Melbourne, but that fellow seemed to be passing out of fashion, too.

He remembered the beach and the three of them (two of whom who *knew*) lying there watching Andrea and her friends parading across the sand with medicine balls and floats and beach umbrellas, thermos jugs and coolers and expensive-looking crystal in which they served up that awful sloe gin. They were friendly enough, Andrea and her friends, but there was a difference. The difference being that the others stood to inherit oil lands or 60-section ranches or stocks or property or family businesses of one kind or another. Even with his own little annuity, Stanley felt oddly resentful. More and more he had come to identify himself with his uncle's half-cropper farm and the pretty cousin praying over that old cow.

"I know one of those boys," John Tom had said, looking up. "He comes from a very good *nouveau riche* family." He had got to his feet and gone over to visit. Then the three of them had been invited for a drink. Old Neil just kept staring at Andrea, and he remembered her returning his gaze, keeping her eyes on him, lowering her lashes occasionally but then always looking up again, reaching for a pack of cigarettes or brushing the sunburnt hair out of her face. "Nobody tans like a rich girl, Stanley," Neil had said. And then: "You've got to be honest about your limitations as well as your gifts . . . But what the hell?" He stood and brushed the sand off his blanket and headed toward the girl.

They had not seen much of Neil for the remainder of the day, but it didn't really matter. John Tom was half out of his mind and putting on a show for the others. He had just begun to paint seriously — and he was good — but he wasn't so much driven by poetic vision as a truly lighthearted conception of life, a sense of vast pleasure and astonishment in what he could do with his hands. You couldn't really say what kind of pictures he painted. All kinds. One day he would be splashing around in the manner of Jackson Pollack, and the next it was Pissarro with sunlight effects and small dabs of pigment and soft harmonies. Stanley remembered once, just after the Korean war started, he had visited John Tom in New York. John Tom had just completed a canvas, an awful thing, yellows and browns and dreadful olive greens, showing a peace dove being disemboweled by a slavering American soldier with a dollar sign for a shoulder patch. Stanley had looked at him helplessly, and John Tom explained that he needed money and that he knew a fellow who would probably pay him fifty dollars for the painting. "He goes around talking about Yankee imperialism all day long," John Tom said.

The afternoon at the beach John Tom had painted everything he could get to sit still for him. He ran up to the old LaSalle and came back with his oils and temperas. He painted beach balls and floats and umbrellas. He molded a figure out of sand and painted it in the uniform of one of the Queen's Guards. He painted a woman's breasts on one of the young men, and at a distance, in a certain light, they were lovely. He wanted desperately to paint a bathing suit on one of the girls. He vanished behind a dune with one of them for a length of time, but it never was established what exactly he might have painted on her.

By the late afternoon Neil and Andrea had gone off walking in the sand and never returned. John Tom loaded their gear in the LaSalle, shaking sand out of his sleeping bag. "The hell with him," he said. "Neil can take care of himself." He told Stanley a story about how Neil had once deserted him on a trip to Biloxi. John Tom had been fourteen years old at the time.

"We'd swiped this old car and it had broken down somewhere in Alabama. I forget where. Neil got out and started walking. Down the road I could see a pickup truck stop for him. He never did come back for me. What happened was that there was a girl driving the truck. It was a Saturday afternoon and they'd gone on into town and had an ice cream at the goddam corner drug and watched some double-feature Western and later passed the evening at the roller rink. All that time I was waiting for him in that broken-down car. The highway patrol finally picked me up next morning. Lucky for Neil he didn't come back. I was fourteen and got off with a lecture and a week in the Juvenile Home. Neil was old enough that he'd have drawn a stretch if they'd wanted to be uncivilized about it . . ."

So they had driven off from the beach in the LaSalle, heading north and west toward the college. Neil didn't appear for three more days. Stanley heard him rattling the window blinds in the quonset hut at five o'clock on Wednesday morning. He was undressing and staring out the window, smiling to himself.

"Hello out there," he said to nobody. "Hello you goddam rosy-fingered dawn."

He padded round the room in his bare feet, whistling softly. It was "Heartaches" — wasn't "Heartaches" popular that year? He was trying to sound like the fellow who whistled with Ted Weems' band, only softly, sometimes in just a light rush of air, and rather badly, too. It was as if he was aware that people were sleeping all over the city, and he didn't want to wake them. But he just by God had to whistle. In a few minutes he took his toothbrush and wandered into the bathroom.

Stanley was wide awake by then, and he got his toothbrush and followed. Neil was immersed in bath water; he lay there with his eyes closed, groaning and hissing to himself, his expression oddly beatific. He looked up, smiling.

"What got you up so early, Stanley?"

"I dreamed Elmo Tanner was in the room whistling that awful song."

"Light me one of those cigarettes, will you?" He lay back in the water. "I feel gorgeous."

John Tom appeared at the doorway, filling most all the space. "I hope you didn't take that little girl across any state lines," he said.

"We drove up to the Hill Country, to a summer place of her family's," Neil said. He soaped his arms and chest and continued to smile. He didn't look much like a war hero. He was slender, with not much hair on his body, and about average height. John Tom had looked twice his size; he seemed enormous there in the small room. But there was a definite resemblance in their soft faces. John Tom moved inside and sat down.

"What was it like?" John Tom said.

"Horses," Neil said. "We rode horses. I met the foreman and watched a hog being slaughtered and chased cattle in a jeep. It was like the army again. But mostly we rode horses."

"All little girls go through a horsy stage," John Tom said.

"And all little boys go through a baby-fat stage. You look like the Goodyear Blimp."

"I feel like the *Hindenburg*," John Tom said. "Stately. Plump and stately. With a sense of impending disaster."

"I'll offer up a toast," Neil said, holding the bar of soap toward them. "To you, John Tom. May all your movements be regular . . ."

John Tom withdrew, lumbering down the hall, talking to himself . . . "All of us standing around at five in the morning, laughing and chatting like we were at a cocktail party at the English Speaking Union. I'm going back to bed . . ."

Stanley had stood there with toothpaste smeared all over his mouth; then he followed Neil back to the bedroom. Neil sat at his desk, looking up at a cartoon John Tom had drawn for him several months before. It was a picture of two young men standing in front of a fraternity house of fantastic size. "But you've *got* to pledge, man," one of them was saying. "It's like an Officers' Club." The cartoon was an enormous favorite. When there wasn't much else on his mind, Neil would just sit and stare at the cartoon.

"How did you get back?"

"She brought me. She has some friends here she visits."

"You plan to see her again?"

"Tomorrow. She's leaving tomorrow. Afraid I'm going to be wearing out that old motorcycle on weekends."

"Go to work and buy a new one. They need some kitchen help at the Swede's. I heard—"

"I got enough of that before and during the war. And all you're fed is cold leftovers. I think I'll get into politics. Run for the Legislature."

"Where in hell could you run for anything?"

"All over. I've lived all over. And I might as well try to get something out of those medals. I'll just pick me a county — a district. We've got plenty of counties and districts. I'll be the goddamdest war hero you ever saw. We'll just pick a county the way those Englishmen used to buy constituencies."

"Be careful you don't pick one with a blind man or a double amputee running for the same office."

"First consideration," Neil said, "first consideration. Got to pick your opponent, too . . . wonder which of my hometowns? They must have heard something about me in a few of them. I put down so many hometowns when I enlisted, the Air Corps P.I.O. went wild sending out stuff on my heroics to all those little newspapers . . ."

"I think you're out of your mind."

"Your family was always in politics."

"They sort of played at it — that's all."

"Fine! You can run the campaign. I'll put you to work. Think of all that patronage after we're elected . . ."

"You're crazy. Listen — you're not going to make any money. The pay is something like ten dollars a day."

"Well. There's nothing wrong with that. And when they're

not in session I'll be able to get me a good job. No goddam dish-washing. Hell! Being a State Representative ought to recommend you for something better than that. I might sell real estate . . . book bands — I might —"

He crawled into bed and pulled the sheet up round his shoulders. "And you've missed the point entirely, Stanley. It's not the motorcycle — it's the girl. I've got to do all this if I expect to marry the girl."

"Listen," Stanley had said to him. "If you ever managed to marry the girl, you wouldn't *have* to work. Her father owns *hotels* or something."

"Stanley, Stanley. You just don't understand. It's my principles — principles running out my ears. I couldn't marry her for her money. It's the money that actually complicates things. If she didn't have any money, I could put *her* to work downtown in some dime store. She could work my way through law school. It's being done all over. It's very big this year. It's these hotels that are messing things up for me . . ."

He lay back in the bed and closed his eyes. Stanley had wanted to ask him about the girl, but he didn't know how to put the questions. He wasn't sure what exactly he wanted to know. And he was afraid it might get him started on that political stuff again. He must have been very drunk the night before. Neil and the girl getting tight driving in from the hills, sipping the family's best wine from paper cups, laughing over the old jokes that had passed between them, stopping the car on the side of the country road occasionally and holding on to each other. Stanley could see her saying goodbye to him on the front steps of some nice home in town, flushed and breathless, with the mist falling on her bare shoulders. The idea struck him as extraordinary. Extraordinary that he should even have such an idea. He'd never done anything of the sort in his life.

Through the blinds that morning he could see the sky all mauve and milk-colored and hear the voices of a few young people on their way to seven o'clocks . . .

Seven

THE BELLBOY was not entirely sure of his ground. Sleepy-eyed and merely sullen in the beginning, an expression of concern and vast bewilderment soon clouded his face as if he half suspected the great joke being played on him.

"Mistah Diz-ray Lee?"

"What?" Stanley stood in his oversized shorts, staring at the boy through the doorway.

"Ben Diz . . ."

"Ben Diz-ray-lee, sir. Are you Mistah Diz-ray-lee?"

"No, for Chrissake. What's all —"

It was some horrible mistake, some monstrous joke played on the young man . . . by the town drunk, maybe, at two in the morning. The bellboy backed off, making apologies.

"Wait a minute," Stanley said. "Hold it a second." He stepped round the corner of the room and reached for a pack of cigarettes. He had not been really asleep — just partly mesmerized by the Mexican music on the radio, lying on the bed and wondering if he ought to switch off the lights. The bellboy had been knocking for only a minute or so. Stanley returned to the doorway.

"Now . . . What's all this again?"

"I'm sorry. Hope I didn't wake you. The radio — I could hear the radio, and I thought —"

"That's okay . . . What were you saying? Just now."

"I had a message for Disray Lee. Or a Ben Raylee . . . It was supposed to be this room. He insisted it was this room and he wouldn't let me call. Gave me two bucks to deliver the message personal."

"Okay. What's the message."

"Are you Mistah —"

"No. But what's the message? Who's it from?"

"He wants you to meet him outside. He wouldn't come in. He's parked out front. He said he couldn't come up. He didn't have any shoes on. And he was wearing Bermuda shorts."

"Wait a minute now. Who wants me to come downstairs?"

"His name was Stevenson."

"Stevenson?"

"He said he wanted to show you his hair."

"Oh! *Ah!* I'll have to dress . . ."

"Yessir." The boy continued to stand in the doorway.

"You said he gave you two dollars?"

"Yessir. I'll give him the message." The boy began backing off again . . .

"Wait a minute," Stanley said. "Come on in here."

The boy followed him into the room. Stanley gathered up the newspapers.

"Give him these while he's waiting."

"All right."

"And this. Can you carry this?"

Stanley poured half a glass of whiskey and handed it to the boy. Then he cleared the top of the desk of change. The bellboy had both hands full, and Stanley dropped the coins into the boy's jacket pocket. Then he began dressing.

The hotel lobby was deserted. Stanley moved between potted palms and Grecian spittoons, the bottle under his arm and the speech folded inside his coat pocket. The desk clerk did not look up and the bellboy was nowhere in sight. The little red car was parked directly in front; Neil was slumped in the seat with the newspapers spread out against the steering wheel. Stanley moved through the revolving doors and stepped out into the warm air.

"Couldn't sleep?"

"Out of the habit." Neil folded the papers without looking up and started the little car. At the first stoplight Stanley refilled the glass and they passed it back and forth.

"You read the stories?"

"Yes," Neil said. "There any later editions? This stuff is okay — what there is of it — but it looks like it got chopped off right in the middle. And there aren't any pictures. They took a lot of pictures."

"There ought to be a morning edition about now," Stanley said. "I guess that's where all the newsboys are. You want to go to pick 'em up wet off the presses?"

"Yes," Neil said. "I'm an egomaniac." They drove off in the direction of the rail yards. Trucks and motor scooters and bicycles were parked at the rear of the old building. There did not seem to be any urgency about getting the news out onto the streets at that hour. The presses made an awful din, but the men and boys moved without enthusiasm, loading the bundles onto trucks, talking quietly. Stanley vanished inside the building and was back in a moment with two newspapers. They drove on a short distance and stopped under a streetlight.

"This is better," Stanley said.

Neil was silent, bent down, squinting in the bad light.

"It's a good picture," Stanley said. "Except that you look like a high school debate champion. Let's start powdering your hair. And painting lines in your face. You look like Andy Hardy breaking into the bank at Bayonne, New Jersey."

Neil grunted. "You see what the Governor did?"

There was a separate story on the Governor. He had apparently called the wire services sometime after his conversation with Neil, announcing that a "Draft Neil Christiansen" committee was being formed and friends of "David McNeil Christiansen" had already paid the $1500 filing fee. "I talked with Senator Christiansen tonight," the Governor was reported to have said. "He wouldn't give us any encouragement. But he didn't say no. We're hopeful we can get a commitment from him before his return to Washington . . ."

"Who is David McNeil Christiansen?" Stanley said.

"An invention of the Governor's," Neil said. "About as authentic as that committee . . . I wonder where he got $1500? I could have used it — I've got an overdraft at the bank."

"Well don't advertise it, for God's sake. You need some money? I've got a few hundred."

"That's your few hundred for going around the world."

"I'll never go," Stanley said. "I never seem to get enough ahead."

"I wonder how far it would get me?" Neil said.

"Owen Edwards finds out you're overdrawn, he'll be going around saying you can't even balance your *own* budget . . ."

Owen Edwards, the State Senator, was also mentioned in the paper. He had made a speech in another city about the need for a return to constitutional government. Tax and tax, spend and spend; the people bled white by foreign giveaways; the courts rewriting the laws; rabble invading our shores. "And our *un*elected representative in Washington never raising his voice in protest . . ." He mentioned the confirmation of an Under-secretary of State, a housing bill, a supplemental appropriation for one of the Mutual Security programs — all of which Neil had supported.

"Thrashing machines," Stanley said. "He's back on thrashing machines for India and India not having anything to thrash."

Neil folded the papers and drove on, heading up into the hills above the city and the winding river, higher even than those better neighborhoods with their Tudor-Gothic circus fronts. Then they circled round and re-entered the city near the campus. Neil tried unsuccessfully to find the old trailer park where years ago they had planted the quonset hut, but half of it was now overgrown in jungle and the other had become an intramural football field. He wondered if the quonset hut was hidden in the jungle or dismantled for bonfire kindling. Neil parked the roadster in a little clearing between the football field and the tangle of trees and vines and weeds now grown man-high. They sat there for a time, passing the glass of whiskey back and forth. Stanley produced two cigars from his jacket pocket and they sat quietly, smoking and occasionally swatting at the insects that came at them in great droves from the jungle.

"This is making me very melancholy," Stanley said. "Except that something's missing. There ought to be a creek running through. I don't recall one, actually, but I feel there *ought* to have been a creek — a place where the wives of all those exservicemen beat their Monday wash against the rocks. Like native women . . ."

"You're getting your images confused," Neil said. "It was John Tom. He used to do his washing around here somewhere. With a tin tub and a washboard."

Again they were silent. Stanley said: "I've got your speech."

"Will I have to rewrite it?"

"No. This time I got the mixed tones licked. I wrote *two* speeches. One with all the right things in it, and one with all the wrong things. You won't have to go through separating one from the other."

"I'll take both of them," Neil said. "I may want to give the wrong one."

At that remote hour the clear sound of young men's voices came to them suddenly from across the campus, soft and melodic, a serenade to a sorority house.

"Oh God," Stanley said. "I may cry . . . My lost youth . . ."

"I remember bringing Andrea out here once," Neil said. "I showed her around and asked if she could live in one of the hutments until I finished law school."

"What did she say?"

"She said yes — if we could run off to her family's summer place up in the hills on weekends. So she could use the automatic washer there and have someone do the cooking."

The singsong voices faded and then rose again, like an old radio receiver picking up a distant signal. Stanley remembered that Neil and Andrea had not really lived in one of the hutments. Stanley and John Tom had stayed on in the little room with

busy wallpaper during the last two years, but Neil had won a seat
in the Legislature on his second attempt, and he and Andrea were
married a few months afterwards. They had honeymooned at
the country place, while Andrea's mother had come to search
the better sections of the city for a suitable apartment. A
carriage house next to one of those phony Norman mansions
was made available when the newlyweds came down out of the
hills . . .

Neil remembered the endless long distance telephone conversations and the weekend motorcycle trips to the summer house.

"I knew it was you," she would say to him. "I had vibrations.
I ruined a pair of stockings getting to the phone."

"Where were you?"

"Outside — fumbling with my date and my door keys."

"Let's get married. It's time we got married."

"Why?"

"Because it's time, and I love you."

"You don't really."

"Hell yes I do."

"Say it again."

"Hell yes I do."

"The other . . ."

"I love you."

"That's nice."

"Sure it is. So let's get married."

"No."

"Then live in sin with me. I can afford maybe a week of really
high type sin. I'm solvent. I've got $500. Collected the night be-
fore election by Stanley and John Tom. I never got around to
spending it."

"Sounds like dirty money."

"That's the only kind there is, honey. You know that. I'll take
you to Mexico for a week."

"No. That's passed. That offer, as they say, was limited. You
never delivered me there on time."

"I was up for office, honey. I was campaigning."

"Did you win?"

"Hell yes I won . . . Don't you read the papers?"

"There's no delivery out here, love. But I knew you'd call. Can you come out this weekend?"

"Yes."

"Good. I need rescuing. There's been a party every night. Pre-debutante parties. I've got to withdraw — absolutely the last group of young ladies I'm presenting to the ravages of society. Got to withdraw from this glittering world and all these faceless figures in white ties . . . You like that?"

"Yes."

"It's hard on one's perspective spending night after night eating caviar and drinking twenty-five-year-old Ambassador."

"I know it is, honey. It's awful. That's why I don't go to debutante launchings any more. I promised myself."

"Will you come this weekend, then? There's a party this weekend."

"I'll try like hell, honey. I'll sure try. You've got the right idea. It's best to ease off these things gradually . . . What's the party?"

"Artist types. Or entertaining the artist types. It's a society we've organized. We encourage the muse."

"I'm only coming to get married . . ."

"It'll be a nice party. Martinis served up lukewarm in milk bottles. They're all a pack of primitives. Neanderthals. Flanked by hairy-faced women."

"Why don't you come here."

"*You've* got to come. I've got a date I can't get out of."

"That's wonderful. You think the three of us will get along?"

"You don't understand. I've got a date, but he won't last the evening. He's a heavy drinker and he always passes out early. Then you'll be my date."

"That sounds awfully tenuous."

"You can count on it. I've never seen it fail. He collapses before ten. He's very unhappy. He works in the family store, but he wanted to study medicine or play the violin or something . . ."

The party was as she described it. The sad young man was unconscious before ten o'clock; the martinis were warm and the guests were a combination of extremes — fine-limbed young people and seedy throwbacks to bohemia. The paintings were hung about like great prime slabs of beef. He moved alongside Andrea from room to room, shaking hands. She introduced him to everyone as her "Representative-Elect." "This is my Representative-Elect," she would say, like the queen and the prime minister. The guests smiled and nodded as if he were in the bond business or was perhaps her desperate young man who wanted to play the violin. The talk was mostly about Truman and Toynbee and Kenton, ranchstyle houses and draft laws and Howard Hughes. Those who could afford it were planning vacations in quaint, clapboard artist colonies, and those who couldn't were already resigned to the endless weeks of working over window displays in local department stores.

Later, she had turned to him and asked if he disapproved.

He remembered saying yes, absolutely yes; that he would be willing to start a subscription campaign just to finance a special, chartered one-way flight to Provincetown. For all the others. With the understanding they wouldn't be coming back. He made an outlandish gesture: "You don't give a damn for all the oppressed peoples of the world."

"Who are all these oppressed peoples?" she said.

"Millions all over. Me . . . right here. I'm oppressed. I want to take you off to some quiet glade and make love and talk about the success of the Berlin airlift, and this party oppresses all that."

She smiled at him. "Get my bag and we'll find this place."

Outside he had said: "I don't know any glades."

They sat in the car, holding on to each other with the trifling medleys of some hotel dance orchestra coming from the radio. There was a period of interminable kissing during which she had got her hand inside his shirt and he was able to push the top of her dress down and touch her small breasts. He remembered the spectacular contrast of dark and light skin. Then she had sat up, touching her hair, and said: "It's too bad."

"About what?"

"About that glade. Now there's no place to go but home, and my folks aren't here this weekend and it'll be such a disappointment you won't get to see them . . ."

She had taken his hand and led him across the concrete walk between banana trees and eucalyptus plants and the Mexican tile floor in the living room and directly up the carpeted stair into a small, girl-smelling bedroom with a view of the garden and a gone-dry creek. She kissed him once, briefly, almost tragically, and began to undress. Next to him in the bed she was trembling violently, but in a moment she was giggling in his ear. "I've read the books," she said, "yet I can't remember any of it. Will you tell me what to do . . ." Later, still smiling with her face next to his, she laughed about not being able to say the right things. "The trouble is I really do feel different . . . I ache all over . . ." And still later, when they had slept in each other's arms for a time, she sat up in the bed, looking like a little girl roused from an afternoon nap. "Don't stop saying it now," she said. "This is absolutely the Wrong Time to stop saying it."

"Saying what?"

"That you want to get married."

"I want to get married," he said, but she had not heard any of it; not even her own question: she was asleep in his arms again almost immediately.

Sitting on the soft leather cushions in the cramped space of the roadster, listening to the young men's voices from across the campus, he was able, finally, to realize his loss, to feel the great gap in himself. Not so much long gone youth as adulthood never quite attained. For all his good intentions, there had been only a kind of chic faithlessness in between, randy and frivolous. If there had once been beauty . . . a fever for life and a search for a code of conduct, those private joys had long since been supplanted by trivial and lighthearted depravities.

He started the engine of the little car. Stanley, sleeping next to him, held on to his glass of whiskey but did not come awake. They bounced across the football field and steered the car toward the commercial district, past darkened dormitories and gray buildings and faintly lit chapels. Moving into the center of the city he smoked the last of his cigarettes and thought about their deeply violated selves.

Eight

SHE WAS AWAKE, suddenly, in the middle of the night, conscious of where she was and remembering why. It was not such a horror as she expected. Merciful oblivion had eluded her, but sleep brought on a condition in which she could at least attempt some kind of coming to terms. It was a curious thing, a small thing — vast hopelessness might descend again by morning, but at that moment in the middle of the night, lying in the strange room, the covers bunched up round her legs and the wet-sheep smell of mattress ticking filling her head, she could look back on the evening and see where she had been. It was not pretty to watch, but there was no compulsion to turn and run. The way she had on the day before when she had seen the small dog, very much like their own but of no particular distinction otherwise, stand trembling and terrified as an absurd, high-fendered Model-A Ford bore down. It was such a comic scene, and so protracted — the old car advancing on the dog, and the dog so clumsy and struggling like an ancient water bird grown too large in evolution for flight — that it did not seem any harm could come of it. Even at the moment when the dog ducked under the front bumper only to raise its head again and strike out at the machine passing over, and the next second with the dog tumbling along beneath the car, fighting back, furious and uncomprehending — she could not believe any violence had been visited. It was all so ridiculous and . . . slow motion. It was not until the dog was released from the infernal thing, dazed and bleeding and staggering toward her, gaining strength and screaming horribly and snapping at its tortured loins, that she was able to grasp what had happened and move herself toward the animal. When she reached it, remembering all the warnings from her girlhood about keeping her distance, the dog was stretched out on the sidewalk, stiff and unmoving and open-eyed. Then she had turned and run; only a few quick clumsy steps, staggering in the high heels, but it seemed she had covered half the block before she turned to look again as the old woman driver of the Model-A stood on the running board and stared from the other end of the street. Then she had walked on, steadying herself, not even breathing hard.

So now she could look back at this last accident earlier in the evening. Perhaps she could retrace her steps and try to help or at least make a prayer as the two of them expired, gasping for air.

Neil would be asking the same question. Or had he even heard the wild cry in the night? Was it all in her mind — some passioned whoop advancing out of the dark fields, ringing inside her head? Perhaps it was she, tipsy all evening and half incoherent in his arms. It doesn't matter — Andy, my friend, you mind not mattering? My mind over matter. Irrelevant is what it is — but so awfully damned relevant is what I am and whether the signal came out of me loud and clear. Look Neil honey you just don't pay any attention to those sound effects . . . But he heard, I know he heard, and he's always been inclined to take things so serious. Oh goddam the both of us, why can't we keep the faith? *Alas a trembling takes me* . . . Who said that? Who got taken

by all that trembling? John Tom and his inevitable seizures: the
Abominable Bookman. The both of us, shaking all over. He
kept his faith one way or another. What were the lines . . . ? *If
ever any beauty* . . . No. That was Neil. Sweet dear Neil and
our dear sweet love for one another. Like eating one's young.
*If ever any beauty I did see, which I desir'd and got, 'twas but a
dream of thee* . . . Was there ever a love, either too much or too
little, that wasn't corrupted by sentiment? And possession? It
would have to be mystical. Or worse, a mere benignancy. Phi-
lanthropists! Why can't you charitable souls leave me alone —
the both of you — and try to do it the right way for a change. By
not *over*doing it, I mean. I wanted some privacy and the two of
you went and overdid it. I remember being wonderfully serene
and self-contained at first . . . but then there was so much to tell
about later and you'd both gone over the hill. I told some others.
Or tried to tell them as best I could, struck dumb and inarticulate,
using the sign language one of you Eagle Scouts had taught me
years before. I wonder if they got the message? Any of them
. . . Any of the messages. I thought the visiting fireman had,
that actor, the aging matinee idol with the changing accents: Oxford and Beacon Hill and the Virginia horse country. But he
didn't get the message. I thought he had. I got his all right.
*Quite the most strenuous good time I've had in years . . . My
manhood stands in salute!* Smutty postcards. He missed the point
entirely. I ought to tell Neil now. He might listen, the way he
was in that ancient vale miles and miles ago when I hadn't really
much to say. I could tell him now, I think I could, I'd do my best,
I'll go to him now and try . . .

She pulled herself from the bed and slipped on the gown she
had dropped in her flight down the hall. She walked barefoot
and shaking into the other room. There was only the empty bed;
the sheets weren't even warm. How quickly these enthusiasms
cool and expire! She inspected all the ground-floor rooms and
finally looked out the front door and saw that the roadster was
gone . . .

Later, in the guest bed, she lay quietly waiting for sleep, waiting and coming wider and wider awake. She thought about a tranquilizer, but then reminded herself that the effect was cumulative, building up over the days, and that the condition it brought on was not so much blessedness as a mere sapping up of nervous energy. She took three aspirin instead and lay there waiting for them to work inside her. In the last stages, just before sleep, she was dimly aware of Neil's footsteps in the hall, but she could not get the words formed on her lips to call out, and she had nearly forgotten what it was she had to tell.

He did not undress, but loosened a button and half unzipped the fly on his Bermuda shorts before lowering himself onto the bed. He did not think much about her; those few thoughts that came through were muddled and confused by the re-creation of emotion, or what remained of emotion, of the gorgeous feeling evoked from his ruminations on the intramural field. What was it he had lost? Beauty, or the illusion of beauty, or the illusion of loss. Real or imagined — that was of no importance. What counted most was the *sense* of loss, a value collapsed or in imminent danger of collapse. Those decaying timbers underneath. How had he let it happen?

He ought not be a politician, he told himself. Nice line of work but requiring a vision . . . a dedication, a certainty of belief in what one is doing. He'd had it once; the trouble was, all those sturdy affirmations began to dissolve. Right before the eyes . . . Front of my eyes? Perhaps a little left of center. You'd had it once, I do believe you did, but you just stopped believing . . . Stopped it altogether . . .

I remember once oh boy you had it, as singleminded and certain and unremittingly earnest as the best of them. Those old pols. That the way the old pol pounces? Old pols! Why is it we have to be so all-fired sure of ourselves? Or at least make like. How come I got the thing dumped on me just now of all times, of all ages, my spiritual prepubescence, when those wondrous self-righteous juices have temporarily ceased pulsing, or gone to vinegar, and I stand here waiting for wisdom or meaning or sweet bliss? They got me at this difficult age — too old and whiskery for playclothes and not yet grown tall enough for cufflinks and striped pants. I lost that vision, that monumental sustaining self-assurance. Just the illusion would be a comfort — perhaps that's what old Arthur Fenstemaker's got himself so high on. The real or the imagined, he's got it, got hold of it good, they all have, all the great ones, like Stanley says, pushed along by that vision, like artists. But those artists are indulged and almost encouraged in their weakness. Because they got the poetic vision. What the hell! They got a different kind? They hold a monopoly or something? Picture an old pol revealing his frailty. Unthinkable. No prayer-meeting confessions please. Get up there like a man and tell 'em how it is you got the cure for all those ills . . .

If I could just see this script old Stanley wrote . . .

Ladies and gentlemen, if you'll bear with me a moment — ten years or so would do nicely — while I grope around in the shadows for a new fuse. Around here backstage. That great hot light in my head seems to have gone dark. Got a match? Perhaps I can scrounge around in these perfumed sheets till dawn and then I'll set us back on course. *Of course!* The one my John Tom charted . . . I know it well, my friends, and him too, that happy navigator. Never a need to spit into the wind with him around. But who the devil got us into these latitudes in the dead of night? Man the boats!

Those two fellows who knew the way seem to have perished at sea, in those sweet-smelling bedsheets . . . You see?

There was this nice lady on board for a time, and she knew the way partly, but the women and children went first and there's no telling where they're drifted now. Who knows? If I could read that script I just might walk on the goddam water. I did it once before. That women and those children might be just over the next swell . . . And of course and perhaps and in any event, all of us and any number of scripts should be visible in the first light of the dawn . . .

Nine

HE WAS AWAKENED by the giggling of the little girls. They stood a few feet away, trying to control their laughter, delighted with the picture of him bunched up miserably in the sheets. The older one held his breakfast in a tray; the younger was laying out silver and an undersized tablecloth. He attempted to smile for them; it felt like an act of contrition.

Their voices were not really coming through to him just yet; they were merely singsong sounds in the beginning. The older girl set the tray in his lap and fled downstairs for salt and pepper. The younger pulled herself onto the foot of the bed and sat watching him, enormously pleased.

"This your mother's idea?"

"No. She's asleep."

"Really?"

"It was *our* idea. Emma helped, but it was *our* idea."

She was silent, watching him. Then she said: "Who do you love?"

"Who do I love?"

"*Yes!*"

He had to think a moment. "You and your sister and . . . your mother . . . and Emma . . . and. I guess those people best of all."

She picked at her nose. He told her not to pick her nose.

Then he said, "Who do *you* love?"

Now she had to think. She yawned.

"The sandman!" she said, smiling, surprised with herself.

"The sandman? That's —"

"And the *Easter* rabbut and the fairies that bring valentines . . ."

"Really? . . . What about Santa Claus?"

"*No!* There *isn't* any Santa Claus." This was stated as incontrovertible fact.

"Well . . . But there's a sandman and a fairy and an Easter bunny?"

"Sure."

"Well then you hold on to those few illusions . . ."

"What?"

"Don't you love any people?"

"Not yet," she said. It seemed a profundity.

The older sister appeared with the salt and pepper. The two of them sat solemnly and watched him eat. Soon they grew restless and ran downstairs to examine the test pattern that preceded the morning television. Occasionally one or both would reappear to let him know Captain Kangaroo was coming *soon* and to *hur-ry.*

On his way to shower he could see that Andrea was indeed fast asleep. Her face was only faintly drawn and her bare arms and legs were lovely. He wore his blue "speechmaking" suit. He wondered who in the world ever coined that awful word.

The girls wanted to know where he was going.

"Speechmaking," he said. They stared at him, uncomprehending. He sat with them for a few minutes and exchanged views on the quality of the television. Emma was banging around in the kitchen. He gave her three phone numbers where he could be reached during the day and started out the back door with the keys to the other car. The morning was clear and sunny and uncompromisingly beautiful, and he began to feel a little better. Emma met him in the driveway at the front of the house to give him a message from Andrea. There was a party somewhere that evening. He could meet her here or there or . . .

Or what? he wondered, driving through the nice neighborhoods toward the Capitol grounds, past the cool, deep-piled lawns and the serpentine walks that were bordered by thick blooms of flowers. He parked the car near the main entrance to the old granite building and proceeded unrecognized toward the Governor's suite. Even the receptionist gave him her No Visitors smile until he identified himself. Fenstemaker met him at the door after the girl had delivered the message.

They sat in the huge, high-ceilinged office; it smelled of good cigars, leather and polished furniture. A secretary was making coffee behind a partition. There were two secretaries — they moved about noiselessly on the thick carpets. Enormous cut-glass chandeliers hung down from the ceiling, and a massive mirror, framed in gold leaf, was set above the marble fireplace, too high even to see one's head, reflecting only and rather pointlessly the opposite wall. One of the secretaries served coffee. She stood waiting, watching them. Governor Fenstemaker blew across the top of the cup. Then he glanced at the girl.

"Ah?"

"You be needing me around noon?"

"Sybil be here?"

"Yes . . . She's having a sandwich at her desk."

"Okay."

"Thanks . . ."

She turned, but the Governor called to her.

"Where're you goin'?"

"Down on the Avenue. I thought I'd buy some shoes . . . It's a good day to buy shoes . . ."

"Oh." The Governor looked at Neil and made a Frenchman's face. Again he called to the girl. "Vydora . . ."

"Yes?"

"Why is it a good day?"

"For shoes?"

"Yes."

"Well, because it's cool and it's supposed to cloud up around noon and . . ."

"Yes?"

". . . And your feet don't swell." The girl bolted through the door.

The Governor looked at Neil, mystified. "Last week," he said, "last week it was the lights — the fluorescent lights. She insisted they were hot and were burning her. Way the hell up there on the ceiling and she was getting heat stroke or something . . . Probably flashes. She wanted to turn out all the lights and stumble around in the dark. We get an appropriation of twenty-five thousand to air-condition these rooms, and she's hot from the lights . . ."

They sipped their coffee. Then the Governor said: "Well what're you gonna do about that fourteen-carat sonofabitch?"

Neil set his cup down and looked at the older man. "Who's this?"

"Edwards. Who the hell you think —"

"What's he done?"

"Haven't you seen the morning papers?"

"I saw 'em about two this morning. Something on Edwards . . . Just his usual."

"You haven't seen this? You're a hell of a politician. I've been up since five reading most of the papers in the state and last Wednesday's *New York Times.*

"I got to bed about five," Neil said. He examined the front page of one of the papers. Owen Edwards, in another city, had finally got hold of a copy of Neil's remarks made at the impromptu airport news conference.

OWEN EDWARDS BELIEVES
CHRISTIANSEN WEAKENING

'Knuckled Under' in Past —
Now Losing Nerve Again?

State Senator Owen Edwards said last night he feels he can win a seat in the United States Senate "practically uncontested."

In an interview following his speech at Miller Auditorium, Edwards assailed Senator Neil Christiansen's "characteristic mental flabbiness" and "noticeable lack of any real conviction — good or bad."

Christiansen is "poorly equipped, emotionally and intellectu-
ally, to hold a position of public trust," Edwards said. "I'm not
telling anything new. Christiansen will probably confirm this in
a few days when he disqualifies himself for holding public office.
This facet of his nature was first apparent when he refused to
stand up on his own two feet and fight like a man for his political
life seven years ago. He didn't give the people the opportunity to
replace him then, as they surely would have done, and I'm certain
he won't let the people judge for themselves now, as I would like
for them to do. He lacks any real qualities of leadership — most
of all he lacks heart and guts . . ."

"I wonder why," Neil said, "they didn't report spitum dribbling
down his chin . . ."

The Governor nodded. "But what are you going to do about
it?"

"Well . . . Like you said last night. Stay above it . . . Ignore
him . . . Jesus Christ, listen to the rest of this . . ."

"I've read it. Several times," the Governor said. "I don't want
you to *say* anything. I want you to *do* something. And the obvious thing is for you to announce as a candidate. Today. Soon as
possible."

"I'm not going to let that baboon make up my mind or push
me into anything before I'm ready . . ."

The Governor got to his feet and paced around, hands jammed
into trouser pockets, breathing hard. He, too, had married into
money long ago, long before he had entered public life. But
Arthur Fenstemaker hadn't resisted the idea of wealth. He had
gone after it, seized it, invested wisely and made some on his own.
He had fought *with* the money and had, therefore, a healthy
respect for wealth and its gorgeous machinations.

"Well," he said, "it's a goddam good day to buy shoes."

"Because it's cool and your feet don't swell," Neil said. And
the mind doesn't boggle, he thought to himself.

"The way I see it," the Governor said, "you've just about got to get into this thing now — whether you announce today or tomorrow or the day after. Whenever. Otherwise —"

"Otherwise he will have put a pox on my house . . . He may be right. Maybe I *don't* have the heart for this sort of thing."

The Governor stood with his back to him, staring through the window, unwrapping an enormous cigar. "I'll tell you something," he said. "You want to know something?"

Neil nodded. The Governor had pushed open a window and through it came the sounds of birds and dogs and children and morning traffic in the streets.

"If you don't get into this, it'll ruin you. As a man. I know you — I've known you for seven, eight years. You're goddam good. You got sense. Hell! I remember the first time I saw you. When I was Attorney General . . . I'd dropped in to visit some friends on the House floor. There was a bill coming up that day. I forget exactly . . . Something that permitted state funds to be deposited in banks without drawing interest. A real jackpot. I didn't particularly like it; not many people did. But it had some solid support and the skids were greased. I was sitting next to the press table and you brushed by heading toward the back microphone, reading the bill and mumbling to yourself. I remember — I heard what you were saying: 'What a lousy goddam bill.' So you got the floor and I sat back and watched you, throwing out a few parliamentary questions, making notes all the time on little pieces of paper. You stood up there and talked and made notes for more than an hour, passing bits of paper to your secretary and whispering to anybody who came near you. After an hour the secretary came back with that pile of typed amendments and then you went after them — you must have tried to change every line during the course of the debate. You stood up there and organized the opposition yourself, operating right out of the seat of your goddam pants, and by God you beat 'em down. It was a real pleasure to watch, Neil . . . what the hell's happened since? You run out of gas at the age of thirty-three?"

The Governor puffed on the cigar. Neil sat looking down at

the pile of morning papers. "I don't know," he said. "Maybe I just got out of the habit."

"Well don't you have any contempt for Edwards? You just can't —"

"That's it," Neil said. "I don't feel much of anything about Edwards. It's like he's been talking about someone else all this time."

The Governor came close. "Then you ought not to feel that way. You ought to despise him . . . You know he's the one?"

"The one who what? What're you talking about?"

"He's the one, goddammit. He's been after you for seven years. He's the one I warned you about in 1950. That's what's behind those statements in the paper. He thinks he scared you off once, and now he figures on doing it again . . ."

"You mean it was *him?* He's the —"

"Exactly . . . So what do you plan to do about it?"

"I . . ."

The phone's ringing saved him from having to force some tortured confession of helplessness across his lips. He did not know what he proposed to do about anything. He'd already lost his navigator, and now, after long months of studying the stars and the tides and the great ocean currents — with all the facts and figures in his head, the accumulated wisdom, the distrees signals — he was piloting a rudderless ship. What the hell *did* he propose to do? Fenstemaker was right. There was only one —

"Yes," the Governor was saying, ". . . tell them I'll be there in a minute. The conference room is a good place. Order them some coffee from downstairs . . ."

He put the phone down and looked at Neil. "I've got to talk to some people . . ."

"I have to leave anyhow," Neil said.

"I'd like for you to stay," the Governor said. "I'd like you to meet 'em when I'm finished. They're money people. Career contributors, you might say. I'm going in there right now and make a pitch for Neil Christiansen. If they're sold, I'd like to bring them in here to meet you. If you're not going to think for your-self, I'll think for you until you tell me otherwise. These people in there — they got no convictions to speak of. They carry their politics in their vest pocket. They just want to go with a winner. I'm going in there now and threaten them with every kind of hor-ror if they don't back my candidate. They know I mean it too. I think I can tap the bloody mother lode if I handle it right. They'll probably put some money on Edwards just to be on the safe side, but I want them to take a look at you. And I want *you,* for my *own* sake if not yours . . . So at least try to *look* like a winner. Get mad . . . Get goddam mad!"

The Governor turned and strode out of the room before Neil could object. He sat sipping coffee. So that was how. Get mad. Get goddam good and mad and look like a winner. He stood and stretched himself so that he could see three quarters of his face in the big mirror. He tried to affect the look of a winner, but the image that gaped back at him merely exuded a kind of vast, be-nign self-deprecation. The dime store Jesus, he thought: Gandhi with a twang. Gray flannel loincloth and button-down lip.

And so it was Edwards . . .

It was curious he had never even thought to ask. The Governor only told him there was someone, the Enemy, lurking outside, faceless and impersonal. But that was exactly the point: It hadn't mattered who it was. He'd never even looked outside to see.

Seven years before — such a melancholy time. All of them, they were all enemies; every man a Hawkshaw, every king sus-pect. Our national malaise. Some few — the pathologists like Arthur Fenstemaker — had seen it coming, but there had scarcely been time to flee the plague, much less sound a warning or stem the virulence in any noticeable degree. "It's the year of the lo-cust," Fenstemaker told him. "These things come and go, like the business cycle. You got to know when to buy and sell. Dump all your holdings — that stuff's out of fashion for a time. It's your brother, don't you see? They're going after him, but it's really you — and these people believe in blood guilt . . ."

Seven years now he had been trying to tell himself it had all been done for John Tom. Was he still not quite convinced? Why else? A man looks after his own. And there *had* been sacrifices — he was still in debt to the bank for the bookstore. It was a long time between campaigns, seven years between, such a time as to cause him to lose sight of whatever vision it was that sustained him. So what the hell if he did come back again to fight another day? He had only Arthur Fenstemaker to thank for that. Washed up until Arthur arrived with a direct commission and an oxygen tank. That was all irrelevant. He had done the thing for John Tom —pulled him off the faculty at the college and set him up in a business of his own. It had been perfect. Who could give a damn if a bookstore proprietor talked a heresy to students?

Then Neil had gone *out* of business for a time.

"It's like this," he had told John Tom, trying to remember how old Fenstemaker had phrased it. "We're facing a bad year. Got to get out from under. Sell before our margin's wiped out. One more campaign and I might be plowed under.

"It's like this," he went on, reversing reality in deference to his brother's feelings, "they come after me, they're liable to bring you down, too. Teaching in a state college is no place to hide during a political purge. I can take care of myself — I got the law practice. Now you . . . You interested in a bookstore? I just bought us . . . you . . . you and me and Andrea — however you want it — I just bought a bookstore."

"I can't run a bookstore," John Tom had said. "Not even a coffee house. All I can do is paint. I'm not even very good *teaching* people how to paint."

"You don't have to *do* anything . . . Just give 'em a book and take their money. The place is right off the campus. You can't add and subtract, I'll get you an accountant. All you got to do is play it straight — wear baggy trousers and hang your paintings around and maybe even grow a beard. Give 'em the crap artist routine. They won't care about your politics . . ."

"For Chrissake, I don't *have* any politics. What's all this —"

"I've got politics then. All over me. And you might lose your job."

"So what?"

"Everything! Me. I care. You understand? Look — I've already signed the papers . . . Come down and see the place. Another month and it's mid-semester. You can give notice today."

Suddenly Neil knew he could not face Arthur's friends. He looked round the big room, blinded by the mirrors and the morning sunlight streaming in through those enormous floor-to-ceiling windows. He wondered if it would ever cloud over and whether one's feet would swell after sprinting across those thick carpets and down the marble halls . . .

He paused at the receptionist's desk.

"Would you tell the Governor I had to run. I've got an appointment at ten-thirty . . . I'll check back with him later in the day."

"I'll do that, Senator. Have a nice Easter."

"Same to you. Nice weekend."

It may cloud over but the lady's feet will swell, he told himself. He was perspiring through the blue suit, and he wondered if he would have to return home to change before the luncheon. The hell with it. He punched on the air-conditioning in the car and drove slowly through the Capitol grounds, circling round the old building several times. Then he turned out into the avenue and headed toward the campus again. What *had* been his motives? Covering his own flank or looking after little brother? And what was it those Hawkshaws had on John Tom? He had never even thought to ask, never known it was Edwards until that morning. John Tom hadn't any politics, not really. He wondered what it was they planned to spill on him, what spleen and feces squeezed from some half-finished lecture note on modern art. He could hear his brother now . . . "The top's hunky-dory but the bottom's rotten, young ladies and gentlemen. Picasso and Rivera knew that — Rivera knew it from firsthand experience . . . But what they don't know is that Communism's just an inversion of the system. Place the botton on the top and a great leavening action permeates the whole. Evolution slips on a banana peel but continues onward, as it must, until that day when absolute zero grips the universe, making quiescent all things for all time . . ."

Once he had heard John Tom in serious discussion with Andrea's father. At least he had looked serious, giving no indication of having tongue firmly planted against cheek. "It's Truman's war," he was telling the fiercely agreeing old man, "but Mac-Arthur will have the boys home by Christmas . . ."

Old John Tom. In that plague season of pursuer and pursued, foul breath in the face and the rending of flesh, traducer and traduced. Who was to guess at motives? Who could speculate on what passes through the backsides of the brain? He had lived to fight another day but serious doubts befogged him now as to whether it had been worth it and who it was he was prepared to fight. Lost that vision, he was thinking; John Tom took it with him when he left. Were there no more possibilities for individual moral achievement? Or was it just unintelligible human savagery. He knew, then, where the sleek dark car was taking him, filling his head with a glimpse of meaning and manufactured ice-cold air.

Ten

THE BOOKSTORE was like a sanctuary, cool and funereal in a second-story loft on the main street just off the campus. Only an hour remained before the luncheon, and he wondered if it would be possible to cancel that engagement also: beg off everything and begin the morning in this gloomy, vaulted chamber, free from disorderly notions, content in the muted chaos of all those endless volumes. There was music coming from somewhere, behind the stacks, an album of Vaughn Williams played on John Tom's old record machine. At first he had thought the place was empty, but then two college girls rounded one of the bookcases, glanced at him briefly, and moved past toward the hall . . . "I lost his black star sapphire ring in the ladies' room at the Club De Pesca," one of them was saying. "We spent all night exploring the sewers of Acapulco . . ."

Then they were gone and only the music remained. He stood for a moment, listening, touching the brown volumes, before heading into John Tom's office.

It was just as he remembered. The same photographs, paintings, clippings, rolltop desk, file cabinet. The place was not so littered as before, but all of John Tom was there — the music and the record machine, the favorite English paperbacks and an old locker-room banner from his football-playing days: "It's Not the Size of the Boy in the Fight but the Size of the Fight in the Boy." There was what John Tom called his memorabilia — a life-sized model of the Arrow Collar Man, a pair of high-topped women's shoes, a poster advertising a steamboat race, and a large, elaborately colored cut-glass light fixture in the shape of a butterfly. It was all there — as if the proprietor had only stepped out for a moment and forgotten to pull the door behind him.

More than a year before, Neil had closed and locked the rolltop desk, taking the key with him. In a moment he had the desk open again and was sorting through the papers. He was looking for the letter that had been sent to him by the magazine correspondent, the one telling about the personal effects being shipped home and enclosing those last notes. He had only uncovered the blurb about pictorial journalism and the few unpublished sketches John Tom had done prior to the revolution. Then he found the notes. He sat down to read them again . . .

Havana teems with gun-carrying police and, from above, lacks the cleancut geometric landscape you come to know over the North American continent . . . Panama at midnight was steamy, with pretty round-faced girls selling the national drink . . . Guayaquil was banana trees and glaring lights, and it was too dark to see anything from the makeshift hut they had for an air terminal . . . Lima gave us all a scare because we had to let down through ground fog, all the while making sure not to hit the Andes, and then there was the flight next morning in the blinding sunlight, up into the mountains, around and across them and over the little volcano pools of water to La Paz. After that we thought we'd never get airborne because the air was so thin, and in Santa Cruz there were children selling devil's faces next to the dirt runway . . . Asunción, we are told, is the only capital in the world without a water or sewage system . . . Thank God no one runs around saying, "Do you like it here? Whattaya think of us?"

. . . At long last, Buenos Aires and the twentieth century, complete with modern plumbing, European styles . . . and Perón. First thing we saw at the air terminal — portraits of Juan and Evita and the usual slogan about being in the land of Justicialismo, National Doctrine, Peronismo, Anti-Oligarcismo, *and so on . . . The correspondent at the American Bar said it was like Germany around 1939. The uniforms are right out of the SS, and they've got the goosestep down perfectly. But then another says it's more like Rome the same year . . . But who the*

*hell cares? Maybe it will be like covering a war in any
event . . .*

*. . . They burned the Socialist newspaper building and the
Jockey Club and two thirds of the churches in the city . . . A
beating of a priest and unimaginably brutal street murders . . .*

*There's something altogether different about these people . . .
Imagine Omar Bradley leading a revolution of U. S. Army garri-
sons on the White House because he disagreed with Eisenhower!
It's the regular way of doing things here . . .*

Neil sorted through the notes. There was another newspaper
article he had not seen before — one more description of how
John Tom had wandered deep into the city where much of the
rioting was going on and how he had been brought down by a
single bullet and pulled to safety by one of the other correspondents who, later on, had gone back again to get the sketchbook.
Neil had his own notion of John Tom shuffling through the center of town, wondering what the hell he was doing there and
thinking about Chick Webb and Alban Berg on the phonograph
and pictures by Thomas Hart Benton; sitting down suddenly,
clumsy and foolish looking, propped on a curbstone and holding
his big stomach in pain and wondering about the regular way of
doing things.

There were two editorials from the magazine that had sent
John Tom south. They described how it was with a brave man dying, going after the news in the best tradition . . . A great
loss . . .

"Crap," Neil said aloud, and then thinking: John Tom . . .
I'm really sorry as hell. But you have to understand the great
soggy heart of the profession. They give you all the glamour and
significance of some young pilot going down in flames over France
and composing a sonnet in his head on the way . . . Journalists!
They got clabber for brains. Operating with all the logic of Har-
old Bell Wright . . . John Tom you would've puked. If you'd
lived to read your obits.

"Goddam!" he said aloud. "Crap and B.S.!"

"What an awful way to talk," said the girl from behind him.

He turned toward the voice, still holding the clippings, the more seasoned phrases of contempt poised inside his head. She had not really startled him, but now her appearance caused his pulse to lurch, as from sugar going to the brain. She was dark and sloe-eyed with hair the color of those burnished woods that shone along the walls of Arthur Fenstemaker's office. She was smiling and seemed to find his presence in the room nothing out of the ordinary.

"I'm sorry," he said. "Excuse me."

"Just words," she said, still smiling. "If you had said bloody or perhaps the same thing in Arabic or Hebrew, I might have been surprised. No matter how well one learns another language, though, it's still just words. The vulgarisms don't have any real impact."

"You must be Elsie," he said. There was no trace of accent in her speech, but he knew this would be the girl Andrea had written him about. She had gone to work in the store earlier in the year, and he had been in touch with the State Department in her behalf. She was an exchange student at the college who did not want to go home. Her father was an English Jew, her mother an Egyptian; they were a Christian family living in Palestine and never quite accepted among either Israelis or Arabs. ". . . a very sweet, confused young girl," Andrea had written, "who feels as if she doesn't belong anywhere . . . But she's wonderful in the bookshop and you must help her get a permanent visa . . ."

In the gloom of John Tom's office she did not seem particularly confused, however. Sweet — yes — and extraordinarily, darkly beautiful, but there was nothing in her manner to suggest her feeling anything but immediate comprehension and self-assurance. The old loft groaned around them as he stood gaping at the girl.

"Yes," she said. "Some of the girls at the sorority house where I'm staying think I ought to change it to Elise . . . More words . . . I really don't understand the difference . . . *Elise* . . .

Elsie . . . ? And you're Neil? Senator Christiansen, I mean."
He nodded.

"I appreciate all you're doing for me."

"We appreciate your work in the shop," he said.

"It's a nice shop," she said, looking around, as if examining the place for the first time. "In New York, two years ago on my first visit, I worked in a bookstore on Christopher Street. Do you know Christopher Street?"

"No."

"I worked there for three months in the summer. It was nice, but not as nice as here. I would have liked to know your brother. His male mannequin thing over there fascinates me. And one night I had a party here and filled his terrible crystal punch bowl with orange juice and Smirnoff's vodka and ice cubes. It was very successful and no one tried to steal books and I think we even sold a few . . ."

"It sounds like a wonderful party," he said idiotically. "John Tom never thought of actually filling the punch bowl. He just liked to have it around . . ."

"It was quite nice. Several faculty members and some older students. I'm older than most, but there are some even more. I would like sometime to visit Washington. Passing through, it is a beautiful city."

"Yes," he said. "Sometimes it's like the outside of an egg — about as interesting."

"Like what? An egg?" She laughed at the idea. "I think I understand. New York City is like chow mein or some oily Middle East dish . . ."

Neil nodded. Did she realize they weren't making good sense? The girl carried a sack from the Rexall's down below. She set it on the desk and unwrapped a sweet roll. "Would you like some coffee? I have a whole pint of coffee."

"No," he said. "I've had coffee all morning. And I'm going to lunch in about half an hour. I've got to make a speech."

"A speech? Where? May I go listen?"

Neil was pleased and a little astonished. He had a theory about the two kinds of people who inhabited his world — friends who listened to his speeches and friends who listened to recordings of Aaron Copland and Samuel Barber. Stanley was one of the few who shifted back and forth from one world to the other. John Tom had been another. But the girl defied classification . . .

"I wouldn't recommend it," he said. "A lot of people sitting around belching and me trying to be vaguely statesman. It would probably seem incomprehensible."

"Oh I like speeches," she said. "I've heard a great many speeches. In various languages."

He told her where the speech would be. She sat across from him, absorbed in thought, nibbling on the sweet roll. She wore white sneakers without socks, a plain cotton skirt and a mannish-looking blouse with three-quarter length sleeves. Yet she seemed altogether feminine. She was full bodied, her movements easy and graceful, and he wondered if any of the young men in school were ever as shaken as he was at that moment by her exquisite face. Had she a lover? Who and how many and where were they now? What kind of speeches had she heard? He tried to picture her wandering around Washington Square in those white sneakers, staring at folk singers and bearded flits in desert boots pulled along by twin poodles; pausing and listening to endless harangues about Civil Defense alerts, sane nuclear policies, Zen Buddhism . . .

The girl finished her coffee and opened a textbook. Occasionally she looked up and smiled.

"Do you know German?" she said.

"No . . . None at all."

"I'm studying German. By myself. I just bought a textbook and started in. No reason. I thought it might be nice to read Rilke's poetry in the orginal German."

That seemed a good enough reason, he told her. He wondered idly what foreign tongue he should study if he were ever to comprehend what everyone was getting at. Andrea, Stanley, old Fenstemaker, the dark girl across the room from him now and possibly his dead brother on occasion — what had they been saying to him? There were so many dialects, most of them unintelligible, and there was so little real communication. Did Berlitz have a course in mystic English? How to translate one's own speeches ringing in the ears — those half-coherent interior monologues set to memory but never fully understood?

". . . I was looking over these old notes of my brother's," he said, pointing to the clutter inside the desk. "Some of them were written just before he died."

She smiled at him brightly, as if he were telling a wonderfully amusing story. He smiled back for no reason.

After a moment, she said: "Do you think I could find a job in Washington? I'd like to live there. I know several languages."

"Yes," he said. "I'm sure we could find something. Soon as we make sure you're not going to be sent home. How much more school do you have?"

"No more. I'm taking courses, but I can leave any time. I've been in college six years, in one place or another. I would leave tomorrow if the opportunity presented itself. Do you really think there would be something for me?"

"Yes," he said. "I might even put you on our staff to translate my speeches."

She stood and walked toward him. "Translate . . . your speeches?" She pulled a chair next to him. "Into what language?"

"English."

"I don't . . ."

"I'm joking . . . A joke on politicians."

"Ah . . ." She did not really understand. But she sat there next to him, smiling, and he felt a sudden compulsion to reach out, to touch, to get through to her in some way.

Instead, not knowing how the thought got across his tongue, he said: "You're lovely."

"What?"

"You're a beautiful woman."

"You're joking? Making another joke?" She continued to smile.

"Not at all. An understatement, if anything."

"You're very nice," she said, touching his arm. "Thank you."

He was going to kiss her then. He could anticipate the lumbering movements toward her and feel her dark face against his. There could be no awkwardness at such a moment; anything could happen in that intimate chamber misted in desire. But as these thoughts passed through his mind, the girl got to her feet and began wrapping books for shipment through the mail. She spoke without looking up.

"Why does Andrea stay here? Why don't you live together in Washington?"

". . . I don't know," he said after a moment. His voice was matter-of-fact, emotionless. What was he trying to say? What was she attempting to uncover? Were all of them doomed to a mere blind staggering, guided by random and unexpected flashes of perception? There was never enough light to see . . .

There was a sound of footsteps in the hall, and he bent down over John Tom's notes. In a moment he would have to leave.

Stanley's face appeared in the doorway.

"Hi. I thought I might find you here . . . Don't ask me how come."

"Stanley, this is Elsie . . ."

"Pivnik," the girl said.

". . . Stanley Elms. You and Stanley ought to get together. He knows all about translating political speeches."

"Are you going to the speech?" the girl said to him.

"Yes," Stanley said. "Now all we got to do is get the speechmaker to go to the speech."

"I'm going," Neil said. "Let me enjoy my last private, golden moments before the world caves in."

"You want to know why I'm here?" Stanley said.

"Why are you here? Why do you come looking for me? Have

they moved the election up to this afternoon or something? What
is it?"

"Old Fenstemaker called me at the hotel. He said you ran out
on him."

"Was he mad?"

"No. Disappointed maybe. There were some moneychangers
in his office and they wanted to look you over."

"I know. Examine my teeth. Poke my ribs. Like a goddam
claiming race. I didn't feel like going through that on this particular morning."

"Well you ought to call the old man. He's been paying for all
the oats."

"I will."

Stanley turned to the girl. "Sell me a book, Elsie," he said.

"What would you like?"

"Something with pictures. Naked girls or Confederate dead.
Cartier-Bresson . . . Matthew Brady . . . Bound volumes of *Play-
boy* . . ."

"We have a Cartier-Bresson," she said. "And a Steichen." She
left to get the books.

"I love her," Stanley said. "And I must have her."

"All you need to do is get her a job in Washington," Neil said.
"Or you can take her around the world with you. She translates
. . . In six languages."

"I need only the language of love . . . Don't look so put upon.
We'll share."

Neil got to his feet. "I'd better run downtown," he said. He
paused at the doorway, smiled at Elsie as she passed. Then he
spoke to Stanley: "You coming?"

"After while," Stanley said. "I'll be there."

Neil moved out into the hall, passed an empty Christian Science reading room, and walked slowly down the narrow stairs.
Coming out of the shadows, he was blinded for a moment by the
sunlight. He stood in front of the drugstore for a moment; looking in at the boys and girls lined up at the soda fountain. One of

the bobbysoxed girls looked back at him curiously. He shortened the depth of his vision then, and understood why the girl stared. The reflection in the drugstore window showed his dumb smile stretched across a face wet with tears. He turned, shading his eyes, and finally reached the car before anyone else noticed.

Get that young face of yours on the television, he said to himself, remembering Arthur Fenstemaker's advice. On the way downtown he thought about the orators, the divines, the Great Caesars, the politicians through the years, across the dynasties of the Egyptian gods, the cult of Isis, the passion of Christ — all of them — the unfolding legends. He pressed the prepared speech inside his breast pocket as if assuring himself against its dissolving into thin air.

Eleven

THERE WAS music coming in on the car radio, and he paused outside the entrance to the underground parking facility to listen for a moment. Then there was a honking from behind, and he drove on, the music fading as he steered the machine beneath the hotel and along a tunnel of polished tile and blinking red and green lights that resembled a hospital corridor. Would he never hear the last of that unfathomable melody? Would it haunt him all the day? An Easter-type song. He tried to imagine it sung in the manner of Abe Burrows. The music still hung in the fouled air of the tunnel. He caught another glimpse of his young face in the mirror, grinning barbarously, as a television pitchman signing off.

He repeated the words of the song aloud — *I said a prayer and played the jukebox* — and the expression of fey content — the happy clutch of doom — stayed with him as he moved past the parking attendant and the elevator boy, through a crowd of slippered bathers heading for the roof, and a hive of white-badged delegates and expensive women bunched in the middle of the penthouse ballroom. They all stared back but did not recognize him, and for an instant at the head table he wondered if he might have strayed into the wrong convention. Or possibly even the wrong hotel. There was a man bent down over a stack of cue cards who could have been a guest speaker, but then he turned and faced Neil, smiling and extending his hand, and identified himself as the master of ceremonies.

"Senator — we were all disappointed you missed the milk punch party."

"The what?"

"Well actually it was highballs. But so early in the day and the ladies and all — we tried to play like it was something else."

"I'm sorry I missed it," Neil said. "I got tied up. Unavoidably."

The master of ceremonies certainly understood how *that* could happen; he understood perfectly. He was a tall, handsome man of about fifty, big-nosed and engaging, a kind of exalted Cro-Magnon species. He wore a tiny, flowerlike lapel ornament which Neil recognized as the Silver Star. God help me, he thought: my hero brethren. He also recognized the man as a former All-American football player from the thirties, but remembered him even more distinctly as an indefatigable lobbyist for veterans' bonuses several years before in the Legislature. He remembered the proposition — $500 for a vote; seven-fifty for working over one or two colleagues — and he wondered if the fellow remembered him. Probably not. Surely there were some others that year who must have told him to go screw himself, in precisely those words or even worse. There had to be — there had been enough votes, at least, to get the bill sent back to committee for study. A long goddam painstaking study . . .

"Haven't we met before?"

"Well now Senator I certainly know who *you* are, but no — I don't think we've ever —"

"In the Legislature? About 1949?"

"No . . . No, I never had the privilege of serving. Made a couple of tries just after the war, but there was a sudden buildup of industry in my district, and the labor boys moved in and organized against me and — well you don't want to hear about *that* . . . I'd like you to meet some of the others at the table here."

The head table guests were strung out the width of the ballroom; they were just now taking their seats. Waiters deposited hot dishes in front of them — creamed something in a pastry shell — and there was organ music coming from behind a veiled stage at the other end of the hall. The song was "Tico Tico."

Neil shook hands with the guests at the table. Toward the end, the pretty little girl from yesterday's airplane flight smiled at him.

"Hi!" she said. "See? I was so impressed I made Daddy bring me along . . ."

"I'm delighted," Neil said. He turned to the girl's father. "Your daughter is beautiful and intelligent — but awfully difficult to put up with when she has a deck of cards. She nearly skinned us alive . . ."

"Where's Stanley?" the girl said. Her father sat there smiling and nodding.

"He should be along soon," Neil said. He waved goodbye to his flying companion and followed the master of ceremonies toward the lectern. He sat next to the wife of an old State Supreme Court justice; she sipped her glass of Scotch whiskey and ignored the plate of food. People he knew only slightly or not at all came by to lean across the table and speak to him. He must have talked with at least fifty of them and drunk three glasses of water during this period. When he had finally picked his way to the bottom of the soggy pastry shell, he leaned back and smoked a cigarette, staring at the crowd of perfect strangers. Then, miraculously, a familiar face floated in front of him. Andrea's father reached across and gripped his hand.

"How are you, Neil? Goddammit boy you're lookin' fine."

"Yes sir, I'm fine. It's wonderful to see you. How've you been?"

"Fine . . . Fine. Proud as hell of you. Saw in the paper you were talkin' here today and I caught a plane to come over and watch."

"Fine . . . That's wonderful," Neil said. He wondered if his mind was slipping, if his brain had ossified. Would he plunge into this speech mumbling *Fine, fine, wunnerful and fine?* Yes, I'm fine, ladies and gentlemen, really fine, and . . . well, swell, I really am, and wonderful, even, and it's —

"Have you seen Andrea?" he asked the old man.

"No . . . I'll call out there later. Brought some Easter baskets for the girls their grandmother forgot to mail. But I came to see you, boy. All of us are proud . . ."

"Really? What have I done?" He smiled down at the old man. They had got along well enough together through the years, but this sudden enthusiasm was entirely new to their relationship.

"Hell! I dunno. I'm just proud of you . . . Maybe it's that sonofabitch Edwards — excuse me, miss, I'm — it's the way he's talkin', I guess."

The Justice's wife nodded sweetly and began to demolish her strawberry parfait.

"It's just politics," Neil said. "He's been saying the same thing for years."

"But not about *you,* by God. I want to see you give that fellow a lickin'."

"I might not run," Neil said. "I just might forget about it."

"You *can't,* boy, you know that. Not after what he's said about you, you can't."

"Well . . ."

"Where's that committee?"

"What committee?"

"The one the Governor announced. Christiansen for Senate. Who's in charge?"

"Well. There's no committee. Not really. It's just something Fenstemaker dreamed up. It doesn't even exist."

"Well it will. Here — *you* take this, then."

The old man handed the check across to him. Neil stared at it for a moment. Then he pushed it back at the old man who stood a few feet off now, as though to retreat if necessary.

"You can't afford this, and I can't accept. I never have, and I can't begin now." He stared at the black-inked figures on the slip of paper. His father-in-law was giving him $5000.

"The hell I can't. You can't stop me. I got a *right,* boy, you know that. One way or another, I'll do it, so you might as well accept it yourself."

Neil smiled at the old man for a moment, his hand covering the check. "All right. But if there's no campaign, I'm tearing it up."

"There'll be a campaign," the old man said. "There'd better damned be. You and I never agreed much on politics — not even half the time I expect — but I'm with you a hundred and fifty goddam per cent in this little deal. You're my kin, and I'm just not going to stand around scratchin' myself while somebody cusses my own people . . . I'll see you later, boy."

The old man turned and headed back toward his table. The former All-American with the Silver Star lapel pin was standing at the lectern, making his preliminary remarks. Neil folded the check and slipped it into his wallet. He thought about the overdraft at the bank; the payments at the bookstore. He looked out over the crowd. Who were all these people — all these enthusiasts? In another time Owen Edwards might have had them gnashing their teeth, wailing, enraged, coming after him and John Tom like a deputized lynch mob. How was it Edwards was suddenly out of fashion and his own young face just as suddenly in? Old Fenstemaker said it was like the business cycle — sometimes you bought and occasionally you had to get out from under to save your margin. They were not for him now — these vigilantes — but they could be if he studied the market and pushed the merchandise on the television. He sang under his breath, unconscious of the words: "I said a prayer and played the juke . . . box . . ."

"What did you say, Senator?"

"I . . . was . . . remembering a part of my speech."

The Justice's wife smiled at him. The ceiling was cloudy with smoke, and he caught a glimpse of Stanley and Elsie heading toward a patch of vacant seats that had been pulled in between him and the luncheon tables. Stanley waved, and the dark girl stared and faintly smiled.

". . . our attractive and able United States Senator . . ."

There was a burst of applause, filling the chamber, and Neil could see the former All-American gazing at him earnestly, smiling, extending his arm, palm turned out, like a variety show announcer. He got to his feet, suddenly tired, mumbling to himself — fine, really fine, and well . . . swell — staring out at the audience which had risen simultaneously, nearly in the same motion with him. He stood at the lectern, adjusting horn-rimmed glasses, pushing them flat up against the bridge of his nose. He held a speech in each hand, looking out and smiling back at the crowd, and when he fixed his stare on Stanley the younger man merely made a shrugging motion, cocking his head and extending his lower lip for just an instant. Neil clipped both speeches to the lectern and began . . .

"I was going to talk to you about Positive Steps in Foreign Policy, and I still might — that's the title of the speech I've got in front of me here, and Lord knows I'd be in trouble with my newspaper friends who've already filed their early leads if I didn't follow the prepared text . . ."

Pause . . . faint laughter . . . a stirring in the seats . . . leatherette padding coming to terms with five hundred distressed recta. He looked down at the empty pastry shells and his slowly dissolving parfait. The absurd thought came to him that, instead of drinking water, he might stand there speaking for half an hour while spooning out periodic mouthfuls of strawberry parfait.

"I keep thinking I'm not really qualified to speak on anything so exalted as foreign policy, though. I was fortunate enough to be assigned to Foreign Relations in the Senate, but up to now at least there hasn't been much give and take. I'm the Very Junior

Senator, and I haven't given half as much as I've taken. I like the Senate. It's a nice place full of good and occasionally extraordinary men struggling with a hopeless and possibly unattainable noble ideal. The fact that the ideal *might* be impossible to realize doesn't undignify the effort. The nobility exists in our conscious efforts to be decent men, to somehow transcend centuries of hopelessness and bad thinking and arrive at some approach to blessedness. That's really all I can say to you today, because politics — and the language of politics — is at best an ambiguity . . . I think it was George Orwell who said . . . Hell, I don't *think* it was Orwell — I know it was Orwell — I just looked it up this morning . . . It was Orwell who used to rail against the language of politics. He was a socialist in England, and I'll now have to file the customary disclaimer about *that* . . . *But* . . . *anyhow,* George Orwell had this to say: 'Political language — and with variations this is true of *all* political parties, from conservatives to anarchists — is designed to make lies sound truthful . . . murder respectable . . . and give an appearance of solidity to pure wind . . .' "

There was a sudden release of tension in the ballroom. Laughter rippled along the press row and the head table and gathered force, moving toward the other end of the chamber. Had they really understood? Or had their minds been lumbering along behind what he was saying, stumbling over his half-coherent phrases as boulders strewn behind him on the trail. Did they grasp that last line only because it seemed vaguely reminiscent of some ancient vaudeville gag? No matter. He told a story he'd heard from Arthur Fenstemaker years ago.

"I could talk to you about Positive Steps in Foreign Policy, but the question sticks in my mind — what steps? What policy? There was this schoolteacher who came into a little country town looking for a job and was interviewed by the superintendent. The superintendent told him, yes, the town needed a teacher, but they ought to clear up a few things first. There had been a good deal of discussion in the town about whether the world was round or perfectly flat — it had developed into a real debate, a controversy. Nearly everyone in the town was concerned and had formed an opinion about this question. So the superintendent wanted to know — how did the young man teach it? Did he teach it round or did he teach it flat?

"The young man thought a moment and replied: 'I can teach it either way you want,' he said . . ."

There was laughter again, and then applause, and Neil waited until just before it subsided before continuing:

"How do you want *me* to teach it?" He looked out and smiled at them. "The truth is, I can't teach it *any* way, because I just don't know . . ." He rambled on into the body of both speeches, picking paragraphs from each. He would be driving the newsmen out of their minds, but he had at least used most of the key applause lines in the text Stanley had distributed to them earlier in the day. He did not stop to ask himself whether he was ruined at this point. He might or might not be — it didn't particularly seem to matter.

". . . the reservoir of great ideas left over from the Roosevelt and Truman Administrations has been just about pumped dry . . ."

There was no response to this. All those registered Democrats out there were Republicans at heart, and he continued . . .

". . . We need both new ideas and old boldness. But our goals can't be achieved by one idea or even by one policy — or a multiplicity of ideas and policies produced by the singleminded purpose of one Administration . . ."

Now there was applause. Old Stanley, he thought. He plays it like the fiddle; beats upon them as a Chinese gong. He knew that line would have to be recovered — he tossed it off, got it back, and more. My resurrector of rash statements.

". . . Our policies have been motivated by sheer reaction, and, as a result, we are inclined to forget just what has been the basis — the moral basis — *of* our policy. We say we send technicians to India because we want to halt the spread of Communism . . .

We say we endorse exchange students because we wish to *spread* our ideas . . . I think we are ascribing ignoble motives to noble deeds. I think we ought first of all to change not our policies — but our attitudes. It's about time for us to proceed on the assumption we do things *not* because they are expedient but because they are right. If we send food to India, we ought to do it because people are hungry and we have a surplus . . . Have we got so befogged in the language of politics — national and international — that we can't even sensibly articulate our own good intentions when we have them? . . ."

He was finished in less than half an hour. He sat down amid sustained applause. He sat there, trying to force some kind of expression of engaging solemnity onto his face, wondering, for no reason that he could determine at that moment, about Andrea and what she and the girls had done all the day. The applause continued, and he stood, smiling, thinking about whether Stanley had noted the number of times he was interrupted by laughter or applause. He was supposed to keep count and pass the information along to reporters. ·

The master of ceremonies was speaking again, bubbling on about Neil's speech, introducing guests who had arrived late at the head table. A question period ensued; the questions were put to Neil from the audience through the master of ceremonies; Neil got to his feet only to reply. They were harmless and well-meaning queries for the most part. He parried a series of questions about oil imports — flabby responses strongly phrased — and he joked with a University student and several delegates who asked him to comment on Owen Edwards' charges of the night before.

"He and I actually have a kind of rapport established," Neil said. "He doesn't think I ought to be in the Senate, and I would regard his election to that body as a disaster of monumental proportions . . ."

"He's just announced," someone called out. "He filed over at the Capitol an hour ago . . ."

There was a general shifting of limbs and chairs and a murmuring response, and Neil could not clearly hear the next question. It came from the back of the ballroom, and the master of ceremonies asked that it be repeated. The air-conditioning was at full strength and most of the women had wraps pulled round their bare shoulders, but Neil was suddenly conscious of perspiration soaking through the back of his coat. The man with the question at the back of the ballroom was making his way through the maze of chairs and tables. He paused after negotiating half the distance. This time Neil heard both the question from the floor and the gasp of astonishment blurted out simultaneously by the Justice's wife sitting next to him. Neil had just got a spoonful of the melted dessert into his mouth.

"I repeat — why does the Senator seem reluctant to put himself up for office . . . ?"

"My God it's Owen Edwards!" the woman next to him said.

". . . Why does he hesitate to plead his case before the court of public opinion . . . ?" Edwards was a stout, happy-faced man with nice color in his cheeks and thick blue-gray hair. He stood in the middle of the ballroom, arms akimbo, in an attitude of indolence and unconcern. Neil waited for a moment and then got to his feet and moved near the microphone on the lectern.

"The question isn't exactly germane to this discussion, but I'll tell you I've frankly put off announcing my intentions because I simply haven't made up my mind." He made a move back toward his seat, but Edwards' next question had followed hard on Neil's reply. The master of ceremonies stood away from the lectern, viewing the scene, and there was no one really at the microphone as Edwards began to speak . . . He had a deep, resonant voice, and there was no need for amplification.

Neil turned and leaned against the lectern, looking out. "What . . . did . . . you . . . *say?*"

"I raised the question whether your reluctance might have anything to do with the fact that the three persons closest to you in life have openly consorted and associated with Communists or suspected Communists?"

"You are out of your mind . . ."

"Am I? Well I have the evidence, Senator, documented, dates and places, that prove —"

"Let's have some of that evidence, then. Document me a date and a place before I come down there and —"

"That won't be necessary, Senator," Edwards said. He was now nearly alone in a circle of the ballroom vacated by the luncheon guests who had moved off a distance to stand and watch. "That won't be necessary until it's a public issue and the people have a right to know just what it is they're being asked to buy, and —"

"All right . . . It just became a public issue," Neil said. "You just made it one, and it'll be official in about twenty minutes or the time it takes for me to get up to the Capitol and file for office . . ." He reached into his coat pocket and produced his father-in-law's check. "I've got the filing fee right here . . . *Now* . . . let's have your so-called documentation . . ."

Edwards beamed. He appeared to be reading from a small looseleaf notebook. "Your closest friend and Number One assistant and adviser — the young man who wrote the Senator's speech here today, ladies and gentlemen — this young man's father was discharged from a major radio and television network several years ago because of Communist affiliation. This is according to reports of —"

"*What* . . . ?" He looked at Stanley who was already on his feet. They gaped at each other, and Edwards droned on . . .

"Your younger brother, John Thomas Christiansen, was frequently in the company of Communists in New York City in 1949 and 1950, once attended a rally in that city protesting the Korean war, consistently voiced heretical and un-American opinions while teaching at the State University until resigning from that institution rather than face the prospect of official investigation that —"

"He's dead!" Neil yelled. "My brother's dead!"

"Slain in a left-wing uprising setting up a revolutionary government in South America . . ."

"Get out! Get the hell out of here!"

"Your wife, Senator, has visited, is *known* to have visited, in the home of Mexico City Communists while ostensibly attending art classes in the summers of 1952, 1953, 1955, and . . ."

Neil did not hear the rest. He had managed to shove one of the tables aside and force his way between the table and the lectern. His movements shook the length of the platform and the microphone crashed to the floor. The groan of the public address system — a tortured blue note — pierced everyone's hearing as Neil headed across the floor. Unaccountably, the memory of a long distance telephone conversation with Andrea, years ago, occurred to him: "Hello, love . . . I'm in Cuernavaca and I want you to come, you'd love it here . . . Just everybody's here . . . Ernest Hemingway's ex-wife and Herman Wouk and every kind of Weirdsville character . . . Will you come, love?"

Then he could hear Stanley's voice, yelling at him; he could see his friend trying to get through the crowd . . . "Hey! Neil! No! Don't, Neil . . . Hey! wait a minute, dammit . . ."

"And in addition," Edwards was saying, still reading from the notes, "you have employed in the bookstore owned jointly by you, your brother and your wife, a young woman of foreign birth, whose visa in this country is about to expire and in whose behalf you have been exerting influence as a United States Senator — this girl is not even welcome — is considered *persona non gratis* — by her *own* people, the Governments of Israel and the United Arab Republic . . ."

He got hold of Edwards in one motion. There did not appear to be a moment's indecision, but for an instant as he moved across the ballroom Neil had not been certain whether he would swing on the man or wrestle him to the floor. It was such an incredible moment — like some improbable scene from an ancient late-late movie show — the good-good man and the bad-bad . . . He got hold of Edwards at the back of the collar and the seat of the pants, feeling like a dim, flickering comedian's image stumbling around in slow motion, scuttling along the ocean floor of the ballroom toward the small lobby at the other end. Edwards neither put up resistence nor spoke out. They skidded round the corner of the lobby — Edwards seemingly content and tractable in his clutch — and bounded off a marble wall. There was not a word spoken between the two of them. Neil let loose his grip and their eyes did not meet again. Edwards walked, erect and stately, into a waiting elevator and vanished behind the automatic doors . . .

Twelve

STANLEY reached Neil just as the doors came together. He had lost sight of the two of them — Neil and Edwards — for a moment just after they had rounded the corner of the penthouse lobby, and he was uncertain as to whether any violence had actually been perpetrated during that short space of time. He assumed not. Neil was breathing a little more heavily than usual, but nothing seemed out of the ordinary. His hair wasn't even mussed.

They came face to face with each other in the lobby, and Neil gave him an idiot's look of fancy meeting. Stanley did not know what exactly to say. Finally, he began to talk. "That was a very strange speech you made in there . . . But they seemed to like it . . . And the reporters were so fascinated I don't think they really cared about your not staying right with the line of the text . . ."

Neil appeared to have something on his mind that he was incapable of putting into words. "You think so?" he said. He smiled enigmatically.

"Yes," Stanley said. He wondered if he should guide Neil back inside or stand there waiting for the next elevator into which the both of them could escape. At that moment, Arthur Fenstemaker appeared. There were some others looking into the lobby, but they seemed hesitant — even the newsmen — about engaging themselves until something or other had been definitely resolved.

The Governor took Neil's arm and turned to Stanley.

"Get inside and hold on to your reporters for as long as you can . . . Try to keep them there until I've had a chance to talk. The roof's caved in but we can get out of this alive and possibly even better off than before . . ."

Andrea's father broke through the crowd and came to them. "God damn good," he kept saying, "goddam good stuff, Neil . . ."

The four of them headed back inside. Stanley moved off toward the press table. It was deserted now, but the reporters would soon be returning if it appeared there would be one final, clarifying revelation. Elsie stood nearby; she came to him and said: "Is he all right? What was all that about, Stanley? Have I got him into trouble? Does this mean my —"

"I think everything's all right," Stanley said, although he was not really convinced of this. He stood watching as Neil and the Governor headed up the middle of the ballroom toward the speakers' table. Fenstemaker looked up sharply at the master of ceremonies, who, after momentary puzzlement, began to applaud wildly: "How 'bout that, ladies and gentlemen, how 'bout that?" Stanley began to applaud, and then Elsie, and fairly soon there was general handclapping and then a roar of approval as the Governor was recognized and the two of them — Neil and the Governor — reached the table.

Neil took his seat, looking down at the empty plates as Fenstemaker babbled into his ear. Then the Governor turned, looked up and smiled: he took the microphone in his hands.

"Here's a man for you — here's a Senator for you!" he said, pointing to Neil. There was tentative applause, but the Governor cut it short. "I appointed him . . . I put him back into office, and I've never had a doubt since that time ten months ago when he took the job that here was a young man of exceptional . . . *ex-*

ceptional ability — and honesty! His speech this afternoon proved that. Here's a young man of unquestioned integrity and principle — and here today you saw he was a good deal more than that! He's a *fighter*. He's got the courage to stand up on his own two feet and say what he thinks and *damn* the consequences. *That* kind of courage stacks up favorably right alongside another kind of bravery demonstrated during the war when . . ."

The sentence went unfinished, lost in applause. They did not know much about the young man, but Fenstemaker had been bearing down hard on the wartime decorations since the day the appointment was announced. That quality had at least got through to them.

"What you saw today, ladies and gentlemen, yes — and you newsmen over there — what you saw was one of the most moving and dramatic human situations you'll ever experience. Here was a man standing up for what he *believes* — ready to fight for his convictions and for his family and friends and for the memory of a splendid young man — his brother — cut down in the prime of life as a member of the *working press* covering the downfall of this hemisphere's evilest totalitarian regime . . ."

There was more applause; this time the Governor let it rise and swell in the big chamber, and when the audience sensed his approval there was another burst overriding the other. Neil was staring at several bright green peas at the bottom of his pastry shell.

". . . And what you've also seen today, my friends, is an end to the kind of vicious, poisonous, witchburning, hate-mongering demagoguery that has *always* characterized the campaigns conducted by Owen Edwards . . . His kind of hatefulness reached a new low today — a new low even for the man who just about *invented* hate — he got so low down in the gutter today he'll *never* get out! I'll tell you folks, and I know you know without my saying, that *that old horse don't run no more* . . . That old dog won't fetch no bones . . . A real man stood up here today and called the turn!"

The Governor poured himself a glass of water and emptied it

in three great, throat-bulging gulps. Neil did not look up. The newsmen scribbled frantically in their notebooks, and the people in the packed ballroom, with more of them arriving every minute, whooped and applauded and stomped their feet. . . . Just the way, Stanley thought, the sons of bitches would have scratched and howled and lusted for the seat of Neil's pants a few years before . . .

"I'll tell you frankly," the Governor said, smiling and touching a handkerchief to his mouth. "I'm glad that fellow came here today — I thank the Good Lord for what happened. It showed you what a real leader, a real fighter you've got for a Senator. And another thing — and for this I'm most thankful — it got us a candidate. Our next *elected* United States Senator! Neil Christiansen wasn't going to run for office, ladies and gentlemen, I'm convinced of that. I'd begged and pleaded with him, but it wasn't until this afternoon that he got mad — he's had enough fighting in the war — mad enough to fight for his friends and the people of the state . . . I don't think he would have sought public office, but now he's in it, and in it all the way, there's no stopping him. Owen Edwards is going to regret with all his heart every word he's said, every minute he spent on this floor today attempting to blacken the name of a decent and honorable young man. Neil Christiansen's in this fight, ladies and gentlemen, and I pity the poor devil who gets in his way now. . . . Stand up Neil! And let these people look at a *real man* . . ."

Now there was a great, animal cry from the crowd. The clapping and stomping and half-moaning reached a pitch of quasi-religious fervor. The roar lasted fully five minutes. Neil stood and looked out at them. Stanley wondered if Neil was sick to his stomach or if the expression on his face was merely the result of a conscious effort to evoke a certain shy, engaging, little-boy quality. He decided Neil was sick. The Governor had not forced him to speak — they could be thankful for that. He hustled his candidate off the platform and out a back exit as the crowd's roar began to subside. Soon there was only sporadic applause and foot-tapping with the organ music, and the delegates — the *crème de la crème*, Stanley noted — stood around and grinned at each other; foolishly and a bit self-consciously. They were the best of people; they might have some uneasy second thoughts about what had happened that afternoon, about what they had heard, first from Neil and then from Edwards, but they could not really ever seriously question the simple, primitive grandeur of those moments when the Governor had them screaming until their throats were dry and pain came to their chests. They would go home now and try to describe those moments to their best-people friends, their employees, their kitchen help. Stanley was staggered by the sudden incredible realization that Neil, for the first time really and truly, was a best-people's candidate. Unless some even better people had serious second thoughts and put up a better-people's candidate from the far-out right. He rather wished they would.

"It's good, isn't it? Hasn't it worked out all right, like you said?"

He looked at Elsie; she smiled up at him. There was a faint glow of perspiration on her face and he was conscious for the first time of his own dry throat and stinging palms. The Governor, he thought, knew where everybody lived.

"Yes it sure is all right," he said to the girl. He looked round at the newsmen: some were writing in notebooks; some were grinning and perspiring; some others simply gaped in awe at the crowd filing out into the lobby. A man carrying a camera hurried toward the press table.

"Downstairs . . ." he said, grinning, showing his poor teeth. ". . . Downstairs . . . In the lobby . . ."

The reporters looked up at him, exhausted, not really wanting to know anything about what was downstairs.

"Old Edwards is holding a news conference . . . Or trying to . . . So far he's just got some photographers and a couple of kids from the college . . ."

"Oh Jesus," somebody groaned.

The reporters got slowly to their feet and headed toward the back elevators.

"Will you do something for me?" Stanley asked the girl.

"Yes . . . What is it?"

"Follow those reporters downstairs and try to get what Edwards says. You have a pencil and paper? Here — just write when you see them writing . . ."

"I can take shorthand. I'm very good at shorthand."

"Fine . . . Take down everything then. I'll meet you in the lobby as soon as I can."

"All right."

Elsie trailed the reporters. He stared after her for a moment, liking the soft shape of her legs, until she had disappeared into the crowd. Then he headed toward the exit into which Neil and the Governor had fled. He had an idea where the Governor had taken them — the hotel management kept a suite reserved for Fenstemaker the year round — and Stanley hurried down the narrow stairs. When he knocked at the entrance, Andrea's father showed his face for a moment, closed and then opened the door. The Governor lay on a couch, a drink in his hand. Neil had his shirt off and a towel slung round his neck. He was pacing up and down and talking aloud, half to himself, partly to the others.

". . . How in the hell . . . How in the goddam hell could I let that jackpine messiah force me into this . . . The last thing I wanted to happen — it *happened*. How come? He picked the time and the place and he *made* me — he practically *owned* me in there. Why'd he do it?"

"He's insane, Neil," the Governor said. He held his amber glass above his head, staring at the ceiling, until an assistant came to retrieve and refill it. "He's psychotic — always has been — it's just that civilization is finally gaining on him . . ."

"He's holding a news conference downstairs," Stanley said.

"Repeating what he said earlier with amplification," the Governor announced, accepting the fresh drink. He pushed himself higher onto the arm of the sofa so that he could get the glass to his lips, although the maneuver was not entirely successful. Some of the liquid dribbled down the corners of his mouth, and he tucked a pocket handkerchief along his collar to stop the flow. "Edwards is just now climbing down out of the trees," he said. "He's way ahead of some of his people, but what he doesn't know is that most of us came into town one Saturday a few years ago and stayed . . . We're urban, by God. All of a sudden the people in the metropolitan areas outnumber the rednecks . . . They come into town — they buy little houses and color television and Volkswagen cars. Edwards is still pitching to the Church of Christers and the pickup truck crowd . . ."

"There's no difference," Neil said. "There's really no difference, though. They'll listen to what he says. Everybody'll listen and they just might by God believe him."

"They would, Neil, they would if he were talking about anybody else but you. But dammit, boy, it's *you* he's saying these things about. Not some quivering intellectual — not some big-nosed, frog-voiced, bucktoothed goon who just stepped off a picket line. Hell! Look at yourself. You're right out of the Coca-Cola ads — the *Saturday Evening Post* covers. You know how long it took for that committee in Washington to convince itself Chambers was telling the truth and Hiss wasn't?"

"No."

"I don't either. But it was goddam long. They couldn't believe Chambers — nobody could — because he wasn't very pretty. And Hiss was gorgeous. A nice Havard type . . ."

"He's right, Neil," Andrea's father said. "The Governor's right — I don't understand half what he says, but he's sure right about that sonofabitch Edwards. Nobody's goin' to believe him."

The old man put a cigarette into a silver holder, then struck a kitchen match on his thumbnail. He wore a two-hundred-dollar suit and there was an antique diamond stickpin in the middle of his handpainted tie. His freckled hands trembled slightly; his red nose was peeling, and he stood there, scratching himself, pulling at his crotch, looking at the others. He had once got himself elected to the Congress — just for the hell of it — until he decided he could send someone in his place to do the job just as well. For many years he had run an empire, a kind of feudal bar-

ony, involving land and cattle and oil wells and sulphur ventures
in Mexico, and if he no longer exercised such vast power it was
simply because he himself had lost interest. He was the last of
them, Neil thought; his contemporaries might resign themselves
to bridge playing and martini parties and bargaining with football coaches, but the old man represented a last thumping flourish
of individualism among them, a reflex, possibly, isolate and exotic: something for the sociologists' exhibit boards.

Neil went into the bathroom, soaked the towel with water and
rubbed his face and neck and shoulders. The Governor was on
the telephone now, on the long distance, talking with editors and
publishers.

". . . I thought you'd enjoy hearing about it, Jake," he was
saying. "It was really something — I'm telling you that boy
grabbed old Edwards by the ass and just trundled him right out
of there like a load of garbage. And Neil — he wasn't mad. He
actually was smiling all the time. He had this hilarious grin on his
face. I mean after all, look what Edwards has been *sayin'* about
him. And today it got down to his family . . . The speech? Well
it wasn't much — it wasn't *supposed* to be, of course. The main
event was Edwards and Neil finally paired off against each other
— and Neil's announcement. He's in it now . . . To hell and
gone . . . It was what you might call a *pretty* speech, a nice sensible speech. It made people think. He talked sense to 'em like
old Adalay. You could play hell out of the whole thing — it's a
natural . . . I *know* it's Saturday afternoon. What've you done
— joined your own damn printers union? Just get your man on
the phone and make sure they get the story right, that's all. Don't
let 'em put those goddam lies of Edwards' up at the top . . . You
don't have some quotes I'll get my man to call you and *give* you
some quotes . . . Don't worry, he's got it all down. We've got it
on tape . . ."

Stanley moved next to the Governor's assistant. They were
about the same age: never really good friends but always aware of
each other all through college. The assistant was named Jay Mc-

Gown. He had a movie star wife, or rather a wife who had left him and subsequently become a movie star. There were some few friends who felt he might ultimately have become Governor himself in ten or fifteen years — if the wife had not outmanned him. He was a quiet and occasionally morose fellow and Stanley regarded him as rather a bore.

"You taped all this?" Stanley said to him.

"Ummn," McGown said. "If we did I wasn't aware of it. He'll have me inventing quotes — re-creating the whole damn scene — if one of those birds asks for it. Jesus, I hope not . . . It *is* Saturday afternoon, and I was up till three this morning."

"Doing what? A party?"

"Yeah, a party. Right up there in that red granite monstrosity. He had me writing editorials. Endorsements. Every kind you can imagine. Conservatives endorsing him, liberals endorsing him, old hard-nosed columnists endorsing him, weekly newspapers, big dailies, free traders, protectionists, segregationists . . . You name it — we've got a pitch already prepared."

"For whom," Stanley said. "Editorials for whom?"

"*Neil.*"

"But this was last night? Early this morning? He didn't even *announce* till half an hour ago."

"The Governor seemed pretty sure of it. I thought they'd probably talked privately and decided on today. That is, if Edwards showed up. It was never really certain whether he would . . ."

"You mean he *expected* Edwards to show?"

"Well, hell . . . *I* don't know. I *think* he did. Who the hell knows what goes through their heads? The Governor keeps his own council."

"But —"

"Jay — you and Stanley come here." The Governor had finished one call and was waiting for the sequence operator to ring back with another. Andrea's father mixed himself a bourbon on ice. Neil reappeared, buttoning his shirt collar.

"Jay — you get the limousine and take Stanley over to the

Secretary's office. They're waiting for you over there. You can park outside the Capitol while Stanley runs in and hands over the filing fee. That'll make it official — they've got the forms all filled out and waiting . . . How much is that check, Neil?"

"Five thousand."

"Write another — you only need fifteen hundred. And I doubt if they have change." The Governor made a cackling sound, choked on his drink and swore to himself, gasping and laughing between breaths.

"I don't have that much money," Neil said.

"What?"

"I can't write a check . . . I don't have fifteen hundred in my account."

"I'll write you one, then," the Governor said. "I'll write you two or three if you want it. I collected a whole piss-pot of cash for you this morning."

"I'll write it, I'll write it," Andrea's father said. He already had his gold fountain pen out and was scribbling on a book of checks. He tore one out and handed it over to Neil.

"Here," Neil said, accepting the one from his father-in-law and offering the other in exchange.

"No . . . No. No. Keep it. Keep it." The old man backed off, waving his arms as if battling insects.

"But I can't *accept* this. You've already given me this one check. I can't take any more . . ."

"Put it in your account," the old man said. He drained off his bourbon and poured another. "So you'll have some. I heard you was overdrawn."

"Where did you hear that? Did Andrea . . . It's all taken care of now and —"

"Christ almighty, Neil . . . I've owned that bank twenty-five years. Didn't you know that?"

"No . . . I didn't . . . And I may just change banks."

"And I got controlling interest in two of the others. You might have a hard time picking the *one* out of *three* I *don't* have any-thing to do with . . . And if you happened to pick that one, I just might buy into it . . . I set the bastards up in business just after the war. Hell! I'm interested in your goddam welfare!"

The Governor was on the phone again. He put a hand over the mouthpiece and motioned at the two younger men. The old man handed over the check, like a headwaiter about to deliver the big surprise. Stanley and Jay McGown headed out the door.

". . . Listen, Howard," the Governor was saying into the telephone, "get up off your ass and do a little work. Have I ever laid down on you? Hell no! This is just a matter of putting a little fire under your own boys. I've got some editorials coming to you Monday, in addition, and . . ."

In the hallway, waiting for the elevator, Stanley said: "I'm supposed to meet a girl downstairs. She's taking notes on what Edwards says."

"We've got a man down there, too." McGown thought a moment. "Listen — do you have to came back up here for anything?"

"Not that I know of. I'm supposed to meet Neil later tonight."

"Well listen — I'll take that thing by the Capitol if you like. And then I can call from there and tell the Man you've gone on home and mission's accomplished and all that crap, and maybe I can get out from under. I mean if I have to come back up here, I'll never get loose. And I won't have to come back up if you don't . . . Understand? This other way, I've got half a chance . . . At least I can get a nap on the couch until the Governor decides something. . . . Okay?"

"Fine."

They rode in silence on the elevator. In the lobby, Stanley waved goodbye but then turned and caught up with McGown.

"Listen . . . What you were saying about Edwards . . ."

"Forget it . . . I've got to run, really . . . I'll talk to you later. I was just popping off — that's all . . . I don't really know."

McGown waved and moved through the swinging doors. Stanley wandered through the lobby, looking for the crowd gathered round Edwards. Elsie appeared from behind.

"Hello," she said. "It's all over."

"What'd he say?"

"The same thing all over again, except a little more. Most fantastic feeling — he was standing there talking about *me*, and I was right next to him taking notes and he didn't know who I was and I kept interrupting and correcting him. He made some mistakes, you see. About my birthplace and my religion and my father's family. Finally, he got impatient and wanted to know how I knew so much and what paper I represented. I said I represented myself and had rather a unique interest in what he was saying. When I told him who I was, all the reporters suddenly wanted to interview *me* and just lost interest in Edwards. Just left him! We all went into the coffee shop and talked."

Stanley stood in the lobby, grinning at her. "Well what finally happened to Edwards?"

"Nothing. That I know about. He started to follow us into the coffee shop but then apparently changed his mind. He just turned around and walked away . . . Is that all right? My notes aren't very good, because I kept listening to what he was saying about me instead of writing. But he didn't really get very far. You think it's all right?"

"It sounds wonderful," Stanley said. He had her by the arm and they were moving through the lobby toward the street. "Would you like a drink?" he said. "My hotel's just across the way, and I've got a bottle. Or there's a private club if you'd prefer that. But we'd probably run into Edwards and some of those reporters. He's probably waiting for them, hoping to buy a round."

"I ought to go home," the girl said, smiling, looking at him with wonderful dark eyes. "Where is Neil? How is he?"

"Up with the Governor . . . What are you doing tonight? Would you be interested in a party? We're going to one — or rather I'm supposed to meet Neil at one. He's supposed to meet Andrea there. We're all meeting — everyone's meeting. You want to come with me and meet everyone."

The girl thought a moment. "What kind of party? I have nothing to wear. Really, I have no —"

"It's not important. In fact you'll be sensational. Wear flat heels and a plain blouse — maybe a man's shirt. They'll like that — this bunch . . . How about it?"

"All right . . ."

Stanley had a rented car parked just outside. There were newsboys hooting the noon edition fictions. Another picture of Neil was on the front page, and they stopped to look. But the stories were those written at eleven that morning — the ones based on the advance text. There was nothing about what happened at the luncheon and only a few lines from the speech Neil had actually delivered.

The Saturday afternoon traffic was thinning, and they stood for a moment watching all the bland faces, all the same people. They were becoming all of a type: the ten-dollar straws with the Old School striped bands, the silk suits and the gray mesh oxfords and the batiste button-downs, the women in empire waist or middy blouse or garish orange print dresses. It would all soon be as jaded and predictable and tedious as all the rest, with only a slight aberration in manner or dress dividing them from, say, Sauk City, Minnesota. Stanley thought about the old man in the hotel room with his diamond stickpin and kitchen matches and Neil trying to hold on to something, overwhelmingly assaulted by the images created for him. He looked at the faces once again as he held the car door for the girl. His own father would have astonished everyone for blocks around with his crazy beard.

Thirteen

"I DON'T like it," Neil said.

"The hell with what you like," the Governor said. "You do what you have to do."

"I don't like it." He continued to pace about the room; he had begun to perspire again. The Governor was going after something inside his ear with the end of a matchstick jacketed in Kleenex. The old man, Andrea's father, had drunk bourbon steadily until falling to sleep in one of the bedrooms.

"Christ almighty," the Governor said, "what in hell is this faint-of-heart business? What do you want? Free the slaves? End the cold war? Institute land reforms?"

"No, no, no . . ."

"You do what you *have* to do, Neil. I shouldn't have to tell you that. You make the best of a not-so-bad bargain. Give a little, take a little . . . The first principle is that you've got to learn to rise above principle."

"But it's too much. Fifty thousand dollars — it's just —"

"You'll need twice that much before this campaign's over."

". . . It's just too much. From the wrong people. I don't even know them."

"All the better. You realize I collected it this morning — and you weren't even around? Skipped out on me . . . I'm beginning to believe I could invent you — just tell the people there was such a thing as Neil Christiansen. And win it all by myself!"

"Not a bad idea," Neil said.

"Look — you want to stay here the next two months and be saddled with a statewide campaign? It's a big state. Runnin' your skinny behind off, making eight, ten speeches a day?"

"No."

"Then you do it on the television. You go back to Washington and work at your job and let yourself be seen on television a few times a week. The TV and the ads and the newspaper support and my own little old organization I'm turning over to you . . ."

"I wasn't even sure I wanted to get into this . . . Hadn't even made up my mind . . ."

". . . Do everything for you. *Everything.* You just show your face occasionally — and collect all the gravy. And don't let it dribble down your shirt front . . . You want to do good? Hey — you want to do good?"

"I want to do goody-good," Neil said, "I really do." He looked at the Governor, unsmiling.

"Well you *can,* don't you understand? Don't you understand that? All you ever wanted to do. Six years . . . Six gorgeous years — I wish I had that much ahead of me. You know what that means? To get elected to the Senate at your age? You're in forever if you got any sense at all and don't rape a nun or something. You're in there for as long as you want and you end up a committee chairman or a vice-presidential candidate and Lord knows whut-all. *You've* got a future . . . I don't know what the hell I've got . . ."

"I understand . . . I appreciate that. But . . . *fifty thousand dollars* — are you serious? Is it that much?"

"That's what they pledged. And they don't ordinarily go back on their word."

"What do they *want?*"

"Who the hell knows? Everything! The goddam moon. That's not your concern."

"The hell it isn't. I'm —"

"You're job is to get elected and stay elected. That's the first consideration. When that's assured, you get good enough, mean enough, you learn enough to fend off the bill collectors. They come around wanting the moon you give 'em green cheese and make 'em think that was what they were lookin' for all the time. *That's* what you do. That's what a professional *has* to do."

"Give it back to them," Neil said, staring out a window toward the hideous rooftops of tall buildings and the green hills beyond.

"The hell I will. I'd keep it myself before I'd give it back. And I haven't even got it yet."

"Fine. Tell 'em to forget it. We'll get by without —"

"*Forget* it? Are you out of your mind? Do you have any *idea* — I know you must because you worked in my campaign . . . you've worked in enough campaigns to know . . ."

"What?"

"What a telecast over the state costs."

"Eight thousand."

"About ten. And radio's half of that. And newspaper ads! And salaries for campaign personnel. *You know.* How can you —"

"All right, all right. But I don't like it."

"Like I said — the hell with what you like. That's a luxury for people elected to office for six year terms. Indulge yourself some other time . . ."

Andrea's father wandered out into the main room. Thin strands of gray hair fell over his face. He had lost a shoe somewhere; his garters were loose and trailed his feet, dragging the carpet.

"What time is it?" he said.

"After five," the Governor said. "Going on six."

"You about finished, Neil?"

"Yes." He looked at Fenstemaker. "I've got to go."

"Sure . . . But remember what I said. Quit behaving like you're having a monthly or something. Take a pill. Feel better tomorrow. *I* get down. God knows I get right down on the basement floor and want to cry and throw a bomb at the next Creeping Jesus who walks into my office with a long face and a longer hand out. But I get over it. It's a little song and dance I go through when somebody plays the secret music. Zip up your fly and go home and think about these things."

The Governor got to his feet and walked slowly into his bedroom. They could hear him in there, on the telephone again.

"Yes . . . Yes . . . Allright, all right, you can knock off. Go get
tight . . . Go get yourself laid . . . Tell Sweet Mama I'll be
late . . . What? I'm taking a nap, that's what . . . And have
someone send a car around and ring me around seven . . ."

Neil and the old man got their coats and headed out of the
suite. The late afternoon papers had arrived and Neil carried the
front sections with him. There were small pictures of Neil speaking and Edwards in his arms akimbo stance, and a larger one of
them slipping sideways on the marble floor of the ballroom lobby.
The caption read GREAT DEBATE — ROUND ONE, although the
story was all in Neil's favor. He could tell himself, struggling
with the emotions of uneasy objectivity and crippled pride, that
whatever advantage achieved was the result of Arthur Fenstemaker's speech to the crowd. There was a brief description of the
scuffling match and the heated words leading up to it, followed
by a lengthy report on all the tributes paid to Neil by the Governor. This carried over into another column on the inside pages,
with more description of Edwards' quick and unceremonious departure. In the last five paragraphs an attempt was made to sum-
marize Neil's luncheon speech, but the quotations were all out of
context and nearly incoherent, and he wondered if there had
ever really been anything to what he had said.

The old man chewed a stick of gum, a precaution, he said,
against whiskey breath, and they moved through the Saturday
evening traffic toward the hills. Neil drove the car, and between
them sat two enormous stuffed rabbits the old man had brought
with him on the plane. The girls spotted them immediately from
the front steps and ran squealing and gasping with delight toward
the open car door. "Grandpa!" they hooted . . . "Easter rab-
buts! . . ."

They stood struggling with the weird animals in the twilight,
attempting to get them pulled inside the house without dragging
bottoms, arguing over colors and rabbit whiskers ("Rabbits have
whiskers?") and the extraordinary length of the ears. Andrea
met them at the door. She was dressed to go out; in the crazy

grandeur of the moment, with the porch lamp on her sweet face and the children screaming and stumbling over one another and whooping instructions at their grandfather, she seemed to embrace and give meaning to all the pretty pictures in his head of what it was he really wanted and how life ought to be. They stood looking at each other with the screen door half open and the girls dancing round them, the old man wheezing and trying to tell a story from his youth about Easter egg rolls on the courthouse lawn of some wornout and forgotten country town.

"I was going out," she finally said. "Cocktails — it's already started — and then dinner downtown and some kind of drinking party afterwards. Can you come with me?"

"Could it . . . be . . . later? I'm just God-awful tired . . . and . . ."

"I heard you announced?" she said. "On the radio. Was it in your speech? I didn't know."

"I didn't either . . . It just happened."

"It was wonderful, Andy. It was the damndest thing I ever . . ." The old man hesitated. The two little girls were tugging on his trousers, embracing his legs. He staggered back for a moment and hoisted each child in his arms.

"Hey, Grandpa!" the youngest one yelled into his ear. "Whoo-dya love?"

"Who do I *love?* Why I love . . ."

Andrea still stared at Neil; her face had gone all soft and inexplicably receptive; she managed a slight smile.

"Whoodja love?" she said suddenly. There was a flash of white teeth and then the smile was gone again, and in a moment she looked on the verge of tears.

His response was nearly automatic, so much that he anticipated the remark and reviled his own contemptuous soul before he had even got the words past his lips.

"The Easter Bunny," he said.

She turned immediately toward her father and explained to him that she was going out for the evening. "S'all right," the old man said, giving all his attention to the girls. He had long since reached a stage of resignation in which the cruel, irrational possibilities of children grown old were accepted as one might get used to brutality in all of life. Now he cared most — and almost only — for his grandchildren.

"I'll try to meet you later," Neil said.

"All right."

Their hands touched and clasped for an instant as she passed and headed toward her car. The instant was unendurable, inexpressible: blessedness and despair, early sorrow and old love and half-forgotten crimes. It was as if each had returned a scarlet nub . . .

After a moment, they all moved inside. Dinner was on the table, and the four of them along with Emma sat for a time and discussed how it was with carrots and broccoli and pot roast and pineapple upside down cake.

"*Up*side *down* cake," the younger one sang.

"But you've got to eat it right side up," the old man said.

The girls sat in their high stools, hugging the extraordinary rabbits, talking incessantly. Neil excused himself and wandered up the stairs to sleep. In the last moments of consciousness he felt he might have glimpsed a sudden truth, a revelation, some forgotten insight from his youth — the best in one and the worst in one, good money after bad, dereliction and desire . . . a harbor in morality . . . an inhuman social order . . . a meek inheritance, the meek inheriting, a general impatience with dullness . . . an unfathomable love for the Easter bunny. He formed the words on his lips . . . Love was not the natural condition of man; neither was decency . . . They were inventions, illusion; and what was needed was not so much cerebration or good intentions as convincing stage props . . . These veiled reflections must have meant something to him as sleep descended, but when he came awake later they seemed insubstantial as shadow, as Cherubim thread . . . ice crystals gone to moisture in the light of day.

Fourteen

IT WAS NOT a very good sleep. Or rather it was more the sleep of
the standing-up, the ostensibly awake, a kind of mesmerized sus-
pension between life and death, perilous and oddly stimulating.

He was aware all the time of the children's voices downstairs
and Emma clearing the table and the old man herding the girls
upstairs to bath and bed. But he was asleep all the same, and he
could not really comprehend what was going on around him. He
wanted desperately for just a moment to pull himself from the
bed and go and give himself over completely, unequivocally, to
the children. What had he ever given them? When had he ever
really made the effort? He could not recall a time. The giving
required a taking, and during those rare moments when he attempted to offer up some little piece of himself, he had never managed to get the girls to understand what it was they were supposed to be *accepting*. He wanted more than anything to make
some gesture, shape some memorable event, invest, just once,
enough of himself and his resources so that the moment might
come back to the children twenty years from now, magically
vivid and graceful and full of meaning.

But he remained on the bed, perspiring a little through the
clothes he had worn all day, asleep and wanting always to rise and
say something, make a speech or paint a picture, knowing without
asking that his tongue was thick and cobwebby and that the
blunt ends of his fingers were dipped in brine.

Soon the house grew quiet with the last giggles of the children
and the old man's wheezing sleep-sounds. He looked at his watch
and finally got himself from bed and began to wash. It was
only nine-thirty when he left the house, and he reached the place

of the party — now wildly and unpredictably underway — a little before ten.

It was a huge, spanishy house, nearly authentic, a restored farm outbuilding around which the city had grown many years before. It resembled one of the original missions a hundred miles farther south, but this quality must have been bogus — a success only for the renovators — for its history was just barely pre-Civil War and the earliest recorded occupants were German agrarian types. Enough of the farmland had been retained to give the place enormous grounds, front and back, freckled with small well-kept shrubs and shaded by huge pecan and flowering magnolia trees. There were cars parked up and down the street, on either side, and half a dozen of them, new and shining, clogged the main drive. Midway across the lawn he paused and looked back, sinking deep into the carpet grass. The cars were like people, or rather they reflected the tastes of the people inside: extremes of one kind or another. There were Alfas and Porsches and a single Carman-Ghia parked next to convertibles and Jeepsters and a couple of twelve-year-old Cadillacs. Even those bent on unpretentiousness seemed to have gone a little too far. The newer, conventional models were as spare and frugal and chromeless as might be found in a Government motor pool, and there were many machines that would be normally out-of-use, beat up and fading, windows splintered, fenders sagging, all of them in a stage of advanced and altogether chic decay, most of them driven by those young people who could put their incomes, earned or inherited, at five or six figures.

There was an awful din coming from inside, and through the windows he could see the crazy circus-shapes of people drunk and dancing, singly and in pairs, talking, gesturing, moving from room to room, peering at bookshelves and record albums and into each other's faces, poking at themselves and dancing partners, pouring whiskey. There seemed to be a great pouring of whiskey, in fact; nearly everywhere he looked through the window glass there was someone with a bottle and a paper cup, even a stunning girl, drinks in each hand, deep in exotic, hip-grinding meditation within a hula hoop. He stood staring at the girl for a moment, from the shadows, until footsteps sounded on the graveled drive and a younger man moved past and paused, struggling with a huge bag of ice.

"Hey! Hey, Neil! Good to see you . . . Come on in."

He grinned and stood aside while Neil opened the door for him. Then they were inside and it was oddly terrifying at first, like walking too close to a locomotive when he was young.

All the noise of which he had been conscious from the outside now seemed only a faint signal from a shrouded wood. Now it came to him in full force, in all its clattering, strident, bass-drum and leper's bell fidelity. But unlike the experience with the locomotive when he was young, there was no sudden impulse to run or stand away. He paused at the door only a moment and then plunged, unaccountably happy, into the chasm of writhing figures.

They were his friends, another kind of *crème de la crème,* the best of another order, and he had spent nearly all of his last ten years in their company, or the nucleus of their company: young people from his first years in the Legislature and the inevitable artist-types Andrea and John Tom had attracted, an irreducible blending of the two worlds, the best of the worlds — a hundred dime store Czars and Michelangelos.

The hosts veered toward him from several directions. There were four of them, all of a type and long-time friends. He had been with them since college, and they had entered the Legislature at nearly the same time. Three of them were wealthy or comfortably well off, the offspring of villainous oil families in the South and West. The fourth had poor-boyed his way to relative security as a full professor at the college. They had been living in the old house for years, scarcely changing in the passage of time, the moneyed three continuing to contribute their share of the rent even when they were campaigning in their districts or making periodic, not to say routine, voyages to other lands. Together, the four of them (with Neil now missing from their numbers) had once represented roughly one quarter of the hard-core Liberal strength in a legislative Lower House that operated with a membership of close to three hundred.

They greeted him, all hands extended; they stood around, remarking with a good deal of enthusiasm about the events of the afternoon, slapping him on the back and shaking his hand for an interminable period of time. They exchanged equally coarse views on Owen Edwards. The story had been spread in the evening papers and by radio and word of mouth, some of it garbled and distorted, and Neil now proceeded as quickly as possible to put straight his part in the whole business of the luncheon. Fairly soon a crowd had gathered round and he began to feel stuffy and a little bored with himself.

"No, hell no . . . I *didn't* flatten him *or* his nose. Our suits weren't even rumpled. I just grabbed him on the behind — and I shouldn't have — and shoved him out of the ballroom and into an elevator . . . Hey, where's Andrea?"

"Not here yet. What'd he do? What'd he say?"

"Nothing . . . Meek as a . . . Where is she?"

"Who?"

"Andrea."

"Not here yet. Bunch of them got started late for dinner. Say —"

"Where can I get a drink? I don't want to talk about this stuff. I want a drink. And move around and look at people. There was a girl with a hula . . ."

He got through the crowd and poured a drink for himself in the pine-walled kitchen. It was real pine; you could smell it. Two students, a boy and a girl who looked to him like high schoolers, stared and smiled and then moved into another room, singing a song from an old *New Faces* album someone had played for them that evening for the first time. They seemed very young; no one ought to be that young, he thought. And no one ought to grow any older — none of them. The parties in this ancient, creaking house would go on endlessly, as they had for ten years now, the young faces appearing from weekend to weekend, passing in the dim light and vanishing into somebody else's old age.

Not theirs. God knows not his. They had all reached mankind's natural condition: long in the tooth and innocent in the head, poised on the brink, falling but never quite fallen into wisdom and decay.

He swallowed half his drink and added more water and whiskey. A girl of about twenty-five came toward him with a guitar slung round her neck. "I want one of these," she said. She was very tall with a nice figure and a tall girl's slump. Or perhaps it was the guitar pulling her shoulders down. She gave him a depraved look.

He searched for a glass or a paper cup in the shelves above the double sink. The floor was wet from the ice sack, and after he had served the girl he stepped outside and found an old washtub. He got the thing in both hands, and when he turned he saw that the girl had followed him. She stood on the back steps, staring moodily round the yard. Then, without warning, she strummed some flattish chords on the guitar and began to sing.

"Sandpiper, housewren, cock of the walk, where do you fly when the Lady Bird calls? Feathers and foodstuffs, mountains of chalk, through bosky dells and evergreen malls . . . Ca-ree . . . ca-raaw, ca-ree . . . ca-raaah, out in the glen, jiggers of gin . . ."

She groaned on insensibly, moving the guitar from side to side in a sawing motion. None of it was comprehensible to him. He thought about the words "jiggers of gin" and "out in the glen." Was that what she had sung? He would never be sure. He stood a few feet away from her with the washtub in his arms, wondering what in the world to say.

When it was ended, finally, the girl seemed to unhinge herself; her eyes came back into focus and she looked at him as if examining a questionable piece of merchandise.

"Very nice . . . Very pretty," he said. "Where is it from? The song."

"I wrote it," she said. "I've composed many folk songs."

"Oh . . . you *write* folk music . . . Compose, I mean. *Well.* That . . . must . . . be . . . "

"They're poems in the beginning . . . I write them as poems and then a suitable melody . . ."

"*Very* nice. Lovely . . ." he managed to say. "Shall we go back inside?" He held the door for her. She shrugged and moved past him, swinging perilously close to his vitals with the guitar, striding on into the pine kitchen and out of it. He stepped inside and hoisted the sack of ice into the tub. Then he took his glass and went into the front rooms.

"I try to get through the day saying as little as possible. So far I've managed with two expressions — 'Scotch and soda, please' and 'How gross' . . ."

"There are some other expressions he uses," Neil said, "but they're almost always inappropriate for mixed company."

Stanley and the girl from the bookstore looked up at him. They were sitting alone together on a couch. A phonograph across the room was at nearly full volume, and the three of them had to bend down toward each other to talk.

"What did you say?" Stanley asked.

"We saw you come in," Elsie said, "but there was such a crowd around we couldn't get through."

They moved over for him. He sat next to the girl, with Stanley on the other side. Conversation was virtually impossible for a few moments against the record music, but someone pressed the rejector button and soft voices of Mariachi singers filled the room. They sat quietly and watched the couples dancing.

"These parties haven't changed any," Stanley said.

"Not a bit."

"I mean *really*. Not just *these* parties — but all of them. I used to sit and watch the ones my parents gave back . . . well . . . way the hell back. No difference. Everyone's still exceedingly clever . . ."

"As opposed to being profound?" the girl said.

"I don't think I've ever known any profound people," Stanley said.

"To be opposed to, he means," Neil said.

"You think everything is imitative?"

"No . . . But the *form's* the same. Not the manner or the spirit exactly. There was the kind of queasy sentimentality that characterized so many things in the thirties and wartime forties — all the enlightened and supposedly significant work in art, politics, the theater — a kind of patriotic, prayer-meeting fervor combined with a men's room snigger. That stuff was pretty bad — look back and it seems *awful,* as garish and obvious as women's shoulder pads, double-breasted suits and collars that didn't button down. But who's to say whether it's really any different — or any worse — than this ersatz sophistication and existentialist gloom it's been supplanted by?"

"Very nice, Stanley. We'll put it in a speech."

"I don't understand any of it," Elsie said.

Stanley looked at the girl. "It's because you don't know the passwords, the catch-phrases. That's what I mean. Those *wise-cracks* are different, but I don't know about the substance. We're still wandering around ready to laugh or cry before a sentence is half out of somebody's mouth . . ."

He turned his attention to Neil. "What about the campaign? What's the plan?"

"We'll just use the wisecracks, the old jokes," Neil said. "The same ones — only on the television. We could do it in our sleep. No sweat . . . No sweat at all. Don't even tax your brain. Big Daddy's goin' to handle everything. He's already rung for the butler."

Stanley was silent for a moment and then said: "I heard something this afternoon I meant to tell you . . ."

Neil was on his feet. "In a minute. I've run out of whiskey. Can I treat the two of you?"

They shook their heads. The girl was uncommonly beautiful. Her hair hung down along her shoulders, dark and undistinguished except for an altogether exciting quarter-piece of earlobe which shone through on one side, milk-white and sculptured looking. She gazed directly at him, and for a moment he was certain of a promise, for whatever advantage he might wish to take of it, but then he could see that Stanley himself was entirely wrapped up in the girl. It would explain his long, compulsive discourse a few minutes earlier, all of it gone for nothing against the girl's uncomprehending gaze. Nobody was getting through; it was that business all over again: thick-tongued and ill-equipped; what they needed was an English-English dictionary. How, then, had he himself got through to the girl on at least one level? Elementary. Elemental. The basic gland persevered. He turned away and went for another drink.

One of the four householders, the professor at the college, was talking on the telephone. He had just set the receiver down as Neil walked by. He turned and said: "That was Andrea."

"What did she say?"

"Well not anything, really. I mean it was Andrea's party. They're just finishing dinner — should be here shortly, half hour at the outside."

He walked into the pine-walled kitchen and made a fresh drink. He was conscious of strange sounds from the backyard, and he bent over the sink and peered through a small window out into the darkness. In a few seconds the moon was clear of the small clouds that had been covering it and the grounds were suddenly bathed in purples of many shadings. The sound persisted — a low, sustained moan, of no particular distinction or emotion, followed by clipped, elegant, high-pitched chants suggesting an absurd and deeply suffering Noel Coward. Then there were those familiar guitar chords and he could see the girl standing beneath a half caved-in grape arbor. There was someone beside her, or rather moving about in the shadows in back of her, and after the two of them had taken several staggering steps in one direction and then another, finally emerging from the cover of the arbor, he could see she was standing with her back to a young man, who was reaching round her from behind, pushing his face up against the nape of her neck and fumbling with the impedimenta of beads and guitar in front. There was a long silence, interrupted by several dull, unintended thonks on the guitar strings, and then a longer silence as the two nuzzled each other in that oddly torturous back-to-stomach embrace.

"Hey Neil — the party's in here, man."

"Hey, Kermit . . ."

"What the hell's out that window?"

"The moon," Neil said. "The grounds are all mauvy-looking.
Pastels . . ."

"Lemmie take a look . . ."

Kermit moved up behind him and peered out into the gloom.

"It's all black, man. You're way out with that mauvy stuff. I
know colors — I've taken up painting this year — and that stuff's
just a buggy black. Black as a Republican's heart. A gypsy's arm-
pit. You like that? *Black,* man."

"Ah, Kermit . . ."

"Ah, yourself . . . For God's sake don't disap*prove,* Senator.
How the hell you been?"

"Fine, Kermit. How about you? You've taken up painting?"

"That's *it* — that's *it.* Yeah. I'm even goin' into the business.
Opening me a little place next week in back of my mother's flor-
ist shop. The Renaissance Gallery . . . The goddam *Renaissance*
Gallery!"

"You don't mean it? What got you onto it?"

"The gallery or the painting?"

"Both. What happened to your books?"

"Gone. Kaput. *Fini* . . . Hell and gone. It was all out of
me — all I had to say in that particular sullen art. Burned 'em.
Every one."

"You don't say? Hell . . . You shouldn't of —"

"Every damned one of 'em. Had to find me a new medium . . .
Spread it around a little . . . That's the way it is with us Good
Doctors. You still my Good Doctor, Neil?"

"I suppose that's for you to decide, Kermit. You're the only
judge of Good Doctors. It takes an honest-to-God genuine P-H-D
to go around conferring honorary doctors of philosophy on people."

"You've got that down, damn sure have. But he's got to be the *right kind,* even if he *is* genuine. Like the P-H-D doesn't really mean a hell of a lot if a cat doesn't *believe* in it. He's got to have that vision. Dig? There's a lot of 'em out there at the college — Doctor This and Doctor That — but I don't know but one or two that's really got the vision. Taking it serious. There aren't really many *Good* Doctors . . . You dig?"

"I think so," Neil said.

"Hey — here's a Good one right here . . ." Kermit grabbed the arm of one of the four householders.

"Kermit . . . Kermit. You conferrin' Good Doctor degrees tonight?"

Kermit's eyes blazed. His hair was clipped short, unevenly. The truth was, he cut his own, and the top of his head suggested a poorly tended lawn, weedy and spotted with crab grass. Although he maintained that the actor Kirk Douglas had ruined Van Gogh for him, he had, all the same, recently grown a scraggly red beard that somehow gave him the look of the movie counterpart, or a trifle more down-at-the heels version. Kermit had recorded the highest grades in the history of the college — had taught school for two or three years before entering into his decline, when he had finally got his vision.

"This Doctor, this Good Doctor," Kermit said, "let me tell you what he did the other day up there in that House of Repscallions."

"What was that?" Neil said.

"Yeah — what the hell was it?" the object of Kermit's attention wanted to know.

"The cats — I mean the fat ones not the swingin' kind — those cats up there were tryin' to pass a bill doubling the tuition at the state-supported schools. Dig? Rather than pass a legitimate tax bill on all the robber-barons so there would be more than enough money to go around — money enough to help those deaf and dumb kids and build hospitals instead of football stadiums and take the niggers out of the shit house and maybe even *end the Cold War* for all I know — rather than do that they were just doublin' tuition at the college. Dig? Well they had the votes. Like always. But you know what this Good Doctor did? He stands up on the floor of our House of Reps, grabs that snortin' pole and offers an *amendment. At the top of his voice!* Ah he was hot, this Good Doctor of mine. He says as long as this lousy bill is going to pass anyhow and since those bums had the votes to double the stinkin' tuition on *something,* why not leave it like it is for most kids but double it for the fratty types. He stands up there and talks about how it was when he was *president* of his own goddam *fraternity* at school — years ago . . . when he was *president* for Chrissake — and how they'd partied all night long, every night, and boozed it up and generally crapped around in a waste of shame. I mean he was tremendous, Neil. It was a *stroke,* a regular *coop,* a genuine-by-God Good Doctor masterpiece!"

"The amendment didn't carry," the young man said, grinning at Neil.

"But you *tried,* man. You stood up there and gave yourself hell . . ."

"What was the vote?" Neil said.

"I dunno. I think we got about twenty."

"How about the bill itself?"

"Same."

"Well, if I'd been around you'd've had twenty-one . . ."

"More than that," the young man said. *"Hell!* A lot more than that. We had some spark when you were there, Neil, workin' that floor, rockin' those bastards back on their ass-behinds. You were always getting us votes — from just out of nowhere. We had some leadership then. Now . . . we're just floppin' around, aimless."

"Tell him about the used car deal," Kermit said. "You weren't aimless then. Hell no."

"It was actually Kermit's idea," the young man said.

"No it wasn't. No it wasn't."

"Yes it was."

"Well you gates did all the work."

"Anyhow, there was this bill pending that was backed up like a sledgehammer by the *new* car dealers. Practically all the gold in Fort Knox behind it. The new car boys were unhappy about the used car boys. A couple of special interests, but the junkies were way outclassed, and it was a really awful bill. It would've stopped car sales on Sunday. You know. *Religion* and all that. And it was going to *pass* for God's sake. Can you imagine? So Kermit gets this idea. He calls me over and says how about amending the thing to exempt Buddhists. Kermit's been practicing Zen and he says he might want to start selling used cars on Sundays and why the hell should he have to observe somebody else's religious holiday? So I put it up and argued and my God it passed! So then some of the others pitched in with amendments exempting Seventh-Day Adventists and Jews and Mohammedans and some oddball sects, and fairly soon the sponsors got the idea. They could just *visualize* all those sharpie used car dealers — all those Rasputins — claiming they were big on Zen or Shinto converts and getting away with it. So they withdrew the bill . . ."

"It all sounds enchanting," Neil said. "I think I'll come back."

"I wish you would. Don't you see? We can block a few things — stop a murder in the streets sometime; blow the whistle on a crime about to be perpetrated in broad daylight, but we're not really *doing* anything. Just throwing spitballs."

"I'll see you Good Doctors." Kermit had freshened his drink and was turning to leave, tugging at his baggy corduroys.

"Where you going?"

"I just saw an absolutely angelic knocked-up woman in there. You know how I am about *them,* man. I dig. I dig all of 'em. The more knocked-up the better. Love 'em every one. Their figures get lovely and they just *glow,* goddammit . . . See you later . . ."

Kermit turned and headed into the other room. They watched him move into the crowd, his dirty cotton sweatshirt, the red beard, blending garishly with his conventional betters.

"I ought to get back, myself," Neil said.

"Hey — do you know Porter?"

"Who?"

"Porter Hardy. The laboring man."

"I've met him once or twice. Isn't he a new one?"

"Yes. He doesn't have any official title. I don't think he **was** ever even a business agent. Jumped right out of college into **labor** politics. He's a kind of pamphleteer — without portfolio — **a** sort of junior grade Mahatma for the pipefitters . . ."

"Ummn."

"He's here. He wants to talk to you."

"What about?"

"I don't know. The usual, I guess. Come on . . ."

They moved through the other rooms of the house. He caught a glimpse of Stanley and Elsie, still firmly planted on the couch, but he could not get their attention as he passed. They wandered through the crowd, past dancing couples and three young men, eyes floating into their foreheads, bending over bongo drums; past the girl with the hula hoop and a man grinning apishly and making Polaroid pictures and Kermit pushing up next to a very pretty and slightly disturbed-looking girl who was enormously pregnant. They found Porter Hardy in one of the bedrooms where the crowd had begun to thin. He was sitting on the edge of a studio couch talking with a nice-looking woman of about the age of all of them. Hardy, aware of their presence, succeeded nonetheless in completing what he was saying to the woman . . .

"Would you do that? Would you do that for me? They are, after all, public records, and I just want to take a look at them overnight."

"I might," the woman said. "I'll think about it."

She looked up at them and began to rise. "Excuse me," she said. She walked across the room, knocked lightly on the door to the bath, and moved on inside.

"Well!" said Hardy, getting to his feet. "Hello, Senator . . ."

They shook hands. Their host departed almost immediately.

"I won't take much of your time . . ."

"Not at all."

". . . I just wanted to talk with you a moment. I wanted to congratulate you on this afternoon first of all."

"It was pretty bad," Neil said. "I suppose it would've been a shambles if the Governor hadn't been there to paste things together."

"Well . . . I'm not *enamored* with Arthur Fenstemaker, exactly, but I imagine you're right. What I meant, though, was the speech. I thought it was a fine speech."

"You think so? You liked it? You were there?"

"I sneaked in after the last course. Swiped a chair at the back. It was a good speech. I liked what you said — what you were getting at."

"Maybe you can tell me then what I *was* getting at. I don't remember much of anything I said . . . Somehow got off the text."

"Well it was all right. *All* right." Hardy did not smile. He seemed to mean everything he said. He was slim and slightly stooped, well dressed and somehow over-earnest in the manner of a bank vice-president. Neil decided he would look more at home in a Merrill, Lynch office rather than a union hall.

"You're very kind," Neil said.

"How do you plan to conduct your campaign?" Hardy said. He had suddenly shifted gears.

"The campaign? There probably won't be much of a campaign. I'm going back to Washington. I'll be down here a few times before the election, make some speeches. I can do most of it practically long distance, though. Films and transcriptions."

"I mean *issues*. What are you going to talk about?"

"Well . . . *You* know. Christ. A little of what I said today. God, Mother and Moderation. But I imagine it'll get pretty bland before it's over." Neil smiled at his little joke, but Hardy seemed more intense and humorless than ever.

"Don't you think you'll need more than that to whip Edwards? A *real* issue. Something clear-cut?"

"No." Neil decided to see who could out-soberface the other.

"No?" For the first time Hardy's radio announcer's voice showed strain. "You don't think so?"

"No."

"Have you thought of pegging it on straight liberal-conservative lines?"

"Yes."

"Well?"

"I think I would lose."

"I don't think you would."

"Well . . . You file in the primary, then."

"No, no, I didn't mean it that way. I want *you* in there. It's just that I think you're going to lose if you go the route you're planning. I've been all over the state. Traveled it all year, from one end to the other. Things are changing. We've never been stronger. And we're gaining strength every day."

"That's good to hear. Best news I've heard all day."

"But I want it to be good for *you*. Have you given any thought to the possibility of campaigning on a labor issue? Against the open shop, for example."

"No . . . No I haven't."

"That kind of campaign would make us very happy, of course."

"I can imagine."

"I think you could win on it."

"I don't think so. I think it would beat me and beat your union shop even worse. You know how long this state's had right-to-work laws?"

"Too long. And there's certainly nothing sacred about them and —"

"Why hell!" Neil said, "Even some of the votes you'd ordinarily count on as liberal would defect on that one. I think *I* might even vote against it if —"

"You mean that?"

"No. But you boys are getting stronger the way things are . . . Why rock the —"

"We're getting stronger for *precisely* that reason. People don't like things the way they are. You have any money?"

"What?"

"Money. Finances. It costs money to run a campaign."

"I've got some."

"How much?"

"Enough."

"How much? A hundred thousand?"

"No. Nothing like it."

"It'll cost you that much to run the kind of campaign you're planning. You know that?"

"Yes. I've got assurances of more."

"What if they bug out on you in the middle? What if they shift over to Edwards? It's happened, you know. Those bastards — boy I can *imagine* where that money's coming from — those birds go with a winner. If you start slipping just a little, why —"

"I don't plan to slip," Neil said. "Not even a little."

"We've got money. We could help you. But more than that, we've got people, votes, discipline. We're *organized*. You'd be amazed. Like shock troops this year."

"As I said, that's great. I want those votes — and I'd welcome the money if you have it. You ought to talk to the Governor. He's handling the —"

"Oh boy, I can imagine how he's handling it. How he'd handle *us*. The first thing, he'd take our money but he'd want it in cash and under the table. He wouldn't want the union label on any of the financial reports. Then he'd tell us to get out and organize our people but for Chrissake be *quiet* about it . . ."

"You needn't. I'm not ashamed of your support. I just meant the Governor was in charge of —"

"I know how he's in charge, mister. Listen — I'll tell you the Facts of Life, revised edition. We're not going that route any more. We're good and tired of being back-door lovers. No more extramarital affairs. No more meetings in the dead of night. We're through with being screwed in the rumble seat. Either you — or any candidate — is good and strong for us in public or we sit on our hands . . ."

"Well . . ."

"We mean it . . ."

"You've put your case beautifully and I sympathize. I'm for you. I'll tell anybody I'm for you. Anybody who asks. But I'm not going to stand up on Mount Baldy in a white vestment and sing about it for the next two months. That's the way it's got to be . . ."

"You'll —"

"I've got to get back to some friends . . ."

"You may regret it, Senator."

"And you may get Owen Edwards. I frankly don't give a damn. And you could get somebody a whole hell of a lot worse than Arthur Fenstemaker if he ever moves out . . ."

"I wish to God he would."

"I enjoyed it."

"Yes."

Neil turned and walked out of the bedroom, leaving Hardy still on his perch on the studio couch. Jay McGown approached him from behind.

"Hey, Neil . . ."

"Jay. Did you get the man tucked in?"

"Think so. I wanted to tell you I appreciate the plug in there. I heard part of it — what you were saying there at the end, at the top of your voice." He stood next to him, smiling, weaving slightly.

"Thanks," Neil said. "But I probably just lost the labor vote in there."

"Nah," Jay said. "Where's your drink?"

"Need a new one, I guess. Must have left it behind."

"Come on," Jay said. "I'll make you one."

They started back into the kitchen. Kermit was standing alone in the middle of the dining room. He grabbed Neil's arm.

"Hey, Good Doctor."

"Kermit. Where's that pretty pregnant woman?"

"Scared her off, man. She quailed on me. Can't seem to get through, make myself clear. How I feel, I mean."

"Shave that beard for a starter," Jay said. "It's that beard that gets in the way."

"Lose my identity, man? Hey, Neil —"

"Yaz."

"You know old John Tom?"

"Yes."

"There was a Doctor. I meant to tell you that. He was an awfully Good Doctor. I meant to tell you . . . How come he split?"

"What?"

"How come he went away?"

"I don't know," Neil said. "I wish I did."

"Good Doctor," Kermit mumbled to himself, walking off alone. Neil and Jay moved into the kitchen. The ice tub was half full of water, and the young man who had taken Neil to see Porter Hardy was breaking open a box of whiskey.

"Look at that host," Jay said. "That's a host for you."

The young man looked up, smiling. "It's the liquor lobby that's host. We take their booze and vote against 'em. They're awfully tolerant . . ."

They poured fresh drinks. Neil took several quick swallows. His throat was dry and then he was suddenly, miraculously, tight. The party raged on around them.

"Grongk," Neil said aloud.

"What?" Jay asked him. The host was still pulling bottles and bottles out of the pasteboard case.

"Dronk," Neil said. He cleared his throat. "If I keep this up I'll be drunk."

"Only way to be round friends," said his friend who was bending over the empty case. "We'll look after you. Won't take any pictures."

"Is Andrea here yet?"

"No . . . Not yet. They were somewhere crosstown. Another party, they said. I'm goin' to lose patience with those people. 'Nother party's no excuse . . ."

"They called again?"

"Yah, yeah, didn't I tell you?"

"I dun know," Neil said. "What she say?"

"Who?"

"Andrea."

"Nothin'. Didn't talk to Andrea. They'll be along. They promised."

There was a silence between the three of them. Jay McGown had got himself seated on the drainboard, his feet dangling, banging against the lower cupboards. The host suddenly sat down inside the empty whiskey case and began slapping his kneecaps in time with the music. Periodically, he took a drink; then propped the glass in his lap and resumed slapping his kneecaps. Neil had got a silly grin on his face. He was aware of how altogether foolish an expression it was, but he couldn't make it go way. With the three of them thus assembled, the effect from a distance was one of great, private merriment — the sort of illusion, chic and exclusive and vastly appealing to passersby, that caused others to wonder whether *they* were having such a good time *after* all. Fairly soon, a large group of people, whooping and shouting and hoping to share in the fun, had crowded into the kitchen.

Now there were several people perched alongside Jay on the drainboard, and others were pushing in close, ducking under can openers and cuptowel racks to see. Some of them sat on the damp floor, encircling the host who was still inside the whiskey case; another of the roommates was lowering himself in the tub of melted ice. "Coo . . ." he said, squeezing his eyes shut. "Oooweeool." Somebody had a bongo drum and was beating on it in a way that irritated Neil but seemed to make the others deliriously happy. They could hardly hear the music from the other room.

Neil finally managed to get through into the main part of the house again. Not everyone had been attracted to the wild, seemingly private goings-on in the kitchen. There were still a good many people about, but the place now gave off an appearance of a *little* more restraint and formality. Not much, but more than had been apparent up to that time. Stanley was dancing with Elsie; there were only three or four couples shuffling about on the living room floor, and the evening had reached a stage at which the soft-music devotees had finally won out over the jazz-ruckus people. Stanley and the girl were a little tight, but they weren't letting each other know about it. Nor were they working at it to any perceptible degree. They were both just a little high; Neil could see that they were.

When one song had ended and before another was begun, he moved in between then, smiled at Stanley, and asked Elsie to dance.

She came tightly against him, and they moved round slowly with the music. He wondered if she had been giving Stanley the same business all evening, and then he wondered whether she was conscious of having any business to give. She was not a particularly distinguished dancer, but then neither was he. They just managed to move with the music, demanding no more than they and the music were capable of delivering. On the third song, just before one of the jazz buffs got hold of the phonograph and announced Brubeck as next up, they were holding close to each other, scarcely moving their feet, silent and suddenly conscious of their own possibilities.

When the Brubeck came on, he returned her to Stanley and the three of them sat together on the couch.

The evening wore on, past midnight, toward some kind of inescapable conclusion or anticlimax. How did it end? How had these parties always expired? Neil could not remember; or he had never taken the trouble to notice. It seemed to him that he *should*, for a change, but there was no indication at that moment of the party's letting up. People had begun moving back into the main rooms from the kitchen. They moved more slowly now, but there was no lessening of their ardor and their eyes still gleamed with the anticipation of something far more desirable and possibly new to their experience coming at any moment or in the next hour or so.

Stanley went to get fresh drinks. There were a few complaints about the absence of ice, but most of those who had gone at the liquor with any seriousness were now numb in the mouth, and they drank their whiskey straight or with tap water. Stanley made exactly that point when he returned with the three glasses; he said it was like having had a local anesthetic in the hard palate. They sat quietly, watching the dancers. Stanley leaned over and started to say something, changed his mind for an instant, and then reversed himself again.

"I was thinking," he said, "does Fenstemaker know much about John Tom?"

"What do you mean?"

"Does he know much about *John Tom?* Did he have anything to do with him before he left the college? Was he even *aware* of him?"

"He sure was," Neil said. "He knew a good deal about John Tom. He was the one who tipped me about what might happen if John Tom stayed on at the college . . ."

"How abut Elsie? Did he know about your trying to help Elsie?"

Neil made a face from the whiskey and set his glass down.

"What you getting at?"

"Maybe nothing. But did he know about Elsie?"

Neil thought a moment. He got hold of his glass and turned it round in his hand and took a drink and tried, ploddingly, methodically, to think. It was like the grinding of poorly meshed or wornout gears.

"Is matterall fack," Neil began, nodding his head. ". . . As . . . uh . . . matter . . . ruff . . . fact . . . I think we wrote to him couple months ago about Elsie . . ." He turned to Elsie, smiling. " . . . We had to get *some*thing — what in hell was it anyway? — we had to get the Governor's — Guffner the State — his official . . . What 'n hell was it? Had to get him to confirm Elsie as something or other, good risk, responrable, *respons*-zable, holdin' job and all that, so the State Department people could go ahead. So we could push on that visa business."

They were sitting up straight on the couch. She was turned toward him and doing something with her hair at the back of her neck. He wanted to get his face in there again.

"I don't know," she said. "What place?"

"I don't know, either. Anyplace. I just know I want to go someplace with you."

"Would you want to go to the bookstore?"

"Yes . . ."

"I've got a bottle of sherry there."

"Yes . . . Come on."

"Stanley?"

"I'll . . . Wait a moment. I'll tell him."

"Tell him what?"

"I'll think of something. Leave him a note."

He left her near the door and went to search for Stanley. He was back almost immediately.

"We're in luck," he said. "Stanley's asleep. Passed out. With Jay McGown."

They started for the door, but at that moment it came open and several faces, misted in drink, appeared. He wondered if this would be Andrea now arriving, right on schedule: the Wrong Time. But it was not Andrea, none of her group. It was, instead, several young men and girls, with Kermit in the lead and three Negroes — two women and a man — in the middle.

The white people were very gay, full of loud and nervous laughter, but the Negroes stood quietly in the middle of the group, not at all sure of the situation.

"Hassah!" Kermit said. "We uz integrated! Ass raht!"

He saw Neil and Elsie as they passed and yelled after them. "Hey Neil. Hey you Good Doctor. Come back, gate. Meet my friends . . ."

Neil turned and waved and hurried on with the girl at his side. Inside the car, he fumbled in his pockets, frantic at the thought that he might have misplaced the keys. Then he found them and got the motor started, although he did not set the machine into motion immediately. Elsie had moved next to him and reached up to touch his face. Before he had half turned in the seat her lips were moving along the edge of his collar and then they kissed. She was directly against him and he had begun to wonder if they would ever succeed in getting to the bookshop when the sound of voices came to them from across the lawn. He peered out the car window and could see that Andrea and her friends had, indeed, finally arrived. They moved into the house, a great shout of approval greeting them. Almost immediately, the phonograph music rose in volume and the scene through the windows of the house was very like the one that had registered in his mind earlier that evening when he had come across the lawn and paused at the front steps. He put the car in gear and headed down the street with the girl next to him.

Fifteen

STANLEY came awake gradually. He lay on his back in what he felt might be a spreadeagle position, although it could have been closer to the attitude of crucifixion. It occurred to him suddenly that it was Easter Sunday — about 3 A.M. on Easter Sunday but Easter all the same. The air was very bad in the small bedroom, and he got himself on one elbow, leaned over and raised a window. He inhaled deeply for about a minute.

Then he lay back on the bed. The party was still going on around him — that would be a small triumph — but Jay was nowhere to be seen. He remembered finding Jay asleep on one of the twin beds, and, failing to rouse him, lying down to rest for just a few minutes himself. He lay on the bed now, uncertain about his own capabilities. He did not think he would be able to stand on his feet for just a while yet. For no apparent reason he remembered the opening lines of a novel he had glanced at in a cut-rate bookstore in 1947. It had something to do with a rather fast young woman coming awake and feeling as if somebody's band of soldiers had marched through her mouth during the night, relieved themselves, and marched right out again. He decided that was precisely the feeling inside his own mouth.

"You better, Stanley?"

"Umnpf."

"Well I'm sorry to hear that."

It was one of the hosts. He grinned at Stanley; he had managed to get a very satisfactory buzz on while avoiding the pitfalls that had victimized all others around him. He was awfully damned proud of himself, Stanley decided.

"Where'd Jay go?" He had succeeded in shaping this question in his head and speaking it aloud, but it had been an awful effort.

"Jay's gone . . . Wandered out of here about a half hour ago. But don't let that give you any ideas. You've got to hang on, wait for a second wind. We've got a whole new group of people coming in."

"Ouuumn."

The interloper turned and went back into the main part of the house. Stanley could hear him repeating his statement, loudly and clearly, in the other rooms. Within minutes, others had begun to repeat it and soon it had evolved into a catchphrase of spiritual uplift for late hangers-on. He raised himself halfway and sat on the edge of the bed. Someone showed a face through the door for just a moment and said: "Hey, don't leave yet. Nobody leaves. There's a whole new group of people coming in."

"Yeah, yeah . . ." Stanley said.

He stood for a moment and then walked very carefully into

the bathroom where he drew the lavatory full of water and washed his face. Then he dried himself and proceeded toward the main section of the house.

The crowd had thinned out some, but there were still twenty to thirty people composing the party, laughing, talking, standing and half lying down in states ranging from ebullience to despair. He looked from room to room for Jay and Stanley and the girl. He saw Andrea and her friends, dancing in the room with the phonograph. The Negroes stood along the wall, watching, and Kermit sat nearby, engaging someone in an impassioned and obviously one-sided conversation. He walked into the kitchen and washed out a glass, filling it with ice and water.

"Howze Washington?"

"Fine. Very pretty this time of year."

He had never seen the person in his life; he was certain of it. The young man had sidled up next to him and begun picking up whiskey bottles scattered along the drainboard, holding them to the light, and setting them down again. "Dead soldiers," he said, smiling, pleased with so apt an observation.

"Yes," Stanley said. "Lots and lots." They had surely never met before. The fellow was a perfect stranger.

"Goddammit. The Scotch is gone."

"There's bourbon," Stanley said. "I see a bottle there." He pointed to where it was, still in its pasteboard carton. "And there's gin in the refrigerator."

"It'll get cloudy," the young man said.

"Perhaps they keep it cold for martinis. It's probably part of their own stock."

"Whattaya mean?"

"This other here is — was — the lobby's."

"Who's the Lobbys?

"What?"

"Who are they? The Lobbys."

"I don't know," Stanley said. He was suddenly very bored with this young man. He stood there drinking his water, hoping the visitor would get himself some whiskey as quickly as possible and leave the kitchen.

Another young man appeared.

"Any Scotch?"

"No," the first one said. "There's bourbon here, and some gin in the refrigerator —"

"Getting cloudy," Stanley put in.

"And this other here was the Lobbys'. All of it."

"I know," the second one said. "But you shouldn't talk about it."

"Who are they? Why shouldn't you talk about it?"

"What?"

Oh Jesus, Stanley thought. He turned to leave, but the first young man caught his arm. "Stanley — do you know Jake?"

"I know Stanley. I've heard a lot about him," the fellow named Jake said.

Stanley searched his mind for something other to say than that he hoped it was all good. He thought of nothing, but only stood there with his glass of water, smiling at Jake and Mr. X.

"Is your boss here tonight?" Jake said.

"He was," Stanley said. "He seems to have given it up and gone home." He wondered about Neil and Elsie in a casual way — about whether he had taken her straight home, for example. He thought of calling at Elsie's but then he knew he might wake her, and that would not be good at all. A foreign girl might not understand or be in any mood to indulge even the best intentioned drunk, and he wanted very much to get started right with Elsie. He had a picture of Neil and Elsie looking in on him and finding him resting comfortably in the bed. They would not have wanted to disturb him. Neil had simply driven her home.

"He must be a great guy," Jake said.

"He *is*, he *is*," said the Unknown. He turned to Stanley. "I envy you. I envy the *hell* out of you."

"Why?"

"Working for Neil. He's a great guy, great guy, just a prince of a guy . . ." The appearance of Andrea in the kitchen temporarily ended that train of thought for the young man. He stood with his mouth open, staring at her. "Jesus," he said under his breath.

"Hello, Stanley. Have you seen Neil?"

"He was here earlier."

"I know."

"I took a nap and when I woke up he was gone."

"When was that?"

"I'm not sure. Around two."

"He must have gone home to bed."

"He must have . . ."

Mr. X turned his back on Andrea and made as if he were mixing a new drink. He looked at Stanley and mumbled something inaudible. Then he hissed through his teeth: "Who-is-she? *Who's she?*" Stanley ignored him.

"Have you met Jake? Jake, do you know Stanley?" Andrea said. Jake and Stanley said they did, indeed, know each other. The other stood off and watched the three of them.

Andrea said: "Was he all right?"

"Who?"

"Neil. He was awfully tired when I saw him earlier."

"He was drunk," Stanley said, smiling. "He was awfully drunk when I saw him earlier."

"Well I suppose —"

Kermit appeared in the kitchen with two Negro girls, one on each arm. They were both a little terrified, and Kermit made an extra-serious effort to introduce them in a civilized way. Everyone was polite. But no one knew quite what ought to be said. It would take years, Stanley thought; years and years. They had grown so used to seeing these people — and not seeing them — behind counters and at the back sections of public conveyances, sullen faces peering from tumbled shacks; unseen, unaware of them even in college classrooms, that it would take years to get any contact established. Even for the young people here who were desperately striving to learn one another.

"These two," Kermit said, "are my models. My first two models for the Renaissance Gallery. We'll have life drawing classes. They have absolutely *exquisite* figures." He turned to his frightened charges. "We'll make a mint, won't we girls?"

Mr. X stood close to one of them, looking as if he would like to take a bite of her. Kermit turned toward him suddenly.

"You dig, man?"

"Wh-at?" He seemed entirely out of breath.

"You dig? This is Rose. She's a real swingin' chick. Earns her bread for college as a dancer. And a model. Take her in there and dance with her, man. It's like . . . It's like, well, like *scorin'*, man."

"*Kermit!*" Andrea said.

"That's all right, Andy. They're used to me, these girls. They know me a lot better than *My Own People*." He laughed and bent down and kissed one of the girls on the throat.

The unknown young man took one of the girls into the other room to dance. Kermit said: "Why'd you let that Good Doctor cut out of here?"

"What?"

"Neil — how come you let him split with that Middle East cunt —"

"*Kermit!*"

"I mean that girl. Hey, Stanley, you know that girl? She's nearly as dark as this one right here."

"*Who* did he leave with?" Andrea said.

"With Elsie," Stanley said. "He took Elsie home. I brought her, but I was too passed out at the time to assume my responsibilities."

"Oh."

They began to move into the other rooms.

Stanley stood in a corner and talked with one of the Negro girls. The other was dancing. Stanley and the girl talked about books. The folk singer appeared; she had got rid of her guitar somewhere. She listened for a moment and then said: "Do you like Langston Hughes? I like him very much."

"No," said the girl.

"I don't either," Stanley said.

"You're a white supremist," Kermit said.

"I like Baldwin," Stanley said. "Won't liking Baldwin clear me, for Chrissake?"

"I like Orval Faubus," someone said. All of them who had been listening roared with laughter.

Kermit talked with Andrea.

"He's a Good Doctor. Neil's a Good one. And John Tom, too. The best."

"Did you know John Tom very well?" Andrea said.

"Oyez. We dug each other right off."

Andrea was silent. Then, half to herself, she said. "I wish I had caught Neil before he left. I was wornout when we got here."

"I'll take you home."

"No, no. There's still a party. And you've got your friends."

"Take my car then. There're plenty cars. Take mine."

"Well . . ." She looked around as if making a decision about something.

"Come on. It's right out front. You know it? It's that green heap. Here the keys."

He dangled them in front of her.

"How would you get it back?"

"I'll be out that way tomorrow. Or tonight sometime, before dawn at least. Just leave the keys in the car. Nobody'd take that machine. Somebody'll drop me off out that way later."

"You sure it's all right, Kermit?"

"Oyez."

Years before, in a more lucid stage in his development, he had once served as Clerk of the State Supreme Court. Andrea remembered seeing him during his first year out of college, standing and announcing the sessions at the top of his voice as the black-robed Justices filed into the chamber: *Oyez, Oyez, Oyez! All persons having business before the Honorable, the Supreme Court of this*

State, are admonished to draw near and give their attention, for the Court is now sitting. God save this State and this Honorable Court . . . She wondered if Kermit remembered; she rather doubted it.

"I'll find the car — that's all right."

She got her wrap and started for the door. Jake moved over and held it open for her.

"Where you going?"

"Home. I'm exhausted."

"I'll take you. I'll get a car."

"I've got a car."

"I'll drive."

"No . . . Really . . ."

"Why not?"

"I'm fine. And I just don't think you ought to . . ."

"All right." He walked outside with her. Kermit's car was an ancient sedan with ruptured seat cushions and flaking paint and a terrible interior smell.

"You sure you can drive this thing?"

"Yes . . . Wait . . . Can you get it started for me?"

He slid in beside her, switched on the ignition and found the starter on the floorboard. The engine groaned horribly until the oil began to circulate. Then he reached over and put his arms out.

"No. No, Jake . . ."

"Why not?"

"I can't. I've got to go, really. Dammit . . ."

She finally let him kiss her and then pulled away, but then he was coming at her again and she relaxed and they thrashed around convulsively in the front seat of the old car for a period of time.

"Enough . . ."

"No."

"Get out of the car, Jake, or *I*'ll get out and start walking . . ."

He opened the door and stepped outside.

"What the hell've I been eating?"

"I've just got to get home. Don't you understand?"

"All right. When do I see you?"

"Call." She gunned the motor; the old car lurched ahead, slowed, gasped, and moved on down the street.

It was a really very old automobile. The smell was not so bad once she had got started and turned the air vents on her face, but she could barely see over the dashboard and the hood seemed enormous, stretching out and up to a fantastic length like the nose of an airplane. The seats were littered, front and back, and she could not bring herself to examine any of the refuse. A fading, years-old *Adlai* sticker clung to the inside of the yellow windshield and flapped in the breeze. Something fell down in her lap from the sun visor, and it made her jump. Paintbrushes. Oils. John Tom, she thought. *"John Tom,"* she said aloud.

A block ahead of her was the old house they had shared for a studio. She slowed and stopped in front of it; a half-dozen rental agents' signs were tacked on the door and windows and splintered columns. It was just an old shell of a house — three rooms — but there had been a skylight and the floors had not been in any imminent danger of collapse. They had shared the studio for several months prior to his leaving town. It had not taken long at all — the memory of it always seemed to amaze her. It was almost like a party; neither had ever taken the other very seriously. *Stop looking, like that,* he had said. *Stop looking at me that way.* But she could not really stop — she had no intention of stopping — and the first time, before anyone had even arranged to have the bathroom cleaned or the old furniture covered, they had ended on that awful sofa, or davenport was what he called it, and it had taken her forever to wriggle out of those paint-spattered denim slacks.

Oyez, we dug each other right off!

How come you let that Good Doctor cut out?

Well how come?

You went off and got yourself killed? 'Cause that old house

had a cuckold's haunt. *Zat all?* They're so serious, the both of them, always taking themselves so serious. He'd of never, my Neil'd never, and if you'd only hung around the old place and let us run our course I wouldn't be half so bitched up now and groaning about your being gone and not coming back and painting your goddam picture all the time, yours and Neil's . . .

She sat looking at the old house until the smell from the seat cushions caused her to drive on down the street. A mile from home, halfway up one of the hills, the old car began to slow. She accelerated, but there was only a pulling-air sound in response. After it had rolled to a stop, she tried for several minutes to get the car started again, stretching her nice legs — such *nice* brown legs — toward the button on the floorboard. She ground the starter until the dashlights grew dim, and just before they faded completely she could see that the gas gauge registered empty.

"Kermit — you son of a bitch," she said.

She sat for a moment and then took the keys and stepped out into the street. There wasn't a sound, not even another car droning in the distance. In the eastern sky there was just a faint coloring, the barest suggestion of Sunday morning. She began to walk up the hill. Before she had covered a block the tears were streaming down her face, and she stumbled along the empty streets with the faint light of the dawn at her back. Walking across the graveled drive toward the house she could see that Neil's car was missing, and then it occurred to her — struggling with the front door latch, fumbling with the keys, Kermit's and her own — that her roadster had been left parked someplace in the city. She could not recall where: some boozy vale. Perhaps it had been turned back into a pumpkin. She lay in her upstairs bed with the light coming in through the windows and the sweet party dress stuck against her feverish skin. She was overtaken by an irresistible weeping, but there was no one in the big house who could hear.

Sixteen

"WHAT was that rumble?"

"My death rattle, honey . . ."

"Perhaps it was thunder . . . What did you say?"

"I like your saxophone player."

"Isn't he nice? You think it was thunder? He's often out there."

"Every night?"

"Nearly every night I'm here to listen."

"Always in the alley?"

"Yes. Always. I've never seen him in the street. He's crippled."

"Is that why he stays in the alley?"

"What?"

"Is it always 'Roses of Picardy'?"

"If that's what it is. Always."

They played John Tom's old records on the phonograph. She had a marvelous figure, and moved back and forth, to the phonograph and to retrieve the sherry bottle, easy and unembarrassed. It was not so easy for Neil; though he felt better after he had got his underwear back on. He lay on a rollaway bed. He remembered helping John Tom pick it out at the Sears Roebuck store. It was about three-quarter width, and with the cheap bolsters it was an adequate studio couch for the back part of the shop. He lay there watching the girl. In a few years she would be getting thickish through the middle and in the upper part of her legs, but none of it had really begun to show. It was a pleasure to watch her, and even more a pleasure to see a woman with large breasts and a big behind who had not yet begun to fatten and decay. So many of those college girls . . .

"I think you will like this."

She sat next to him and they shared the glass of sherry. He tasted it.

"Very good . . . It's always 'Roses of Picardy'?"

"The same every night."

"*There* was a song . . ."

"What?"

"I had a record of it once. Sidney Bechet."

"Bechet?"

"Yes. Perhaps someone will bring it back and record it. With a beat. And a hipster choir in the background. Let's hope so."

"Yes."

They lay nearly sideways together, his head up against her breasts. He turned and kissed the flat of her stomach. She said something — Yiddish or Arabic — he could not tell what.

"Hmmn?"

She laughed. "I don't think it's translatable."

"Do you like John Tom's records?"

"Oh, yes."

"Do you have any of your own?"

"Yes. But you might not like them."

"Ah! Let's see. Petrouchka. Prokofiev . . . Vaughn Williams?"

"No. They're mostly sixteenth century."

"And you've been reading Thomas Hardy."

"Only the poetry."

"You're unhealthy — that's what you are. You're not falling into any of the recognizable patterns for the healthy, American brain-girl fresh from . . ."

"Healthy? I'm unhealthy?"

"No. Not how you think."

He turned on his front side and rested his chin along the curve of her middle. Then he pulled himself up toward her face and they kissed for a time. There was still some easy responsiveness between them. It had not been a spectacular thing; she was neither matter-of-fact nor especially fevered about it. But it was something out of the ordinary, and he guessed, like everything else, it could be attributed to her being a foreigner. A function, a need fulfilled. With some poetic imagery to sustain the illusion.

"Is this old couch often put to such uses?"

"What? This couch . . . ?"

"Have you any lovers?"

She thought a moment. "I don't think so." And then: "Oh! The *couch*. No . . . And not this way. I've spent some nights here. And kissed men here."

He felt unaccountably, queasily jealous. Did those juices ever stop flooding the darkened pools of the ego? He was overwhelmingly assaulted by vague notions of crime. It was a tyranny, and he felt somehow unmanned.

"I'm sick," he said.

"You're feeling badly?"

"In the head."

She stroked his temples. He supposed it was as good a therapy as one could find. It was miraculous how much better he felt already. He got his face down between her breasts.

"Ah!"

"All right?"

"Wait . . . There."

The mechanism ground along, resuming, slowly at first, undemanding, nearly aimless, and then the dark passages loomed up ahead of them and they were lost for a few moments in glimpses of each other and the dawn coming through the windows at the far side of the room. His thoughts were incoherent and all out of context: remembering the crippled saxophone player in the alley and the feel of Owen Edwards' damp backend and an edifice of triteness used to describe somebody's one-man show —- the one posthumously staged by Andrea in John Tom's behalf — *"the palette caked, the brushes dry . . ."*

He slept for a little while. When he awoke she was still next to him, her head propped against one of the bolsters, smoking a cigarette.

"Do you like this?" he said.

"Of course I like this. Don't you like this?"

"Yes. Perhaps I just need reassuring."

"Strange . . . Do you feel better?" She did not smile; she was altogether serious.

"Yes."

"I may come to Washington."

"Really? That would be very nice."

"Stanley asked me."

"Stanley's very nice."

"He said he could find me a job."

"I imagine he could. You marry Stanley, by the way — or anyone for that matter — and your problems are ended."

"What an odd thing to say."

"Why?"

"Americans are always trying to end all their problems. When the trick is to use them to some advantage."

"I mean the passport, the citizenship business."

"Oh yes . . . I suppose they would be."

He dozed for a moment, his face resting against her dark shoulders. He heard her talking.

"What?"

"I wouldn't want to do that, though. For a while at least. Stanley is a very good person and I would want to live with him and no one else . . ."

He was dimly aware that she was articulating some kind of fundamental approach to life, but he fell to sleep again while she was talking and he could never remember the rest of it. He came awake again about an hour later, and Elsie was now sleeping soundly beside him. He got to his feet and dressed and then stood for a few minutes looking at the girl. He found an old yellow bedspread in a closet and covered her before turning to leave.

The sun was well advanced. The tower clock at the college chimed a half hour, and he looked up to see the time. There were lowlying clouds circling the horizon in the east and they lit up the sky with streaks of amber and blue and fading browns. Driving toward home he began to pass cars crowded with people in Sunday dress and occasional good citizens on foot, and as he approached a church he had to stop for a procession of children, fresh-faced and beautiful in vibrantly colored smocks and gowns and vestments. They passed by, strung out in ones and twos, not talking though irresistibly tempted, vastly excited by the hour and the promise of an Easter Sunday. A pair of scrubbed and faintly smiling nuns tagged along. He thought about his two little girls and how he would have to start in immediately upon his arrival at the house to hide all their beautifully colored eggs. For no reason — and only for a few seconds, really — he began to cry.

Seventeen

HE RESOLVED to give the day over to the children. This would be their day — he would dedicate himself to the proposition. Everything in him would be offered up. He had got to leave them with something.

He searched the kitchen for the eggs. There were some candied ones hidden in a basket, wrapped in colored cellophane, on a shelf next to the liquor supply. The ones Andrea — or Emma — had dyed for them earlier in the week were stored in the refrigerator. He would hide them all in the backyard, in the deeper growth beyond the swings and the sandpile. Then he would wait for the children and they would wander outside together and hunt for the eggs. When every one was found they would take turns hiding them all over again. He would stay close to them and they would talk; he would tell them a story, spin out a parable on what it was all about, improvise, make a speech. Surely he could think of *something* — anything — to say to his own lovely children. The old house was silent and the day grew warm.

He wandered out back and hid all the eggs. Then he made himself some instant coffee and sat for a time at the kitchen table, trying to read the Sunday paper. But the front page was full of politics — himself and Edwards and Fenstemaker — and it oddly failed to hold his interest. And besides, he would be cheating on the girls if he got his mind to working in that direction again. He finished off the coffee and set the paper down, rubbing his eyes. The old house rumbled with the sleep of others, and he experienced a momentary sensation of utter fatigue. He looked out a window, feeling lightheaded and a little boozy in the lambent morning air. If he had ever really got to bed that evening, he knew there would have been a terrible hangover later on. But he felt perhaps a brief rest might do him some good; not sleep — he felt no need for sleep — but just a temporary cessation of the demands he had been making on himself, the calling upon resources no longer his to give. He wandered into the study and lay quietly for a time on a narrow couch. Then he was conscious of nothing until he awoke with his father-in-law bending over him.

"Neil . . . Neil, boy . . ."

"Wha . . . What is it?" He sat up suddenly, looking around. "What's the time? Are the girls—"

"I wouldn't of waked you for anything else. It's the Governor. He's on the phone."

He rubbed his eyes and got to his feet. "What time did you say it was?"

"I don't know what he wants," the old man was saying. "Doesn't sound especially urgent, but I couldn't get it out of him . . ."

The old man walked with him into the hall and handed over the telephone receiver. Neil held the instrument for a moment — carefully and a little away from him as if it were a particularly distasteful laboratory specimen.

Then he was conscious of voices in the main room, sounds of displeasure, cross and tiresome. He looked in, still holding the telephone receiver. Andrea was arguing with the girls; the two of them sat together in small chairs facing a blank television screen. Someone else stood nearby — he had to push his eyes into focus to see that it was Andrea's mother. He could not imagine where she had come from.

"Hello, Neil dear," she said.

He said hello but could not manage to get any surprise or pleasure into his voice. Andrea turned and faced him. The children, visibly irritated, paid no attention.

"What's trouble?" he said.

"The eggs," Andrea said. "The eggs are gone — all of them — and I know these two must have sneaked them out and eaten or buried them or something. And now they expect me to go buy them some more."

"Have the girls been to Sunday School, Andrea?" her mother said. "They really ought . . ." Her voice trailed off and she made an empty gesture with her hand, smiling at everyone.

"Maybe . . ." Neil began. "Perhaps . . . one of those big Easter rabbits came downstairs last night and hid them for the girls. Have they been in the backyard yet?"

Andrea looked at him furiously for an instant and then turned big-eyed toward the girls. "*That's* it. That must be it. Let's see if there's anything in the backyard."

The girls were transformed. They gave a whoop, sprang from their chairs, and piled past him down the hall toward the rear of the house. Andrea followed them. "Sorry," he said. She only shrugged and walked on after the girls.

He started in the same direction, turned to replace the phone receiver and remembered suddenly that there was somone on the other end. Andrea's father appeared from the kitchen, stirring a cup of coffee.

"What did he want?"

"I haven't found out yet."

He said hello. There was a silence and he repeated it and then a voice came on.

"Just a moment, Senator. Governor Fenstemaker . . ."

"Neil? Neil, you all right?"

"Yes."

"I just wanted to check. Have a good Easter?"

"Yessir. What time is it? Can you tell me?"

"Little before twelve. Eleven-forty. See the papers?"

"I glanced at them. I just woke up."

"I've got 'em all here. All of 'em. Ten or fifteen. We did all right, by God. Listen to this . . ."

He read from several editorials.

"That one's front page . . ."

He read from several more, and then from the news stories, the majority of which had quoted the Governor's unscheduled post-luncheon address at great length. Edwards had obviously got very much the worst of it. The reports treated Neil with a good deal more respect, although there was a certain indirectness in the printed accounts. Almost with the reverence shown for the dead. Everybody seemed bent on speaking well of him, but he was hardly a felt presence, scarcely a public image for anyone to rally round.

"I think we're in good shape," the Governor said. "I'm having some surveys run, and we should know something fairly soon. They'll probably show Edwards out front at first, but —"

"He'll be ahead?"

"Imagine so. He's been politickin' this state for years. He's well known. But not particularly well liked. Not by a damn long shot. What we need is to let people take a look at you in contrast. If we're not more than four or five percentage points behind him I'd say we got the cotton halfway to the gin. Just a matter of

time. Ole Owen's got all the votes he's goin' to get — shot his
bolt of uglies a long time ago — and we haven't even tapped our
possibilities yet. He's had his and it's never been quite enough,
and you've got noplace to move but straight up. Just time, that's
all."

"How about the money?" Neil said. "Any coming in yet? Do
we have enough for some broadcasts?"

"Yes. And I think you might plan one this week sometime.
When are you going back?"

"I'm not sure."

"Well, it can be handled here or there. The thing is to get the
time — a good time slot — bought and paid for now. Otherwise,
they'll slip you in behind the Mickey Mouse Club or put you in
the place of something everybody'd rather hear than you. You
got to study these things . . ."

"I'll talk to Stanley about some speeches . . ."

"Good. You might use a little of that egghead stuff . . . That
sounded pretty good yesterday."

"You think so? Really?"

"Well I don't mean over*do* it. I mean it just looks good up
next to Edwards. Keep your virility for God's sake, but make
yourself some pretty speeches if you want. Just make sure you got
some *wholesomeness* in there. You know — Eric Sevareid eating
apple pie. Like that."

"What about labor?"

"What about it."

"I had a talk last night . . ."

"So I heard. Jay told me. Appreciate what you said. You did
all right."

"You think they might lay down on us?"

"They'll come around. When they see they either got to fish or
cut bait."

They talked on for a period of time until the Governor grew
impatient of the silences and rang off. Neil headed for the backyard. He could see the girls with their baskets full of brightly
colored eggs. The phone signaled in the hall.

"Wait a minute," the old man said. "That thing's been ringin' all morning." He returned in a moment. "It's for you."

Neil headed back to the phone. He kept wondering whether the girls had found all the eggs. He was the only one who knew where they were hidden.

"Hello."

"Senator — this is . . ."

It was someone from another city wanting to place his advertising.

"I'll let you know. We haven't selected an agency. We'll have to make a decision . . ."

The next time he had got as far out into the yard as the sandpile and was just beginning to say something to Andrea and her mother when the old man yelled at him from the back door. A newspaperman was on the line.

"We're trying to get our Monday leads in early," the fellow said, "so we can go home and enjoy the holiday. Would you have some kind of statement? Could you give us something?"

Neil said he would ring him back. Then he got Stanley out of bed at the hotel.

"Can you come out and eat with us? . . . And bring your typewriter. Try to think of something harmless to say so we can be in the Monday papers. And maybe it ought to be simple and nonpolitical . . . It's Easter *Sunday*, that's why . . . Yes . . . Elsie? Who . . . ? Oh! That's right . . . You get home okay? Well listen, try to drive out here soon as you can . . . We'll call the wire services . . ."

When he reached the backyard again, the girls had fled into a neighbor's house to show their loot to friends. Andrea was upstairs, changing, Emma in the kitchen preparing lunch. The mother-in-law wandered abstractedly around the backyard, brandishing a butterfly net. He stood there under the shade of the big trees, wondering about the older woman. She offered no explanation, so he returned to the house.

The telephone continued to ring. He got Emma to answer them and take the names down, most of which were garbled and some of which had to be given a return call. The Sunday papers still did not interest him and neither did the old man who followed him from room to room talking about the crazy goddam Eisenhower budget. He put a record on the phonograph, but even old Bunk Johnson seemed strident and overbearing on a Sunday afternoon. He stood around, picking at the open pots of food in the kitchen. Andrea's mother came in from the backyard.

"Neil, dear, would you help me a moment?"

He said yes. She led him into the dining room.

"I've been doing this thing . . . Nature photography. Several of my friends and I. We've become rather good at it and —"

"She even bought a goddam three-hundred-dollar Leica," her husband said.

". . . We take these lovely pictures. *Nature* pictures. We get insects and bugs and animals and freeze them and —"

"*Freeze* them?"

"Yes. And —"

"Freeze *an*imals?"

"Yes. Well not large animals. I mean . . . see these?"

She unfolded her net enough to show him several trapped insects of no particular distinction, along with a gorgeous brown and yellow butterfly and a rather large bee.

"Just a moment — I'll go get my case."

She disappeared into another part of the house. He stood there looking at the net with the butterfly flapping desperately inside it.

"Watch this," the old man said, grinning conspiratorily. His wife returned, smiling gaily. They both looked quite mad. She opened a small overnight bag and set out several bottles and dabs of cotton and a plastic container one might use for leftover foodstuffs.

"Here, will you help me? Dad won't have anything to do with it."

"Damndest thing I ever saw," the old man said.

"What are you doing?"

"It's an anesthesia. Here — can you just . . . We get the loveliest color photographs . . ."

She went after the insects with the dabs of damp cotton. Neil held the net for her.

"Careful . . . We don't want to soil their little yellow fur . . ."

When all had been gently etherized she slipped them into the food container and asked Emma to set it inside the freezer. Emma started to say something to Neil about a job for her eldest daughter, but then gave it up. "Specimen jar?" she said, uncomprehending, but still uncomplaining, accepting the container and taking it with her into the kitchen. Andrea's mother produced a picture she had made of a katydid. At least she said it was a "pretty little" katydid — to Neil the color close-up rather resembled some primitive throwback, a Martian or a rocket ship or possibly a prehistoric mammal. He stood looking at it for a few minutes, making sympathetic sounds, and then wandered half crazed up the stairs to the children's rooms.

There was an erupting toy box which he picked over for a few minutes before he began to examine the cartoons and paintings on the walls. John Tom had done them for the older sister several years before. They were imaginary animals, mainly, being led around by amoeba-shaped people. I ought, he thought, to get them an enlargement of that goddam kaytdid. He heard the children's laughter from next door and moved over to a window, hoping to catch sight of them. Andrea came into the room while he was standing there.

The phone jangled incessantly downstairs.

"I'm sorry about the eggs," he said.

"That's all right. I just didn't know. It would've been a real job trying to keep the girls occupied and out of sight while we hid them, and you saved me that."

They talked about the girls, the drawings on the walls and the picture of the katydid. Yes, she said, she had seen the katydid. He decided she must be avoiding the subject of the night before and his late return, so he brought it up himself.

"What time did you get in?"

"I don't think I even looked," she said. "Kermit lent me that awful car of his and I ran out of gas on the way home. I just collapsed. Why were you so late?"

He wondered how much she knew and whether she had been aware of the hour of his return.

"I took that girl home — the one from the bookshop — and then came here. Then I couldn't sleep so I went out driving again. I just rode around until dawn. Saw all the early mass and sunrise service types filling up the city and came back home."

"She's the loveliest girl . . ."

"Who?"

"Elsie."

"Oh . . . Yes . . . Very. I think Stanley is interested in her."

"Too bad he passed out."

"I couldn't budge him. Neither of us got much sleep the night before — or the night before that. When did you get to the party?"

"It must have been just after you left."

"How long did it go on?"

"On and on," she said. "It was a pretty bad party."

"Yes. Everyone was misbehaving. I got into an argument with some . . . How was your party? The one earlier."

"Oh it was nothing. We had drinks and then a late start for dinner. We looked in at one other place before I finally got them started in the right direction. I'm sorry we missed all the way around."

"I should've waited. Who were you with?"

She named several people.

"Is that all?"

"There were some others I don't think you know."

They were silent.

"I didn't even know them very well."

"Who?"

"The others in my party."

"Did you see Kermit's colored people?"

"Yes. They were nice."

"I just saw them. We passed going out as they came in."

"I thought they were all rather nice . . . But I suppose it's just as well you missed them."

"Why?"

"If that idiot Edwards heard about it. I told my father this morning — I shouldn't have — and he was almost out of his mind. God! With our crowd, you forget what other people are like."

"Other people are all right," Neil said. "They collect katydids, trot off to Sunday School. Sing hymns instead of folk songs."

"What's she like?"

"Who?"

"Elsie."

"I don't know. Does she sing folk songs, too?"

"Probably. She looks like she would fit in that bunch."

"I didn't think so."

"Really? What did you think?"

He sat on one of the children's beds and propped his back against the wall. "Not much. She was hard to talk with. I really think Stanley is interested in her."

"Did they talk?"

"I supose. I left them alone most of the evening . . . Do you mind if he comes for dinner? We've got some work to do here."

"Fine. I haven't even seen Stanley this time."

"That's right."

The telephone continued to ring downstairs. He had a picture in his mind of all the unanswered and garbled messages piling up.

"When do you have to leave?" she said.

It came out of him without his even thinking about it.

"Tonight."

Her face seemed to fall.

"Oh hell. I'm sorry, Neil. We should have stayed home to-

gether last night. I've hardly seen anything of you . . . *Damn!*
Could you put it off another day?"

"I . . . don't think so. We've got a good deal of work ahead of
us."

"Neil?"

He looked up at her. She sat down next to him.

"I'm sorry. I really am."

"What about?" He looked at her innocently and groaned to
himself. One or the other was always throwing up the barricades.

"Please, Neil . . ."

"Well . . . I'm sorry, too."

"What's going to happen? What's going to happen to us?"

"I don't know. I can't even tell you what's *happened* to us."

"I wish one of us could."

There was another silence.

"I love you . . ."

He looked at her, trying to keep the right expression on his
face.

"Well, I'm certain I feel pretty much the same way."

"Lie down with me here. Would you? For a little while?"

He slid down the length of the bed and lay against her. Her
breath was sweet and he knew his must be a horror. She put her
arms round his neck and moved around so that her skirt was
nearly up to her hips; he could catch a glimpse of her nice skin as
he put his face against hers. The sun was streaming in through
the blinds, and in this nearly perfect audaciousness they were
conscious of the children's voices ringing in the streets and the
pots and pans being knocked about in the kitchen, Morton Gould
on the radio and her mother and father sitting quietly together
downstairs waiting for them to appear. She opened the front
of her blouse and brought his face down against her small, soft-
curving breasts. He was reminded of years past, years long forgotten, and the splendor and recklessness and intensity of late
afternoon loves . . .

Eighteen

"ANDREA . . . Andrea, dear. There's some company to see you . . ."

Her mother's voice sang to them, footsteps hesitating on the stair. Andrea rolled over him.

"All right — I'll be down ⁚ . . ."

Then she rolled back and they lay side by side trying to recapture whatever special emotion there had been for them. It seemed to be passing them by, just barely, and they clung to the heavy languor of the moment as if it had been the real thing and they had won it for themselves.

Presently, she leaned over and kissed him on the side of his face and got to her feet, straightening her clothes. Her throat and forehead shone in the withering heat of the early afternoon and small streaks of perspiration were coming through the back of her blouse. She looked at herself critically in the mirror.

"God! I can't go down there looking like this. Could you see who it is?"

She looked lovely with her face and forehead shining and her hair damply matted, and he told her this. But at the same time he slipped his shoes on and started downstairs.

The sound of Stanley's voice was a relief, and it was not until he had reached the bottom and turned into the main room that he realized Elsie was with him, talking with Andrea's mother about the insect pictures. Stanley looked like death, but it was apparent he had come to terms with the condition. He wore a fresh suit and was making an effort to keep his mouth from going slack, and he did not complain. He stood a short distance away, staring at Andrea's painting — the amalgam of Neil and John Tom — her cosmic lover, her legendary poet-politician folk hero.

He turned to greet Neil. The complaint — the early call, the hangover, the business with Elsie the night before: which was it? — showed only in his eyes. He could not get them quite into focus.

"Hi, Dads."

"Hello . . . Hello, Elsie." She looked up, smiled nicely and nodded, holding on to the katydid photograph. It probably made absolute good sense to her.

"I've written you something," Stanley said. "Want a look?"

"Yes."

They sat on a couch and Neil made penciled notations on the copy. They did not hear Andrea reach the bottom of the stair, but he immediately detected the surprised and faintly disapproving quality in her voice. She was already being entirely *too* nice to the girl, telling her that *of course* she should dine with them; they would *love* having her. The phone business started again, and Andrea's father looked in.

"It's the Governor, Neil. He must of just finished his consommé." The old man had a terrible laugh, possibly the result of it not quite being a laugh but rather a contrivance of high-pitched grunts put together in sequence, wheezing and dreadful. He seemed determined not to show his teeth for fear they might shoot right out of his head.

"Neil. Any plans yet?"

"Some. I'm going back tonight."

"Ah. You been bothered much this morning?"

"Yes. The goddam phone . . ."

"I've been getting some for you the last hour or so and having them transferred out there. Anything interesting?"

"No . . ." He thought a moment. "The papers. I'm working on a statement to give them now."

"Anything particular you wanted to say?"

"No. Not really."

"Then I'd suggest you hold off. Go out of business for the day . . ."

"All right."

". . . Piss on the fire and go home . . ."

"Okay . . ."

"Unless Edwards comes up with something. I don't think he will. He's trying like the devil. I understand he's been calling the newsmen, instead of the other way around. See? You're ahead without even opening your mouth."

"That's fine. I didn't much like the idea of popping off anyhow after so much in the papers this — "

"Well listen — what I called you about . . . There's a Mexican going to call you. Probably soon as we hang up. He called me and I gave him your number, but then I got in ahead of him."

"Who is it?"

"A *Mex*ican."

"From Mexico?"

"No, goddammit, hell no. American of Spanish descent. You like that better? Enrique García López. Henry. You know Henry?"

"Yes." He remembered Henry in the Legislature and as a city judge and later as a *patrón,* a new political leader of the machine-vote counties to the south.

"Well listen — you be careful what you say to that slant-eyed bastard. He'll probably want to make a deal."

"What kind?"

"I don't know. But be careful. He's a goddam bandit."

"Do we need him?"

"Hell yes we need him. Every goddam vote we can scrape up. But don't promise to make him Secretary of State or anything. He's just liable to ask for that. For a starter."

He gave a great laugh of satisfaction.

"All right," Neil said.

"Hey — one other thing. You really leaving tonight?"

"Yes."

"Could you get by here to see me in the next hour?"

"Oh, hell — *listen* — This is my *last day here.* You understand? I've been tied up every minute of — "

"Okay, *okay.* Can I come by there?"

"Well . . . sure. Happy to have — "

"Be about fifteen minutes. That all right? I won't stay long."

He could hear the children being summoned from next door and the dinner being set out on the table. In another room Andrea was still full of false enthusiasm for Elsie. Elsie was giving it to her right back, playing the innocent.

"You can't talk about it on the phone?"

"No."

The Governor rang off. Before Neil had reached the other room they were called in to eat. Andrea stood at one end of the table and advised where they should take their seats. The girls were quietly stuffing themselves in the kitchen, and he went in to say hello. They showed enormous appetites, dead tired and emotionless from the excitement of the morning, scarcely interested in any dinnertime conversation. He tried desperately for a few minutes to tell them something, but even if he had known what it was he wanted to say there was some doubt whether he would have ever got through to them.

"You find all the eggs?"

"Yes."

"Where were they hidden?"

"Yard."

"Did you have a good Easter?"

"Yes. Grandma froze a butterfly."

"Yes," he said. "She sure did."

"And a bumblebee!" said the younger sister.

The older set her fork down and began suddenly to cry. Neil was frantic.

"What's wrong, honey? What is it?"

"There's nothing to *do*."

"Yes there is . . ."

"What?"

". . . There's . . ."

"*Nothing!*"

"There's the park. After the naps perhaps we can all — "

The older one continued to cry.

"I want to freeze a bug," the younger one said, looking up impatiently. Andrea came into the kitchen to speak to the children for a moment. Then she looked at him.

"I think that's very nice."

"What?"

"Elsie. You didn't tell me she's going to Washington . . ."

She went back to her seat at the dining table. Neil joined them and served himself. He spoke to Stanley about the decision against any statement for the papers. The old man discussed cattle and the dubious quality of the beef they were being served. The grandmother described her new Leica camera. The phone rang again.

He tried to get Andrea's attention, but she avoided his gaze. He wondered if it were possible to get past the loneliness, the little terrors that isolated them all and were now nearly beyond comprehension. They had perpetrated such violences against one another — was there some twilight court where sentences for these crimes were miraculously, blessedly commuted? Just when you had thought a healing had set in, one of them laughed or coughed or hiccuped and the tissue tore away . . . He reached for the phone.

"Hello."

"Neel? Neel Creestawnsawn?"

"Hello, Henry."

Enrique García López bragged on him some. They talked about the time they had worked together, years ago, on legislation — never close to passage — setting up minimum housing requirements for migratory farm laborers.

"Neel?"

"Yes."

"You got it wrapped up dawn here, boy."

"Good . . . Good."

"Mawst be like that ahverwhare."

"I hope so, Henry. I sure hope so."

"You think you'll be needing my votes?"

"Well . . ."

"Ah doan think so. Ah think you could do without us. Spicking frankly."

"I'm not so sure. I thought you said . . ."

"Sure. We're for you, Neel. Hawndred per cent. Tell me what you need and I'll get it for you."

"I don't know what *amount* I need, Henry. It's just that — "

"That prick Adwards — he's struck gold or sawmthing."

"What?"

"He wants-a deal with me."

"What, Henry?"

"That prick Adwards — he's damn fool, Neel, you know that? — he's offer me five thousand."

"For what?"

"The votes. To deliver the cawnties."

"Well, damn, Henry . . . I don't think I could make it without you. Or perhaps I could. But I'd like to have you with me."

"Ah'm with you, boy. All the way. You can be sure of that thing. But I was figuring if you got any to spare you might make it without some of mine. That way I could accept that crazy man's money — and I need it, Neel. Ah got a little debt."

"What do you mean?"

"I mean you got the votes here if you need them. But they goin' to Adwards, otherwhise. And if it gets too close I can always ring in a few thousand more votes Ah got. Secretly registered. Just for you. We got great pawtential down here."

They talked some more and then ended the conversation without anything being definitely decided. The others had moved back into the main room, and Emma was clearing the dishes. The children had been taken up to bed.

"Godalmighty," he heard the old man say. "It's the Governor again."

Arthur Fenstemaker came through the door, grinning hugely at everyone and looking as if he might at any moment circle the room in a compulsion of handclasps and vault up the stairs to kiss the children. He did kiss Andrea on the side of the face and squeezed her mother's arm until the older woman began to turn red at the neck and laugh, nervously and for no reason, at everything the Governor said. The Governor stood glaring at Elsie for a moment, repeating his promise to visit her in the bookstore and make a purchase.

"But she won't be there," Andrea said gaily. "She's leaving us just as soon as Stanley finds her a job in Washington."

"Cut that stuff out, Stanley," the Governor said. He took Neil's arm and they went into the study. They sat in two big chairs and lit cigarettes.

"First thing when you get back, I want you to see some people for me."

"All right."

"First thing. Otherwise, we've got a disaster on our hands."

"What's it all about."

"A lynchin'."

"*What?*"

"Well. Almost." The overstatement and then the qualification seemed to make Fenstemaker feel a little better. "Not really, but pretty much the same thing. A month ago this sheriff and two or three deputies and some others tied a colored man to a tree and beat him to death. With chains."

"I haven't heard about *any* of this. *Last month?* How did — "

"Only because I been sittin' on it five weeks. I heard about it soon's it happened. They were tryin' to hush it up down there, but you don't really ever hush up anything like that. I sent some people in to look around and then I got a couple Rangers to make an investigation. It didn't take them long. They had the whole story for me in about a week. It's a goddam mess. I'd like to go down there and lay some chain on a couple of those sonsofbitches . . ."

The Governor went into further detail. He explained how they had documented the case and were prepared to turn it over to the District Attorney.

"What do you want me to do?"

"I want you to see these people in Washington. They've heard about it, too. We came across a couple of their investigators asking questions all over the town. The Rangers told them they had the case nailed down and sent them back. So they know about it there."

"What's the problem?"

"The problem is that nothing's going to happen. No charges, no nothin'. Nothin' at all. And when they hear about it up there they'll raise an awful goddam stink."

"I should think so. What do you mean nothing will happen?"

"Well, nothin' right off. The thing is, there's this Judge and this D.A. and I don't trust either one. They're liable to put the case before a grand jury and recommend they forget all about it. They're not exactly in mournin' over that nigger."

"Well for God's sake, Arthur . . . What do you plan to do about it?"

"I'll get 'em. One way or another — those two and the whole damn bunch of them are going to pay and pay and pay . . ."

"But what about a *trial?* Isn't there even going to be an *indictment?*"

". . . And pay," the Governor said. "I'm going to turn them inside out. Maybe the whole goddam town while I'm at it. There may be an indictment — I *think* there will be. Who the hell knows? Maybe even a conviction. But it's going to take time to get the thumbscrews tightened on them. And there won't be time for anything if those people in Washington start screaming at me. You get some more of their investigators down here and we'll have a riot. And if I don't get some action taken in court, we're going to have some mean goddam legislation jammed down our throats or up our behinds or however you prefer to look at it."

"You want me . . ."

"To talk to those people. You can do a sellin' job for me. They'll listen to you. *Explain* it to 'em for Jesus sake."

"All right. I'll try. They might understand."

"Yes . . . I wish the hell I understood."

"Understood what?"

"Just what the hell my part is in all this," the Governor said, standing to go. "I got no business. I just jumped in like a damn fool. I don't even know why. Right reasons or wrong reasons — who the hell can say?"

He stood and began to walk toward the front of the house, then stopped abruptly and turned back to Neil. The vitality so noticeable on his arrival had nearly leaked away; his face sagged and his eyes were clouded over.

"You think this is the right thing to do?" he said. "I've searched my head and . . ."

Before Neil could reply, or even begin to search his own head, the Governor's expression firmed.

"The hell with all that," he said. "I can't worry about motives. Let the rest of them worry about that . . . They'll have me doing the right thing for the wrong reasons anyhow. You do what you have to do."

He turned and took another step and then faced Neil again.

"What'd that fellow want?"

"Who?"

"The Mex . . . Henry . . . He call you yet?"

Neil told about the telephone conversation.

"Well it could've been worse. And you said the right thing. He's a bandit, like I said, but he's honest and he'll do what he says. Let him take old Edwards for a ride. I'd prefer to see the money go that way. Edwards'll be lucky to get a vote for every five dollars he throws around. And he hasn't got much to throw."

"You think those people you've talked to will stay with me all the way? Even if I begin to sag a little?"

"Who knows?" the Governor said. "They're *all* a bunch of bandits when you get right down to it. We could win without their money. But this way it's easier. You can go back up to Washington and vote that economic aid and lower the interest rate and maybe even get a nigger bill through. You'd prefer that, wouldn't you? Like it a lot better than rampagin' around here tryin' to outtalk Edwards and bein' something you ain't?"

"Yes," Neil said. Then he put the question to the Governor.

"You know where Edwards got all that information — on John Tom and Elsie and Stanley?"

Fenstemaker began unwrapping a cigar and looking for a waste-basket in which to throw the cellophane. Not finding one, he stuffed the wrapper in his pocket, stared blandly at Neil, and said: "From me."

"Why? Why in the world would you — "

"I did it because old Edwards was pokin' around all over town, asking questions. He's a crazy goddam campaigner, but he's good at that sort of thing. He would've got all of it sooner or later, and I felt as long as I had some control over how and where he'd use it you wouldn't get hurt any. I passed the word along to a few people he was talkin' to, and it worked. You *weren't* hurt. The poor dumb bastard fired all his barrels and brought down the house. It was a good performance — funny as hell — but only that. He didn't even *touch* you. Otherwise . . . How'd you like to go through this campaign pickin' out buckshot from your behind?"

He smiled, and then said: "Talk to those people up there for me, will you? They'll believe *you*. You obviously got no guile . . ."

Then he was gone, through the main room with an extravagant wave toward the others, striding down the driveway to his limou-sine. Neil stood at the door and watched him go.

It should have been John Tom, he thought. John Tom would have been far more successful at this business — he could have been the epic poet-politician, with a knowing, no-nonsense approach to how things were and how they ought to be and a com-pensating awareness of the terrible underpinnings of the system that supported them. He never took himself too seriously, and yet he had been one of the few serious persons he had ever known. A very Good Doctor. He had made a speech to a bunch of them one night at one of the parties in the big spanishy house across town, standing there, lecturing them, the vitality coming to him as all of Neil's began to drain away: "Bums, hacks, medicine show evangelists . . ." he said. "Liberals! You're all hysterical Tories at heart — Wobblies playing the bond market. Simpering, powdered old pros from Flitville — worrying about bad breath and lip hair while the world caves in. Go ahead! Get right with your Zen-Buddha! Walk softly and carry a goddam badminton racquet . . ."

The trouble was, they had no stomach for it — John Tom's awful compulsion to look at reality — they could not bear to watch for too long a time. Stanley still carried a little of it with him; it was what he called his mixed tones. But all the others couldn't possibly stare the truly monstrous in the face . . .

The afternoon wore on. Stanley and the girl went out for a ride in the hills. Andrea and her parents sat talking about a summer trip to Taos or Acapulco. Neil talked incessantly on the phone and stood around waiting for the children to come awake. When they finally wandered down the stairs, cross and perspiring, he attempted to engage them in conversation. But it was about as brittle and meaningless as cocktail party patter, and they soon grew bored with him and followed their grandmother outside to chase insects.

Toward evening, Stanley returned with Elsie and began transferring his luggage from one car to the other. Neil stuffed clothes in his bag upstairs. Andrea brought him some freshly laundered shirts. They sat quietly, talking about the house and the children and their personal finances, trying obliquely to recapture a little of the magic that had just barely passed them by earlier in the afternoon. Clouds gathered and a noisy rain began to fall.

"Perhaps the flights will be canceled," she said.

"We'll have to go out and wait, in any event."

There was one last phone call. The pretty little girl who had accompanied them on the flight down wanted to know if he would like a ride back the following morning. He told her no, wanting desperately to stay one last evening with Andrea and the children but certain at the same time there would be her parents and possibly one last unavoidable party getting in the way. It could get a lot worse, he thought, before it got any better. The girl's singsong voice droned on interminably, rising and falling. Listen, he wanted to tell her, Listen . . . Quit trying to be something you've invented. Forget about your Village parties and your folk dancing and those contrived plans to romance with Negroes and Senators and misunderstood artists. Get out of those goddam bulky skirts and those awful quarter-heel shoes . . . Put your hair up sometime; get it out of your face. Quit chewing your nails and take a bath every night and keep your underwear laundered. Ease off all that *posturing* and wait for something really *genuine* to happen.

He told her thanks-very-much and give-his-best-to-her-father and have-a-good-trip-back.

Then he left the phone off the hook and got his bags from upstairs, kissed his children and left a twenty-dollar bill in an envelope for Fat Emma the maid. It had been like a weekend with friends in some gay country house spooked by forgotten assignations. They loaded the bags in the back of the car and drove slowly through the gleaming streets toward the airport.

They stood on the ramp, rain falling all around, rattling the shed above their heads. Andrea watched Stanley and the girl talking and then bending toward each other to kiss. She wavered a moment, looking up at Neil who seemed either half asleep or in a mild state of shock. She put her arm through his and their shoulders touched lightly and finally they were able to turn their faces to each other and kiss. They mumbled insane, insensible goodbyes and then Neil and Stanley made a run for the plane. The folding stairway swallowed them up and the big motors began to groan. She and Elsie looked at each other glumly and turned to leave. Her name came across the public address — there was a number to call. She dialed the number from a booth and Kermit's voice shrieked at her.

"Hey, Miss Lady, where's that car of mine? Old Jake and I are out here at your digs, and somebody's split with my heap."

She told him what had happened with his car. He found this unimaginably funny.

"It's the *gas* gauge, Miss Lady. I never think to look. Listen — old Jake and I are giving a little party tonight at my new Renaissance Gallery and we got absolutely to have you with us . . ."

She began to feel a little better and promised to meet them there for a drink.

Nineteen

HE SAT in the huge leather chair, head back, hands clasping armrests, spine brushing somebody's Great Seal, spinning round slowly, unobtrusively, in ponderous half circles, following the debate, the dark voices, the magpie deliberations that filled the fluted chamber. Lights, faces, shone above his head — the voices raged on below and around him. Occasionally, he read from a pamphlet. He wheezed a little song under his breath, tapping his foot: *You feet's too big . . . Don' wawncha 'cause you feet's too big . . . Mad atcha 'cause you feet's too big . . . Ah really hate ya cause —*

(The United States Senate meets in a Chamber of quiet dignity and rich tradition. Details of the renovated Chamber are much like the original, but every effort has been made to make this one a model of perfection in lighting, acoustics, comfort and convenience . . .)

He wondered how long. The voices seemed to fade, droning, like slave minstrels, like fraternity serenades, rising and falling.

He banged on the big desk and mumbled some-some-sumpin' . . . "will be in order . . ."

If he weren't, he thought, stuck up there on the throne and forced to rule, he could have slipped inside the cloakroom for a drink. That was where the others were — he could hear their occasional laughter through the swinging doors. Could he risk a vodka? Right out here in the open? A watered vodka with a couple ice cubes. Who would know?

I'd try it, he thought, I'd try so hard, like she said. You do what you *have* to do, mah boy — and Gov'nahr Ah just *have* to have a watered vodka. The Very Junior Senator needs relief. What the hell is this? Pledgeship or something? Where'd all those other Juniors go?

Am no presiding officer.

Wasn't meant to be.

I'm the goddam *Prince!* An easy tool.

You Pro-Tem there or you Mister Leader — hey fellas! — get me down off here, look in that back room and round up some more Juniors. *Doan wawncha cause you feet's too big.* . . . Where was Stanley? Where was old Stanley, my old Junior? Out counting returns? He was supposed to be back — he was definitely supposed (after the mail was signed, the office locked tight) . . . definitely supposed to be back here to — *There* he is, raht above mah head, up there with that lovely dark girl with the hair that smelt so good last evening. Knew you'd make it, boy. Happy you could bring a friend. She hasn't changed much — your girl, yours and mine — still pushing the myth of herself: black-eyed and un-lipsticked with that batch of hair pulled over the little ear that might have been sculpted right out of creamery butter. *Hey, Stanley you lump!* Git down heah and fetch youah Massah a vodka-water. With a handful of that little lady's hair to paste over my heart. Can't seem to catch his eye. Got hers — not his — got hers, we're exchanging looks in this great gilded cham-

ber. All this quiet dignity . . . rich tradition . . . Get me a
pint of Quiet Dignity, kid . . . hundred proof.

(. . . Senators elected to America's highest legislative body
conduct their part of the Nation's affairs against a background of
cream and dark-red marble, gold silk damask walls and the rich
gleam of mahogany desks . . .)

Well it is — it certainly is, gentlemen. That's gold silk damask
if I ever saw gold silk damask, and it goes real pretty next to that
little girl's rich mahogany face up there and I'll stake my reputation on *that*. Soon's I'm legally elected to this highest legislative
body. Hey Stanley! Get me some returns. Don't just sit there
rubbing bums with that girl — push the clock up, close the polls,
stuff a ballot box. Gimmie a vote and a vodka and a deep-froze
butterfly for my children. Give a little attention, for God's sake,
to your presiding *officer* . . .

(. . . As President of the Senate, the Vice-President sits behind the mahogany desk on a rostrum at the north of the Senate
floor . . .)

Well, now. This the north side, is it? Something to tell my
grandchildren, my children's children . . . Girls . . . you won't
believe this, but . . . your granddad used to keep the Vice-President's chair warm. Warm as could be.

(. . . Framing the Vice-President's rostrum is a background of
red Levanto marble pilasters centered by a heavy blue velvet
drape embellished with a gold embroidered border . . .)

Now what in hell's a pilaster? Let's see here . . . let me just
. . . There. *Structurally a pier but architecturally a column.* So.
So? Sounds phony to me, but those draperies are definitely blue
— they got that right. Now . . . if I can just go get myself pi-
lastered —

(Directly behind the Vice-President himself is a huge, silk American flag . . .)

Roger. But where's Himself and why don't he come back here and give me some relief. Goddam Republicans . . .

(. . . The motto *E Pluribus Unum* . . . is carved in Hauteville cream marble above the rostrum . . .)

Take their word for it. I turned round to look, somebody might pass a bill or call a quorum or clear the calendar and then where'd *I* be? Examining Hauteville cream marble, that's where. So they ought to get me down off here before I let our Doomed Republic slip right through my fingers. *Ten* parliamentarians couldn't help . . . Where's that party? Those party? What's doing at the Embassies? Lost track with these night sessions. Ex*cuse* me, Countess — thought that was my wife I was goosing . . .

(. . . here sit the official reporters of all proceedings . . . During a spirited debate these reporters have to move from place to place, taking notes while they walk or find a seat near the Senators engaged in the discussion . . .)

All right, Official Reporters of All Proceedings! Get up off your rusties! Don't you know a spirited debate when you hear one? What was it that fellow said earlier? About these parlous times? *My constituents, Mr. President, are pissing Strontium 90.* Well now I wonder if in putting the facts together or the statement together that my distinguished and dear friend just made (his feet's *too big*), in what I think is rather a partisan manner, he has considered a few points of interest, among which is the fact that I happen to be of a generation that was permitted — and was proud to do so — to serve some time in the service of my country, during which time our generation — which is now the succeeding generation — and you, my friend, are, of course, talking about

another generation — is the generation that made no profit from
the war — and was proud to do so — and, well, my friend, my
high-spirited friend . . .

(. . . desks are modified replicas of those used in the Old
Senate Chambers; a few are originals brought to the new Chamber in 1859. Two historic desks still serving today's Senators are
those once used by Daniel Webster and Jefferson Davis. A small
block of wood inlaid on the left side of Davis's desk marks the spot
where a Union officer reportedly thrust his sword . . .)

Now let's not deal in hearsay or histrionics, gentlemen. Either
the Union officer did or he didn't and. . . .

(. . . Two tiny snuff boxes of black lacquer, adorned with
Japanese figures, rest on marble ledges flanking the rostrum.
They are kept filled with snuff, and, though never used, they re-
main a tradition of the Senate . . .)

Never *used?* My God we'll call in the Hoover Commission!
Waste, duplication, bureaucracy . . . And how about that other?
That *Japanese* stuff. Foreign imports, unfair competition —
wait'll the Tariff Commission hears . . .

(. . . Another custom carried over to the Senate today is blotting sand . . .)

Blotting sand? And who was it got the contract for *that?* Bil-
lions for defense, I say, but not one more red cent for blotting
sand. And I say — and I think all reasonable men will join with
me in saying — *Up in Harlem . . . Table for two . . . They was
four of us . . . Me . . . Your big feet . . . And you —* join me
in saying, in asking, in *demanding* . . . unanimous consent to
take me down off this rostrum framed by red Levanto marble pilasters. Let me withdraw from this glittering world of gold dam-

ask and Hauteville cream marble. I remember a time we withdrew, for all of two weeks one spring when the azalea bloomed
along the back fence of that little house and Andrea had that little
miscarriage. Of Justice. Missed that goddam carriage house, lost
it somewhere between the patch of heather and the flowerless
turf . . .

(. . . Beyond the Lobby is the Marble Room, a private chamber for reading and consultation. The entire interior of this
comfortably furnished room is of various hues of marble. Two
large, gold-framed mirrors placed at each end reflect and re-re-
flect the room's magnificent crystal chandelier and create an illusion of endless halls and countless chandeliers . . .)

Well! Give a cheer! Home at last with my misplaced illusions,
my endless halls, my chandeliers. Ready for some reading and
consultation. Thought the time would never come — those fellows out there, they don't understand, never had to meet a pay-
roll. But now I'm here, what's a Very Junior Senator to do? Belt
a whiskey from a paper cup? *Hah do, hah do . . . Hah do,
Senter, hah do . . .* All my betters. I could place a call on the
long distance and (make it a *conference* call, Operator) talk with
Andrea and (failing at that?) all my other friends, three-quarter
million of 'em, just back from votin' their conscience. Ought to
explain how awfully nice it is to be here, folks, and I appreciate
the great mandate you give me. Only what in hell was it now?
Seems to slip my mind. I could do that, place that little call, or
maybe check the supper clubs to see what's doin' in town, deciding between Paul Desmond and Lefty Frizzell . . .

He stood staring at the others. The older men moved past,
smiling, pausing to inquire about the early returns, clapping him
on the shoulder and moving on. He examined news ticker bul-
letins, but it was too early to tell . . . primary elections in the
South . . . tantamount to election . . . only token Republican

opposition expected in November . . . near-record turnouts . . .

Stanley and Elsie waited for him at the entrance, standing in the vaulted reception room (. . . east end of the Lobby, where visitors may consult their Senators . . . outstanding example of the artistry of Brumidi . . . beautiful frescoes and murals by the Italian artist . . .). They walked into the hallway and waited for the elevator. Outside, it was nearly dark, and the Air Force band was playing in an open space in front. They paused, listening to the music for a few moments, and then caught a cab to the hotel, brass and bass drum fading as they rolled along.

There was a huge crowd present, spread through the suites of rooms. A cry of approval went up when he entered, and he worked his way round the room, shaking hands, the beaming faces, young and middle-aged, faintly awed, grinning their confidence. They talked about the campaign for half an hour. He stood there with an oversized drink in his hand, making the words come, nodding, tilting his head, grinning back. All kinds of faces floated past: housewives, lobbyists, displaced provincials, soldier boys, people from other staffs, union agents, Negroes (extra-warm handshake, clap 'em on the back, had to avoid 'em during campaign), old pols, Mexican bandits. After half an hour he slid away through the crowd and found an empty bedroom where he lay down and fell immediately to sleep, thinking about news tickers and pilaster columns and somebody's feet bein' too big. Stanley woke him with the report about the very early returns — only a few counties reporting, most of them incomplete. He blinked his eyes in the bedside light, squinting at the figures.

"Slight lead, hah?"

"Holds the trend, be more than slight," Stanley said.

Elsie came in to say the Governor was on the telephone. He lifted the receiver and said hello.

"Feelin' better?" Fenstemaker's voice was like a cannon in his ear.

"Not especially," Neil said. "I'd hesitate to make a victory speech on the basis of —"

"What've you got? What's the count you got?"

Neil told him, reading from the report Stanley had received.

"Hell! Goddam and hell! No wonder! I've got a real tally for you — been receivin' reports from my county men last two hours. They're way ahead of that election bureau. Listen to this — you got fifty thousand on him up to now, with two hunnerd thousand cast and reports from most of the counties. You like that? Listen — that's a real trend. That knocks 'em in the goddam plexus. It'll hold even when old Edwards' snuff dippers are still tryin' to stuff boxes out in the boondocks . . ."

He told Stanley and Elsie. They went to tell the others. He talked with Fenstemaker several minutes more and then rang off. He could hear Stanley reading the report in the other room and the great whoop of pleasure going up as the figures were chalked on a blackboard. There was some singing and a demand that he come make a speech. He put this off until the next report from Fenstemaker, letting Stanley take the figures from Jay Mc-Gown, and when it was an obvious runaway — so far outdistancing Edwards that opposition campaign managers were conceding even before Edwards himself gave in — when his *election* to the Senate was unmistakable, only then did he come out front and make the speech. They clapped and howled for more, but he moved inside while the friends began passing whiskey bottles back and forth and organizing a snake dance through the suite of rooms. He sat on the side of the bed and tried to get Andrea on the long distance.

Fat Emma took her time answering. He could hear her coming on, finally, and giving the operator another number. He broke in to ask if he could talk with the little girls but changed his mind when Emma said they were already asleep. There was a pause and then another series of rings and then it was like being forced back into the party underway just beyond the door. There was a great deal of confusion at the other end, and he told the operator he would speak with anyone there.

"Hey! Hey, Neil! Congratulations man. Great . . . Great . . . How 'bout that?"

He thanked the younger man and asked if Andrea was present.

"Yeah — hey — just a minute — hey — you know you pulled us all in on your shirttail?"

"You didn't need any help," Neil said.

"Hell we didn't. Listen — hey, listen — our majorities were bigger than ever. That's one thing. And we pulled in a bunch of others — new kids we never expected would win. It was you did it. You talked by-God sense and pulled in the youngsters because you were such an apple-pie type yourself . . ."

Apple pie-eyed type, he thought, and then said, "Well that's fine. You ought to have a good session next year . . . Andrea around anywhere?"

"Yeah . . . Yah . . . Just second . . . She was here . . . second ago. Listen, how about I get her to call you. Hah? What's number?"

Neil asked the young man to look around. He tapped his foot to music coming in from the nightstand radio. The music ended and the announcer came on. "Colonaid!" the fellow exulted. "For aging colon . . . The colon muscles lose *tone* and *strength* . . ."

"Hey, Neil . . . Neil?"

"Yes."

"She was here minute ago. Ought to be back. What's your number, I'll have her . . ."

He gave the number and said Thanks, thanks again, and rang off after the young man invited him to join them at Aspen for the weekend. They were all flying up. Chartered a plane. Big ski trip. "We think we got Andrea talked into it . . . Why don't you fly up there, hah? It's great up there, it's . . ."

He said he just might do that. He would take it under advisement. He set the receiver down and lay on the bed. "Aging colon?" he said aloud, rubbing his eyes. The colon muscles lost *what?* He stood and slipped on his coat and left by one of the doors that opened onto the hall. They had stopped singing inside and switched to dance music . . .

On the fiercely lighted, half-deserted street he began to walk.

The white Capitol dome was spectacular, veiled in mist. He walked the several blocks, toward and past the big white dome, pausing finally in front of the Library to stare back and around him. The Library building was lost in shadow, but lights shone softly on the fountain in front. He stood looking at Neptune's Court, conscious suddenly of the rush of water and the coiled snakes the size of a man's arm, spewing liquid, dark and glittering, toward the bronze figures. The Great King stared back, moody, contemplative, his tarnished face and beard catching the light. The King sat on rocks, thinking, ignoring the impossibly muscled young men on either side who trumpeted wild-soundless tunes on conch shells. The towering women were at right and left of the young men. They sat astride rampaging seahorses. All of them were washed in greens and blues, and Neil stood in front, thinking he loved the heavy-thighed woman at Neptune's right most of all. She was majestic — storm-tinted and lonely — her huge blue-green breasts swaying slightly in the rush of water, her face clouded by streaks of dark decay. He stood there peering through the bad light and was suddenly transported toward her, into the water, onto the moss-slick bottom, cold liquid filling his shoes and ballooning the air inside his trouser legs. He staggered, sliding sideways on the green bottom, and gripped a snake's head for balance. The spray fell all around him and he walked along, squish-squash, shoes sucking feet, moving deeper into the King's chamber. He staggered once again, brushing the weathered bronze of the seahorse, got a grip (on a hand? a foot?) and hoisted himself up behind the big wonderful woman. She was magnificent! Primal, content, constant, quietly abused. There was no other like her — he was certain of it. He sat astride the gleaming horse hips and held on to his lady, reaching round her swollen ribcase, marveling at the curve of her bare stomach and the way her big legs joined the trunk. He had never felt such love.

He held on for a moment longer and then began pulling himself around toward the front so that he could get his face up next to the cold blast of her breath and kiss her lovely, barely parted, rain-rusted lips.

Lights shone at him. He ignored them at first, thinking they might go away. But then the two Capitol policemen got out of their car and stood at the rail separating the sidewalk from the pool of water. They yelled something and he held on tight. One of them got down into the water and came toward him, flashing the light in his eyes.

". . . Senator . . . ? That you Senator . . . ?" He turned back and yelled at his partner: "It's Senator Christiansen." He turned round again, keeping the light low. "You all right, sir?"

"Hello," Neil said, smiling. He began to climb down. He steadied himself against the younger man. A wad of papers, shaken loose from his hip pocket, floated nearby. He bent down and retrieved them, shaking the water off. "I was up there," he said, pointing to the stairs that circled above the fountain. "I lost these papers. Very valuable papers. Had to go into the water to get them."

"You should've given us a call," the young patrolman said. "We give you a lift, sir? You ought to get home and take off those wet clothes . . ."

Neil said that would be fine; it would work out perfectly. The policemen remembered the primaries and asked about the vote, and he told them and they were real happy for him. The three of them climbed into the patrol car. He was borne through the quiet streets, past row houses and ruined balustrades and awful-smelling basement entrances to the apartment he shared with Stanley. He could hear the phone's ringing halfway up the stairs.

He slipped off his trousers and wet shoes and socks and talked with newsmen on the phone. Yes, he was quite pleased . . . He had expected to win, of course, but not . . . not so overwhelmingly as it now appeared . . . What was the latest count? *That* much? Well, now . . . Well. It was all very something something something.

He pulled off his clothes and got himself dried and bathrobed, thinking he would have to call Fenstemaker first thing next morning (they would plan some victory dinners for the fall, clear some federal appointments in the home state); thinking that with such a showing in the primary he might very likely get by without an opponent in the general election; thinking he should call Andrea (should he fly home [avoiding Aspen] to stare at his children?), write some letters, thank-you notes to contributors, a good long note to Andrea's father who'd come through with twenty-five thousand — Thinking he should make a film for television, give old Stanley a raise in pay and a month off (soon as he's written the script); raise Miss Elsie, too, hoping to get one last breath of her nut-smelling hair. He thought about these things, reminding himself he had six years — a full term — to advance on the committees, secure his position, pursue his blue bronze ladies — tarnished and faithful — in the fountain, saving their storm-violated world. He lay in the bed, watching the great white bulk of the dome grow dim, sorrows and joys oddly approximated by the incredible fact of success.

Country Pleasures

I wonder by my troth, what thou and I
Did, till we lov'd? Were we not wean'd till then?
But suck'd on country pleasures, childlishly?
                                        — JOHN DONNE

Here at the last cold Pharos between Greece
And all I love, the lights confide
A deeper darkness to the rubbing tide;
Doors shut, and we the living are locked inside
Between the shadows and the thoughts of peace:
And so in furnished rooms revise
The index of our lovers and our friends
From gestures possibly forgotten, but the ends
Of longings like unconnected nerves,
And in this quiet rehearsal of their acts
We dream of them and cherish them as Facts.
                                        — LAWRENCE DURRELL

One

VERY EARLY that morning the official party had come down out of the mountains and begun to move across the flat, sun-blasted land. The mountains reappeared from time to time on either side — reassuringly close in the beginning so that one could see the winding goat paths and the stubble of mesquite on the lower slopes; then from a distance of a great many miles that turned the ridges into slagheap shapes, purple and rumpled looking in the low, clouded light of the early hours. The limousine came through and out of the passes, and the lesser ranges gave way to sandhills and these into gray dunes. Then there was only the tortured prairie grass, dust-bleached and brittle, and the perfect stretch of highway with the dark folds of the mountains always out front or in back or on either side, shimmering in the new-visited heat, rising off the floor of the ranchland and collapsing again.

"I keep thinking we're going back into the mountains," Sweet Mama Fenstemaker said. She had been sitting quietly in back and studying the bald landscapes for nearly an hour. "I keep thinking we're going back," she said, "but we never seem to get there."

Jay McGown turned sideways in the jump seat and stretched his legs. He was an exceedingly tall young man with a bland and perpetually happy freckled face that reflected none of the discomfort he experienced during the morning's drive. He had been up late the night before, drinking with the Governor; he had risen earlier than any of the others that morning, checking travel routes, juggling luggage in the car trunk, loafing in the lobby of the Paisano Hotel and reading historical tracts on Pancho Villa's border raids. Now he sat in the jump seat, sore-eyed and sleepy, his long legs grown stiff in the cramped space. He was delighted to turn sideways for a few minutes and talk to Mrs. Fenstemaker: "It's because we're driving between two parallel ranges. It looks like they come together up ahead, but they don't really — it's all an illusion. Like going down the middle of a railroad track and thinking the rails come together on the horizon."

"Fascinating," Mrs. Fenstemaker said. She made clicking sounds in the back of her throat.

Jay started to elaborate on this thesis. He could make effortless conversation with Sweet Mama for hours at a time; and at this point he welcomed any opportunity to change positions in the jump seat — but the Governor, who had been napping alongside his wife, opened his eyes and said: "All an illusion, all a goddam illusion." He smiled and pulled on his nose and added: "Let's have a little drink — little of that Scotch whiskey, Jay. Before our ice becomes an illusion. Let's all have a little tot."

Jay opened a zippered bag at his feet and removed whiskey and soda and plastic tumblers. Another bag contained ice cubes. Sarah Lehman, riding in front with Hoot Gibson Fenstemaker, leaned over the seat to fish out the bottle opener for Jay. Hoot Gibson took his eyes off the highway for a moment to examine Sarah's behind.

"Sarah — you pour the whiskey," the Governor said. "Jay can fill the glasses with ice. Let's everybody get organized. Hoot Gibson, you just keep your mind on the goddam drivin'."

Hoot Gibson laughed and moved his big shoulders around. Sarah was still bent over the seat, her skirt pulled tight round her hips. Hoot Gibson finally shifted his gaze back to the highway. "Jus' remember old Hoot Gibson," he said. "On the rocks in that amber glass, Jay. I like that amber glass."

"Isn't it awfully early yet?" Mrs. Fenstemaker said. "Maybe we could stop for coffee or a soft drink . . ."

"We're out in the ranch country, Sweet Mama," the Governor said. "Day's half over. Sun's been up for hours. Hours. Primitive goddam country. Man needs to be fortified."

Jay and Sarah filled the glasses and passed them around. Hoot Gibson adjusted the air-conditioning and turned the dial on the radio. There was only static and an occasional fading wisp of rock 'n roll music. He gripped his drink and concentrated on the driving. Sarah switched on the phonograph and played a Morton Gould record. The Governor jiggled his phone receiver.

"Hell of a country," the Governor said. "Hell of a goddam country. Can't even rouse an operator."

"Perhaps you can phone when we get there," Sweet Mama said. "They'll have phone lines, won't they?"

"Half-dozen calls I needed to make . . ." Fenstemaker mumbled. "We ought to investigate the cost of installing shortwave radio."

Jay wrote "shortwave" on a yellow pad and reached over to refill the Governor's glass. Sarah Lehman asked Sweet Mama if she would like a soft drink.

"No . . . No, I think I'll wait," Mrs. Fenstemaker said. "Until we get there. It should be soon, shouldn't it? We've been driving nearly three hours."

Jay nodded. "Not far now," he said. "We ought to see them a good distance ahead. They're supposed to be set up not too far off the highway."

"I can't imagine," Mrs. Fenstemaker said, "I just can't imagine it."

The big car drummed along the smooth surface of the highway. The Governor leaned back and closed his eyes again, holding his drink with both hands against his chest. Mrs. Fenstemaker read a magazine. Hoot Gibson opened a window vent to dispose of a cigarette, and they all shifted uneasily in the blast of desert air. Sarah turned to Jay and said: "Suppose you're excited."

"More anxious than excited," Jay said. "They're bringing Victoria Anne out for a few days. I haven't seen her in nearly a year."

"Oh . . . You've talked to the mother, then?"

Jay leaned over and rested his arms on the top of the front seat. He shook his head.

"No. The Governor talked to her. He did all the talking. I got to speak to the girl, though. She told me she was coming out here to visit her mother. She'll be here a week."

"I'm happy for you," Sarah said. Jay traced a line with his finger along the curve of Sarah's arm until she shifted in the front seat and stared ahead.

"She called me Daddy," Jay said.

Sarah looked back at him. "That's an enormous improvement over the last time," she said.

"Yes," Jay said.

"There it is!" Hoot Gibson said suddenly. "Godalmighty . . . That must be it up ahead."

Everyone strained to catch sight of the prefabricated Victorian mansion towering above the floor of the ranchland. The mansion loomed on the horizon like a great landlocked whale, ginger-bread bas-relief against the backdrop of bleached dune and mountain and gunmetal sky. Then as they moved closer the whole fantastic scene came slowly into focus: the Mexican village, simulated adobe huts, plaster on plywood; balsa outbuildings and ersatz oil derricks chained to railroad flatcars; tents and trucks and tractors and trailers, buses and vintage cars and the endless, milling mob of carpenters and technicians and tourists. Off to one side there were perhaps half a dozen handsome beeves huddled together, grazing from a mound of store-bought silage.

"Destruction upon destruction . . ." Fenstemaker gasped. "The whole goddam land is spoilt . . ."

"It's incredible," Sweet Mama said. "What will they do with it when they're through here?"

"They already sold the big house to the fella owns the land," Hoot Gibson said. "Gonna use it for a cow barn."

"They even dyed the grass green near the mansion," Jay cried. "It wouldn't respond to the water they piped in, so they dyed it green."

Hoot Gibson slowed the car, weaving in and out of stalled traffic, moving past the crowds gathered along the highway: ranch hands and motorists and women in slacks and straw hats and bobby-soxers on horseback. The limousine came to a stop at a wire gate. Hoot Gibson lowered the window and smiled at the guard.

"Guvanah Fenst'makah's pahty," he said.

The crowds moved in closer as the guard lowered the wire gate. Hoot Gibson steered the car through the entrance and down a dirt road toward a huge commissary tent and several large trailer houses parked nearby. A press agent flagged them down midway, caught hold of the door handle and tried to ride on the lip of the running board; he held on for a few seconds and then stumbled into the dust. Another studio official got astraddle a front fender and proceeded to direct them, with a flourish of arm and hand movements, toward the trailer houses.

"They're mad — they've all gone mad out here in the heat," the Governor said. "I'm beginnin' to think maybe our comin' here was a mistake."

No one said anything. They all stared in wonder. The limousine came to a stop in front of the main trailer.

"Jay, you get out and see if they're ready for us," Fenstemaker said. "Get everything organized. So we can leave soon's the work's done." Jay got out of the car. "Keep that goddam air-conditionin' on, Hoot Gibson." The Governor touched his forehead with a pocket handkerchief and blotted at a film of dust on his blue suit.

Sarah joined Jay outside. The two of them engaged the press agent, attempting to get the visit organized. The press agent assured them everything was arranged.

"Miss McGown and Mr. Shavers are inside the trailer house,"

the man said. "They're expecting the Governor right now."

Jay signaled, and Hoot Gibson switched off the motor. The Governor and Sweet Mama began moving out of the car. The press agent said: "You say your name was McGown?"

Jay nodded. He introduced Sarah. The press agent nodded.

"McGown, hah? That's quite a coincidence. Too bad you're not the Governor."

Jay said yes, it was too damn bad. The press agent led the way to the trailer house and showed them inside. The trailer was enormous. They stood on the thick carpet of a large reception room while the agent explained that the doors on either side led to the dressing quarters of the actress and the director. The agent knocked lightly on the director's room and Edmund Shavers appeared almost immediately. He was a tall, thick-shouldered man with a youngish sun-burned face that betrayed middle years only when his smile dissolved into pink folds. He was smiling now, showing remarkable white teeth. He wore cowboy boots and starched khakis; he pulled a red bandanna round his neck and moved about the room, clasping hands.

"Wonderful . . . Wonderful . . ." Shavers was saying, and Fenstemaker was saying it right back: "Goddam happy to be here . . ."

"How long can you stay?" Shavers said.

"I'm afraid —" the Governor began.

"I understand," Shavers said. "We'll try to get the picture-taking over with as quickly as possible. These publicity people . . . you've got to stay right on them."

The press agent asked if he should see about Miss McGown, and Shavers nodded. He turned back to the Governor and said: "Maybe you'll stay long enough to see us shoot a scene after we've finished with the publicity pictures. We've got a scene with Vicki scheduled in just about . . . Ah! Vicki, dear. Come meet the Governor . . ."

Vicki McGown stood in the doorway for an instant, spectacular in the soft light, vibrantly colored. Her blond hair and painted eyelids and the glow of her young skin combined to produce such an effect of voluptuous good health and vitality that the press agent, standing alongside and gawking at her bare legs, appeared in contrast to have risen just recently from a sickbed. Vicki wore white shorts and a faded blue cotton workshirt. She smiled and walked directly over to Jay and kissed him lightly on the mouth. Then she turned to the others, holding on to Jay's arm and nodding to each of the guests as Shavers introduced them. The press agent began to describe the photographs of Vicki and the Governor that were planned for the morning. He produced a folder, a "press kit" on the Governor's official visit, and commented briefly on the news releases and feature stories already prepared.

Arthur Fenstemaker glanced at the material without interest and passed them to Jay. Jay stared at the stories, aware of nothing but the pressure of Vicki's hand on his arm. Vicki said, "I'll have to change for the pictures. Only be a minute. You come with me, Jay-Jay?"

Jay looked at Sarah and then at the Governor and then at Shavers, who was flashing his incredible smile. Fenstemaker nodded soberly; Sarah stared out a window. Jay followed the actress into her dressing room.

Vicki pushed the door shut, and then, leaning with her back against it, opened her arms to her husband.

"We bein' social?" Jay said. He stepped close and Vicki kissed him again, a kiss that began as the one before but soon became something else entirely, stirring another season's love, an ancient distress signal. Her hips shifted slightly and Jay pulled his head back a few inches, looking at her.

"Godalmighty," he said.

"You like being social?" she said.

"I guess I do," he said.

"Long time, Jay-Jay."

"Long time, all right."

She let loose of him and moved to her dressing table and

looked at herself for a moment. "I liked your Governor," she said. "He's better looking than I thought he would be."

"He's thinking of having his nose bobbed," Jay said. "He's a great, vain king."

Vicki unbuttoned her denim shirt and threw it across a chair. She reached for a Western costume on the clothes rack, held it up for him to see, and then began pulling off her shorts and underwear. Jay thought at first he would not look, but then, realizing it now was all the world's prerogative, he came close and circled round, examining her as he would a prize beefstock.

"You got your figure back," he said.

"It *has* been a long time. Haven't you seen the pictures?"

"How could anyone avoid 'em?" he said. "Was all that stuff necessary?"

"It was at first," she said. "It helped a lot in the beginning. It made all the difference in the world."

Jay pulled a string on the window blinds and looked out on the bare land, at the carpenters and camera crews and technicians milling about shirtless in the morning sun. There now seemed to be a veil of lilac suspended in the distance, between the motion picture set and the purple roll of mountains miles away. He said: "When is Annie coming out? I'd hoped she would be here today, hoped I could get a look at her before leaving."

"Victoria Anne," Vicki said. "Call her Victoria Anne. She'll be here in a day or two. Can't you get the Governor to stay awhile?"

Jay shook his head. "I think he wants to leave right now. He gets uneasy. He gets restless when he's suddenly dropped into a social order that doesn't make sense to him. He's used to running things."

"He could probably run things here," Vicki said. "God knows no one else is. He doesn't like this particular social order?"

"He thinks it's no order at all. He's ready to go home. When could I see her?"

"What?"

"Annie. When could I see her?"

"I'll bring her to the party if you like," Vicki said. She had the cowgirl costume pulled over her head and now began to brush her hair. "Tell me something about this crazy party."

"It's the whole point of his being here," Jay said. "Give a little, take a little. He wanted you to come to his party, and Shavers made him come out here first to endorse the picture. He didn't like it, but at least he could understand it. The party's a very big deal. Press, radio, television — and now the movies. About a thousand people coming from all over. Impressing the rich and powerful. For his re-election campaign."

"Was it your idea?"

Jay shook his head. "He has a big party every couple years."

"I mean my being there," Vicki said.

"No. It was the Governor's idea. He was obsessed with the notion."

"Really?" Vicki seemed delighted. "Is he a picture fan?"

"I doubt if he's seen a movie in fifteen years," Jay said. "He's just interested in his employees — and he's always been fascinated that I had a movie queen — a love goddess he's been calling you — for a wife."

"And how about you?" Vicki said. "You fascinated?"

Jay managed to smile. "I'm pleased you're such a success," he said.

"Who's the girl?" Vicki said suddenly.

"Who?"

"The girl you're with."

"One of Fenstemaker's secretaries. Sarah Lehman. I've been dating her some."

"Doesn't bother her that you're married?"

Jay sat down on an ottoman, wondering if he would be able to avoid an argument. He thought a moment and said: "No more, I suppose, than it's bothered you that you're married." The actress was applying fresh lipstick and did not reply.

Jay went on, "How about it, now that we're on the subject? When do I get loose? When are you going to be sensible about a divorce?"

"Any time you're ready, Jay."

"I'm not ready on your terms, Vic. Goddam. I want to see Annie a few months out of the year."

"Then you ought to reconsider," Vicki said. "If you love your daughter so much, come live with us. It's not such a bad life these days, you know."

"I . . . don't think . . . I could do it," Jay said very carefully. "I'm not sure I could survive any more of those evenings. Waiting up to shake hands with your boy friends."

"You exaggerate," Vicki said. She brushed closeby and took his arm, smiling. "I'm not going with anyone special. I'm just a lonely, misunderstood career girl."

They moved into the reception room. A few minutes later, out in the open, in the murderous heat of the midmorning sun, the sweet faint smell of her still clung to his face.

Two

THEY ALLOWED some of the tourists and ranch hands through the front gate to witness the picture-taking; they let through as many as were needed to provide an audience for the ceremonies. The crowd followed Vicki and the Governor, watching their movements as if the two of them were high priests, gathering round one of the balsa wood oil derricks in the beginning and then moving on to the preposterously bright green lawn of the gingerbread house. The mansion was authentic and convincing in every detail, like a wondrously well-engineered replica, an outsized child's toy put together between desert sandfaults.

Jay followed the crowds, keeping at a distance, standing just close enough to watch Vicki and the Governor move through their routine with the easy and stoic assurance of those long impaled by the public gaze, striking their poses, shifting to good sides, smiles coming on and vanishing again as the photographers requested. Jay asked himself if he exaggerated and got his answer: Yes, 'deed I do exaggerate; I am exaggerated, overblown; all my life, front and back, magnified and foreshortened, my papier mâché visions sullied by balsa wood and vegetable dye. He stood a short distance away from Vicki and the Governor and stared in wonder. They were not quite people, those two. They were a little hard to believe; each of them heightened by special technicolor effects.

Fenstemaker was a handsome contemporary figure, but his appearance evoked for Jay the memories of a tinted matinee idol found in the picture frame department of a dime store. His face was unlined and beautifully tanned, and his expensive white teeth, whiter even than the movie director's, were emphatically, unimaginably regular. And Vicki no longer seemed quite real. She had not been so altogether perfect when he had married her. Now she seemed the product of an expensive engineering process. Basic research. American ingenuity. Both of them — Vicki and the Governor — had undergone refurbishments to make them as close as possible to physical perfection. But the technicians who labored over their willing remnants — the surgeons and dentists and hair stylists and masseurs and manicurists — had demonstrated something less than consummate skill; had never quite got them put together again. They were hardly people, these two, but synthetic equivalents, albeit a pair of comely and brightly packaged ones.

The picture-taking was nearly ended, and Hoot Gibson stood beside Jay, sucking on a piece of ice. Sarah and Mrs. Fenstemaker had returned to the cool interior of the trailer house.

"Look here!" Hoot Gibson said. "Look over here!"

Hoot Gibson pointed to the flatbed of a truck parked nearby, stacked with desert brush. "You know what that is?" Hoot Gibson said. "It's tumbleweed."

Jay nodded thoughtfully. Yes, it certainly was tumbleweed, he said. No denying it.

"Tumbleweed," Hoot Gibson repeated. "Imported. Brought all the way here from Burbank, California. Ain't no tumbleweed out here — ain't nothin' left out here after the drought — so they brought their own goddam tumbleweed . . . An' you know what else?"

"What else?" Jay said.

"It don't tumble," Hoot Gibson said, overjoyed. "Even when there's a good wind. It just don't tumble. So they brought out some big blowers — big 'lectric fans — to make the tumbleweed tumble when they shoot the moom pitcher."

Jay felt a little better. He smiled at Hoot Gibson and Hoot Gibson smiled back, vastly pleased. The photographers were putting away their equipment and the crowds were being led back behind the wire fence. The Governor, Vicki and Edmund Shavers approached. Hoot Gibson left immediately to get the limousine started and the air-conditioning primed. Arthur Fenstemaker, perspiring, mumbling a vague exhortation from the Old Testament, shook hands gravely with the actress and the director. He turned to Jay.

"Everything ready?" he said.

Jay nodded. The four of them began walking toward the trailer house. Fenstemaker paused midway, his eyes fastened on an ancient, finely polished touring car parked under a dusty, flapping tent.

"It's the Dusenberg," Vicki explained. "It's the one I drive in the picture. I love it. In fact, I'm going for a ride right now — before we begin shooting. You join me?" She looked at the Governor and then at Jay and Edmund Shavers. "Anyone?"

Fenstemaker hesitated; he mopped his face and smiled. He appeared to have been visited by a new surge of vitality.

"Come on, Governor," Vicki coaxed. "I'll show you around in the car."

Fenstemaker followed Vicki toward the Dusenberg. He stopped midway and called back: "Jay, you and Hoot Gibson get the drinkin' equipment and come with us."

Vicki had the motor running when Jay and Hoot Gibson arrived with the whiskey and ice. The Governor sat in front alongside Vicki, looking as if he were on the verge of discovery. Shavers called to them: "Be careful with that car, Vic! We can't afford to let anything happen to it. Or to you. Or to the Governor, especially."

"Don't worry 'bout thing," Vicki yelled. The Dusenberg shuddered as she raced the engine.

"We're shooting in forty minutes!"

"Plenty time!" Vicki called out. "Here we go . . . Flappers and sad birds!" The big car started off, lurching across the open fields.

Jay and Hoot Gibson sat in back and tried to hold the whiskey bottles steady. They poured drinks for the four of them and passed the tumblers around. The Governor raised his in a toast, and Vicki laughed and looked wonderful, her white hair streaming out behind in the wind. Jay could not imagine her motives, but every delay, every weakening of Fenstemaker's determination to leave, brought Jay closer to the moment he might see his daughter. He did not know when she would arrive; he could not begin to hope for so much time; he could only live from one interruption to the next, hoping they would somehow manage to stay on till Annie appeared. Vicki pulled a scarf round her head and raised her voice above the drone of the engine: "We'll drive down to the Mexican village. Not the one we built, but the real one — over this way on the back road."

Fenstemaker nodded and smiled and finished his drink. He passed his glass back for another. Jay sat on the hot cushions, gazing at the fold of mountains miles away. Hoot Gibson took over the mixing. They banged along the dirt road, turned down a stretch of macadam and off again to the right, leaving the pavement for a second time and heading toward the rising foothills. Hoot Gibson was kept busy with the drinks. They all had another round.

"You got to stay after this stuff, honey," the Governor said to Vicki. "Otherwise, the ice melts. You got to toss it down fast."

"I wish we had gin," Vicki said. "You like gin?"

"Ah, yes," the Governor said, rolling his eyes. He could not abide gin.

"Gin and rose petals," Vicki said. "You ever had gin and rose petals?"

"Never the pleasure," Fenstemaker said, tossing down his whiskey, cold.

"Gin and rose petals," Vicki repeated. "And champagne splits at breakfast!" She turned and looked back. "You remember, Jay-Jay?"

Jay nodded and looked off toward the mountains. The reminder was like an old debt caught up with him.

"Where was all this?" Fenstemaker said.

"College," Vicki said. "Freshman year. Never known anything so glamorous as gin and rose petals and champagne splits for breakfast. Jay was president of the student body, and I was seventeen years old. Seventeen! First-class seduction — ranked with the best . . . my lost sweet innocence . . ."

Jay sat in the back seat, smiling to himself, Scotch whiskey splashing down his shirtfront, wondering if he had ever succeeded in violating anyone. Sweet innocence. It was what he missed most in life and wanted more than anything to recapture — and he wondered if it really ever had existed for the two of them, even in the beginning. He could not remember Vicki as she had been then, but he was certain it was not so much innocence that defined her as a dumb-struck happy acceptance of life's infinite possibilities.

Fenstemaker turned and looked at him, his big face gleaming in the sun. "What you do to Miss Vicki, Jay?" he said. "How come you ruined this little lady?"

Jay spread his palms, balancing the drink in his lap. "We were both helpless," he said. "Trapped in the cruel vise of the System."

"Whut's all that 'bout vice?" Hoot Gibson said.

"Vise . . . Vise," Jay said.

"Hoot Gibson and I had some good times together at college," the Governor said. "But we never had any champagne for breakfast. Only a little jug of sour mash whiskey now and then." An expression of vague melancholy came on his face. He raised his glass. "Gimmie a little of the Scripture, Hoot Gibson," he said.

Hoot Gibson smiled blandly. "Mah virgins an' mah young men," he said, "are fallen by the sword."

"We are all stricken in years," the Governor said.

They passed round the whiskey again.

Jay tried to think about Vicki as she had been several years before. He could remember the college clearly, but he was unable to put together a convincing picture of Vicki. There had been too many conflicting images risen in the interval. It had not looked much like a college. In the moonlight, in the cold of an open car, approaching it from a distance, moving across the wild countryside, you could have mistaken it for a great, shapeless circus that had somehow broken down on the edge of the city. Once, years before, it might have looked like a college — there was still a thin, defeated frieze of ivy on some of the older buildings. Huge stone amalgams of what was identified as Spanish-Grecian had risen from the cotton fields, alongside the Gothic imitations of the past, and later still there were the hutments and the frame and tarpaper lecture halls. It had become a sprawling, gerrymandered maze of dull brick, stucco and yellow pine, suggesting the decline of a painted harlot in her middle years. Though in the cold of an open car with Vicki at his side, approaching the campus on a winter morning at mid-century, riding through the quiet, tree-lined streets, past the feeble expanse of grass along the Mall and the stone gargoyles out front of the Main Building, it had seemed an altogether lovely place.

"They were serving gin and rose petals at this party," Vicki said. "I remember once Jay and I had to drive to the other county to buy more gin — and on the way back stopping at a florist shop and waking the owner and ordering more rose petals."

Jay tried to remember a time when they were uncorrupted. Once, farther south, they had parked on a levee, across the river from the Mexican whoretown, and kissed for a long while. There was that old Mexican. He remembered the Mexican, crawling out of a mud hut to relieve himself, and the way he jumped in the headlights of the car.

"We were married by a one-legged justice of the peace," Vicki said. "What you'd call a ceremony of quiet and dignified simplicity."

The heat was awful on the desert road, but Vicki's sweet drunken laughter had them all feeling better. Hoot Gibson lay back in the leather cushions, grinning at everyone. The Governor had a beatific smile on his face.

"Ah feel relaxed and beautiful," Hoot Gibson said.

"We've been gone nearly an hour," Jay said. "Did Mr. Shavers say something about —"

"There it is up ahead!" Vicki yelled.

The old Dusenberg had topped a rise and now they all strained in their seats to catch sight of the village lying between the hummocky sandhills.

Three

SHAVERS and Sarah Lehman and Sweet Mama Fenstemaker were crossing from the trailer to the limousine, transferring small overnight bags, walking off their impatience, when they caught sight of the Dusenberg returning, stirring up dust, moving obliquely in a random, zigzag manner toward the camp. The three of them shielded their eyes from the sun and watched the approach of the old touring car. Lunch was being served to the location crew underneath one of the big commissary tents, and the studio people turned away from the tables to stare. The car veered off at a sharp angle and began a long, erratic, lazy circle of the campsite. Shavers and Sweet Mama appeared to sag in the heat. Sarah hesitated, wondering if she could reach the coolness of the trailer house before the others arrived and caught her up in the general derangement. Shavers pulled out a handkerchief and rubbed it along the back of his thick neck. His starched khakis were streaked with perspiration.

"She's driving that old car too fast," Shavers said. "It's a wonder it didn't break down on them. It's just a damned expensive antique."

The Dusenberg went into another sharp turn and then moved directly toward them, slowing suddenly and proceeding on a relatively stable course to a point midway between the trailer and the limousine. Vicki's delirious laughter could be heard above the rumble of the motor, and the others — Jay and Hoot Gibson and the Governor, the three of them flushed and dusty in the midday heat — sat upright in the car flashing tortured smiles. The Dusenberg came to a stop and Vicki got to her feet and stretched, standing on the floorboard and holding on to the top of the windshield for balance. She waved her free arm.

"It was wonderful, Ed," she said to Shavers. "You should've been there . . . Never seen anything like it before."

Shavers came closer. "Seen what?" he said. Sarah and Sweet Mama stood and looked.

"We just gave everything back to the Mexicans! All of it! We had a little ceremony." Vicki turned and yelled at the people eating lunch under the big tent: "You white men got twenty-four hours to clear out!"

The studio people had all turned to look now. Sarah and Sweet Mama moved closer, following Shavers. Hoot Gibson pulled himself absolutely erect in the backseat; he folded his arms, squinted in the sun, and regarded the campsite with disapproval. Arthur Fenstemaker sat in front next to Vicki, staring at the dashboard, shaking his head. Jay tried not to look at anyone. He continued to sit upright in the backseat, and from time to time batted his eyes.

"What're you talking about, Vic?" Shavers said.

"We gave it back!" Vicki repeated. "The whole damn state — every heathen's square mile of it. To the Mexicans. We signed the Treaty of San Felipe Dolores del Rio. Governor here signed it over to the Mayor. Back there. Mexican Mayor. Deeded it over to him. Mayor promised to give it back to the Indians first chance he gets."

She turned to Arthur Fenstemaker, who continued to stare at the dashboard. "What was the Mayor's name, Arthur? I forget already."

Hoot Gibson got slowly to his feet. "Ah got copy of 'greement raht here," he said, pulling a piece of brown wrapping paper from his back pocket and flapping it above his head so that all could see. Everyone turned to stare at Hoot Gibson. "Name was George Washin'ton . . . Herrera Ebahn-yez . . . George Washin'ton Herrera Ebahnyez . . . He was part nigger Ah thank." Hoot Gibson smiled at everyone and sat down.

The Governor fumbled with the door handle, suddenly moved to action, and, looking at no one, got out of the car and walked directly to the trailer house. Sweet Mama broke off from the others and followed him, asking, "What happened, dear? Where on earth did you go?"

"Vicki . . ." Shavers began again. He hesitated; his shoulders slumped; he appeared to have given up the interrogation as hopeless. "Come on inside with me, honey. We got to get you fresh again for the scene we'd planned to shoot." He opened the door and took Vicki by the arm, attempting to guide her toward the trailer. Vicki came along, unprotesting. "It was priceless, Ed," she was saying. "I've never seen anything . . ."

Hoot Gibson was next to climb out of the car. He stepped down off the high running board and wandered toward the big tent. Some of the studio people stared at him for a moment and then turned back to their plates. Hoot Gibson sat down on a bench and waited to be served.

Jay McGown lay back in the seat. The ancient leather was murderously hot against his skin, but he could not bring himself to move. Sarah walked to the car and Jay finally pulled himself up again and began fishing around in the ice bucket. He filled two glasses of water and passed one to Sarah.

"It really was something," he said, looking up and smiling and shaking his head. "Like a bad dream. When you know it's only a dream and not really so bad. Sort of a cheerful nightmare quality."

"Well there's certainly some of that quality about your Miss Vicki," Sarah said sharply.

Jay struggled to his feet, wiping his face. "Let's get out of this heat," he said. They walked together toward the trailer.

He tried patiently to explain to her, but Sarah never seemed really to be listening. He tried, all the same, explaining that it had not been Vicki's show; not entirely. The Governor had been very much a part of it for a time. It was he, in fact, who initiated the business about Good Neighbors and Brotherhood, explaining how the very sandhill on which they'd all planted themselves, all the goddam state, most of the western half of the continent, might be Mexico's to this day if it had not been for a few quirks of fate, vagaries of history he called them. And Vicki had come in then and said let's give it back, let's deed it over — deeds, not by-God words, was what we needed — hand it all back to them for friendship's sake. Like Good Neighbors. Neat stroke of institutional public relations! And everyone agreed. Or rather nobody objected. And that fellow Ibáñez went to his ice barrel and brought out the Mexican beer and the others in the village, the ones who'd been afraid to show themselves when the Dusenberg first appeared, those people came round and peered shyly through the grubby windows of the storefront, watching Fenstemaker raising his bottle and sealing the bargain with a toast. The fellow Ibáñez called himself the Mayor, the Judge, the *Alcalde,* though there couldn't have been more than twenty or thirty Mexicans in the village: tenants and ranch hands mostly and most of them living on the Alcalde's credit. The Governor called him Roy Bean, called Ibáñez that, called him Judge and pointed to the modern Lily Langtry poster that had been pasted across the mirror above the bar. It was the awful photograph of Vicki — Jay had seen it plenty times — old Vicki stripped naked, sitting crosslegged on a bearskin rug, holding a pink lapdog, a spitz with its fur dyed, just a pup and just large enough to cover the parts of Vicki that surely everybody and his dog had seen before anyhow.

And they'd attempted to explain to Ibáñez, communicating in stilted English and nearly incomprehensible Spanish, that the girl right here and the girl in the calendar were one and the same: Miss Vicki McGown the motion picture actress. Arthur kept introducing himself: "I'm Arthur Goddam Fenstemaker," he'd say, pumping the Mexican's arm, trying to make it clear who he was and what he represented — and Hoot Gibson kept trying to help, repeating over and over again, *"Regardez una Governar!"* Ibáñez would smile and nod and go back to his ice barrel for more beer. Then he plugged in an ancient jukebox and they all danced, Ibáñez first, doing a fantastic mambo-rumba thing with the blond-haired woman, then the Governor and then Hoot Gibson and finally Jay — they'd all insisted on it; they'd even invited some of the Mexican cowboys inside to dance with Vicki, bought them beer and given them money and tried to explain how they'd just turned back the land; and fairly soon they were all drunk, helplessly drunk before noon in the desert sun. A great tragicomic goodbye was said to the cowboys on the ruptured steps of the Ibáñez store, with the Governor trying to remember the words of his Inauguration Speech and the Mexicans whooping and hollering and banging on two-stringed guitars as the Dusenberg groaned off down the road.

The ride back had been interminable. Several times they were not sure of the way, and he could see Fenstemaker, beginning to sober, wondering what in hell had gone on back there and whether they were now lost in the ranch country. But then Vicki had got her bearings from the mountains on either side of them, and Hoot Gibson passed round the tumblers full of ice and whiskey and soon the location camp came in sight, sprawling out ahead next to the pre-fab mansion.

"I suppose," Jay said to Sarah, "that a little of the magic goes out of the episode in the telling."

"You had to be there, etcetera," Sarah said. She handed him a towel to wash his face.

Jay blotted at his forehead and scrubbed his neck. He wondered about disillusion and whether it ever came to Vicki. He'd told her once, years before at college, thinking he was bringing enlightenment to an innocent, that life could be a great all-satisfying bacchanalia for anyone who did not allow tradition and convention to smother the impulse. And she'd bought the idea right off, though the funny thing was it did not seem to matter. There had to be an awareness of having sinned a little if the debauching gesture meant anything at all, and for Vicki there really never seemed anything to be liberated *from*.

They moved out of the reception room and into Shavers' quarters, where the Governor and Sweet Mama had come to rest.

"Jay," the Governor said with great weariness, massaging his eyes, pulling on his nose, probing his face as if conducting an examination, "we signed something out there . . . What exactly did we sign out there, Jay?"

"There were a couple of things being passed around," Jay said. "You dictated something to me — a kind of proclamation — but then you didn't sign it. You signed the sheet Hoot Gibson was waving at everyone, something very simple like 'I hereby give this land back to the Meskins.' Hoot Gibson's got the copy if you want to take a look at it."

"No — there was something else. There were two copies. I signed two copies. I'm sure of it."

"Oh, Arthur . . ." Mrs. Fenstemaker began, but immediately subsided.

"What you think, Jay?" the Governor said. "You think there's any chance of that little proclamation ever gettin' into the papers?"

"There aren't any newspapers out here to speak of," Jay said.

"Didn't ask how many newspapers out here. I can see there ain't any newspapers out here — nothin' out here. Listen to the question. Nobody listens to questions any more. I asked if you thought —"

"No," Jay said.

"Good," the Governor said.

"Dear . . ." Mrs. Fenstemaker began again.

"And if it does happen to turn up, we can deny everything," Fenstemaker said.

"Arthur," Sweet Mama said, "you're getting tired and you need some rest. You're tired and short tempered and I think we ought to consider returning to town as soon as possible. If we don't leave soon, we'll have a night flight back home and the pilots don't like night flights, remember."

"Hell with the pilots an' their night flights," the Governor said. "Let 'em miss some sack time . . . I'm feeling fine . . . *Fine* . . . I want to stay here awhile. That fellow Shavers mentioned some scenes they were shooting. I want to take a look at what it's like. He mentioned the possibility of including me in one of the scenes. He said I had a good face — face of a leader, he said."

"Really? Did he really?"

"Said I was photogenic. Wants me to play a part in the picture. Playing myself. What you think about that, Jay?"

Jay wanted to say the right thing, but he hesitated, knowing he should tell the Governor that it was an awful idea, worst idea he could imagine. He stood there wondering if he should tell the Governor what he *ought* to hear or what he *wanted* to hear, hesitating, miserable in his indecision, not so much because he feared Fenstemaker but because he rather imagined they each wanted to stay over — and the hell with the consequences. Another twenty-four hours and Jay's daughter might have arrived. And the Governor was obviously fascinated by the prospects of appearing in the motion picture. Jay attempted to weigh the amount of trouble they might get themselves into in another twenty-four hours against his desperate need to see the little girl.

"Not really playing myself exactly," Fenstemaker said. "Playing Governor of the State, though. Can't really be me. Story takes place twenty-five years ago, during the oil boom. Who was Governor twenty-five years ago, Jay? Sarah? Anybody know?"

Jay told him who was Governor twenty-five years ago.

Fenstemaker looked unhappy. "Don't know if I want to play that sonofabitch or not," he said.

Jay finally came to a decision. He said: "You ought to base your judgment on what exactly the part involves. You want to make it clear from the start that you reserve the right to approve or disapprove not only your role as the script shows it but the overall film itself. The finished product, I mean. You can't trust these people. I can tell you . . ."

"*You* sure can't!" Fenstemaker hooted. "You fought this war long time ago, didn't you Jay?" He seemed to think this enormously funny. His big shoulders were still heaving from laughter when Vicki and Shavers entered the room.

Four

SARAH LEHMAN was not ordinarily so reserved as she had been on this day. She was acutely conscious of the fact and she resented it; though her resentment was vague and notably groundless. She resented Arthur Fenstemaker for allowing such a spectacle as had developed through the morning; resented Jay for not attempting to avoid it, not making some kind of defiant gesture. And she thought she resented Vicki McGown most of all for the unsettling, graceless effect she had on those around her.

All through that morning Sarah had felt helpless and dumb-struck in the clutch of Vicki McGown's world. She was nearly inarticulate; she felt dull and witless and absurd, and the admission only confirmed her sense of defeat — leaving her painfully aware of the distance between the drab fact of her present conduct and her normally dazzling potential. That was the frustrating thing. She was a handsome girl, and well educated; she could see for herself that her looks were of a more enduring and flawless quality than the actress's — and it was obvious that she had better sense. But there was something else that got in the way. Sarah had achieved very early in life a rare combination of beauty and intelligence, and now the intimidation of Vicki McGown's presence — even the prospect of it — had dulled her head and clouded the glow of her pretty face. She wanted to cut Vicki with a word, bring her down to life size with a turn of crushing phrase, but she could not seem to bring it off against the weight of the woman's vast and careless self-possession.

She was furious with herself, having finally to admit she was helpless and ineffective in contending with another woman. And worse, the main threat was something ubiquitous and indefinable. What was it? Pride, repose, luxuriant vitality? How could one isolate the elements? Where had it all begun? She thought of Arthur Fenstemaker's transformation from timorous, picknose politician into . . . whatever it was that currently passed for greatness. The Presidency makes the man? Perhaps the movie queen story, drummed and repeated, endlessly recited, over and over again, had made its impression on Vicki McGown's muddled intellect, advancing from some dark tendril of the brain, as in a post-hypnotic suggestion, to a point where Vicki could assure herself that she *was* a queen.

The charged atmosphere of Vicki's presence was all round them again, subtle and fantastic. Shavers looked exhausted; Fenstemaker's eyes were bloodshot; Jay and Hoot Gibson and Sweet Mama seemed collapsed in a heap on the small couch. But they came suddenly awake as Vicki moved across the room, generating her wondrous resilience. She walked to the couch and draped a dark arm over Jay's shoulder.

"I've just talked with Victoria Anne, Jay-Jay," she said. "They're flying her out this afternoon . . ."

"Really?" Jay said. "I wish you'd let me speak with —"

"It shouldn't be long now," Vicki said. "They'll have her here in the morning at the latest . . ." She turned to Arthur Fenstemaker and went on: ". . . So now you really should consider spending another day — give Jay a chance to visit Victoria Anne and give yourselves an opportunity to see some of the other stars."

Fenstemaker spread his hands and said, "Well . . ." before Vicki broke back in.

"You can spare the time, can't you? I hope so. Ed told me he wants to get that handsome face of yours in front of a camera. I think that's wonderful . . . You could get the shooting done tomorrow, couldn't you Ed?"

"I think we could," Shavers said. "Matter of fact, I've had a couple of writers working on your scene, Governor. I think we've got it worked out. We had a problem at first — most of our tight

shots and interiors are filmed at the studio. But I think we can
handle it out here in the open."

"You'll do it won't you, Governor?" Vicki said. "You ought to
make the most of your visit . . ."

"Who're the others coming out?" Sweet Mama said.

"Picture stars," Hoot Gibson said. "More of 'em."

"Greg Calhoun is one of them," Shavers said. "He's Vicki's co-
star. I think you'll all like Greg . . . He's fine boy." He looked
at Sarah and Sweet Mama as if for confirmation. "You ladies
heard of Greg, haven't you?"

Vicki talked about Greg Calhoun and some of the players who
had been cast in character parts. Sweet Mama nodded; Sarah did
not comment. Vicki turned back to the Governor.

"It's such a waste of time to come all the way out here and then
just stay a few hours," she said.

"What about it, Governor?" Shavers said.

Fenstemaker looked at his wife. "How you feel about it, Sweet
Mama?"

"It's up to you, dear," Sweet Mama said. "You're exhausted —
I'm worried about you . . . I feel fine."

Fenstemaker nodded gravely at the suggestion that he might
need rest. "Jay?" he said. ". . . Well I know you'd like to stay
. . . Sarah, how 'bout you, honey?"

"I just work here," Sarah said hopelessly. "It's — whatever
you think. You've got some appointments to —"

"Where'll you put us up, Ed?" Fenstemaker said.

"No problem at all," Shavers said, waving his hand, as if inventing solutions. "All we do is bring in two more trailers . . ."

"I got to make about a hundred phone calls," Fenstemaker said.

"We'll have the trailers wired for calls before dark," Shavers
said.

Fenstemaker pulled on his nose. He walked round the room
for a moment and then paused to stare out a window, examining the country like a speculator about to buy. "Then I suppose . . ."

"All settled, then," Shavers said. "I'll have everything arranged. Trailers be here before long — you'll have your own rooms then. We'll all have a fine time . . ." He looked at the others, vastly pleased. "You'll excuse me now . . . We're little behind schedule, and we'll really have to push it if we're going to get Vicki out of here for the Governor's party this weekend."

"By all means then," Fenstemaker said cordially. "Step it up!"

Shavers spoke to Vicki: "We'll shoot that scene in just a few minutes. Don't take any more rides . . . Please."

"I'll be along," Vicki said, and Shavers left the room.

Vicki stepped between the Governor and Hoot Gibson, touching their arms lightly. "I've got to change again," she said. "It won't take long. And when I'm through I want you all to come join me for a drink."

"Ah'd be for that," Hoot Gibson said immediately.

"Governor?"

"I'm not so sure, Miz Vicki . . ."

"You ought to take a little nap, Arthur," Sweet Mama said. "Right over here on Mr. Shavers' couch."

"Mebbe so," Fenstemaker said. "I got a good deal of work waitin' for me later . . ."

"Governor, I understand entirely," Vicki said. She smiled; Hoot Gibson smiled; Fenstemaker bent his head down, took Vicki's hand and kissed it. "And I thank you, Miz Vicki," he said.

Vicki clutched Hoot Gibson's arm. "It's just the four of us, then," she said. "Miss Lehman and Hoot Gibson and Jay and myself. I'll be ready for you in a few minutes. We'll have that drink. I've a maid in there who mixes an exquisite whiskey sour. Uses egg whites. They're *good* for you." She let loose of Hoot Gibson, reached out and tapped the end of his red nose. She waved at the others and walked out of the room, across the reception area and into her own quarters.

"Bourbon!" Hoot Gibson exulted. "Haven't had bourbon — haven't had anythang but Scotch whiskey — since th' goddam 'nauguration . . ."

His mouth was flapping at the refrigerated air. None of the others was listening. The Governor had already moved away and settled himself on the couch. Sweet Mama was pulling a pillow and blanket down from a storage bin. Jay stared absently in the direction Vicki had gone. He turned finally to Sarah, smiling. "Godalmighty," he said. "How long does it take to fly here from the coast?" Sarah did not answer him; her mind was plodding ahead in time, attempting to adjust, to equip itself for the drinks they would have presently and the nightmare that was surely due to engulf them before another day was ended. She realized suddenly that it was just as Jay had described it to her, months ago, and at that time she had not believed what he said. He had talked morbidly of his life with Vicki, but it had never seemed altogether real for Sarah. It was as if Jay had taken real situations and people and dramatized them, inflated them all out of proportion, given them such embellishments that the empty episodes he described lost all the breath of life.

But it was true; all of it. It was all true, what he said, and now she could see it for herself. She tried to remember everything Jay had said to her in describing the horror off which he had been feeding. "I liked it," he had said. "That was the awful part. Maybe I'm still drawn to it. Even now I get a perverse pleasure out of Vicki — all her sexuality. My head tells me one thing, but I can't really hear it for all the whooping going on back and forth between my balls." She had been offended by the admission, and he was never so candid with her again. Though now she understood what he had been getting at. She wished that she could tell him now that it was comprehensible, finally; that she had at last come through to visualizing what up to that time had seemed only a sort of imagery, a sleight of hand that Jay made with mirrors. Jay had described Vicki, but in fashioning a picture of his actress wife for Sarah the assembled impressions had amounted to no more than the cracked-glass reflections of Sarah herself and those few women who had ever seized her interest. And Vicki was like nothing in her experience — she was the authentic, the genuine article.

She had been mistaken about Vicki, blundering along on false assumptions, thinking the Vicki that Jay had pieced together in his own imagination was a farce — and she belabored him for not recognizing the fact. But now she could see Vicki was no farce, no sniggering exaggeration, no crude burlesque of the merely carnal. Vicki's special quality had been communicated to all of them in the room: in a look, in a casual shifting of the limbs, in a movement or a gesture or a rhythm of the pulse. Sarah knew it had been communicated. In the crackling sensuality of Vicki's presence Sarah herself had felt very like an animal tasting the air.

One weekend, years before, returning from a college party, she had shared a pullman berth with a girl she had known only casually. In the middle of the night she had come awake in the girl's arms, only half aware that it was the girl, not wanting it to end and wishing she were still asleep. Another time, later on, during Arthur Fenstemaker's first campaign, she and the Governor had been riding in the backseat of an automobile, returning from a rally in another city. Fenstemaker had begun to slump sideways against her, exhausted. She had held on to him, attempting to make him comfortable, and presently his big arm had come round her middle and his hand moved over her breasts. She had not wanted the drive ever to end or Fenstemaker to shake himself from sleep.

Such episodes were like wild carryings-on in a back room, blinds pulled down against daylight convention. It was horrific, all a darkness, and seemed to have nothing to do with the other, the methodical push-pull of seduction. There had been the business with Jay a few weeks before; that had given her a taste of it. But that had been before she had gasped out the meaning to herself of Jay's nether world, all the stopping points along the way that Jay had attempted to describe. Now she wanted desperately to tell him that she understood, and more: she wanted to move closer for a better look. There had been the business with Jay, she thought, but even in the darkness of his room there were bright stalks of sunlight that shone through the blinds . . . I must have acted awful, she thought, I must have —

A Negro maid in a uniform of pale blue polished cotton appeared at the door.

"Miss Vicki say she dressed now and would like ver' much to have you come join her for a drink."

The Governor sat on the edge of the couch, poking mercilessly at his swollen eyelids. "I think I'll have that drink after all," he said.

Sweet Mama helped him to his feet. There were the five of them then, moving toward Vicki's room, and Sarah could not do anything about her feeling of their all being borne off to slaughter.

Five

IN THE SOFTLY LIT, caramel-colored dressing room, Vicki held court, stretching her golden legs along the deep carpet, seated on a short stool facing a many-sided mirror, talking to the others through the reflections, turning occasionally to supervise the pouring of the cocktails.

Presently they heard the grinding of gears and the groan of the trucks coming toward them up the road from the highway.

"That'll be the trailers," Vicki said. "Now you'll have your own rooms and you can freshen up if you like."

The Governor and the others stood and looked through the blinds as workmen directed and assisted in setting up the staggered line of trailer houses.

"Are there telephones in those things?" the Governor asked.

"Oh yes — or there will be in a few minutes. We've also got a little intertrailer communication system. If you need anything, just pick up the pink phone. It'll ring in Ed Shavers' office, and somebody there will help you."

"I've got some phone calls — there's some work I have to do. No — no Sarah, you needn't come. Just some calls. I'll try to get it over with in a hurry, Miss Vicki, so I can watch that scene of yours they're shooting."

He turned and raised his glass to the others, finishing off the drink; then headed out the door. Mrs. Fenstemaker began to ask Vicki about movie stars. Jay and Sarah sat quietly while Vicki patiently answered her questions. Hoot Gibson followed the maid into another room and managed to have her serve him the bourbon straight — "raht on top uh them rocks."

Arthur Fenstemaker found a small writing table in the other trailer, where he seated himself and placed the call. It was close and uncomfortable at first in the stale air, but then the generators began to throb and the draperies moved silently in the coolness of the room. The draperies were splotched with half-moons and shafts of bright colors and spindly-legged martian creatures with clocks for faces. Arthur Fenstemaker looked at them, fascinated, until the call came through.

"Arthur — you all right?"

"Well, they are running hell out of me. They won't give me any rest, and now I'm out here in no man's land trying to —

"Arthur, you are a pretty tough customer — one of the toughest. Do you want to come up here tomorrow. Is that it?"

"I can't come tomorrow. I want to come before you do this terrible thing that I heard this morning you are getting ready to do."

"I'm not going to do anything to you, Arthur."

"Well somebody's after me — haven't I been square with your bunch?"

"You've been more than square, Arthur. What is it you want?"

"I want you to get a sixty-day extension. That'll give me time to —"

"Extension on what?"

"You know what. Hell and goddam — if you do this terrible thing —"

"What can you do in sixty days?"

"I don't know. But we can reason together. You do this thing now and you'll have a mess on your hands. You'll defeat me, and the kind of fellow taking my place will have promised everything short of civil war to get in. I've been what you bastards up there call *moderate*. They'll be calling me a Communist down here if you do this thing. You'll crucify me, beat me, and there'll be nothing moderate about whoever happens to be the next Governor."

"I didn't even know you were running for re-election."

"Well somebody up there does — you can bet your sweet life on that. First I heard of this was sprung on me this morning, just before I was leaving for this no man's land —"

"Where the hell are you, anyway?"

"Never mind about that. They called me and told me what you people were about to do in the courts. I didn't know any action was even being contemplated. My God it would kill me. You realize that?

"Yes, but —"

"You know what my position is. I want to cooperate in any way I can. I want to abide by the law. But you get somebody stirring up the people and I'll have a riot on my hands. And then pretty soon you won't have me here to smooth things over. For example — there are a bunch of segregationists down in —"

"Wait a minute, Governor . . ."

"There are these segregationists and they're bringing in this bird from — Well you know who he is. It's been in all the papers. He's making a speech tomorrow night, and they've got these special buses taking members of the Legislature down —"

"Wait a minute, wait a minute. Let me ask you a question or two. I don't know whether I can get this postponed. It'll take some work, I can tell you —"

"I appreciate that . . ."

"I don't know if I can. If I do, I don't want any credit for it, and if I don't, I don't want any credit for it."

"Neither do I. I'm not talkin' to anyone. My staff doesn't even know about it . . ."

"There are a lot of things I can't do. And messing around with the courts is one of them."

"I know that. But this was instigated by your people. Who they are I don't know. But you can take the pressure off. Sixty days is all I ask. Somebody up here's trying to defeat me."

"The way you say it, I belong to a giant conspiracy."

"No, no. The wicked fleeth when no man pursueth. I'm ready, willing and able to do the right thing — in sixty days. I need a stay of execution."

"I'll see what I can do."

"You're a good man. God bless you."

"Well you're all right yourself. I'll call you."

"When?"

"I don't know — when it's settled."

"Call me at the Capitol. My office will know where I am."

"All right."

"All right."

Six

ARTHUR FENSTEMAKER sat quietly for a few minutes after he had broken the connection. He stared round the room, not seeing any of it, thinking of the conversation, going back over it sentence by sentence, reassembling the phrases in his mind. He thought casually of having a drink brought to him. He smoked a cigarette, one of the five he had rationed himself for the day. The other telephone, the pink one, made a buzzing sound. He picked up the receiver.

"Governor?" Vicki's voice came to him, twinkling and insistent; the emotions it aroused in him were unsettling. He wanted to keep his mind on his business.

"Yes, Miss Vicki?"

"Would you like another drink?"

"Well now you must be reading my mind. I —"

"Or would you like to take a walk over the hill with us and watch that scene?"

"Perhaps I should — just to see how this business is done. I'm a little frightened about what I've committed myself to."

"Nothing to be frightened about. Come along and you'll see how simple it all is."

He agreed to meet the others outside. It was now midafternoon but the sun was still nearly directly overhead; the reflections came at them from every direction. They did not have far to go to reach the set, which was hardly any set at all. One of the wooden oil derricks had been hoisted off the railroad flatcar and placed near a fence that was only a few hundred feet long. A dirt road paralleled the fence and several hundred yards up the road the Dusenberg was parked. Vicki was driven to the Dusenberg in a jeep; the others stayed behind and watched the cameramen and technicians going over the scene with Shavers. One of the men stood in the middle of the road, paying out a tape measure to a camera boom. Others stood around under the wooden derrick, looking up dubiously at its insides.

Then the area in front of the cameras was cleared except for a single person, a stand-in for Greg Calhoun someone explained to them, who climbed halfway up the derrick and straddled one of the cross timbers. The boom camera moved up and around like a cobra's head, and Shavers climbed on top for a moment to satisfy himself about something; no one was quite sure what.

They could hear the rumble of the Dusenberg, idling down the road, and then someone signaled Vicki to proceed. The old automobile moved ahead, and the cameras swung with the approach. It was rather an anticlimax for the visitors. Vicki approached in the Dusenberg; then the fellow hanging on to the derrick waved at her and the Dusenberg stopped and Vicki waved back and rested her arms along the open window of the car, her chin on her arms. They ran through the scene again, and once again, shifting the cameras occasionally, and Vicki had returned up the road for still another attempt when the Governor, Mrs. Fenstemaker, Hoot Gibson, Sarah and Jay gave up in exhaustion and headed back to the row of trailer houses.

The Governor and his wife went directly to their "suite." Hoot Gibson wandered on across to the mess tent. Jay and Sarah stood and talked for a few moments outside one of the trailers. It all seemed very formal and painfully remote. There had been little real communication between them since the week before when Arthur Fenstemaker had arranged the trip in exchange for a personal appearance by Vicki at his party. They talked idiotically outside the trailer house.

"It's hot," she said to him.

"Yes."

"Is my nose blistered?"

"Yes. Is mine?"

"You look like a lobster."

"We'd better go inside."

"I— They don't seem to have cared whether we share the same trailer."

"I can find another if you like."

"No, it's not — I just — Oh come on, let's get inside."

The arrangement was similar to the quarters shared by Vicki and the Director. They examined the furnishings in both rooms. "Which do you want?" Jay asked pointlessly. The rooms were nearly identical.

"This one's fine. I want to shower . . ."

"I'll get the bags," Jay said.

They stood looking at each other uncomfortably, like ancient players on a grade school stage, lines long forgotten, prompters vanished from the world, as the ceaseless, shifting desert wind gnawed at the trailer walls.

He had wanted to kiss her then, but turned instead and went to get the bags. They had not touched each other since the week before when Arthur Fenstemaker brought the business with Vicki out in the open. He remembered the look Sarah had given him when he agreed to help the Governor get his "movie queen wife" to come to the party — a look reserved for some alcoholic husband about to come down off the wagon for a first drink . . .

He remembered the newsstand, later that day. He had slipped into the narrow stall out of the afternoon sunlight, pushing past piles of outdated papers and rows of withered fruit laid out in thin wooden boxes. He paused before a display of pocket fiction, thumbing through several selections, before moving to the magazine rack. His fingers moved over the magazine covers, eyes searching for the familiar face and platinum hair. Twice he was fooled by comely imitations (they simply did not interest him) and once he came across an old copy of *The Vicki McGown Story* that he had purchased two months before and destroyed almost immediately.

He took the magazine down from the shelf. There was a half partition toward the end of the stall, and from beyond that came the "thwack" and "thwack-thwack" of a domino game.

He examined the cover photograph. They had done something with her faintly irregular front teeth — he could not tell what — and there was the inevitable stretch of bosom cleavage; otherwise, except for the white hair that never seemed to photograph the same color twice, scarcely any change was discernible in the months since he had begun averting his eyes from such things. Across the top of the cover the editors exulted: "Six New Intimate Portraits of Vicki McGown!"

He found the section with the color photographs. They had Vicki lying in what appeared to be a field of clover in exquisite disarray, and the expression on her face ranged in stages of arousement, from bemused interest to vague pleasure to the teeth-grinding ecstasy of orgasm. On the facing page there was a full-length nude of her, laid out in the grass in deep, untroubled sleep.

It meant nothing to him now, he told himself, although there had been a time when the caterwauling memories of her pursued him everywhere he wandered, when it had been impossible not to think or talk about her or react to the mention of her name. That had been in the early days when she had become a "person-ality" with no visible means of support. She had been a phenom-enon, all right, a household word before she ever made a picture.

So many photographs . . . There had been so many. The first had been the "Miss Rocket-Launcher" thing while he was still stationed in Japan, and there had been a maddening succes-sion of others, but the one that really got her career underway was after he had returned, when he was living in San Fran-cisco and seeing the little girl, Victoria Anne, on weekends. Vicki had called him from Los Angeles one Friday.

"How would you like to keep Victoria Anne for several days?" she asked.

"I could arrange it. Why?"

"I've got a free ride to Cannes for the Film Festival. It's a tremendous opportunity."

"Cannes! Good heavens, Vic, that's —"

The several days stretched into several weeks, and Jay, unable to hold down his new job in the interim, had sat in the silent heat of the furnished room with the little girl, teaching her the new words (Eyes . . . *Ice* . . . Nose . . . *Noss* . . . Mouth . . . *Mouse*) until the predictable photographs preceded Vicki's return, pictures of Vic stripped down to the bottom half of a two-piece suit, stand-ing calf-deep in the surf in the arms of an aging, out-of-fashion male star. An unretouched version of it appeared the next week in a news magazine, and it had done both their careers some good. There were a succession of substantial character parts awaiting the older fellow; for Vicki it was her long-awaited "discovery."

But he did not really mind about the pictures; he had begun vaguely to enjoy them. It was the image he had of Vicki in his mind that nagged and badgered his emotions. There was the scene set in his head at college, the evening they announced their secret marriage to the others, with the celebration that followed and Vicki tight on champagne, swinging on the arm of his roommate, the two of them standing together in some dim corridor of his brain, the roommate kissing her lightly on the lips and Vicki laughing and unconcerned, dizzy with the wine, returning the kiss with more meaning than he thought possible. There were the other episodes in the months that followed, and always Vicki unable to fathom his objections, mentally or morally incapable of grasping the distinctions, until he began to feel slightly limited and priggish himself, like an old woman crabbing after her husband's muddy shoes.

There was the episode with the Kruegers. They had been to a dinner party that had begun to disintegrate like so many of the others, the guests drunk on rum and dinner never being served. He had seen Vicki leaving with Ben Krueger, and out of self-defense or possibly a last, thundering avowal of his manhood, he had begun to flirt with Evelyn Kreuger. The others left sometime afterwards and the two of them remained in the darkened house, Jay and Evelyn Krueger, and whatever it was they sought from each other was realized in one of the front bedrooms.

When the door came open they lay terrified together, unable to move or reason or crawl out of their perspiring bodies, agonized by the searing patch of flesh where their hips touched. But then there was only the darkness and presently the sound of Vicki's muffled laughter.

"They've all gone."

"Without us? They couldn't have gone without —"

"Well, it's twelve-thirty. It's —"

"I wonder where Jay-Jay went?"

"With the others probably. . . Will I see you tomorrow?"

"Oh yes, yes, I —"

"God you're great . . ."

"I'm worried about Jay-Jay."

"You shouldn't be. Why bother about Jay? Jay doesn't possess you. How can any person possess any other? How can you possess a nymph?"

"It's not that. I just wonder where he went."

"I'll take you home. Come on . . ."

There was the sound of the door being pulled shut and then the enormous silence of the house, with Evelyn next to him sobbing in her pillow.

It had come to them suddenly, and with finality, that there was nothing to be done, nothing to savor, no moral bludgeon, even, with which to flail the other lovers. They had been denied something, furthermore, something terribly important, whatever it was that at least could have made the moment seem significant for themselves. There was nothing for them — no hope or want or simian grace; they were left defenseless by an awful knowledge, while Vicki and Ben were carried along in the animal heat of renewal and discovery.

All the fun was suddenly gone out of revolt. Where had they been wrong? They had strewn the altars with garbage, but now the bedsheets smelled of coffee grounds as well. Was it because there had been no moral tradition to begin with — no real values to revolt against? Was there only the intense gesture in the empty air? Perhaps all of it was first generation: new rich, new smart, new wicked, as gauche and false and phony as the oil wealth around them, which wasn't wealth at all but a kind of stage money used for buying unpronounceable brandies and football coaches.

The thing between Vicki and Ben Kreuger soon collapsed, but the precedent was there and was subsequently resumed, in one way or another, after college and in California, from that time to this. Jay had hoped he could pass it off philosophically, but it did not get any better for him — and soon the sensation was very like discovering Vicki in bed with another man, other men, ten or twenty of them, hundreds and thousands, and the cumulative effect of the photographs, the stories, the endless chatter in the Hollywood columns, the images in his head of the early days, pursued him like some king-sized cuckold in stereophonic sound.

And the truth was that he had begun to enjoy it, in some twisted, despairing way, deriving an awful pleasure from lying awake nights, comforted in his indifference toward other women — evoking the picture in his mind of Vicki in coitus, with one sideshow performer and then another, thousands of them, standing around in disorder, stamping their feet and clapping their hands, hooting and whistling and pawing at their loins . . .

Seven

Now THE SUN began to descend, slowly at first as if it were unwilling to give up the promise of the morning, and then in a headlong thrust toward the distant hills, the heat rising off the floor of the desert, blistering the pavement of the highway, bathing the colorless dunes in sudden refractions of violet light. The shifting crowds of people outside the camp, no longer repopulated by late arrivals, began to disperse. They came together in one last vicarious enthusiasm at the approach of a studio car, which scarcely acknowledged the witnesses as it turned quickly off the highway and moved toward the tents and trucks and trailer houses.

Several teenagers in the crowd thought they had recognized Greg Calhoun in the car, but they could not be sure. Several others said a little girl's head was visible next to the young man in the backseat; they were fairly certain about the little girl.

Studio employees sat under the big mess tent, talking together at the wooden picnic tables, puncturing cold cans of beer and passing them around. Others showered in newly constructed stalls near the tent and talked about driving into the nearest town for the evening. Edmund Shavers was going into town to watch the rushes. There was an ancient theater in the town — open only on weekends — at which he had arranged to have the rushes run. Shavers wore fresh khakis and examined his face in the marble bathroom of the trailer house he shared with Vicki McGown. Vicki examined her face at her dressing table in the other end of the trailer. She felt curiously void of any feeling. She was not a calculating person; most of the time she was pushed along on impulse. Now she waited for something, anything, an idea or an event, to seize her.

In another trailer Sarah Lehman stood in her shower stall and watched the beads of water move down her marvelous little breasts. Here in the pink-tiled privacy of herself she was not reminded of any of the people around her. She could have been in her own shower in her own bathroom in her own apartment, anywhere away from the moment. She had not wanted to come here; she had not wanted to stay: now she wished she could remain in the shower stall with the mist falling on her perfumed body. Jay McGown lay on his bed in the adjoining room and listened to the water running in Sarah's quarters. He had fallen asleep thinking of Vicki, had dreamed of her fitfully, none of which he could remember on awakening, but still thinking of her now he concentrated on the sound of the water running in Sarah's apartment. He tried to picture the way Sarah might look in the shower stall; but she kept looking like Vicki.

Arthur Fenstemaker was on the telephone again. His wife lay asleep on the bed and shifted in the covers only when the Governor raised his voice. His wife lay asleep wearing only a half-slip. Arthur Fenstemaker wanted to move over to the bed and put his hand along the sweet curve of his wife's neck and shoulders, but he could not get off the phone.

". . . Well a lie will go round the world several times, my friend, while truth is tying its shoelaces.

"Well it's a bad business — it's —"

"How many members of the Legislature went down to hear that nigger-baitin' son of a bitch?"

"Well we ain't learnin' nothin' on the telephone. See if you can get an advance copy of his speech and call me back . . ."

In the studio car Gregory Calhoun (né Rabinowitz) put on a miner's helmet. He turned to the little girl.

"How does it look, Annie?"

The little girl giggled, shifting sideways in the seat and reaching for the helmet. Greg Calhoun took off the miner's helmet and set it on the little girl's head. Now she laughed aloud and clapped her hands together.

"But what are you going to *do* with it?" she said. "Are you going to wear it in the picture?"

"If they'll let me. What it's really for, though, is for jackrabbits."

The little girl thought this was hysterically funny.

"*Jack*rabbits!"

"Jackrabbits. Not these little Easter bunnies you read about in your picture books, but ugly, buggy, long-legged jackrabbits. Jackrabbits bug me, Annie. I'm goin' to shoot 'em all dead."

"With the helmet? You can't shoot a *rabbit* with a *helmet*."

"With a gun. A forty-five gun. I wear the helmet at night so I can see the rabbits in the dark."

"You've got forty-five guns?"

"No, no. A *forty-five* automatic. That's a type of pistol. I just bought it. And the helmet. For the rabbits."

"Are there rabbits out there?" Victoria Anne McGown looked

out the window, at the scarlet sun and the range of mountains miles away and the strange pile of tents and trailers up ahead.

"There are ten thousand jackrabbits out there, Annie. You can bet your life on that. You can smell 'em. You smell 'em?"

"*Smell* rabbits?"

"In their native habitat. They smell worse than the rabbits. The habitats."

"My mother's an actress," the little girl said abruptly.

"Oh no she isn't. You shouldn't go around talking like that."

"She is too! She *is* an actress. That's what —"

"No, no, you're getting it all mixed up. Your mother's a *star*. Your mother's a moom-pitcher star!"

"Oh."

"Exactly."

"Are you an actress?" Victoria Anne McGown asked.

"Yes. I'm an actress," Greg Calhoun said.

"You're not a *star*?"

"No. I'm an actress."

The little girl subsided and the two of them sat quietly as the studio car moved toward the trailer houses. Edmund Shavers sat in an aluminum folding chair in front of his trailer, and he pulled himself out of it as the car approached.

"You're early," Shavers said. "I wasn't expecting you until — what the hell is that on your head, Greg?"

"It's a miner's helmet," Victoria Anne said. "A miner's helmet for shooting jackrabbits — only you shoot the rabbits with forty-five guns. You can smell the rabbits out here." She turned toward the young man. "You smell any rabbits, Gregory?"

"I smell 'em. Out there ruttin' around . . . You smell 'em, Edmund?"

Shavers looked around him in brief confusion. "What? There aren't any — Hey, Victoria Anne, we've got a big surprise for you." He bent down toward the little girl, taking hold of her hands.

"Have you got some jackrabbits?"

"No . . . No jackrabbits. Something else though. Your father. Your father's here, and I bet he wants to see you."

"My *father?* Oh good! I want to see him because I don't remember what he looks like!"

"I don't remember what mine looks like either," Greg Calhoun said.

Jay heard the voices, but not-listening, lying on the chenille bedspread trying not to think, conscious of only himself in the gathering darkness of the trailer, conscious of the weight of his body on the bed, the feeling gone out of his arms and legs, not-listening and not-thinking, the voices did not really come to him.

There was that old Mexican.

There was that old Mexican who must have symbolized all he'd left undone, all the forgotten promises and vague resolves. So many promises to himself and to others and so much promise. Before he had turned away, shifting his horizons from the murderous social forces around him to the narrow perspectives of inward observation and dislike. Now there was only a certain vapidity of the spirit. Once there had been so many alternatives. There had been the commitment; the French would call it that. There had been that old Mexican, and the next day at the tennis courts, bending down at the water fountain, mopping his face with a clean-white towel, examining the specks of clay clinging to the dampness of his legs, the picture of the old Mexican stooping in the headlights of the car, showing his broken smile, had come to him again. He remembered looking around the courts, at the other young people, brown skin, white shorts, all of it seeming gorgeous; and the old Mexican pissing in the rain. Ten years ahead in time Mr. and Mrs. Jay McGown would have been entertaining at LaGloria Country Club. He remembered thinking that, and making the promise, *no they won't; no they won't.* There was the commitment, and it was easy afterwards because he had all the gifts, all the graces, all the emotional and mental equipment, to get the job done.

Before the balls conspired to disable the intellect.

Coming back from California he had thought it might be possible to be seized by some of the old enthusiasms. All the bright young people were coming home to help Arthur Fenstemaker, all the dedicated people moving together to put the man in office and bring in the new day. But he had not really been seized by any of it — not the way Sarah was, back from Wellesley for the summer with all those shrill ideas in her head; not the way any of the others were, caught up in the crazy rush of a "crusade," most of them a little envious of Jay as a former student body president and of the intimacy with Arthur Fenstemaker such dead glories gave him.

None of the old urgency was there. It was all a little flat — an ashes in the mouth. There was that old Mexican, but the memory of him was dim in his head now, diluted by his own despair. *Dear Mister Governor,* the letter said, *we live on a farm and dont make any money and we have a beautiful little girl who has the palsy. She cant do anything for herself, she cant talk or is able to hold up her head, and she likes to hear music and take baths. It costs us a thousand dollars a year in treatments, and that's more than we make some years. I cant stand the thought of putting her away, but . . .*

Was there a limit on your sympathy or a boundary to despair? How did you involve yourself in mankind? If there was anything to what the Frenchmen were saying, that each is guilty toward each for everything, then perhaps there was something to the rest of it — that all are bound to each other in suffering and in love. Jay hoped not; he was sorry if it were true. There wasn't enough in him now to go around.

But was this being honest with himself? Somewhere off in the boondocks of his reason the idea rebelled. Another toadying up to the horror that had been consuming him. How much, for example, was there of Arthur Fenstemaker to go around?

There was Kermit Abrams who had come to see him the week before. Mad Kermit — brilliant, mercurial, quixotic Kermit had come to the Capitol, his red beard blazing, seeking him out as if to get in touch with reality. When did Mad Kermit come? The day Arthur got Victoria on the telephone, the afternoon of which he and Sarah had gone to the apartment and — Mad Kermit came that day; there was plenty of Kermit to go around; there always had been, even at college. I mean man let's *do* something, Kermit and his red beard and awful breath and worn-over shoes, like I mean what are you *doing?*

I've been up all night, Jay told him, working on a speech for the Governor. I've —

I mean if you'd just listen to me, gate, just take me serious, we can end the cold war, usher in the new age of ecumenical progress and peace, and — Jay, man, was your wife a good lay? Tell me that. I mean —

I've been up all night, Jay explained to him wearily, working on this speech the Governor's supposed to give before the Jaycees. I've been trying to get some applause lines in, and I've been up all night, and —

I often wondered, Mad Kermit said, *what liberal politicians like you stay up all night for. I always thought it was to get milk for the slum kids —*

And Kermit had gone raging through the halls of the Capitol building, down the front steps and past the portico and through the park and hanged himself with a coathanger in his apartment closet two days later. There was that business with Sarah in the afternoon; there was Arthur Fenstemaker on the phone with Victoria and Jay talking with the little girl later on . . . Victoria Anne? How are you sweetheart this is your daddy . . . Your father . . . Yes I know I'm in Texas . . . I'm calling from Texas . . . How are you honey . . . Your father, yes that's right . . . Are you coming out here to see me? Wait . . . Wai — Hello . . . Victoria Anne, hi sweetie, are you — Your mother? Where's your mother? Out . . . where? Her picture took . . . taken.

Daddy, she had said to him, I know what you are Daddy I heard someone say . . . I heard someone say you're a prick,

Daddy, why are you a prick, Daddy, is that like an iceprick or a toothprick? Yes I'm coming to visit you goodbye Daddy.

There had been Kermit before that and the business with Sarah afterwards. Why did Kermit — Kermit couldn't understand that while he was out drowning the slum kids in milk it was up to Jay and the Governor to work at it more realistically and see that there were simply no more slums. Why couldn't he understand that?

There was that old Mexican.

There —

He pulled himself off the bed and felt his way across the darkened room in the trailer house to answer the knocking at the door. Vicki was standing there — he could see Sarah's face across the narrow entrance way looking out at them from her bedroom — and next to Vicki was Shavers, holding the hand of a little brown-haired girl, and next to her was a good-looking young man wearing a miner's helmet.

Eight

THE LIGHTS of the location camp had vanished behind a silver dune. The four of them — Jay, Sarah, Vicki and the little girl — followed the young man with the flashlight on his head.

"The idea," Greg Calhoun was saying, "is that you pot 'em while they got their mind on other things. They're out here rutting around, trying to make babies — this is the season; I've been reading up — and you let 'em have it with the light and then the gun. Bing-Bang!"

"A nice way to die," Sarah said. She was closest to Greg Calhoun. Jay and Vicki flanked the little girl.

"Only way to die," Greg said. "In a last, thumping flourish."

"If you can time it for the morning papers, it would be pretty good," Jay said.

"It's not perverse enough," Sarah said. "That sort of thing happens every day. You need something grotesque to really expire in the grand manner these days."

"You could catch him with a bed full of jackrabbits," Vicki said. "That's grand — that's absolutely —"

"Where are the jackrabbits?" Victoria Anne said, tugging at her parents' arms. "You smell 'em yet, Gregory? I wanna smell the jackrabbits."

They wandered between sandhills and baked arroyos, with the little girl breaking loose now and then and running a short distance ahead to wait for the others. No one could be sure how far they had walked. The sky was enormous and all around them; the world seemed infinitely remote.

Sarah was beginning to tire. There was sand in her shoes, and the first flush of excitement she had felt in the night air had faded. Now there was only a dull ache in the calves of her legs. She began to perspire slightly in the fresh dress. She looked at Vicki, who seemed carried along by a boundless vitality. Vicki had her hair piled on top of her head, and there was a glow of moisture along her shoulders and the back of her neck; but she did not slacken her pace.

"Couldn't we stop and wait for the rabbits to come to us?" Sarah finally said.

"No sport in that," Greg Calhoun said. "You've got to keep pushing ahead, going out to meet the rabbit on his own terms."

"What exactly does that entai —"

"Hey!" All of them stopped suddenly, half off balance in amazement. No one was ever sure afterwards just how many rabbits stood petrified in the dim light from the miner's helmet. There seemed at least a half dozen staring at them, tense and blind-eyed. Victoria Anne squealed with delight and then she screamed and could not stop screaming, even after Greg Calhoun's arm came down and the dust the bullets kicked up had settled and the explosions echoed across the desert floor.

"Missed! Missed them all!" Vicki exulted. Jay had hold of Victoria Anne and was trying to pull her to him, but she kept breaking away and standing a few feet off, her fists clenched, screaming at the darkened sky. "I think we'd better head back," he said. He finally got the little girl next to him, and she subsided.

"I can't go back now," Greg said. "By God I've stood the charge of a jackrabbit and now it's in my blood."

"I'm going to take her back," Jay said. "It's late anyhow." Sarah started to join him, but Vicki took the little girl's hand and said something about bedtime. Then Sarah knew she would have to remain behind with Greg Calhoun. She regarded the prospect with a mixture of exhaustion and unaccountable relief. All day long she had felt herself pushing along toward the darkness, certain there would be something to be faced in the evening with Jay. She had wanted to tell him she understood what it was he had been trying to tell her. The compulsion was still there, but now it somehow filled her with dread. The massive effort necessary to re-establish communication intimidated her, and besides, it did not seem the time or place. Perhaps she could talk with him later in the evening. Perhaps there was some reverberating truth she could get from Gregory Calhoun. She stood quietly beside the young man as Jay, Vicki and the little girl moved away toward the camp.

Greg Calhoun turned to her. "I'm glad you stayed behind," he said. "It wouldn't have been any fun without somebody to play the game with." She was nearly his height, and he did not have far to move, bending toward her, his hands held behind his back, not touching her anywhere until his lips brushed hers. There had been only his nice face coming at her and the faint smell of whiskey and cigarettes on his breath. It had not been much of a kiss, but the nearly nothingness of it left her trembling.

Greg Calhoun sat down abruptly in the sand. He was right at her feet and he stared through her legs at the open country. It was as if he were talking to himself. "We'll have a party," he said. "We'll have a picnic with refreshments. We'll all get drunk and bury our heads in the sand." He produced a pocket flask and held it up toward her.

"What is it?" She bent down and unscrewed the top.

"Brandy. Cognac. Try it . . . You like it we'll send out for a case."

They sat crosslegged in the sand, passing the flask back and forth. After a time they lay back in the sand side by side and stared up at the sky. The trembling in her legs had moved into her chest; she wished terribly that he would touch her and knew she would scream out like the half-terrified little girl if he did.

She was finally able to talk.

"Tell me about your work," she said.

"Very serious. Very serious about my work. Shavers is serious about his — Vicki's serious about hers. We're all dedicated artists except me because I really am."

"Really are what?"

"Making a great deal of money and taken seriously by the critics. It's tremendous, it's nothing like it was on television, it's — It's something seeing your face looking like a slice of rare roast beef, magnified as big as hell on the screen like a goddam Navy blimp . . ."

"I've never seen any of your pictures."

"I've only made two. This one's the third, and it's going to be a bitch — one of the worst in modern times. And I wish I had a stake in it because they're going to clean up."

He rolled over on his stomach and lay next to her, and she thought Ohmygod and remembered all the clichés about her heart thumping in her ears, and then he kissed her again, very lightly on the lips.

"Do you like this? Zis nice party?"

"Yes."

"Why are you trembling?"

"I'm terrified."

"Why?"

"I've been that way all day."

"Even before I came? Perhaps in anticipation of — No."

"It's just all this . . . A kind of nightmare. Vicki's part of it I suppose."

"Ah! What I've always maintained. She affects women the same way. I knew it."

"She's the real thing."

"Yes she is. The real honest-to-God thing. That poor guy."

"Who?"

"Jay."

"Yes."

"Would you like to make love?" He was lying on his side looking into her face, and she had been so absorbed in the conversation that her response was nearly automatic.

"Someday," she said. Then she pulled herself back into the crosslegged sitting position and began to laugh.

"That's a marvelous answer," the young man said. "Best I've ever had!"

"What I mean is . . . I . . . Well someday, sure."

"But not with me. Tonight."

She was still laughing. It was partly some kind of hysterical release from the awful images that had been in her mind most of the day. The actor had done this for her, and now she bent down and kissed him. She pulled back and said, "We could sit out here and neck."

"Yes we could. We will. But what about the other? I'm fascinated."

"Well there's the sand, and . . ."

"Wonderful!"

". . . and I don't know how."

"No! I don't believe it."

"Well it's true."

"You could learn . . . You could —"

"This is no place to learn."

"You're right. Let's have a drink. I'll drink to your sweet and blessed . . . Your . . . You're a remarkable woman, Miss Sarah, and you'll always carry a little piece of my heart."

They stood and stretched and brushed the sand off their clothes and began the long walk back, arm in arm. She was glad she had stayed behind with Gregory Calhoun. She felt somehow cleansed; the experience had been a kind of absolution, and outside the trailer house she was able to enjoy the sweetness of her young body against his, the two of them together in the evening air.

Presently she entered the trailer house. And now, she thought, now would be the time to talk with Jay, bringing herself to him all whole and honest and lovely. There would be no horror now at the thought of his hands against her boiling skin. She could explain it all to him, really, for the first time. She bathed her face quickly with a damp towel and hurried to his door at the other end of the trailer house. When there was no response to her knock, the fear coming to her already, she opened the door and switched on the light to survey the empty room.

She stood there for a moment, agonized, and then moved to a window where she looked out across the punished expanse of desert grass at the other trailer. There was no light showing at either end. Perhaps he had gone for a walk; possibly he and Hoot Gibson had — There was the Governor's trailer. She left his room and stepped outside, all the promise vanished from the moment when she had stood there only minutes before. She rounded the corner and saw the Governor's trailer was dark. There was a light showing in the empty mess tent and in Greg's trailer, and as she stood there watching, Greg's room went dark.

Back inside she lay in her bed listening for Jay's approach. She fell asleep still listening and then came awake suddenly an hour later. She examined her watch and pulled herself from the covers to look once again at Jay's empty room. This was how he said it was; she remembered now: the pictures coming at her, just as it must have been for him, the grotesques in all their grisly detail, the sights and sounds and smells of it, carousing through her heart and head. There seemed no escape. She thought briefly of going outside and waking Greg Calhoun, but then she could tell herself there was nothing more he could give her, scarcely anything she could even now accept.

Nine

ALL THE WAY back there had been no real communication between the two of them. Whatever needed to be said was conveyed indirectly through the child, who walked in the middle, holding on to their hands, providing the only tangible connective. It was astonishing, Jay thought, what little adjustment was necessary on both their parts to bring their conversational needs down to the level of the child's. All that had gone before between them had been articulated in a kind of child's talk anyhow, and there seemed no good reason why they could not have gone on through life together remarking about the blueness of the sky, the vastness of the day, inquiring if either of them needed to use the potty.

They talked through the child on the way back to the camp, avoiding the shadows of the dunes, attempting to guide each other toward the level spaces where the moonlight shone. Soon he had to carry the little girl; she fell fast asleep clinging to his shoulder and there was not much said between them after that. They concentrated on the walk through the packed sand, absorbed in the simple and immediate need of getting from one place to another, hay-foot straw-foot, over the dunes and away from the shadows and toward the camp. Absorbed in these mechanics, it was some time before Jay realized they were lost.

It suddenly came to him that they had been walking too long a time, a time all out of proportion to the period during which the original party of five had sought and found the rabbits. He looked at his watch and knew that by now they should be well past the camp; beyond, away, to the side or in back of it — there was no way to determine. He stopped on a little rise and shifted the child to his other shoulder.

"We're lost," he said.

"What? Are you joking?"

"No. We're lost. I don't know where we are." This last admission reverberated in his head. This sudden acute responsibility seemed unfair. He had got them lost, and now it was up to him to get them back home safely again. Arthur Fenstemaker was nowhere around to instruct him; there was no one to call, no help from any source.

"Well what do we do?"

"I don't know," he said.

"Which direction were we away from the camp?"

"West . . . A little southwest, maybe."

"Can't you look at the stars or something and tell which way we've been heading? What about the North Star?"

"I wouldn't be able to find the North Star — I can't remember the last time I looked at stars. If I found it even, I'm not sure it's always in the north."

Vicki flopped down in the sand, stretched her long legs and kicked off her sandals.

"We're really lost, then?"

"Yes."

"I like it. I'm glad we're lost. I wish Victoria Anne weren't here, of course. But I like being lost with you."

"Really?" He had tried for a note of impatience.

"Yes. I want to be lost with you. I want to be lost *in* you . . . Do you like that? I think it's from a line I had."

Jay looked about in all directions, attempting to get some kind of bearing from the mountains. But only the larger ranges were visible against the purple sky. He finally selected a course he was not at all sure about and set the perspective of the mountaintops in his mind to avoid the possibility of moving in circles.

"Do you want to rest some more?"

"I'm enjoying it. I'm not tired, really. I'm just enjoying it."

"We'd better get started."

They moved off again in the direction Jay had chosen. He needed to keep his eyes on the mountains, but occasionally he would slip back into the numbing absorption of every step. Vicki did not falter or weaken or speak out against him. Several times she offered to relieve him of the burden of the child. There were pauses, mounting in frequency, in which he shifted the little girl from one shoulder to another. After half an hour he began to think seriously of spending the night in the dunes.

Soon now, he was certain of it, the others at the camp would begin worrying about them. Sarah and Greg Calhoun would be returning without them, and there were bound to be questions and some concern. Perhaps Hoot Gibson would have returned from town with Shavers, and the two of them would come looking. The Governor might even take charge of a search party. What he needed now was to stay in one place and build a fire so the others would have some signal to guide them. He should stop plodding senselessly across the sand; there was a good possibility he had been heading away from the camp all this time.

It was Vicki who sighted the shack. Even after she called it to his attention it was difficult to tell it from one of the dunes. It was a shapeless, shambled thing, collapsed at one end, with a growth of mesquite bunched all round.

Vicki held the little girl while he pried loose the weathered wooden slabs nailed across the entrance. He examined the dirt floor and then led his wife and child inside.

Afterwards, he built a fire beyond the entrance, testing the direction of the wind to avoid the smoke, building it with cactus leaves and cattle droppings at first, the way wornout pioneer brides had collected buffalo chips on this treeless plain fifty years before, and then with loose planking from the sides of the tumbled shack. When he had the fire roaring in his face, blistering his forehead and singeing the hair on his arms, he sagged against the door in exhaustion while Vicki's cool hands moved over his cheek, her vacant voice rising and falling in allusions to wiener roasts and toasted marshmallows.

Soon the sounds of her words trailed off in his consciousness and he fell asleep. He lay alone for a period of time and then there was the warmth of Vicki's body against him. In his sleep he knew it was Vicki and not Vicki; he was aware only of the warmth and the nearness and the smell of her perfume in the desert air. When he came awake suddenly they were together in the half-light of the fire, his face buried against her neck. He stood and began gathering more wood for the fire. Vicki was sitting awake when he returned.

"Please come home," she said to him.

"What?"

"Please come back with Victoria Anne and me. I want you to live with us again. I know I've been bad. I know some of the things I've done are nearly unforgivable. But I think of you all the time and I need you all the time. Both of us need you. Do you think you need us?"

"I don't know. Of course I need Anne. I guess I need you — or something of you — in a way. It's just — I can't believe it would be any different than before."

"I think it would. I think I'm different than before."

"You probably are. But if there's any improvement I'm not sure it has any bearing on us." He lay back in the sand and closed his eyes.

"Hold me like you were." She was on her knees leaning over him.

"I can't," he said.

"You were. You were all over me for a while."

"I was asleep."

"What difference does that make? It just shows . . . something, I don't know, but it was so nice to be with you again."

She lay beside him. Jay lay on his back with his eyes closed trying to think of sleep, release, escape, of shaking loose and giving in, of headlong flight and boozy, luxuriant fulfillment. Where were all the gay places? Where were —

"I'm looking forward to the Governor's party," Vicki said. "Will you ride up with me?"

Where was all the fun and —

"Will you ride up with me?"

It was out there somewhere, remote and unattainable. It was out here in these landscapes. It was at the Governor's party it was —

"We can leave day after tomorrow, Jay."

"Try to sleep," he finally said. "Lie next to me if you want, the way you were, and try to sleep."

He could lie next to her here and ride up with her on the day after tomorrow and they could fly home together when the ranch party was ended and — It was all a madness. The whole crazy idea would turn to vinegar once it was daylight. There would be Sarah standing in the sun, the white down on her arms, her skin all glowing . . .

He liked to think he had been pushed toward Sarah from the beginning, but it was just not true. There had been too much pestilence in his head at the beginning. What stale enthusiasms remained were directed toward his work with Arthur Fenstemaker, and it was some time afterwards that Sarah had begun to poke around in his dead remains.

He had thought, frankly, it would be hopeless, but the capacity for love had not vanished entirely. He loved Sarah; surely he must love her; he had not gone out of the business after all; and it had all been going so perfectly until the evening the week before when they had been together at the apartment. In the dark heat of the room she had just begun to perspire, faintly beneath the softness of hair that shaped her face, lightly through the blouse and along the folds where her exquisite breasts began. They were a little heap in the middle of the bed, and she whispered in his ear *I want to yes I think I want to,* and from where he was lying he could see the blistered paint on the door facings and the preposterous bathtub with the elaborately gnarled legs. The draperies rustled quietly as she brushed past, folding her clothes carefully over the back of a chair; there were dust motes suspended in the stalks of light coming through the blinds and the fuzz from the bedspread tickled his neck. She had come toward him, her olive skin glistening, pausing and regarding herself with astonishment in the rippled mirror; her back and shoulders made lovely lines in the soft light, and as he moved toward where she was sitting on the side of the bed he could see that she was trembling slightly. It was not until he had kissed the back of her neck that he realized she had the magazine laid out in her lap, open to the picture sequence of Vicki in the haystack, and by then she had begun to sob convulsively.

Afterwards, he could not fix it in his mind just how long they stayed there. Thinking back there was only the shapeless space in his memory: only the two of them in the dark room, in the rumpled bedclothes, with Sarah crying quietly to herself. Sometime during the night he had driven her home, and since then they had not talked about it. They had been together nearly all the waking hours, but it had been impossible to discuss: there had been only the private, hopeless insistence to themselves that it never really happened.

Where was she now? The shifting desert wind reminded him that he had left her with Greg Calhoun, pursuing the phantom rabbits across the sand. Was she back now and had she set out with the others at the camp in search of him? And how was he ever to articulate his feeling for her once she had found him? He felt sleep coming on again, and now in exhaustion he turned toward Vicki, regret and resistance gone out of him, submerging himself in her enormous warmth, remembering nothing in his dreams but the great, swelling, unaccountable pleasure of her presence. His next conscious moment was when he opened his eyes in the daylight and saw Hoot Gibson grinning at him fiercely from the doorway of the shack.

Ten

"IT WAS ONE of those evenings," Edmund Shavers was saying, "one of those magnificent summer evenings, flaming with color, suffused with all the magnificence and simplicity of the love we feel when we're young. Everything was rose, then pink and cream and then rose again, and the air — my God! the air. Well you could taste it. There was a texture to it, and you could taste the sweetness, and the sun was dropping down behind an old stone farm building; its roof looked as if it was on fire; and there was a rusting Nehi sign across one of the windows and there were a couple of kids playing in the grass out front. It was about this time of evening — right now — and I thought you couldn't write it or paint it or photograph it; not and convey all the movement and emotion. So I knew then I wanted to direct pictures."

"How very poetic, Mr. Shavers," the Governor's wife said.

"Well it's a little hard to describe, but it's what I felt at the time."

"I believe it, Ed, by God I believe it," Greg Calhoun said.

"Well why shouldn't you believe it? It's what I felt. Why should I be trying to —"

"That wasn't why I tried to get into pictures," Vicki said. She was a little tight, and although her face retained all its color and expression, the languor had gone out of her voice and she had become sullen. The others shifted in their aluminum folding chairs and watched the sunset.

"I was just tired of living in one-room apartments and not having enough money to go out and that awful window fan drumming away next to my head night after night. It was that window fan. You remember that window fan, Jay-Jay?"

"Yes," Jay said.

They sat quietly for a time, attempting to recapture or sustain the feelings Shavers had evoked in them. Jay watched the sunset and tried not to think about the window fan, but he could hear it again, drumming away next to their bed; it kept coming back to him. The night he left Evelyn Krueger crying to herself in the front room he had returned home to find Vicki already groggy with sleep. She rolled toward him in the bed, grabbing him round the middle and kissing his back. "Where've you been?" she said. "We had something to eat," he said. "Evelyn and I had something to eat . . . Where did you disappear to?" "Went furrh ride," she said. "Jus' went furrh ride." And she was asleep again, almost immediately, with the window fan going next to the bed, the sound of it set in his memory that night during the hours he lay awake, listening to the rhythm of the fan and Vicki's even breathing.

In California the evenings were cool; he could still hear the fan; they had a three-room apartment then, with a nursery for the little girl, pink walls and pink asphalt tile on the floor and the Mother Goose figures he had strung on a mobile; the fan still drumming in his ears even when there was no fan and Vicki out past midnight all the time, coming in half drunk and giddy with delight over the parties her agent had given her. He heard it in Japan, in the officers' quarters, the window fan grinding away in his brain. There was that phone call from the States, his old commander being very frank about it . . . *It's not just that she's going out with some of the men on the base, Jay, but she's borrowing money from them.* It was something about clothes, party dresses, and something else about a photographer's bill, and there just wasn't enough in the allotment to cover it all. There was the window fan roaring in his ears after he had got back and then moved out and then moved on; where was that town? Where he had worked at a radio station, selling commercial time to car dealers and appliance store operators and substituting occasionally for the wheezing, bucolic disk jockey; it was quiet there, on the street where he lived in the rooming house, elm and oak trees along each side and dusty-leaved petunias lining the walks and the wisteria and queen's wreath winding in and out the lattice-work on the porch.

It was quiet there, except for the —

"Let's take a walk, Sarah, while there's still some light."

Greg Calhoun was bending over her, his hands gripping the armrests of the folding chair, his face a few inches away.

"I don't know," she said. "The Governor may need me. I —"

"He's on the phone again," Mrs. Fenstemaker said. "Go ahead, you two. If he needs anything I can take care of him."

"He's going into town with me shortly," Shavers said. "We're going to take a look at the rushes. We can all go in and see how his shots turned out."

"We'll be right back," Sarah said. She stood and moved off with Greg Calhoun.

Arthur Fenstemaker struck a match with his thumbnail and lit a cigarette. He frowned into the mouthpiece of the phone.

"They're going to *what?*"

"March on the Capitol. That's the word here. They're comin' from all over, expect to get at least a thousand, maybe fi'teen hundred."

"Now wait a minute — what the goddam hell are they marching *for?*"

"I'm not sure. It's not certain to happen, of course. But there are a lot of rumors, a lot of talk. It all started down there when that guy made his speech."

"What rumors?"

"There's just some talk. It's all very vague. That there's going to be some kind of action taken in Washington. It all started down there when that guy made his little speech. Now they're all comin' back, demanding you call a special session."

"Special session for what? Hell and damn, what can they —"

"Legislation to get around whatever action is taken."

"How are they so sure there's going to be some action."

"Nobody's sure. There's just a lot of talk."

"No danger of a demonstration if there's no action, is there?"

"I wouldn't think so."

"All right. Now . . . Just try to sit on this thing if you can. God Almighty will have us by the hand if we get out of it. I don't know what's happening. But the blind man knows the Lord, and we may just . . . Take it easy. I'll call you."

In the stillness of the evening, with the soft light beginning to fade, Arthur Fenstemaker stood outside the trailer house for a moment before approaching the others. When he got close, they turned in their chairs and greeted him.

"Let's have a drink. I'm hungry for one," he said. "I get these terrible pains in my chest and back and there's too much on my mind, and it takes either a pill or some good Scotch whiskey to get me unwound. I prefer the whiskey."

"Would you like me to get out the Vibrator, dear?"

"Later. I want to sit here and have a drink."

"There are the rushes," Shavers said. "You want to take a look at them, don't you?"

"Yes. I don't feel like it, but I'm fascinated about this stuff and of course that's why we agreed to stay another night . . . Wouldn't mind spending the goddam summer."

"You don't want to go back, dear? Why don't you want to go back?"

"Just hate to face all that madness."

"Trouble at home?" Jay said. "What did you —"

"No. Nothing serious. Let's have that drink, Jay. Where's Sarah? Where'd Sarah go? She knows how I like 'em."

"Sarah took a walk," Mrs. Fenstemaker said. "I'll fix you one."

The lights of the limousine flashed in their eyes for an instant before moving around to the back of them. Hoot Gibson and Vicki emerged. They left the car doors open; the music was turned up full volume on the phonograph.

"We went riding," Vicki said. "We got as far as the highway and I discovered the record machine. We decided to come back and dance . . . Will you dance with me, Governor?" She had her head thrown back and was moving to the music, her bare feet sliding softly in the sand, her hips shifting in rhythm, circling round the others.

"In a minute, Miss Vicki, in a minute. I'm going to have a little drink first. Then we'll dance the rest of the goddam night."

Vicki danced with Hoot Gibson, who swung her over the sand. He had his shoes off and his pants legs rolled up and was very light on his feet. "Smooooth," Vicki hummed.

There was a silence while another record fell on the turntable.

"Allright, Jay," Vicki said. She had planted herself in front of him, her legs apart, her hands on her hips. "S'ure duty dass with your wife. Dass with me, Jay."

He stood and danced with her. They moved through several numbers, the others sitting quietly, looking up at them occasionally. Hoot Gibson stood around in his bare feet, sorting through records, waiting his turn. Vicki had both arms around Jay, and they danced close together.

"What are you trying to do?" he finally said to her.

"You like that? Hoot Gibson did."

"I'll bet he did."

"Wait till I get hold th' Governor."

Sarah and Greg Calhoun returned at that moment; Jay stood

away from Vicki and then led her back to Hoot Gibson. He moved to Sarah's side, but she did not speak. There had been the agonizing silences since the morning, from the time he had greeted Hoot Gibson at the entrance to the shack, waking Vicki and carrying the little girl out to the waiting limousine where Sarah and Greg Calhoun were waiting.

No one had missed them until well after sunup, when those at the camp were awakened for the shooting of the Governor's scene. They had even sent Mexicans on horseback out looking for them then. Sarah sat quietly in back, holding the little girl in her arms, while Vicki described the long walk the night before and asked about the reaction at the camp when the three of them had not returned.

Sarah had sat quietly, holding the girl, and there had been nothing he could really say to her since the morning. It was impossible to explain or to make righteous assertions of his innocence. Had it all been an innocence? There was something that Sarah sensed between Vicki and himself — some vague, voluptuous aura that she could not identify. It was as in a dream, or waking from a dream, and being haunted by the unreality that lingered afterwards between the dreamer and those dreamt about. It had taken him most of the day to rebuild any aggression toward Vicki. At first he had felt only softness and acceptance. They had lain in each other's arms half the night: Now it all seemed a monstrous infidelity which both possessed and repelled him. The whole memory of it was an awful poetry compounded of innocence and blasphemy. How was he to explain this to Sarah or even to himself?

Now he sat next to Sarah in the sand, watching Vicki dance with Hoot Gibson and Greg Calhoun. He kissed the exquisite curve of her arm. "We need to talk," he said.

"The Governor wants us to go into town with him soon," she said.

"Let's take a walk."

"I'm tired of walking. I just got back from walking. I nearly walked myself to death last night . . . . Seems you should've had enough too. If all you did was walk."

"Isn't there any place we can go?"

"Well, there's that shack. I wonder if you could find that shack again. I wonder —"

"All right, forget about it." He stood and moved to one of the wooden picnic tables where the bar had been set up. He returned with drinks for the two of them.

"Are you uncomfortable here," she said to him, "with Vicki caterwauling around? Is that it? Is that —"

"I said forget it. I'm sorry I even —"

"What is it — you jealous? Or perhaps a little itchy yourself. You weren't jealous of me, though. It's not very flattering."

"Jealous of you? What about?"

"Damn you Jay! You're so wrapped up in yourself — you and all you like you . . ."

"Why should I be jealous?"

". . . with your aimless, selfish, introspective agonies. 'Oh God save me — all life is a despair.' Bunk!"

Vicki and Greg Calhoun approached, holding their drinks and dragging folding chairs across the sand. Vicki was breathing hard and there was a glow of perspiration on her face and shoulders.

"How about a little rabbit hunt, hah?" Greg Calhoun said.

"Let's leave the rabbits to their own amours tonight," Sarah said. "It's a small comfort for them in this awful place."

"What have you two been talking about?" he said.

"Jay's been telling me how depressed he is. It's his way with girls."

"Now wait a minute — that's not —"

"He's right. You are all a depressed generation. You may quote me."

"Let's not talk intellectual talk," Vicki said.

"We shouldn't," Sarah said. "But it's *such* a lovely, lofty plain we're on."

"*De*pressed, *re*pressed, *op*pressed, *sup*pressed. All that analysis stuff. I believe in acting natural. I just want to be myself."

"Normal as blueberry pie, Vic," Greg Calhoun said. "Stay as sweet as you are."

"You're very nice. But I can't be as nice to you. You got problems, Gregory."

"Have I got problems," he said, lowering his eyes. "It's because I'm a mystic. I am concerned with the human condition, the human situation." He opened his eyes. "I'm very strange and tropical to be perfectly frank, Vicki . . . I will show you death in a handful of bust." He reached for her, but she brushed him aside.

He turned suddenly toward the others. "What about you, Sarah? You say Jay's depressed. Aren't you depressed?"

"Never going to get depressed again. All I have to do is look at the sad faces of the men; that'll cheer me up."

"Not *all* the men, Sarah. Surely there must be a few who —"

"But only a few," Sarah said. "Just a few — men like Shavers over there . . ."

"And the Governor. Don't forget the Governor."

"The Governor most of all," Sarah said. They're the proud, exceptional types. The rest of us are just hanging on for dear life."

"Watch it, now," Jay said. "You'll be saying all of life's a despair in a minute and —"

"Did someone mention my name? We heard someone mention our names." The Governor was approaching, with Shavers and Mrs. Fenstemaker close behind. "I'm fortified for that dance now, Miss Vicki." Vicki stood and took his arm, but he was not yet ready to go. "Who mentioned our names? What have you young people been talking about?"

"We were just saying," Sarah began, and hesitated . . .

"That men like you and Ed Shavers are the proud, resolute individuals of our time," Greg said, "and that the rest of us are just along for the ride. At least that's Sarah's theory."

"Sarah is being both kind and ungracious, then," the Governor

said. "I just don't know what I'd do without the people around
me. I couldn't do without Sarah, for instance. Or Jay. Or my
Sweet Mama Fenstemaker here . . ."

"Don't forget your Vibrator, dear," Mrs. Fenstemaker said with
a little laugh. "What would you do without the Vibrator?"

"Damned sexy vibrator," the Governor observed. "How 'bout
you, Ed. What would you do without Vicki and Greg here — and
all these people helping you make pictures?"

"It's nice to think that I could," Shavers said.

"Could what?" Vicki said.

"Get along without you, sweetheart . . . Will you dance with
me later?"

". . . the night away," she said in a singsong, pulling the
Governor toward the dancing space near the limousine.

The others sat quietly for a time; then Greg asked Sarah to
dance, and Shavers danced with Mrs. Fenstemaker. Jay was left
alone, except for the company of Hoot Gibson. Hoot Gibson
strolled round the circle of dancers, singing to himself: "Ah covah
th' watah*frawnt* . . ."

Jealous of whom? Jay thought. What was she talking about?
Because she had taken a walk with Greg Calhoun or because
Arthur Fenstemaker was some kind of father image to her — to
them all? She thinks she knows, but she could not possibly; she
had never sunk so low as to comprehend the horror that possessed
him. But couldn't she at least appreciate the relativity of the
thing? The responses she expected in him were all out of proportion to the nightmare of his experience. How could she think
anything so thin and insubstantial could — It was as if she had
asked the drug addict if the needle hurt.

The moon passed behind a bank of clouds, and the flapping of
the tents nearby signaled a change in the wind. A chill came into
the night air, and Jay was seized by a near paroxsym of trembling, a thing that had begun faintly in his chest, in the beat

of his heart, and, swelling inside him, pounding in his head, expanding finally to every part of his body. Weak in sickness and in terror, he stood and watched the others for a moment: they seemed not to notice him or anything around them. Then he fled toward Vicki's trailer where the little girl lay sleeping.

She lay there in the middle of Vicki's enormous bed, pink and defenseless and incredibly beautiful, part of him on the bed, the best of him, sprung from the womb of some benign and beatific monster. What part was him? How much of himself had he given — to the little girl lying there or to Sarah or Vicki or to any of the others? To that old Mexican relieving the pressure of his insides in the headlights of the Chrysler — had there been a little girl lying on the mud floor inside the thatched hut? He had not stopped to see.

He crawled across the bed, still trembling, whimpering quietly to himself, and laid his man hands on her shoulders. She came into his arms, pulling the bedclothes with her, and she remained with him, not waking, while the mad thumping in his chest subsided until at last he could trace the convulsions from his limbs to his heart and finally to the tiny pulsebeat in the little girl's wrists. After a time the rain began and he rose to close a window, listening to the sounds of the others scurrying in the sand toward the car; heard them calling for him in the dark. He returned to the bed and lay beside the little girl, hoping they would not find him, concentrating on their not discovering where he fled. There was the sound of the limousine pulling away, and he began to fall swiftly to sleep.

The rain was falling with more intensity now, with a volume of sound that filled the room. It had not been more than a few minutes since the others had departed, and he had come awake conscious of Vicki's presence. He could see her shadow against the window, pulling off her clothes, and then she was next to him in the bed, her arms around him, consuming him.

"Oh Jay, Jay, I wanted you to be here, I love you so much, Jay, hold me like that . . ." Her voice was muffled for a moment as she got his shirt front open and buried her face against his chest.

"Oh it's so good you're so good to be with here Jay hold me like that, you're coming with us aren't you love, coming back with Victoria Anne and me . . ."

"I don't know, I don't know . . ."

"You've got to Jay, I'll die without you love, hold me close closer I'm going to die love I'm going to die right here I'm . . ."

He could not breathe and his head was spinning with the length of her against him and great convulsive sobs begun inside him. She lay tense and electric against him and said, "Don't move just yet, don't move love, but in a moment we'll go into Shavers' room and we won't wake Victoria Anne and we can be in there to-gether, only don't move just yet, just hold me like that while I die a little and say you'll come with me say yes you're coming back with me, Jay, say yes . . . yes . . ."

". . . Yes . . . Yes . . ." he began, and ". . . Yes . . . No, I —no . . . God help me no! I can't I won't I never will." She still held onto him, but he began to pull himself from the bed, and she had not heard him clearly yet, her arms following his movements, Vicki rising with him, holding on to his waist, and mumbling . . . "Ed's bed in there he won't mind."

"I'll just bet he won't," Jay said. "Has anyone ever really cared in whose bed you landed? Have you? You ought to know that one in there pretty good by now, and what about the others . . ."

"Others . . ." Vicki mumbled.

"Gregory, for instance, or whatever well-muscled, suntanned ditch-digger happens to pass outside the trailer . . ."

"Gregory . . . I never, I . . ."

She still held on to him. "Jay . . . I . . . Jay, please say . . ." The weight of her had pulled him off balance and now they sat collapsed in a heap on the carpeted floor beside the bed.

"All I want," he began softly, "all I want is Victoria Anne. If a divorce is too much let me have Victoria Anne. She can come live with me, and you'll have all that freedom, away from re-sponsibility completely. You don't need her; you never see her . . ."

"Oh I do, I do, and I need you Jay, the three of us together."

"No you don't. No. I don't understand what it is all about with me, but if you're suddenly that way again I'm sorry. You practically held the door the first time I left. But now all of a sudden — I want her, Vic. I can take good care of her, give her love and attention, a lot of things that —"

"I need her, too. I can give her all those things and more — advantages that . . ."

"Do you care? Do you really care?"

"Of course, love, believe me, love, I need her and I need you, please Jay hold me like that again . . ."

He sat and looked at her loveliness for a moment, seeing her clearly in the soft shadows; then leaning forward he kissed her lightly on the lips and helped her to her feet. "We'll talk about it tomorrow," he said. "We'll talk about all of this tomorrow, about you and me and Victoria Anne. I've got to go."

She slipped under the bedcovers and lay silent, watching him as he turned and headed out of the room.

He stood for an instant at the door and then raced across the open area, with the huge raindrops pounding the sand like the bludgeons in his head, toward the trailer he shared with Sarah. The sound of the rain falling lulled him to sleep before the others returned, and he did not awake until Sarah knocked on his door the next morning.

She was in her dressing gown and stood at the door, regarding him coolly. "You'd better get dressed and get your bag packed," she said. "We're leaving in an hour."

"Oh. Really. I hadn't realized that —"

"About time, too. I'm nearly out of my mind in this place."

"I suppose you are. Well, you'll be rid of these people for a —"

"No I won't. They're coming with us. He's sent for a plane."

"What about the car?" He half feared, half anticipated driving it back, hoping Victoria Anne could go along with him.

"Hoot Gibson and Mrs. Fenstemaker left in it early this morning. She wasn't feeling well last night, so she stayed in town at the hotel. They left early, driving alone."

"How did his scene turn out?"

"All right. He wants us over there with him when we're dressed." She turned and moved back into her bedroom. Jay dressed quickly, packed his small bag, and waited for Sarah. She let him kiss her briefly at the door, but all her young warmth was restrained, and he held her arm as they ran in the rain toward the Governor's trailer.

The others were gathered in the room with Arthur Fenstemaker: Vicki and Greg Calhoun in bed with him, the three of them under the covers, half sitting, half lying, wearing sunglasses; Edmund Shavers lay sprawled on a nearby chaise, dark glasses perched at the end of his nose also. All of them had tumblers of iced tomato juice in their hands.

Jay and Sarah stood at the entrance to the room in amazement, while the others gave a simultaneous greeting. Jay paused and turned his head, listening to the sound in the room. There was the rain coming down on the roof of the trailer, but there was something else, a deep, rhythmic humming that came from everywhere and nowhere.

"It's the vibrator, Jay!" the Governor said. "It's that damned vibrator — it's tremendous I tell you."

"It's absolutely marvelous," ·Vicki said, her eyes half-lidded, staring at the ceiling. "I've never experienced such a sensation."

They came closer, the deep drumming of the Vibrator filling their ears and faintly tickling their feet against the floor, the ends of bedposts trembling, appearing blurred and diffused. Edmund Shavers was purple in the face, holding his sides with laughter.

"Now you know all my secrets," the Governor said. "What keeps me going, puts color in my cheeks and a spring in my step . . . All my deep dark secrets. Vicki, dear, this is the perfect hangover cure — your vodka and tomato juice and my vibrator."

"And the sunglasses!" Vicki said. "Don't forget the sunglasses."

"Yes, yes," the Governor said, touching lightly at his forehead. "I'd almost got used to them. Perfect . . . Gregory, I must ask you to get off my machine, my friend, temporarily of course, while I get another lovely lady in here beside me. You will naturally understand . . . Sarah, my sweet, put your bag down and crawl in and I'll give you a ride you'll never forget."

Sarah looked horrified. She stared around in confusion.

"Come on, honey, don't be afraid . . ."

"It's not that; it's just —" She approached slowly as Greg Calhoun slipped out of bed and the Governor held back the covers for Sarah. "Edmund, my friend, see if you can fix one of those red drinks for Jay and Sarah."

"Turn it off first," Sarah said.

"For you — anything."

Sarah slipped out of her shoes and got into bed; she and Vicki now flanked the Governor; Shavers brought her the red drink.

"Ready? Off we go!"

The three of them lay in the bed with their heads propped against the end. Sarah's lips began to tremble slightly, and Jay could not tell whether she was about to cry or if it was merely the vibration of the machine.

"This — this," said the Governor, "is what gives a man a social conscience. You lie here on this machine with a red drink in your hand and handsome women on either side of you and you wonder what all the poor people are doing . . ."

Eleven

MOVING EAST from the border country toward the populated areas, past the dying, wornout towns and homesteads and abandoned silver mines, the colors do not change so much as the topog-

raphy, the mountains on either side and the dead places in between becoming a graying sameness of routine foothills and
feeble, half-verdant river valleys. The newborn and ephemeral
mountain streams feed down into these low sections from time to
time, suggesting a better season for next summer, spring or fall,
but never quite fulfilling the promise. It is an ersatz Eden, a
mere accommodation to what lies farther east, but it is life all the
same, even in its atmosphere of half-death, and the very lack of
long, lush summers has produced a fierce people from the grim-
faced German farmers who settled here a hundred merciless summers before. Game does not abound as it subsists, and the
dwarfed liveoaks continue to push their roots into the blistered
hillsides just as the patient farmer-ranchers stay on to make their
living off the land.

Arthur Fenstemaker was not one of them, but they were
proud to claim him as a neighbor. It was here where he was born
and grown to manhood. He had not stayed on, but he had done
the next best thing. He had come back.

He had come back with such luster and flamboyance that he
was very nearly left bankrupt by the gesture, but it remained a
monument to him nonetheless. From the earnings of his first oil
strike he had returned to claim the few acres that were his family's, expanding these holdings and constructing on the land a
replica of an ancient Federalist mansion which had been a subject
of fascination for him during a brief invasion of the Virginia
horse country some years before. It was a truculent, appalling
structure, huge and gloomy against the bald landscapes, complete
with outbuildings, brick stables, slave quarters, stone fences, and
an antique Federalist Eagle that frowned toward the distant hills
from atop the main gable. Then Arthur Fenstemaker assumed
his dream of infinite magnificence, retiring to his country place
after his second big strike, at thirty years of age, bent on becoming a public figure esteemed for his good works (which were
eventually many) and his dedication to the liberal ideal. That he
had been successful, realizing the full measure of his ambition,

was manifest in his present eminence; his election to the governorship had seemed the consummation of all that was right and
exalted in man, as inevitable as the triumph of good over bad in
some Western epic from the films.

Now his guests wandered through the lush gardens, down the
promenade festooned with lengths of flowering shrubs and paper
lanterns, past the brick terraces and the outdoor tables brought
in for the party, lingering beside the imitation marble swimming
pool. They seemed unwilling for the moment to give all this up
for the brooding interior of the country house.

"The grounds are gorgeous, Arthur," Shavers said to the Governor.

"It'll be a wonderful party," Vicki said, "it'll be a marvelous
party out here in the garden and all around. What kind of people
are coming?"

"Nice people," the Governor said. "Gay and enchanting and
extraordinary people, all of them, all come to see you Miss Vicki.
It should be an interesting party."

"All come to see me?"

"The center of attention, the principal attraction . . . I wish
Mrs. Fenstemaker were here to show you the place. She enjoys
showing people around for the first time."

"She'll be here for the party?"

"Oh yes."

"And Hoot Gibson? I'm mad about Hoot Gibson . . ."

"Sooner even. Tonight or in the morning. He's bringing in
some papers for me to sign."

They moved back toward the house, beneath the flowering
trees. Vicki walked arm and arm between Shavers and the Governor. Sarah, Jay and Greg Calhoun remained beside the pool
for a few minutes before joining the others. The little girl lay
asleep in one of the upstairs rooms. Sarah looked at Greg and
said: "What do you think of it? All of it."

"I'm disappointed actually. I'd rather hoped for a portcullis
or at least a moat . . . Try to imagine one right over . . ."

They strolled on toward the house. "Mine will definitely have a moat . . ."

"Yours?" Jay said.

"Yes. I'll go back and build one on the desert, a cheap imitation of the Governor's, doing him one better. Mine will be an imitation of the Governor's which was an imitation of one he saw in Virginia which was possibly a mutation of something someone saw in Europe or possibly out of Walter Scott's books, both of which were probably imitations. This is all very sad. Am I making you people sad?"

"Oh yes," Sarah said gaily.

"Good."

Jay moved ahead of them, quickening his step on a signal from the Governor.

"I'm really feeling much better," Sarah said to Greg.

"Why is that?"

"Away from the desert and those terrible trailers."

"I thought it was Vicki who intimidated you out there."

"How did you know? I mean — Well she's still with us, but I'm feeling better. It was the trailers, I think, the whole place, confining the spirit."

"It never seemed to confine Vicki's, did it?"

"Perhaps she's just irrepressible, is that it? That's being nice . . . I'm looking forward to the party. Like Vicki, I can't wait until the party begins."

"Will there be any women? I mean enough women." The others were far ahead of them now, past the entrance to the house and beyond, standing in the graveled driveway.

"Lots of women. All sorts of women. Women and girls, sisters and mothers and daughters and just all kinds."

"I like all kinds. That's the kind I like best."

"Oh . . . Oh . . . Steel yourself."

"What's wrong?"

"The organized activities are about to get underway . . ."

A stripped-down Army command car had appeared from behind the house. Jay steered it out of the driveway and pulled up next to the others. The Governor turned and motioned for Sarah and Greg.

"Organized activities?" Greg said to her.

"Yes. First you'll take a long ride across the ranch. He'll show you the cattle and horses and irrigated farmland and maybe even the old fish hatchery. Then you'll come back and take a swim or play shuffleboard or badminton and then you'll go in for drinks before dinner and afterwards he'll insist you try the brandy and then there'll be some more drinking and then a hell of an awful long walk out into the woods and back again and by then . . ."

"That's enough," Greg said, raising his hand. "Couldn't we just take a ride on that vibrator, instead, just you and me?"

"It's too late," Sarah said. "Here they come . . . And I just remember I've got some work to do. Besides, I've been on this tour." She waved at the others and left Greg Calhoun standing there; she walked quickly toward the back of the house.

Inside, the place smelled of damp stone and stale air, reminiscent of something from her childhood, she could not remember, not entirely, searching for pillbugs possibly, in the cool dark earth beneath the front steps of her home. Lying under the steps, herself against the ground, Chinamen underneath if you dig deep enough, watching the dust motes rise and fall, searching for pillbugs and doodlebugs and dirtdobbers' nests, I found one here, watch out for snakes and scorpions, I found one, too, right here, right where? Right here. No go away no I don't want to see you no and you haven't been circum — No I haven't one and no yes maybe yes I want to feel yes, someday I'll have breasts and you won't and maybe you can feel.

The servants had arrived from town early, and now they moved quietly through the big rooms, dusting the furnishings, mopping the insides of ashtrays. From the kitchen she could smell the steaks cooking. Up the carpeted stairway, past the enormous tapestries, she paused finally at the entrance to the bedroom where the little girl lay sleeping. Victoria Anne's eyes fluttered and she looked up in heavy-lidded pleasure.

"Hello Sarah." She smiled and closed her eyes and opened them again. "Where are all the others?"

"Out for a ride. Jay and I will take you for a ride later. All right?"

"Yes . . ."

"Have you ever hunted for pillbugs, Annie?"

"*Pill*bugs . . . What's a —"

"Never mind, sweetheart. Finish your nap and we'll take a ride or go for a swim when you wake up."

"All right."

She smoothed the covers on the bed and left the room quietly. In the privacy of her own bedroom she unpacked her bags and then lay down and closed her eyes. She thought of Jay next to her; not grabbing or feeling but next to her, not breathing or talking but just the two of them in love together, next to one another, each to each, all others excluded. Would there ever be such a time, such a place, and could there ever be beauty and ease and grace? How did it go? How did the phrase go? Convention and tradition work blindly for the preservation of the normal type and for the extinction of . . . Well who were the normal types? Extinction of . . . Extinction of . . . Where was beauty and grace? Where was it? She had asked Arthur Fenstemaker just the week before, on an evening following that business in Jay's apartment; where was it, she asked him; would there ever be beauty and ease and grace?

My dear, he began, and hesitated, and she half expected some dumb German farmer lecture on sweat and toil and sorrow. Sweetheart, he began, and hesitated, moving toward his window, looking out, his back to her, over the darkened Capitol grounds. You have to look for it, he said finally, you have to look for it. Look out here, he said, pointing toward the trees and beneath them, an old Negro woman bent in ancient pain, standing alone and calling to the birds . . . cheeree . . . chee-ree . . . she sang, and the birds sang back. You have to look for it, he said.

Was that all? Was that really all there was? The rest an illusion and a monstrous joke. If Jay would only — If Jay only . . . Jay could be sweet; Jay could be proud and resolute and sweet when he wanted to, when the other wasn't on his mind, he could be a dear sweet dear the way it was at his apartment; it had all seemed so fine, the two of them in the room, in beauty and grace, Jay next to her, his cool hands on her skin, and *I want to yes I want to* and then the other. Those awful Vicki pictures in the magazine, Vicki pictures was what they were, like the books hidden under the front porch with the pillbugs, and the scalding thought that it was Vicki, not her but Vicki, not her but any transferable female would do, on the bed with him, naked and alone with him in beauty and ease and grace.

"I'm ready, Sarah," the little girl said, standing in the doorway in her bathing suit, "I'm ready for the swim."

Sarah stood and moved toward Victoria Anne and put her arms around her. "Do you like it here, sweet?" Sarah said. "Do you like it here with Jay and me?"

"Yes, yes," the little girl said, holding onto her neck. "I like it here with you and Jay . . . I want you to come sleep with me sometime. Daddy slept with me last night; I remember he came in and slept with me until Mommy came and they fussed and he left. Will you sleep with me tonight, Sarah?"

Sarah was trying to hold back the sobs from her voice . . . "If I can, Annie, if I can . . ." She took her suit and undressed quickly in the bathroom. There was a faint, last summer's line of darkness running round her and she wondered if the new suit would —

"You're beautiful, Sarah," the little girl said in awe, standing half into the bathroom with her great sad eyes staring. "You're so pretty all over."

Sarah smiled back, but then she had to turn her head as the tears flooded her eyes.

Twelve

JAY MOVED among the crowds of visitors, nodding his head, clasping hands, gripping arms, the names of near-strangers falling from his lips and Fenstemaker's wisdom rattling round inside his head: *For the lips of a strange woman drop as an honeycomb and her mouth is smoother than oil . . .* He repeated it, trying to keep the words arranged as they had come to him, first from Hoot Gibson and then the Governor . . . *But her end is bitter as wormwood, sharp as a two-edged sword. Her feet go down to death and take hold in hell . . .*

The party is begun, he thought. At last, finally, begun. All these gay enchanting people, marvelous people, all come together, salt of the earth. It'll be a nice party. Nass potty. What was it Sarah said? Be a man, Jay. Be a man, for God's sake, don't whimper — wipe your nose — like that. Be one like Arthur. There . . . he goes with another carful. Of people. Nass people. I'm upset. That you won't get hold of yourself (people are looking). All these nice people are looking, Jay. Be a man!

But Sarah I forgot. I forgot how. Seems I used to know — why'd it slip my mind? All those places. Misplaced it. She's just never been there with me in all those dark places. She just don't know. What it's like. I'll tell you Sarah what it's like, it's — Well it's — Well it's really not so bad sometime, all cool and luminous. Like vaults and cellars and basement rooms. I lived in a place once, ancient bloodbrick downstairs crypt in Frisco; had a job at a dry cleaner's just round the corner where I learned Oh God about the two-bath system for treating blue serge. Lived down there nights thinkin' of Miss Vicki and the girl. It smelled awful, smelled of sewage, and you know what?

You get used to it. The smell, I mean. The other not at all.

Be a man? She's got that right — yes — that's the tick — But not too large a one, and hulking. Otherwise it's difficult to slip back into the womb of this gay-mad reminiscence. I should take Sarah sometime. We'll go there, stroll down memory lane and — It's all cool and mossy down there like I said and it could be made into a really gay place for the right sort of people. Look!

Here they come again in that old command car, they're having a time.

What a time!

Lust not after her beauty. Neither let her take thee with her eyelids . . .

Let's have a drink on that before this party gets too far gone, we've only seen the first of these nice people. Very earliest arrivals. Let's get Greg and Shavers and Hoot Gibson, and there's Mrs. Fenstemaker — hah yew, Miz Fenstemaker, me tew Miz Fenstemaker — and have a drink here beside the pool before the crowds make it impossible and Victoria Anne's still sleeping upstairs. You know she damn near drowned today? Damn near. While all of us were inside drinking in that crazy solarium, I heard screams. Godalmighty they were awful. The screams. You ever heard child scream? Like death? She'd sneaked off for a swim and I was sitting there drinkin' with all those nice people and trying to figure what's on the Governor's mind (he's got a problem, I can tell, I got a gift) and I kept hearing them. The screams. And not certain what exactly it was, thinking it was just maybe the usual clangin' in my head, I put my drink down and went quietly to see. Very quietly. Not wanting to be obtrusive, understand. Or panic. Or believe they were screams. And she was half drowned when I got there, damn near, and we stood sopping wet on that phony alabaster and had a good cry. Just the two of us. Hope it doesn't give her the trauma, you think it might? Her teeth were chattering and she was still blue with cold when I put her into bed. I love her . . . And her love is better than wine . . . whine . . .

Ah, here comes that grand lady again — Nice time, Miz Fenstemaker? Jus' fine, Miz Fenstemaker — and here oh boy come the Mariachis with the guitars and all that spangled stuff. Those spics are really — That old Mexican, wettin' in the rain. Whatever happened to that fellow? I should ask sometime. But I know, I remember now, he picked cotton on my daddy's farm and amassed a great fortune and went back across the river and bought the Emperor's Palace. Old Max's place. Including Carlotta's mirrors. And all the silverware. And a purple swimming pool. Like Fenstemaker's. I'll have to tell Annie that story sometime, next time we sit shiverin' together next to the three-meter board.

Here comes Sarah again — there she goes — thumping my jukebox heart. You'd like it down there Sarah, you really would, all green and grassy. We'll leave tomorrow. Tomorrow I'll take the limousine or maybe that old stripped-down Army command job, and you and I and Annie we'll remove, cut out, encamp elsewhere. Arthur won't mind. Least he could do for young lovers. Leave this vale of tears. You like that? Nice phrase? I got a gift, honey, such a gift. So many gifts; so many tears (be a man!). I remember once how it used to be when (what was that old-fashioned expression?) I was a leader of men, way back the way it was when all of us were so goddam sure of ourselves. We were going to . . . Let's see. Going to (oh, yes) usher in the new age of ecu . . . ecumenical progress and peace. How's that Kermit? You heard any good applause lines lately? You been out hustling milk for the slum kids? And end the cold war, too, that's right. Old Kermit. You old mad dog you, why'd you go off that way and hang yourself for? All bah yersef. You should've waited for the rest of us, or better still we should've found you a place here, a productive place in society as they say, shaved off that awful beard and cleaned your nails and got you some cordovans and some soft white button-downs. You'd have loved it, I know you would, you old mad dog, got used to it, adjusted, the way it was with me and that smell of sewage.

Those Mariachis! Hot damn see what you're missin', man

they're *great* and I'm going to dance cha-cha, if I can only (let's see) where's Sarah gone. Let's — There she goes, too bad, all squared away with that Gregory person, old Gregory what's-his. Well let's see. Lots of people. Lots and lots of nice people. Niz pipple. And such a gay party, fabulous gay place really, and look there goes the actress, what's her name (what bubes!), and there goes that wretch of her husband, estranged you know, he's very estranged and very down and very out and the Governor's wiper what's more. The world owes him a living — one of those birds — and he doesn't care for the one it has come up with currently. The living. Is easy. I'll ask her, by God, I'll ask her once more and dance with her not too close and perhaps, just possibly maybe perhaps she'll act sensible about this divorce business and . . . my God! she smells good, the way it was the first time . . . *For there is no faithfulness in their mouth; their inward part is very wickedness; their throat is an open sepulchre; they flatter with the tongue* . . . I could very nearly forget the way it was afterwards, remembering the first time, with those paper lanterns coming on now and the sun all violet in the hills and Vicki's sweet face suspended here for a moment. Poignant. I can't stand it. Poinnnyant. Like that. Mischiefs of whoredom! Yea, on every hill and under every green tree she lay down . . . *Let her breasts satisfy thee. Let thy fountain be blessed and rejoice with the wife of thy youth. Be thy ravished always with her love* . . .

Where did it go, oh Jesus where did it all go? How did we lose beauty and honesty and innocence, and who the hell substituted this carrion of strident heat and human parts on us? It was Vicki who . . . It was Vicki she . . . Was it me? My own upper lip all these years? No matter. What matters is now, so look here and now Vic and be sensible about our mutual misunderstandings and — what'd she say? Grow up love and talk about something else (isn't this a nice party?) and enjoy it while there's time. Grow up? Now she's on it too, and is everyone here a thousand years old or something? The hell with all that, I'm going back down to my vault, my crypt, my basement room. It's cool and glossy down there like I said: green and mossy, with a river of old hope running through. I'll go find Sarah, she'll want to come, and Victoria Anne: we'll take that stripped-down Army job and — Where is she, where's she wandered off to? Where? With that Greg, with that nice people. Here beside me on the dance floor just a mile ago, last week at the apartment her dark skin burning . . . There they go, I see them *there,* just ducking into the arbor behind the wisteria blooms, those two together, I see them now, revealed just barely in the pastel light of the lanterns. Old Greg. Maybe he's me! It ought to be. Beside her in the honeyed air. I ought to leave them there, my man arms pressing Sarah's flesh. They ought to be left alone, those two, Sarah and me, but I like the picture of them together, her gray eyes lifted toward mine, favoring the kisses . . . I really can't stand here gawking, though. I hear the little girl screams again; I'd better move along. Don't they hear them? The screams? I'm coming, love, jus' tread water or something while I wander through these crowds of niz people without causing too much commotion. I'm coming, like I promised, like the last time, so don't stop screaming or I'll know you've gone. Under. I can't seem to get under this fence. Or through the field of bamboo shoots and new mown hay . . . the way . . . they photographed your momma in the nude. There's a creek near here, I remember it as a boy of twenty-six, just over this rise and down — Ah! Home at last! Damn near broke my neck but I made it and it's not such a bad place as mud flats go and a southeast breeze in summer. You can't beat that, and it's really very awfully nice to be back, and finally find myself.

Thirteen

"WE'LL GO SEE Dead Man," Arthur Fenstemaker said. "That's it. I knew there was something I hadn't shown you. Dead Man. Good Old Dead Man."

The party ranged around them, people filling the downstairs rooms of the main house, pushing out into the softness of the night, trampling the carpet grass and slipping off into the fish-pond, their numbers multiplying on the promenade and in the garden. Arthur Fenstemaker and his friends sat closely together on a second-story balcony overlooking the pulsing scene. Something had brought them together here in the middle of the evening — the Governor, Shavers, Vicki, Sarah, and Greg Calhoun — as old and good friends pulled toward each other to recount all those happy times of some forgotten year. Sarah thought of Mr. Thurber's moth: "Who flies afar from the sphere of sorrow is here today and here tomorrow." There seemed no escape from this time, this place, these people.

"Dead Man?" Shavers said. "What is this Dead Man?"

"Whatever it is I'm ready for it," Vicki said. "People are beginning to grab downstairs."

"Dead Man," the Governor said, "is a friend of mine lives down the road. Old friend. He's meant a great deal to me. Let's go."

They made their way down the back stairs and across a small patio between rows of high hedges. From either side came the sounds of the party; on the graveled drive they came upon Hoot Gibson and Mrs. Fenstemaker sitting together in an iron loveseat. The Governor roared his mock rage at them: "At it again! All the time behind my back . . ."

Hoot Gibson giggled and hiccuped. "Yew know bettah 'n that, Awh-thik!"

"He's got the hiccups," Mrs. Fenstemaker said. "The poor dear — he's got them terribly."

Hoot Gibson kept his mouth closed, smiling at them tight-lipped, the silent convulsions coming on him at regular intervals.

"A little walk," the Governor said, "will put an end to Hoot's distress. Come on . . . We're going to see Dead Man."

"Not now, dear," Mrs. Fenstemaker said. "The caterers are cleaning up and I've got to supervise." Hoot Gibson joined them and Mrs. Fenstemaker headed back toward the house.

They walked quietly along the hard road now. Vicki removed her slippers, and she and Sarah walked on either side of the Governor. Hoot Gibson, Shavers and Greg Calhoun were in back of them. The Governor suddenly remembered: "Jay — where's Jay? I haven't seen him since the afternoon."

"Out on the dance floor for a while," Sarah said. "I saw him once."

"I danced with him once," Vicki said. "He was hanging around those Mexicans when I left."

I saw him once, I saw him twice, I saw him through the day, Sarah sang to herself. I must have seen him six thousand times, but mostly not at all. As through the wrong end of a telescope: minute, remote and inarticulate, his nice mouth flailing air. What had he been saying? Even the sound of his voice had faded from her memory. She could see his nice mouth and teeth, the half-moon scar on his forehead and the golden hair on his knuckles reflected in the sunlight — blinded by all the crazy touch-stones of desire, she could see these things and not see Jay. He himself seemed to have retreated into some gray miasma of the soul. They had been together with the little girl earlier in the afternoon, strolling, just the three of them, through the silent gardens: Victoria Anne skipping ahead of them, returning and running ahead again. Be a man, Jay, she had said to him, be a man and quit mumbling your troubles to me. Be a man like Arthur; give me a cheap imitation if nothing else. Can't you get a little of it through osmosis? So she won't talk with you about the girl — you're making no progress on the divorce. Don't come to me with it — don't ask me what to do. We'll do something, work out a way, but don't ask me why it can't be better. I don't know.

Anybody around here know? he said to her. We'll ask Arthur sometime, he said, his dead face staring, continuing the walk through the garden, pointing out the names of shrubs and plants and flowers to the little girl.

He had been a whole person in the beginning, nice-talking nice-kissing like Greg, nice-dancing in his arms at garden parties months ago, nice whiskey breath in her face and nice drunken laughter intermingling over wines and books and broken salad bowls. It had all been so pretty in the beginning when —

"Dead Man," the Governor said. "Not much to look at, but awfully good company."

The only sounds that came to them were the night noises from the dark creekbed and the faraway music of the Mariachis. The shadow of the frame cabin was up ahead. They came through the gate and paused to examine the tombstone in the yard.

"Look here," the Governor said, striking a match so they could read the words.

JOHN HERMAN JACKSON
1898–1935

"He's inside," the Governor said.

A set of vague questions was paused in the mouths of the visitors, but they hesitated now and waited to see for themselves. The Governor shook the front door and then stepped inside and switched on a light.

"Dead Man!" the Governor shouted. "Hey, Dead Man!"

There were muffled, shuffling sounds from another room, and then the old man appeared at the doorway, blinking his eyes and smiling, his white hair in his face. The Governor made the introductions. Sarah nodded and took his hand when her turn came.

She had been here a dozen times before, but Dead Man Jackson did not remember names or faces. He knew only Arthur Fenstemaker.

"Dead Man," the Governor began, stretching in the length of a ruptured, faded sofa, "we've been havin' a party . . ." He described the events of the past several days, the visit with the moving picture people in the desert, the shooting of his scene, the trip back culminating in the party now going on up the road. The old man smiled and nodded:

"How about a drink, Dead Man!" the Governor shouted. The old man came alert, a broad gummy smile on his face. He rose and went into one of the darkened rooms, returning in a moment with a pale bottle.

"Bootleg hootch," the Governor said, looking satisfied at everyone. "It's Dead Man's . . . It's the best." Old jelly glasses were brought out, and everyone had a taste of the whiskey mixed with tap water. The Governor finished his before the others. He stood and stretched.

"Goodbye, Dead Man," he said, and then raising his voice, "I said goodbye, Dead Man!" The old man gripped his hand and waved to the others.

"Okay Hoot Gibson," the Governor said. "How 'bout a little benediction."

Hoot Gibson weaved unsteadily in his cowboy boots, holding his jelly glass just above his head.

"Hoot Gibson — I should have told you folks before now, Hoot Gibson used to be a preacher," the Governor said.

"Minuhstah th' Gospel," Hoot Gibson put in, smiling at everyone.

"He was a hellfire good one around here," the Governor continued, "Nothing that would shake you folks up, but a good one for the people around here. Simple, straightforward sermons everybody could understand. Dignified. All that . . . But it got so he couldn't get himself out of bed on Sunday mornings. He'd get drunk Saturday night on Dead Man's whiskey and was paralyzed next day. So he came to work for me so we could feed him twenty-five-year-old Ambassador . . . Okay Hoot Gibson."

"Deahleh Buhloved," he began . . . "we awh gathuhed heah to —"

"No . . . No . . ."

Hoot Gibson rambled on, the words tumbling out of him: "See howuh good an' howuh pleasant it is fah breathahren to dwell togetheh in . . ." He made a kind of sign in the air with the jelly glass, and they filed wordlessly out into the open. The visitors still waited for some explanation, and Arthur Fenstemaker finally began to talk about Dead Man.

"Dead Man," the Governor said, "was a famous bootleg whiskey maker and salesman in these hills when I was a youngster. He made the best. Everybody came to Dead Man — they called him Herman then. But the Federals got on to him after a time and they began closing in. That was when Dead Man died. He simply expired up here in the hills. His family had a funeral for him, pine casket, tombstone, the works. Everybody forgot about it then. The only time they thought about Dead Man was when they were reduced to swilling the inferior grade stuff that came into circulation after Dead Man died.

"Then one night there were a bunch of folks sittin' around, passing a bottle back and forth between them. Someone said, 'You know, that tastes like Herman's.' 'Damn fit dudn't,' another one said, and before long everybody knew he was back, somewhere in the hills, turning it out again. Well it got so there was a lot of talk and jokes and stories, and the Law heard about it and went lookin' for Dead Man again. That time they got him and sent him off to the pen. When they let him out finally, he came home to find most of his family gone or died off and all his equipment destroyed. He was an old man then, so I asked him if he would like to come live on my property. He said 'sho' but first he headed straight for the cemetery and dug up that damn tombstone and put it back down there in the front yard. He paid for it, you see, and he was going to keep it for his own."

"There's a scenario for you, Ed," Greg Calhoun said. "Use a bunch of Spanish peasants in the cast, write it in Japanese, dub it in Greek, and throw in your English subtitles. You'll have a classic that'll take all the prizes."

They walked along the road back toward the house. A spectacular silver moon had now appeared from behind a distant hill, and the soft light bathed the land.

"Is there a part in it for me?" Vicki said. "You forgot girls."

"Lots of girls," Greg said, "all running around with their dress-fronts open. You know those peasants, they —"

"At the funeral," the Governor said. "There were a good many girls at the funeral. Dead Man was very popular in those days. What a funeral! It was the real thing, with mourners and bunches of flowers and all the women crying. Everything was gray — it rained and rained and we never saw the sun and even the flowers were sick and pathetic looking. I remember when they carried that pine box off and the family followed in beat-up jalopies, I never felt so mortal. I knew I was going to die then . . .

"And then old Dead Man came back, and it was like the redemption. Old Dead Man came back and I wasn't ever going to die. All the high and mournful music was ended, and we were all going to live forever like the Gods. We — what the hell's that up ahead?"

Jay had been attempting to pull himself from the mud and up the craggy side of the creekbank for what seemed an hour to him. He had lain at the bottom for a time, soaked in the thick dampness, the water coming through the back of his dinner jacket and under his arms. There was a gaping hole in the knee of his trousers, and he had struck his head on something. When he raised his hand to touch the sore place he had left a smear of mud across his cheek which was beginning to dry against his skin. He had not seen the others approaching until he reached the top and tried to stand.

He stood in front of them, weaving, regarding the sky.

"Jay — it's Jay," Vicki said. They moved toward him.

"Damn — what happened to him?"

"Look at him."

"He's hurt . . . Oh Jay you're hurt."

"What happened?" The authority of the Governor's voice came at him.

"Nothing . . . really," he said. "I was just . . . just trying to take a shortcut. To catch up. You take a walk to Dead Man's?"

"Yes. What happened?" Sarah said.

"Just fell off in the creek, trying to find a shortcut."

Shavers and Greg Calhoun got hold of his arms and helped him toward the back of the big house. Upstairs they watched him undress and change, and then Sarah, Vicki and Mrs. Fenstemaker moved in close to look at his head.

"He ought to have stitches," Mrs. Fenstemaker said. "He really ought to have stitches."

"He ought to have his head examined," Sarah said grimly. She turned and moved back downstairs with the others. Mrs. Fenstemaker and Vicki remained behind, and then only Vicki.

"You were drunk," she said to him, smiling. "You were beautifully, gorgeously drunk. Do you remember? Do you remember any of it — dancing with me? You weren't even making sense."

He turned on his side and stared away from her.

"Yes I was. All I said was . . ."

"I know what you said. Is that all that's on your mind? Do you care that much? I thought . . . we might be able to make one more run at it. But you just seem . . . Is it all gone between us?"

"No," he said. "It's all there, everything that was in the beginning. It just doesn't amount to much."

"I love you," she said.

"How can you say that? Lord help us, how can you?"

She turned and headed toward the door. "Forget it," she said.

"Wait a minute, Vic, I want to . . ."

"Tomorrow," she said, and pulled the door behind her.

He lay on the bed for a period of time and then stood and

looked at himself in the mirror. "I love me," he said. "Out of the glade, Orpheus comes, bearing his misery under his arm." He took a damp rag and wiped the crusted blood off the side of his head. He thought of looking in on Victoria Anne. And then a little drink, he said to himself, a little drink will —

Arthur Fenstemaker pushed open the door and looked at him. "How you feel?" he said.

"Fine," he said. "I was just dirty."

"Well, the sky is falling . . ."

"What?"

"We're in a hell of a fix. You feel like driving into town?"

"Sure. I guess. Why? What's —"

"I thought we could get it put off," the Governor said, half to himself. "Now I just don't know . . . There's going to be trouble in town tomorrow. There are going to be a thousand mad fanatics coming after me and I'm not going to be there but you are. You're going to have to handle it until I can . . . I just now heard by phone. Haven't had time to think. Got to *think*. Get packed and get ready. Sweet Mama's got to go back, anyhow. You can drive her in . . ."

Fourteen

THEY LEFT some time after midnight with the music of the Mariachis echoing in the hills. There had been only a few early departures: the very old or the very young, returning to the city at a respectable hour, and a brace of radio, television and newspaper people who had to prepare scripts, write stories, or process film. Most of the others stayed on, wandering through the house or in the gardens or racing their cars down the moonlit graveled roads. A sobering buffet breakfast was being served on the main patio as Jay and Mrs. Fenstemaker headed out the driveway.

Jay had tried to find Sarah; there was something he had to say to her, though whatever it was seemed only a shapeless phrase in his mind. Perhaps he had wanted merely to touch her hand, but she was nowhere to be found. He had caught sight of Vicki once, looking down on her from the balcony above the patio. She was dancing the mambo with someone, and a crowd had gathered to watch. The Governor was at a desk in one of the upstairs rooms, talking on two telephones, unable to discuss anything, waving Jay and Mrs. Fenstemaker out the door.

Edmund Shavers had stopped Jay in the hall, wanting to talk. It seemed as improbable and out of context as all the rest of it when he offered him the job. "You don't know anything about making pictures, but you don't have to," Shavers said. "I need someone with me . . . I'd like to have you with me. You'd be living close to your daughter, and perhaps you and Vicki can even patch things up. She's been talking about the possibility."

"I don't know," Jay said to him, dizzy with the shortness of time and the urgency for decision.

"Think it over," Shavers said.

He had thought it over. He thought it over now, steering the big car through the hills, toward the city, with Mrs. Fenstemaker asleep in the back seat. He had looked in on Victoria Anne; it was the last thing he had done. The little girl lay bunched up in the middle of the gigantic bed, deaf to the sounds from outside: whoops of Mexican musicians and the crash of breakfast trays. He kneeled down and pulled the covers up round her pink shoulders, thinking that if he could remain in this darkened room beside her, the sounds coming through the window and the silk draperies stirring next to him, everything would somehow be fine, absolutely peaceful and secure.

For several years the absence of the girl had not really touched him. He thought it had in the beginning, but it was nothing comparable to the sense of loss that now filled his chest. The first loss of the girl had been very like the loss of love. There had been some dull shapeless pain during those years; the ceaseless, stultifying laying on of everyone's drugstore therapies had even been a part of it. But now the girl was back and love was back — at least the promise of it was back — and the possibility that all this could be lost again, irretrievably lost, came to him with searing finality.

They reached the deserted, wet-washed streets of the city at two in the morning. Mrs. Fenstemaker began to stir as he drove up the steep incline of the driveway in front of the Governor's mansion. She was nearly incoherent with sleep as he walked her to the door. She would be awakened at seven for a breakfast downstairs with some Junior Leaguers; there would be a ceremony at somebody's tomb later in the morning and at noon she would address a businesswomen's luncheon. There were a half-dozen other appointments on her schedule in the afternoon, and she might conceivably get involved in this march of the segregationists. There was Arthur Fenstemaker sitting in a padded room at his ranch in the hills, talking on two telephones, the big vein in his forehead purple and distended. The Governor would be trying to hold his world together, thousands of madmen at each other's throats, and here I am, Jay thought, attempting to keep my small spheres all of a piece and contain the confusion in my head.

He drove the car through the winding Capitol grounds, the trees and lawns and statues glistening under the moon; he stood for a moment before the granite building, looking away from it toward the trees. Old Kermit, he thought, Old Mad Kermit had wandered on these grounds a week ago and gone home to hang himself. There was a story about Kermit and one of the jobs

he held after college. The placement office had found him a
teaching fellowship somewhere in the Middle West, and he had
lasted five months there. His dismissal came one midnight in the
bedroom of the president's wife. "She was old and terrible looking," Kermit had told him once, "but man I loved her. You know
why? 'Cause nobody else did. It was a great passion — one of
my greatest. I crawled into her bedroom window one night and
stood there in my pajamas, loving the old smell of her. I hadn't
even put on my clothes. I'd just been lying in my own bed and
the idea occurred to me. So I just took a walk in my peejays and
stood there in the middle of her bedroom and declared my love.
'I'm in love with you, Mrs. Pennington,' I said. 'I can't help it.'
Then the president of the college came in and canned me on the
spot. I mean, man, nobody *loves* anymore . . ."

They forgot how, Jay thought; it seems to have slipped the
mind. Vicki seemed full of it, an excess of it so that it became a
self-worship, an indulgence. Sarah was endowed with it, but the
spectacle of his own struggle against short supply had distorted
the emotion for her.

There had been a time, he reminded himself once again, when
hope and assurance and large intention trumpeted in his ears,
when the future shimmered before him so colossal and limitless
with promise, that . . .

He tried to go back in his mind to how it was, but now he
wondered if it had ever really been that way. He questioned
whether this, too, was a joke played on himself — the fond inventions and embroiderings of time. He had long since given up his
dream for the future. Had he now ceased believing in the past?

The ideal man! Innocence become imbecility; reduced to
sniffing leftovers.

Halfway down the marble hallway of the Capitol building he
shook a guard awake and had him run him up on the elevator.
The Governor's reception room was thick and sticky with stale
air. He opened some windows and tried to place a call to the
country house. Sarah's voice presently came on the line.

"He's asleep," she said to him. "He was exhausted."

"I was supposed to get a call from him," Jay said. "I'm not sure how to handle this thing in the morning."

"He's asleep. Everybody's asleep. The party's over."

"Let's get engaged," he said. "Can you be engaged to a person when you're still married?" He had tried for a note of levity, but it somehow sounded hysterical.

"I don't know," she said. "Some people can do anything."

"What do you mean by that?"

"Oh *Jay* . . . I just don't *know*. I'm tight I guess. Everybody out here's tight. 'Cept Arthur — he just looks like death."

"What the hell's going on out there?"

"All sorts of things," she said, "all sorts. I got a half-dozen propositions during the evening. A record for me, I think. Some of them very attractive."

"What?"

"The propositions. Vurry 'tractive."

Now he was beginning to feel a little boozy himself.

"Must be quite the fashion. I got a couple of those things, too."

"What?"

"Propositions. What you said. Two of 'em."

"That's what I heard," Sarah said. "Ass whata heard."

"What did you hear?"

"Lots uh things."

"What? What did you hear?"

"You 'n Vicki. Unnerstan' you two might get together 'gain."

"That's not true? Where did you hear that?"

"One uh the innersted potties. She tol' me all 'bout it. I was outside under the arbor neckin' with old Greg — that's a nice person that Gregory — and she came up to tell us all about it. All 'bout how it might happen. Vicki. She's a peach."

"Sarah . . . Sarah . . . What's going on out there? What are you doing?"

"I'm sittin' here, my sweet, drinkin' Scotch. The twenty-five-year-old stuff they keep locked in the closet. Hoot Gibson's passed

out in another room. Arthur's asleep. So're the others, I s'pose,
doin' I don't know whut-all."

"You go to sleep, too, Sarah. Get to bed and try to rest and I'll
talk to you tomorrow."

"Na minute. Have a little drink first. Bye see you . . ."

The disconnection was immediate, and he sat staring at the
phone receiver as if the instrument itself had failed him. Sometime later he stretched out on a leather couch in the Governor's
office and slept fitfully until he was awakened by the iceman come
to fill the cooler. He ran an electric razor over his face and applied a fresh dressing to the place on his forehead. By nine he
had not heard from the Governor and he placed another long-distance call. This time there was no answer.

Secretaries and staff members had begun to fill the outside
offices. He sat at the Governor's desk, and within a few minutes
the reporters began calling to inquire about the team of Federal
investigators and the report filed in Washington.

"What's he say, Jay, what's he say?"

"Well it's not so bad," he began. "We've been showing good
faith, making progress. The Courts should certainly understand
that —"

"I don't care what you think, Jay. I wanna know what *he*
thinks."

"He's not here," Jay said. "He's out of the city."

"We know that. We already called out there. No answer.
What's he tryin' to do — hide or something? It's not going to get
any better . . ."

"It's very unusual for the Federal Government, the Justice Department, to take an action that . . . It's —"

"We know that. What's he say? What's the statement? He'd
better do something or this knocks hell out of his re-election
plans."

"We need time to study the case. We —"

"When he gets in, you call us, dammit."

"Okay. Okay."

He tried the country house again without success. As soon as he had put the receiver down, the incoming calls resumed. There were inquiries from other newsmen from other cities and from members of the Legislature.

"Is he gonna call a special session, Jay? Just tell me that."

"I don't know, I don't know."

"He'd damn well better. He'd better close the schools. We got the votes to do that."

"No you haven't."

"What!"

By the middle of the morning reports were coming in about the demonstration planned, the "march" on the Capitol. There were calls from other cities from people planning to drive in, inquiring if the Governor would be there to talk with them.

"I guess we'll just have to close the schools."

"I don't see how."

"Why not? Why not?"

"Half of them are desegregated already," Jay said. "And what are we going to do without schools?"

"You've lost your mind."

Hoot Gibson appeared in the office early in the afternoon. Jay pulled him into one of the back conference rooms.

"Where is he? What's happened?"

"I don't know, Jay. I been gone since early this mawnin' runnin' all ovah, runnin' round all ovah. Had to 'range to get the servants back into town fah Miz Fenstemakeh's pawty. Had to get those pitcher people on the plane."

"They're gone? They're all gone?"

"All 'cept Miz Vicki."

"She's still there? What about Anne? The little girl. They weren't supposed to —"

"Little one went with the others. Vicki stayed on. Said she'd take a later plane. I don't know when."

"What about Arthur? What did he say?"

"Nothin'."

"Nothing? Nothing at all?"

"Nope."

He tried to make some sense of this and found it impossible. It was like talking in another language. And it was all a nightmare. Be a man! he thought, and was shaken by half a giggle, half a sob. He tried to call into the country again, but there was no answer. Another phone was ringing, long distance from the Governor's campaign manager.

"Where the hell is Arthur? What's he going to do?"

"I don't know where he is — or what his plans are."

"Well this is murder. They're going to have us whipped before the campaign even gets started. You have any ideas? Jay. Don't any of you people have any ideas?"

"I haven't had an idea in two years. The Governor usually has all the ideas."

"He'd better come up with a good one this time."

Hoot Gibson stood looking out a window, scratching himself. The girl, Jay thought, why did they take the girl? If there had only been time to think or plan. Now the departure of the little girl seemed to have left a great gap in him, an irreparable loss of imagination and vitality. And Vicki. Had she stayed to talk with him? Why hadn't she called? Why didn't they answer the phone out there? He searched his mind for a course of action. Be a man? There was some small fiber of it left in him, but now the brain seemed to have boggled at the prospect of exertion. Part of myself is expired; too late for the resuscitator, bring the wagon. Too much of me is — Dead. *Old Dead Man* — he might know something! Worth a try, he thought. If he could make himself understandable on the telephone, Dead Man could take a message to the house. He reached for the phone.

Hoot Gibson stood staring out the window, and then turned at Jay's sudden movement.

"Ah heah they's goin-a be a mawch round the Capitol buildin' this aftahnoon. Yew mind 'f ah go down an' watch?"

"No," Jay said, dialing the long-distance number once again.

If only old Dead Man can hear me, I'll have to shout, I'll have to — "Hey!"

Hoot Gibson turned at the door.

"Sarah. What about Sarah? She come in with you?"

"She was dronk," Hoot Gibson said with a grin.

"All night? I talked to her last night, and . . ."

"She slept a little, ah thank. In the front room. She was havin' another when I left though. · At it prutty early. Ah nevah seen that sweet thang carryin' on that way. She can put it down when she's uh mind to." He turned and wandered out of the office.

The conversation with the old man was not as bad as he expected. The trouble was that he had to shout. He had to scream whole sentences into the phone, long and involved explanations pitched at the top of his voice, and in the middle of this one of the secretaries stuck her head through the door, looking at him in amazement. "That's right Dead Man! Just walk up to the main house if you can! See if anybody's there! Ask them to call me! This is *Jay*, Dead Man, this is *Jay*! Ask someone to call into town! Ask Arthur to call . . . *Arthur!* All right? . . . All right! . . ."

Outside on the Capitol grounds, groups of people were gathering beneath the trees. It looked very much like a huge old-fashioned picnic for a time, but then these early crowds were swollen by later arrivals carrying placards and banners, painted bedsheets and pasteboard signs. There were women and children sprawled out on the grass, watching from a distance and joining occasionally in erratic, short-lived marching formations and crazy snake dances. There were some old men with cymbals and an ancient bass drum and a tarnished trombone. There were several clusters of people grouped around speakers, who stood on the hoods of cars waving their arms. Jay watched fascinated from the second-story window.

Another newsman called: "You going out to greet them? They're a sweet bunch. You ought to get to know them."

"No thank you," Jay said.

"I've got a little thing here that needs some comment."

"I told you. The Governor's not here. I don't know where he
is."

"I know, I know. It's not that. There's a Mexican here says
he knows you and the Governor. Says you and Fenstemaker visited his place of business out in the ranch country a few days ago
and had a party . . . a party at which, let's see here, you deeded
the state back to the Mexicans —"

"What?"

"Isn't that a dilly? He says you had a little dancing party at his
bar and the Governor signed this proclamation — he's got it
right here, on brown wrapping paper yet — signed this thing giving the state back to the Mexicans."

"He's out of his mind," Jay said flatly.

"He says he knows you."

"I know a lot of Mexicans, but he's not one of them. The
fellow's got the paranoia. Treat him nice."

"Okay. Just checking. We'll show him the tenderest solicitude. All these minority groups are neurotic. You know?"

He returned to the window and watched the march around the
Capitol building. There was a kind of cheering section being
organized in front, and there were calls for Arthur Fenstemaker.
He talked to more reporters and state officials by telephone. Evening began coming on, and the crowds out front were thinning,
ready to disperse, threatening to be back on the following day and
the day after until Arthur Fenstemaker made an appearance.
The office help cleared off desks and went home. Two or three
staff members remained with him for a time, but they soon followed the others. Jay sat in the Governor's room; he sent out for a
sandwich and poured himself some of the Governor's whiskey.
Mrs. Fenstemaker called. She had not heard from Arthur all day
and was worried — there was no answer to the calls to the country place. Jay said yes he knew; he had been trying since the morning and would continue to check. He would call her back.

He sat at the Governor's desk and drank the whiskey. He

switched on the television and watched films of the demonstration in front of the Capitol occurring earlier in the day. They had shots of the women and children and bedsheets and bass drums, and then there were clips from the party of the night before — the Governor with his arm around Vicki, waving at the cameras, Vicki flanked by two minor state officials, both of whom appeared to be competing for the best vantage point from which to look down the front of her gown. Another set of clips, better quality film, apparently furnished by the motion picture people, showed the Governor, Vicki and Edmund Shavers standing outside the prefabricated Victorian mansion on the location set in the desert. Then there was even a years-old photograph of him, Jay McGown, flashing across the screen, an old, grinning visage from out of the past, from his student body president days. Jay McGown, the announcer explained to him, was Miss Vicki McGown's estranged husband and the Governor's personal assistant.

Jay sat back and sipped the whiskey, stuffing potato chips into his mouth, hypnotized by the screen. The personal catastrophe of Governor Arthur Fenstemaker seemed complete — total, absolute and final. Arthur couldn't have done better if he had tried, Jay thought. Had he tried?

He thought about the telephone. He had become so fond of the instrument during the course of the day, and now it had not signaled to him in more than an hour. He ought to call someone, he thought. Anyone. He called the country house, and there was no answer. He remembered Dead Man — Dead Man hadn't called back — and he asked the operator to dial Dead Man's number. Now there was no answer at Dead Man's. He tried to think! Who could he call? Mrs. Fenstemaker? No, she was no fun, all sincere and defenseless. Who could he call — who in the whole wide world? He wished he could call Kermit. Old Kermit would have enjoyed hearing all about what had happened since he hanged himself. There was that fellow Ibáñez, the Mex; he could call him now but where the hell was he? Look here Old Mex, I'm really very sorry about this afternoon. I just didn't know it was you, the real Ibáñez. Let's have a look at that proclamation now. We might be able to make some adjustment.

There was Victoria Anne. He would call old Victoria Anne, Annie, his sweetheart, his love, his unquestioning lover. Light a little candle, Annie, say a little prayer for me. He put the call through.

"Yes?" said Shavers. Jay wondered why anyone would possibly say "Yes?" in answering a telephone ring. The thought of it evoked a vague antagonism in him.

"Why should anyone possibly . . ." Jay began, and then hesitated.

"Yes?" said Shavers irritatedly.

"Victoria Anne McGown, please," Jay said.

"Who?"

"Annie. My little girl. Part of me . . . The best of me."

"Who is . . . Jay? Jay is that you?"

"Ed! Ed Shavers! How in the world are you? How's Victoria Anne."

"She's fine, Jay, we're both fine. Just been in a couple of hours. Doing a little baby-sitting. She's taking a nap. Just a minute and I'll —"

"No. No. Don't wake her. I just . . . I was just . . . wondering if you got in okay."

"Fine. Everything's fine."

"When are you expecting Vicki?"

"Well don't you know?" Shavers said. "Haven't you talked to her?"

"Haven't seen her," Jay said.

"Oh. Well. Say . . . you been thinking about that offer, what I talked with you about last night?"

"All day long, Ed. Thought about nothing else all day long."

"Good! Good! What did you decide?"

"I'll tell you, Ed, it's . . . it's . . ."

"Yes?"

"It's somehow slipped my mind what I was going to tell you,

Ed. Call you back when I remember." He broke the connection.

He sat in the Governor's leather chair and drank the whiskey. Be a man! What was it Sarah said? "Even if it's a cheap imitation of one, be one. Can't you get a little of it through osmosis or something?" He sat in the Governor's chair, rubbing the seat of his pants against the soft leather, thinking about osmosis. Could you make a love, manufacture an emotion, the same way?

The nice phone rang for him.

"Yes?"

"Speak louder I cain't heah yew, who zis speakin'?"

"Dead Man! How are you, Dead Man!"

"Speak louder. Who zis speakin'?"

"It's me! It's me, Dead Man! *Jay!* Jay McGown!"

"Yew th' one that called?"

"Yes! That's right, Dead Man! I'm the one!"

"Yew bettah get out heah."

"What's the trouble, Dead Man? What did you —"

"Yew bettah get out heah, boy . . ."

Fifteen

THESE DREAMS . . . like whiteshrouded men carousing through me, like great fat bears. Pursue me, through me, purple and swollen. I always forget on waking. Get up now (right now) and put it all down the way the psych prof told me (hold me!) else it will vanish in the light. Extract a lungful and impale the stuff on some exhibit board. For the authorities to see. All there

is of me. Big bears and snails and tornado tails. And don't forget the small dogs sniping with teeth like barracuda. Who'll
come to look? There's a charade. Who in the whole wide world
qualifies as my interpreter after it's put down in black and white?
These lapdogs munching and spangled wishbones growing from
my breast? There's Arthur, he'd know, he knows everything. I'll
write him a letter. I'll lie here and write him a good one . . . I
lie here now on my cushioned ledge, composing. Where to begin?
Begin at the beginning — a little description first. It's pleasant
here, very *très* and very gay, my high blue vaulted room with the
white stalks of wornout sunshine coming — No. At the beginning. Farther back, try to remember. There was this place some
time ago, somewhere west of my love, those dreary wastes those
trackless sands . . . How was that? Best I can do. I lie here now
on my snug soft silken ledge, myself beside inside me. Sometimes
I am like this and sometimes the other, straddling the ledge, my
skirt pushed up, my navel showing. That's when they come; I
think they are several people, burrowing in the luxuriant folds of
me, like bugs and slugs the way it was when we were digging toward China under those lovely latticed porch steps. Sometimes I
feel down there and I am all soft and mossy, so pretty all over like
the little girl said. When they come they come very softly, cats on
fat bear's feet; they're very quiet about it and nice in a way and I
only cried out once. And that was in the beginning. It was funny
how I got here, I don't think I've ever told myself. I'm on the
ledge mostly, my clothes pushed up over my head, but sometimes
I get down and walk around. Some. Times. There were times
I remember thinking Jay would come with the others but he never
found the ledge. Such a nice place really, a really lovely ledge
with a view of the lake and the olive farms and bluebonnets
painted on the ceiling. There was this sweet man brought me
here; he's beside me now as I write; I feel the length of him
against my legs. He always goes first before the others. And he's
the only one who ever really gets inside, crawling back on his
hands and knees, gasping for air, like a nice baby. I remember
Jay used to try. But he never had such a nice ledge as this one and

there were always people watching. I'll bring Jay up here with me sometime soon and hold him against my breast, my heart thumping like the first time, and he won't have to know about the other; this other, he must be leaving soon, taking the bears and lapdogs with him. Sometimes I get down and walk around and mix myself a gin, but this other doesn't. He just lies here next to me, sleeping. He's been strangely inarticulate of late. Perhaps that's how it's supposed to be, (I'm not sure; I'm new around here like I said). I'm wide awake. Those dreams. I don't remember any now and I was going to write them down, pulsing through me, inside-out me, all those scattered buttends. I recall a little of the first time. There was that blond girl, she wanted up here with him I know, the way she was hanging around, and he chose me and was nice, the way I know Jay would be if he could only find himself a ledge. It's very quiet now; I can hear this old house groaning and a night bird outside my window, serene and peaceful, and feel the silk pajamas against my skin, my skin all Vicki-perfumed. You have to look for it, Arthur told me, you have to look for beauty and grace, and I tried, I tried so hard with my eyes closed and the sweet taste of somebody at the corners of my mouth . . .

Sixteen

THE DRIVE through the hills seemed interminable. Jay sat hunched over the steering wheel, his eyes straining into the darkness. He raced ahead on the straight stretches and braked the big car hard on the turns. The night was moonless, and the head-

lights revealed little of the gloom. He had to look carefully for
the cutoffs, and even with the extra effort he missed the first one
and had to come toward the Governor's house from a backroad
that took him by Dead Man's shack. Dead Man stood leaning on
the gate, looking toward the Federalist mansion that was black
against the hills. Jay stopped and called to him through the car
window.

"What's the trouble, Dead Man? What happened?"

"Go see fah yosef," the old man said. "I nevah been 'round
theah all day long." He turned and moved to his porch.

Jay sped toward the darkened house, the wheels of the car
slipping and losing traction on the graveled road. Halfway there
the limousine spun off into a culvert and crashed along crazily
with the right fender churning up topsoil for a hundred feet.
Jay accelerated the big engine for a moment, but then turned
the ignition off when he smelled the rubber of the tires burning
against the sides of the culvert.

He pushed one door free and ran the remaining distance to the
house. Folding chairs and aluminum picnic tables were stacked
neatly on the stone porch. Only the paper lanterns, strung along
the promenade, floating in the evening air, gave an evidence of
the party the night before. The house was open and he moved
quickly through the downstairs rooms switching on lights.

Servants had worked until dawn that day, cleaning up; save
for an empty gin bottle in the middle of the enormous dining
table, there was no sign of disorder. The house seemed as life-
less and undisturbed as some Etruscan tomb, silent with the gods.
Jay stood for a moment in the dining room, remembering his
first visit here in the early weeks of the Governor's campaign.
They had been served an incredible meal, and Arthur Fenstemaker sat in the big chair, stretching and talking: "This is what
you have to watch out for, Jay. Remember it. You sit here in
these carpets up to your ankles with a fire crackling in a corner and
these black men serve you red wine and rare roast beef — and
there's crêpes suzettes comin' later — and tell me, now. Can you
get all wrought up about the poor folks?"

Jay turned and took the steps of the elegant staircase two at a time, turning on the first landing and feeling along the damask walls for the light switch. White fluorescence flooded the broad hallway, and he hesitated for an instant, listening for a sound, a merest whisper, the rustle of window blinds in one of the bedrooms. He moved down the hall toward the sound, and then, fumbling for the lights once more, the pile of clothes alongside the bed caught his feet and he slipped against the mattress, his hands coming down on Arthur Fenstemaker's cool flesh and jerked back as in a spasm. The gasp of unfamiliar terror caught in his throat. He finally got the lights on.

Arthur lay on the bed, covers bunched down at his feet. He wore red silk pajama bottoms, pulled tight against his thick waist; the sparse hair on his chest was speckled gray and black, and there was a faint stubble of beard under his neck and along the jawline. His expression was no expression — neither peace nor pain — although a mild annoyance might have been suggested by his scarcely parted lips. He seemed an insane shade of powder blue; perhaps it was the fluorescent light against the tanned flesh.

Jay felt for a pulse, but the utter lack of warmth in the body discouraged even this gesture. Lifting the wrist he could see the whole length of arm responding to the pressure. He sat on a leather hassock and smoked a cigarette, looking at the man on the bed.

"I'm sorry, Arthur," he finally said. "Goddammit to hell I'm sorry."

He went into the bathroom and washed his face with cold water. The vial of Vicki's perfume was on the dressing table. He picked it up and looked in amazement. He examined the bathroom closely and then moved into an adjoining bedroom and found Vicki's overnight case near the door. He sorted through the jars and bottles and small boxes to be sure, and then in a rush he searched through the empty closets. He returned to Arthur's room and sat down again. Then he stood and moved to the opposite side of the bed and found a half-slip on the floor, a thin-wispy wad of silk lying at his feet. The rumpled bedclothes

smelled of Vicki's perfume, and he could make out the impress
on the vacant pillow where her pretty head had lain. He walked
back round the bed and sat on the hassock.

"Well I'm still sorry," he said to the dead man. "Sorry as hell.
You should've stayed with that vibrator."

He walked downstairs and poured himself a drink, and then
carrying the bottle with him, he returned to sit with the Governor. There were the telephones — the Governor had two of
them in his room — those nice phones. He sat and thought for a
moment and then dialed the rural operator. It took some time to
get her out of bed and on the line.

"Yes?" She's been talking to those fashionable California people, Jay thought.

"You have a sheriff or a deputy or a justice of the peace you can
send out here? This is the Fenstemaker place."

"You want all three? What's wrong?"

"Any one of them or all three — I don't care. Just send 'em out
here," Jay said.

"Don't you want to talk to 'em?"

"I could but I don't. Just send somebody out here, it's —"

"I'm not supposed to do that. I'm —"

"Just do it for me, will you please? It's an emergency."

"All right."

"And get me this number in town . . ."

Mrs. Fenstemaker's voice came on the line in a moment.

"Jay? Have you heard anything? I've been worried so . . ."

"Is anyone there with you, Mrs. Fenstemaker?"

"A few friends, yes. They're just leaving. We've been sitting
out on the front gallery all evening."

"Could I speak to one of the men?"

"There *aren't* any men, Jay . . . Just some girl friends of
mine."

"Well one of the ladies, then."

"What is all this about, Jay? What's wrong?"

"Well . . ."

"Is it . . ."

"He's dead, Mrs. Fenstemaker . . . I'm sorry. He died out here sometime today . . . I'm at the country place. I'm sorry, Mrs. Fenstemaker. It looks like a heart attack of some kind."

"Who, Jay? Not Arthur, you don't mean Arthur do you? You're not sure are you?"

"Yes ma'am."

"You sure he's dead, you sure he's not just —"

"Yes ma'am, I'm sure. I'm sorry."

"Oh oh oh oh. Oh Jay! Oh, what . . ."

"I'll take care of everything. I just want someone there with you. Can your friends stay?"

"Yes, of course, yes. Oh oh oh. Where was he, Jay, where did you find him — no don't tell me, I don't want . . ." Her voice trailed off and he could hear the mumbling of her girl friends, and then one of them came on and he explained what needed to be done. "Don't call anyone. Don't tell anyone. We'll annouce what's happened in the morning when everything's settled. Otherwise, we'll have news people running through the house out here and calling Mrs. Fenstemaker at the mansion all night long."

He put the receiver down and thought for a minute. Then he stood and began cleaning the room, picking clothes off the floor and smoothing the bed; he locked Vicki's overnight case in the linen closet. He returned once again to the telephone table.

"Did you get someone sent out here?"

"Yes. The constable and the jaypee. What's happened? Can't you tell —"

"Now I want to call California," Jay said.

"Just a minute," the operator said. "I've got a call comin' in on my other line. It may be for you . . ."

Mrs. Fenstemaker's voice came to him again: "Jay? Jay? Do you know anything yet? Do you know anything about —"

"No, nothing at all. There's a justice of the peace coming out. And a doctor. We'll need a doctor — I forgot that . . . You call a doctor, too, Mrs. Fenstemaker, or one of your friends call. You ought to have a sedative."

"I'm coming out. I think I'll come out."

"I don't think you should . . . There's nothing you can do here, and you'll have a rough day in town tomorrow. I'd advise against it."

"All right, Jay."

"Fine."

"Will you get time and charges on all these calls, Jay, so we can make them official business . . . Oh oh oh what an awful thing to say. I'm in shock, I must be in shock." Once again one of her friends came on the line and advised him a doctor was on the way to the mansion.

The rural operator came back on. "I need a doctor now," he said to her. "Will you call a doctor?"

"I've already called him. What's goin' on out there?"

"You ought to know if you've been listening in."

"Is he really dead? Arthur really dead?"

"Yes. Get me an operator in town now so I can call California."

There was a delay of several minutes, and he kept the phone to his ear, sipping whiskey mixed with water from the bathroom tap. Occasionally he looked at Arthur Fenstemaker. The Governor's face seemed to be constricting into a terrible grin.

If I can just bring this off, he thought. If my mind doesn't sag, if I don't turn to jelly . . . Arthur would have been the man for this job, this little business. There was a man who — Sarah. Where the hell was Sarah? She must have . . .

"Yes?" There was Shavers again, damn his soul.

"Ed, this is Jay, I —"

"Oh! Jay! You calling about what we talked about? I hope —"

"Not exactly. I was wondering if you've heard from Vicki."

"Sure have. She's right here . . ."

Here comes my heart, he thought.

"Jay. Jay, doll, it was sweet of you to call . . ."

"I just thought we ought to have a talk."

"You haven't changed your mind, have you?"

"No."

"I stayed behind a few hours today, thinking we could talk.

Then I thought it wasn't any use. I reached a kind of decision . . ."

"You left some things behind," Jay said. He had a swallow from the bottle. The dead man on the bed seemed to sigh a little.

"I know, I know," Vicki said. "I remembered when I boarded the plane. My overnight case. And some perfume in the bathroom. Did you find the perfume?"

"I found it," Jay said. "All over the Governor's bed."

"What? What did you find, Jay?"

"The bedsheets reek of it. The perfume. And the Governor's dead. Did you know that, Vicki? Or didn't you even stop to look when you crawled out of the sack?"

"Dead!" He heard Ed Shavers say "What's that?" and then repeating the question to Vicki, coming nearer the phone.

"Jay, Jay, wait a minute. You say Arthur's dead? You're kidding, you're making a joke."

"He's dead, all right. Expired. Gone. That's the way I found him tonight. Lying in bed in his pajamas in an empty house and your stuff strewn all over it. Police and newspaper people are on their way over now, and I thought I ought to tell you about it . . ."

"Oh God! Jay! Get my things out of there. Are they going to involve me in this?"

"The implication ought to be pretty strong in the story. I don't see how they could resist it."

"Well then get my things out. Hide the bag. And I think I left a bra and panties hanging in one of the bathrooms. Get everything. You'll do that for me, won't you Jay? Thank God you called. Do you have to tell them I was there this morning? It was just part of the morning. When did he die?"

"I'm not sure," Jay said. "He's been dead for some time."

"Well do this for me, Jay. Do it if you can. At least don't *volunteer* anything about my being there this morning. I can't afford to get involved in anything like this. I've got to be careful — the studio warned me. That's one of the reasons I'd hoped we might be able to get together again. That and just wanting you with me again. Jay . . . Jay? Are you listening? Will you help me, Jay?"

"I'll help you if you'll help me," he said.

"Well sure. Fine. Eye for an eye, all that. What is it you want?"

"I want a divorce with none of this 'he left me *prostate*' business to the papers, and I want Annie to come live with me."

There was a silence during which his lips moved in a gabble of incoherent prayer. He looked over at his friend Arthur Fenstemaker, who had done this thing for him. Arthur smiled back fiercely.

"All right," Vicki said, all the gold gone out of her voice.

"All right? You say all right?"

"Yes. If you let me see her when I want to, let her come visit me when I've got time off from work."

"That's fine by me. It's heaven. But how will I know you'll keep your word?"

"If you were going to engage in blackmail by long-distance phone you should have thought of that. I can't tell you how. I'll just keep my word — that's how."

"Well . . . now this has all worked out nice. You've been very decent, Vic."

"Oh yes. Now will you get my clothes and bag out of there please. Hide 'em, burn 'em, mail 'em to me or something."

"It's already taken care of. I cleaned up before I called."

"That's a cheap trick." She seemed to think this was funny.

"Well, I could have always hauled the stuff out again for the newspapermen," he said.

"You know," she said, "you went to a great deal of trouble yourself to bargain for something you already had."

"What do you mean?"

"I had decided — I decided this morning before I left — to let you have the divorce and even part custody of Victoria Anne. I thought it was the least I could do."

"Least you could do?"

"You've got enough troubles already."

"What do you mean, Vic?"

"Well . . . I'll get to work on the divorce tomorrow. I'm in a hurry for it, actually. I'm thinking of marrying Greg Calhoun for a while . . . He's been very nice.

"You're *thinking* about it? For a *while?*"

"Well, you know. Wear the green hat. You taught me, doll."

"I hope not."

"Jay. Jay love."

"Yes?"

"It wasn't me, love."

"Wasn't you? Wasn't you what?"

"It just wasn't me, love. All I said to the Governor this morning was goodbye. So goodbye, love."

After she had broken the connection he stood staring at the bed until he saw the headlights of the approaching cars. He left the bedroom and walked along the hallway toward the stair. He did not know why such an idea occurred to him, but he moved past the stair to the end of the hall. He reached round the door facing and switched on the lights in Sarah's room.

Her fallen face turned to him, red eyes staring. She lay on her side in the bed, the covers pulled up round her shoulders, clutched at her throat. For a moment he could only stand and regard her in dumb-struck innocence, his own sweet innocence, forever inviolate. When he finally moved toward the bed the fine lines in her face began to work in little spasms and then the face contorted and collapsed, with tears swelling and flooding her eyes.

"I'm sorry," she said to him, her bare arms reaching out "Oh Jay I am so sorry. I couldn't help it, I really just couldn't help it, and now I've killed him — have I killed him Jay? It should have been you — it was supposed to be you and making you all live and whole the way I felt. It was going to be so pretty with you, beautiful with you . . ."

Her bare arms blinded him, and he dropped down on one knee next to the bed and buried his child's face in her hair. He could hear them downstairs, ringing the chimes, pounding the door; soon they would realize the house was open and they would make the ascent to the second floor. He did not much care. They could ransack the house, haul his friend Arthur Fenstemaker away in a shroud, set the place afire. All he wanted now was the room and the bed and Sarah's young warmth.

"Beauty and grace," she was mumbling in his head, "beauty and ease and grace . . . We'll have it now, won't we Jay? Such a sweet thought. But look at me —" She pulled back the covers. "All mussy. They kept coming and feeding on my lap, straddling me like bears and bugs and cows, burrowing like crabs, when all I wanted was you. I have this ledge, I have this lovely ledge for the two of us now. With a view . . ."

He could hear them coming up the stairs now and he stepped away and turned the light down and walked into the hall to wait. He led them into the other room and they all stood a short distance from the bed and looked at Arthur, pale blue in the soft light, bathed in the faint fragrance of woman, grinning over some great vague private joke.